ROMANCE

It begins in 1789, in France, and climaxes in the newborn State of Alabama, in 1834, with the building of the stately mansion, "Windhaven Plantation."

This is an epic journey that encompasses all of the world-shattering events of this torrid era. But more, it is the proud and passionate story of one man—Lucien Bouchard. The second son of a French nobleman, a man of vision and of courage, Lucien dares to seek a new way of life in the New World that suits his own high ideals. Yet his true romantic nature is at war with his lusty, carnal desires. And four women in his life reflect this raging conflict: Edmée, the high-born, amoral French sophisticate who scorns his love, choosing his elder brother, heir to the family title; Dimarte, the ingenuous, earthy, and sensual Indian princess; Amelia, the fiery, free-spoken beauty who is trapped in a life of servitude for crimes she didn't commit; and Priscilla, whose proper manner hides the unbridled passions of her true desires.

ADVENTURE

From the somber fields of Normandy, alive with the rumblings of the oncoming French Revolution, to the deep and darkly treacherous reaches of the Alabama frontier, *Windhaven Plantation* presents the determined struggle of one man to build a family and a home.

Lucien Bouchard's life is robust with excitement and continuing challenge. He is a man who keeps himself physically strong by tilling the rich, black soil that has become a part of him. His adventures through the wilderness; his overcoming the dangers of unrelenting nature; his surviving the cruelties of the savage Creek Indian laws and the deviousness of the Yazoo Land Company—all combine to make *Windhaven Plantation* a bold, glittering saga of the "Cotton South."

HISTORY

A bold era, as it was lived, unfolds in this sweeping panorama. Covering over four decades, a territory is settled, the state of Alabama is born, and a world is reshaped. History comes alive, and we see it not only through the eyes of the men who make it and become a celebrated part of America's heritage, but also through the eyes of those who are forgotten, some of whom rose to the occasion, others who were crushed by it.

Windhaven Plantation is a compelling drama that holds the throbbing pulse of a young nation through its early tempestuous years of political and economic crisis.

Windhaven Plantation is a story of people who loved and lusted, fought and retreated, won and lost, as they hurtled toward their destiny. You will be there among them, experiencing the excitement and the drama, the heartbreak and the triumph.

And you will return to Windhaven again . . .

Pinnacle Books by Marie de Jourlet:

WINDHAVEN PLANTATION
STORM OVER WINDHAVEN
LEGACY OF WINDHAVEN
RETURN TO WINDHAVEN
WINDHAVEN'S PERIL

Windhaven Plantation

by Marie de Jourlet

PINNACLE BOOKS   LOS ANGELES

ACKNOWLEDGMENTS

No author who delves into the past can be successful without the thoughtful help of historians and research aides who can ferret out the obscure details which help flesh the bones of the story. I should be ungrateful if I did not pay tribute to the following: Milo B. Howard, Jr., Director of the Department of Archives and History of the State of Alabama; J. Evans and B. Benson of the Montgomery City-County Public Library; Ingrid H. Nichols of the University of Alabama Press; my good friend Rich Padnos, history minor at the University of Illinois; Collin B. Hamer, Jr., Head, Louisiana Division of the New Orleans Public Library; Rosanne McCaffrey, Research Coordinator of The Historic New Orleans Collection; I. W. Allen, retired schoolteacher and chessplayer of Montgomery, Alabama, who provided many realistic descriptions of the locale; and Victor Levine and Cheryl Upchurch of the Capitol Book & News Company of Montgomery, Alabama. Their combined enthusiasm and perspicacity in tracking down verifications and sources to authenticate the framework of my novel were inspiring stimuli to make my task worthy of their efforts. Finally, grateful plaudits to my typist-transcriber, Mrs. Doris Samuels, who herself contributed some valuable suggestions to the work.   THE AUTHOR

WINDHAVEN PLANTATION

An original Pinnacle Books edition, published for the first time anywhere.

ISBN: 0-523-40642-8

First printing, February 1977	Seventh printing, May 1978
Second printing, March 1977	Eighth printing, August 1978
Third printing, March 1977	Ninth printing, February 1979
Fourth printing, April 1977	Tenth printing, April 1979
Fifth printing, May 1977	Eleventh printing, June 1979
Sixth printing, December 1977	Twelfth printing, September 1979
Thirteenth printing, December 1979	

Cover illustration by Bruce Minney

Printed in the United States of America

PINNACLE BOOKS, INC.
2029 Century Park East
Los Angeles, California 90067

CHAPTER ONE

It was not the cold, dry wind of the *mistral,* but the ominously damp, bone-chilling wind from the English Channel which surged over the coast of Normandy and moved southward over the town of Bolbec and the provincial village of Yves-sur-lac. Though it was the first week in May in the year 1789, the gusting wind twisted and shook the boughs of the apple trees in the flourishing orchards of the *Comte* Étienne de Bouchard, the *seigneur* of this pleasant village and an honored member of the court of fat, well-meaning Louis XVI of France.

Beyond the orchards, to the west, the fields of young spring wheat were ruffled by that same wind, and onward to the hills where the Comte's herds of Guernseys and Holsteins passively grazed on the thick, rich grass; the clappers of their copper bells stirred and tinkled as the wind swirled over them. The white-haired herdkeepers, old Jacquinot and Rizarde, leaning on their staffs, looked up at the somber sky and shook their heads, then moved among the lowing animals to herd them back safely to the barns before a storm should break.

"It is a strange wind, that one," squat, bearded Jacquinot observed to his taller, wiry companion. "In forty years I do not remember such a wind in May, *mon ami.*"

"Nor I, *mon vieux,*" Rizarde uneasily agreed, again glancing at the sky. "My father, who began his service with the father of our good *seigneur,* who was little more than a stripling then, used to tell me that such a wind in

1

May carries evil news with it." He quickly made the sign of the cross, then cupped his hands and called to the cow which led the herd to and from the grazing land: "*Holà*, Mathilde, *allons-y!*"

The squat, bearded herdsman made the sign of the cross also as he moved beside his companion, squinting now and again at the stragglers and calling out their names. He, like Rizarde, had begun as a stableboy half a century ago in the service of the good *Sieur* Roberte, whose only son Étienne was now his sovereign lord and master. And he prided himself that he knew the name of each cow in the herd, her idiosyncrasies and how many liters of good rich milk she would yield. "Yet 'tis also said, Rizarde, that even an ill wind blows some good," he vouchsafed as if to quiet his own uneasy presentiment.

"Are you thinking it might be poaching weather, old friend?" Rizarde grumbled as he stooped to right a young calf whose wobbly legs had crumpled as it lustily sucked from its mother. Then, straightening, he put two fingers to his mouth and directed a shrill whistle at one of the meandering Guernseys which had strayed down the slope leading to the apple orchards. With a tinkling of her bell, the animal turned and trotted docilely back toward the rest of the herd. "*Diantre!* You know as well as I do that old fool of a Louvier is still setting his snares over the hill by the lake. One day Jouvert will catch him and then—pouf!" He made the gesture of cocking his fist into a gun and pulling a trigger with his thumb.

"But he's not caught him yet, Rizarde," Jacquinot said; "it's a little game between them all these years, *tu le sais bien.*"

"Just the same—" Rizarde gloomily shook his head— "it's the law and Jouvert is in his rights if he shoots the old fool."

"Perhaps one day such a law will be done away with," the squat herdsman muttered.

"Have a care what you're saying, man!" Rizarde glanced angrily at his friend. "That's treason, and the king's provost will have you clapped in irons if he should hear you talk that way. Come on, I don't like the looks of

2

the sky, let's get these cows back to the barn, and then I'm for a mug of hot wine and my bread and cheese!"

"Just the same," Jacquinot began, and then, seeing the troubled look on his friend's face, shrugged and finished, "well, no matter. Ah, there goes the little one again—I'd best carry it back to the barn. Its four legs aren't yet as steady as my two old fat ones, eh, Rizarde?" Dropping his cudgel, he stooped to lift the bawling calf in his arms, and then, seeing Rizarde's harsh features soften, cleared his throat and strode onward as the sky grew still darker with the advent of twilight.

The elegant Swiss ormolu clock on the mantelpiece had just finished chiming four when the liveried footman, deferentially inclining his head, led *Père* Auguste Morlain into the sitting room of the *Sieur* of Yves-sur-lac. The latter rose from his goat-legged writing table, ornate with Watteau panels and heavily encrusted with silver, to welcome his priestly caller. "It's good of you to come, *mon père*. Gervaise, a glass of Burgundy for his reverence!"

"I won't say no to that, my son," the bespectacled priest chuckled as he smoothed his cassock and seated himself on a sumptuous Louis Quinze chair. "It will help settle my old bones, rattled as they have been astride my balky jennet. Ah, thank you, my son . . ." He turned with a beaming smile to accept a glass of wine from the footman, who again inclined his head, then hastened to his master to serve him with another glass.

"I shall ring if I need you, Gervaise." The elderly *Comte* nodded dismissal, then, leaning forward, he demanded, "What can you tell me of the feeling of the village about the latest news from Paris, *Père* Morlain?"

The stocky little priest grimaced, then shrugged. "One hears rumors, of course. But I do not think that Yves-sur-lac will be much endangered. After all, you and your father have been benevolent lords of this domain, you have been just and honorable in your dealings, and they hold you in esteem."

Étienne de Bouchard, resplendent in a scarlet coat with the Order of Saint Louis on his breast and a billow of lace at his sleeves, thoughtfully sipped his wine before reply-

3

ing. "That's true enough, *Père* Morlain. You as my confessor and God as my judge know that I've tried to live in peace with my vassals as with my *rentiers*. But this madness of a few hotheaded revolutionaries may spread like a plague even to the most peaceful villages."

"And yet, my son—" the little priest earnestly leaned forward—"out of that calamity has come much that is good. You know that when the king recalled *Monsieur* Necker when our country was on the verge of bankruptcy, he gained great popularity by recommending the calling of the States-General. Though there are courtiers who would have him dismissed again, there is talk of establishing the commune as the city government of Paris and of organizing the National Guard."

"True again, *Père* Morlain, but the deputies of the Third Estate, joined by many members of the lower clergy as well as by a few opportunistic nobles, have demanded such sweeping political and social reforms that neither the assembly nor the king has the power to grant them. From this comes, as I see it, nothing but anarchy." He rose, scowling, to pace the room, a tall soldierly figure of a man, though in his early sixties, his powdered wig and the silver sword at his side accentuating his military bearing. "The National Assembly meets three months hence. God alone knows what their decision will be, one that may well affect the lives of all of us in this industrious village which my father and I and our forebears have worked so hard to perpetuate."

The priest fumbled with his rosary, troubled and not certain of his words. "But the justice of God must prevail, my son," he said at last. "I know that there are many of my brothers who are ambitious for power—which Heaven forbid that I should be!—and I do not share their views. All I can tell you is that while there is talk of the peasants' revolt in Brittany, here in Yves-sur-lac those I number in my flock of a Sunday are well content with their noble master—yourself, my lord *Comte*."

Clasping his gnarled hands behind his back, the elderly nobleman moved toward the fireplace, stirred one of the burning logs with the poker and then turned to face the priest. "Normandy is loyal to the king, *Père* Morlain. It

4

has been so since the year of 911, when Charles the Simple gave this region as a duchy to Rollo, the leader of the conquering Norsemen. The Normans accepted Christianity and all the French customs. Over a hundred and fifty years later, the great Duke William II conquered England. Then, after the English had taken Normandy back under Henry Plantagenet, Philip II recovered it for France in the thirteenth century. This rich, fertile country was devastated in the Hundred Years War when England conquered it once again, but in 1450 it once again became French."

"This I know, my son."

"Of a certainty you know, *mon père*. And pardon my lecture in history, but perhaps you do not know that one of my ancestors fought with William II, and another was a war lieutenant for Philip II, and still another led a great force against the English when Normandy was at last returned to France. Here in this province there is all the history of my ancestors, and I have two sons to preserve my lineage. Can you wonder that I am troubled by what takes place in Paris even now? If defiance against the King of France himself is not halted—and by military means if need be—then lineage and the work of generations to bring thrift and industry and prosperity to our nation will be cast aside as nothing;" He thrust the poker with a clatter into the fire and flung himself back into his chair, his face working with emotion.

The priest reflected, nursing his chin with a pudgy hand, his forehead creased with thought. "Perhaps, my lord Count, if you were to reduce the tithes, amend some of the outmoded feudal rites—"

The old nobleman stiffened, glared at his interlocutor. "You would admit the Third Estate to an equal vote not only with myself but with all the lords of all the provinces of France? Take care, *Père* Morlain; what you even hint at is intolerable; it smacks of these revolutionary notions born out of the meetings of the rabble who cry out against their betters when not a man among them would have the stomach or the knowledge to replace what we have built for centuries. What would they give us in place of what you see here in Yves-sur-lac? Bloodshed, infamy and dishonor, little else. As for the tithes, I am foresworn as *seigneur* of this village to transmit all such taxes to the king. I would be stripped of my office and would be deserving of it if I did not maintain what you call the outmoded feudal rights. No, *Père* Morlain, I cannot agree to that. I have groomed my elder son, Jean, to take my place when my time is up, and he, as I, must and will be loyal to the throne."

"And your other son, my lord Count?"

Étienne de Bouchard scowled and shook his head. "He's a dreamer, I fear me much. Oh, he has a feeling for the land and he seems to know more of animal husbandry and the planting of crops and their harvesting than even I or my chief steward, Blaise. I am certain his saintly mother spoiled him when he was a child, letting him browse among dusty books and hearken to poetry and the romantic tales of knighthood. But then, it is only natural that I concern myself most with Jean, since it is he who will inherit the title."

Père Morlain rose from his chair. "I will pray for you and your good wife and Jean and Lucien, my lord Count. And also for the sanity of the National Assembly in August. Meanwhile, I would hope you do not think ill of me or that I harbor seditious thoughts against the king."

"Of course not, *mon père,* I know you too well for that. You have lived all your life in this peaceful village and you have done good work. You are not to blame for the malcontents, be certain of that. And for your poor, here are twenty gold louis." He took a little velvet purse from the pocket of his red coat and handed it to the bespectacled priest.

"When I speak of this munificence at my sermon Sunday, my lord Count, all will praise and bless your generosity as I do."

"I count on your blessings, *mon père.*" For the first time, Étienne de Bouchard allowed himself to smile. "It may well be that within a week or two I shall ask you for a more specific blessing—to be directed to my son Jean, who, unless I am much mistaken, will plan to take unto himself a wife. His mother and I will rejoice in this, since it is but to perpetuate our line and it will be an alliance

6

that will bring joy to the village as to ourselves. But of this, you will learn in good time. May your journey back to the village be less arduous."

"I fear me not, my lord Count, for my jennet is vexed with me that I take her from her stable and her oats through this sudden angry wind that has fallen upon the land. But again, may He who died for the salvation of all mankind grant His blessing to you and yours, *monseigneur*." He made the sign of the cross as the elderly nobleman bowed his head, and then left the sitting room.

Jean de Bouchard had halted his bay mare at the edge of the orchard not far from the well-worn road that led from the little village to the two-story red brick chateau of his father. He had seen the little priest uncomfortably jogging along on the spirited little jennet and smiled mockingly at *Père* Morlain's ineffectual tuggings at the reins. Then, glancing back at the two square towers which flanked the flat-fronted chateau, he clucked to his mare and headed her toward the outskirts of Yves-sur-lac.

Six feet tall and blond like his father, he was insolently graceful as he bestrode his mare in his full-skirted coat of lavender velvet laced with gold, in a peach-hued velvet waistcoat, with elegant black silk breeches and hose. He wore a pair of short, polished black leather boots with spurs, and his powdered hair was bound at the neck with a broad ribbon of watered silk. From his side, a thin, silver-hilted dress-sword swung to his rhythmic gait in the light saddle.

His features were cold and supercilious, with dark-blue eyes that had little warmth in them, a strong Roman nose whose nostrils were perhaps a trifle too sensuously flaring, and a full-lipped moist mouth which gave further proof of his sensual nature. Six months from his thirtieth birthday, smugly assured that his father's title and powers would inevitably pass to him, Jean de Bouchard rode with the air of a man who savors the bounties of well-born privilege.

Like most scions of wealthy noblemen, he had attended the University of Paris, but he had given little time to his studies. Having been quickly welcomed into the clique of

7

snobbish and affluent young gentlemen who, like himself, were being trained to succeed their fathers as custodians of French aristocracy and all that it entailed, he had reveled in all of the distractions which Paris could offer a blue-blooded youth with an unfailing supply of golden louis in his purse. Knowing himself to be physically well-favored, he had begun by seducing a pretty little *midinette* who had lost her post when her employer discovered that she was with child. Deaf to her tearful entreaties, Jean de Bouchard had contemptuously paid her off with a handful of louis and warned her that if she persisted in importuning him, the heir to a count of France, she would soon find herself in the Ursuline Prison, where prostitutes and female thieves and vagrants had their hair shorn and were taught to sew, their rations being bread and water and liberal applications of the strap wielded by the holy sisters.

Like most of his companions, he had taken fencing lessons at a *salle des armes,* where, for a munificent fee, a noted swordsman deigned to give lessons to aspiring pupils, who, to be sure, practiced with his less illustrious assistants until they had demonstrated sufficient skill to engage blades with the master himself. Jean de Bouchard had pursued his proficiency till the master himself, one Chevalier Jacques de Brivaut (who had fallen out of favor with the king and thus been obliged to gain his livelihood like any humble tradesman) had declared that there was nothing more that he could teach the young profligate. But if the old *Comte*'s elder son had acquired a virtuoso skill with the rapier, it was not only because it was the fashion for a nobleman to be able to defend himself; it was a kind of anticipatory precaution for the purpose of extricating himself from unpleasant situations which he perceived might arise from his own inflammably lecherous inclinations.

His next conquest had been a handsome young widow who, his affable and equally dissolute friends had assured him, was notorious for her chastity. It took him two months of diligent wooing and romantic courtship to bed her with the honeyed promise of marriage—despite the fact that he was seven years her junior—because he could not conceive of life without her. Once he had made her his mistress, he callously exhibited her garter and her nightshift to an admiring and envious throng of friends, collected his stakes of a hundred louis from the disgruntled, plump and pimply son of a marquis who had wagered against his amatory success with the widow and suggested that the loser seek to console himself by returning these intimate articles to the lady and offer himself as replacement.

Before he had ended his studies at the University of Paris, he had seduced a dozen more, all of them women of quality, if only to prove his own fastidious taste. And three of them supposedly faithfully married. Out of these transient liaisons had come three duels, the first with an elderly guardian of a demure brunette who had been dazzled by Jean de Bouchard's haughty manner and splendid physique. They had met at dawn in the Parc des Invalides, and after the third parry, Jean de Bouchard had thrust his rapier through the old man's lungs. The other two duels had been with outraged husbands, and the sneering blond son of Étienne de Bouchard had killed the one and given the other a crippling wound in the muscle of the thigh, which left him unable to walk for the rest of his life without a grotesque limp.

He found life on his father's bucolic estates tediously dull and took himself off to Paris at least twice a year, where he maintained as his mistress the auburn-haired leading *soubrette* of the *Comédie Française*. He had visited her only last month and been chagrined to learn that she was contemplating marriage with a shipbuilder in Toulon. It was high time, he knew, to satisfy his crotchety old father's constant urgings and take himself a wife. To be sure, since he would be the old man's successor to the title, it would be as well to have an heir of his own so that his milksop of a brother, Lucien, could inherit nothing more than half of the *rentes* of the estate.

He halted his mare on the road to take a silver snuff box from the pocket of his waistcoat and to tap the fine powder into his nostrils. Then he chuckled to himself. For the joke would be on Lucien, to find out whom it was that he had at last decided to marry. That bookish fool

9

thought himself in love with her, but he knew her better than Lucien ever could; better, indeed, than she did herself. The alluring prospect of being *Madame la Comtesse* de Bouchard would carry more weight with her than all of Lucien's sonnets and pledges of eternal devotion. Besides, the wench was full-blown and hot for plucking, even if she was of high quality and, he had no doubt, still a virgin. That his brother was as yet unscienced in the art of taking maidenheads he had no doubt whatsoever. Yes, it would be an amusing jest. And he had already told the old Count that within a few days *Père* Morlain might be summoned for news of the banns, which he would read aloud in church of a Sunday.

But meanwhile, between that time and the altar and the bridal bed, there were still diversions to be had, even in this miserable little village. One of them was Madelon Rovier, the piquantly innocent seventeen-year-old orphan girl who had been adopted by old Auguste Rovier and his barren wife, Hermione, when she had been found as an abandoned baby wrapped in swaddling clothes in a basket laid on the steps of *Père* Morlain's rectory. Rovier was blacksmith and stablekeeper for the little village and, Jean de Bouchard knew, almost fanatically loyal to the throne. And with her creamy skin that even a marchioness would have envied, her tumbling, glossy black hair and mouth-wateringly ripening bosom and hips, Madelon Rovier had already inflamed him to desire. Now that he could not quench his brooding passions in the amiable and competent embrace of his Parisian mistress, Madelon would make a splendid surrogate.

Only a week ago, riding into the village to have new shoes fitted onto his restive mare, Jean de Bouchard had managed a few moments of clandestine conversation with the wide-eyed, blushing young girl and pressed a coin into her hand, murmuring, "Buy yourself a ribbon and wear it as my favor, but say nothing to your old fool of a father." And now, on this dreary storm-threatening afternoon, he knew that Rovier and his wife had gone to Bolbec to visit a critically ailing relative.

Riding up to the back of the stable and vaulting from his saddle like an athlete, he tied the reins to a sturdy wooden rail and, pausing to take another pinch of snuff, moved toward the door of the stable where he knew that Madelon would be bringing oats to the horses this time of day.

He saw her leaning into a stall with a heavy wooden bucket and making soft, encouraging sounds to a spirited black stallion. Her gray kirtle tightened over the luscious *rondeurs* of her buttocks, and his eyes narrowed with concupiscence. *"Ma belle, me voici!"* he announced in a hoarse whisper.

With a startled cry, the young black-haired girl whirled, dropping the bucket and clapping a hand to her mouth. Her eyes widened at first with fright, then with almost fatuous admiration for the elegant cavalier who stood before her, preening himself, a smile of anticipation on his fleshy mouth. *"Monseigneur,* I—I didn't dream it was you—oh my, here I am in my oldest clothes and you so elegant!"

He chuckled softly, triumphantly, as he came toward her. Then, as if she had been a duchess, he took her hand in his, bowed his head and brushed her trembling fingers with his lips.

"Ohh! You—you mustn't, you shouldn't, *monseigneur!"* she gasped, awed at so lordly an attention.

"N'ayez pas peur de moi, petite," he murmured as he took her in his arms and brushed his lips against her creamy cheek. "You know, do you not, Madelon, that soon I shall be the *seigneur* of this village? My father has not many years before him, and it is within my power to do great things for you if you are gentle and obedient, *comprends?"*

"Please—you mustn't—my f-father—" she stammered, feebly thrusting at his chest with her little fists, her face scarlet with confusion and shame at his sudden boldness.

"But don't you understand, little one? When I am *Comte* of Yves-sur-lac, the law permits me to exact from you the *droit du seigneur*. It means that you must come to me; yes, Madelon, to my bedchamber when I will it. Be gentle now, and I shall bring you presents and soon you will be my *jolie maîtresse."*

"But—oh no, my lord, it—it is a sin—*Père* Morlain has said so, a girl must be wed before she can let a man

11

take such liberties with her—yes, you are my noble lord, I know this—but it's not right—please—let me go—"

"*Mordieu!*" he swore under his breath, his face darkening with lust. "By the ancient feudal law, I can force you to yield yourself to me, Madelon. But don't you see, *petite?* I want you willing and eager for me. I know how to make you die of pleasure. Come, over to this empty stall, I'll be very tender with you because I know you are *pucelle.*"

"No, no, oh, please don't—oh, you mustn't, *Monseigneur*. I'm a good girl—you mustn't—stop—you're tearing my blouse—oh, no—oh, I am so ashamed—"

He had dragged her, half-fainting with her conflicting emotions, into the empty stall and flung her down upon a pile of hay. His hands had ripped off her blouse, baring the magnificent, blooming round globes of her creamy breasts, which rose and fell tumultuously, their dark-coral tips quivering. Swiftly, he unbuttoned his long-skirted coat and then his waistcoat, undid the belt of the dress sword and tossed it carelessly to the hay-strewn floor of the stall beside him. Madelon Rovier shrank back against the partition, huddling her arms over her naked bosom, her eyes enormous and filmed with tears.

As he opened his breeches, Jean de Bouchard heard the stable door open and a boy's voice, anxious, call out, "Madelon? *Es-tu là?*"

The elder son of the Count whirled, his face mottled with fury and passion, and snarled between his teeth, "Get out of here, young *vaurien!* And don't come back, or I'll give you a drubbing!"

"Oh, Antoine! It's—it's all right!" Madelon sobbingly called from the stall.

The boy, no more than fourteen, lanky and with his dark-brown hair almost as long as a girl's in ringlets over his nape and ears, hesitated a moment, then moved forward, but away from the furious blond nobleman who turned to confront him. With a cry of alarm, he saw Madelon lying back on the hay at the rear of the stall, her arms still clutched over her bare bosom, tears flowing down her cheeks like rivulets.

"You—you've hurt her—you've made her cry! Go

12

away and let her be!" he cried out and flung himself on Jean de Bouchard.

"You would strike a nobleman of France? You filthy little *canaille!* I'll teach you to lay hands on your betters!" He stepped back to the opening of the stall, stooped to retrieve his sword belt, drew out the short dress sword and, baring his teeth with sadistic fury, thrust the shining blade into the boy's heart. Madelon uttered a piercing shriek of horrified consternation, tried to rise, but could not, petrified by the unexpected savagery of the nobleman's retaliation.

With a choking little moan, the boy sprawled face down on the ground and lay still. Jean de Bouchard contemptuously wiped the bloodied blade on the ragged trousers, then dropped the sword and turned back to his prey. "Now then, *ma douce aimeé,* there'll be no one to disturb us now."

"N-no—you've killed him—he was only a little boy— oh, please—let me go—I don't want you to—aahhh!"

The girl's despairing cry was muffled as his lips brutally fused to hers, his wiry fingers ripping away her *jupon* and the batiste drawers beneath, and then he flung himself upon her as she writhed and shuddered under his brutal penetration.

Lucien de Bouchard smilingly waved aside the eagerly proffered aid of gawky young Edmond, the Count's stableboy, as he saddled the superb, spirited Arabian palomino. "He's too used to me, *garçon.*" His quick smile softened the hurt to the boy's zeal. And, to compliment Edmond, whose ambition was to become the first groom of the estate, he added, "It was thoughtful of you to change his straw and to give him an extra ration of oats. If it doesn't storm, I'll be back by suppertime."

"Very good, *monseigneur.*"

Lucien mounted the magnificent cream-colored stallion, a present from his father on his last birthday, patted its neck and murmured gently to it as he gave a slight tug at the reins. With effortless ease, the cream-colored Arabian broke into a canter, and Lucien de Bouchard turned its head toward the south, along a little road that would take him over the hill where his father's cattle grazed and down past the clear, shimmering blue lake from which the village took its name, set between two hills and thus protected from the cold, damp wind that so ominously blew across the fields and orchards and beyond.

At twenty-six, the Count's younger son was tall and wiry, his skin tanned from the sun, his black hair cut shorter than was the fashion and bound at the back with a simple kerchief. In his brown coat and sturdy riding breeches and scuffed boots, Lucien de Bouchard, by contrast with his brother, did not look like a nobleman. The truth was, he felt uncomfortable in frills and lace and all the gewgaws of the nobility. His face was angular, as weatherbeaten as that of his father's herdsmen, with a humorous curve to his frank, firm mouth, a straight and undistinguished nose, strong, deeply cleft chin and large, dark-brown eyes in which there always seemed to lurk a twinkle of amusement at the world they surveyed. His body was muscular and lean, his hands callused from working on the land. If the Parisian rabble which had stormed the Bastille had cornered and stripped him, not even the most fanatical anti-Royalist who had bellowed along with the rest, *"Liberté, egalité, fraternité!"* would have had the least suspicion that he was one of the accursed aristocrats against whom all the nation was rising in an upheaval that would pit brother against brother, class against class.

Like Jean, Lucien had been enrolled in the University of Paris, but where his older brother had frittered away his time with wenching, dicing and dueling, Lucien had steeped himself in philosophy and history. He had read Rousseau, Voltaire, Descartes and Montaigne, as well as Plato and Socrates. He had even read the letters of Thomas Paine, whose *Common Sense* had hastened the Declaration of Independence and whose *The American Crisis* had heartened patriots in their struggle against George III. And he had thought that this man, this firebrand with the conscience of a nation as his own restless demon, had very likely foreseen if not even prophesied what now seemed inevitable in all of France.

14

If Jean called him a milksop, it was only because of his interest in books, music and poetry and perhaps too because, at offhand moments, he would pen a sonnet or a rondeau to Edmée de Courent, the exquisitely lovely black-haired daughter of the king's provost-marshal in Yves-sur-lac. The old Count had more than once rebuked Lucien for demeaning himself by working in the fields beside the peasants and caring for Arabe, his palomino, instead of leaving such earthy tasks to the groom and the stableboy. Yet Lucien had withstood his father's constant grumblings and disarmed the old man by acquiring such astute knowledge of the crops and cattle on the estate as to have the expert knowledge of a veritable overseer. Indeed, bookish as he was, Lucien would often urge the aging *seneschal* to let him enter the ledgers and balance them so that his father would have an accurate accounting of the profits of the harvest, the milk and cheese and butter, the foaling of the cows and the mares, as well as the payment of tithes from the villagers. These, in turn, were remitted to Louis XVI to maintain Versailles and Fontainebleau in all their baroque luxury when in many regions of France as in Paris itself there were those who did not know when their next scrap of bread would be provided.

He wore no sword, except on those formal occasions when guests were dining at the chateau. He felt more comfortable with an axe or a spade or even, on more than one occasion, handling the crude plow to break up an acre or two of ground where barley or millet or wheat would be planted. He would share the workers' simple *déjeuner* of bread, cheese and sausage and a sourish wine of the province and enjoy it as much as one of the Lucullan banquets which the old Count often staged in honor of a visiting king's minister from court or a neighboring nobleman. And many of those workers often said of him, in the privacy of their own cottages, that he would make a far better successor to the old *seigneur* than Jean—though of course they did not openly dare voice such a sentiment. Besides, Lucien knew as well as they the inexorable law of primogeniture; only in the event of Jean's death could he aspire to the title and the lands of Étienne de Bouchard.

Though at an age when most men were married and begetting their first heirs, Lucien, for all his romanticism of spirit, had shown little inclination toward the opposite sex, with the one exception of Edmée de Courent. First, he had always idolized his mother, the *Comtesse* Laurette de Bouchard, the only daughter of a minor nobleman of Rouen, whose self-effacing, gentle ways and still discernible brown-haired beauty his father had unerringly detected thirty-two years ago and promptly wooed regardless of the paltry dowry which had accompanied his choice of a wife. Now fifty-four, though gray had streaked nearly all of the soft brown ringlets of her hair and the passing years had wrinkled her brow and neck, her sweetly melodious voice and round, gentle, heartshaped face still recalled to the old Count the rapturous days of their young passions and her unswerving fealty to him as wife and sweetheart. And to Lucien, the serene, guileless outlook of his mother had set from the very first a kind of criterion by which he had come to judge most women.

Not that he had not known the agonies of the thwarted flesh, in his adolescence and even now more keenly, but only once had he assayed the temptations of a light o'love and that in Paris in the week that had followed his completion of his studies. The students had held a masked ball, and he had found himself the partner of a saucy-tongued, slim, black-haired girl who had twitted him about his scholarly and almost monkish behavior. She had called him an old sobersides, doubted that he had ever mustered enough *élan vital* to kiss a wench, and, goaded by her piquant loveliness as much as by her saucy tongue, he had seized her and kissed her passionately on the mouth. She had laughed softly, knowingly, and the two of them had slipped out of the hall above a popular bistro where the students had been carousing, and gone to her room. He had had no doubt of his manhood, he knew also the dangers of yielding to such temptation. His brother's duels were fresh in his memory, and when one of his close friends had told him the next day that Vivienne—his passionate young initiatress—was the wife of a stodgy old professor at the University, he had been horrified at his own folly.

Eight years ago, the then newly appointed provost-marshal had acquired the somewhat smaller lands to the southwest of his father's estate, across the hill on the other side of the lake, and it was then for the first time that Lucien had met Edmée. Though she was only ten at the time, the impertinent bravado and precociously flirtatious airs she displayed toward this serious young man had made Lucien think of Vivienne. Thereafter, he had visited the chateau of the provost-marshal many times during the ensuing years, and last year, after Edmée had reached her seventeenth birthday, he determined that he would ask her to wed him. It was true that he could not offer her the title of *Comtesse* nor this fine estate; yet by the law he would be well off so long as his father continued to pay the expected tithes to the throne. Besides, if it came to that, he had learned enough skill about farming to earn an honest livelihood in any other part of France. And if Edmée loved him, as he had begun to think she did, the matter of a title was one of sheer vanity when all was said and done.

So, at least once a week for the past several months, he had been riding this tortuous road up the hill and down, around the lake and up the other hill to the Courent chateau, paying a formal visit to the provost-marshal and his buxom, cantankerous wife, who had been born in Paris and was homesick for the excitement of it in comparison with the drearily rustic life to which she felt herself now condemned. And then at last, Edmée would make her entrance into the salon, and he would tremble with an ill-disguised excitement as he bowed to her as to a duchess, kissed her hand and then almost diffidently slipped a folded sheet containing his latest effusion into her soft, slim hand.

Last week, his eyes brightened to recall as he urged the palomino up the hill where the cattle had been grazing, they had been left alone for a whole half hour, and he had actually dared to take her in his arms and kiss her and to stammer that, if it pleased her, he would ask to speak to her parents very soon on a matter of the greatest

17

importance to them both. And Edmée had smiled and moved out of his embrace, cocked her head and whispered, "Dear Lucien, always so gallant and faithful, I truly did not know you could kiss a girl like that! Take care, before you turn my head! Now I must go back to my parents—and I long to see you again!"

The wind tugged at his rough brown coat as the palomino attained the crest of the hill, and he looked back toward his father's chateau, then to the left, where the little village sprawled far beyond the orchards and the grazing land and the fields. He did not envy Jean, except for this land, knowing that his brother would never have the feeling for it that he himself had learned so long ago. And what troubled him most was that, having delved into the philosophies of mankind as he had at the University and thereafter, he could not share his father's and his brother's unswerving belief that land such as this must always rest with the privileged and that those lower in the scale of birth must be denied the joy and creativity of its ownership and working.

Then, bending to the head of the palomino, he urged it down the slope. *"Viens donc,* Arabe, *mon ami!"*

At once the wind lessened, for here in this little valley the two adjacent hills formed a kind of *asile du vent,* a haven against the wind. Beyond the lake and ascending halfway up that other hill, was a thick forest of birch and poplar. Now, as he lightly touched his booted heels to Arabe's belly, the palomino moved with certain footing down toward the still blue lake.

He saw a shadowy figure creep suddenly out of a clump of poplars and stoop toward a wriggling rabbit taken in a crude snare. And then he heard the boom of a musket. Twisting to the left in his saddle, he recognized his father's gamekeeper, florid-faced, nearly bald Émile Jouvert, who had just lowered his musket and was hurrying toward the fallen figure of a little man in ragged waistcoat and breeches, with a gray cloth cap pulled down over one side of his face.

Lucien de Bouchard galloped the palomino toward the far edge of the lake, dismounted and ran toward the fallen man.

"He's dead this time, *monseigneur*," Jouvert complacently chuckled, planting the stock of his musket on the moist earth. "This time I didn't miss, as I promised him I wouldn't."

"But why, Jouvert?"

"*Monseigneur*, you ask me that?" The gamekeeper's jaw dropped and his eyes were blank with stupefaction. "But it's the law. That's Pierre Louvier, and even your father, the great *seigneur*, will tell you he's been poaching the estate these last ten years."

"But to kill a man over a rabbit—we can spare such provender for a man who needs food, Jouvert." Lucien's voice was choked, and he clenched his fists to restrain the fury that swirled inside him. The little poacher lay sprawled, face down, his hands grasping the still struggling rabbit, a trickle of blood oozing from the horrid wound in his neck.

"That's not for me to say, your lordship," the gamekeeper sullenly growled, squinting down at his musket and shifting his booted feet. "All I know is, poaching's against the law, and don't you think old Louvier didn't know it all these years. He's got a little hovel on the other side of that hill, but he works when he pleases, hires himself out to the blacksmith now and again. But mostly, he's been living off the *seigneur*'s land. And it's more than rabbits he's poached, I tell you."

Lucien de Bouchard drew a deep breath, controlling himself. "And his family? Does he have one?"

"Oui, *monseigneur*, an old hag and three brats. But then, they can hie themselves off to old *Père* Morlain, he'll find charity for them. That's not my concern."

"Then, since you know so much, I want Christian burial for this man. Do you understand, Jouvert? And I myself will give his widow some money and my promise to fend for her and her children. Get you gone to the priest then, and see to it that this poor fellow's taken care of as I ordered, *comprenez-vous*?"

"I'll do it, *monseigneur*. But I still say, it's the law. I was only doing what your father had me do. Don't blame me for it, *monseigneur*."

19

Lucien de Bouchard mounted the palomino, glanced back a last time at the sprawled, lifeless body of the little poacher. "No, Jouvert, I don't blame you. I blame the laws that led to such a waste of human life."

CHAPTER TWO

He looked back a last time at the dead poacher to see the stout gamekeeper bend down, grumbling, and roll the inert body onto its back. With a shudder of revulsion, Lucien de Bouchard turned Arabe to the winding, narrow pathway through the thick forest which led up to the hill beyond whose peak he could see the not far distant chateau of André-Charles de Courent, once a Paris *avocat* and now resplendent in the title of Lord Provost-Marshal of Normandy. The chateau, to be sure, was smaller than that of Lucien's father, but its interior was far more luxurious, undoubtedly a result of the influence of Madame Lucette de Courent, herself the daughter of a wealthy wine merchant who had served both Louis XV and his grandson who now sat upon the throne of France.

As Lucien attained the top of the forested hill, he felt the cold, damp wind tug at his coattails. The sky was still more ominously gray, darker still because twilight was at hand. For a moment Lucien halted the palomino and thrust his hands into the pocket of his coat to assure himself that his newest verse for Edmée lay neatly folded. In it, he had spoken of the *"demoiselle avec des beaux yeux qui me fait rever,"* and gone on in amateurish but ardent Alexandrine lines to relate to her how those laughing, bewitching eyes had emboldened him to wish to gaze into them for the rest of his days. He thought to himself that he had watched her grow from flirtatious child-woman to a young enchantress who, even though she might take on

21

the staid role of wife, would still retain her verve and wit and charm, and so keep him ever constant and desirous of her. Though his own mother was almost self-effacing in contrast with Edmée, he nonetheless could understand how his gruff, blustering old father had remained faithful and devoted all these years. Well, he could pledge to Edmée the same kind of devotion. Yet he wished that he had chosen a better afternoon than this, already haunted for him by the unforgettable sight of the little poacher's death and by the raw wind and the dreary sky. Nevertheless, he had told her last week that he would call on such and such a day at such and such an hour, and it had been all that he could do to endure the week of waiting until at last he would ask her to marry him. All that he could be sure of at this moment was that she had given him back his kiss and told him that she longed to see him. Well, that augured good fortune even on such an afternoon as this.

A stableboy hurried out to take Arabe's reins and to nod deferentially to the sturdy young man in the brown coat and riding breeches who strode purposefully to the porticoed door of the chateau. There he was admitted by a grave, liveried footman, dressed even more colorfully than his own father's servants, for Madame de Courent sought wherever possible to retain her memories of the elegant luxury of the French and the finest fashions in both decor and costume. He was introduced into the salon where Edmée's father sat, with one gouty leg resting on a thick cushion placed upon a little footstool before him, sipping a glass of excellent Malaga from the Canary Islands from an exquisitely wrought crystal goblet.

"Ah, Lucien, my boy, it's a pleasure to see you again," the provost-marshal greeted him, gesturing with his glass to the footman. "Another glass for my guest, François."

"Thank you for your hospitality, Your Excellency." Lucien bowed stiffly. He observed that the provost-marshal's fat, faintly pockmarked face expressed a greater conviviality than he had previously observed at other meetings. This time, the king's officer in Normandy was actually beaming at him, even chuckling, as again he lifted his glass as if to toast Lucien.

"Why should I not extend the warmest hospitality to the fine son of a family with whom I look forward to having the most felicitous of alliances" was André-Charles de Courent's effusive explanation of his jovial mood.

Lucien permitted himself a hopeful smile. This was better than he had hoped for. He knew, to be sure, and well in advance, what obstacles there might be to his proposed request for the hand of Edmée; by the laws of primogeniture, Edmée would not become a countess if she married him. Yet so sure was he of her affection for him and of his own even deeper feelings for her that he had not allowed that impediment to overcome his inward assurance that such matters were only superficial and that the heart would decide rather than the calculating mind. "You do me a great honor, Your Excellency," he inclined his head, this time with a grateful smile.

"Come now, no false modesty, my boy!" the provost-marshal boomed, setting down his glass on a lacquered tabouret. "It's not often that an old man gains two fine, nobly bred sons by uniting the one with his only daughter. Yes, Lucien, once the banns are read by your village priest, you shall see how warmly Madame and I shall receive you here at the chateau."

"Why, Your Excellency, I want nothing better than to be your son, once I've married Edmée. For so wonderful a girl could not have come about had it not been for two such estimable parents as yourself and Madame."

The gouty provost-marshal scowled, beckoned to the approaching footman to fill his glass after the latter had tendered one to Lucien, and then squinted quizzically at the young man before him whom he had still not bidden to a seat. "Marry Edmée?" he echoed. "But you are having your little jest, Lucien, are you not? I had thought that your brother would be here ahead of you, and so I assumed—"

"What did you assume, my lord Provost-Marshal?" Lucien stiffened, his fingers tightening around the stem of the goblet and staring uncomprehendingly at the king's officer.

"Why, *morbleu*, that you'd come here to pay your respects, *bien sûr*."

"And so I have, as well as to ask you for the hand of your daughter Edmée in marriage to me, my lord Provost-Marshal."

"Can it be—no, I believe you are not informed, then. What a pity—how unfortunate—if I had only known—" the fat little man reddened with embarrassed confusion.

Lucien's eyes narrowed and his lips tightened. "Are you trying to tell me, my lord Provost-Marshal, that you did not expect me to ask for the hand of your daughter? But I have visited your chateau many times these past years, as you and Madame well know, and it was my intention this very afternoon to announce to you my heartfelt desire in the matter."

"This is really regrettable, my boy. Do you mean to tell me that Jean hasn't already told you, or your parents either?"

"No one has told me."

"I regret this infinitely, my poor Lucien. But that was why I welcomed you as another son, don't you understand? You see, your brother, scarcely two weeks ago, did us the honor of asking us to bless the union between himself and our daughter."

Lucien turned pale and with only a great effort kept from breaking the costly crystal goblet. Recovering himself, he turned and set it down upon a sideboard. "I regret having disturbed you, then, my lord Provost-Marshal. If you would indulge me in one last request, a boon out of the hospitality you offered just now, might I talk with Edmée alone?"

"But of course, my boy. Well, one would say that we were back in Paris, n'est-ce pas? A romance and a broken heart, all in the same family and neither knowing it—it's like something out of Molière, isn't it?"

"I do not see the humor of it at the moment, but you will pardon my sentiments, I am sure, my lord Provost-Marshal."

"Yes, I understand. I deeply regret this. I wish you might have known it so that I was not the one to give you such unhappy news, Lucien. Ah, here's Edmée now. Take her into the little salon across the hall, my boy. I'm sure you'll understand when she explains to you."

24

Lucien turned and saw a slim, dark-brown-haired girl elegantly clad in a crepe de Chine frock over which she had drawn a furred pelisse. Her face was oval, a delicate cameo, with high-set cheekbones and a dainty little Grecian nose and a small but ripe and—he realized now with a sense of tortured loss—extremely kissable mouth. As he turned to confront her, Edmée de Courent quickly put a hand to her mouth and then, recovering, curtsied. "It's good to see you, dear Lucien," she said in a sweet, clear voice.

"Edmée, you've my permission to talk to Lucien in the salon across the way. He has something to say to you, *ma belle pigeonne,* and I count on you to bring the smile back to his face again," the provost-marshal solicitously urged.

"Thank you, Your Excellency. My apologies for disturbing you. If you will do me the honor, *Mademoiselle?*" He offered her his arm, and Edmée took it, glancing back at her father with widened eyes and heightened color in her creamy cheeks, then whispered to him, "I couldn't get a message to you before this. But we'll talk about it once Papa can't hear us. Come along, dear Lucien."

She opened the door and drew him inside, then swiftly closed it and moved close to him, a provocative smile on her red lips. "I couldn't tell you before this, not even last week. You see, *m'amour,* Jean asked me to keep it a secret until the banns could be read."

"Then you knew—even when I told you last week that I had something most important to tell you when I next came—you had already pledged yourself to my brother?"

"Shh, Lucien! Don't look at me so coldly!" She reached up a hand to touch his cheek and then, with a soft little laugh, pressed her lips to his. "Don't you remember how surprised I was when you kissed me the last time? How I told you that you might turn my head? And so you have, *mon cher.* And it doesn't mean that we shan't be the very dearest of friends even if I must marry Jean."

"That cold wind from the Channel seems to have dulled my wits, Edmée. I don't follow you, it seems."

"Oh, Lucien, you're the wise one, you've all the schooling and no one can write such wonderful poems to me—I know Jean never could or would. But don't you see, *m'amour?* It's a great honor for a girl to become a countess, to marry into one of the oldest families in all of France. My mother and my father will be so proud—father's title of nobility is so new and it's only because the King created the post for him here, you see."

"Let me understand you, Edmée. You are going to marry my brother to become a countess? I thought you understood that if you and I wed that would not be possible. So that's the prize you seek?"

"You put it so badly, *m'amour.* Think of the lovely poems you've written to me—and I'm sure you brought one today of all days, didn't you?"

"I did. But of that, no matter now. I want an answer."

"But I've given you one and I thought you understood beyond it. Must you shame me by asking more?"

She stepped forward, in the same movement shrugging off the loosely draped pelisse so that her dimpled bare shoulders and the almost too brazenly displayed cleavage between her high-perched, firm, round creamy breasts were displayed. Her slim hands grasped his shoulders almost urgently as she whispered, "You who are so wise in book learning and so naive in worldly things, Lucien—can't you guess what I mean—do you wish to shame me by explaining?"

His face flooded with crimson; the nearness of her, the spicy scent of her perfume, made his senses swirl, and it was only with a strong effort at self-mastery that he was able to respond, his features unrelentingly stiffened: "I am afraid I do not quite catch your meaning."

She made a wry face, and, coquettishly, lowering her large, glowing eyes, murmured, "Either it's that, or it's that you don't wish to, *m'amour.* Reflect a moment—my mother is unhappy here in this wretched little village, far from her friends and the gaiety of the court to which she has *carte blanche,* because my grandfather has catered to two kings and is well received by royalty. And as I am her dutiful daughter, I sorrow with her that we are isolated here in this rustic province. But if I should marry and become a countess, link myself thus with one of the oldest and noblest families in all France, *cher* Lucien, then *Maman* will feel that at last we are restored to high estate."

Grudgingly he conceded, "I can comprehend that. But what does it have to do with you and me, Edmée?"

Her fingers dug into his shoulders as again she grimaced, this time with annoyance. She moved even closer, till her firm young bosom brushed his chest, as she whispered, *"Mais tu es vraiment imbecile, je pense!* Even your brother is more tolerant and he is older than you. Oh, I am truly furious with you, Lucien. So I shall marry him and give him the heir he wishes for the title, but after that, you may be sure he will take his pleasure where he will, nor will it greatly matter to me. For then, don't you see, you unsmiling great bear, that we can have our own little amusements."

He stepped back now, disengaging himself from her almost feverish embrace, stunned by the divination of what she was saying, for it was at violent contrast with the concept he had created of her. This was no budding delectably ripening girl on the threshold of womanhood, retaining all the charming caprices of adolescence and childhood with the more inscrutable promise of rich maturity and lasting, devoted union to the man she chose. Instead, he might have been conversing with one of the calculating if highborn courtesans of the court. And the knowledge sickened him, knowing Jean for what he was, a cynical opportunist, amoral with those beneath his aristocratic rank and with all women whom he regarded as mere purveyors of lustful pleasure to his selfish needs. His voice trembled as, collecting his thoughts, he at last managed: "Then even last week, when you returned my kiss and encouraged me to visit your father—when you must have guessed what I would have to say to him—you were even then betrothed to my brother?"

Edmée de Courent's eyes narrowed with impatience. "Are you no more than a clod of a peasant then, with all your fine learning, your endless poems, your show of caring for me?"

"Show?" he uttered a bitter laugh. "You appear to have misread my feelings as much as I seem to have misread yours."

"Ohh! Was there ever such a leaden-minded man as you, Lucien!" she exasperatedly burst out. "Of course I care for you. It was—it is still—exciting to know that for all your stiff-necked, awkward manner, you desire me. But I must be practical too, *chéri*. I'll marry Jean even if I do not love him—though I admit—" this teasingly, with a provocative little smile that made him tremble with suppressed fury—"he is more direct with a woman than you are. Till you were bold enough last week to kiss me as I want to be kissed, Lucien. Then I knew I hadn't mistaken my feelings for you—and when Jean tires of me and I've fulfilled the function for which, I'm told, girls marry, why then I'll be yours. Now do you understand at last, you wicked, heartless bully, to force a girl to be so shameless?"

"Yes, Edmée, I understand at last, as you say. But that was never my desire or intention. I want—I wanted—to marry you."

"I shouldn't mock you so, *chéri*." Now she was all contrition, cloying sweetness, as she wound her supple arms round his neck and brushed his lips with hers. "You're the very soul of honor, everything Jean is not. All the more reason, then, why I want you as my lover. But I can't marry you. It would break *Maman*'s heart—"

Lucien slowly disengaged her arms, his hands gentle but insistent on her slim wrists. "As it would break yours not to be the Countess de Bouchard. Yes, Edmée, I understand it perfectly. I don't judge you for it—who am I to judge, knowing that I could never give you that title unless my brother died? But you were right in speaking of my honor. I should discredit it, as I should my father's and yours as well, were I to agree to such a *ménage*. And so, I thank you for your frankness, and I take my leave of you, *Mademoiselle* de Courent."

He bowed to her, then strode out of the little salon and out of the chateau. Outside, as he waited for the stableboy to bring Arabe to him, the sky was now as dark as the melancholy, bitter anguish that filled his soul.

"You've hardly touched your food, Lucien, *mon fils*," old Étienne grumbled as he impatiently nodded to his footman to pour more Burgundy into his twice-emptied glass. "Doesn't Lemaire's treatment of the partridge meet with your approval?"

Lucien, seated across the table from his brother, did not look up as he took a sip of wine, then grimaced as if he found it sour. "It's quite good, actually, *mon père*," he agreed. "But it's a rabbit that has turned my stomach."

"But we've had no rabbit served this evening. What the devil are you thinking of?" The old Count's shaggy eyebrows arched quizzically.

"Of a rabbit in a snare that cost the life of a man. The price was much too high, and it was a very small rabbit," Lucien said slowly.

"It appears that you are speaking in riddles this evening," Étienne de Bouchard testily retorted, scowling from his place at the head of the long table at his younger son. "What's all this of rabbits and snares and too high a price, if you please, Lucien?"

"Late this afternoon, I saw Jouvert shoot poor little Pierre Louvier."

"Oh, is that it, now? But I'll have you know that Louvier has plagued my estate for a decade and more, and Jouvert was certainly within his rights. Have you forgotten that it is the law of the land that poaching is punishable by death if the *seigneur* so rules? I assure you, Lucien, that it was a game that the rogue played, and he knew the stakes very well. Of course I am sorry for him, and, no doubt, his widow and brats, but he knew the risk he ran."

"The price was still too high, my father. And now of all times, when there is unrest in France, unrest against all of us who are born to privilege—"

"Mordieu!" The old count slammed his fist down upon the table and the plates and silverware clattered to its impact. "You begin to sound like one of the rabble, Lucien. Do you tell me to my face and at my own table that you find my rule over my fief unjust and inhuman? By comparison, *M'sieu* the student of the University of Paris, I assure you that even our little village priest considers me benevolent. There will be no uprising of our peasants here in Normandy. And if there are those who feel that I have dealt harshly with a poacher, they have only to refer

29

themselves to the edict which came from the throne itself. Let them blame Louis the Carpenter. If his grandfather were still alive, we should have no rebellion in France today."

"On the contrary, my father, it was exactly the extravagance, the corruption and immorality of Louis XV which brought about our present catastrophe. One cannot blame his grandson, who by nature prefers hunting and his workshop to his royal duties. And there is also the matter of his unpopular queen, Marie Antoinette, whose intrigues led to the dismissal of able ministers like Turgot and then Necker. It is much too late to have summoned Necker back; the damage was done long ago."

"Heaven deliver me from this revolutionary cant!" the old Count exploded. "All of this outburst over a rabbit and the stupidity of a poacher who was clumsy enough to let himself be caught. Let me have an end of it, if you please.

"Perhaps I understand Lucien's *morgue,* my father," Jean suavely interposed. "It is not the rabbit which concerns Lucien, but the affections of a certain *Mademoiselle* Edmée de Courent."

Lucien turned pale and stiffened, his eyes fixed on his handsome brother, who had changed his attire for the evening meal and under his fine maroon waistcoat wore an elegant silk shirt with ruffled sleeves and collar, which his long aristocratic fingers narcissistically touched even as he spoke.

"May the devil take me if I understand what either of you means to tell me," the old Count growled, glowering first at Jean and then at Lucien.

"Why, it's quite simple. You know, my father, you've been after me to marry and present you with a grandson. Well, since I have already obtained the consent of the provost-marshal and his charming wife, as well as that of their daughter herself, you may have the banns announced between myself and *Mademoiselle* Edmée," Jean indolently drawled. "As to my brother, he has had quite a poetic and romantic infatuation for her—which does credit, I hasten to assure him, to his good taste. But of course the young lady was practical enough to choose me over Lucien because he cannot make her a countess. Also, I am older and more mature in such matters of the heart, whereas Lucien mistakes the scribbling of verse for *la grande passion,* you see."

With a visible effort, Lucien controlled himself. Forcing his voice to remain steady, he ignored his brother's smirking look of triumph as he addressed his father: "It is true that I permitted myself the small hope that *Mademoiselle* de Courent would favor me, though I also knew why she would prefer my brother. But that is not what distresses me so much as it is to find you oblivious to what you call a rebellion of the rabble. Who will defend Louis XVI if the revolution sweeps over all of France—perhaps the Swiss Guard and a few hundred mercenaries who will be tempted by the booty that would fall to the more powerful conquerors. My father, the feudal age is dying, and it may die more violently than any of us here tonight dare believe or imagine. When it dies, all your rights will be swept away if the Third Estate is granted an equal vote with those of the aristocracy."

"Nonsense! Do you forget the centuries by which my forefathers held this land against war and oppression, plague and famine, religious persecution and insurrections?"

"I forget nothing, but we learn so little from history, my father," Lucien soberly replied. "In the Middle Ages, when only the priests and the high nobility could read and write, there were grievous wrongs done to the poor peasants who toiled on their rich lands. But today the people are no longer so ignorant and superstitious as in those medieval times. And if, as I am certain, Louis XVI is overthrown, what will become of your right to command forced labor, your right to the first vintage of all wines pressed from the grapes upon your lands, the taxes which you levy, not only for the King of France but to maintain this vast estate?"

"You go too far, Lucien! Take care!" the old Count thundered, again clenching his gnarled fist and pressing it down hard against the table as he glared at his younger son.

"I know the history of our forebears, my father. I know how they fought to hold these lands. But they were given through the grant of a king many hundreds of years ago, before men could dream of liberty and equality."

"*Tais-toi!* That's enough, Lucien!" His father half-rose from the table, his face mottled with rage.

"But although the people have changed, the rights of the aristocracy, of those born to privilege, have not been altered by one jot or tittle," Lucien calmly went on. "Men and animals are called to field labor, taxes are put upon bridges over streams, over wells that are sunk upon land to bring water to the peasants. Even the humblest villager here at Yves-sur-lac must pay a tax on his own hearth, for the right of dovecot and of fire, and he may not fish or hunt, it being a capital offense—as poor Louvier learned this afternoon."

"Will you ally yourself, then, with the scum of the Paris vagabonds, the riffraff who are as changeable as the wind itself and who have loyalty neither to king nor law nor to themselves if truth be known?" Étienne de Bouchard trembled with ill-concealed fury as he glared across the table at his defiant younger son.

"I say only, my father, that it is high time we learned from the pages of history that men should be free and given the chance to earn their livelihood as in a kind of commune, a brotherhood which recognizes their dignity as it does their toil and does not take all from them in the name of taxation and the king. Yes, by birth, by education and by your own wisdom, my father, you have earned the right to lead this province, to guide it wisely. But with the storm that gathers over France, you would do well to give freedom to the peasants and to hire them as honest workers, and—"

"I will hear no more in my own house! And you dare preach loyalty to me, you, my own flesh and blood, who defend these base revolutionaries who would bring us to anarchy and destroy the nation? Spare me your quotations from that dangerous madman Voltaire, for I recognize his sentiments only too well in your mouthings this evening, Lucien."

32

"I will do more than that, my father." Lucien stood erect, his face grave, as Laurette de Bouchard, at the other end of the table, uttered a stifled cry of anguish, tears glistening in her widened blue eyes. "To prove to you that I have no ambition save to make my own way to the best of my own natural abilities with which God has endowed me, and so also that my brother may have no fear that I stand between him and his ultimate succession to you as Count of Normandy, I will seek a new land that has neither king nor rabble to shape its future, but only the spirit and the energy of those who come to it to begin a new world."

"My son, oh, Lucien, you cannot mean what you are saying—no, you mustn't think of leaving France," his mother sobbed.

He turned to her, his face gentle, his voice apologetic. "But I must, dear mother. I haven't yet earned the privileges which come with birth, you see. When I work with the peasants tilling the soil, when I see old Jacquinot and Rizarde bring in the herds, then I feel there is purpose in my existence on this land. I would rather be my own man, farming my own land, a stranger in a new country, than an usurper."

"Am I, then, an usurper too, Lucien?" the old Count demanded, his voice shaking with suppressed fury.

"No, my father, and it is true that you are kindly and compassionate to your peasants in the main. But once Louis XVI is stripped of his powers, so will you be of yours, you and all the other nobles. It may be that you will even be condemned for your fidelity to the throne and to the ancient feudal laws which can no longer prevail in an age of enlightened reason when men everywhere seek an end to oppression, whether it be by taxation or coercion. Do not be angry with me, my father. There is still time before this storm breaks upon France to weather it. Let your land be parceled out and given in free title to your villagers, and let them share their earnings so that the tithes to the king or whatever governing body will one day rule France may be paid honorably and without exorbitance."

"I will hear no more, I tell you! Go then, to your brave new world, your mythical domain where there is no king and no law—and where will it be, Lucien?"

Again Lucien stared gravely at his father. Then, very softly and gently, he replied, "To the untouched frontier which lies beyond the new thirteen colonies of America. Many have gone there already, my father. The Marquis de Santerre, the Vicomte de Treves-sur-mont and many others."

"Cowards and traitors to their king, those two, and all who follow like the rats that would desert the sinking ship, when as yet there is no danger," his father angrily countered. They stared at each other like two adversaries across the table, the old Count glowering, his black-haired son grave and silent. The Countess de Bouchard had buried her face in her hands and was silently weeping. And then, bowing his head, Lucien murmured, "I did not mean to make you unhappy, my dear mother, or you either, my father. I ask your pardon. But my mind is decided upon the matter, and I shall leave for Le Havre as soon as I have made my preparations."

"Go, then, since you are so stubbornly determined to abandon your family, boy!" Étienne de Bouchard's voice wavered to belie his scornful mien. "But if you go, you are no longer my son. I have only Jean, my first-born. I will not give you a single *sou* to make a cowardly *émigré* out of you."

"I have not asked you for alms, my father, nor shall I ever. And now I have the honor of bidding you a very good evening," Lucien said as, with a stiff bow to the old man, and a lingering, almost contrite look at his sorrowing mother, he left the dining salon.

At the sound of the faint tap on his door, Lucien rose from his writing desk, a half-finished letter lying before him. Setting down his quill and with a somber face, he opened the door to admit his mother. The Countess Laurette de Bouchard wore an exquisite white satin peignoir, and her large, reproachful blue eyes which she dabbed at with a lace kerchief, were swollen with tears.

"I am distressed to see you so, mother," Lucien solicitously said. "As you can see, I was writing a letter which perhaps will better explain to father the sentiments which prompt me to leave the chateau. But I intended to talk with you before my departure."

"I cannot believe it, to this moment I cannot believe it, dear Lucien!" the Countess groaned as she seated herself and twisted her kerchief between her soft hands. "I know—you're in love with that forward little minx, who isn't really worthy of you, dear Lucien. But surely you can't think of leaving us just because she's ambitious enough to marry your brother? You will find a girl worthy of you, one who knows your honesty and goodness of heart. I beg of you, don't grieve me for the rest of my days by abandoning your father and me. He's too proud to say such things to you, but I—I who bore you and watched you become a man, it will kill me not to see you again!"

He bent and kissed her on the forehead, and for a moment his eyes misted with tears. Then straightening, almost impatient of his emotion, he said calmly, "It's not just Edmée, dear mother. I meant every word that I said at the table tonight. And you would do well to think of your own safety by leaving France. You can go to England, or to Flanders. For what is coming will be a terrible, bloody uprising that will change the very nature of France, level the old feudal laws as it will the fine chateaux of the nobility."

"But, dear Lucien, the people of Normandy are industrious, gentle and undemanding. They will not turn against us. Even old *Père* Morlain has told us how much we are loved in Yves-sur-lac."

Lucien shook his head. "Once Louis XVI is made to abdicate, as I know he will be, there will be ungovernable mobs throughout every province of France, those who will loot and kill until their saner leaders bring about a balance to a new nation. That is what I fear most of all for you and father. But as for myself, I do not leave France as a coward, but rather to begin a new life where my love for the land and for the people on it will have useful harvesting."

"Where will you go, Lucien?"

"By ship from Le Havre to New Orleans, where, as you know, there are already many *émigrés* as well as the Acadians who were returned to France from Canada many years ago. Once there, I will make inquiries and find my way to free land upon which I can settle and farm and begin a new life."

"And—and you mean to go alone?" His mother's voice quavered with her anguish as she stared poignantly at him.

"Young Edmond, the stableboy, has begged me to take him with me. I shall take Arabe, you see. Father will not miss him. Our groom, Bertrand, whom Edmond hopes to replace, is in his early thirties. Besides, Edmond's parents died last year of the flux, and his only kin is a drunken uncle in the village."

"Then, if your mind and heart are set upon it, Lucien, I cannot hold you back. All my prayers and my love will go with you. And this also—for you will need substance in your new world." The Countess rose, drew a magnificent cabochon ruby ring from her finger and placed it on his ring finger. "It was my grandmother's, Lucien. Honoré, the famous Paris jeweler, valued it at two thousand golden louis. It will perhaps not bring so much in your new world, but it will at least keep you from starvation. And before you go, I will give you a purse of a hundred golden louis. That is your share of the *rentes*."

"I will keep the ring in constant memory of you, my mother. The gold I will take as my hire for the work I have done on this estate. And I shall repay it to father many times over."

Laurette de Bouchard burst into tears, and then, clinging to him, buried her tear-streaked face against his chest.

CHAPTER THREE

It was noon of the next day, and this time the sun shone brightly without a cloud to hide it over the fields of Yves-sur-lac. Lucien had packed his effects—and these were few, comprising only a few necessary changes of clothing for the journey—into a leather *sac de nuit* and attached it securely to the back of the saddle which he himself had fixed upon the spirited palomino. Beside him, Edmond Vignon, only a few months past his eighteenth birthday, slender, with curly light-brown hair and an engaging, innocent face, was adjusting the cinches on a docile piebald mare which Bertrand had given him as a parting gift. And with it, too, a word of advice, basking as the Count's groom was in the strengthening of his own post: "*Va t'en donc,* boy, it's the wisest course for you to follow. You're a moonsick calf over that *petite* Madelon in the village, everyone knows that. Going with your new master to a distant land may make a man of you. And he will be a fine master if you'll but follow his counsel."

Edmond had blushed and mumbled an inaudible acknowledgment of both gift and advice. It was true that whenever he had been sent to the village on one errand or another for the count, he had dallied in his return until he could catch a glimpse of the pretty foundling who had been adopted by the old blacksmith and his wife. But he knew only too well what little chance he had of marrying her, with only paltry wages and his keep and his apprenticeship as a virtual serf to the old *seigneur*. That was why he was even now speechless with gratitude at Lucien's having brought about this seemingly miraculous freedom. And all because, late yesterday afternoon, when he had taken Arabe to the stable he had impulsively exclaimed, "What I wouldn't give to ride with you, my lord, to look after you and Arabe!" And Lucien had stared at him oddly for a moment, then uttered a bitter little laugh and replied, "Even if it meant leaving France, would you still follow me, Edmond?" And now, he who had never been a league beyond this little village was about to accompany his kind young master to the port of Le Havre and thence across the great ocean to the new world of America. For a moment, he had suddenly remembered Madelon, but with the bright optimism of youth, he had consoled himself by thinking that there would be other girls, perhaps even prettier. And then too, if he worked beside his master and was industrious and loyal, he would be paid wages which he could save until he could afford a wife. It was a glorious day, with all the adventure of the unknown awaiting him and a journey to that distant land of which he knew so little!

Lucien de Bouchard laughed softly as the beautiful palomino whinnied and thrust its nose, snuffling, against his chest. "You smell the carrot I brought you, don't you, Arabe? Well, here it is, then. It's the longest journey you'll have made for me, good friend. And there'll be miles of new countryside for you to race upon when I give you your head. Now, I've packed lightly so as not to tire you too much before we find our new home." The palomino tossed its head and whinnied again. Then, vaulting into the saddle, Lucien turned to the eager stripling: "We'll stop at the rectory for a moment, Edmond. I've said my goodbyes, but I want *Père* Morlain's blessing. After that, we'll take the road through Bolbec. There's no great haste, we'll make the port by early afternoon tomorrow, and the *Guerrière* sails with the evening tide."

He rode ahead, Edmond following at a deferential distance behind, the boy still awed not only by his good fortune but also by the thought that he had been chosen to serve the son of the great *seigneur*. And Lucien's last words had made him quiver with secret delight; perhaps there would be time for a meeting with Madelon, perhaps when he told her of the wonderful destiny that was to be his, she might even agree to wait until he could return to France with his fortune made. And perhaps a kiss for the sake of *au revoir*.

Lucien turned in his saddle to look back at the chateau, to remember it standing so sturdily amid the green of the fields and the slopes of the hills under the blue sky. How dourly resolute it was, commanding the stretch of fields below it, two stories of the finest red brick, with a tower flanking it at each end. The long, rectangular windows with their shining glass panes provided an unhampered view of the orchards and of the grassy incline toward the hill along which cattle grazed over toward the right of this peaceful landscape. Before the entrance was the imposing portico with its heavy white-oak pillars and its roof like an isosceles triangle, with three broad stone steps ascending to its porch. But it was from the towers that, as a boy, he had always surveyed this beautiful country. At first, when very young, pretending that from its height he could make out the ocean so many miles beyond and see the masts of the Viking ships or, even more romantically, those which flew the black flag of the freebooters. Later, he watched from there to feel himself at perfect kinship with the toilers on the rich, gentle land and to know an abiding love for that land from which the priceless bounty of the food that meant life would come.

One day, he promised himself, with God's help and his own purposeful strength, he would build a home for himself and whomever fate decreed should share his life . . . a home that would be exactly like the chateau of the old *seigneur*. In that way, perhaps, he could continue the proud lineage of the Bouchards, and this time without the hampering obstacles of ancient servitude imposed upon those who would toil with him to build the home and to help him work the land.

He told himself that it was not out of impulse that he took this sixty-kilometer journey to what would be the finite end of his life in France. True, Edmée's inconstancy had staggered him more than he cared to admit; he had believed that with her wit and charm she would take the long view of life and foresee a happier one with him than with his shallow, pleasure-seeking brother. Yet for the past few months, ever since the uprising in Brittany and the other signs of discontent throughout the land, Lucien had kept himself informed of sailings from the great port. And indeed, if Edmée had chosen him yesterday, he would have poured forth all his persuasive and sincere eloquence to urge her to come with him on the *Guerrière* to begin a new life and to care nothing for the trappings of this doomed aristocracy which could surely not survive the hate-festered poverty of those whom his father had so contemptuously called the rabble.

Just before the road turned along the orchards, Lucien reined in Arabe for a last look at the chateau, as well as to make sure that the leather saddlebag was securely tied and no burden to the palomino. He felt drained of emotion. His father had made short shrift of his farewell; the old Count had coldly wished him well and irately refused to listen to his plea that the family earnestly consider leaving France before it was too late. So, cut off short and flushing with agonized embarrassment to have been so summarily dismissed by the sire he had loved and respected all his life, Lucien had left the letter he had written the night before on his father's *escritoire* and then, alone with his mother for the last time, he had repeated his deep concern for the future of this entire province, urged his mother to prevail upon the old Count to read his letter and, forgetting all concern for its writer, to consider in all practical wisdom the imperative need to anticipate the coming holocaust and to escape its inevitable destruction.

Finally, he had gone to his brother's bedchamber, where Jean indolently was consuming a late breakfast of fruit, *café au lait* and *croissants*. His blond brother had cynically greeted him: "So you're really going, after all? But if it's because of Edmée, after all, there's no real need, my sentimental brother. She's already hinted at a certain interest in you, and when she's served her purpose and given me an heir, by then I'll have entered the Royalist service with the King's own commission and will doubtless serve him in Paris. As you know, I'm fond of that city and its delightful and obliging women, so I shan't mind too much if you and Edmée amuse yourselves in my absence. Within limits, of course, for I should detest learning from others that my own brother has cuckolded me, you understand."

If Lucien had for a moment thought of turning back upon his resolve to leave France, his brother's amoral parting speech would assuredly have driven away all such indecision. Very coldly, masking the sudden unreasoning fury which had seized him, Lucien had retorted, "I should be the last one in the world to give you cause to impute such infidelity to your future wife. I wish you both all happiness, though I myself could not be too hopeful of this commission of which you speak. It may last no longer than Louis's days upon the throne, which I believe to be numbered. Well then, Jean, I bid you *adieu*."

With a heavy sigh, Lucien nodded to the bright-faced stripling behind him. Half an hour later, he dismounted in front of the rectory and bade Edmond hold the reins. He could not help smiling to himself at the way the youth glanced around, obviously eager to catch a glimpse of pretty Madelon.

"My son, it's good to see you!" The little priest came forward to greet him. "I was sorry to have missed you yesterday afternoon on my visit to your father."

"I've come to take my leave of you, *Père* Morlain, and to ask your blessing."

"Take your leave of me? What do you mean, Lucien?"

"Tomorrow I shall sail on the *Guerrière* for New Orleans. I mean to cultivate my own garden, just as Voltaire advised."

The little priest crossed himself. "Then you do not share my view that even if the king should be deposed, sanity will prevail?"

"I cannot, *mon père*. But I came also to ask this; when I reach the new land I seek, you will send me the news of my father and mother and of my brother Jean as well. My destination is New Orleans, and I am not certain what it will be thereafter, but I am sure that if you write the governor-general there, your letter will find me. And I ask you also to advise my parents to leave France as soon as they can."

The priest sighed and lowered his eyes, again making the sign of the cross. "Yesterday, I should not have agreed with you, my son. I am not a worldly man and my creed is to render unto *le bon Dieu* and to the Louis who is our Caesar that which is his upon this earth. But when I returned from my visit to your esteemed father, I found tragedy here in our little village. Madelon came to me weeping to confess her great sin and to beg absolution for it. She accused herself of the death of the young stable-boy."

"He died? But how?"

"It appears—" the little priest's voice shook—"that your brother claimed the *droit de seigneur* with poor Madelon, and that when the boy attempted to stop him, your brother ran him through with his sword. I have told myself that this is the feudal law of France and has been so for centuries, but in the eyes of God it is still murder and lust. Madelon has locked herself in a little room in this rectory and I must try my best to comfort her. I can only pray for your brother and the boy. He was, as you may not have known, a foundling, like Madelon herself, and adopted by the same good people who took her as their child."

"My God, it's monstrous!" Lucien felt a sudden rage take possession of him. He was abandoning Edmée to the possession of a man who thought so little of life that he would kill an innocent child who sought to circumvent his sensual pleasures. Then, humbly, bowing his head, he at last murmured, "It is another frightful proof that the old France is dying and that it is time for a new order of justice and equality among men, *mon père*. I can only add my prayers to yours and ask you to take this little gold to say mass for the boy's soul and as a token to his foster parents in their grief." From the purse which his mother had given him, he counted out ten golden louis and pressed them into *Père* Morlain's hand.

"It is a sad leave-taking you make now, Lucien, my son. But I will carry out your wishes, especially as regards your mother. I can only hope that the news of Jean's cruelly thoughtless deed will not reach her—I have no doubt her losing you is bitter blow enough, my son." He shook his head sadly and then made the sign of the cross over Lucien's bowed head.

Lucien and Edmond rode through the gates of Le Havre and down the cobbled streets toward mid-afternoon of the next day, having stopped for the night at a little inn which marked the halfway point of their journey. As they rode toward the quays, the young stableboy gawked open-mouthed at the throngs. There were sturdy fishwives carrying baskets of herrings on their heads, their thick petticoats showing bare legs and feet, shrilly calling their wares. There were watermen with coarse woolen caps and loose, shaggy trousers rolled to the knees, as well as peasants in goatskin coats whose wooden shoes clattered on the round kidney-stones of the cobbled street. One could see shipwrights and workers from the docks, peddlers of all sorts of goods mingling with tradesmen in sober garments and merchants in long, fur-lined coats. At times the crowd made way for a two-horse cabriolet, warned by the whip-crackings and the loud shots of *"Gare!"* from the coachmen who conveyed rich merchants to the offices of the shipmasters. There was also the imposing carriage of a nobleman, with its escutcheoned panels and two white-stockinged, powdered footmen in vivid liveries hanging on behind. There were monks and priests in somber brown and black, and there were the usual wary *gendarmes* in blue coats and gaitered legs who moved about to make certain that order was preserved.

There were sailors, too, the *matelots* from Brittany, Rouen, Nantes, most of them French, but some of them English, Spanish and Dutch as well, who would put to sea on the tall, full-rigged ships whose proud masts Lucien could see beyond in that azure stretch which swept to the very horizon and beyond. And once again the sun shone brightly, as if there were not a shadow of doubt or gloom or despair to be seen in all of France.

From a surly *gendarme,* Lucien learned the location of the dock where the *Guerrière* lay at anchor and bade his young companion to follow his lead. One would not have taken Lucien de Bouchard for an aristocrat on this May afternoon, not in the modest, caped riding-coat of brown cloth with matching waistcoat and breeches, his knee-boots splashed with mud and his hair neither powdered nor bewigged. He wore the ring his mother had given him, the stone turned inward lest it attract the eye of some cutpurse.

When he reached the dock, he and Edmond dismounted, and Lucien made his way up the gangplank to seek the ship's purser, who stood on deck, legs straddled and studying the manifest.

"A good afternoon to you, *m'sieu*. Can you take two more passengers and their mounts?" he pleasantly asked.

The purser, a stocky, red-faced Breton, eyed him and appraised his worth in a single casual glance. "There's room if you've the passage money."

"What will you charge us, then?"

"Let's see now. For the two of you, unless this rogue of a boy with you eats like ten, say thirty golden louis. And for the horses, add another five and they'll be well quartered in the hold. It's not a full cargo we're taking to Havana and New Orleans on this journey, but mainly fancy aristocrats."

"I'm not one of those, *m'sieu*. Thirty-five louis, then, I believe you said?" Lucien smiled, drew out his purse and counted out the coins into the purser's pudgy hand.

By his reckoning, he had fifty-five *louis d'or* as his stake in the new world, plus Arabe and his own energy and skill. Well, there were doubtless many others before him who had set sail with far less of the world's material goods and yet they had persevered.

In the hold of the three-masted ship, he worked with Edmond to improvise rude stalls for Arabe and the pie-bald mare. And by then the shrill bleat of the boatswain's whistle announced the hour of departure.

Standing with Edmond beside him at the rail, Lucien stared down at the quay and the nameless faces of those, of all quality and degree, who watched the *Guerrière* draw anchor and move slowly away out to open sea. Then, when he had had his fill of all those sights, he

44

turned his head in the direction of Yves-sur-lac and in his mind's eye, saw for the last time the sturdy chateau where he had been born and which he was leaving behind forever.

CHAPTER FOUR

When Lucien signed the manifest of the *Guerrière*, he did so simply as "Lucien Bouchard of Yves-sur-lac." By this dropping of the preposition "de," he symbolized his own abdication of any hope of the title which his father presently held and which his brother must by French law inherit. He did it unhesitatingly, since in his own mind he had already abandoned any such aspirations on the fateful evening when Edmée de Courent had rejected him as a husband. Beyond that, however, he foresaw the practical value of Americanizing his name in this fashion, a feeling reinforced about two weeks after sailing by a chance conversation with Jabez Corrigan, the second mate of the vessel.

Jabez Corrigan was of sturdy, medium height, with an unruly shock of red hair, in his early forties, yet he spoke such excellent French that Lucien's curiosity was piqued. One evening, before supper, as was his wont, Lucien descended into the hold along with Edmond to feed Arabe a ration of oats and the palomino's favorite treat of a carrot. The second mate, at the suggestion of the purser, had descended below to inspect the cargo, and he grinned broadly when he saw the blackhaired young Frenchman affectionately nuzzled by Arabe in search of his expected carrot.

"What a superb animal, *m'sieu*," Jabez Corrigan volunteered. "One doesn't see many Arabian stallions like that and surely not on the *Guerrière*."

46

"Ah, you know something of horses, then, *mon ami.*" Lucien turned smilingly to the red-haired second mate.

"When I was a boy in County Cork, I was a champion rider," the second mate began, then scowled as if irritated with himself for revealing what was apparently his secret.

"I did not think that you were French by birth, *M'sieu* Corrigan," Lucien engagingly replied. "Indeed, I've been meaning to ask you how it is that you speak my native tongue so ably. I myself, at the University of Paris, made fair acquaintance with the English language, and I know a few words of Spanish as well."

"That will serve you well in the new world, *m'sieu.* Well, since you've as shrewd an eye for lineage as I have for horses, I'll say only that I was impressed into the British navy when I was scarcely older than this young friend of yours here," gesturing at Edmond. "I didn't much care for the rations or the cat-of-nine-tails, and so one rainy evening when we landed at Calais, I deserted and hid away until my ship had sailed off without me. I made my way to a farm in Brittany, worked in the fields there for some years until the old farmer gave me a small piece of land and I married his youngest daughter. Then, the love for the sea came back to me, and I signed on the *Guerrière* when she was first launched from the shipyards in Brest six years ago."

"That accounts for your fluent tongue indeed, *M'sieu* Corrigan. And your wife, and your children, are they still in Brittany?"

Jabez Corrigan's face darkened and he shook his head. "No, *m'sieu,* Blanchette died in childbirth. I've no doubt it was that which led me back to the sea. But you, *m'sieu,* I can see you're a man of quality. It's none of my business to ask why you're leaving France—though as you've seen for yourself, we've a few counts and marquises among our passengers who, like you, are bound for New Orleans. As for myself, I'm certainly not English, not with my Irish blood still hot in me, and I'm not a Froggie, either. This king of yours isn't long for his throne, I'll say that and hope you're not offended."

"No, you're quite right. Like you, *M'sieu* Corrigan—"

"It'll be Jabez to you, and here's my hand on it," the second mate interrupted as he offered his hand to Lucien.

"Then I'm Lucien to you, Jabez. As I was saying, I'm a farmer at heart, just as you were once, except that what's happening in France is likely to bring a harvest not of crops but of terror and bloodshed. I thought to myself, having read of the courage of those thirteen colonies which revolted against the tyranny of the English king, that I'd come to this new country and find land not yet settled upon, land where there's no need for politics or the choice of one king or one leader over another."

Jabez Corrigan pensively nursed his chin with his thickly callused hand. "Well now, I've set foot in New Orleans and Mobile several times these past six years, Lucien, *mon ami,* and I've seen and heard things about the country you'll be going to for the first time. Mostly, of course, it's under the Spanish now. Both New Orleans and Mobile, and then northward from Mobile is Indian country. But there's a cunning, clever man by the name of Alexander McGillivray, who has the ear of all the chiefs of the Creek Confederation, the tribes settling on that land now. It's country where a man could hide himself and make a new beginning—if he could get McGillivray's permit to trade with the Creeks."

"That might well suit my purpose, Jabez. These *sauvages rouges,* as we call them in France, were the very first settlers. I should think they would have little concern for politics, only the desire to thrive and to survive their adversities against the elements and the beasts of the forests."

"It's not all that simple, Lucien," Jabez Corrigan wryly chuckled. "First off, McGillivray's in the pay of the Spanish, and the Spanish have their own notions about trading. Also, they've more gold than your French king at the moment, and so they can give fine presents to the chiefs. Still and all, there's news that the Americans are making up to McGillivray to get him to allow their own white settlers to live in peace with the Creeks. So, as I say, if you could get to his ear and get him to like you, you'd have a powerful friend to start you off on your new life."

48

"I'm grateful for your advice, Jabez. How do I get to Mobile?"

"By flatboat from New Orleans, a journey of about two days. I've no doubt you'll be wanting to see the sights of New Orleans, though. And there are pretty girls there if that's the sort of adventure you fancy." He winked knowingly.

Lucien laughed delightedly. There was a refreshing honesty to the second mate, a good omen indeed for this new world which he sought. "Why, as to that, I certainly shan't mind looking at them after long weeks of nothing but sky and ocean, Jabez. And when we reach New Orleans, you will honor me by being my guest for the finest dinner we can find in that city. I confess that the bill of fare on the *Guerrière* is likely to become monotonous before we reach port."

"That's true enough, and I know many a place in New Orleans where you can dine like a king, Lucien. But about the pretty girls, there's one aboard already—or haven't you noticed?"

"I saw a young woman on the quarter deck the other afternoon, talking with the purser. Who is she?"

"She's bound for Havana, where we stay three days to take on fresh water and supplies and also discharge some of our cargo. We'll take on rum and molasses and spices and a few slaves."

"Slaves?" Lucien wonderingly echoed.

"A few Arawak Indians from the island of Cuba, but mostly blacks. They bring good prices in New Orleans, some to work the sugar cane north along the Mississippi from New Orleans, some to serve in the households of the rich aristocrats."

When he saw Lucien frown, Jabez Corrigan added, "To my way of thinking, there's not much difference between slaves in the new world and what we've had here in France, what with the peasants at the beck and call of the high nobility, not daring to call their souls their own because of all the old laws. The difference is only that they're bought and sold, and the owner puts the slave to work and takes care of him. There aren't enough whites yet in this big country beyond the thirteen colonies to do all the work that's needed to build towns and roads and trading posts and the like."

"Yes, I've no doubt you're right. But the very word slavery galls me, Jabez. Just as with my father—" he caught himself in time—"just as in France, if a man's born to a peasant family, that's what he is. That's another reason I'm coming to America to work land and to make a life that I can build with my two hands and my strength and my brain."

"I'll not disagree with you on that, Lucien. But about the pretty wench you've noticed, she's on the manifest as Inez Castillar, and it's said she was an actress at the theater in Paris and Tours and Bordeaux, and she's returning to visit an important Spanish officer in Havana. She's Spanish herself, dark and fiery and I wouldn't mind being marooned with her if this ship should founder." He quickly put his right hand behind his back and crossed median and forefinger to ward off ill luck, then grinned and winked at Lucien.

"I'm in your debt, Jabez, for all you've told me. We'll talk again. And whenever you like, come down and see old Arabe here. Making a new friend will perhaps distract him from Edmond's old mare—though as you see we've separated the stalls so he can't show too much interest in her."

Jabez Corrigan shared Lucien's laughter and shook hands again, then continued his inspection of the hold. Lucien went up on deck to enjoy the air and the calm beauty of the ocean. The wind had slackened during the day, and the sails hung limply. Beyond was the endless sky and sea and the feeling of loneliness and mystery which accompanied one who had left his home and did not know where his next would be.

Indeed, Lucien had already noticed Inez Castillar from the very first moment of her boarding at Le Havre. Wearing a brocaded green cape over a fashionable blue silk gown whose daring cut exposed her shoulders and the cleft of jutting, closely spaced round breasts, she had been effusively welcomed by the ship's purser, who had made a great fuss over her and kissed her hand, then had one of the sailors usher her and the little ten-year-old blackamoor who accompanied her, carrying a small scrolled oaken chest, to her cabin near the foredeck. Only the day before his first encounter with Jabez Corrigan in the hold, he had seen her standing at the rail and had politely nodded. She had turned to greet him in Spanish-accented French, with a coquettish smile that showed perfect, small white teeth, and her expressive, large dark-brown eyes had swept him from head to foot as if instantly appraising his virility as a male who might be of consequence to her. In the same instant, seeing his drab garb, that quickened interest had as suddenly faded. He had cynically thought to himself that if he had worn his mother's ring with the stone uppermost, she would have been still more attentive.

But young Edmond Vignon had not only seen her but had also been smitten by her, often staring in awe-stricken, adolescent desire after her supple figure, seeing the lustrous black hair combed back high from her forehead and bound in a thick psyche knot at the back of her head, with rows of little curls tumbling from it in piquant disarray. Her full, sensual mouth and her warm olive skin, as well as the provocative little black beauty patch high on her left cheekbone had intoxicated the young peasant, whose concept of desirable females had gone no further than ingenuous Madelon, who had been of his own age and lowly class. And the strong, cloying scent of her Parisian perfume, wafted to his nostrils, had left him flushed and trembling as it stirred his young manhood for the first truly carnal time.

Noticing the youth's infatuation, Lucien had warned Edmond midway through the voyage: "A woman like that is not for you, *mon gars*. She's the kind who goes to the highest bidder, and she's not likely to be faithful for long even to him. There will be time enough to find you a willing, useful helpmate once we settle ourselves and sell our first crops. Remember, boy, it's not physical beauty alone a man desires in a woman—though I'd be the first to admit that he can be attracted by it, the proof being your own state whenever *Mam'selle* Inez hoves into view. No, in a wife, Edmond, you want steadfastness, the kind that brings her to your side with the notion that she'll

51

stand by you through bad days as well as good, lean years as well as fat, building with you something that's worthwhile at the end of your days. At least—" he had permitted himself an ironic little smile—"that was my original philosophy."

"Oh, *monseigneur,* I know I'd have no chance with someone like that—but she's so beautiful, and she smiles at me and I can't help wishing she were my sweetheart!" the curly-haired youth blushingly avowed.

"Well, there's no harm in wishing. Just don't get too friendly with her, or you'll find yourself eating your heart out all for nothing, and she'll amuse herself telling her wealthy Spanish protector what a conquest she made of a country bumpkin," Lucien had chuckled, nudging Edmond in the ribs to make the youth see the joke of it.

The *Guerrière* had good fortune in this sailing, for there were no harsh gales to drive it off course. There were, however, many days of almost windless calm, when the sails on the tall masts hung idly and the ship seemed hardly to move upon the blue Atlantic. After the first days, Lucien found his sea legs, as did Edmond, though time seemed to crawl for Lucien as he impatiently awaited his first glimpse of the new world of which he had read so much. Scarcely thirteen years before, the peoples of thirteen small colonies had banded together to defy the king of what was assuredly the most powerful nation in the world, and they had secured their independence. There had been a war, it was true, but with comparatively little loss of life when one considered the dreadful slaughter of the Hundred Years War. He would, he knew, out of his own choice in seeking untenanted land as yet not colonized, condemn himself to an almost primitive life of survival against elements and beasts and the savages who roamed that southern expanse of the new United States. From what he had studied of European history, Lucien did not believe that the Spanish could long maintain their rule over so vast a territory. And to maintain it by force would mean mustering thousands of soldiers, as against the few military garrisons which presently. showed as only a scant number of color-headed pins upon an only partly charted map.

Moreover, if Louis XVI should indeed be deposed, as every sensible indication led an intelligent student of history to infer, it was likely that France would not only endure internecine warfare, but also stand in grave danger of being attacked by the neighboring nations who had long been jealous of the territorial possessions of the Bourbon dynasty. And all of this could only mean that, ultimately, the hold of both Spain and France in this virtually limitless new world would be ceded to those courageous colonists who had already braved George III and proclaimed a new nation that might well one day defy all the world with its vigor, untapped natural riches and the indomitable spirit of its settlers. To think upon such a prospect was to hearten his own innermost resolve.

Throughout most of the voyage, Lucien took pains to converse with Jabez Corrigan whenever the opportunity presented itself. More than that, he insisted that the second mate speak in English most of the time, in order to refresh his own theoretical but necessarily sketchy knowledge of the language. For it was quite likely that, although there might be many Frenchmen who, like himself, would seek a new beginning in America, the intrepid pioneers who had settled the original thirteen colonies would surely push westward and southward to expand the frontiers of so vast a land. And doubtless, although the Marquis de LaFayette had been one of the most enthusiastic allies of the young United States, there would be many hard-grained colonists who would look suspiciously and even inimically on neighbors who were, in language and habits, so obviously strangers from a foreign nation. It was still too early for the world to accept the concept of the universal brotherhood of man, no matter how much Voltaire and Paine and Rousseau preached that Utopian doctrine.

Besides, he found the red-haired Irishman unabashedly candid in speaking his own mind, and, since he himself knew something of the ancient quarrel between the British and the Irish, Lucien could appreciate Jabez Corrigan's stubborn determination to become his own master and to shape his own destiny as circumstance and opportunity provided. It was not a lesson, he reflected soberly, that one necessarily learned by attendance at the University of Paris. Looking back, it was almost ludicrous to reflect on the thought that when he had been an eager student in assimilating all that books could teach him he had not once thought that one day soon he might be preparing to settle upon a land where the only inhabitants were Indians who would be hostile to nearly anyone born with a white skin. There was a kind of ironic pattern to it all, he mused philosophically, because just as the French aristocrat would look down with contempt and even hatred at a base-born peasant, so might a local brave who dwelt upon virgin land that had never known the footstep of a white settler be ready to kill at the sight of one on the grounds that not only was he the original squatter but also because he would inevitably regard himself as the superior of anyone not born to his own tribe or with his own pigmentation.

From what Jabez Corrigan could tell him of his occasional sojourns in Mobile and New Orleans and from gossiping at taverns and on the wharves, Lucien learned that the Creeks were reputed to have a highly advanced civilization, though at the same time they had proved to be more warlike than their neighbors, the Choctaws and even the Cherokees. "If you really intend to settle among those redskins, Lucien," the second mate once remarked as both men were admiring Arabe's prancing about in his stall in the hold, "you might find yourself having to learn their heathen tongue. Mind you, I don't really mean by heathen that they don't believe in a God—from some of the things I have heard, though they call Him by some name I can't even begin to try to pronounce, they've a pretty fair idea that somebody arranged the scheme of things and is looking out for them way up in the sky. And I imagine if you're honest and deal fairly with them, once you can make yourself understood even a little, you've a chance to survive their knives and tomahawks and their guns—oh yes, they've guns, all right. The Spanish have seen to that, because they want them as their allies, and McGillivray gets them weapons as part of the trade goods he exchanges with them for skins and pelts, beeswax, bear oil and fresh vegetables and such-like. And then there's this, Lucien—even if you get McGillivray to take a fancy to you and send you into Creek country, either to trade or work for him in his agency office, you'll have to know how to defend yourself. Have you ever killed a man?"

"God forbid!" Lucien had impulsively retorted.

"Amen to that, but it's one thing to stand here and talk as you might in church about the Fifth Commandment, and quite another when you're out on the trail and out of nowhere and without warning one of those cunning devils comes at you with a knife or what you'd call in French a *casse-tête*. The fact is, I think the French term is much more to the point than the word we use, tomahawk, because it means to break a head, and that's what a tomahawk will do in the hands of a powerful brave."

"No, Jabez, I've never struck a man down in cold blood, though I'll admit there've been times when I've thought of it. I only hope I shan't have to do it. But the instinct of self-preservation is so strong in all of us that I suppose that if we faced extinction otherwise, we'd bring ourselves to it in a fight where only one man could be the victor."

"That's as good a way of looking at it as any, Lucien. But let's talk now of more pleasant things. Now this palomino of yours is a beautiful, magnificent horse, but I don't see much future for it along the Indian trails, fording the creeks or the rivers, going through the forests where you have to cut your way ahead of you. You'd do better with one of those sturdy little packhorses or even a mule. But I've no doubt that once you meet up with McGillivray, you'll find out about these things first-hand. Now maybe if I go to the galley, I can pilfer another carrot for Arabe here. We're just about out of them now, but we'll be in Havana soon enough to pick up supplies, especially fruits. That's one thing they didn't treat you to in an English ship, I can tell you, Lucien."

And so the days passed instructively for Lucien, who mulled over the bits of information which the second mate so readily furnished and which he began to piece together in his own mind to try to find a sensible pattern to this jumble of bits and pieces that went into the making of his future life.

From time to time, when the ship's passengers met to take their meals, Lucien had occasional conversation with several of the French *émigrés,* but, apart from their being his own countrymen, he found little in common to share with them. One of these, a slim, rather effeminate-looking Gascon in his mid-thirties, *Comte* Raoul de Langlois, who ostentatiously strolled along the deck in ruffles and saffron waistcoat with matching ribbons and laces and took snuff out of a costly golden snuffbox every quarter of an hour, confided that he had been so disturbed by the mutinous revolt of his peasants under a new tithe which he had imposed for the purpose of embellishing his wardrobe that he had simply decided to abscond with the tax money owing to the king and take up his abode as a fashionable gentleman of leisure in the Creole district of New Orleans. Another, an arrogant mid-fortyish marquis from Saint-Azeres, had found the duties of maintaining order in his fief too onerous to permit him sufficient time to spend with his young mistress, whom he had sent on ahead of him to New Orleans. As for his wife and ten-year-old daughter, he had deprecatingly commented, "Madame my wife has had the good sense to take a lover who dotes on her, so much that he does not much care whether her child is to be cared for also, and so I have really no ties to hold me in a France that is not what it once was for an aristocrat who prefers to indulge himself—since after all, my dear fellow, that is why we were to the manner born, is it not?"

And at times, also, the black-haired actress deigned to address a banal question or two to him across the table, to which Lucien made polite if guarded answers, having no wish to involve himself. Yet even on such occasions, it seemed to be young Edmond who hung upon her every word and who, gaping like an infatuated schoolboy, seemed to drink in the sensual enticement of her face and the insinuatingly vibrant drawl of her soft contralto voice.

Quickening breezes off the island of Santo Domingo

hastened the *Guerrière*'s approach to Cuba, and toward the middle of the fourth week in July the vague outlines of that Spanish-ruled island were at last sighted. After the noontime meal on the Saturday of landing, Lucien went down to the hold to inspect Arabe, after having told Edmond that during the three days of loading provisions the two of them would go ashore and see the sights of Havana, if only to stretch their legs after the confinement of a long ocean voyage.

Edmond, excited by the prospect of visiting this exotic port, which the sailors with whom he had chatted during the voyage had extolled in the most glowing and licentious of terms, had hurried to his young master's cabin and put on a fresh shirt and tidied himself for the landing. He had tossed his paltry belongings into a little sack which had been contained in Lucien's saddlebag and was opening the latter when Inez Castillar silently entered the cabin. Her eyes glistened with avarice as she caught sight of Lucien's purse. She wore a flamboyant red silk gown, daring in the display of olive-sheened shoulders and the provocative hollow between her lush breasts, the skirt flounced with expensive Alençon lace and a yellow ribbon band along the top of her bodice. The boy straightened, conscious of her presence from the wafted scent of her tangy perfume, and turned scarlet to see her standing only a foot away. "*Mam'selle*—madame—I—" he stammered, numbed by her tantalizing nearness and the sight of palpitating, soft woman-flesh.

"Inez to you, *mon brave garçon*," she huskily murmured, her slim hand touching his flaming cheek. "But you're trembling so, *mon cher!* As if you were afraid of me, but there is no reason why you should be."

"My—my master's in the hold—I mean—" he stumbled, at a total loss for words. Even with Madelon, whom he had idolized, he had been unsure of himself and hesitant with words; before this gaudily gowned adventuress, he stood as an innocent rustic would have done before the sudden reincarnation of the goddess Venus herself.

Her hand rose to caress his curly hair and to confuse

57

him still more as her red lips, maddeningly close to his, curved in a flirtatious smile. "But it's not your master I was seeking, *chéri*. Don't you think a woman knows when a man desires her? At the table all these long evenings on this dreary ship, don't you think I've noticed you looking at me and wanting me?"

"Oh please, *mam'selle*, I—I didn't mean to be rude, truly I didn't—"

"But of course you didn't, *m'amour*." She uttered a soft, husky little laugh and brushed his lips with hers. "It's the nicest compliment you could pay me, and you were the only one who did, too. Listen, little one. While your ship remains in Havana, would you like to come to see me? Perhaps tomorrow night—in the village of Regla, you will find me at the *Casa de Los Tres Cruces*. You've only to ask in the city where it is and you can ride there to me on the mare you have in the hold—"

"But—*mam'selle*—I swear to you—" he was trembling violently now, his adolescent lust suddenly wakened and conflicting with his consternation at finding himself so incredibly involved with this elegant, delectable and yet grand lady so far above his humble station.

"I shall be very disappointed if you don't come to see me," she murmured. Her hand now descended along his hip, and then slyly and wantonly moved across his breeches. Edmond uttered a choking cry, shaken to his very marrow by that brazen caress, and clutched her bare shoulders as his mouth fused to hers. Dazed, shuddering, believing himself with a heavenly houri as might a devout Mohammedan who has earned the paradise of the Prophet, he did not see her other hand dip into the open saddlebag, draw out Lucien's chamois purse and conceal it behind her back.

"*Muy guapo, muy hombre*," she whispered as she sinuously broke away from him. "You will come to see me tomorrow night, then, *joli gars?*"

He could do no more than nod, staring at her as if he could not quite believe this ecstatic carnal communion. "Yes—oh, *mam'selle*, I don't know how you could care for me, I'm only a stableboy, I—"

"But you are a man, a man who desires me, young and handsome. When we are alone in my bedchamber tomorrow night, you shall be as bold as you wish, and I shall love you all the more for it, Edmond. I shall wait for you. Do not keep me waiting, *amorcito!*" Adroitly, as he stood staring at her, still bemused, Inez Castillar retreated toward the door of the cabin and then disappeared. He felt the edge of the bunk against the backs of his knees and slumped down upon it in emotional reaction, as if drained of all his strength. Then he drew a deep, unsteady breath, wonderingly shaking his head, his smile fatuous and his eyes wide and staring after that vision. Only after a long moment did he at last recollect his senses and go back to his preparations.

"We'll give the horses some exercise, once they've moved the cargo for Havana and before they take on fresh supplies, Edmond," Lucien smilingly told his young companion. "Aren't you listening, Edmond? *Ma foi,* you look as if you've just come back from the moon."

"Oh—I—I beg your pardon, *monseigneur*—"

"The devil with that, haven't I told you a thousand times already?" Lucien expostulated. "It's *M'sieu* or just Lucien. And when we reach New Orleans, I'm going to teach you a little English. It'll come in handy in our new life, that worthy Jabez assures me. Now then, I see you've put on a fresh shirt and tidied yourself. And tried to use my razor, I'll be bound, judging by that chafed look of a newly born baby's bottom you've around your jaws and cheeks. Go to, for whom are you primping yourself? I shan't let you consort with the *putaines* of Havana, you may count on that; they're sure to have the pox."

"Oh, but I wasn't—I mean—it's just that after all these months on the ship, I wanted to look respectable," Edmond self-consciously stammered, blushing again and lowering his eyes.

"I was only teasing you, Edmond. Don't take it so to heart. Now, is everything in order? My saddlebag—what's this now?"

"What, *m'sieu?*" Edmond looked up, startled.

"My purse—I kept it here—haven't you seen it?"

Edmond's jaw dropped and he uttered a strangled little cry. "It must have been—oh no—I can't believe that—"

"What are you talking about? Who must it have been?"

"I—I know—I was a fool—she stole it—that woman, the actress from Paris who—"

"Inez Castillar? Stole my purse? What are you saying, boy?"

"She—she was here while you were in the hold with Arabe, my master. She asked me—she wanted me to visit her at her house in Regla—oh what a fool I've been! I'll find her, I'll make her give it back—"

"Wait, I'll go with you—"

But Edmond, with a sobbing cry, had already rushed out on deck.

A longboat, with two black oarsmen and two Spanish soldiers on whose polished morions the bright sun gleamed had drawn up alongside the *Guerrière*. As he leaned over the rail, Edmond was just in time to see one of the soldiers carefully hand down the little blackamoor, who hugged the chest to him with one arm, while Inez Castillar was already seated in the longboat.

"Mam'selle!" Edmond cried, staring down at the dangling rope ladder. "My master's purse—it's all the money he has for the new world—please give it back!"

She looked up, bent to one of the soldiers and whispered something, at which the swarthy, bearded man burst into a mocking guffaw.

"Oh, *mon Dieu,* what have I done?" Edmond despairingly cried out. Then, before Lucien could stop him, he vaulted over the side of the ship down the rope ladder and dove toward the already receding longboat.

"No, come back, Edmond, it's too dangerous—come back!" Lucien called out.

But the boy, floundering in the still blue water, his arms thrashing to speed himself toward the longboat, whose gunwales were painted with the red and yellow of the flag of Imperial Spain, had eyes only for the taunting smile on the moist red lips of Inez Castillar, who tilted back her head and burst into jeering laughter.

He managed at last to reach up one hand and grasp the gunwale. The swarthy, bearded soldier lifted his musket by the barrel and brought it down on Edmond's head with a sickening thud. With a gurgling cry, the boy sank and disappeared from view. Only a few bubbles rose to the surface of the glassy water.

Tears streaming down his cheeks, his face contorted with agonized rage, Lucien turned to find Jabez Corrigan at his side. "The thieving bitch," the red-haired second mate growled. "But if you've any thought of pursuing her to an accounting, Lucien, you'd be going to your own death as assuredly as that poor boy did to his. She's the sweetheart of a certain *Capitano* Pedro Escobadura, and he's one of the most vicious and also most powerful brutes in all Cuba."

"Then I shall go to the Spanish governor there to demand justice!"

"What justice? What proof would you have, you a French *émigré*, to bring accusations against one of His Most Catholic Majesty's most valiant officers and a woman who is the toast of all Havana, besides being that officer's doxy? You'd find yourself in the stocks at the least and perhaps even sent to the *garrote*. No, Lucien, you can't avenge poor Edmond with your own useless death, I'm afraid. Best to say a prayer for his soul and go on with your quest. Look you, he willingly gave his life to help you succeed in it, didn't he?"

Lucien watched the longboat grow smaller in the distance as it headed toward the wharf. He stared at the grim towers of the Morro Castle in the distance and the ominous cannons of the Cabañas which vigilantly guarded the seaward approach to the harbor. Beyond were the dazzling white traceries of villas and the vivid contrast of purple bougainvillea and scarlet frangipani.

And below, the water was glass-smooth, its colors varying as far as the eye could follow from somber indigo and clear sapphire and then a pallid green.

His lips moved in a silent prayer for the boy who had looked so eagerly for a life where humble birth and servile duties would mean nothing as against courage and purpose and who had found so shabby a death. "If I have a son," he vowed to himself, "he will be named Edmond after you. That much at least I promise you."

CHAPTER FIVE

It was early afternoon of August 8, 1789, when the *Guerrière,* having entered the Balize and avoided grounding in the dangerous passes at the mouth of the Mississippi, completed its torturously slow journey of a hundred miles against the current to the town of New Orleans. During the fortnight between Havana and this, his first sight of the new country he would henceforth call his own, Lucien had been torn between moods of agonized despondency and indecision as well as by an even fiercer determination to achieve his quest, if only for the sake of young Edmond Vignon. If it had not been for the companionship and advice of the friendly second mate of the French ship, he might well have been crushed by the sudden fatalistic feeling of ill omen which had come with watching Edmond's heroic but futile death.

But common sense told him that since he had burned his bridges behind him, returning to France would be the act of a cowardly fool who did not have the stamina to stand by his own decisions. He might, having read Shakespeare's *Hamlet* in the French translation at the University, have clung to the melancholy prince's self-pitying declamation that a spiteful fate had chosen him to set right times that were fearfully out of joint. Yet despite his streak of romanticism, which he had manifested, as he now knew, to little purpose with Edmée de Courent, Lucien was innately a pragmatist and of a practical bent, which he had proved more than once to his father's discontent in his greater concern for the land and its harvests than the upholding of ancient traditions and ceremonious rituals. The actual and inescapable fact was that he was arriving in New Orleans without a *sou,* save for Arabe and poor Edmond's mare and his mother's costly heirloom ring, which strong filial sentiment alone kept him from considering as an immediate source of money. And again it was Jabez Corrigan who, the day before the docking of the three-master, pointed out the way to retain the ring and to gain the vital stake Lucien would need before he could effect a practical means of livelihood in a territory to which he was utterly foreign and unused.

"I told you before, Lucien, that your palomino can't stand up to the kind of journey you'll be making once you find McGillivray in Mobile and go up into his country, assuming he lets you. If you could be sure that he'd be in the hands of a good owner, who would love him and appreciate him as much as you do, wouldn't that ease the hurt of having to sell him? Well, I know just such a man in New Orleans. If you like, I'll arrange for him to see Arabe. As to the mare, perhaps you can get about twenty-five *piastres*—that's about five of your *louis d'or,* in Spanish silver."

"I understand."

"There's a wealthy Creole who lives on Dumaine Street, and he makes a tidy profit betting on horse races against his rich friends. He'd be the man to buy Arabe, I'm thinking."

"It'll break my heart to give up Arabe, Jabez, but there's no help for it. And again, I'm greatly in your debt, *mon ami.* I'm thinking that you've a better heart than most of my own countrymen can boast of these days," Lucien replied with a bitter little smile.

The *Guerrière* anchored at two hundred fathoms in the stream and several hundred yards above the huge quay. As it ended its journey up the Mississippi, Lucien had seen Spanish moss and cypress along the banks and from time to time the sudden slithering of brownish-green creatures with hideously long snouts and short, powerful clawed feet in the stagnant waters. Curious at these last, he had pointed them out to Jabez Corrigan, who had chuckled and explained, "We call them the scavengers of the town, Lucien. They're caimen, and they'll eat anything from a dog to a man. Along the levee where you'll find traders and thieves and whores peddling their wares on the keels, rafts and flatboats, many a fellow's had a knife thrust into his belly and been tossed into the river. The caimen aren't fussy."

"How horrible! And that miasmic smell—it's from the dead, then?" Lucien had queried.

"Partly that and the mud and the moss and the slops, and then there's the heat and the dampness of this almost tropical land," the red-haired second mate had whimsically explained, grimacing as he sniffed the humid air. "There's the customs quarantine boat putting out to inspect us for *la fièvre jaune* and any other maladies we may have brought with us from *la belle France*. After a bit, we'll lower the gig out with four good *matelots* to row her, and you and I will go find this Creole who might take a fancy to your Arabe."

"This is quite a crowded harbor." Lucien stared toward the willow-crowned levee, then back down the watery inlet they had come up so slowly on the last stage of their journey. "I see at least half a dozen other ships."

"That you will, and more at certain times of year than now. There's a Spanish bark, and a British brig, and there's a schooner-rigged coasting vessel from Pensacola, right off. Oh, I didn't mean to frighten you, Lucien, about the caimen. As to that stench which makes your nostrils wrinkle as it does mine, it's because you've got hogpens and open sewers here, and the wind brings it all this way. Still, it's the only way to come to New Orleans. Once you get past the levee and the vendors and the hawkers on Tchoupitoulas Street, you'll see how well the Spanish have rebuilt New Orleans in little more than a year."

"Rebuilt it?"

"Oui, mon ami," the second mate nodded. "Last year, on Good Friday it was, New Orleans had a great fire. And because it was Good Friday, the priests wouldn't al-

low the church bells to be rung, or the townspeople would have saved a great deal more than they did. But under His Excellency, Governor Esteban Miro, who, to my way of thinking, is a great improvement over ambitious young Galvez—that one took his father's place as viceroy of Mexico, four years ago—there's profit enough to be made for our ship in making so long a voyage. You see, Miro's civil and military governor of the provinces of Louisiana, Mobile and Pensacola. He's a just man, and the only trouble is that his Spanish masters across the ocean don't understand how this country's going, and they impose all sorts of taxes and restrictions on trade—but you'll learn that in Mobile soon enough."

An hour later, Lucien and Jabez got into the gig, passing the small cargo-ship which was approaching the *Guerrière* to claim the cargo it had brought from Le Havre and Havana. The river was a muddy brown, nauseous, the moribund sight of it in ironic contrast to the activity of the vessels moving about the quay. Jabez and Lucien clambered up the levee, and the Count de Bouchard's younger son looked round him bewilderedly at the strange sights and sounds that were his introduction to this new world. Just as the gig had reached the levee, he and Jabez had been accosted by a white-haired Choctaw squaw in a *pirogue* who held up oranges and sassafras, gesticulating to them on the low price of her wares. And when Jabez had smilingly shaken his head, she had flung an orange at him and cursed him roundly.

"This is the Place d'Armes, Lucien," the second mate edified him. "It's not a place to find yourself alone at night, but you can guess that for yourself. I've told my *matelots* not to be fools enough to relieve their hunger for a wench with any of these sluts you see here doing their business right in the boat. See that brazen-faced girl, the one with the skin like *café au lait* and her gown pulled up to her *tetons*? She's a free quadroon, out of one of the cribs, and when a ship like ours docks in New Orleans, she and her kind hurry down to the levee to earn all the *maravedis* they can. Like as not, I'll lose at least one or two men who won't have the brains God gave them to re-

66

alize that the least they'll get will be the pox and at the worst will find themselves dumped into the river for the caimen to feast on."

As they reached the street next to the levee which Jabez Corrigan had described, Lucien saw merchants standing in the doorways of little shops, their goods displayed for sale on the *banquettes*, the sidewalks made from old flatboat gunnels, calling out at passers-by to halt them for inspection of their goods, eager to haggle over their prices with the seamen, who, they knew, were bringing new gold and silver into New Orleans. Jabez Corrigan, it was evident, knew New Orleans like the back of his hand.

"This town was first hewed out of the forest, and the engineer in charge of the first colony of the Sieur de Bienville was the one who laid out the streets. As you can see for yourself, it's in flat, swampy ground fit for growing rice, but wretched for tobacco and vegetables. River water comes to the soil, and so do the crayfish. Bienville's engineer had four houses built to each city square, and there was a deep ditch for each square, and here you see the *banquette* between the fence and the ditch. In certain parts, you don't dare leave these gunnels, or you'll sink up to your waist in stinking mud. But there's beauty here, too, and it's a thriving town of five thousand and more coming every week from where you and I did."

"I can see that the architecture isn't French," Lucien proffered, looking to right and left of him, drinking it all in, feeling a tingle of excitement at his first steps on land since setting sail from Le Havre. He had taken the second mate's advice about not going ashore in Havana, not trusting his own blind instincts to seek vengeance for the wanton murder of poor Edmond.

"Of course, the French were here first, so New Orleans was the capital of the French colony. Then Spain got it about twenty-seven years ago. At least here, the Spanish and the French get along peaceably enough, maybe a good deal more than they do in Mobile. You can tell that by what they call their streets—we've just passed Chartres, called after the Duc de Chartres. Now here's Royal, the main street for most of the merchants, not those fly-by-night hawkers we just passed. Then there's Bourbon, after the kings of France. Where we're going, Dumaine Street, was named after that duke who was the bastard son of Louis XIV by de Montespan."

Lucien admiringly glanced at his new friend. "For a second mate, you know as much about French history as I think I do," he complimented the red-haired Irishman.

Jabez Corrigan, flushing, brushed the compliment away with a gesture of his hand. "When my duties aren't too heavy on the *Guerrière*, I dip into a book now and again," he sheepishly admitted. "But if you tell any of my *matelots*, I'll denounce you as an aristocrat and that's a promise, Lucien!"

Lucien laughed heartily and clapped his arm around the second mate's shoulder, and it seemed to him that with this staunch advisor and friend, he had recouped much of the spirit which had gone out of him in Havana.

"Before the fire," Jabez Corrigan volunteered, "many of the houses were built with a framework of cypress logs and held together with a mixture of mud and Spanish moss. They had gardens surrounded by white-washed high picket fences. But there's much to be said for the Spanish style you can see now—ah, here's the house we're after."

It was built flush with the *banquette*, the generously proportioned windows and doors closed with heavy batten blinds of cypress, made of brick and plaster and with a tiled arch over the heavy door. On the second floor, a balcony railed with delicate wrought iron overhung the street, and standing at the rail was a tall, wiry, dark-brown-haired man in his late forties, with only a trace or two of gray at the temples. He wore trousers and an elegant frockcoat of white linen.

"Mon ami Jabez! *Entrez ici, je vous prie,"* he called down to the second mate. "You and your friend are welcome to New Orleans. Come take a glass of madeira with me, and I'll tell you the latest news."

He disappeared then, and Lucien heard the tinkling of a hand bell. A moment later, the door was opened by a stout, beaming Negress in bright calico, a red bandanna tied over the top of her head. Curtsying, she invited them, in a dialect in which Lucien recognized only a few French words, to follow her to her master.

She led the way through a narrow, dark corridor into an elegantly furnished salon at the back of the house. Lucien could see through the bars which crossed the large fan-shaped window a courtyard in which banana trees, oleanders and *parterres* of flowers provided a sylvan touch of beauty against the ugliness of the muddy streets. Near the window was a writing desk of exquisite rosewood, with Flemish-scrolled legs, a comfortable divan with damask covering, and *pouf* cushions at each end. In the center of the ceiling, two huge palmetto fans hung, with pulley-cords to move them back and forth. Already a grinning little brown-skinned boy, perhaps twelve years old, wearing red breeches and jacket, was drawing on the cords to cool the oppressively humid air.

Their host appeared, extending his hand at once to Jabez Corrigan, who shook it warmly. "Lucien, this is *M'sieu* Jules Ronsart, who fancies horses. *M'sieu* Ronsart, I present to you Lucien Bouchard."

"*Enchanté, M'sieu* Ronsart." Lucien smilingly inclined his head.

"A countryman!" The tall brown-haired Creole beamed as he seated himself at the writing desk, waving his two visitors to the divan. "Clotilde is bringing the wine and some little cakes which she baked only this morning. Ah, here she is. She's the best housekeeper in all New Orleans and as good a cook, as I learned in Port-au-Prince, which is where I found her."

Lucien accepted a glass of madeira and one of the little sugar cakes, tasted the latter and nodded his gustatory approval.

"*M'sieu* Ronsart owns a sugarcane plantation in Haiti, Lucien, and I brought him to New Orleans last year," the second mate explained.

"So you've just come from France, *n'est-ce pas?*" The Creole planter turned to Lucien. "Then you've the latest news of the court. How goes it with Louis XVI?"

"Very badly, *M'sieu* Ronsart," Lucien gravely replied.

"I am certain that the people will force him to abdicate. There is considerable unrest throughout France and uprisings in Brittany and other provinces."

"As bad as that, eh? If what you say is true, the French colonies will be seriously endangered. And where do you come from, yourself, *M'sieu* Bouchard?"

"From Normandy. Yves-sur-lac, to be exact."

The Creole planter's alert dark-blue eyes widened with interest. "I know that village well. Wait a minute—I know the name Bouchard even better. Isn't there an Étienne, who is *Comte* in that province?"

"My father, yes, *M'sieu* Ronsart."

"*Diantre!* What a small world it is, after all! I myself am from Mézières in the Ardennes. My father was a very successful draper who had scores of villagers spinning thread for the weaving of cloth for him. But he also enjoyed raising horses as an avocation, and that is why my good friend Jabez knows how the passion for racing obsesses me. I recall having met your father some twenty years ago, in Paris, on his way to Versailles. *Ma foi*—" he slapped his knee as if pleased at the recollection after so long a time—"I remember how he talked of his cattle and of the fine horses he had. He was a man of bearing and dignity, the kind one does not forget over the years."

"You are kind to speak of him so, *M'sieu* Ronsart."

"But you do not refer to yourself with the preposition of nobility, *mon ami*. How is that?"

"My older brother will succeed to the title, but I am not certain that titles will much longer matter in France, *M'sieu* Ronsart, not after the State-General convenes this very month," was Lucien's answer. "At heart, I feel myself to be a farmer who loves land more than politics, and so I have come to America to find a brighter future than France can yield me."

"*C'est bien possible,*" the Creole soberly admitted. "But we've news here in New Orleans which neither you nor Jabez has heard. The thirteen colonies have now a president, that same brave General Washington who led the Continental armies against the British. It was on April 30th of this year that he took the oath to defend the Constitution."

"That's heartening news indeed," Lucien answered. "From the colony of a monarchy to a republic is a great achievement for so young a nation."

"That is true enough, *mon ami*," the Creole interposed, "but you must not think that what has taken place in those thirteen colonies will necessarily claim the rest of this vast continent. Many British sympathizers refused allegiance to this brave new republic and settled in Western Florida. You may know, of course, that by the Treaty of Paris of 1763 England was granted all French territory east of the Mississippi River and Spanish Florida in exchange for Cuba. And then, six years ago, by still another treaty signed at Paris, Spain regained both east and west Florida with the 31st parallel as the northern boundary from the Mississippi to the Appalachicola. That is the rule we are under now here in New Orleans, though thus far we French can live in amity with the Spaniards. Perhaps it is because our monarchies are so much alike in so many ways," he concluded with a wry smile as he lifted his glass to toast Lucien.

"My friend was robbed on the voyage, *M'sieu* Ronsart," Jabez Corrigan now broke in, with a sympathetic glance at Lucien, "and so he finds himself here in New Orleans without a *sou*, except for a magnificent Arabian palomino which is still in the hold of the vessel. I had thought that perhaps you might wish to see this glorious horse, for I am certain it would win many races and many hundreds of *piastres* for you."

"You know my weakness only too well, Jabez," the Creole smilingly twitted him. "Can I not lure you from your ship this time and make you assistant to my overseer at my plantation?"

"Thank you, but I still prefer the sea," the second mate answered.

"Well then, my English overseer has nothing to fear of being replaced. With such a one as you, his post would surely be in jeopardy." Ronsart smiled. "But if ever you change your mind, you've but to tell me. You'd like Haiti, and there are such beautiful women there too. My *petite maîtresse* was born there, and if her skin had a touch

71

more white, I swear I could parade her at Fontainebleau itself and all the court would think her a true princess of beauty. But now, I am at your service *M'sieu* Bouchard and I'm eager to see this palomino of yours."

CHAPTER SIX

It was nearly twilight when Lucien and Jabez, together with Jules Ronsart and two sturdy, liveried Haitians who served the Creole as handlers of his stable as well as bodyguards in this disreputable section of New Orleans, were rowed back to the *Guerrière*. Once the sun-bronzed plantation owner had seen Arabe in his stall and observed how affectionately the palomino whinnied at and then nuzzled Lucien, he enthusiastically exclaimed, "But my good friend Jabez did me a great service in telling me of such a *cheval magnifique! M'sieu* Lucien, I am all envy and greed in an instant—and that means that I suspend my nominal judgment as a banker and allow you to set your price. I can only hope that it is not too dear. How old is this beautiful animal?"

"It was a year old when my father gave it to me on my birthday last December," Lucien answered. "And if I had not had my purse filched from me by that scheming wanton in Havana, assuredly you would be looking at Arabe only to praise him, my dear Jules."

"*Entendu!* Thus one might say that your misfortune is my great good fortune." The Creole gave Lucien a sympathetic look. "But for an Arabian horse, known to be the swiftest in the world, a horse that will guarantee my winning every race and add to my already sizeable capital, I should be a rogue if I offered you less than two hundred golden louis. As I have told you, I operate a private bank here, issuing my own notes and scrip. The sugarcane and

73

rum which are brought from my plantation near the city of Port-au-Prince are sold here, sometimes bartered for other goods which I need back in Haiti as well as for my own enjoyment in New Orleans. If you like, therefore, you may have this in the new American currency of what would be a thousand dollars, or a thousand *piastres* or the *louis d'or*. I tell you in all honesty that golden coins are becoming rarer here, and hence of greater value than the Spanish money. As to the American dollars, they are accepted, but not quite so eagerly, the country being new and its banks a far journey to the northeast, as you know."

When Lucien pondered for a moment, the Creole went on: "I should say it would depend on what you intend to do and where you intend to go—unless of course you are thinking of settling down here in New Orleans? I should be honored if you would be my guest during your stay, and since you have told me of how you have toiled like a veritable peasant upon your own father's estate in Normandy, I might even consider offering you a post in Haiti, just as I did Jabez a little while ago."

"No, *M'sieu* Jules, that offer I should not accept because I want land of my own. Another reason also—however strong your hold upon that land in Haiti, it may be weakened by the events taking place in France at this very moment, which becomes the same reason that caused me to leave Yves-sur-lac."

"Of course, I had forgotten for the moment of your determination to become a pioneer in uncharted territory. Forgive my little joke—it is one of my worst habits. But then, if you do not stay in New Orleans, do you think of going on directly to Mobile?"

"I do, from what Jabez has told me of this man McGillivray. Can you tell me anything about him?"

"Yes, a good deal, for I've met him and admire the man. He has great ambitions and equally great power. Perhaps he was born to both, for he is the son of a rich Scotch trader, Lachlan McGillivray, and his mother, Sehoy Marchand, is a Creek. He spent his early years at his father's trading post on the banks of the Tallapoosa, and when he was about fourteen, he was sent to Charleston to

74

learn the merchant's trade. He was a loyalist and fought on the British side during this war which gave the colonies their independence, you see. So the Americans confiscated his property, and when the war was over, he returned to the Creek country and his plantation near Fort Toulouse in Mobile, which the French of Mobile built near the meeting of the Coosa and Tallapoosa rivers. He inherited the plantation from his father. He holds the rank of colonel in the British Army."

"Then assuredly he is a man who knows this part of the country better than most and can foresee its future," Lucien decided. "I had already made up my mind to go to see him, from all that Jabez told me. What you have said decides me even more strongly."

"In that case, since his trading post in Mobile, which is called Swanson and McGillivray, will honor my notes, I shall write you out a draft for a thousand *piastres*. Hercule and Daniel will see to Arabe in the morning. And now, *M'sieu* Lucien, after we have returned to my house to complete this little transaction of ours, will you and *mon brave matelot* Jabez do me the honor of dining with me?"

"It will be my great pleasure. Don't forget, you'll make Arabe a true friend by feeding him an occasional carrot."

"That is not always so easy here in New Orleans. But I think he may enjoy a taste of sugarcane now and again. Never fear, I'll care for that beauty as if I were in your place, my word upon it! And, *ça va sans dire,* if you visit New Orleans again after you have found your land, as I assuredly hope you will, you have only to call upon me and you shall ride Arabe as in the happier days in France."

Refreshed by the luxury of a bath in a tin tub to which the beamingly solicitous Clotilde carried bucket upon bucket of water, into which she dropped stones heated in the oven, and then fortified by a superb dinner of jambalaya and roast duck prepared by the tireless Clotilde herself, Lucien plied his gracious host with many questions during this, his first night in the new world. Jules Ronsart, thanks to his own holdings and his role as a private banker, was astutely informed on the commerce and the politics of this vast southeastern portion of the new continent. It was his opinion that it would take at least a generation to incorporate so much of what was still a wilderness into the framework of the thirteen colonies, and that it could hardly be done with the presence of French and Spanish settlers and armies who greatly outnumbered the still sparse population of American settlers, who were mainly in Georgia and the Carolinas and West Florida. "Don't forget, Lucien," (the conviviality caused by his delight in acquiring the palomino and his admiration for Lucien's intrepid departure from France had led him to dispense with the formal *"M'sieu"*) "that many of these settlers fled the thirteen colonies when it was unpopular and dangerous to remain a British Tory, and they will not take kindly to giving up their leanings and becoming American citizens. And there is the not inconsequential matter of purchasing these millions of acres of untouched land from the Spanish. If what you say about the downfall of the French monarchy is true, then France will be unable to maintain its holdings in this new young continent. That is why this Alexander McGillivray does not entirely break off his former association with the British, and why he is still so greatly catered to by the Spanish court and their administrators here. There is no doubt that the American officials will seek to court his favor as well. You may yet find yourself drawn into a far more dangerous whirlpool than you predict will take place in France."

"As to that, I must take my chances, Jules. But if a young republic is strong enough to defeat the strongest British troops against overwhelming odds and to establish its independence through loyalty and purpose in the cause of freedom, then I do not greatly fear the final outcome."

"I will drink to your optimism, Lucien. Tell me, what do you think of this *taffai?* It is a rum made from molasses, better refined on my plantation than here. The cruder and rawer kind sometimes finds its way to the *sauvages rouges,* and then they become quarrelsome and murderous." The Creole lifted an exquisite silver cup to toast his guests.

Lucien took a cautious sip, then shuddered at the burning glow left by this potent rum. "I'd say it was strong spirit, Jules, strong enough to turn a gentle scholar into a bold adventurer in the wilderness. And I should not like to try the less refined vintage. To your very good health, and to yours, Jabez, my friend!"

It was almost noon of the next day when Lucien awoke, summoned by maternal Clotilde, who informed him that Hercule and Daniel had already brought the palomino from the ship's hold and conveyed it safely to a comfortable stall in her master's stable on the outskirts of New Orleans. He was there even now, she assured him, eager to ride Arabe and accustom himself to the stallion's speed. This next Sunday, indeed, he proposed to race Arabe against the bay of *M'sieu* Victor Marivault, an affluent shopkeeper of Royal Street who was his favorite adversary at both chess and horseracing.

After breakfasting on baked red snapper with Clotilde's own secret tangy sauce, cornmeal cakes and a strong coffee liberally laced with chicory and West Indian rum, Lucien turned to the red-haired second mate and asked, "When do you go back to France, *mon vieux?*"

"Ten days from this morning, Lucien. This time we'll dock at Port-au-Prince with cargo and several passengers, one of them being *M'sieu* Ronsart. He's going back to inspect his sugarcane and visit his girl. She doesn't like New Orleans, and since he dotes on her, he's faithful to her wishes."

"Fidelity is a rare trait in both a man and a woman, Jabez. Sometimes it's fidelity in love that matters, sometimes it's fidelity to a cause, such as these Americans had against the might of George III. Sometimes it's as Shakespeare says when he has old Polonius say to Laertes, 'To thine own self be true, thou canst not then be false to any man.' But haven't you truly thought of going back to the land, Jabez?"

"Yes, I'd be a liar if I said no to that, Lucien. But you see, there's a freedom to the sea. I didn't have it when they pressed me onto a British ship, true enough, but I've got it now. The master of the *Guerrière* is a good man, and perhaps one day I'll be master of my own ship. Who knows—one day I may even haul your cargo across the Atlantic."

77

"If that happens, there is no man I'd rather entrust it to, Jabez. But will you do me one favor when you go back?"

"You've only to ask it."

"*Merci bien.* I'd like to send a letter to let my father and mother know I'm safe here. I'll send it to them in care of the rectory at Yves-sur-lac. Perhaps you can find a courier or some coach going along the road to Bolbec— it's not far from there."

"I'll see to it, you've my word for it, Lucien. And now, are you off to Mobile? I can inquire for you at the quay when there'll be a flatboat going there. They journey several times a week, because there's much commerce there. It's such a rich soil for growing fruits and vegetables that they often send supplies here to New Orleans in exchange for some of the things we bring from France."

"Yes, I'd like to leave as soon as I can. I must say goodbye and a thousand thanks to our host, of course. And I want to see Arabe for the last time too. But you remember, I promised you a fine dinner, so this evening you're to be my guest. Will you tell me where I may take you?"

"I'll tell you what. There's a Madame Rambouillet on Isola Street, that's a good mile past here and on the very edge of town. She makes the finest gumbo I've ever put a spoon to, and she can take a scrawny pullet and make a feast worthy of Louis XVI himself out of it."

"Then that's where we'll dine tonight."

"I'll meet you there at six o'clock, and now if you'll write your letter I'll be getting back to the quay to see how they're handling our cargo off the *Guerrière*. And I'll inquire about the flatboat. I'll pick a boatman who's not likely to cut your throat for the draft *M'sieu* Ronsart has given you, or for that ring, either. You're wise to keep the stone turned inward. And another thing—that end of town is safe enough before it gets too dark, but you've no weapon."

"No, that's true. I can fence well enough, but I seldom wore a sword back in Normandy and I've never had to defend myself against a man who wanted to take my life."

The red-haired second mate scowled and shook his head. "You'll need more than your bare hands if McGillivray sends you into that wilderness and a Creek brave who's had a drop too much of *taffai* takes a notion to tomahawk you, Lucien. Have you ever fired a flintlock or handled a knife?"

"No, but I daresay I can learn if I must."

"You needs must, be sure of that. Now go write your letter. I'll get Clotilde to bring you a quill and some parchment and sealing wax."

Lucien seated himself at the rosewood writing desk and hurriedly addressing the letter to his mother told her briefly of the successful end of the voyage and his intention to go to Mobile, from which it was his hope to be directed to the land he sought. He did not speak of his sale of Arabe nor of Edmond Vignon's tragic death; there was no reason to have her agonize over the theft of the money she had given him nor over the pathetically useless death of that naive but courageous boy. When he had finished, he shook sand over the letter to dry it, then carefully rolled it tightly into a narrow scroll, made it fast with three round seals of sealing wax and addressed it to *Père* Morlain at the rectory of Yves-sur-lac.

"There, Jabez, and once more I find myself thanking you for having done more for me than I could ever truly repay. I will wait here to say my *au revoirs* to Jules, then perhaps stroll about the streets a bit and meet you at Madame Rambouillet's at six as we agreed."

Lucien had freshened himself before Jules Ronsart returned, making use of the finely honed straight razor, made in Augsburg and another gift from his father, who had purchased it at the shop of the Parisian jeweler Honoré, the very same from which his mother's cabochon had come. Its silver handle bore the heraldic crest of Normandy: a mailed fist above a shield embossed with the *fleur-de-lis* of France, and with the motto *"Pour Dieu et le Roi."* For God and King—but now in this new nation which had revolted against another king, it would be for God only. Here, Lucien believed, each man might shape his own destiny with the help of a just, all-seeing God and be the more faithful and unswerving in his devotions, since—as was assuredly true in France—the laws of a temporal king often went counter to Divine edict. All of Europe had been nurtured for centuries on the tradition that the will of a king was also that of God Himself; during his studies in Paris, Lucien had already learned otherwise.

At about two o'clock that afternoon, Jules Ronsart returned home, bathed in sweat from neck to thigh, but radiant, his riding boots mud-flecked. "Never in all my life have I ridden so intelligent, so swift and beautiful a horse, *mon ami* Lucien!" he exuberantly exclaimed. "I do not even need my riding crop. I tell you, that Arabe of yours—alas, of mine, rather—has more intelligence than his new master. He is responsive to the slightest touch of the reins. I shall win back everything I have lost from my boasting friend who believes that he stables the finest horses in all New Orleans. Oh yes, I had forgotten to tell you, Lucien. I'll take that mare of yours as well, and give you twenty-five *piastres* in good Spanish silver. You'll be needing some pocket money for your journey, at least for the flatboat to Mobile. Don't pay any boatman over four, especially if you're traveling alone, and choose an honest type—but I daresay our good Jabez will see to that for you."

"If Arabe has treated you thus, Jules, I can rest assured he's in good hands and my heart isn't nearly so heavy. And I think that I've already said my last goodbye to him yesterday. To see him again now, after you've ridden him so well, would only make me regret having had to sell him in the first place. But I was about to tell you that I have exceeded your hospitality by far. I'm taking Jabez to the house of a certain Madame Rambouillet this evening to stand him the dinner I promised on the *Guerrière*."

The wiry Creole chuckled and winked. "I applaud his taste and your decision to indulge it, Lucien. Her cuisine is nearly the equal of Clotilde's. Besides, she has something to offer which I cannot at this moment—a bed wench. Indeed, she has several, and I add quickly that these are of more circumspection and charm than the *sales putaines* you find at the levee."

Lucien gawked at him, uncomprehendingly for a moment, then flushed hotly. "You mean that hers is a house of assignation?" he finally stammered.

"*Holà!* You remind me of the *Chevalier* Bayard, *sans peur et sans reproche*. Yes, in a sense it is that. You see, Marthe Rambouillet came to New Orleans ten years ago as the wife of an utter scoundrel who had been discharged for his peculations on a plantation in Santo Domingo. Once arrived here, he proceeded to open a little salon where he ran games of chance like *chemin de fer* and *vingt-et-un*. The captain of a Spanish brig from Mobile found him palming an extra queen up his sleeve one evening and made Marthe Rambouillet his widow. For a time, she became a seamstress, and then gave shelter to a few *demoiselles* abandoned by their lovers or husbands for one reason or another. Now she is in debt to no one, and four delightful young ladies of complaisant virtue are quartered in her establishment. I have it also on good authority that she herself is *hors de concours* from any amatory pursuits, since she herself is the mistress of one of my good friends. Yes, Lucien, if it's dalliance you want after an excellent repast, there's no better place in all New Orleans at this moment."

Under his host's amused look, Lucien fought against the adolescent blushes which he inwardly damned. "Quite simply, I've never thought of paying for love," he contented himself in saying.

The gumbo and the *poulet au vin* were all that Jabez Corrigan had predicted, and Lucien counted out only two of the silver coins which the Creole had given him for Edmond's mare as payment, mildly surprised at the lavish fare which such a token sum had purchased. Marthe Rambouillet herself served him and Jabez, as well as three other elegantly groomed Creoles at the other tables. She was in her middle thirties, Lucien estimated, but still admirably preserved, buxom, chestnut-haired, with a round, sweet face and appraising hazel eyes. After she had served the two men a plate of fruit and some little *gateaux* and gone to the other tables to converse in a tone too soft to be heard, Jabez eyed the young Frenchman and whispered, "I've found a flatboat to Mobile for you, and if you'll be down at the quay by noon and ask for Pierre Durand, you'll find him as reliable a boatman as you dare trust your life to these days. Now, are you going back to Jules's?"

"No, Jabez, I'm going to ask Madame Rambouillet for a room for the night. A room alone, I may add. You hadn't told me about the lovely doxies she boards here."

Jabez Corrigan leaned back and gaffawed with unashamed merriment till tears stood in his eyes. "Devil take me if you're not some knight of the Holy Grail himself come to this wicked city to purify it! I'm thinking it will be a harder job to do that than to cross the wilderness and keep your scalp safely perched on that handsome head of yours. I'll speak to Marthe, then, for you. But as for myself, if it won't change your opinion of me, I've asked for Roxanne to help me to slumber this night. She's a winsome lass, that one is, and she reminds me a little of my own poor Blanchette."

"Heaven defend me from sitting in judgment over any man, least of all you who have done so much for me," Lucien vehemently declared. "I confess to being an incurable romantic, but I don't for a moment suppose that everyone should follow my example. Moreover, looking back now, I begin to wonder if my romanticism wasn't a trifle misplaced. But of that, no matter. I think, after this luxurious banquet, which has made me quite forget the viands aboard ship, I shall take a little stroll and enjoy the night air."

"Very well, Lucien, but be careful. Even at this end of town there are rogues who lie in wait for men with well-laden purses. And you've still no weapon to defend yourself with. I'll get you a good knife tomorrow to take to Mobile. You can remember me by it, if you will."

As Jabez Corrigan rose to walk to the back of the room to talk to the attractive widow, Lucien stretched his legs, then rose and left the house. The night air was humid and very still, and only a few distant stars twinkled in the dark panorama of the seemingly moonless sky.

Beyond the house of Marthe Rambouillet stood the charred ruins of two houses which had been almost razed by the great fire the year before. Some of the timbers stood at crazy angles, like gaunt black skeletons in a graveyard unearthed by a supernatural command, and Lucien caught sight in them of two shadowy figures who seemed to be holding a third between them. Muffled oaths came to his ear as he turned to stare and listen: "Damn if this perky little filly isn't getting me primed to poke her good, playing like she's so pure and holy—hold still, you tricky bitch you, try to bite, will you now—grab her arms and twist them a little, Josh, I'll peel her raw and then we'll fooferaw her like she really wants!"

"No—stop it—damn you—my aunt will have you jailed in the Cabildo for this—in the stocks and whipped—ohh, you're tearing my dress—help, please—no!" It was a girl's voice, vibrant with revulsion and fear, and Lucien, oblivious to his being unarmed against the unknown girl's two assailants, hurried forward, calling, "Let her go, let her go, I tell you!"

Now he could see them, one a lanky, black-bearded riverman with a dirty red bandanna round his head and a silver earring pierced through his left ear; the other, burly, naked to the waist, his breeches already open, matted grayish hair on his chest like some dank jungle growth, his face scarred and leering. Their intended victim had crumpled to the damp ground, sobbing softly, her low-necked dress of blue jaconet muslin ripped at one side down to her waist to expose a surprisingly ripe, round breast covered by a thin pink chemise, one of whose straps had been ripped also and bared a dimpled, carnation-sheened shoulder.

"Wal now, Josh—" the lanky man grinned obscenely at his burly confederate—"here's a pretty macaroon wants to save this purty piece of pokemeat. Let's you and me rip out his tripes for his pains and see if he's carrying gold or silver before we have our fun!"

"I'm for that too, Hughie," the half-naked older riverman savagely avowed.

"Look out, he's got a dirk!" the girl called to Lucien, who had crouched with his hands clenched, ready for any attack. The lanky man, called Hughie, had suddenly come at him from his left, whipping a heavy, long-bladed pirate's dagger with narrow hilt which he had drawn from the belt

83

of his dirty breeches. As he lunged at Lucien, the young Frenchman leaped to the left, his left hand clamping on the riverman's wrist and adroitly twisting it till Hughie screamed and dropped the dirk, stumbling back, his face a ghastly mask of agony. "He's fair broke my wrist, Josh, kill the bastard!" he screamed.

At almost the same moment, the burly ruffian, with a roar of rage, had leaped toward Lucien. In almost the same, unthinkingly reflexive movement of his supple body, Lucien kicked up his right foot with all his strength, driving the toe of his heavy boot squarely into the burly riverman's crotch. A frenzied bellow of unspeakable agony rang out as Josh fell heavily on the ground, rolling over and over among the charred bits of timber and planking which had once been the floorboard of an elegant little French-built house.

Lucien bent to retrieve the dirk, then drew the sobbing girl to her feet. "Into the house, quickly, if you've the strength, *mademoiselle*," he urged.

"Yes—oh thank you—I was going there—she's my aunt, you know—but they followed me, those beasts of the levee, and they caught me before I could enter—oh, if it hadn't been for you—oh, God—" she sobbed hysterically as he hurried her faltering steps, his right arm round her slim waist, toward the door of Madame Rambouillet's house.

The buxom widow, having heard the commotion outside, was already there to open it for him and to utter a cry of alarm: "My little angel—what's happened—are you hurt—has this man dared to put his hands on you—"

"Oh, no, *Tante* Marthe! He—he's the one who saved me from the rivermen—and one of them had a dirk—he was *magnifique, vraiement!*" the girl gasped as she flung herself, still sobbing into her aunt's compassionate embrace.

As she stroked the girl's quivering shoulders, Marthe Rambouillet stared gratefully at the tall, black-haired Frenchman who faced her, gripping the pirate dirk in one hand, breathing heavily, his face still taut and flushed from the furious energy he had been so unexpectedly called upon to exert. It had happened so swiftly that Lucien had had little time to think of anything save self-survival; he had been fighting for his life and yet now, as he drew deep breath upon breath, he realized how close he had been to taking a human life in the instinctive reaction to the threat of losing his own. *"M'sieu,* I shall be eternally grateful for what you've done for my little Eulalie," the widow huskily murmured. "Are you hurt?"

"No, madame, I don't think so."

The girl turned her tear-stained face back to look at him, and in the candlelight which flickered in the room, Lucien could see how intensely lovely she was, made the more so by the ripped dress and chemise, her lustrous dark-brown hair bound in a huge psyche knot at the back of her head, her slim neck and the vivid warmth of carnation-tinted, satiny-soft skin. Her face was heartshaped, with a dainty straight nose whose thin, sensuous wings flared and shrank, and her mouth was generously ripe, the lower lip fuller than its red twin. Her eyes were large, wide, narrowly spaced and cat-green, fringed with short but very thick lashes. "Oh, he was so brave, *ma tante!*" she gasped. "I thought they would kill him, but he took away that dagger from one man and kicked the other— *mon Dieu,* what a huge brute he was!—and hurt him badly. If it hadn't been for him, dear *Tante* Marthe, I— I—" and again she burst into tears, burying her face in the widow's ample bosom.

"Is there any danger that those men will try to come after your niece, Madame Rambouillet?" Lucien asked.

"Oh no! the *guardia civil* patrol along here this time of night, they'll find those *vauriens* and clap them into the *Cabildo,*" the widow reassured him. Then, to her niece, "Go to your room, my little one. I'll send Francine in to look after you."

"Oui, ma tante," Eulalie tearfully agreed as she disengaged herself from her aunt's protective clasp. Glancing back at Lucien, she turned and hurried to the back of the room and out the narrow passageway leading to a staircase.

Lucien saw that the other three men had left the tables, as well as Jabez Corrigan. Marthe Rambouillet moved toward him, her eyes soft and concerned. "Are you sure you aren't hurt, *m'sieu?*"

"No, thank you, madame. My heart's still beating very fast, but I'm sure that's normal under such circumstances. I think a good night's sleep is all I need. I'm leaving for Mobile tomorrow."

"You shall have the best room in my house, *m'sieu*. And if you wish, it would be my pleasure to send Julie to you—she's my newest and youngest girl, still very fresh and sweet. And I assure you, *m'sieu,* it will be done in love and there would be no question of recompense."

Once again Lucien Bouchard found his cheeks reddening with a virtuous confusion that had already gripped him on more than one occasion and long years before this night in New Orleans. Choosing his words carefully lest he give offense, he replied, "But, madame, I only did my duty, and the thought of being rewarded never occurred to me. Besides, I suddenly find myself exhausted—I've been in New Orleans just two days and I don't know what awaits me in Mobile. If you could show me to the room, it would be I who should be in your debt."

"You're a most gallant man, *m'sieu*. But then, your friend *M'sieu* Corrigan has told me a little about you. You mustn't think that Eulalie is—how shall I say it—one of my girls."

"I assure you that I didn't."

"She's come to stay with me only since a month, you see. She was married a year ago, but her husband, who was Henri Villefranche the sailmaker, died of *la fièvre jaune*. That is one of the maladies we fear most here in New Orleans. And Eulalie could not bear to be alone after that."

"I understand. I'm only happy I was able to be of some small service to her, then."

"Come with me, *m'sieu*. I'll show you to your room. Would you like some wine or rum?"

"No, it's best that I keep a clear head for tomorrow. I've two days in a flatboat ahead of me and it's an experience for which I may need all my strength and wits about me," he whimsically countered.

The buxom widow led him up a narrow stairway and down the hall to the last door on the right. She carried a lighted candle in a pewter holder, opened the door and went ahead of him to place the candle on a little table beside a sumptuous four-postered bed with a multicolored quilt as cover.

"There are two mattresses, *m'sieu*," Marthe Rambouillet proudly boasted, "each filled with goose feathers. They, like the bed, were brought two years ago from France on *M'sieu* Corrigan's fine ship. You will sleep like a king, I promise you."

"I'd much rather sleep like a man who's had a most exhausting day, madame, since I very much fear that the king who rules over the country from which this magnificent bed came may not be sleeping at all these nights. I think there is a quotation covering that—let me see now—oh yes, 'Uneasy lies the head that wears a crown.' But I shall sleep, and again, all my thanks."

"Then I shall leave you to the sleep you so bravely earned, *m'sieu*. And I wish you good fortune when you leave New Orleans." Marthe Rambouillet gravely curtsyed to him and then left the room, softly closing the door.

Lucien Bouchard uttered a weary sigh and began to undress. He laid the dirk on the table beside the candleholder, eyeing it with a shudder. He'd been very lucky tonight. If that older, bigger scoundrel had been armed, he might well be lying with candles at head and feet instead of preparing to sleep on an even softer bed than he had enjoyed in his father's chateau.

When he was down to his underbreeches, he drew back the quilted cover and flung himself down with a groan of comfort. It was still oppressively warm and his heart was still pounding from the violence he had so luckily managed in circumvent. There were no sounds wafting to him from the street below nor from the other rooms. He leaned toward the candle and blew it out, and then fell back, his arms pillowing his head, and was at once asleep.

It was past midnight when the door opened and closed silently. Eulalie Villefranche stood a long moment, till her eyes could make out Lucien's almost naked body on the huge bed. Then, an enigmatic little smile played around the corners of her full moist lips, she slipped off her cream-colored satin peignoir and let it festoon her slim, exquisitely chiseled bare ankles and moved toward him. As she reached the bed, she put her hands behind her to the thick knot of hair and undid it so that it poured down in a silken, soft, shimmering cascade below her shoulder blades. Straightening, she cupped her high-perched, widely spaced, round firm breasts, then glided her palms down the sleek contours of her lithe, amphora-curved hips. Ascending the little Jacob's ladder, she sinuously stretched herself out on her side, reached out a hand to caress Lucien's lean, weatherbeaten cheek, then his high-arching forehead, and then at last, his firm, incisive mouth. Her right palm lingeringly caressed his vigorous chest, her fingertips playfully tweaking the sprigs of sparse black body-hair about his paps.

Lucien stirred and moaned again, as Eulalie gently naked young woman beside him consolingly murmured, "Shh, *m'amour*." Her right hand moved downward over his belly, sinewy and lean, then over his muscular hips. Her breasts swelled with a mounting excitement and she sidled even closer to him. Then, bending her head, she brushed his throat with her lips as her hand grew bolder still, moving along the insides of his thighs and then against his wakening manhood.

Lucien stirred and moaned again, as Eulalie gently nipped his pap with her small white teeth, then flicked the tip of her tongue against it. Suddenly he woke, uttering a hoarse cry of surprise, swiftly thrusting out his hand toward the little night table to retrieve the dirk.

"No, *m'amour,* it's I, Eulalie," she gasped, for he had flung his other arm round her waist in a crushing grip.

"What—you—but how—" still partly drugged with sleep, Lucien eased his hold, his hand drawing away from the table, groping in the darkness to brush against the rich, satiny curve of a swelling naked breast.

"I came to thank you, *cheri,*" she whispered, propping herself up on an elbow, her glossy, unbound hair tumbling down to cover a breast, its soft mass tickling his side.

"*Mam'selle*—Eulalie—I didn't seek such thanks—"

"*Tu te moques de moi, vraiment!*" she fiercely whispered. "I wanted to, don't you understand? And you've nothing to fear—I haven't been with a man since poor

88

Henri died, *tu comprends?* Besides, I just had *mes temps lunaires* so you won't get me with child, if that's what you fear—" then her voice became husky-soft with desire, "though I shouldn't mind at all being made with child by such a strong, brave man as you, *m'sieu!* And now, please, before you make me feel ashamed of behaving like one of *Tante* Marthe's girls, won't you take me?"

Again her hand strayed down between his thighs, and Lucien shuddered at the sweet, blinding lust that seethed through his sinewy body. He could smell jasmine on her skin, in her hair, and the warmth of her bare flesh on his was maddening torment. With a hoarse cry, he gripped her by the shoulders and drew her down beside him, then swiftly husked his underbreeches and flung them to the floor. *"Oui, prends-moi, vite, avec tout ton force, m'amour,"* Eulalie panted as she arched to receive him.

His lips came down hard on hers, bruisingly, fiercely, demandingly. With a soft little satisfied laugh, she wound her pliant arms round his shoulders, her legs nimbly crossing over his, as she granted him total access to the warm, pulsating core of her.

In the darkness, on the featherbed, Lucien Bouchard conjured up the vision of his beloved *demoiselle* Edmée, as he had dreamed their wedding night might be. There was tenderness and tortured yearning, but with it also, there was the vision of the insolent adventuress Inez Castillar. And as Eulalie groaned and sobbed, her body leaping and shuddering to his virile thrusts, there was blended the triumphant power of avenging male lust as well.

CHAPTER SEVEN

He was at the quay well before the appointed time of noon to seek out the boatman Pierre Durand, carrying the lightly packed saddlebag which he had brought all the way from Yves-sur-lac. Into the bag he had tossed the dirk which he had wrested from the bearded ruffian who had tried to kill him with it. Marthe Rambouillet had brought breakfast to his room, almost angrily refused to take a single *piastre* for his night's lodging and had again expressed her gratitude for what he had done for her niece. Of Eulalie herself, there was no sign; Lucien, with a flash of insight newly taught, understood that she wished to spare him any possible self-recrimination or embarrassment, which her presence would assuredly have caused. But he told himself that one day, somehow, he would send her back some worthwhile keepsake that, though it would not be insultingly meant as fee for the tremendous release she had given him, would tell her that he would not soon forget the generous candor of her body's exquisitely passionate bounty.

"Over here, Lucien!" He turned to see the red-haired second mate squatting down on the edge of the wharf below which the muddy water lapped at a wide flatboat. Standing, hands on hips, was a grizzled, squat man in his fifties, his face as sun-darkened as that of a *nigra* in a tattered shirt, red sash wound round his corpulent paunch, and buckskin knee-breeches. Lucien made his way through the swarm of prostitutes, sailors and traders to reach his friend, while the boatman stared at him with suspicious, squinting eyes.

"This is my friend Lucien, Pierre; he'll be your passenger to Mobile," Jabez Corrigan smilingly explained. "And if you think he's a Parisian dandy, get it out of your rum-sotted noggin. Last night, this fine gentleman took care of Josh Peters and Hughie Warren, two bullies who've probably put at least a dozen bodies in the Mississippi since they deserted the Continental Army at Valley Forge and made their way down through Indian country to earn their filthy living here in New Orleans."

"*Tiens, c'est une merveille!* If that's the case, *m'sieu,* I'll not charge you more than three *piastres* to Mobile," Pierre Durand declared. "What's more, I'll even man both the oars."

"Not at all, *mon ami,*" Lucien laughed, "I'll pull my fair share along with you. The exercise will help ease the pain in my ribs and muscles."

"Hmm," Jabez Corrigan chuckled softly, "are you sure you're sore from that fight last night, or did one of Madame Rambouillet's doxies take a fancy to you after I fell asleep with sweet Roxanne? Go to, man, that color in your cheeks isn't only from the sun. Now I meant no harm, Lucien, just my little joke. The fact is, I'll miss you. Chances are the *Guerrière* won't make another trip here to New Orleans till next spring, for the Atlantic's much too rough in the winter months. So I'll say my farewell to you now and wish you Godspeed and perhaps by next May if you come back here, you can look me up at Madame Rambouillet's house."

"I'll remember, Jabez. I shan't ever forget you. I only hope our paths cross again when I am able to help you a little for all that you've done for me."

Lucien extended his hand and Jabez gripped it as the two men stared smiling at each other for a moment. Then the red-haired Irishman scowled. "Now take a piece of advice and when you see this fellow McGillivray, don't be too proud to let him know you can handle yourself in a fair fight. He's got no use for milksops. There's something about an Indian, say what you will that many of them are murdering red devils, but he knows when you've a straight tongue and a good heart quicker than most men I've met on this side of the Atlantic. I've seen to it that Pierre has enough provisions so you won't starve. But you'd best be rubbing some bear oil into that handsome face of yours or the sun'll blister it."

"Thanks again. So far, every piece of advice you've given me has been right, so I'll not chance ill luck by refusing to take it now, Jabez. *Dieu te garde, mon brave.*" Lucien's voice was husky as he took hold of the edge of the old wharf and deftly lowered himself into the flatboat. "There's jerky here, and leather bottles of water and some dry corn. It's not a feast, but it'll keep your belly full till you reach Mobile, *m'sieu*," Pierre Durand drawled.

"Jerky?" Lucien echoed the unfamiliar word.

"Yes, it's beef that's cut into strips and dried in the sun. You'll get used to it, and if you're on the trail, you'll bless it, especially when you can't kill any game to feed yourself. Well now, let's shove off, if you've done with your business."

"I have for now," Lucien said, and as he lifted one of the heavy oars, he turned to look back at the wharf. Jabez Corrigan stood, raising his hand in farewell.

It was mid-morning of the second day when the flatboat passed through the widening thirty-mile-long funnel of Mobile Bay's union with the Gulf Coast and entered the thin passageway between the offshore strip of Dauphin Island and a low marshy peninsula. In the year 1702, the noted French explorer Jean Baptiste LeMoyne, the youngest of six brothers of Quebec-born Iberville, who was to be ennobled as the *Sieur* de Bienville, had driven his vessel through the narrows and founded a colony north of the mighty bay. It was a settlement known as Fort Louis de la Mobile in joint honor of Louis XIV of France, who had authorized the expedition to give France a hold for trading and eventual colonization, and of the friendly Alabama Indian tribe known as the Mabila.

Though the fort had now passed under the aegis of the Spanish, nature had created a defense stronger than any manmade fortification: the great delta, an enormous labyrinth of marsh and bayou fabricated over the centuries by the rivers emptying Mobile Bay. Lucien, standing now to stretch his aching limbs after the two days of hard rowing, could see broad stretches of mangrove and saw grass, clumps of towering pine trees and overhead a swarm of mallards taking flight in an arrowlike dark cloud that momentarily blotted out the blazing azure sky of this hot August day. On the other shore, a white-tailed deer peered from behind a gnarled cypress tree, then scampered off, as if the sight of the two occupants of the flatboat threatened its peaceful grazing. From afar he could hear the bark of an otter. Under the sun by day and the stars by night, he had found Pierre Durand an amiable companion, full of tall tales of the river, the Indians who inhabited the lands beyond, the comings and goings of notorious and gaudy personages. There was none of Jabez Corrigan's gently chafing wit on the subject of the daughters of Eve, however. Old Durand was a misogynist. As a youth, he had been the older son of an Acadian family who had settled above New Orleans, married a flighty girl who, as he had glumly and only briefly explained, had put horns on his head a scant week after the wedding and who had run away with an Indian trader bound for Pensacola.

When Lucien had explained his purpose in seeking out Alexander McGillivray, Pierre Durand had snorted and shaken his head. "And suppose he takes a fancy to you and sends you to one of the Creek cities, what then, *homme*? Will you breed with a Creek squaw? You'll need to, whether you marry her or not, for 'tis sure you'll find no white settlers at those points."

"I hadn't thought of marrying, Pierre. It'll take me time enough to get my land, to farm it and to make it prosper. A man doesn't marry until he knows he has enough provender to support a wife as well as himself."

"That's one way of looking at it, I'm thinking. Oh, you'll find a squaw to share your bed, likely enough, for they've hot blood in them—though I've heard tell they're whipped before all if they're caught at their nasty little games, and worse yet if they're married and give their braves the horns. Well, here's the wharf, and you've been a good passenger, *M'sieu* Lucien. I wish you well and may I never see your scalp on a tepee."

"Amen to that, Pierre," Lucien laughed as he tossed his saddlebag onto the low ramp and then leaped after it. He turned to catch the tarred rope the old boatman flipped toward him, and made it fast several times round a heavy post.

"I'll go back as soon as I've loaded up with jerky and fresh water. Though maybe if I stay a bit, there might be a passenger bound for where I just brought you from, *M'sieu* Lucien."

"Jabez was right about your knowing your trade, Pierre. And right about that bear oil too, though I'll be wanting a bath as soon as I can get one. I don't think even an Indian squaw would find me to her fancy with this stink on me. Here, I'll give you a hand. And when you go back, give Jabez my best and tell him I hope to see him perhaps next year, if God wills it."

"Oui, ça sera mon plaisir," the grizzled boatman solemnly nodded as they shook hands again.

Slinging his saddlebag over his shoulder, Lucien trudged toward the trading post, nodding pleasantly to helmeted Spanish soldiers, who eyed him curiously and returned his greeting with answering smiles.

He could see at once a kind of architectural kinship with New Orleans. The trade town of Mobile was situated on the easy ascent of a rising bank and extended nearly half a mile back on the level plane above. The fort, erected very near the bay and across from the lower end of the town, was made of brick. Beyond, within the town itself, he could see buildings made of heavy notched and pegged logs, and some of brick, one story high but on an extensive scale, four square, encompassing on three sides a large area or courtyard. There were others, evidently belonging to those of lesser wealth, made of a strong frame of cypress, filled in with brick, plaster and whitewashed on the outside.

Directly in front of him stood the trading post of Swanson and McGillivray, a wide, plank-structured edifice with a wooden lean-to with inclined roof flanking it on each side and with windows of oiled paper. Beside one of the lean-tos stood a nine-foot wax tree, its berries the size of cherries and covered with a thick scale of white wax. It was hot and sultry, and there was no wind to stir the branches with their glistening white fruit. Along the front of the building was a wooden porch with heavily timbered roof, and on it stood a Spanish garrison officer talking animatedly with two braves in moccasins, doeskin leggings and jerkins. As Lucien made his way toward the entrance, ascending the two steps to the porch, they turned to stare at him.

It was the first time Lucien had seen Indians, and he could not help staring with an admiring curiosity. One, who held a large melon in his hands and had evidently been offering it in trade to the Spanish soldier, was rawboned, six feet tall, his coppery-tinted wiry bare arms bedecked with beaded bracelets, his high, broad forehead daubed with vermilion in cabalistic signs which proclaimed him of the Choctaw tribe. The other, a Creek, was sturdier and perhaps an inch shorter than Lucien himself. A turkey feather was thrust through his coarse black hair, which was braided at the back of his neck, and his ears were slit at the lobes and adorned with shells. Neither brave was bearded; indeed, their faces seemed more naked than those of any white man Lucien had thus far encountered in the new world.

The Spanish soldier turned to confront Lucien. *"Que pasa, hombre?"* he demanded, his narrowed eyes sweeping Lucien from head to foot.

Summoning the few Spanish words he had at his command after so little practice, Lucien replied, "I have come in search of Señor Alexander McGillivray."

"Sì esta aqui, señor." The soldier gestured toward the door of the building.

"Gracias," Lucien nodded in acknowledgment. Shouldering his saddlebag, he entered the door and was at once assailed by the varied odors of the trading goods, piles of deerskins in a corner, baskets of maize, millet, beans, potatoes and watermelons. Elsewhere, Lucien saw stretching racks of raccoon and bear skins, piles of muskets, and hogsheads containing balls, powder, as well as others filled with knives and tomahawks. It was in effect a warehouse

95

of trading goods and supplies within this squat building with its shingled roof. And to his right, nailed onto the rough-finished wall of plaster and mud, was a strip of bark the size of a flag, on which in varicolored dyes there appeared a map of Mobile and the territory upriver and beyond.

There were half a dozen Indians and citizens of the town near him intently engaged in haggling over goods. But he had eyes for only one who stood behind a heavy, square wooden table, clad in buckskin and wearing moccasins, but with the epaulets of a British colonel at his shoulders. He was six feet tall, but spare and almost frail-looking, superbly erect in carriage. Lucien was struck most by his large, dark, piercing eyes and by the hugely expansive forehead, which began seemingly at his very eyes and broadened at the top of the head, lofty and spacious.

Behind him, whispering to each other, stood a young half-breed and a muscular, pleasant-featured black man, also wearing Indian leggings and jacket.

Seeing Lucien, Alexander McGillivray frowned and beckoned. "You have business with me, sir?" he demanded in impeccable English. But even in that short sentence, Lucien was conscious of the vibrant, magnetic tone of the man, of his indomitable personality and the shrewdness of his appraising eyes.

"I speak English only passably, *Monsieur* McGillivray." Unerringly, he knew that this must be the famous trader-agent, for no one else in this room emanated the authority and dominance of this tall, spare, yet still young man who was not more than thirty, his dark-brown hair in the style of the Creeks, with braid at the back and a turkey feather thrust through it. "And my Spanish is meager, I fear."

"You do passably well, sir. Then you are French. And you have come to see me for what purpose?"

Lucien approached the table, laid his saddlebag upon it, opened it and took out the draft which Jules Ronsart had given him, unfolded it and handed it to the tall, imperious man who confronted him.

"Ah, yes, my friend Jules, who fancies horses just like

96

Charles Weatherford. A thousand *piastres,* to be claimed in trade or in cash as you choose upon my house. But you could have had this accepted anywhere in New Orleans, sir."

"That's true, *M'sieu* McGillivray. But I came to Mobile expressly to ask you to allow me to settle upon land, to farm it, to live upon it and to be of use as a citizen of this new world."

Alexander McGillivray's handsome face was bland as he glanced smilingly at the half-breed and Negro to his side. "Do you come as an agent of the French king, *M'sieu* Bouchard? I do not speak your tongue, though I studied Greek and Latin at Charleston. But Creek was my mother's tongue and I speak it best of all."

"This I've been told. But to answer your question, no, I have no politics. Indeed, I left France because the people are rebelling against the king and the aristocrats, and perhaps even as I speak to you, the king himself may be overthrown and a government of the people created to replace the throne of France."

"I have had from the newspapers in Charleston some little news of the unrest in your country, *M'sieu* Bouchard. In your own experience, what is it? Do you come here as a trader, a settler or a spy?"

"Never the last, I swear to you. If you must know, I am the younger son of a Count of the province of Normandy. I did not agree with the feudal laws which governed the province, and there were other matters which persuaded me to seek my fortune here. I was happiest when I worked upon the soil with my father's peasants, *M'sieu* McGillivray. That would not have been possible, and if indeed the king has been overthrown, the aristocrats will no longer hold the land."

"That much is true. You see, when I was a boy and schooled in Charleston, I was avid to read books of history and government, so that in time I might have wisdom to bring the tribes in whose veins there flows the same blood as my beloved mother's. And I will tell you directly that I am besieged not only by the French and the English, but also the Americans, to allow trading and settling upon the lands held by the Creeks. They will not sell their land so readily, a man must earn it. To do that, he must live with them and be a blood brother. If you have stomach and courage enough for that, then perhaps I may test your zeal."

"I see no objection to that, if you have none, sir. From what Jules Ronsart and also the second mate of the cargo ship *Guerrière* have told me about you and this part of the country, I understand that those who were the first settlers of all upon the land should have some first right of disposal."

"You talk at least like an honest man. But now I have some business with these gentlemen. My servant, David Francis, will show you to a house where you may have food and drink, and he will tell you more of my enterprises that you may better understand my dealings with those who come here to settle or to trade. But first, it must be understood that the Spanish, who control Mobile as they do New Orleans, and whose agent I am as spokesman for the Creek nation, have of necessity imposed restrictions upon all commerce. It is conceivable that, if you should be accepted by my people, you would respect all such Spanish laws."

"There is a saying that when in Rome one does as the Romans do, *mon colonel*," Lucien smilingly countered.

A bleak smile curved the lips of Alexander McGillivray as he beckoned to the half-breed. "My problem, sir, is that those who come to Mobile and the lands surrounding it often try to do far more than even we who are the masters here by tolerance of the Spaniards. And that leads to bloodshed, which I will not foist upon the Creeks. They are gentle, honest people, but once they are betrayed or angered, their vengeance is swift and merciless. Now go you with my servant, who will better acquaint you. Then perhaps tonight I shall talk further with you." The half-breed moved round the table toward Lucien, who understood that the interview was over. Alexander McGillivray strode from the table toward one of the Spanish officers and led him toward the back of this squat warehouse, pausing among the heavy wooden counters to show gourds containing medicine bark and beeswax, crude wooden bins in which cured tobacco leaves added their

98

aromatic fragrance to the multitude of odors which filled the humid air.

Lucien Bouchard had spent only a few minutes in this trading post in a town about which he had read only the scantiest of historical detail during his studies at the University of Paris. And yet, as he accompanied the half-breed out onto the wooden porch and saw once again the mighty bay of Mobile, he knew that he had already decided to meet whatever test Alexander McGillivray would set before him so long as the stake for which he played would be the virgin land his very soul coveted.

CHAPTER EIGHT

David Francis led Lucien down toward the end of the town, to a frame house on the corner of the street surrounded completely by a picket fence, with kitchen and garden outside. The house was set between posts and covered with bark five feet above ground, and the half-breed proudly remarked, "The cellar below has a brick wall which makes it cool for the keeping of milk and fruits." The house comprised two rooms, a hall, two closets, a double chimney, with a gallery all around. At the door, a pretty teen-aged Creek girl wearing doeskin petticoat and jacket and moccasins, a circle of beads around the top of her head and her black hair thickly plaited, genuflected to her husband and then smilingly gestured to Lucien to enter.

"It is one of my wives, Kitanda," the half-breed explained. "She will bring us venison, corncakes and coffee. The house is owned, of course, by my great master, who kindly allows Kitanda and me to use it when he is away on his business."

"You speak English well, much better than I," Lucien complimented him.

"That too is my master's doing. Even as a boy, he read many books and he learned the deeds of great men so that he could surpass them and bring the knowledge they had to shape it into good things for his people, the Creeks. While we eat, I will tell you about Alexander McGillivray."

"He called you his servant, did he not? And the *nègre, l'homme noir?*" Lucien inquired.

"That is Paro, and yes, he is a servant also as I to the great leader. He too was taught to read and write, and because of his learning saved many white settlers from the tomahawks of the Creeks. Eight years ago, when the British General Campbell was defeated and the whole of West Florida was given over to Spain, more than a hundred British settlers and their slaves set out for friendly Georgia by way of the Cherokee nation. When they crossed the wide Coosa River and approached the Creek town which traders call the Hickory Ground, the braves came upon them. From the saddles of the settlers, which were like those of the Georgians, the Creeks believed they were Americans, whom the Creeks have reason to hate. Had it not been for Paro, who took an old letter from one of the settlers and read from it, making it up out of his head, a full account of the journey of these settlers, they would have been massacred."

"That was a noble deed."

"My master does not wish bloodshed unless it be that of a faithless enemy. Ah, here is our food. Kitanda has prepared the best part of the venison in your honor, sir."

Lucien had tasted venison in France, but this version, simply prepared, seemed even more delicious, and he smiled and nodded his thanks to the young Indian girl. David Francis turned to address a compliment to her in the Creek tongue, and she inclined her head toward Lucien in thanks.

These people have a culture and a dignity which surely elevates them above the contemptuous term of sauvages rouges, Lucien thought to himself. Aloud, he prompted: "Your master seems very young to have such great powers as I am told he enjoys over the Creeks. I am eager to hear from you how he accomplished all this."

"It is a tale I am proud to tell, truly. His father, Lachlan, when he was but sixteen, had read of the wonders to be seen in this new land. He ran away from his wealthy parents to board a ship bound for South Carolina. It was in Charleston that he landed, with nothing more except a shilling in his pocket and a suit of clothes upon his back."

101

"That was courageous indeed, if foolhardy," Lucien interposed.

"But he was driven by the Great Spirit which has the power to touch a man's heart and guide him to his destiny. I, who am partly Creek—my father was English, my mother of one of the neighboring tribes near the Coosa—also have felt this touch me, but not as this has touched my Great Master. But then this boy Lachlan saw the traders packing to go into the wilderness and asked to go with one of them. He was given a jackknife as a reward for helping the trader, and that jackknife he sold to an Indian for two deerskins. When he returned to Charleston, he sold the deerskins for silver, and that was how he laid the ground for his great trading posts and his fortune."

"A beginning after so little to come to so great an end—it is an example to spur me, who has so much more to start with, to great things also," Lucien mused aloud. As David Francis eyed him curiously, he apologetically flushed and explained, "There is a parallel here, David Francis. My parents are wealthy, as were those of the father of your master. I, like that courageous man, came here because I did not trust the future of that wealth to which I had done so little to contribute. In France, where I lived, my father had good land and good cattle. When I worked with these, I was happy. When I thought of the misery of the poor people who were taxed to support the luxury I had not myself earned, I believed I could fulfill my manhood only by beginning again upon new land that I should earn."

"My master will understand that and I think he will admire it. Now let me tell you about his father's destiny. He wed Sehoy Marchand, who was then sixteen and the daughter of the very captain who once commanded that Fort Toulouse and was killed by his own soldiers because of a mutiny which was brought about by British traders who urged them to desert and flee to Charleston. Perhaps that is why my master is not greatly fond of the Royalists—though he has himself even stronger reasons."

"I am grateful to you for telling me all these things in confidence, David Francis. You heard me at the trading post, how I said that I am no agent for any country, only a man who happens to have been born a Frenchman and who willingly gives up his birthright for the chance to live in freedom and in honesty."

"If your deeds are the equal of your straight, honest words, then you will have nothing to fear from the Creeks or my master or any of us who serve him," David Francis gravely replied. "Now, after my master's father had wed Sehoy Marchand, whose mother was a full-blooded Creek of the Tribe of the Wind, which is the most powerful in all the Creek nation, he began a trading house at the Little Tallase on the east bank of the Coosa. The Creeks aided him, and thus he could extend his trading till he owned two plantations upon the Savannah River, besides stores filled with many goods in the towns of Savannah and Augusta. When my master was fourteen, his father took him to Charleston with the consent of his wife—you see, sir, among my people, the children always belong to the mother. Yet my master had no great love for the counting house at Savannah, where he was sent after his schooling and he began to study the histories of Europe. A man of the church taught him Greek and Latin."

"And I, who thought myself well schooled at the University of Paris, know now how little I have learned of this world in which I am about to live," Lucien ruefully admitted.

"My master has said that books are valuable only insofar as they guide a man to meet adversity when it comes upon him," the half-breed averred. "The British made my master a colonel, for they were anxious to secure his influence with the Creeks to help their trading. But because he fought on the British side during the War of the Revolution, the Americans seized the plantations and the black slaves belonging to his father. Lachlan went back to Scotland, where he still lives. It had been his hope that Alexander, my master, his wife Sehoy and his two daughters would inherit those plantations. Happily, a good man, William Panton, also from Scotland like my master's father, had founded a trading post at Pensacola and made a treaty with the Spanish when they became masters of that territory. It was Panton who called my master to him and befriended him to the Spanish authorities of West Florida. Five years ago, my master signed a treaty of alliance with Spain as the spokesman of the entire Creek and Seminole nations. And one of the laws set forth in that treaty, sir, is that no man may come upon the Creeks to cause rebellion against the King of Spain."

"Then you may be certain that I have no such desire. I look upon myself not as a rebel but rather as a humble pioneer ready to learn the lessons which this land and its peoples can teach me." Lucien stared intently at his host.

"I feel that you speak from the heart. This evening, after my master has dined and finished with his business, I will take you back to him and tell him that I believe you may be of service to him."

"My servant David Francis gives me good report of you, *M'sieu* Bouchard. He has told you, I believe, how my father's destiny was guided to the Creeks and how thus I was born with the proud boon of my mother's royal blood and my father's natural skill at commerce. Discount his praises of me—I am but a servant of my mother's peoples from Florida to Mobile and throughout this land which many seek to take from them. What he may not have told you is that the settlers of Georgia, whose forebearers came with Oglethorpe and were of British sentiments and greedy designs upon that and neighboring lands, even now try to discredit me and to remove me from my post as one puts tongue to the words that leap from the heart of every Creek. But this new President, the good General Washington, has written to me, entreating that I meet with his commissioners next month in Savannah, there to parley upon a treaty that will allow honest American settlers to come upon the land of the Creeks. I do not know yet if the tribes will agree to this, but it would make for peace and enable my people to pursue their trading, their hunting and fishing and their begetting of children who will perpetuate that which the Great Spirit wills for the Creek Confederation."

"Knowing no more than I do now, Colonel McGillivray, I would at once agree that land which is sown in blood often reaps a grisly harvest. It is what I fear most for my own unhappy country."

"Well then, to our business, sir. I will give you this piece of bark which has my sign upon it. If you will take it to the *Mico* at Econchate, and you will tell him that I leave to parley with these commissioners, you will be made welcome at this village of the Creeks. The *Mico*—the chief—will help you to meet Charles Weatherford, who is married to my half-sister and who holds a trading house on the first eastern bluff below the meeting of the Coosa and Tallapoosa. Perhaps you will wish to be of service to him, for in so doing you will serve me also. Or if life among the Creeks seems good to you, as you will observe during your stay at Econchate—that is the Creek word for Red Ground—and if you are worthy, you may become a blood brother of the tribe. All depends on your own skill and honesty and your ability to face hardship, danger, even the loss of your life."

"I've faced greater dangers in France, and I do not fear what awaits me in this land, Colonel McGillivray." Lucien stiffened, his eyes meeting those of the tall trader. He felt himself swayed by Alexander McGillivray's magnetism and eloquence, and he sensed also a driving and keen ambition which had its dangers for its owner—and perhaps, too, for himself.

"But because you have never lived with any Indians, *M'sieu* Bouchard, you will enter a totally uncharted world by yourself and with very little aid. Foremost, know that we Creeks do not understand the private ownership of land or houses as you whites do. One may own—the word is not even in the Creek tongue—a field or a house as long as he uses it. When he leaves it, it no longer belongs to him. Land belongs to the entire tribe, and not even a chief has the right to sell it or sign it away by treaty unless all the nations of the Creek Confederation do so agree. It is this, of course, which the new President of the United States hopes for in sending his commissioners to talk with me."

"I understand what you have said."

"Very well then. Do you see this bark map on the wall?" He strode toward it, pointing with his finger. "Here is Red Ground. You are here." His finger swept downward. "You will take a flatboat to the other side of the delta, and your journey will be on land northeast to a distance of some hundred ninety miles. Such streams as you may encounter are fordable. If you follow the course of the Alabama River, you will come without error to Red Ground."

"What provisions will I need, Colonel McGillivray?"

"I will honor your draft and open an account for you. If Weatherford accepts you as an aide, you may use it to purchase such things as you need for your own comforts as well as trading goods with my people. For the journey, I will give you a packhorse and enough jerky and dried corn to nourish you. The water from the river is good. There are berries and fruits you will come upon. Have you weapons?"

Lucien smiled, opened his saddlebag and drew out the pirate dirk he had taken from the lecherous attacker of Eulalie Villefranche, and then a hunting knife with bone handle sheathed in a hand-tooled leather scabbard sewn to a sturdy belt—the present of Jabez Corrigan.

"There are bears in this land, and however valorous you may be, I do not think you can kill one with either of those weapons. I will give you a musket with flintlock, powder and balls, a tinder box to make fire, and a compass. My servant David Francis will make you a copy of this map. With good fortune and if you do not tarry upon the trail, you should reach Red Ground certainly within a fortnight. And one thing more—there are poisonous snakes in the creeks and they often drop from the Spanish moss and the cypress trees upon unwary travelers. When you camp, do so upon high ground and away from the water."

"For all of this, much thanks, Colonel McGillivray."

The tall man's shrewd dark eyes reflectively studied Lucien's eager face. "You have spoken much to my servant and to me of freedom and equality. These I know are the tenets of your French philosophers, for I myself have read them. But you may not know that the Creeks hold slaves, the *nigras* from the Guinea Coast. I myself have them toiling for me at my plantations. Yet they are

106

well cared for, they have a better chance of survival than if they remained in their jungles, with their tribal blood feuds. Often we free them when they have proved their trustworthiness and our Creek women sometimes intermarry with them. Does this, I wonder, alter your concept of freedom, *M'sieu* Bouchard?"

Lucien frowned, knowing from the intensity of his interlocutor's words how important his answer would be. He knew also that neither guileful hypocrisy nor excessive adulation for the formidably vital man who faced him would ring true. Indeed, almost uncannily, Lucien found himself likening Alexander McGillivray to the crafty Armand Jean du Plessis, duc de Richelieu, that great Cardinal of France a century and a half ago who had founded French absolutism and, through his own ingenious conspiracies, managed to suppress the ceaseless intrigues of the recalcitrant great nobles of the realm. Young though this new land was, this tall spare man with the enormous forehead and the magnetically piercing eyes and the compelling voice, progeny of an Indian girl and a Scotch merchant, appeared to him to have the same cunning sagacity and ruthless determination which had characterized that immortal French statesman.

And that was why he said, choosing his words more carefully than he had done in his final examination before his professors at the University of Paris: "But, sir, you have already told me that the Creeks do not own in the same sense that we whites know the word. If that be true, these *nigras* you call slaves are perhaps more laborers guided to diligent toil by wise masters. Just as I regarded my father's peasants at Yves-sur-lac never as my inferiors simply by accident of birth—for that is the will of your Great Spirit and of my own God—but as men with emotions, hopes and dreams such as mine who unhappily had not the means nor perhaps even the skill to achieve them. Well, then I should not like to think that I myself would ever hold another man or woman in bondage to me by ruthless might or treachery, but if I should come to live among your people, I would abide by their laws insofar as I can reconcile them with my faith in the dignity of a man to shape his own life."

Alexander McGillivray's thin lips curved in an approving smile. "You might have made a greater diplomat, had you stayed in France, *M'sieu* Bouchard, than you may make a farmer or a trader here. But, as you yourself have said, it remains upon you to shape this destiny, this ambition which has driven you across the ocean to seek your fortune and to find me out. Go, then, you will sleep this night at the house of David Francis. He will bring you back here in the morning, to provide you with your needs for the journey to Red Ground."

"I thank you, Colonel McGillivray. I will deliver your message as you have instructed me."

"A moment. When I asked you whether you had weapons, you showed me this knife and this dirk." As he spoke, he idly reached his hand toward an iron tomahawk. "This is a *casse-tête à pique,* and it is perhaps somewhat amusing to reflect that it was made by the French and shipped to Mobile to arm their Indian allies against the English. In the olden days, we Creeks used stone hatchets. Can you wield one, I wonder?" As he finished the last words, he suddenly grasped the sturdy wooden handle of the weapon and sent it flying in an underhand toss toward Lucien Bouchard. Almost reflexively, stepping to one side, the young Frenchman deftly caught it by the handle. And then, in almost the same fluid movement, he whirled it overhead and flung it at the bark map. The sharp edge of the blade buried itself in the very part which was marked Econchate.

The black, Paro, and two vermilion-bedaubed Creeks who stood nearby grunted in admiration. Alexander McGillivray chuckled, and nodded. "You are strong and quick, qualities you will need for your journey and for your life once you reach Red Ground. Go then in peace among my people, and if any brave accosts you, you have but to show him that piece of bark on which I have put my sign that you are a friend."

Replacing the dirk and the belt-knife in his saddlebag and closing it, then shouldering it, Lucien Bouchard inclined his head toward the leader of the Creek Confederation and left the trading post, David Francis at his side.

Alexander McGillivray turned back to stare at the huge

bark map, then pulled the tomahawk free and tossed it to a tall Creek brave wearing leggings and moccasins, his bare chest bedaubed with vermilion and black in signs of the turtle and the bear, his ears pierced with shells. "Let him have two days' start, Ecanataba. Then track him." He tossed the tomahawk to the brave, who caught it as deftly as had Lucien.

The dark eyes glowered. "I kill?"

Alexander McGillivray shook his head. "No. He will show you my sign, of course. But you will take him prisoner, and when you do, you will bring him to Red Ground and he will be a slave of the Creeks. We will see then if his fine words can explain away his doing the tasks the women must do, such as planting corn, doing the cooking. And if he is a slave, he will wear the deerskin petticoat of a squaw."

The brave's eyes glistened, his lips curled at the demeaning jest. "Ecanataba will bind him over the tail of his own packhorse and lead him as a weeping squaw-slave to the *Mico*."

CHAPTER NINE

Compared to Arabe, the pack pony which David Francis led down the little ramp and onto the flatboat seemed small and frail. But when Lucien questioned the half-breed, the latter smiled and explained, "You need have no fear that this pony cannot carry you and the saddlebag on your journey. I have often seen such beasts loaded with three bundles of sixty pounds each, two suspended across the saddle and the third atop it, the pack covered with a skin to keep off the rain. My master has carried kegs of *taffai* on this one, even chickens and ducks in cages made of reeds which are strapped upon its back. And the one I have given you has several times made the journey from Mobile to Econchate."

Then, taking the oars himself, the half-breed rowed across to the eastern shore where the brick-constructed Spanish fort rose, across the estuaries of the delta by which entrance was effected into the great bay of Mobile. "You see now the high grove of the fort." David Francis pointed toward the Spanish garrison. "Northward is the high ground you will follow along the Alabama to the Creek village of Red Ground. There are enough provisions in meat and corn, if you eat sparingly, for ten days. With your flintlock musket, you can easily kill game if you should run out of provender."

"Yes, the map and the compass, and the knowledge that this pony will find the trail familiar will aid me greatly, David Francis. Thank your master for me, and be assured of my own deep gratitude to you, David Francis."

"I have marked the map to show you landmarks to look for, *M'sieu* Bouchard. Remember, now, to keep that pass which my master gave you handy at any moment, for if you are met by a brave who thinks you have come unbidden into the land of the Creeks, you will need it to save your life. Yet there is some assurance you may know as you set forth; the forehead of this pony has been marked with a strong dye, one which comes from the trading post of my master. Thus any member of the tribes along the Alabama will be familiar with it. Your danger would lie only from a renegade or a wandering party of hunters who may have strayed beyond their boundaries and who do not at once recognize the sign. But even for them the pass of Colonel McGillivray will be enough."

"Again, my thanks, David Francis." They had reached the eastern shore now, and Lucien, stepping onto the little dock, drew on the reins of the docile pack pony, to which he had attached his saddlebag, a pouch of provisions and a large leather water bottle. The flintlock musket he had strapped to the horn of the saddle along the side for easy access. The half-breed had shown Lucien how to load it with powder and ram it, how to place the ball and the flint, and Lucien had fired three or four rounds to familiarize himself with the weapon.

He turned now to David Francis and extended his hand, and the half-breed smilingly shook it. "May the Great Spirit guide your footsteps, *M'sieu*. Be wary on the trail always. Remember to camp on high ground away from the snakes. If you make a fire, keep it small, and when you have finished, try to conceal the signs of it from any who may pursue you." He uttered these last words slowly, his dark intelligent eyes intently fixed on Lucien's smiling face. Then, with a last nod, he got back into the flatboat and began to row it back toward the trading post.

Once, thousands upon thousands of years ago in the Upper Cretaceous times, the land of Alabama was submerged to receive deposits of sand, gravel, clay, chalk and volcanic ash. Roaming those prehistoric shores and swimming in the waters of the great Cretaceous sea were the last of the dinosaurs. In the Tertiary epoch, the seas returned again, to deposit, with the caprice of nature, more sand and gravel and clay and limestone, then retreated to their present place in the Gulf of Mexico. From this titanic alteration of nature upon its own handiwork came Alabama's Piedmont, the roots of the ancient Appalachian Mountains, the valley and the ridge provinces. From all of that, too, the evocation of luxuriant vegetation and monstrous insects. As the years passed and these plants and insects perished to be submerged beneath the waters of stagnant swamps, formations of vital coal were created—as yet unknown, but lying there for the far-seeing pioneer to unearth as part of the wealth of the land he would one day make his own.

To Lucien's awestruck eyes, the beauty of this land which began at the bluff near the fort and continued beyond his ability to see was wondrously green and rich. So beautiful, indeed, that its hidden dangers of serpents and animals did not disquiet him. Already, though he was nowhere within sight of land that would one day be fertile with the great crops that would make the South a power unto itself, his instincts for the soil and its potential told him that here bounteous harvests could be taken from the land by dint of tilling and planting and sowing. Here in this new land, as yet so sparsely inhabited, there could be no thought of poverty or starvation, none of the ills of an old royalty which he had left behind him. Even the harvested wealth of the province of Normandy, granted times of peace and diligent toil, could offer nothing unto what such land as this could provide for those who had the energy and dedication to pursue the task.

By nightfall, he had covered twenty miles along the route which David Francis had indicated on the rough map, and he had seen the lush growths which ornamented the lower reach of the Alabama. It was part of the vast Southern Floodplain Forest, in which grew the tupelo gum, the bald cypress and pecan, the shumard and laurel oaks, the swamp chestnut oak, and the picturesque water and willow oaks. There was the swamp privet, the red bay and the water elm, the cabbage palm and the sugarberry. Now in this sun-drenched land so near to water, the humidity of the soil itself fostered thick growth and dazzling pigmentation among the flowers and the trees, the bushes, the grass itself. He camped for the night on a little grassy knoll, a mile from the river, from which he could see in all directions. There was a majestic hush to the forest, broken by the twittering of night birds, the rasp of crickets and the buzzing of other insects he could not identify. But it was dry here, and with his gun lying beside him, loaded and primed, he ravenously attacked his provisions. He had resolved to use the dried beef strips and corn sparingly, but there would be no problem of finding water when the large leather bottle was emptied.

There was an exhilaration in him which made him lie for a long hour staring up at the distant glint of stars made tinier still by the branches of the trees above which sometimes obscured them from his view. A blanket under him, his head pillowed against the saddlebag, he thought of all that had happened to him in this incredibly brief span of time between the afternoon when he had ridden out to call upon the Provost-Marshal and to learn that Edmée loved him in her fashion but not as he had dreamed she might. It was as well. Pampered and used to the luxuries of Paris and all the attentions which her doting father and mother lavished upon her once they had come from that great city to take their abode in the rustic backwaters far from where revolution was breeding, she could not have had the fortitude to accompany him on a journey such as this. What he had done had been to look within his heart and, having found there an adoration for the true beloved, embellished and endowed her with all those attributes without really discerning that she in no way could possess them.

He could look back now and smile almost sheepishly at the pompous rhetoric of his verses, the lofty sentiments therein expressed, dedicated to her whom he had placed upon a towering pedestal and revered as the epitome of all that was gracious, beautiful and desirable in woman. No, his feelings of romanticism were not wrong, only his naive assumption that since he was drawn to her, she must inevitably possess all those qualities he cherished. Now he saw that these were only words, fine-sounding and yet empty when once applied to a creature of flesh and blood, of

113

capricious whims, of innate selfishness and all the feminine cunning of the female who, knowing herself desired, contrives to extract the utmost in self-gain from those who woo her.

It was startling to Lucien to discover how, across an ocean from Edmée de Courent, he could discover the pitiless, selfless power to look back at what he had been and how he had acted these past years and see that he had actually been more in love with love itself than with any woman of flesh and blood and thoroughly feminine characteristics. Yes, there could be no doubt of it now: he had been a kind of intellectual Pygmalion who had yearned so passionately to find a Galatea. And because Edmée had been virtually a neighbor and also because in that little village there had been no opportunity to meet other women and to ponder them and choose, he had concluded that because he found her desirable, she must necessarily be that divine model for all that was commendable, virtuous and praiseworthy in womanhood.

His breakfast, after a refreshing sleep, was only a swig of water from the bottle and a handful of the dried corn David Francis had packed for him. The pony, reins tied to a gnarled oak tree, placidly contemplated him as he looked around the site of his first night's camp. Lucien climbed into the saddle and set out along his course to the northeast. By midday, he had found one of the landmarks David Francis had marked on the map: an Indian burial mound, topped with shells, stone tomahawks and wild turkey feathers. Another hour and he passed near a little stagnant creek. Halting the pony, he looked around at the landscape, which seemed to change with miraculous new formations of trees and plants and grasses, and even in the merging, rustling, whispering sounds of birds and insects and the hidden animals that dwelt here where no man had his habitation.

As he stared down into the little creek, he saw a black-and-white banded king snake sunning itself on a wide flat rock beside the bank, and he shuddered with an instinctive revulsion, then headed the pony along the trail. Now the vegetation grew more dense, the trees cypress and some small dwarfed pine, and the intensity of the sun seemed to filter down even through the leafy branches and touch him with its burning fingers. He had smeared the malodorous bear oil liberally over his neck and face and hands, but his skin was already harshly reddened from the intense sun. As the shadows began to fall at last and to burnish the many shades of green vegetation with somber patterns, his pony suddenly shied and reared with a terrified whinny. Taken by surprise, Lucien was nearly thrown from his saddle. Something had brushed past him as it dropped from the overhanging branch of a huge cypress beside an almost dormant little stream that had edged away from the bank of the river and wound its way toward the trail.

The pony sidled, kicking and whinnying, and as it turned, Lucien saw in the grass a black-tailed, orangeish-scaled snake, its head drawn back to strike and its mouth open, the inside of its mouth milky-white. Wrenching the musket free, controlling the plunging pony as best he could with the clamp of his knees and calling out soothingly to it, he propped the heavy wooden stock against his shoulder and pulled the trigger.

The shot had the sound of a whipcrack, crisp and sonorous and reverberating in the still, forested area. The snake threshed and twisted and then was lifeless, the heavy iron ball having nearly ripped its head away. Lucien dismounted, feeling himself trembling with nervous reaction, and, a quick glance telling him that he had no more to fear from the first water moccasin he had ever seen, concentrated on calming the terrified pony.

As dusk fell, the immensity, the almost tropical lavishness of vegetation, thickly forested bluffs, flowers in profusion and riotous coloration enthralled the senses, and once again, with the eye of an esthete, Lucien marveled at the subtle and imaginative alteration of those colors applied by the palette of shadows. Such visual beauty defied the talents of a Watteau or a Botticelli; not even the manmade grandeur of the Louvre could begin to equal the artistic wonders of this seemingly primeval wilderness.

By nightfall, again choosing a camping place on higher ground and in a small clearing surrounded by clumps of pignut hickories and bitternut, with a single tall, lightning-scarred pine rising majestically above these others—

another of the landmarks David Francis had indicated for him—Lucien had his frugal meal of jerky and corn washed down with water. He thought of the Lucullan banquets at the chateau, especially when his father sought to impress a visiting dignitary or nobleman with the inspired improvisation and variety of his own kitchen; this plain fare now seemed far more palatable to him. The sharpening of his senses, the feeling of utter isolation and—though he knew it was not really so—the sensation of being the first to traverse this winding trail through country that resembled nothing in all France had made welcoming demands upon his sturdy young physique. Even more than in those afternoons when he had accompanied the old herdsmen with their cows or himself helped to prune the orchards Lucien felt a singular sense of belonging now to what was about him and what lay ahead of him.

He needed no fire again, and as he thought about it, the advice of David Francis came back to mind. Blandly helpful though the half-breed's words had been, they held nonetheless some greater concealed warning than he had at first perceived. To obliterate the signs of any fire so that no one might pursue him—could that, did that mean that someone would? From what he had read of the *sauvages rouges,* he knew that they were hunters and trackers unparalleled on any other continent. True, he had the *sauvegarde* of Alexander McGillivray himself to show the Indians that he came in peace and under the protection of their renowned spokesman. Yet was it not possible that there might be braves from other tribes who bore no firm allegiance to the trader-agent and who would see in him only an interloper to be slain?

He estimated that he had come nearly fifty miles in these two days, a not overly strenuous pace, and one that if maintained should bring him to Red Ground some six or seven days hence. From a distance, he heard the low, faint rumble of thunder, and he turned his head in its direction. It was not unlike the sound of cannon firing in battle.

Was it a symbol of what was taking place across the Atlantic, perhaps at this very moment? In mid-August, the States-General were meeting in Paris to decide the fate not only of a king and his court of aristocrats and empowered

116

nobles, but of an entire nation. Were the peasants still devotedly loyal to his father? Had Jean already married Edmée? His letter would not reach *Père* Morlain till sometime in November, and if the country were delivered up to revolutionary turmoil, perhaps never. Even granting that the letter was safely delivered, there could be no reply until at least the end of February or March of the next year.

He slept at last, after offering up a prayer for the safety of his mother and father, yes, even for Jean and Edmée, and even more than those last two, for all the humble, kind and loyal villagers of Yves-sur-lac.

He woke a little after dawn and, breakfasting swiftly, resumed his journey, determined to advance as many miles as he could before the intense heat of the midday sun.

It was indeed a hunter's paradise. There were flocks of wild turkey and woodcocks, quail and nutria, and as he followed the winding course of the Alabama at times he saw mallards soaring in an arrow-shaped cloud over the tops of lofty pine and cypress trees. Looking down from a small bluff, he could see the whiskered, comical face of an otter peering up at him, half submerged, its paws gripping a broken tree-branch lying athwart the river and its bank.

If Lucien had been traveling northwest instead of northeast, he would have arrived just beyond the Spanish fort of St. Stevens along the Tombigbee. By the end of the day, he estimated that he had come nearly seventy-five miles, into country which was part of the Southern Mixed Forest with its profusion of magnolia, cucumber trees, sweet gum and beech, red bay short leaf pine, loblolly pine and ironwood. There was timber enough here to build many a mighty fortress, or, much better still, many a thriving town whose inhabitants could live in peace. If the colonists of those original thirteen valorous states expanded their new republic and strengthened it, this new land, too, would surely within his own lifetime become a part of that heroic union.

His evening meal was made festive this third night when he discovered that he had camped near a clump of wild blackberries, and he slept dreamlessly. Before dawn, however, he was wakened by a sudden thunderstorm, and he

117

hurried to move his musket out of reach of the sudden driving rain. When the storm ended, the sun blazed more brightly than ever, and Lucien broke camp and followed the narrow trail to the northeast again.

Once again, a little after noon, the sky suddenly blackened and the jagged flashes of lightning punctuated by the furious claps of thunder made him take shelter under the projecting bank of a deep ravine. It was nearly an hour before the drenching rain abated and the sky again took on its serene blue. He was delighted with the calmness of his pony; even Arabe had shown nervousness during such violent storms. He fed it with a handful of corn and led it down to the banks of the river to drink its fill, then mounted and resumed his journey.

About an hour before twilight, the forest seemed to dwindle, and there were many stretches of clearing and little hills and ravines beyond. Because of the storms, he estimated that he had come perhaps a dozen miles along the way, and at best he would have another two hours before making camp for the night.

Somewhere to his left there was a strange, harsh coughing sound. The sturdy little pony snorted, moved to the right and momentarily lost its footing. Tugging at the reins, Lucien tried to direct it back upon the trail but found himself descending into a low ravine. The pony tossed its head and pawed the air with its right hoof, its eyes rolling. A few feet away, on a termite riddled whitened log, a little black bear cub was lapping its pink tongue against an already half-consumed comb of honey. Lucien chuckled at the little cub's antics and was about to urge the pony back up the edge of the ravine onto the trail when a hideous growl made him turn in his saddle to the left. Charging at him, eyes red with fury, was a full-grown black bear, the mother of the straying cub.

Lucien tugged the musket loose, having loaded and primed it that morning after the first early storm, aimed at the charging bear's head and pulled the trigger. But the flint was wet and there was no igniting spark to set off the charge. By then, the bear had leaped at the pony, raking its belly with savage claws. Its agonized scream chilled Lucien's blood as, clutching the useless musket's stock with

118

both hands, he drove the barrel between the bear's gaping jaws. Already the pony was stumbling, floundering in its death throes. Lucien flung himself off to the right and landed in the ravine and regaining this balance instantly, he drew the hunting knife Jabez Corrigan had given him from the belt-scabbard strapped round his waist.

The wounded bear, blood gushing from its muzzle, stood up and with its sharp-clawed paws seized the musket to tear it out of its torturing impalement. Lucien agilely leaped behind it, his left arm clamping round the bear's middle, as he drove the sharp knife repeatedly into the bear's heart.

The ferocious roars deafened him and the dying bear, twisting, slashed with its paw, ripping his waistcoat along the left side and drawing blood. As he thrust home a last time and then leaped away, reeling with pain, he saw the bear totter and then fall heavily on its side in a welter of blood.

The pony, its entrails spilling out onto the moist dark earth of the ravine, still screamed and kicked. Weak though he was, Lucien bent to it and ended its agony with a swift slash across its throat.

Sinking down on his knees, Lucien fought the waves of nausea and pain as he loosened the straps of his saddle-bag, fumbled for the tinder box and stumbled up out of the ravine. The river was not more than two hundred feet from him, but every step was a battle against the swirling black waves of sickening exhaustion, of the agonized pounding of his heart. Reaching the river bank at last, he unbuttoned his ripped, blood-soaked waistcoat, slowly eased it off his shoulders, grinding his teeth against the sudden blinding flash of lacerating pain in his side. Tearing off his shirt and discarding it, he winced at the ugly sight of the raked furrows of raw flesh which the bear's claws had left from just below the armpit nearly to the hipbone.

Wincing, he pressed the torn shirt against the bloody stigmata. Fortunately, they were not dangerously deep, but he must cauterize the wound as best he could. Tearing up a fistful of dry grass, he wadded it into a pile at his feet, struck a spark from the tinder box and watched its smoke till the little pile burst into flame. A bent, dried twig would be the cauterizing agent; holding it into the little fire until it kindled, and setting his teeth with every iota of his waning strength, he forced himself to touch the burning twig all down the ugly gashes. Sobbing groans escaped him, his chest heaving spasmodically, till at last it was done. Retching, sick unto death, he bowed his head until the spasm at last passed. Then, crawling to the water's edge, dipping his hands into the mud, he laved his tortured flesh, patting and rubbing and caking the black moist earth over the lacerations.

When it was done, he rolled onto his back and lay like one dead. An inquisitive bluebottle fly buzzed round him, settled on his forehead, then flew off. The soft lapping of the river, the still of the forest fringing it and the darkening of the sky were all that stirred now, save for the little cub back in the shallow ravine whining pitifully and pawing at its unresponsive mother.

CHAPTER TEN

He wakened to the soft sounds of the twittering of birds above and the gentle murmur of the river. As he moved, there was pain and he groaned aloud with it. Sitting up cautiously, he saw that the raking claws had left livid wounds but the mud had, together with his improvised cauterizing, puckered the raw flesh together, and there was no bleeding. He got to his feet with an effort, after first crawling to the water's edge to bend his head and to drink greedily and gratefully. Then he retraced his steps back to the ravine.

There was no help for it now; he must go on foot the rest of the way and he could not have come even halfway by now. The little bear cub was gone; only the carcasses of the bear and the pony remained. His saddlebag was partly pinned under the side of the pony. Exerting all the strength he could muster, he managed at last to drag it free. Once again swirling blackness clouded his eyes and he bowed his head, groaning again at the stabbing torture along his side. The greatest danger was in the festering of the wounds; his waistcoat and shirt had slightly protected him from the sharpest excoriation, which might well have caused him to bleed to death.

He forced himself to chew and swallow two strips of the jerky and gulped his water bottle empty. Then he went back to the river, knelt down and laved his side with the cooling mud. To carry the saddlebag the rest of the way would slow him grievously, and its contents, except perhaps for the razor which had been his father's gift and bore the crest of his own lineage, could be sacrificed. He would take a fresh shirt and waistcoat; the balls and powder were useless now because the musket was ruined. The pouches of corn and jerky could be put into the pockets of the waistcoat well enough and the dirk into his boot. He would strap the water bottle around his neck, first refilling it from the river and, of course, he would keep the map and compass as well as that piece of bark which was his passport into the country of the Creeks.

He went back to the river to fill the leather bottle and to press more wet mud against his throbbing side. There was nothing more he could do for his wounds. Fortunately, he still had the use of both arms and he could only trust to Providence that the bear's claws would not cause a dangerous festering that would devour the flesh and bring death after agonizing fever. There had been a villager in Bolbec who, riding toward Dieppe to be at the bedside of his dying sister, had been attacked by a pack of wolves and clawed so ferociously by the leader that he had died weeks later in unspeakable agony.

After he had dried himself a last time with the tattered shirt, he put on the fresh one and then the new waistcoat, flinching a little as each movement aggravated the lacerated flesh. But it was bearable, and it made better sense to forge on ahead and reach Red Ground, where perhaps the Creeks would have herbs and poultices that might aid him to recovery rather than wait here and hope that all his strength would soon return.

He stuffed the tinder box into his already bulging pockets and took a few steps along the trail to the northeast. His muscles ached sorely, but that was only natural; he had lain for long hours there beside the river, for when he stared up at the sweltering sky, he saw that the sun had reached its position of near-noon.

A little farther on, he found a gnarled, heavy branch which had fallen from a dying pine tree, and, setting one booted foot on one end, he tugged at the other with all his energy to break it into a kind of walking stick. Testing it, he found that it eased the torture of his side and steadied him. And then suddenly he halted, as an idea struck him.

He remembered having seen the Creeks at Alexander McGillivray's trading post in Mobile, their ears decorated with shells, their bodies daubed with meaningful signs. He would come into the Red Gound as an intruder, even though he carried the trader's imposing credentials. If he wished to live among the Creeks in order to earn his land, would it not be wise to prove to them that he could be a hunter too, coping with danger on a trail he had never before taken?

Though what he had to do made him grimace with nausea, he grimly turned back toward the shallow ravine. Using Jabez Corrigan's hunting knife, to which he owed his very life, he compelled himself to cut away the claws of those monstrously large front paws and to put them into the case with the crested razor. Then he went back to the trail.

A few hours later, he rested and had some of his corn and a draught of water from the bottle, then forced himself to rise, to forego the temptation to lie on this little grassy knoll and stare up at the sky and hope that the throbbing in his side would disappear. The soreness of his muscles, however, seemed greatly to have eased, and that was heartening.

At nightfall, he made his camp again, found that he was hungry enough for two more strips of jerky and more of the corn. His thirst worried him, however; it might be the sign of an approaching fever. His lips moved in a silent prayer to Him whom the Creeks called the Great Spirit that he might be granted time enough to know the end of this journey, its meaning and purpose, to learn if his resolve to leave France and all that he held dear behind him had been only the impulsive and overly romantic—yes, perhaps even cowardly—gesture of a dreamer instead of the will of a man who wanted to shape his own life by the principles he believed could alone justify it.

Just at dawn of the sixth day, when a faint pink luster began to dapple the darkened blue sky, the tall Creek brave, dismounting from his pony, saw the charred pile of grass and the twig. Squatting, he studied them carefully, then moved along the trail, his black eyes glittering and narrowed as he scanned the landscape. He came upon the shallow ravine and the carcasses of the bear and pony, and, a few yards distant, the discarded saddlebag. The Frenchman had done well for a novice, having lit no fires before this one. But the droppings of his pony and the indentations in the grassy knolls where Lucien had camped at night were signs enough for the alert Ecanataba. He paused long enough to let his pony drink its fill from the river, to feed it a handful of corn, then vaulted into the saddle and kicked his heels against its belly, his keen eyes following the trail ahead. There was no hurry. Let the Frenchman think he was safe from all pursuit, and then his enslavement would be the more crushing to his pride. Yet he did not intend to underestimate a man who had killed a bear with a hunting knife and taken its claws. For if the white stranger could reach Econchate before he did, he would be greatly honored once he showed the cruel claws of the she-bear.

The edges of Lucien's wounds had drawn together, the pain had somewhat subsided, and he was no longer feverish. To move his left arm, however, still caused torturing twinges which made him set his teeth and wince.

At the first shadows of twilight, drenched in sweat, his muscles aching, Lucien stretched himself out on his back on a small hilly patch of ground near a tall white hickory tree. He chewed two strips of jerky slowly, ate sparingly of only a half a handful of his remaining corn and washed it down with a long swig of water from the bottle. He reasoned that since his trail was always near the river and within occasional sight of small creeks, there was really no need to carry the bottle round his neck. It was an impediment which slowed him, and it could be discarded without danger.

As evening fell, he carefully eased off waistcoat and shirt to examine his wounds. They were jagged, purplish-blackened traces, but there seemed to be no suppurating matter from them. Each long breath that he drew sent a flash of pain along his torn side, but the crude walking stick had helped him. Still and all, he did not think that he had come more than a dozen miles this day.

It was peaceful tonight, not a cloud in the sky only the round ball of the full yellow moon and the orbit of tiny stars. If anything, the air seemed slightly cooler than on any night before, and it was a blessing. Beyond, he could hear the chirping of nightbirds, and from a greater distance, what sounded like the hooting of an owl. Suddenly he felt the back of his neck prickle, as if some subconscious presentiment were warning him not to yield to the overwhelming urge to close his eyes, relax all his muscles and seek the blessed Lethe of sleep.

He forced himself to move back against the tree and to prop himself up against it, the tree branch which had served so well as walking stick close to his right hand, and Jabez Corrigan's knife in its scabbard at his left. He fumbled for the piece of bark on which Alexander McGillivray had made the sign of peace and waited. As if the forest knew the taut intensity of his nerves now, it seemed more silent than ever of a sudden, but once again the hoot of the owl was heard, and this time nearer.

There was a sudden rustling overhead and, startled, he looked up to see a squirrel scurrying along one of the leafy branches up and out of sight. He exhaled a sigh of relief, and then once again he heard the hoot of the owl. Straining his eyes into the darkness beyond the trees and clumps of bushes, he could make out nothing. Even the light of the moon did not help there where all the trees grew so thickly to protect the animals as well as their predators who took refuge in them. And then suddenly, without warning, out of the darkest shadows sprang a tall, wiry brave, naked to the waist in his buckskin leggings and moccasins, his chest painted with the marks of turtle and bear, his ears pierced with shells—and Lucien Bouchard recognized one of the Creeks he had seen at the trading post.

"Friend!" he called anxiously, holding up the piece of bark.

The Creek approached slowly, crouched, a stone tomahawk in his left hand, rawhide thongs dangling from his right. "I not kill, you I take to Econchate," he said in a deep guttural voice.

"No, no, see this? Friend, friend of your chief McGillivray!" Lucien insisted, waving the bark again toward the brave.

But Ecanataba shook his head. "I say again, I not kill, I tie hands and take you with me. Make no trouble, no hurt. Put hands out and stand up!"

On his lips there was the contemptuous smile an adult might have for an errant child, and Lucien stared at the dangling thongs and understood. It had been a test indeed, except that Alexander McGillivray had shortened the odds in his favor. And, having heard him speak so loftily of freedom and how even a slave would have incentive to achieve it, the trader had with ironic casuistry determined to let him taste the gall and shackles of servitude for himself. And once he was led with thonged wrists to Econchate, there would be an end to his dreams of new lands on which to settle and to till and sow and reap.

"I cannot move—the bear—my side hurts too much—come, tie me then as I sit here," he called to Ecanataba, gesturing toward his left side.

The brave moved forward, confident now, gripping his stone tomahawk and lifting it to warn Lucien of the futility of resistance. Lucien, his right hand having edged stealthily toward the broken piece of branch, now seized it and flung it into the Indian's face.

Taken by surprise, Ecanataba stumbled back with a hoarse grunt, dropping his tomahawk. With a supreme effort, Lucien lifted himself from the ground and leaped forward, his arms wrapping round the brave's slick, greased waist, and flung him heavily to the ground. They rolled, twisting, entangled, the brave trying to thrust his free hand down to the hunting knife sheathed in the belt of his leggings, but Lucien gripped his wrist and twisted it with all his strength till a stifled groan was torn from his assailant. The agony of his side seethed through him, but there was no time to think of that now. He had never killed a man before, but now he was inexorably compelled to do so if he wished to save his own life; he could read the hatred in the black glinting eyes of the man on whom he lay, holding him down as best he could, preventing that hand from reaching the lethal knife.

Drawing up his right foot, his left hand still clutching

the brave's right wrist, Lucien thrust his right hand down to his boot and drew out the pirate dirk. Then, as Ecanataba lunged with his left hand to thrust thumb and forefinger against his jugular, Lucien thrust home the dirk between the Creek's ribs.

There was a gurgling cry, Ecanataba stiffened, his eyes rolling, and then he slumped in death.

The hot torment of his wounds washed over Lucien like scalding water, bringing tears to his eyes, as he crouched, fighting for breath, exhaling stertorous gasps. He felt the warm trickle of his own blood through shirt and waistcoat, as he tugged the dirk free, wiped it on the grass and replaced it in his boot.

For a long moment he stood looking down at the dead Creek, whose face was twisted in the rictus of violence and hatred, the lips curled back, the teeth bared, the eyes wide, staring, accusing. Again he fought the nauseating pain, trying to think clearly. The Creek must have come on a pack pony as he had; it was certainly unlikely that he had come by foot all the way from Mobile, since he had no pouches for supplies strung about him. Somewhere in that forest, his pony must be tethered. And with that pony, Lucien could reach Econchate, perhaps in time to have his wounds treated; to walk the rest of the journey was unthinkable now with the pain he was enduring.

Gradually accustoming himself to the darkness, he moved cautiously forward, through trees and bushes, till at last he heard a soft nickering and uttered a cry of joy. The pony stood, a musket tied across its saddlehorn, pouches of jerky and corn on each side, and a leather bottle of water. He had killed a man and these were the spoils, and in such a wild, strange land the victor took those spoils without scruples or afterthought.

He led the pony back to the clearing, tying the reins to the hickory tree, then put the razor case into the dead brave's pack. Then, feeling his strength wane, he grasped the saddlehorn and bowed his head, trembling as the violent reaction swept him. At last, steadying himself, he eased off waistcoat and shirt and groped his way to the river, where, after avidly gulping as much water as he could take, he scooped mud up with both hands and

127

pressed them against his bleeding side. When he had caked the wounds until he could no longer see the ooze of blood, he rolled over onto his back and let exhaustion and sleep claim him.

When he woke it was well past noon of the next day, and at first he opened his eyes, dazed, till he remembered. The slightest breath now sent flashes of pain all down his side, but at least the bleeding had stopped. He plunged his face into the water at the river's edge and then made his way back to the pony. This time he forced himself to down four strips of jerky and two handfuls of corn, and then, emptying his pockets of all but the map, compass and McGillivray's fateful piece of bark, untied the reins and painfully mounted Ecanataba's pony. It was docile and did not rebel against this strange rider. Under the bright sun, without a backward look at the stiffened body of the dead Creek, Lucien turned to the northeast and toward his goal.

Four noons after his encounter with the Creek who had trailed him, Lucien came in sight of the village of Econchate. It was near the bank of the river, and heading it was a mound on which rose a spacious timbered house, whose dimensions his practiced eyes estimated at about 120 feet by forty. To one side stood another edifice almost as long and as wide, its roof covered with split pine cones. After that, there were smaller timbered houses, and then scores of wigwams. These houses were made of notched and pegged timbers, covered with palm and straw and reeds, daubed with clay between the uprights. There was a wide corridor from the central and largest house down to the end of the village. He saw mongrel dogs, young girls clad in doeskin breechclouts and moccasins, gray-haired squaws drawing water in clay gourds from the river bank. At the entrance to the largest house, four tall Creek braves stood with arms folded across their chests, staring at him with impassive gaze. Slowly he dismounted, his legs shaky beneath him, for he had a touch of fever just the night before and his body was drenched in sweat. Once again the edges of the wounds had drawn together, but he had discovered matter in them, and he realized the danger.

Nonetheless, straightening with a visible effort, holding the reins of the pony, he moved toward the main house guarded by the four braves, the bark *sauvegarde* palmed in his left hand for them to see.

"Do you speak English? I come to see the *Mico*," he said in a thick, hoarse voice.

Two of the four braves guarding the largest and foremost house at once disappeared into the entrance, and a moment later there emerged a tall, stately Creek, wearing a mantle of interwoven bark and flax ornamented with shells and painted with stripes of varicolored dyes. Two eagle feathers were thrust through his topknot, the rest of his iron-gray hair being formed into a short braid which reached only to the back of his neck. He carried a long wooden spear pointed with flint, and behind him came two shorter, stockier Creeks who wore mantles also, but less imposingly ornamented, and with only a single eagle feather in their topknots.

Lucien righted himself and stepped forward to face the three evident dignitaries of this Indian village, holding out the marked piece of bark. "Friend," his voice wavered. "This is from Colonel McGillivray to the *Mico* of Econchate. I come in peace to your village."

The tall gray-haired mantle-clad Creek advanced, his two companions standing impassively and watching as he reached out to take the piece of bark from Lucien's faltering hand. "I am Tunkamara and I am *Mico*. I speak your tongue, our great one who speaks with many tongues for all the Creeks has helped me know it. You come from Maubila?"

"Yes. And to tell you that Colonel McGillivray goes to Savannah to meet with the American commissioners for the treaty of peace between the settlers and your people."

"That is good if the Great Spirit so wills it. But you lead the pony of the son of my war chief Tantumito. How is this? Is Ecanataba not well that he does not ride it?"

Lucien saw the second mantled Creek, his face wrinkled and grave, stare intently at him, and intuitively he realized that this must be the father of the brave he had been forced to kill. As again the sick nausea made him tremble, he compelled himself by sheer will to stand as straight as

129

he could and to say in as steady a voice as he could command, "He will not come. He tried to bring me prisoner to your village, we fought, and to my sorrow but to save my own life, I killed him."

There was a simultaneous gasp of surprise from the four guards of the *Mico*'s dwelling, and the father of Ecanataba looked upward at the sky and held his hands clasped at the top of his forehead as he murmured words which Lucien did not understand.

Tunkamara put a hand to his heart, looked up at the sky and then answered, "It was the will of Hisagita-imisi, the preserver of breath, who willed it. As he who is the supreme god of the Creeks willed that you be a mightier warrior than the son of my war chief. As *Mico*, I welcome you to Econchate. No man here and no squaw or child either shall lift a weapon against you, or the deed will be punished. This is our law. But you are wounded—look to him, Tisarte, Munarta!" he swiftly turned to call to the guards.

For Lucien Bouchard, standing before the *Mico* under the fierce midday sun, had suddenly fainted.

CHAPTER ELEVEN

When he woke, it was to find himself lying on a blanket, his waistcoat and shirt having been removed so that he was naked save for breeches and boots. He was in a little house built of logs and poles with walls of reeds and canes, plastered with thick coatings of sand and clay, and a thick thatch roof above. The floor was of sandy earth. Beside him knelt a girl of startling beauty, her black hair drawn away from the top of her high, smooth forehead and thickly plaited almost to her waist. She wore a loose, wide doeskin petticoat from waist to ankles, her small shapely feet thrust into beaded moccasins of the finest deerskin, and a doeskin jacket, also ornamented with beads and bits of shell. Her feet and hands were dainty and small, and as she knelt she cupped between her small slim fingers a wooden bowl containing some kind of stew with bits of dried venison, squash, corn, cabbage and peas.

Her soft coppery skin glistened from grease and the juice of an herb, and her scent was strange to Lucien but not at all unpleasant. Her soft, expressive brown eyes were closely spaced, large and wide with solicitude as she stared down at him. Her nose was straight, small, with delicate nostrils, her cheekbones high-set, her mouth small and firm. On her slim bare arms she wore copper bracelets, on which, by some kind of rude chisel, was engraved the head of an eagle. Though she could not have been more than seventeen or eighteen, so far as Lucien could estimate, she had the quiet almost regal dignity of a mature woman.

The pain seemed to have left him. He glanced at his left side and saw that straps of deerskin had been wound round him, and he could feel under them a kind of moist bark pressing tightly against his wounds.

The girl smiled shyly, then held the bowl closer to him, nodding her head as a sign that he was to eat. "Do you speak French or English?" Lucien asked in his native tongue. The girl stared back at him uncomprehendingly, and he rephrased his question in English.

"Some I speak, not like my father. You eat now."

"How long have I been here?"

"Twice the sun has risen and set. Our *Windigo* has made strong medicine. But you must eat."

He raised himself to a sitting position, trembling with a kind of giddiness, then took the bowl from her soft hands and began to eat. It was tasty and nourishing, and he emptied the bowl before he spoke again. "My name is Lucien. How are you called?"

"I am Dimarte, daughter of Tunkamara, who is of the Eagle clan and *Mico* of Econchate."

"Dimarte," he repeated. "It is a name pleasant to say."

She looked down, then murmured, "It means, she who serves."

"I would talk with your father, Dimarte, for I have come to live among your people on the land if I am allowed"

"You are not from Maubila?"

"No. I have come from across the great ocean because there will be great suffering there, perhaps even war."

Her eyes again considered him. "You do not flee from war because you are a coward. You cannot be such, if you have slain Ecanataba, for he was the son of the war chief who is of the Snake clan."

"I did not want to kill him, Dimarte. But he meant to take me prisoner and bring me here as a slave."

"There are slaves in this village. Their skins are black and they too come from across the ocean."

"This I was told by the man who sent me from what you call Maubila, the Colonel McGillivray."

She rose with an exquisite, supple movement, holding the empty bowl and staring down at him. "When you are well, my father will hold council. The old men will talk and they will say if you are to stay here. Now you are in the house of a warrior whose spirit passed years ago. Here you are safe from all danger, for my father himself has said this. The *Windigo* will come soon to see if your wounds are healed." She turned and left the little house, and he lay back, an anxious frown on his handsome, pain-drawn face. What if they rejected him? This primitive hospitality had been gracious indeed, and yet it might mean no more than what one would have found in Europe: even an enemy who partakes of your bread and salt is your guest until he leaves your house, and then you may in all conscience slay him. The brave he had killed would surely not go unmourned, and there would be those who would want his life because he had taken Ecanataba's. There was no doubt in his mind now that Alexander McGillivray had meant to trick him, and if the order had been given to enslave him, might it not be carried out here in this village where he was for all intents and purposes a captive?

Yet at least his wounds were healing well, and if it was fated that he was to become a slave or even put to death, he would meet the test with regained strength and courage. For Lucien Bouchard still could not forget that his father had addressed him as a coward because he had expressed the will to come to a new land where there would be no politics or feudal privileges to determine how a man could decide how he wished to live his life.

Thanks to the medicine applied by the *Windigo*, a wizened whitehaired Creek named Tsipoulata, Lucien swiftly regained his strength. The medicinal bark which was used as a compress against the claw scars of the bear was, he was given to understand, much in demand at Mobile, and the Creeks traded it there along with deer and bearskins. Since the majestic Alabama River ran downstream toward the trading post of Alexander McGillivray, the trade goods were floated on pirogues, canoes hollowed from the trunks of larger trees, or on log-constructed rafts or flatboats, a journey of from six to ten days. These crude but useful vessels could not move upstream, and so supplies were taken by pack ponies from Mobile to Econ-chate.

The lovely Dimarte had given Lucien to understand that he had the freedom of the village, and out of curiosity alone, as soon as he found that he could walk about without pain, which was the very day after his first meeting with the *Mico*'s daughter, he walked out into the Indian village and saw the disposition of the houses and wigwams. Here too, just as in France, there was every sign of rank and status: the wigwams at the far end in this long square were those of the untried braves, who had not yet distinguished themselves in battle. With greater skills and prowess came the log and pole houses, and then the more imposing dwellings of the members of the council, the war chief, the dignitaries of the various Creek clans who formed this branch of the great tribe. Even in the attire of the Creeks, this difference in rank was exhibited: most of the braves wore only breechclouts and moccasins of deer-skin, while others like the *Mico* and the war chief donned ceremonial mantles—as they had done to receive him at the gates of Econchate—or buckskin jackets and the same long combination of breeches and leggings which he had observed garbing Alexander McGillivray himself. The women invariably wore short protective leggings from in-step to mid-thigh, a protection against snakebites, though Dimarte herself at ceremonial rituals wore knee-length boots of the finest treated doeskin, short soft leggings which covered her loins under the beaded petticoat. The children, who he could see at first glance were doted on by their mothers (and he remembered how David Francis had told him that the Creek mother must decide the future of her child), went about naked except for moccasins till they reached the years of puberty.

To the east of the village were the cornfields and some patches of indigo, others of potatoes and vegetables. There was a smoking house for the treatment of venison and bear meat, this latter a great delicacy among the Creeks.

That second evening, as he was going back to his little house for the evening meal which Dimarte would bring him, he decided to shave his bristly black beard. The razor case lay beside his blanket, and he opened it just as the

134

Mico's daughter entered. When she saw the bear claws, dark with the animals dried blood, her eyes widened and she sank down on her knees, placing the bowls of food carefully to one side of her, and bent her head down toward the sandy floor. "You are great hunter and great warrior too," she avowed, straightening and staring intently at him.

"It was a bear I met on the trail from Maubila, Dimarte," he told her. "Luck was with me, for my musket did not shoot and I used this hunting knife." He touched the scabbard-belt.

"You killed a bear with just that knife? Then indeed you are a great hunter. My father must know this at the council. Will you not give me the claws of the bear to show him, Lu-shee-ahn?" (He thought that he had never heard his name so exquisitely pronounced!)

"Willingly, Dimarte. And now, if you will help me, I would shave my beard. With this, which is a razor." He lifted the silver-handled razor from the case. "But I will need soap."

"I have never seen that done. Here, the braves pluck the hairs from their face and brows with clam shells."

"That would be too painful for me," he chuckled, enchanted by the sudden roguish smile which curved her soft lips. "Do you not, perhaps, have soap—it is something one uses to rub upon one's face when one wishes to clean it."

"I will see." She rose quickly, then very nearly blushed as she knelt down again to tender him the bowls of his supper.

"You must not kneel to me, Dimarte. You are the daughter of the *Mico*," he gently remonstrated as he reached down to take her by the hands and lift her to her feet. "I will put the bowls on that little bench and it will do very well." He retrieved them, walked over to the low bench in the center of the little house and set them down.

"But I am the one who serves, and you are the guest of my father and all his people," Dimarte softly countered. "I will try to find what you wish." And again, to his secret delight, she pronounced his name with the lengthened vowels and the lingering accent which was almost like a caress. He watched her go, entranced. Her naturalness, her dignity, her wonderful maturity despite her youth wêre wedded to a piquant coquettery which had, however, nothing of the courtesan or of the schemingly ambitious female who excuses all she does on the grounds of her prized virtue. In this short time, she seemed to epitomize for him the most enticing qualities of both Edmée and the Cuban adventuress, yet with none of their flaws. Perhaps indeed fate had guided him to this unknown Creek village from across the ocean, where, with God's help and his own determined strength and willingness to learn the new lore of this land, he could begin his life again and achieve more than ever he could have done at Yves-sur-lac.

She returned with a gourd containing wood-ash lye and lumps of bear fat rendered into slimy lumps which looked to be more abrasive than cleansing. At his behest, she brought a bowl of water and then stood watching at the entrance of the little house, fascinated by his novel act. He would have sworn he heard her giggle when, soaking his beard in the water and then cautiously rubbing one of the lumps from the gourd against the thick, moistened hairs, he swore under his breath at the stinging harshness of that crudely made soap against his sunburned skin.

But at last he shaved his beard as closely as he could without making his skin painfully tender—this soap indeed was strong enough to cauterize a wound!—and then he turned to look at her and smilingly said, "You see, it is much easier to do this than to pluck each hair, Dimarte."

"Yes. I must tell my father about this new way of taking off the hair from one's face."

A sober, disturbing thought suddenly seized him: "Is the father of the warrior I slew upon the trail angered with me, Dimarte?"

"He understands the will of the Great Spirit. But the wife of Ecanataba, she who is called Shehanoy, is said to mourn in anger and in grief. She has shorn off her braid, and by Creek law may not marry again until the next corn festival, which is eleven moons from now. But she knows that you are under my father's protection, Lu-shee-ahn." As he watched her soft lips form the musical, unique pronunciation of his name, he had an irresistible impulse to kiss them, and he found himself crimsoning just as he had done when he had penned his sonnets to Edmée de Courent—how long ago that now all seemed!

He pondered the rest of the afternoon over the startlingly advanced culture of the Creeks, the more absorbing because their spokesman was a man whose father had been a Scotch trader and himself the pampered son of extremely wealthy parents. He recalled not only what he had read of the Spanish conquest of the Indians during his courses at the University of Paris, but also the charmingly fanciful musical tableau composed by Jean Philippe Rameau as a diversion for the King of France. Rameau had endowed the "red savages" with the same kind of romanticism which he himself had applied to his courtship of Edmée, while the accounts of the Spanish attempts to "Christianize" the Aztecs and the Incas as well as the Indians of southeastern North America had abounded in pious declamations, suggesting that these benighted savages were in sore need of the true faith to redeem their barbaric souls. It was Hernando de Soto who, just 250 years ago, had come from Cuba to peninsular Florida with merely 600 soldiers, 200 horses, and thirteen hogs and marched into this very territory where Lucien was enjoying hospitality of the Creeks. In the battle which had ensued, only 82 Spaniards were killed as against 3,000 of the Alibamons and the Muscogees. Whimsically, the historical references which Lucien had read of this great battle mentioned that de Soto's thirteen hogs had bred into thousands, more than enough to provide his marching troops with the meat they needed during all their time of exploration and conquest.

From that victory, de Soto had found what he named the "Rio Grande," the Great River, which was actually the Mississippi. It was gold he sought, but he found only frustration, fever and finally death three years after his conquest of the Indians, and his body was sunk at midnight in that same "Rio Grande" which he had discovered, so that the Indians might not claim it and be heartened enough to drive back the white intruders.

The Indian tribes had not yet united, but after the terrible extermination De Soto and his soldiers had wrought

137

upon them, their ranks were filled by braves of Mexican origin who had been driven out of their country by still another intrepid Spanish explorer-conqueror, Cortez. These warriors had formed the Muscogee Confederacy, and when they defeated the French some sixty years ago in this very century, they became the most formidable tribes in this southeastern portion of the country. This confederacy was called "Creek" because of the many beautiful rivers and streams which wound through the territory occupied by these fierce warriors. Dimarte had already told him that her people had conquered the tribes upon the Chattahoochie and all the rivers from there to Savannah, even overcoming those tribes who lived in the territory of South Carolina. This, then, was where his journey had led him, and he would live or die now by the edicts and the simple primitive creed of those who were now his hosts.

What he had already seen in these few short days of the peaceful life of this village near the banks of the Alabama River was indeed at variance with the stirring legends of Creek warfare against the white invaders from across the Atlantic, those who came for gold, others who came in the name of the Holy Church and those who came, perhaps like *Sieur* de Bienville, to broaden the horizons of the Old World by finding new boundaries where there might be trade and friendship between the youngest and the oldest nations in this still not fully charted world. It had been a wise impulse to take the claws of the mother bear with him to Econchate, as well as the pony of the son of the war chief. The agricultural life he saw extending beyond this village in the well-cultivated fields of corn, of indigo and of vegetables and even some fruits was one he knew from France; the world of war and cruelty and bloodshed was one he had tried to flee in advance, only to find himself, by the trick of fate, plunged into it headlong.

He had already determined, in the event that he should be summoned to attend this council of the *Mico* and his advisors, to offer as proof of his sincerity an eagerness to learn the Creek language not only so that he might better understand their way of life, but also so that he might communicate to them the things he had learned in working upon his father's estate across the ocean. And he knew whom he wished to be his teacher: the gentle, sympathetic young daughter of the *Mico,* who, when he had first opened his eyes after his fainting spell before the gateway of the Creek village, had appeared to him as a kind of ministering angel.

It was a pleasant thought which occupied him for the rest of the day, and by the time twilight fell, he was almost impatiently awaiting her bringing him the evening meal. He marveled at the friendliness thus far shown by all of the inhabitants of this evidently well organized and smoothly run Indian village. There had been no derisive jeers or taunts, not even gawking curiosity at his appearance and his walks in the square to observe how the houses and wigwams were constructed and placed and to inspect the fields of growing crops beyond the village. No matter how bloodthirsty the Creeks were reputed to be— and what history he had read seemed to verify the legend—he had been treated like an honored guest with a respect and dignity which, though perhaps it lacked the ostentation of Versailles, was assuredly genuine.

He rose to his feet as the supple, black-haired young girl entered the little house. He went to take the wooden bowls of his supper from her hands, placing them on the low bench and asking if she would not share the food with him. Her eyes lowered, her voice soft, she agreed.

"Will I be allowed to come to the council with your father, Dimarte?" he anxiously demanded.

"That is not yet sure. There are those who wish to send you back to Maubila to say to our great leader that we will wait for the news of the parley between the Americans and himself before we allow more white strangers to come upon us. Others argue that if you have been cunning and strong enough to kill the she-bear and defend yourself against Ecanataba, you would have wise words for the council. It will be decided when the sun has run half its course in the sky."

So he could only wait and hope and, now making idle talk with her about what he had seen in New Orleans and Mobile and something of the land where he had lived before his journey, to glance covertly at her from time to time to observe the loveliness of her features and to guess at the lithe, graceful body which her finely wrought and beautifully beaded doeskin garments concealed.

"If you will, tell the *Windigo* for me, Dimarte, that I am nearly well now and that I am grateful. Already most of the pain has gone from my side, and I would not trouble him to visit me tonight. Tell your father too of my gratitude for all the kindness everyone has shown me," he said as she was taking up the bowls and preparing to leave the little house.

"I will say to the *Windigo* and to my father what you have told me, Lu-shee-ahn." Once again he watched, almost spellbound, the charming way in which her soft lips moved to approximate the French pronunciation of his name.

His heart was strangely light, despite the troubling concern over what the council might decide tomorrow. Somehow he felt that in Dimarte, the closest and therefore the dearest to the mighty *Mico*'s heart, he should have a strong advocate on his side when his case was heard. And when he told her of his desire to learn Creek so that he could understand her people and speak his own thoughts clearly in that tongue, she had smiled and nodded, though she had not otherwise responded to the offer.

He sat staring at the empty room of this house in which, though a guest, he was still isolated, still an intruder, veritably on trial. He could hear the barking of a dog, the call of a squaw to her child, the faint crackling of a fire beneath a crude spit on which a rabbit was turning near one of the wigwams halfway down the square of the village. He had walked out to look, not too quickly after Dimarte had gone, lest she perhaps turn back and see that he was staring after her—but already the absence of her gentle, candid presence in this little house had made a sudden almost self-pitying stab of loneliness pierce the pleasure he had known during his convalescence.

And the sight of that rabbit turning on the spit had served, also, to bring back the memory of the dead poacher who had fallen victim to the ancient and inexorable feudal laws which had become so intolerable in France, since they had approached total despotism. Here in these original thirteen colonies, men had banded together, oblivious to their religious and genealogical differences, to overthrow another kind of Old World despotism: that of a British king who believed that his subjects ought to be grateful to pay tithes even though they might not utter a word in the imposition of them.

There was silence at last in the village of the Creeks, and a three-quarter moon hung in a partly clouded sky as he turned, somewhat morbidly pensive, back to the blanket which would be again his simple comfortable bed. There was a heaviness and stickiness to the night air, and the thongs around his half-naked body which held the medicinal bark against the ugly claw marks of the bear chafed him. Carefully, he loosened them, drew off the bark and saw that the angry purplish-red and blackened marks were fading, though the unmistakable furrows of those savage claws would never totally be effaced. He drew and exhaled several deep breaths, finding hardly any pain at the effort, and then, smiling as he remembered Dimarte's charming amusement over his shaving away his beard, lay down to sleep.

But this time, though he seemed to fall almost at once into sleep, he dreamed. And it was as if all that had happened in so short a time since that fateful May afternoon paraded in swift, unstaying images before him: the ride down into that little valley, that little *asile du vent*, to find his father's gamekeeper standing with a smoking musket over the body of the little poacher; the affability of the Provost-Marshal and then Edmée's unexpected parry to his honorable offer of marriage and lifelong devotion; the taunting hostility of his own brother across the table and his abrupt decision to leave the chateau forever. Then in swift procession the journey on the *Guerrière*, the unexpected friendship with that rogue of a red-haired Irishman, poor Edmond's wasted death, and then the sale of Arabe and the unforgettable night with Eulalie Villefranche. And after that, with hardly a pause in this kaleidoscopic flashback of his subconscious mind, the meeting with Alexander McGillivray and the beginning of his trek into an unknown wilderness. The snake that had dropped upon his path from an overhanging tree branch, then the bear—

the bear and the musket that would not fire, and the knife
—the knife—

He opened his eyes to find that he was trembling and sweating, and in that same moment a shadowy form flung itself down on him, a hand thrusting down to his left side in search of that very knife in the scabbard-belt which he still wore strapped around his waist. A warrior in a breechclout, slim and lithe and strong—

Not a warrior, a woman, her hard, round closely spaced, firm-nippled breasts mashing against his chest, and the hiss of her voice in his ear: "*Chetato durtatimisi! Gusadio Ecanataba migadra!* (Dog of a white man, I avenge my husband Ecanataba!)"

She had managed to grasp the handle of the knife, but his left hand grasped her wrist and dragged it away. Now with her other hand she clawed at his eyes, hissing like a snake, spitting vitriolic curses which, though he could not understand a word, told him at once that this was the widow of the warrior he had slain along the trail.

He turned his face to one side, but not until her nails had drawn blood all down his cheek and perilously near his right eye. Groping for her in the darkness, his right hand at last caught hers and now he had both wrists, and swiftly he rolled her over under him, pinning her with all his weight and staring down into her harshly sensual, high-cheekboned, ripe-lipped face. The braid of her dark-brown hair had been shorn off, and her nape was bare, and there was a small topknot at the back of her head, and the belt which held a brave's breechclout over her loins was made from the tanned skin of a cottonmouth.

Her body was satiny, but hard and muscular, taller by several inches than even Dimarte, the top of whose head came to his shoulder. Her hips were leaner, too, almost like a boy's, but the strong, firm thighs and the round muscular calves jerked and flailed under him as, her face warped in a rictus of implacable hate and revulsion, she spat at him, then, like a snapping-turtle, darted her head upward and tried to bite at his chin, her small white teeth clicking together. Her fingers spread out like the talons of a hunting hawk, trying to reach up to rend and tear him, as she twisted and writhed ceaselessly. Panting, he needed

142

all his strength to hold her wrists out on the sand, while he continued to pin her with his legs and loins, looming over her to stare down into that venomously lovely face as he tried to explain to her—knowing how useless it would be because she would not understand his words in the first place—"I did not want to kill him, believe me. It was not my doing. He would have killed me instead. Forgive me."

Again she spat at him, her spittle landing in his right eye, and as he blinked and instinctively released one hand to try to brush it away, she instantly thrust her freed hand down toward the scabbard-belt again. This time she drew it nearly halfway out before he managed to grip her wrists and pull the knife free, then, with a squeezing clasp that made her gasp and wince, forced her to drop the knife to the sandy floor. Then, lunging away from her and grasping it, he flung it toward the doorway of the little house and as her nails again raked his cheek pinned her wrists out on either side and immobilized her once more.

In her frenzied struggles to seize the knife and his checkmating that attempt, the breechclout had been torn away, and she was naked beneath him. She had come barefoot and by stealth, wearing that breechclout so that in the darkness any guard nearby would think her a warrior and not the vengeful widow of the son of the Creek war chief.

But now, the nakedness of her, the tangy smell of the oil and the paint she had daubed on her supple body, the involuntary friction of her thickly thatched pubis against his loins in this relentless duel, had wakened Lucien's maleness to an intolerable pitch. The first time he had known a woman during his student days had been out of a tortured curiosity and almost adolescent desire, but still chaste; the second, that unexpected boon of the emotionally overwrought girl in New Orleans, had been perhaps a kind of uplifting sublimation over his loss of Edmée de Courent mingled with his contemptuous loathing for the Cuban adventuress. But this time, it was out of primordial, atavistic, blindly unreasoning lust.

Suddenly, with the quickness of a cat, she turned her head and sank her teeth into his left forearm. With a reflexive snarl of pain, Lucien balled his right fist and struck

143

her on the side of the jaw, then, arching himself slightly over her, opened his breeches to liberate his ferociously turgid manhood. Her left hand momentarily free, Shehanoy thrust median and forefinger forward, stiffly poised, to gouge out his eyes. He had time only to turn his face to one side when her nails again scraped the edge of his cheek, and then he caught her wrist again and once more pinned her arms, lowering himself against the writhing sweat-and-oil glistening body. His turgid phallus rubbed against the thick crisp fleece of her sex, and she uttered a strangled cry of loathing and rage, as she arched her supple body and again turned her head and bit at his left wrist.

Doggedly, impervious to the pain, Lucien thrust again and this time entered her. Her eyes widened, rolled to the whites, her mouth gaped in a yelp of frantic shame and revulsion, as he thrust again, hilting himself in her tight warm sheath and lowering himself till his heaving chest flattened the hard yet wonderfully satiny-smooth mounds of her young breasts, his right cheek pressed hard against her left to prevent her biting. And now he was fully the master of this naked, murderous, beautiful adversary.

Her body stiffened, then jerked fitfully as he pitilessly foraged with deep rapid thrusts that involuntarily shook her as she writhed and groaned. Her teeth were bared now, her eyes revulsed, her nostrils flaring and shrinking, and her fingers futilely clawed the air, then tore at the sandy floor in her extremity.

He had no mercy for her now. The retaliatory weapon of his furiously aroused manhood took its conscienceless reprisal for her murderous attempt upon his life. Her bare heels dug at the sand, then her knees rose and her legs straightened and lunged out as, by every means left to her, Shehanoy battled her unwanted ravisher. He could feel the hard straining jaw and cheekbone pressed against his tighten in supreme muscular defiance as she strove to command her body to be impervious to his onslaught. Unslackeningly and pitilessly, he delved, receded, thrust again into the deepest core of her until a shattering, explosive force drained him and he sagged, shuddering and gasping, over her moist warm nakedness.

As she felt the volcanic fury of his spasm, Shehanoy uttered a gurgling shriek, her body quivering inordinately in answering tumult, against all her will and instinct, forced to it by the frenzy of hate and lust which had blazingly consumed them both.

The light of pine torches suddenly illumined the darkness. In the doorway stood Tunkamara, flanked by two of the braves who had been guards at the entry to Econchate. He stared at the entwined couple, then down at the knife of Jabez Corrigan, and he scowled with anger.

"Take Shehanoy to the hut of captives, bind her with rawhide thongs. When the sun is high, the council will pronounce her punishment!"

CHAPTER TWELVE

When Lucien awoke, it was to find Dimarte bringing him his morning meal, her face grave and her eyes downcast. After the *Mico* and his guards had taken Shehanoy away, he had slept like one drugged, vitiated by the fierce, relentless battle the young woman had waged against him. Now, with that inevitable self-searching which a man feels after he has taken a woman against her will, he was filled with a kind of self-flagellatory remorse.

"What will they do to her, Dimarte?" was his first question as, ignoring the bowls of food placed on the low bench, he looked anxiously at the lovely Creek girl.

"They hold council even now, Lu-shee-ahn." Her voice was low and sad as she turned toward the door of the hut.

"Wait, please, don't go, Dimarte! I want to go to them and tell them not to harm her, I have no anger against her. What she did, she did out of love for her husband, whom I killed."

"It is not for you to say, Lu-shee-ahn. You are guest here, the council is forbidden to all except the highest elders of the clans. Although my father as *Mico* rules for life, he must rely on the wisdom of those who speak for all the other clans who dwell in this village. No one may come into the meeting house unless he is so bidden by the elders."

"And you, Dimarte? Can't you speak for me?"

She shook her head. "The council is for men, and this time I am not bidden to it. I have told my father that it

146

was her grief which led her to your dwelling, but that will not excuse her. He had given his word that no one should harm you while you dwell with us, and she has broken that law."

She left him then, and Lucien, distracted by the thought of what retribution might be exacted from that striking, handsome young woman who had fought him like a warrior but whom he had used as he might have done the lowliest *putaine* of the streets of Paris, paced the sandy floor as he pondered some way to save her.

About an hour later, he heard the sounds of excited voices outside in the village square, the long aisle-like clearing on each side of which the houses and wigwams stood, as well planned by the unknown Creek architect of this thriving village as any hamlet of his own France. Leaving the little house, he stood transfixed as he saw the squaws and children, the old men and the untried striplings congregate outside their dwellings, crowding to see the spectacle. Before the meeting house, which was to the right of the imposing dwelling of the *Mico* himself, four stakes had been hammered into the ground, and beside each lay a rawhide thong. Now, even as Lucien stared, he saw four braves lead Shehanoy out of the council house. She was naked, her wrists thonged behind her, pale and yet with head erect and lips firmly compressed to meet her fate. Behind her walked Tunkamara in his most elaborate mantle, and beside him the war chief Tantumito, the father of the man Lucien had been forced to kill on his journey to Econchate. The other elders and advisors followed, some wearing mantles of scarlet, blue, green, fancifully decorated round the borders with tiny round brass bells, others wearing short cloaks which covered only shoulders and chests, made of feathers which had been dyed to the colors of their own clan. On one gray-haired Creek, Lucien espied a large silver gorget suspended by a ribbon round his neck; his arms were ornamented with silver bands and a similar collar hung round his neck. The guards who led Shehanoy toward the clearing and the stakes wore only breechclouts and moccasins, their chests adorned with the figures of animals, stars and crescents, and of the sun, a kind of tattooing (as Lucien

147

later learned) effected during their adolescence by pricking the skin with a needle to the blood and then rubbing in a bluish, permanent dye.

Lucien saw also that the father of Ecanataba held between his hands a deerskin sack whose top was bound with a sturdy rawhide thong.

Spellbound as he was by this ceremony which presaged what he fearfully divined was to be some kind of severe punishment, he did not notice that Dimarte had come up beside him and put her soft hand against his lips as if to warn him to silence. He started and turned toward her, his eyes questioning.

Tunkamara moved now to take his place between the four short stakes and, raising his voice, began to speak with a solemnity which increased Lucien's fears for the condemned, naked young woman around who the guards formed a circle behind the *Mico*.

"What is he saying, Dimarte?"

"That Shehanoy has broken the law of all the tribes by coming to the house of a guest by stealth and at night to kill him, and that for this she is to die."

"*Mon Dieu!*" he ejaculated with a gasp of horror. "No, they mustn't do that to her—I wanted to be at that meeting, to tell them that I understood why she hated me. No woman who loved a man who had been killed by a stranger, even though I had no wish to kill him, should be blamed for acting as she did."

"They will not listen, the judgment has been made."

"Now what is he saying?"

"That since Ecanataba and his father, our great war chief, are of the clan of the Snake, and because Shehanoy dared to wear the skin which is the sign of that clan, her death will be by the snake itself."

"No—it's horrible—I must stop them—"

"You dare not. My father has given orders that the guards—do you see them over there across the square?— are to take you back into your house if you try in any way to stop that which must be done."

Tunkamara now moved out of that square bounded by the four stakes and turned to his elders. All of them, including the war chief, nodded silently. He lifted his hand,

and the four guards took Shehanoy by the shoulders and
elbows and forced her into the center of the square. They
thrust her down on her back, unbinding her wrists only to
drag them to the two front stakes, while the other two
guards thonged her ankles to the other pair, spread-ea-
gling and stretching her naked under the sun. She had
closed her eyes and her lips moved silently, her body
quivering. Lucien stared as if by hypnotic compulsion at
her coppery-toned magnificent body, and when he glanced
to one side, he saw two braves holding stone tomahawks
and vigilantly watching him from the entrance of the
house directly across from his.

Tunkamara spoke again in Creek, and the war chief
walked slowly round his daughter-in-law's tensing naked
body, murmuring some kind of incantation, lifting the sack
and lowering it several times. Then, at last, he walked beyond her, about ten feet away, squatted and, laying the
sack on the ground, carefully unknotted the rawhide thong
which closed it.

Lucien uttered a stifled cry of horrified stupefaction.
Out of the sack, slithering in a kind of jerky motion, there
emerged a snake about three feet long, its body coppery-
red in hue and marked with darker bands. Its head was
long and blunted, and in the sudden stillness which
gripped the watchers, Lucien could hear a sibilant hiss as
the snake moved clear of the sack, its head pointed toward
the condemned prisoner. Lifting her head, Shehanoy saw
it approach, her eyes widening with unspeakable terror.
Then, in a veritable frenzy of revulsion and dread, she
tugged her wrists against the rawhide thongs. But they
held fast, as did those which bit into the finely chiseled
ankles as her feet twisted, her toes clawing and clamping
in convulsive movements.

"It's too horrible—I can't let them—Dimarte—will it
kill?"

The lovely Creek girl beside him nodded, watching the
scene, a kind of distressed pity on her exquisite face. "Yes,
it is a copperhead, its bite is deadly. And it has been
starved for a week, kept in the sack. Sometimes the people
of the Snake clan keep it so, that they may say prayers to

149

its spirit which is in the sky above and in forests, to bring them good fortune in their hunting."

With its characteristic, hideously undulating movement, the copperhead moved toward the feet of the helpless prisoner. Lucien could endure the sight no longer. Stealthily, he put his right hand to the scabbard-belt, only to remember that the knife had been appropriated by the *Mico*'s guards last night. Then he remembered the dirk in his boot. Stooping swiftly, he retrieved it, grasping it by the point between right thumb and forefinger, and ran forward. A startled cry broke from the guards and the elders, and the two braves who had been appointed to prevent his interfering with this terrible mode of Creek justice raced toward him from the other side of the square. He drew back his arm, and just as Shehanoy uttered a gurgling cry of utter terror, flung the dirk with all his strength.

There was a loud shout of wonder from the onlookers. The dirk had sped unerringly to pin the ugly blunt head of the venomous snake to the earth. Its glossy-scaled coil threshed and jerked, and then at last was still.

Tunkamara stared accusingly at the half-naked young Frenchman, then extended his arm to point at Lucien and to utter a command. The four guards started forward, but already Dimarte had run to Lucien's side and, holding up her right hand, called out in Creek, "No, his heart is good. What he has done shows that he does not take life in vain!"

"He has interfered with our law, daughter," the *Mico* answered her, shaking his head with disapproval.

"Dimarte, tell him that I bear no hatred for this woman. Tell him that there is grief in my heart that it was I who brought her to this terrible punishment because I was forced to kill her husband. Tell him too that I admire her, I respect her. I left my own land across the ocean because the woman I loved could not possibly have had so great a love for me as to give up her life for mine. This woman here acted in loyalty and love and that is no crime in the eyes of my Great Spirit, who surely is one with yours."

Dimarte's eyes softened, she nodded, then turned back to her father and translated his words into the Creek tongue.

For a long moment, Tunkamara stood considering, while Shehanoy, having fainted in terror, lay inert, her face turned to one side. Then at last he spoke, and it was Dimarte who turned to Lucien to translate her father's words: "What the white stranger has done is very brave. He has shown the courage of the eagle, the boldness of the wolf, the cunning of the snake. His heart is good and he can be pardoned for breaking our law for the reasons my daughter has told me that made him act as he has done. But Shehanoy has broken the sacred law and therefore it is my judgment that she be banished from this village. She shall be given corn and water only for a day's journey, and if she returns to Econchate, she will be put to death by stones from the hands of the women and the children. I, *Mico* of Econchate, have spoken."

The four guards, first warily ascertaining that the copperhead was indeed dead, slashed the rawhide thongs binding the naked young woman's body to the stakes, lifted her in their arms and carried her to the last wigwam of the village.

Then Tunkamara spoke once more, this time in English: "My daughter Dimarte will come with you to put what you may say into words which we understand. You shall speak to all the elders of the council, to tell us what you would do here on our land."

After the evening meal, which Dimarte again brought to him, Lucien prepared for his summons to the council. The *Mico*'s daughter had, to his pleased surprise, brought him a kind of jacket made of buckskin, which fitted comfortably and concealed the ugly marks of his healing wounds. But even more to his surprise, Dimarte halted him at the door of the little house and, her face suddenly, exquisitely grave, placed about his neck a necklace made with plantain and root fibers on which the claws of the she-bear had been ingeniously strung. "The elders will see this and know that you have the skill of a great hunter, Lu-shee-ahn."

"It is thoughtful of you, Dimarte. I thank you once again."

Her eyes were demurely lowered as she murmured, "I strung the claws together myself. I bring it to you as a gift of thanks now for what you have done for Shehanoy, for she and I were good friends. You were brave to do what you did. You did not think of yourself, even though they might have killed you for it."

He put his hands on her slim shoulders, as she looked up into his eyes, and he felt her soft skin quiver at his touch. Perhaps, unlike a French girl, she did not actually blush; but all the same there was an air of piquant embarrassment on her lovely features. "I think your people respect bravery and truthfulness, Dimarte. But now I must depend on you to tell them in your tongue what I will say to them in my own but from the depths of my heart. And it is strange now to tell people I had never known until these last few days all that I believe in and what I live for, seeing that I could not even convince my own father that in my view the land gives life, sustenance and the feeling of being useful in one's life by working upon it and bringing forth crops which will sustain the lives of others and those to come after them."

She moved away now, a little self-consciously as again she lowered her eyes. "My people know when someone speaks with a forked tongue. They have watched you here and they have seen how you have looked upon our village and our customs and found them good, how you have not mocked them or thought yourself better than them. And they know that you have compassion, as you showed for poor Shehanoy today. I will put your thoughts into our words and I think they will believe them, Lu-shee-ahn."

And thus it came about that the younger son of a French nobleman who could trace his lineage back to the fierce Norsemen of the tenth century stood in the center of the meeting house where sat Tunkamara as *Mico*, the father of Ecanataba, the *Windigo*, two men whom Dimarte described to him as Tascamingoutchy and who were the lieutenants of the war chief as well as Sokinata, a corpulent, white-haired elder who bore the title of *Tichoumingo* and whose role was that of assistant to the *Mico*. Sokinata arranged for all ceremonies, feasts and dances and sometimes acted as speaker for the *Mico*.

152

But it was Tunkamara himself who spoke to Lucien, beginning in his guttural voice those words of English in which he stated the case before the council. Before he began the interrogation of the young Frenchman, he added, "Our women of the village may not by our law be heard in council, only those who are known as 'the beloved' and these may raise their voices in matters of war and peace. Dimarte, who stands beside you, is of that number, and she will make your words known to my elders."

The lovely black-haired Creek girl turned to him and murmured, "The elders wish to know of your life before you came to Econchate."

Briefly, then, heartened by the knowledge that this gentle, wise and remarkably mature girl would sense his fervent beliefs and interpret them honorably to those who might be inimical toward him, Lucien narrated the events that had led him to leave France. It was his wish, he told the council, to be allowed to serve in whatever apprenticeship they would choose for him, and to earn the right to have a piece of ground on which he might sow and harvest crops, to one day marry and have children who would toil to make this new nation strong and just, with peace for all the different tribes and clans among the whites as there were among these gracious hosts who had received him here as a stranger, cared for his hurts and permitted him to speak to them as a free man speaking to others.

As Dimarte translated, he could see the wrinkled, coppery faces ease their guarded vigilance and the dark eyes fix on him with greater tolerance, and he saw the father of Ecanataba turn to whisper to the old *Tichou-mingo*, who approvingly nodded.

When he had finished, they deliberated among themselves, ignoring him, and Lucien looked round the meeting house. It was whitewashed inside and out with coarse-chalk and white marly clay and decorated with oyster shells. The elders of the village sat tailor-fashion on a kind of low dais which occupied nearly half of the space of this edifice. On the walls, hanging from pegs, were trophies of the hunt and of war, tomahawks of enemy tribes whom the Creeks had defeated in battle, headbonnets and

153

mantles, ceremonial robes, longbows and doeskin quivers of arrows. On one section of the wall above the elders, Lucien saw the symbols of those allied clans dwelling here at Econchate, the turtle, the bear, the rabbit, the snake, the wolf, the eagle.

At last Tunkamara rose and moved to the edge of the dais to declare to Lucien the will of the council. "We have thought upon your words, we find your heart good, your spirit brave and honest. My daughter says you wish to learn our ways and our tongue. This I say then to you, stay still as guest at Econchate till you have learned our tongue. You will meet other whites who trade with us, they will show you how it is done. Perhaps they will have you go with them to Maubila and take part in the changing of goods for our people."

Lucien inclined his head. "I am willing and grateful, Tunkamara. And I thank the council."

"The white man Weatherford, who is married to the sister of our great leader in Maubila, has already said to our elders that as trade prospers it would be good to have another storage house and dock upon the river. It is a place we have seen ourselves and find good. The land is rich for the growing of crops there. Tomorrow, two of my braves will take you there in a pirogue. Then you will tell us if it is pleasing to you. Now we will smoke the pipe to pledge our word to you and you, yours to us."

It was a journey of no more than twenty miles southwest, and when the two braves dragged the pirogue onto the bank, Lucien was already rapt with excitement. Here indeed to his own practiced eyes was rich soil, and a century later geologists and agriculturalists would record the fertile limestone and clay soils of the "Black Belt" in which this land was sited. It was lowland, but not eroded from the river. It was at the bend of the Alabama, with a huge bluff towering to his right as he stepped onto the ground, and to his left and beyond, a lower, gentle hill. Thus within these two landmarks was a kind of valley, a true *asile du vent*. Yes, it was as if he had been taken from his native soil and set down, with some as yet unknown but planned purpose, into its very counterpart here in this brave new world.

And as he stared at that verdant land, he saw in his fancy the red brick chateau with its twin towers of Yves-sur-lac . . . a chateau whose replica, if God would so grant, he might one day erect here for himself and his destined heirs.

CHAPTER THIRTEEN

Lucien had no way of knowing that on the very day he had set out for Mobile to meet Alexander McGillivray, that exultantly proud spokesman of the great Creek Confederacy had sent a letter to his partner and benefactor William Panton in Pensacola, which he had requested was to be privately exhibited to the Spanish authorities in that territory. After commenting that there had been no pack-horses going to Pensacola for many months, he had finally found a courier to whom he had promised two kegs of *taffai* in return for conveying this urgent message. In it, he wrote:

> In order to accommodate us, the American commissioners are complaisant enough to postpone the meeting for our treaty until the 15th of next month. Pickens returned in the hopes of the Cherokee treaty; but in this I took measures to disappoint him, for those Chiefs would not meet. In this do you not see my cause of triumph, in bringing these conquerors of the Old and masters of the New World, as they call themselves, to bend and supplicate for peace at the feet of a people who shortly before they despised and marked out for destruction.

In that same letter, the wily trader-agent declared that he would shape this intended treaty to his own purposes.

I will, as you observe, confine it to the fixing of our limits and the acknowledgment of the independence of my nation. This I deem very necessary, as the Americans pretend to a territorial claim and sovereignty over us in virtue of the late peace made with England. You well know how customary it is in all treaties with the Indians to agree to a commercial one also, it being absolutely necessary, as it more firmly attaches them to friendships formed; for without stipulations of that sort in a treaty of peace, none will be lasting. However, in this instance I will agree to none, as you have a prospect of being able, by the favor of the Spanish government, to supply this trade on as moderate terms as the Georgians can do. Here let me observe to you, that in the affair of trade the Americans will push hard for it, and it will be for us the most difficult part of the negotiation. But I will risk the breaking off of the conference before I will give in to it. On the whole, if I find that these commissioners insist upon stipulations that will in their operation clash with those already entered into with Spain, I shall not hesitate to cut short the negotiations, and support the connection which we have with Spain, it being more safe and respectable than the Republicans can make one.

He explained to Panton that if he had made an earlier treaty of any kind with the Americans, the Creeks would have been driven into hostility with Spain. He also complained that the ammunition and guns given to him by the King of Spain had greatly disappointed him, for his people, who had always been accustomed to the best English guns, found these Spanish weapons unfit for the purposes of hunting or war.

Finally, he intimated to Panton that the American commissioners had hinted at wishing to have a private conversation with him prior to the meeting for the treaty, which to McGillivray's mind meant that they might give him back his house and lands, which were worth in the amount of 30,000 pounds sterling. And he declared to his benefactor that for years he had been dependent on him and wished to repay the debt. "Here on the one hand," he noted, "I am offered the restoration of my property, of more than 100,000 dollars, at the least valuation; and on the other, I have not the wherewithal to pay an interpreter. And I find that letters are still addressed to me as agent for his Catholic Majesty of Spain, when I have some time ago renounced the pittance that was allowed as being a consideration disgraceful to my station."

It was the declaration of a proud man indeed, but between the lines as within them, there could be no doubt: Alexander McGillivray would hold above all else the well-being of the people from whom his beloved mother had come. And meanwhile, it would be the settlers of Georgia who would be most cruelly harassed by the vindictive power of the tribes under McGillivray's control, for in this way he would vent his brooding resentment upon the banishment of his father and the confiscation of his patrimony. If Lucien had spoken to the elders at Econchate of wanting to live in peace, he himself was to learn that peace would be on the terms which the Creeks themselves would make as it suited their proud spirit, one which imbued the very ethos of Alexander McGillivray, in whose veins their courageous blood ran.

But meanwhile, all unknowing of the fomenting disputations that would lead to doubts, misunderstandings, accusations of treachery and, finally, warfare, Lucien himself was enjoying the most absorbing and rewarding experience of his life. A few days after his appearance before the council, he was summoned to the stately dwelling of the *Mico* to meet with the trader Charles Weatherford, who maintained a post near Wetumpka on the first eastern bluff below the confluence of the Coosa and Tallapoosa rivers. He was a stocky, pleasant-faced, brown-haired man in his early thirties. And he had brought with him on his way to Mobile to meet with Alexander McGillivray (and thence to act as emissary in the American treaty conference) his beautiful wife and his alert, highly intelligent seven-year-old son, William. Tunkamara in introducing Lucien to this white ally of the Creeks who had become a blood brother through marriage to the half-sister of Alexander McGillivray, humorously declared,

158

"Our friend has built a racetrack and himself lives upon it, and the Spanish are angry with him for having stolen fast horses from their fort in Mobile."

"I wish—" Lucien smiled wistfully—"that you could have seen the Arabian palomino I brought from France, *M'sieu* Weatherford. More than that, if I had been able to keep Arabe, I should at once challenge you for high stakes and thus make my fortune, for there is no faster horse in all this new world."

"I take it, then, that you were obliged to sell him—was it in Mobile?"

"No, in New Orleans, to a Creole by the name of Jules Ronsart."

"I have heard of that man," Charles Weatherford chuckled and nodded, "He is as good a judge of horse-flesh as I, but it is far too distant to go into New Orleans to steal your horse back for you. The *Mico*—honor to his great name—tells me that you wish to become a blood brother of the Creeks and to trade for them. Also, he has pointed out the land which was shown to you, and you found it good."

"I think it will raise superb crops, *M'sieu* Weatherford. But I must first earn the right to settle upon it."

"You will, man, you will. If our great leader at Mobile has sent you here to enjoy the hospitality of the *Mico*, and I am told how well you have already proved your courage, you will have powerful friends in the Alabama territory. When I am returned from Mobile after my errands for our leader, we will talk again of horse racing, Mr. Bouchard."

A day later, Lucien met a still more fascinating man, Abram Mordecai, a native of Pennsylvania, who four years before Lucien's departure from France had founded a little trading house two miles west of Line Creek. Mordecai was a cheerful, stout little man with a graying beard, married to a Creek woman whose father had been a warrior and whose mother a *nigra* from the West Indies brought into slavery and eventually freed by the Creek tribe to which she had been bound. Proud of his Jewish faith, Mordecai sat one evening in Lucien's little house while Dimarte brought them cornmeal cakes and broiled catfish and learnedly dissertated on his belief that the Creeks were originally descended from his own people, one of the ten lost tribes. "Look you, sir," he eagerly asserted, "I have witnessed many of their Green Corn dances and they utter in grateful tones the word 'yavoyaha!'—and many of the elders have told me that this means Jehovah, or the Great Spirit, and their utterance of it is a return of thanks for the abundant harvest with which they have been blessed each year. Yes, you do well to leave a decaying aristocracy to seek your fortune among the purest and oldest of the children of God."

But what interested Lucien more than this scholarly analysis of religion was Mordecai's remarks on the various crops he had seen in his travels from Pennsylvania down through the southeastern part of this new country. "In Georgia and the Carolinas," he declared, "I have seen how they grow cotton. Now you well know, good sir, that in your country of France the commoners as well as the fine noblemen wear garments made from that plant once it has been properly fabricated. I foresee—and mark my words, it will not be long—that one day even these Creeks will learn to grow it for their profit, to be shipped across the ocean to the countries of Europe, where it will be in great demand at excellent prices. I have been told already that in the West Indies fine Sea Island cotton has been planted with most rewarding results. Many of the Georgia settlers have had seed from their own and the Carolina plantings, and if they are ever allowed to come here, they will doubtless bring it with them. Rich soil such as this will make cotton thrive; take pains to remember what I tell you, good sir."

"That I will, you may be certain, *M'sieu* Mordecai."

He was not to forget that conversation and he was to see Abram Mordecai again, to his own great good fortune, after the turn of the new century. . . .

"Yes, Mr. Bouchard," his garrulous new friend went on, "I have lived many years with the Indians, and I have traded the goods of my pack for pink root, hickory-nut oil and pelts of all kinds. I have taken those to New Orleans and Mobile in boats, and to Pensacola and Augusta on pack-horses."

"Hickory-nut oil? Yes, even in France I recall it being served as a great delicacy at the table," Lucien offered.

"The Indians make it very simply. They boil the cracked nuts in water and they skim off the oil as it floats on the surface, you see," Mordecai explained. "I have prospered, thanks to the kindness of Jehovah, and the Indians accept me as one of them. Well, you see over there by the fire with those other squaws my own lovely and loyal Shulamith, who has within her the blood of Ham as well as that of one of the ten lost tribes. She is my help-mate."

Then, with a soft ingratiating chuckle, he leaned forward to whisper to Lucien, "But look you, you are young and handsome. Take care the Creek maidens don't flock to your house or the *Mico* will be vexed. Get yourself a wife. You may have more than one—the great McGillivray has two and he would have more but for all the business he does with the Spanish and Americans and his own people. Only, if you are amorous, as I am, take care not to entice the squaw of one of the warriors—that could be most dangerous for you."

Lucien burst out laughing. "I am appreciative of your advice, *M'sieu* Mordecai, but I assure you that you have no need to fear for my welfare on that score. I am not a philanderer by nature; what I seek most is constancy." The smile left his lips as he said those last words, for he was again remembering Edmée de Courent. . . .

Now being an accepted ally, though to be sure still regarded as an apprentice, Lucien had unhampered opportunity to observe the intricacies of the life of this thriving Creek village. At the far end and to one side, there were timbered warehouses where the Creeks stored the goods which men like Weatherford and Mordecai would take to Mobile, as well as the goods that would be brought back in exchange for them. And he saw that now, just after the last great Corn Dance, which had celebrated a bounteous crop of vegetables and fruits and successful hunting forays which had brought back many deer and raccoons, several bears and a never-failing supply of edible fish, the Creeks were not unmindful that they must be strong against their enemies. There were formidable quantities of

161

muskets, ball and powder, the iron tomahawks McGillivray had shown him, knives, and strong bows with metal-tipped arrows that could speed to the heart of a man as to that of a deer.

Weatherford had depicted to him the raised levee, or loading platform, on the bank of the Coosa to which supplies would be carried, placed upon the log raft or flatboat for the journey to Mobile. Lucien remembered this description, and determined to pay a visit to that trading post by rowing a pirogue there himself. Weatherford had genially consented to this tour of inspection and promised to invite Lucien to his house once he had returned from his business with McGillivray.

He spent time too in the cornfields, mingling with the women, smiling and nodding at them, watching how they irrigated and cultivated the precious crop. He conferred with Tunkamara, with Dimàrte as his translator, to inform the *Mico* of improved methods of planting and cultivation which he himself had utilized in the orchards and fields of Yves-sur-lac, and the *Mico,* delighted at the white man's knowledge, gave orders that these suggestions be carried out. Each day, immediately after the morning meal, he and Dimarte began his study of the Creek language. It was musical, with a hint of Spanish derivative in the vowels and the long, gracious-sounding names of places, of animals and of intangible things, which gave him further insight into the creed and outlook of the Creeks. The lovely daughter of the *Mico* used the most elementary method of teaching: she would hold up an object and say the Creek word for it and he would repeat it. Each morning, he learned at least twenty new words, and before the lesson was over, she would hold up the objects—but in different sequence—to hear how well he had retained those terms. He made swift progress, being not only an excellent student in his own right but, as might be well imagined, drawn more and more to his enchanting, young and yet so obviously mature instructress.

After a week, he casually asked, "How does a man marry a girl among your people, Dimarte?"

"First you must know that marriages are never made between members of the same clan, Lu-Shee-ahn. But it could be done in several ways. A young brave who favors a maiden of another clan may ask one of his relatives to go to one of hers and learn whether she might accept him. Or sometimes, he may toss a pebble two or three times at her feet. If she ignores it, he knows she is not for him. But mostly, it is our custom that a man who wishes to marry with a girl of another clan first harvests a crop and builds a house for her. Of course, he will tell her father of his intentions."

Then, almost mischievously, with a sidelong glance and her thick lashes fluttering, she murmured, "Have you so soon forgotten the maiden you loved across the ocean, Lu-shee-ahn?"

"I shall never forget her, Dimarte. But she was my first love. As a man grows older and wiser—and not always just with the years, but with the new things he experiences and the new people with whom he comes into contact— he learns that love is not only first attraction or desire or that which may be unattainable to him. Often it comes from being frequently in the presence of one he finds good and sweet and helpful, such as I find you."

"You must not speak of such things to me, Lu-shee-ahn!" she quickly interposed. "You have known me not even a moon, nor I you. And besides," she added teasingly, "you have already had your first woman at Econchate. Have you forgotten Shehanoy?"

He gasped, and then found himself blushing violently. "How could you have known of such a thing?" he stammered.

"You are forgetting that she was my friend. Now we shall go on with our lesson and we shall not talk of marriage again." Her face was suddenly prim as a school teacher's in the act of reproving a wayward student and her voice was cool. But even as he watched her hold up the bowl in which she had brought his breakfast, he saw her take a quick deep breath and he would have sworn that he saw also a flush on the coppery satin of her cheeks.

The four commissioners sent by President Washington to bring about a treaty with the Creeks, General Andrew

Pickens, David Humphreys, Cyrus Griffin and Benjamin Lincoln, had sailed from New York and arrived at Savannah on September 10th, bringing with them abundant provisions to feed the Indians while at the treaty site. Their destination was Rock Landing upon Georgia's famous Oconee River, where Alexander McGillivray, with two thousand warriors under his leadership, had been encamped for more than a week on the western bank. The commissioners pitched their camp on the opposite bank and spent the first two days in private conferences with the wily trader-agent, who showed them exceptional courtesy. He brought with him most of the chiefs, who also exhibited a friendliness which greatly encouraged the four commissioners.

On September 24th, these four intrepid men crossed to the camp of McGillivray and were led with great pomp and ceremony to the place of council. Believing that their mission would be successful in view of the cordial reception by the Creeks, they proceeded to an immediate reading of the treaty. It stipulated that the boundary made at Augusta, Shoulderbone and Galphinton should remain; that the United States would guarantee the territory west of that boundary forever to the Creeks; that free trade should be established with the Indians from ports upon the Altamaha, through which the Indians could import and export upon the same terms of the citizens of the United States; and, finally, that all Negroes, horses, goods and American citizens taken by the Indians should be restored.

Following that reading, the four commissioners went back to their own camp and all through the night McGillivray and his tribal chiefs held their own private council. The next morning, he sent a letter to the commissioners that the terms they proposed were not satisfactory and that the Creeks had resolved to break up the meeting and go home, since it was now the time for hunting. In the letter, McGillivray pledged to meet the commissioners again at some future time and meanwhile to keep his warriors from committing acts of hostility during the following winter. General Andrew Pickens knew that no treaty could be made without liberal compensation for the valuable lands which the Georgians were cultivating, and as he had been instructed by President Washington's new government to pay the Creeks a fair equivalent for the territory, he sent back word urging Alexander McGillivray to remain and to state his personal objection to the draft of the treaty.

But McGillivray had already retreated to the Ockmulgee River, from which new camp he sent on September 27th this discouraging reply:

Gentlemen—I am favored with your letter of yesterday, delivered to me by the hand of Weatherford. I beg to assure you that my retreat from my former camp on the Oconee was entirely owing to the want of food for our horses, and at the earnest entreaty of our chiefs. Colonel Humphreys and myself at different interviews entered deeply and minutely into the subject of the contest between our nation and the State of Georgia. I observed to him that I expected ample and full justice should be given us in restoring to us the encroachments we complained of, in which the Oconee lands are included; but finding that there was no such intention, and that a restitution of territory and hunting grounds was not to be the basis of a treaty between us, I resolved to return to the nation, deferring the matter in full peace till next spring. I am very unwell, and cannot return. We sincerely desire a peace, but cannot sacrifice much to obtain it. As for a statement of our disputes, your honorable Congress has long since been in possession of and has declared that they will decide on them on the principles of justice and humanity. 'Tis that we expect.

Washington's four commissioners had nothing else to do but return to Augusta greatly discomfited. There, meeting with Georgia's fiery Governor Walton, they sought an explanation for the impasse which had so unexpectedly detoured their efforts to bring about a peace and the establishment of beneficial trade.

To this, Governor Walton declared that the Creeks and

Cherokees, prior to the American Revolution, had ceded lands in the territory of Wilkes County, but that during the war that area had been attacked by the Indians and they had been called upon to make restitution. In the spring of 1783, the Cherokees had come to Augusta and signed a treaty, the Lower Creeks coming in the autumn of the same year and signing a similar deed, which thus in his opinion ceded to Georgia their respective rights to the lands described in those two treaties. The Georgia legislature, after examining the treaties, had surveyed, sold, settled and cultivated the lands in peace. Moreover, he pointed out, the Indians had made these treaties voluntarily and had received presents of comparable value in return. Yet in view of all this, many settlers had been killed and their property stolen.

And thus while Lucien Bouchard learned the language and the customs and the laws of the Creeks and became more and more enamored of his lovely young instructress, the storm clouds were gathering, as they had already gathered over the land he had left forever. When the four commissioners returned to New York, President George Washington's first impulse was to wage a war of invasion against the Creeks and compel them to make a peace and give up the Oconee lands. It was true that he had been drawn to this decision against his own private judgment by the urgent demands of the Georgia delegation and Congress. But when he found that the expenses of such a war would amount to at least $15,000,000, he abandoned the project, knowing that the newly created government of a republic still in its infancy could not sustain such an expense while it was still coping with the costs incurred during the victorious war against the British.

He determined therefore to send a secret agent to visit the Creek Nation by circuitous route and attempt to bring Alexander McGillivray back to New York—for at the time that was the site of the Congress.

The news of the Americans' unsuccessful attempt to effect a peace treaty with the Creeks reached Tunkamara by the middle of October, when Charles Weatherford and two braves rode into Econchate on their way back to

Weatherford's trading post. Lucien himself was permitted to attend the council of the elders as Weatherford explained what had taken place. The young Frenchman was saddened by the news. He earnestly felt that the future of the struggling young colonies which had become an independent republic could ultimately prosper only if these rich lands were open to them with friendly commerce between the settlers and the Creeks, but in no way a settlement such as the conquering Spanish would have attempted. In his own direct mind, Lucien considered that his hosts were the pioneers of this land and that they should be automatically granted the right to maintain what they had carved out of the wilderness without bloodshed or connivance.

What he had seen thus far at Econchate convinced him that it was possible for all men to live in peace and to follow a communal pursuit: that of building a prosperous future by cultivating the land and sharing its harvest with all who would contribute to the well-being of a strengthening new country. He had already been disillusioned by class struggles between aristocrats and peasant: surely here there was the God-given opportunity to pursue the dream of a universal brotherhood that would not separate men because of the color of their skin or the differences in their birth. Had not their stirring Declaration of Independence pronounced the solemn words, "We hold these truths to be self-evident, that all Men are created equal, that they are endowed by their Creator with certain unalienable Rights, that among these are Life, Liberty, and the Pursuit of Happiness—"? If those words were still to ring true with the passing of the years, then those who had formulated them must see to a wholesome compromise between the rights of the Creeks and the understandable broadening of the still narrow frontier of this new nation built on a concept of freedom.

With October, the oppressive humidity eased, there were cool evenings and it was the season of hunting. As Lucien's proficiency in the Creek language grew, he was delighted to find himself invited to take part in an occasional hunt. Nanakota, a tall, lean warrior of the Turtle clan, whose rank was that of *Hatakholitopa* ("beloved

167

man"), had befriended him and made him a present of a strong bow, a beaded doeskin quiver and a dozen feathered arrows. Nanakota had himself designed the arrows, with a keen sense of the balance and carrying power these missiles must have to hit their mark with force. Lucien accompanied him and four other braves who were known simply as *Tasca*, each of whom had killed an enemy but was not yet considered valiant enough to be numbered in the lofty ranks of Nanakota himself.

"Now that we have the white man's musket," the tall genial warrior explained to Lucien, "there is good hunting. But when we enjoy most the sport of stalking our quarry, we use the bow, for it is a better test of skill."

By early afternoon, the little hunting party had reached a dense pine forest some fifteen miles to the east of Econchate, in which Nanakota had often hunted with great success. He fitted onto his left hand the skin and frontal bone of a deer's head, dried and stretched on elastic chips, with the horns ingeniously scooped out. Wagging his fingers, he illustrated to the young Frenchman how this device was used as a decoy to lure bucks toward the hunters. "The only danger," the Creek warrior added with a twinkle in his dark eyes, "is that it is so like the deer that sometimes another warrior will shoot at you, thinking that you are the buck. If we place ourselves wisely, we prevent this danger. And now we will make the call of the doe to its mate, and perhaps it will draw a fine buck for you to shoot at."

The other braves had moved to the left in a broad arc, taking up their places behind trees and clumps of bushes, while Lucien squatted down beside Nanakota behind the shelter of a large blackberry bush. Lifting his left hand and waggling the deer's head, Nanakota took a hollow horn fitted with a wooden mouthpiece which, as he showed Lucien, contained a small brass vibrating tongue. "Blow this, and move the palm of your hand over the opening of the horn. It will sound like the cry of a fawn or a doe," he instructed.

Greatly intrigued, Lucien obeyed. A few moments later, Nanakota held his forefinger to his lips, then nodded toward the slight clearing ahead. A young buck had moved from behind a huge pine tree and warily approached the clearing. Once again Nanakota lifted his left hand and moved the device of the deer's head, and the buck took a few steps closer toward the blackberry bush.

"Now!" the Creek hissed to Lucien. Notching the arrow and drawing at the bow, Lucien swiftly rose, took quick aim and sped the arrow. It struck cleanly and deeply below the shoulder, and the buck snorted, turned, and began to run for shelter, only to crumple and fall on its side, kicking convulsively for a few moments.

"Aiyee, you are indeed one of us, Lu-shee-ahn!" Nanakota exulted. "The buck is yours, you may do with it as you will. One of the squaws will skin it and make you a jacket if you like."

"May I not give it as a gift?"

"But that would be a fine deed, yes, yes. You learn our customs quickly, Lu-shee-ahn."

"You, who are of the beloved men, must surely know the heart of Tunkamara," Lucien carefully sounded out his friend. "I would know whether his daughter Dimarte is pledged to some warrior."

Nanakota permitted himself an amused grunt, his eyes shrewdly appraising Lucien's eager face. "You aim high, but you may yet hit the mark as you did with the buck, Lu-shee-ahn. The beloved woman, the daughter of our great *Mico*, is not yet bound to any man."

"It would not be against the law of the Creeks if I were to offer my suit for her hand, then, Nanakota?"

"Why, no, and you have already proved yourself to be one of us in many ways. The claws of the bear, your fight against Ecanataba, and how you spared his squaw— these things are remembered by all of us. Now you speak our language well for a white man, and we read in you no evil or deceit. But you must build your house and you must till your land before you can be ready for marriage."

"Then I will bring this deer to Tunkamara as a gift, not only in my gratitude for the hospitality he and all of you have accorded me, but as the first of many gifts by which I shall make known to him my desire to wed with Dimarte. Alas, I must first have land on which to build this house for her. Although it was shown me, I am not yet sure the time is set for me to claim it."

Again Nanakota grunted with amusement. "When you bring the deer before our *Mico,* be bold enough to ask for what is in your heart and he will understand. If he accepts you as her suitor, you will know at once. If he does not favor you, you had best know it quickly, I think."

"You are my good friend, Nanakota, and if he looks with favor upon my suit and I win Dimarte, I will make you the gift of that gleaming knife which you have long admired, the knife with which I shave my beard."

"Ho, ho, for such a gift I will even speak on your behalf to Tunkamara. Dimarte's mother is with the Great Spirit these ten years, and Tunkamara is both mother and father to her thus, and perhaps this is why he is slow in granting her hand to any warrior of the clans. But I myself have seen that she looks on you with soft eyes like the doe. I tell you in truth, there is no other warrior she so favors, Lu-shee-ahn."

And that night, when Lucien and the braves returned to Econchate, the young Frenchman carried the carcass of the buck to the dwelling of the *Mico* and, laying it down before the entrance of the dwelling, waited until Tunkamara emerged in his ceremonial mantle.

"My gift to you, oh mighty *Mico,*" he said. "The first of many such, I promise, to show my heartfelt thanks for the kindness you and your people have granted me at Econchate. And one thing more, if you will pardon the zeal of a stranger."

"You are no longer a stranger to the Creeks. What would you say to me?"

"That I love your daughter Dimarte, and would marry with her, once I have built the house and tilled the land that was shown to me, Tunkamara."

"I had foreseen this, and it does not displease me, nor my daughter. I give you leave then to go upon the land by Pintilalla Creek, and I will give you two black slaves as the gift of this village in your endeavor. You will build a depot near the bank of the river for the trading post our friend Weatherford has said will bring more bounty to our

170

village. When this is done, I will wait to have you speak to me again and you shall have your answer."

As he rose, saluting Tunkamara with the Creek hand-signs for deferential thanks, Lucien felt his heart swell with joy, for he knew that he had fallen deeply in love with the gentle daughter of the *Mico*, a love in which, this time, he had not invested her as he had Edmée with virtues she did not have, but rather born out of undeceived recognition of her gentleness and goodness of heart.

CHAPTER FOURTEEN

It was on a Monday of the third week of October that Lucien Bouchard, accompanied by a soft-spoken, tall, Ashanti black named Ben and the latter's wife, Ellen, a pretty, small, industrious Kru girl of about twenty, paddled a large pirogue to the bend of the Alabama River and that towering bluff which framed one side of the extensive valley-like land which Lucien had already been shown and which, despite its flourishing trees and bushes, flowers and wild grass and shrubs, had brought back so strongly to his mind the view between those hills of Normandy where he had ridden that fateful May afternoon.

Ben, nearly thirty, and Ellen had been captured during raids on their African villages a decade ago, brought by a Portuguese slaveship to Santo Domingo and sold there to a French plantation owner. Three years ago, needing money for his return to France after a disastrous crop and the mysterious fire of his house, the owner had sent them to Mobile, where Alexander McGillivray had bought them and had them sent as a gift to Tunkamara at Econchate. As a child, Ellen had worked as a slavey in the plantation owner's kitchen, while Ben had labored in the sugarcane fields. They had fallen in love during their servitude with the Creeks and had been permitted to marry. They spoke no English, but were fluent in a mixture of French *patois* and Creek, which Lucien could readily understand.

At first he had demurred at the thought of owning human beings, for the term of slavery itself could only recall to him the pitiful, oppressed lot of peasants under the intolerable rule of many bigoted French aristocrats. True enough, his father had dealt with relative kindness and justice with his peasants on the fief of Normandy, but that did not alter the inescapable fact that through the circumstances of birth and wealth, one man might arbitrarily control the lives of others.

Moreover, it was the first time that Lucien had come into contact with two human beings who had actually been shackled, transported from their primitive homes, forced to work in a strange country for a strange owner who had the power to have them flogged or branded or mutilated or even put to death if they disobeyed him. It was true that at Econchate he had seen several black slaves, both men and women, working in the fields, helping skin the game and drawing water and doing other domestic tasks usually allocated to the Creek women. It was true also that their Creek owners had treated them kindly and seemed to be on genuinely friendly terms with them. But now he had a husband and wife bound to him by Tunkamara's decree for whose lives he would be henceforth responsible. To have refused the *Mico*'s gift was unthinkable, but he had already decided what he would do when the three of them worked together on this land where one day he dreamed of constructing a house that would be the very twin of his father's durable and comfortable chateau.

But what Lucien's studies had not told him and which had remained for the surprisingly well-informed and cynical Charles Weatherford to reveal was that the French had been the first to introduce black slavery into Alabama, at the urging of the *Sieur* de Bienville because he needed labor to develop the area around Mobile. "It seems odd indeed, my good French friend," Weatherford had told him, "that you would turn your back on the land of your birth because you could not stomach the feudal laws, when this slavery which your nation has brought about is much more tyrannical as well as profitable in terms of gold and silver. Do you not know that the first slaveships arrived in Mobile in the year 1721, and that slaves were so numerous that your own King Louis XV issued an edict on the black slaves in Louisiana three years later? As I

173

recall, it was that all slaves were to be instructed and baptized in the Roman Catholic faith and that any other religion was forbidden. It held also that marriages between slaves and free persons were forbidden——and that is certainly not true of our Creeks, as you have seen for yourself. The slaves were to be fed and clothed, but they might not own property and they could not testify in any court of law. Tutors for a master's children could be set free, and I do not think that slavery will ever be abolished so long as men can see a handsome profit in obtaining captive free labor in this way. Some twenty-five years ago, the English took over where the French had begun, and they still bring in slaves from the ocean-going vessels in Mobile Bay to smaller boats that can go upriver to the villages of the Creeks. Be grateful for what you have received from Tunkamara, and tell yourself that your house and the depot will be built the sooner because of their aid."

Lucien thus had to wrestle with his own conscience, and this, of all the temptations set before him in his newly chosen path, seemed the most troubling of all. He could look in retrospect at his fight to the death with Ecanataba and justify it on the grounds of necessity to survive; his rape of Shehanoy had been a retaliatory act of blind animal instinct, which in the cold sobriety of afterthought and because of his own innate continence, he could still regret with a secret shame, the only mitigating ease of it having been in the knowledge that he had saved her life when it had been forfeit by her having raised a weapon against him. But the acceptance in bondage of a man and a woman who would toil for him under his orders was quite something else; from the pragmatic viewpoint, he dared not offend Tunkamara, and he did not know whether the transference of ownership permitted him to manumit Ben and Ellen back into the freedom they had known in their native Africa.

As the tall Ashanti took the axes and provisions out of the pirogue, Lucien turned to him and said softly, "The *Mico* has told me that you are now my slaves. Is this true?"

Yes, master, it is so. He has said that we are to serve

you as we should any of the Creeks, and that you will look after us and punish us if we disobey."

"Since I shall live with these people and I have hopes of marrying the *Mico*'s daughter, Ben, I do not know that it would be wise to set you free and let the Creeks know what I have done, or they might think it an insult to their chief. But between you and me and your wife Ellen here, I tell you that I shall never think of you as slaves. If you will work with me and help me, I will see that you are well rewarded for your labors, and you will have your own life and I will do all that is in my power to make it good and comfortable."

The tall Ashanti took Lucien's hand and brought it to his lips, and the young Frenchman flushed with furious embarrassment as he tried to disengage it. "You have said I have the right to punish you if you disobey me, and so I will ask you never again to do what you have just done, for it will offend me. In my eyes, you will be my friends and work beside me. In France, I worked on the land with my father's peasants, and I did not look down on them, nor shall I upon you. Know this, even if I cannot declare you free because I am still a newcomer to Econchate and must depend on their tolerance of me to survive."

"I'll work for you, master, and Ellen will cook her very best for you, depend on it," the Ashanti gratefully promised. He turned to his young, shy wife, whispered something to her, then hugged her. Lucien watched them, envying in that moment the constancy which had brought them together, two blacks from different tribes in distant Africa, thence to a French plantation and finally to the village of the Creeks. Their adversities had only strengthened their love for each other. Yes, he was grateful for Tunkamara's gift; Ben and Ellen would share his life and enrich it with their devotion for each other, a devotion which he now could see as a steadfast love which had nothing to do with fanciful sonnets or sighing at the moon for a lady's favor.

By the end of the first day, Lucien and the tireless Ashanti had cut enough logs, plastering the spaces in between with mud, to make a crude shanty to provide enough shelter for the night. Jerky and corn and water from the river was their bill of fare, and after a day of chopping trees and notching and pegging the rough logs, nothing had ever tasted better to Lucien. Ben had brought along tobacco and a long pipe, and he and Lucien took turns puffing at it and savoring the strong rich taste of tobacco, with which Lucien was not at all familiar. At times his father had permitted himself cheroots imported from the West Indies, but Lucien had not found them particularly pleasant. Now, with the sounds of the nightbirds and the crickets and the lapping of the river just beyond this narrow little shack, there was a kind of camaraderie between the white man and the black, while Ellen busied herself outside with collecting the provisions and wrapping the axes in a blanket so that the cool night air or a sudden rain might not dull their sharp edges.

"Tomorrow, master—" Ben passed the pipe to Lucien—"we find some rocks and I build Ellen an oven. Then she can make you some corncakes and cook the jerky in some batter to make it tastier."

"Of course. I want to build a little house, and one nearby for you and Ellen, Ben. And then we'll have the storage depot for the trading goods to ship downriver to Mobile. We can go back to Econchate by the end of the week for more food. And it will take almost a week to hoe up all the weeds and brambles and clear a little plot of land we can plant on. About the best we can hope for this late in the season is some squash and a few beans and potatoes. Ben, you've been here long enough to know the seasons. Are we to get much rain in the months ahead?"

"No, master, in the autumn it's mainly dry."

"I'd just as soon you wouldn't call me master, Ben. If you like, *M'sieu* Lucien, that'll do well enough. I suppose when we're back in the village, you'll have to show them you're a slave, but not out here when we're alone and working together, do you understand?"

"You're a good man, *M'sieu* Lucien. I wouldn't be ashamed to call you master, to tell you true. Back in Haiti—that's the west part of Santo Domingo, you know —I met a man who said that nobody should be called master unless he could lead the people to freedom. He

176

said it was wrong in the eyes of *le Bon Dieu* for only a few cruel men to force gentle people into bondage."

"I agree with him, Ben. What was his name?"

"He was a slave like me, *M'sieu* Lucien. His name was Francois Dominque Toussaint."

By the last weekend of November, Lucien and Ben had completed the notching and pegging of logs and their joining together with clay to make a sturdy cabin, and about twenty feet away another in which Ben and Ellen would live. They had begun to prepare the first timbers for the storage depot which would be on the levee to form a new trading post in ample time for the early spring exchange of goods between Mobile and Econchate. Lucien had rowed the pirogue back to the village several times for supplies, and each time he had had a treasured few moments with the lovely black-haired daughter of the *Mico*. Each time, too, he had brought Dimarte's father gifts of fish and raccoons which he had shot with bow and arrow and had reported on his progress.

But this weekend was to be a festive one, a kind of harvesting festival which would celebrate the good season, the coming of winter and the aura of peace which was still within this land—though it was a peace of inaction, as if all men waited for the events of the coming year.

The squaws were busy with preparations of tasty viands, since Tunkamara had invited warriors from the village of Wetumpka to enjoy his hospitality and to compete with his own warriors in games of marksmanship and *tokonhay*, the original Indian version of lacrosse.

There would be dances, too, the cermonial dances of both villages, and the chants and prayers to accompany the rituals by which the Creeks thanked the Great Spirit and the elements of fire and air and water and soil for the good life they enjoyed. There would be delicacies from puddings made from dried sunflower seed and hickory-nut meats, persimmon cakes from a foot to a foot-and-a-half wide and made from the pulp of ripe persimmons, which, once dried, would keep indefinitely. There would be dumplings, cooked beans, potatoes, chestnuts, wild turnip roots and the inside of the maypop, to accompany the venison, the raccoon, the fish and the bear meat which would be lavishly served to the guests. And there would be gambling, too, on the outcome of the *tokonhay*; Tunkamara had told Lucien of a game in which the ownership of the land between the Warrior and the Tombigbee rivers had been determined by the outcome of such a contest—although, as he had added with a wry smile, neither side had kept its part of the bargain.

Never before had Lucien looked so fit and wiry, radiating energy and confidence, particularly when his eyes rested on Dimarte in her ceremonial boots, jacket and elaborately decorated petticoat. With an eagle feather thrust into the thickest part of her braid near the back of her lovely head, her dark eyes flowing with the pleasure of this conclave and of the tributes paid to her father by the arriving guests, she had never seemed more desirable, more lovely.

He had not yet fulfilled the wedding terms demanded by Creek custom, he knew, but the long arduous days spent clearing the few acres of land he had determined to plant, the building of the two little houses and the foundation for the depot had made him realize how much he missed the warm, gracious companionship of this gentle girl who was already a woman. Of course, he had planted at the wrong time of year, in his enthusiasm to achieve his goal and win Dimarte; Ben had pointed out, with all deference, but with a quiet grin on his face, which indicated that he well understood Lucien's reason for such excessive zeal, that springtime was the proper season. Yet, careful to please his new master, he had also speciously declared, "It is well to cultivate the land which has never before known the hoe or the plow, *M'sieu* Lucien. Now you have made a truck patch near your house, an especial one for pumpkins, squash and potatoes, with the larger cornfield in those acres you have marked off already. That is good, and while the weather remains good, I will help you clear those acres. But the time would be better spent finishing the levee, for I know how eager the *Mico* is to have it finished once the river flows quickly down to Mobile in the spring."

Even with their few provisions and the lack of real conveniences, Ellen had wrought wonders as a cook. Ben had built her a rock oven, and both he and Lucien had watched her make cornmeal, using a mortar which had been fashioned from a small log hollowed out by burning and scraping. Filling it about two-thirds full of dried shelled corn, she had then poured about a pint of water onto the corn before she started to pound it with the pestle. The friction of this pounding made the grain warm and dry, softened the corn and loosened the husk. When it was fine and dry. she sifted it, pouring a small amount in a sifter like a flat-bottomed basket. As she tossed the meal around, she blew out the husks, and then it was ready for use in breads and stews. And she had baked bread in "pones" on the hot stones or part of an earthen pot, or again, wrapped in leaves and dropped into hot water. The stew she had made him of a catfish and herbs and cornmeal had been, to his taste, a gustatory treat that rivaled anything he had known at his father's chateau.

At noon on the Saturday of this final week of November, there having been a great feast and many speeches of welcome and ritual dances the night before, Tunkamara invited Lucien to take part in the *tokonhay*. "I have wagered the *Mico* Entinalda twenty muskets and fifty tomahawks that our warriors of Econchate will best his in the game. You are strong and quick—I saw how you killed the copperhead, and the beloved man Nanakota told me how swift you were with the bow a moon ago—and your skill will surely help defeat Entinalda's warriors."

"I shall be glad to take part in representing the mighty *Mico* of Econchate." Lucien inclined his head. "Am I, a white man, permitted to wager on the outcome?"

"There is no law which prevents it, and you are already our ally, as you know well. What wager would you make, my son?"

Daring greatly, Lucien smilingly regarded Dimarte's father as, taking a deep breath and aware of his audacity, he declared, "If by my skill I aid your warriors in defeating those from Wetumpka, let me find favor in your eyes as the mate of your daughter, oh Tunkamara!"

"Hiyee! You are not only quicker than the striking serpent, but bolder than the deer that runs toward a pack of

179

wolves, my son!" But Tunkamara's dignified, grave face showed no signs of displeasure. "The man who would mate with Dimarte must be bold and quick and strong and good of heart, and these things you have shown me that you are. I will take your wager—but if we are defeated, ask me not again till the sun of the summer sky blazes down upon us. Be it so understood."

West of the village of Econchate was a strip of prairie-like ground which had been prepared the day before by the unfledged braves, the *atac emittla*. These were young men who had not yet counted *coup* over an enemy or brought back a deer or a bear to prove their valor. The playing ground, from which all trees had been cut down and stumps uprooted and the soil leveled, was a quadrangle some ninety yards wide by a hundred and fifty long, with two tall poles six feet apart forming goals at each end. The object of the game was to drive the ball between the opponent's goal post. Each time a goal was scored, the team registered a point and won the game when it had reached the total of twenty. When *tokonhay* was played between rival clans of a village, sixteen points sufficed to proclaim a victor; but in the competition between villages, the larger total was set, not only as a greater test of skill but also to prolong the festivities for the enjoyment of the spectators.

To one side of the playing field there stood a long open shed with a blanketed dais, on which the two *Micos* sat in the center, the elders of Econchate at Tunkamara's right, those of Wetumpka at their chief's left. The game was played with forty to a side, all the contestants wearing only breechclouts and moccasins, their bodies streaked with black and vermilion designs which showed the signs of their clan. Many of the Wetumpka braves had rings of bone or of brass pierced through the cartilage of their noses, others adorning themselves with large broad brass or copper bracelets round their arms and wrists, their plaited hair bedecked with strings, shells and feathers. Nanakota explained to Lucien how the game was to be played and aided his white friend in preparing for the contest, himself painting on Lucien's chest and back the sign of the bear, signifying that this white ally of the Creeks had, in killing such an animal, earned the right to represent that powerful clan. Bronzed by the sun, muscular and trim as he had never been before, Lucien was nevertheless seized with a kind of adolescent modesty about wearing only a breechclout, particularly when he observed that squaws and children had lined up on both sides of the playing field to watch . . . and among them was Dimarte.

In its way, *tokonhay* was like a war game: it was played with tremendous gusto and vigorous bodily contact, a game in which endurance counted as much as skill and cunning. Each player held a racket about two and a half feet long made of hickory wood and covered with deerskin. Lucien had stationed himself near Nanakota, in the second rank of players on the Econchate side. Now, at a sign from both chiefs, old Tsipoulata laboriously rose from the dais inside the shed and with great dignity and solemn face, making ritualistic signs with one hand, approached the center of this playing field, holding the ball in his right hand, which he first held up three times to the sky, murmuring a formula meant to pay honor to the Great Spirit. Then he flung the ball high in the air and moved with understandable alacrity despite his advanced age, beyond the boundaries. A young war lieutenant of Wetumpka in the front rank followed the flight of the ball and, catching it with an arcing swing of his racket, which he held in his left hand, sent it speeding sideways to be caught in the cup of a racket of one of his companions, who began to run toward the Econchate goal. Three of the rival players converged upon him, and at the last moment, before what seemed to be an inevitable collision of these painted, glistening, coppery-skinned male bodies, the Wetumpka warrior whirled his racket to send the ball looping far back toward the Econchate goal. A sturdy young Creek named Micasata, in the exalted ranks of the "beloved men," ran swiftly back and, while speeding toward his own goal, caught up with the ball and backhanded it over his head toward Lucien, who swiftly struck at it to send it flying back toward the Wetumpka goal.

A burly Creek, whose ears were ornamented with pieces of red- and blue-dyed shells, with a fierce grunt, caught the ball deftly in the cup of his racket and ran toward the

Econchate goal, flanked by three tall shouting braves. Lucien saw two of his own comrades hurl themselves at the trio and fell them like logs to the ground, while the burly Wetumpka brave, with a neat side-step, avoided the lunge of a slim young Econchate warrior and made his way toward the coveted goalposts. Lucien broke ranks and ran back with all his speed, overtaking the Wetumpka warrior just before the latter could draw back his arm and send the ball flashing over the boundary mark set off by the two upright poles. Neatly tripping him so that he sprawled headlong, Lucien scooped up the ball and flipped it to Nanakota, who in his turn, seeing himself confronted by four circling Wetumpka braves, lobbed it overhead to a war lieutenant. The latter, looking back over his shoulder and catching the ball in flight, continued with a burst of speed which outdistanced the Wetumpka men and crossed the goal amid wild shouts of "Aiayee!" from Tunkamara and his elders.

A lesser luminary, this time from the Wetumpka village, entered the field and tossed the ball in the air as the *Windigo* had done to start a game, a procedure repeated after the scoring of each goal. Nanakota, grinning at Lucien, patted him on the back and nodded his approval of the young Frenchman's swift resourcefulness, and Lucien, breathing hard to get back his wind, glanced over at Dimarte and with a sudden surge of joyous exhilaration, saw that she was smiling at him and nodding. It was in a way playing the role of schoolboy, trying to show off before a pretty young girl, Lucien well knew, but the fierce rivalry of this energetic game had kindled exactly that reaction from him. And besides, there was the matter of the wager with Tunkamara.

The tide of fortune swayed from one side to the other as the afternoon wore on. His body glistening with sweat, his heart thumping fiercely, feeling the soreness of his calf muscles increase as the furious pace of the game went on unabated, Lucien saw the Wetumpka team score three quick goals in succession before his own comrades could equalize matters. Then, for another hour, both teams seemed to score alternately, till at last, as the sun neared the demarcation which would soon bring twilight's rich

lavenders and reds into the serene blue sky, the score stood at nineteen for each side.

This time, because the very next goal would bring victory to either side, the old *Windigo* lofted the ball into the air and stepped quickly back. The war lieutenant of Wetumpka himself, who had shaved his head except for an arrow-like patch of black hair down the center, caught the ball and swung it back to one of his own players at his left side. The latter, dodging and leaping this way and that to avoid the Econchate braves, swept it back to him across the field as the Wetumpka lieutenant caught it in turn and raced down the sidelines. Lucien, avoiding the lunges of the two Wetumpka warriors, caught up with him and struck out with his racket to disengage the ball, scooped it up and turned as the Wetumpka lieutenant slipped and fell trying to retrieve it. Lofting it to Nanakota, Lucien called upon his failing strength for a last burst of speed and managed to outrun the last two Wetumpka braves in his path as Nanakota, with a Herculean swing, lofted the wobbly deerskin ball in Lucien's direction. He caught it, stepped forward and collapsed over the Wetumpka goal line, amid roars of encouragement from the onlookers.

He was pummeled exuberantly by his teammates as they pulled him to his feet and more dragged than led him in triumph before the dais, where Tunkamara, his wrinkled face wreathed with pleasure and pride, rose to hold out his arms and receive him as the hero of Econchate—and, no doubt, the man who had earned the village much bounty from the many wagers between the elders of each village.

"You have brought great honor to Econchate, and our hearts are full of thanks to our white brother," Tunkamara declaimed as he clasped Lucien by the shoulders and gave him a benevolent nod and smile.

Lucien wearily returned the tribute, and then, turning h' head, saw his genial hunting companion Nanakota a' called to him. The almost strutting "beloved man" hurr' toward the dais. "Speak to the *Mico* for me, Nanakot' ask it as your friend. I have no relatives in this village you said you would stand by me. And I will give yo' gift of which I spoke in the forest."

Nanakota granted assent. Then, bowing low to the *Mico*, he said in guttural Creek, *"Oh he Dimarte nagalla inochante dimisi, o Tunkamara."*

Lucien uttered a stifled cry of joy. Nanakota had just asked that Dimarte be taken in marriage by his friend who was as brother to him. And he saw Tunkamara smile and nod, and reply, "So let him speak for himself unto the maiden he desires. If she accepts, then will I, *Mico* and father both to her, give my consent also."

Too overwhelmed to speak, Lucien could only shake the hand of Nanakota and squeeze it eloquently. For now he was looking to the other side of the field, where Dimarte stood, and she was still there, arms at her sides, watching intently.

"Go to her, be quick now, as you were at the *tokonhay*. But till she accepts you, even the word of the *Mico* does not bring her to your marriage bed, oh Lu-shee-ahn," the "beloved man" teased him.

Lucien forgot his exhaustion and his almost nakedness as he strode across the field to the slim black-haired girl in doeskin and boots. Remembering the custom of the Creeks, he stopped and groped for a pebble on the sandy ground, found one and tossed it toward her feet. Dimarte glanced down at it, then folded her arms and awaited him.

"What was said to my father, Lu-shee-ahn?" she demurely inquired.

Taken aback by the question, Lucien tried to recall the momentous words which Nanakota had uttered, words which now brought him before his heart's desire. "I think—yes, Nanakota said, *'Oh he Dimarte nagalla inochante dimisi',*" he replied, his voice hoarse not only with emotion but from the strenuous exertion of that prolonged game.

Dimarte's dark eyes widened, then she put a hand over her mouth and turned to one side.

"Dimarte, what is wrong? Do I offend you by asking your father for you to be my wife, with Nanakota speaking in place of the relative I do not have here in this village?"

She shook her head, and then, very slowly, turned back to face him. Her eyes danced with a saucy merriment, and with that too was a dark glow which made him quiver with

184

a sudden sensate longing. "I had thought you were a better pupil, Lu-shee-ahn," she softly replied. "Do you know what you have just made Nanakota say to my father?"

"Yes, that he speaks for the friend who is as his brother to take you in marriage, Dimarte."

"Oh, no! What you have said to me is that the friend who is like brother to me wishes to take Dimarte into the bushes."

Lucien's face turned crimson from temples to throat, and as he struggled to find words with which to extricate himself from this hugely embarrassing linguistic error, he saw that Dimarte's exquisite face was crimson as his own.

Stepping closer to her, his hands gently grasping her shoulders, he whispered, "Well, that is true also, my beloved. But only after the *Mico* has married us."

CHAPTER FIFTEEN

Dimarte had consented to wed Lucien on the very day of his twenty-seventh birthday, December 18th, and there was much to do within the scant three weeks before the festive ceremony which would be celebrated in the village of Econchate. On the day after the memorable game of *tokonhay,* after having first told Tunkamara of the date which his daughter had agreed upon, and after promising Nanakota that he would bring the razor in its handsome case back to the village as a present to the "beloved man" for having interceded in his favor with the *Mico,* Lucien returned to the beautiful but lonely strip of ground between the bluff and the hill near Pintilalla Creek. There was much to do, indeed. Puncheon floors for his cabin and that of Ben and Ellen must be finished and as much work done on the little loading depot by the river's edge as possible in order to satisfy his future father-in-law.

Ten days before the wedding, as he and Ben were fortifying the roof of the cabin which he and Dimarte would occupy to keep the inside dry against the occasional severe thunderstorm which visited this region in the winter, Lucien heard a man's voice hail him from the river. He hurried outside to see Charles Weatherford stepping out of a pirogue which his gaudily painted Creek companion was making fast in a tiny cove just beyond the towering red bluff.

"Welcome, Mr. Weatherford," Lucien exclaimed as he shook hands with the trader of Wetumpka. "Will you

186

share the noonday meal with me? Ellen has made a fine fish stew and there is plenty for you and your companion."

"Yes, I thank you." He turned to beckon to the Creek. "Beniwoy, bring the jug of *taffai*. We shall all drink in honor of our white brother's coming marriage to the beautiful Dimarte."

The brave nodded, went back to the pirogue and returned with a clay jug, grinning as he held it up and shook it to indicate that it was full. "Very strong, make fire in belly," he volunteered.

"I came back from Mobile last night, Lucien," Weatherford, like all the Creeks, used the approximation of the nasal sound of the young Frenchman's name. "There is much news from France. A three-master arrived in New Orleans the end of last month, and its captain, whose wife's relatives are Spanish and live in Mobile, sent a courier at once to the town."

"News from France—what is it, Mr. Weatherford?"

The affable trader chuckled. "Since we are now both on the same side and working for Colonel McGillivray, and since you are about to take yourself a Creek wife as I've done, let there be first names between us, Lucien. Well, it appears you were a wise prophet when you left France. The Bastille fell in July."

"*Mon Dieu!* How did it come about, have you learned, Charles?"

"You know, I'm sure, that when you left your country your king was to call the States-General. They met at Versailles in May, demanded reforms which the king would not grant, and the following month proclaimed themselves the National Assembly and took an oath not to separate until they had made a constitution."

"Yes," Lucien said slowly, "that was indeed to be foreseen. And then?"

"At last your feeble Louis yielded to their demands, but then he dismissed the minister Necker, and it was then that the mob of Paris stormed the Bastille. So, to save his own skin, I've no doubt, poor old Louis gave in again and recalled Necker. They established the commune as the city government of Paris, and they organized the National Guard."

"All those things which I felt in my heart would happen have then apparently taken place," Lucien said aloud as if to himself.

"But there is more. Early in August, the Assembly abolished all feudal privileges. There are rumors that the mob may even depose Louis and his extravagant and insolent queen."

"Then it is revolution indeed in France. I would to God I had news of my father and mother, of my brother and of the girl—but, Charles, did the courier bring news of any uprisings throughout the provinces?"

"That is all we have been told. Naturally, if there is a revolution in your country, there will not be many French ships, unless of course they bring those who flee the dangers of this revolution against the monarch."

"This revolution against the monarch, as you put it, Charles, will change the history of all Europe and before much longer," Lucien Bouchard gloomily declared. He thought of the letter which Jabez Corrigan had taken back to France and wondered if by now it had reached kindly old *Père* Morlain. It was possible that all ports would be closed; if terrorists should take over the power which poor, well-meaning Louis had never known how to muster for the general good of his people, then there would be blockades, and the *émigrés*—especially the nobility—who tried to escape France would be halted, their property doubtless seized by what was certain to be a vindictive and retaliatory legislation and perhaps even their lives forfeit. For France had never known a democracy such as had been created in this country; here, the very newness of the land and the inspired vitality of its settlers who sought freedom from religious and political oppression of all kinds had brought about a republic with minimal bloodshed. But in France, it was the story of an old world in its death throes, one in which the greedy and the bloodthirsty opportunists would plunder and pillage to reverse their lowly stations and to pay back all those of aristocratic birth, rank and estate in their haste to be done forever with feudal tyrannies and the boundless differences between the empowered rich and the embittered poor.

He could only pray that *Père* Morlain had somehow been able to persuade his crochety old father and his gentle mother that their safety lay in leaving France, even if it meant abandoning the lands and the chateau. At first, a few years ago, when he had had the first presentiment of the stormy clouds slowly and ominously gathering over the land, Lucien had idealistically supposed that his father might be able to preserve his heritage by freeing his peasants and then hiring them to work upon the land and to establish a novel but practicable commune which ultimately would satisfy those who denounced the monarchy. Now he saw how hopeless such idealism had been. For if the mob of Paris could storm and capture the fortress-like prison of the Bastille, which for centuries had been the impregnable place of confinement for the enemies of the king, then the die was cast. He could do no more now than say a prayer for the lives of his family . . . and for Edmée, who would be his brother's wife.

Charles Weatherford tapped him on the shoulder. "Don't look so sad, Lucien. It's true that your country is lost, but now you have a new one and you're about to wed the prettiest Creek maiden in all Econchate. I gather that you've found a brave who will stand in for you as relative."

"Yes, Nanakota was kind enough to stand before Tunkamara in my behalf, Charles."

"Good! But now there's the matter of gifts and all the ceremonials for the wedding."

"I have brought Tunkamara fish and raccoons from this land which he has been kind enough to let me settle on."

"But that won't be enough, not for a wedding!" Weatherford chuckled. "You must make a fine gift to Tunkamara himself just before the ceremony, and at the wedding itself, you must bring forward a bag of meat— that Nanakota can do for you. Just as Dimarte's father will place a bag of freshly baked bread beside her once the two of you face each other upon the marriage ground."

"What should I give the *Mico?*" Lucien worriedly asked.

"Colonel McGillivray has told me that you have a draft for a thousand *piastres* on deposit with him at his trading house. I can provide you with the gifts you will require and, if you will sign a note, myself deduct the amount from that draft when I return to Mobile."

"That will be most kind of you, Charles. Tell me what I'll need. And one thing more—when you return to Mobile, might I beseech you to carry a letter from me to my family in France which perhaps can be put aboard a ship returning there?"

"I'll arrange that for you. I shall be back in Mobile by Christmas, and it's possible that the French ship *Destreyère*, which brought this news I have given you and went on to New Orleans to unload much of its cargo and to pick up new stores, will have returned by then to collect its final cargo before returning across the Atlantic."

He would send another letter to *Père* Morlain, Lucien thought to himself, with the news of his forthcoming marriage to Dimarte, asking for the little priest's blessing and for that of his father and mother as well. Also he would entreat the priest to dispatch him news of his parents by the swiftest way. Aloud, he replied, "You are most kind to me, Charles, and I shall repay the favor."

"You have earned it. Now you are in my master's service, and you are well thought of in Econchate. Your marriage to Dimarte will strengthen your acceptance by the Creeks, and they will doubtless bring you many goods for trading. My own post is now so large that I should find it difficult to serve them as well as I serve my own village of Wetumpka. But now to the gifts for the *Mico*—I have a fine pair of handtooled Spanish leather boots with spurs and the plumed hat of a Spanish grandee which Tunkamara would surely fancy. And since he is fond of strong spirits—especially at times of great celebration such as your marriage—a cask of Spanish wine would please him greatly."

"Then by all means, Charles, I shall buy those gifts from you at the value you set and without question as to the price."

"You are an honest man, Lucien, and I shan't try to make a profit this time between friends," Weatherford grinned. "Authorize me to deduct 175 *piastres* from your draft, and I shall have my braves bring these gifts to Tunkamara on the morning of the wedding."

The sun shone brightly on the morning which was both Lucien's birthday and his wedding day, and two grinning, sturdy Creek braves from Wetumpka had landed their pirogue at the bank of the river near Econchate and brought the boots and plumed hat and the cask of wine to the entrance of the *Mico*'s house, where Lucien impatiently awaited them. He was dressed in jacket, breeches and leggings of the finest buckskin, beaded and fringed, the beaded pattern on chest and back showing the head of a bear, of which powerful clan he was now acclaimed a member. From Nanakota had come a pair of soft doeskin boots, almost knee-length, and in return, as a token of steadfast friendship, the young Frenchman had given the "beloved man" his treasured compass, which had brought him safely to Econchate, where his life seemed ready now to recommence toward a new and brighter destiny.

The night before, Ben and Lucien had killed three raccoons, and these were brought to the dwelling of the *Mico* as a contribution to the wedding feast. Ellen had baked a huge persimmon cake and made two huge bowls of sunflower seed and hickory nut puddings, these being toothsome favorites of Tunkamara himself.

At noon, the elaborately ritualistic ceremony of a Creek marriage began. The marriage ground itself was an intermediate space between Econchate and Lucien's own dwelling place, some five miles to the southwest of the Creek village. The lesser braves and women had cleared this ground and set up platforms with thatched roofs, where the *Mico* and his elders would witness the ceremony. Nanakota and Lucien had already set out for the marriage ground, and the villagers followed an hour later. The "beloved man" had instructed the young Frenchman in the procedure of this joyous yet solemnly traditional ceremony. Once the elders had taken their places on the platform, Tunkamara himself led Dimarte forward by the hand, while Nanakota, his arm around Lucien's shoulders, urged his "relative" forward till Dimarte and Lucien stood facing each other at a distance of a hundred yards. Then the *Mico* gestured, and Migardo and Eschtola, two warriors in their mid-thirties and cousins of Dimarte—since she had neither sisters nor brothers—walked toward Lucien and, each taking him by a hand, led him toward a blanket spread upon the marriage ground. It was then Nanakota's turn to walk toward Dimarte and draw her to the blanket and seat her beside Lucien.

The beautiful Creek girl was clad in a soft doeskin petticoat, moccasins and jacket, an eagle feather thrust through her braid. Her eyes downcast, but her lips wreathed in an exquisite smile, she took her place beside Lucien. Nanakota leaned over to his "relative" and whispered, "Do not be alarmed now if she runs away from you. It is the tradition." And as Lucien looked up, startled, Nanakota grinned and added, "Never fear, she will be brought back. She will not run too far or too long, I promise."

At that moment, Dimarte sprang to her feet and ran toward the east and away from her father and his elders. As Lucien started to his feet with an exclamation of surprise, Nanakota restrained him with a soft chuckle, "Ho! That is not your work, not yet. Tonight if she runs, then you may catch her—but now it is for her cousins to bring her back to you! Besides, did I not tell you she would not run too fast or too far? Already her cousins have caught her, and now they bring her back to you, and that is the sign she has chosen you as her mate."

It was true indeed. Dimarte, her eyes twinkling with merriment, but her lips compressed as if in the semblance of helplessness, allowed herself to be led by the wrists back to Lucien and seated beside him. Her two cousins returned to the other side of the marriage ground and carried back sacks of freshly baked bread which they placed beside her. In his turn, Nanakota carried a deerskin bag in which the carcass of a skinned raccoon was contained and laid it beside Lucien.

It was not a marriage by priest in church or chapel, yet to Lucien it seemed as powerfully symbolic as any ritual of the Holy Church. For these bags of provisions were traditional symbols of the ancient days when man was the hunter and it was his task to provide the household with game, while his squaw was to raise corn for the bread and the hominy which would nourish the children she would bestow upon him. He glanced obliquely at Dimarte and found that she had turned to look at him with a radiant little smile and a soft nod of her head. Her arms were folded across her bosom, and he could see the color heighten in her coppery cheeks. Then she turned to look toward her father, and Lucien quivered with the knowledge that this wise, gentle, lovely girl, who perhaps would never know the fripperies and the flounces of elegant Paris, possessed what was far more important to him, a sympathetic devotion and an understanding of the differences between them, as well as the knowledge of sharing her life with one who, till a few months ago, had lived and been educated in a totally different land.

Nanakota had retreated well behind them, taken up a doeskin sack, and now came forward. Opening it, he proceeded to shower Dimarte with trinkets which Charles Weatherford had given Lucien as his own wedding gift to the daughter of *Mico*: ribbons, trinkets, leg-guards made of sturdy buckskin to ward off the bite of a snake and a rectangular coverlet in the shape of a small blanket into which dried corn shucks had been strewn as a kind of soft mattress for the bridal bed.

Dimarte's two cousins, standing nearby, quickly snatched up these tokens and, leaving only the coverlet before the *Mico*'s daughter, returned to the platform to distribute these gifts among the elders, who in turn would bestow them upon their wives or daughters, as was the custom.

Nanakota, standing behind Lucien and at his left, bent now to whisper, "Now you must take her right hand with yours, her left hand with yours, and rise, first facing each other to bind your coming together and then facing the *Mico* and the elders."

Lucien turned to Dimarte, reached out his hands and took hers, as both rose. Supple and willowy, with a fluid grace that was instinctive and would have put a practiced

193

dancer to shame with its exquisite simplicity, the Creek girl rose to face him. Her face was serious, her eyes wide and searching as she stared into his face. Lucien had been told that not a word should be spoken between them till after the ceremony, and he implicitly obeyed this instruction. But in his mind, as in his heart, the lovely word "Dimarte" resounded again and again and yet again.

They turned to face Tunkamara and the elders, and both bowed low. Then it was that Lucien's beautiful young wife murmured, "Now you must open the sacks and distribute the food for the feast they will have to honor us, my husband, my Lu-shee-ahn."

With the food, there were dances, and there were orations by the *Mico* himself and several of his elders, including the wizened *Windigo,* who, shaking a little pouch which contained the feathers of an eagle, the claws of a bear, the head of a cottonmouth, the shell of a turtle and all the other symbols of those clans which comprised the village of Econchate, blessed their marriage and asked the Great Spirit Hisagita-imisi as well as Ibofanaga ("the one sitting above" who bore a close relationship to the sun but was not the sun itself) to grant long life and many strong sons and good hunting and happiness to the new couple.

And then as dusk began to enpurple the sky, four of the strongest braves of the village rowed Lucien and his bride back to the little house of logs and clay, that new dwelling between the towering red, thickly wooded bluff and the gently rolling hill which was the haven against the wind of this land on which he would now settle.

Ben and Ellen had strewn wildflowers of the season about the puncheon floor and on the thick pile of neat blankets in one corner which was to be the bed. Beside the cabin and near the smaller one in which the Creek slaves would live, Ben and Lucien had built a roofed shed with a stone oven and an improvised flue to carry off the smoke and the heat. Ben had made a little table of hickory wood, and the bowls and gourds atop it were filled with flowers too. On the table stood a rude candle made from tallow drippings and bear fat. Lucien struck his tinderbox and with a dry twig lit the coarse wick. The flickering, eerie light illumined this his first house, built with his own hands and the aid of Ben's, thus more precious to him than all the ornately furnished rooms of the chateau at Normandy. There were two little stools beside the table and these Lucien himself had made.

As Dimarte stood beside him, inspecting the first home she had ever known away from Econchate, he took the doeskin coverlet from her and laid it upon the blankets. Then, as she turned to look at him, her eyes modestly lowering, clasping her hands before her, he came swiftly to her, took her in his arms and kissed her on the forehead and on the cheek.

"What do you do, my husband?" Her voice was a soft whisper.

"It is a custom among my people, beloved. In French, we call it *un baiser,* a kiss, to signify that you are my love."

"It is sweet yet strange, Lu-shee-ahn. Will you not teach it to me, and your other customs of which I know so little?" she demurely asked, her eyes still downcast, so standing before him with clasped hands as if not yet sure of her acceptance by him.

He turned the stone of his mother's cabochon ring, then drew the ring off his finger and taking her left hand, placed it upon her third finger, which, in the little church of *Père* Morlain, would have signified his pledge before God and man. And the wonder of it was that at this moment he did not think of Edmée de Courent, nor regret that it was not she who stood beside him now. This love was sweetly strange and new: it was based on trust, on sympathy and understanding, and on the deepest respect for what this gentle Creek girl could teach him of a culture and a way of life perhaps centuries older than his own. And most of all, upon her unhesitating and loyal trust in confiding her life to him, a white man and an interloper on the land of the Creeks, she who had the virtual rank of princess in her tribe and who, as one of the "beloved women," the honor of appearing in council with the elders and the *Mico.*

"Oh, it is beautiful, Lu-shee-ahn!" Dimarte exclaimed, examining the ring, turning it this way and that, holding her hand up to her face, then looking at him with a radiant, grateful smile.

"It was my mother's. I will ask it back only if one day this land might be no longer ours and we should have to buy it from those who would claim it from the Creeks," he responded, his hands caressing her slim shoulders, his lips brushing the high arch of her lovely forehead.

That enchanting face, whose every line he knew now as he had once known Edmée de Courent's, was momentarily shadowed and grave: "I too have the feeling that one day the Creeks will be driven from this good land, Lushee-ahn. Even the *Windigo,* who has read the signs, has said that one day the white man will come with many guns and drive us away, into a land where there will be no hunting and no rich earth in which to plant and harvest the crops our people need."

"May your Great Spirit and my God, who may well be one and the same, Dimarte, grant that such a day will never come to pass," he murmured as he kissed her once again. And this time it was her lips his own sought, softly and gently so as not to terrify her, for he knew that she was a virgin. Even so, at the first touch of her sweet mouth against his, he could not suppress the swirling tide of physical desire that rose in his virile body at the knowledge that he would be her initiator, her lover as her husband, the father of the children for whom he would toil to make this land abundant in its bounty. Mingled with his desire was a great humility and also a secret apprehension. With Jean, he suddenly and bitterly reflected, such a situation would never have arisen; his brother would have seen in Dimarte a desirable woman to be taken and enjoyed with no concern to her own pleasure or the quieting of her virginal fears.

And so, when the kiss was ended, when he had felt her instinctively press against him, putting her hands to his waist to support her first troubling sensations to this all too urgent kiss, he released her and moved away, uncertain, suddenly as shy as she.

Dimarte moved toward the bed of blankets and the doeskin coverlet and then turned and calmly began to remove her doeskin jacket. As it fell, the magnificent young

196

beauty of her round firm breasts dazzled him, and the flickering shadows cast by the candle traced mysterious patterns on the warm, coppery-satiny skin. He trembled at the sight of the dusky-coral aureole, narrowed round the pert buds of her virgin nipples, and the graceful, slim waist which flared under the doeskin petticoat into lithe, enchantingly rounded, supple young hips.

Crimsoning, he turned toward the candle, but Dimarte's soft voice stopped him. "No, my husband. A warrior is to see the body of his squaw, that it may be pleasing in his eyes, that he may make a child upon her and that she will have the strength to bear him a fine warrior like himself."

Her shoulders straight, a gentle, almost proud smile on her lips, Dimarte unfastened the doeskin petticoat and let it fall to the puncheon floor. He caught his breath at the sensual beauty of her body, so beautifully muscled, so firmly wrought, yet with all its alluring, secret promises of soft, feminine allure. Then, as she stooped to pull off her boots, his eyes feasted on the smooth, deeply hollowed back, the lissome shoulders, the rounded, young opulence of her haunches, and the enchanting swaying of her firm breasts.

Then, still proudly and joyously, her dark eyes glowing with love, Dimarte lay down upon the bed of doeskin and blankets, the cornshucks rustling suggestively as she awaited her mate. Lucien uttered a choking cry of rapt desire and poignant anguish, stricken to his very marrow by the touchingly candid, beautiful compliance of her act of yielding. Then, swiftly, divesting himself of jacket and breeches and boots, he blew out the candle and found his way to the Creek girl's arms.

Fiercely, he told himself to be more gentle than he had ever thought a man could be lying beside the warm, quivering, desirable body of this Indian girl who had displayed such an eloquent nobility of spirit, gracefulness and kindness in the few short months he had known her. Yet in even so brief a span of time, he knew her better than he had ever known Edmée de Courent. Dimarte was not capable of deception or artifice or dishonest emotions; they might dispute over differences which arose out of

197

their different worlds, but he could never hope for a mate whose elemental honesty and goodness and loyalty were indeed, as some historian had written of the Chevalier Bayard, *sans peur et sans reproche*.

His lips brushed her warm, herb-scented shoulder, his hands reverently stroking her sides, her flanks. Dimarte sighed gently, turning to him, linking her arms round him, drawing him down upon her. "I have never been with a man, Lu-shee-ahn, but as your squaw I have been taught by the old women what would please you. Take me as your squaw now, so then I will know that I please you as much as you do me. Warrior of the Bear, pierce my body with your weapon, so that we are truly wed!" she whispered in the darkness.

There was no world other than this, confined within the walls of this narrow little cabin. Truly this day he had been reborn, and yet from his old life he had retained the sensibility of the great gift and the deep, comforting and fiercely thrilling joy Dimarte had accorded him. His lips brushing a turgescent nipple, his left arm under her shoulders, his right hand reveling in the satiny smoothness of her hip and thigh, he drew a long, shuddering breath of speechless gratitude. There had been no words, there could never be words, to express to the young woman who lay beside him the miracle of their coalescence, the timeless, immeasurable ecstasy which had begun so hesitantly and almost fearfully on his part, only to find himself flatteringly and ecstatically made welcome and no longer a stranger far from home and parents and those things which he had loved. There could be no way of telling Dimarte how in the simple act of union she had both consoled and abetted him, never wanton but ever eager, learning his own urgencies as she discovered for the first time her own, matching him with delight that brought him ever new delight till flesh and nerves could not bear such cumulative passion.

He felt her soft hand touch his cheek, then his lips. "Is Dimarte pleasing to her mate?" came her soft, throaty whisper.

"There is no woman like Dimarte. She is more than pleasing, she is adored, my sweet, my wife, my beloved."

"Do I please my lord more than the one in France?" Now there was the faintest hint of an adorable wifely jealousy, which enchanted him and made him laugh with exultant pride as he whispered back, "I do not even remember her name or what she looked like now. I remember only Dimarte."

And as he moved upon her again, feeling her quivering, pliant thighs make eager way for him, as he felt her arms lock round his shoulders to draw him upon her and as he heard her gasp of pleasure, Lucien Bouchard knew he had not lied.

CHAPTER SIXTEEN

During this last fortnight of the year, Lucien's life took on what was for him an idyllic simplicity, one of serene contentment. Given to introversion as he had often been, he found himself philosophizing over his good fortune in finding the lovely Creek girl so willing to share his life. But exactly because of his intellectual bent, there were times even during this primitive honeymoon—for such it was—that he experienced a twinge of remorse in thinking of his father and mother. For in one sense, he could not forget the old *seigneur*'s scornful reference to him as a cowardly *émigré*. Now that the monarchy had been overthrown, his father's accusation rankled in his mind. What if he had remained in Normandy and done what he could to avert the coming catastrophe that was now engulfing all France? Could he have assured the safety of his beloved father and mother, of Jean, even of Edmée? Or had he acted, when all was said and done, when all the high-sounding principles might be more accurately judged as mere rhetoric to hide his real motive, because of Edmée's rejection of him? If that were true, then he was not nearly the philosopher he had always deemed himself to be, but instead little more than an adolescent wanting to make a grand gesture out of pique to his own self-esteem.

He could not help this spiritual self-flagellation, exactly because these first weeks with Dimarte in that little cabin had brought him the kind of happiness that went far beyond poetry and moonlight and romantic posturings. Yes, he clearly saw now that Edmée could never have given him the same kind of totally trusting love of which this Creek girl of the untamed wilderness was capable. And if it had been the choice between these two women in his life, Lucien Bouchard would have been supremely content over the sudden decision he had made to turn his back on the chateau of Normandy and come across an ocean to a continent of which even the history books he had read at the University of Paris had told him so very little. Thus, in the night, as he held Dimarte's warm body against his own, brushing her eyelids with his lips as he watched her smiling in her sleep after their lovemaking, he found himself returning again and again to the thought that he had heedlessly abandoned his parents and, just as the fierce, proud old man at the table that last night in Yves-sur-lac had said, deserted a sinking ship even before any danger to himself. But now there was no turning back; all he could do was pray to a just and loving God not to punish his father and mother because of his own obsessive desire for land and the freedom to live upon it as he chose.

Yet the uplifting joy he gleaned from observing how Dimarte so eagerly adapted herself to her own new life served to banish these haunting specters of remorse. From the very first morning, when she firmly bade Ellen show her their provisions stored in the oven-shed and the way in which her white husband made the fire from his tinder-box, and at once assumed all the menial duties of a faithful squaw who leaves the valorous deeds of hunting and fishing and building and tilling the land to her mate, Dimarte made Lucien marvel at her unflagging zeal and industry. She who had been the most beautiful girl of the village and admitted to the council of elders because of her wisdom now went to the river for water, polished the boots he had brought from France with bear grease till they gleamed like new, tidied their little cabin, prepared his meals and served them with a self-effacing concern for his approval that made him feel as if he were a king—or, here in this new world, the *Mico* himself.

And at night, in the stillness of the dark and the enclosure of the four walls of this cabin which did not even approximate the relative size or comfort of her father's dwelling, Dimarte became all women to him: shy and submissive to his male ardors at times, again eagerly curious to learn what would please him most with her caresses and endearments and, most excitingly of all, when the sweet flash of mischievousness seized her, teasingly exhorting him to treat her ruthlessly, as he had done Shehanoy. And when those capricious moments came upon her, she became a primeval Lilith, feigning resistance and evasion, then sweetly submitting, only, in the very next moment, to writhe away and to pretend with simulated ferocity that he was not permitted to possess her. And in the tumultuous, savage ecstasy of their inspired and imaginative lovemaking, Lucien felt himself purged and appeased, consoled and fulfilled as he had never believed any woman could bring about for him.

It was after one of those rapturously embattled nights, toward the end of their fortnightly *lune-de-miel,* that Dimarte whispered to him, her voice vibrant and choked with ecstatic sobs, "Oh, my husband, I am certain that tonight you have made a child within my belly, and it will be a strong one, as mighty as his father whom I love with all my heart and my body!"

Wordlessly, Lucien had brought her left hand to his lips, kissing his mother's ring, which had become the pledge of his devotion to this exquisite Indian girl, and then he had kissed her forehead and at last her mouth, cradling her in his arms as they lay at peace in the little cabin, their clamoring senses at last lulled by the sweet dreamless sleep, the restorative boon of ardent love.

Shortly after the first week of the new year, Lucien returned to Econchate to report to Tunkamara that the loading depot, and the levee were ready and that he wished to serve the *Mico* and the village. Tunkamara commissioned him to take many deer- and bear-skins to the trading post in Mobile and told him what goods the village required in return. That next morning, Lucien carried the piles of cured pelts to a flatboat, saw to his provisions for the estimated week-long journey down to Alabama, and by noon, using his long pole as he had seen

202

the boatmen in New Orleans do, headed the flatboat toward Mobile.

On the morning of the seventh day, securing the flatboat to the low dock near the trading post, Lucien, weary but exhilarated by having made the long journey successfully and without aid, carried the tightly bound piles of pelts into the plank-structured trading post of Swanson and McGillivray. The half-breed, David Francis, was the first to recognize him, and he came forward with an enthusiastic greeting, helping him carry the largest piles onto a broad counter. "I am glad to see you, *M'sieu* Bouchard! We've heard how well you proved yourself at Econchate, and how you've managed to wed the *Mico*'s daughter."

"My prayers must have been heard, David Francis, and I am happier than I thought a man could be. This life is new, but it excites and tests me, and I am eager for it. Is Colonel McGillivray in Mobile now?"

"No, my good friend, he has gone to Pensacola, and I shall join him there in a month or two, for as you possibly have heard, we are to meet with the American commissioners again in New York this time," the half-breed explained.

"I hope a peace treaty can be brought about. Thus far, I've seen only the harmonious family life of the Creeks, and I've made friends in the village. It would sadden me to think that any of them would die in battle."

"The Creek warrior looks upon death in battle as a reward for valor, *M'sieu* Bouchard. But I too pray there will be peace. However, my master fears that the ambitious Georgia settlers will not be content with any peace, wanting as they do to extend their boundaries and to take the lands of the Creeks. He asked me to congratulate you on what you have done in so short a time."

"I have passed his test, thanks in part to your advice," Lucien retorted.

The half-breed's eyes widened, and then a thin smile briefly appeared on his lips. "We need say no more. But Ecanataba had orders not to harm you, only to capture you. It was my master's belief that a man who speaks of freedom so loftily before he has truly earned it should

203

taste for a time the shackles of a slave so that he will better understand the priceless nature of that freedom."

"I bear him no malice for that. He did not know me from any other man, and I foresaw there would be a trial of my worthiness. I regret that I killed so brave a warrior."

"I have heard also how gracious you were in sparing the life of Shehanoy. That was a good thing. But now, to business. These are prime pelts, and Charles Weatherford has already told us how much you can aid the village of Econchate. As time progresses and you become more skillful in our ways, my master intends you to stock such necessities as are found here at your own trading post, so that you can effect immediate trade with the Creeks and earn advantageous wages for yourself."

"I should enjoy that. And I look forward also to the spring, when I may plant crops that will feed the village."

"That is good. Tunkamara has need of pack ponies, as I see, and you shall go back on the trail with them, bearing the goods for Econchate. Tonight, if you so wish, you will be my guest at the house where you stayed before."

"I thank you, David Francis. Your wife is well?"

"Yes, quite well, I thank you. You will return tomorrow to Econchate?"

"Such is my plan. I have no other business in Mobile. But wait—are any boatmen bound for New Orleans this week, David Francis?"

"Why yes, I think so."

"I should like to buy a present for a young lady there, one who was kind to me. I will purchase the gift here and pay the boatman for his trouble."

"That can be arranged, *M'sieu* Bouchard," David Francis smiled.

And so, the next morning, old Pierre Durand, the same boatman who had taken Lucien from New Orleans to Mobile, made the journey back to that newly rebuilt city on the Mississippi, taking with him a bolt of fine green damask which had recently come from Spain and accompanying which, addressed to *Madame* Eulalie Villefranche at the house of her aunt on Isola Street, was a note in which Lucien had gallantly expressed his unforgettable memories of a certain eventful night.

At about the same time, Lucien and his pack ponies laden with supplies, began the trip across the mouth of Mobile Bay. Once ashore, Lucien mounted his pack pony, with six other sturdy animals of burden harnessed in single file behind his. With a last wave of his hand to David Francis, he began his return journey to Econchate and thence back to her who was truly in his heart, the "beloved woman."

Custom demanded that he remain during a village festival dance and feast which took place the day after he had entered Econchate leading the six pack ponies behind him, amid the welcoming shouts of the braves, who recognized this blood brother of the Clan of the Bear who, as Tunkamara had stoutly declared to all of them, spoke with true tongue from a heart that was good and who was the more welcome now because he was the mate of Dimarte.

At the feast, his Creek more fluent now and his mind keenly able to cope with the complexities of the language and especially the shades of hidden meaning which many a simple phrase usually concealed at the council, Lucien discussed with the *Mico* and the elders the prospects of the treaty which it was said their great leader would sign in that unknown and far distant city of New York when the warmth of spring again blessed the fertile fields and the wide river of the Alabama. It was on the second day, after the feasting and the dancing, when the foremost elders met with the *Mico* to plan hunting forays for the early spring and the planting of the crops, that Tunkamara turned to his white son-in-law and gravely asked, "What does the mate of Dimarte say to the war drum if it beats and if it summons him to fight against the white-eyes like unto himself, now that he is our blood brother and honored by all clansmen of the sign of the bear?"

Lucien pondered a moment, for he too had often thought of this question on his journey up the trail from Mobile. He had already shown the people of Econchate that he was no coward; nevertheless, once a member of this clan, if that clan should be summoned by the war drum, he would have no choice but to fight for the village. At last he answered, "I will give my life for my beautiful squaw, whom I honor for herself as for her kinship to the great *Mico*. I will defend my friends here and my brothers against unjust attack."

"Ho, that is good," Tunkamara grunted and handed him the ceremonial pipe to smoke.

He knew that he was bound in honor by the laws of these primitive but honest people whose life he had adopted as his own and now it was the most tangible bond of all, for he was truly bound in blood by the ties of marriage to Dimarte. And yet he could not help saying a silent prayer as he rowed the pirogue back to that red bluff and that little cabin which meant more to him now than the stately chateau at Yves-sur-lac that he would never be compelled to kill any man, whether white or red, in cold blood because of the exigencies of war.

He had bought presents for Dimarte and for Ben and Ellen too; a Spanish comb for his lovely wife, salt and flour for Ellen as well as a colorful shawl, and for the staunch, tall Ashanti who had labored side by side with him to build these cabins and the loading depot at the river bank a sharp hunting knife affixed in a deerskin scabbard to a sturdy belt. It was very much like the knife Jabez Corrigan had given him, that knife which had killed the bear and which Shehanoy had tried to use against him for the slaying of her warrior husband. When he had bought it from David Francis at the Mobile trading post, he had remembered the red-haired Irishman and fervently hoped that one day soon he would meet him again to tell him what had happened since their friendship had begun on the *Guerrière*.

Dimarte, hearing the joyous welcoming cries of Ben and Ellen, had hurried out of the cabin to meet him. And although he had been told that most Creek women were undemonstrative, he was overjoyed to see her hurrying to him, the happy glow in her dark eyes, that unforgettably radiant smile on her soft lips as she came to him and laid her head against his breast and murmured, "It has been so long, Lu-shee-ahn, so very long, and how I have missed you! And tonight I have something to tell you which I hope will please you, my husband, my warrior."

Inside the cabin, she clapped her hands with glee as a child might over the lustrous Spanish comb, playfully fixing it here and there on her thick braid or at the top of her head, adopting piquant poses which made him laugh for very joy in their reunion. In her look, there was a deeper, warmer regard, a sweeter eloquence than he had seen even on their bridal night or when they had been seated side by side on the marriage ground and she had stolen quick glances at this white man whom she had chosen over any Creek warrior to be her mate. And then, after the lavish supper which Ellen had insisted on preparing as a welcome home for the master—a word which she continued to use despite Lucien's embarrassment at all its connotations—when once again Lucien and Dimarte were alone and lying side by side on the doeskin coverlet and the blankets, Dimarte whispered, "Last week the time of the moon did not come for me, and so I know I am with child, my beloved husband. It was made that night when you conquered me as you did Shehanoy, I know it well. And it will be a boy, a strong healthy cub for my man of the Bear Clan, I promise." And when he had kissed her tenderly, too full of emotion to be content with mere words, holding her close and quivering with the delight which her nearness always brought, she teasingly whispered, "I am afraid you must be ready to give up certain things, Lu-shee-ahn, according to our law."

"So long as I needn't give you up, Dimarte, I shall obey the law. What must I sacrifice?"

"Why, when a squaw is with child, her mate may eat no salt or pork until the child is born. Will you hate me for this, my dear husband?"

"They will be easy to give up, my dear one. I have eaten no pork since I left France, and as for salt, the herbs you use in cooking for me are far tastier. So it will not be a great loss and therefore I cannot hate you. I shall hate you only if the law says I may no longer hold you thus and kiss you thus also," and, punctuating his words, he set his mouth to hers as his hands slid under her supple hips. With a happy little sigh, Dimarte arched to him, welcoming him to the exquisite haven of her lithe young body.

By April, Lucien had made three more trips to Mobile, pleasing Tunkamara with his shrewd trading and making a profit of some four hundred *piastres* for himself, which was added to his account at Swanson and McGillivray. Between those trips, he and Ben tilled more acres and planted corn. Again by Creek law, once the seed was in the ground, the crops were to be worked by the women, and Dimarte and Ellen tended the growing stalks. Lucien and Ben had killed several water moccasins, those poisonous snakes indigenous to the area which beset unwary travelers in the creek or river as on the land near the river. When the young corn began to sprout from the rich earth of limestone and clay, they put up a kind of picket fence made of broken barrel staves to enclose it and minimize the danger of those venomous reptiles. On his third trip, Lucien brought back eight pack ponies laden with supplies like hoes, spades, blankets and trinkets for the women, which could be kept in the spacious depot and thus be speedily taken to Econchate. The pelts which paid for them would be stored there also, and when the demand was high and the stock ample, Lucien would make another journey on the flatboat to Mobile.

All these weeks of energetic labor and of travel occupied his energy, while he watched Dimarte grow still more beautiful with her advancing pregnancy. It was not yet too noticeable, but the gentler, calmer and even graver attitude which she displayed told him that this young girl was already disciplining herself to the full maturity that had made her worthy of being called to council and would make her an incomparable mother of this his very first child. And he had not forgotten his vow to name that child, if it were truly a son as Dimarte believed it would be, after the courageous stableboy Edmond Vignon.

Each time he had visited Mobile, Lucien had paid a boatman to go to New Orleans and to the offices of the governor-general to ask for any letter that might be addressed to him. And each time the answer had come back that no letter had yet been received. Surely by now

Père Morlain had received his first letter, and if the kindly old priest had responded to it at once, an answer would have been waiting at New Orleans by now. It might have been that the courier whom Jabez Corrigan had sent from Le Havre had not been able to reach Yves-sur-lac at all, or the letter might have been lost or stolen. Yet again, if the angry uprisings of the peasants in many other provinces of France had infected the people of Normandy with this revolutionary madness, the priest himself might have had to flee for safety—unless he had joined the revolutionaries. And God alone knew what had happened to his father and mother in such a case. As before, all Lucien could do was pray that those two people dearest to him next to Dimarte had been adjudged on their merits as mindful of the welfare of their villagers and so left in peace on their estate.

George Washington had determined to bring Colonel Alexander McGillivray into his presence and settle the difficulties of negotiation which had so disappointingly marred the meeting of his commissioners with the Creek trader-agent the previous fall. He selected Colonel Marinus Willett, who had been a distinguished officer in the Canadian War and the American Revolution, to visit the Creek Nation by a circuitous route and to try to effect a private meeting with McGillivray, doing his utmost to persuade the Creek leader to return with him to the home of the Federal Government. Willett had been warned to keep his mission a profound secret from everyone except General Andrew Pickens, to whom he bore Washington's own personal letter.

Colonel Willett sailed from New York and fourteen days later arrived at Charleston; he continued on by horseback to the home of General Pickens on the Seneca River.

By April 19th, 1790, Washington's secret emissary, accompanied by an Indian guide, set out for the Cherokee town of Santee, a village of eighteen houses and enclosed by mountains. From there he went on to Pine Log, escorted by Thomas Gogg, a friend of General Pickens who had been a trader among the Cherokees. There Willett met Chief Yellow Bird, who held a game of *tokonhay* in his honor. The next day, Yellow Bird took Willett to Eustenaree, a city of refuge to which any criminal could flee for honored sanctuary, for it was the law that no blood could be shed within its boundaries.

The two chiefs of Eustenaree, Badger and Jobberson, welcomed Colonel Willett, who bore letters from General Pickens to them, and they agreed to accompany him to Ocfuskee on the Tallapoosa River, where it was learned that Alexander McGillivray was visiting. Washington's agent had spent ten days since leaving the borders of South Carolina in his march over a wilderness country which was the constant scene of murder and robbery, not only by marauding Indians but by renegade whites who lay in wait for settlers attempting to find more peaceful country for their homes.

On the 3rd of May, Colonel Willett at last met Alexander McGillivray, whom he described in a letter to President George Washington as "a man of an open, generous mind, with a good judgment and very tenacious memory." Two days were spent in earnest conversation, and Colonel Willett witnessed a religious ceremony of the black drink. It was a ceremony which invariably accompanied Creek oratory when serious matters were being decided by the council and each elder or high-ranking warrior wished to speak in his turn. A square area was set off on clear ground, bounded on all four sides by long open sheds under which, upon a platform of canes raised three feet from the ground, the elders reclined or sat crosslegged or lay back propping themselves on their elbows, all wearing those elaborate costumes which were prescribed for council meetings. In the center of the square was a fire over which was suspended from a cross-stick a large earthen pot which two braves tended, using long ladles to skim off the froth which profusely rose to the surface of the black drink. Then each brave proceeded to opposite sides of the arena and handed the ladles around. As each elder or warrior drank from the ladle, the two braves commenced a song of one note, "Ah-ah-a-a," prolonged with a shrill key without drawing breath until the drinker finished his task. Then in turn, each elder would rise and speak his mind upon the issue at stake.

After many ceremonies, Alexander McGillivray, accompanied by his nephew, and his servants Paro and David Francis, set out with Colonel Willett from his home at Little Tallase for New York, stopping first at Stone Mountain in Georgia to be joined by the chiefs of the Cowetas and the Cussetas. Thence to North Carolina and on to Philadelphia, and finally to Elizabethtown Point, where they boarded a sloop which took them to New York. There the Tammany Society, in the full dress of its order, marched them up Wall Street by the Federal Hall where Congress was in session and then to the house of President George Washington to whom they were introduced with pomp and ceremony.

On August 7, 1790, with Dimarte but a month away from coming to full term with her child, Henry Knox negotiated the all-important treaty with Alexander McGillivray and his delegation, who represented the entire Creek nation. It set forth that a permanent peace was to be established between the Creeks and the citizens of the United States; that the Creeks and Seminoles should be under the sole protection of the American Government, and that they should not make treaties with any other country; that they should surrender at Rock Landing all white prisoners and blacks taken during the recent hostilities, in default of which the Governor of Georgia was authorized to send troops into the nation to claim and liberate them; and finally, that the boundary line between the Creeks and Georgia was to be that claimed by the latter in the treaties made at Augusta and Shoulderbone.

Thus the wily Richelieu of Alabama had surrendered the Oconee lands on which so much blood had been shed and so much negotiation wasted for a paltry $1500 to be paid annually to the Creek nation as well as goods to be distributed among the Indians from the Augusta warehouses. But, secretly, beyond this treaty, Alexander McGillivray agreed that the commerce of the Creek nation should be carried on through the ports of the United States and that the Creek chiefs of the nation should be paid an annual tribute of $100 and handsome medals; fi-

211

nally, that he himself was to be constituted an agent of the United States with the rank of brigadier general at the pay of $1200 a year; and that the United States should feed, clothe and educate Creek youths in the north.

A trusted lieutenant was sent on a packhorse bearing $2900 in gold to be paid to the chiefs as a pledge of good faith to keep the treaty, and instructed by President George Washington to remain with Alexander McGillivray to be sure that the latter would carry out the provisions of the treaty in restoring the liberty of all prisoners and establish the boundary line between the Creeks and the embattled Georgians.

On the face of it, the treaty seemed to promise peace and the growth of this southeastern part of the new country, to offer opportunity to colonize and eventually to create states that would join the original thirteen. In reality, it was to be the prelude to bloody outbreaks of Indian attacks upon the settlers, of countless deceptions and ambiguities, and was destined to change the life of Lucien Bouchard in a dramatic way that even his wildest imagination could not have conceived.

Even as the news came slowly out of Mobile on the progression of Alexander McGillivray's triumphant tour to the young nation's capital, news that seemed to augur at last peace between the fierce Creeks and the white settlers in their midst, Dimarte, her face pale and drawn with the pangs of imminent labor, made her way into the cornfield, almost indignantly refusing Ellen's aid. It was her duty as a Creek squaw to bring forth her child—and never in any cabin or shelter—without assistance from anyone. In the hot sun of the late morning of September 17th, while Lucien paced inside the cabin and swore a thousand useless oaths to speed his young wife's hours of agony and liberate her child, Dimarte's stifled cries of pain made Ben and Ellen cling to each other as they stood beside their cabin and called upon the gods whom they had worshiped in Santo Domingo to bring a swift and merciful end to Dimarte's suffering.

But it was only at twilight that the daughter of the *Mico*, tottering in her weakness, her bloodstained petticoat torn by the rending of her slim fingers in the atrocious pangs of difficult travail, bore her son to the river bank and, slowly kneeling, washed him in the river and then as totteringly rose and moved, step by painful step, like an old arthritic woman, back to the cabin where Lucien awaited her.

Ellen had made a cradle of cane and at Dimarte's own earlier instructions had made one end of it two or three inches lower. It was into this rude support that Dimarte now laid her son, its head lower than its body. Lucien uttered a sobbing cry: "My beloved, you're suffering! Come, let me carry you to the bed, and Ellen will bathe you with cool water and bring you nourishing stew."

"I have given you a son, Lu-shee-ahn. I have given you your Edmond. I am not a good squaw, it took too long to bring forth your son, my beloved husband. I do not know how it is, for I was always young and strong and my body obeyed me. Can it be that the Great Spirit could not decide whether to give my little son breath? Have I sinned against the law in some way by loving you so, my Lu-shee-ahn?"

Gently lifting her in his arms, kissing her sweat-dampened, pain-creased forehead, he laid her down gently on the doeskin coverlet and blankets, saying "Oh no, Dimarte, it is I who have broken some law and offended, to cause you such pain! I would to God I might have endured it myself and have you spared it!"

She had closed her eyes and lay very still. Now she opened them and put out a trembling hand to stroke his sun-bronzed, taut face. "I think the pain was punishment for my jealousy of that woman you once loved in your far country, oh my husband," she sighed.

Ellen had crept into the cabin now, and she stood beside Lucien, anxiously watching the exhausted young woman. "Look after her, Ellen. Each time she cried out in the fields, it was like a knife being driven through my heart," Lucien said softly. When Ellen glanced down at his opened hands, she saw that his nails had drawn blood.

He turned to the crude cradle and stared down at the whimpering infant. It was sturdy and well made. It would be the more loved because of its mother's Spartan agony.

213

Besides, it was the child born out of their undying love for each other.

He knelt down beside the cradle and reverently touched the baby's forehead. "Edmond, my son, my heir, born from the mother who welcomed me to this new land, where, if God so grant, she and I will live to watch you grow to manhood and to the fulfillment of those dreams which I have always had but may not myself accomplish."

CHAPTER SEVENTEEN

Dimarte seemed to have recovered from her arduous labor and was able to suckle little Edmond almost from the first. He had her dark eyes and black hair and was in every respect a perfectly formed, healthy child. Lucien, his anxiety over his young wife's health greatly relieved as he saw her take full charge of the infant, was startled to see her continue to dip it every morning into the river. But Dimarte explained, "Soon I will let him sleep on the floor of the cabin, Lu-shee-ahn. You see, the Creeks believe that the body of a child must be made no more sensitive to the cold than its hands and feet. It will make our little Edmond strong and vigorous like his dear father. I promise you will be proud of him, as I am, my dearest one."

And so, some two weeks after little Edmond's birth, Lucien saw that Dimarte had indeed carried out her plan of inuring the child to the hardships of this lush but still savage frontier. Carefully laying it on the puncheon floor, a slight blanket under its body so that again its head might be lower, she insisted that this discipline would strengthen the child's bones and give him stamina, which would be of great use as he developed into boyhood and then sturdy manhood.

In the middle of October, Lucien made a trip to Mobile on a flatboat, taking more pelts for trade. By this time, the Spanish had appointed Captain Manuel de Lanzos as commandant of the town with the thriving trading post which faced the great delta of the bay of Mobile. Lucien had dinner with Lanzos and found him an affable, sophisticated and well-traveled man who had come from Valencia to Peru before his appointment at Mobile. He expressed delight at his appointment and indicated that he would do all in his power to stimulate trade among the Creeks. The problem was, he pointed out to Lucien, that the Indians seemed to prefer English-made goods to Spanish, and his government understandably preferred to keep its monopoly. He went so far as to intimate to Lucien that since there were numerous American settlers not happy with the new republic, it was feasible that Spain might seek to have this southeastern part of the continent become either a part of her Gulf provinces or else an independent country under a Spanish protectorate. Governor Miro himself, Lanzos informed the young Frenchman, had himself engineered just such a plan. Indeed, Miro had even considered the Spanish annexation of the territory of Kentucky.

This time Lucien took back with him several cows, some gauze and colored linen, plates, sugar and bottles of Spanish wine. Under the arrangement of Swanson and McGillivray, Lucien received a sizable commission on the exchange of Indian goods for theirs, so that the account kept for him in his name constantly grew in monetary worth. He had been impressed by Lanzos, who had been extremely candid with him as one man of the Old World to another; he perceived very clearly that so long as the Creek trade flourished, the new commandant would close his eyes to the fact that James Mather of New Orleans, who was in partnership with William Panton, had been given authorization by the Spaniards to sail two vessels under the Spanish flag and supply all that was needed for the Indian trade at Pensacola, yet loaded them at London. It was obvious from this fact also that Alexander McGillivray was the strong silent partner of these men, and that so long as the former retained his power as spokesman for his mother's people, the Spanish government would do everything possible to woo his favor and continue its stronghold at Mobile. And that might well lead to war, a war that could end the serenity of Lucien's just-begun new life and engulf all of the Alabama territory.

How ironic it was that he who had left France so as not to defend a parasitical monarchy against the imperious needs of the common people should settle with the first pioneers of this New World, only to learn that they in their turn were influenced by yet another monarchy whose rivalry with France, since the two countries were geographic neighbors, was in some ways more intense and embittered than the hostilities between his homeland and England. And if France was truly in its death throes, how would the other nations of Europe act toward this neighbor who had been the sponsor of the arts and of sophisticated culture and gracious living? Would they, like ravening wolves who turn on one of their wounded mates, seek to partition or devour France? And as yet he had had no word from Normandy: Lanzos had promised him to make inquiries among his friends in New Orleans and dispatch to him at Econchate by the very next Creek courier to that area any letter or other news of the events in France which might concern him.

This time the journey back to Econchate took eleven days. The cows were frightened twice by snakes, and he killed a copperhead, smashing the butt of his musket against its evil head as, partly concealed by a piece of driftwood which had rolled onto the edge of the river bank, it struck at one of the cows' hind legs just before twilight on the second day of the journey back. It had taken fully an hour to quiet not only the cows but also the pack ponies, and by then it was time to make camp for the night. On the morning of the fourth day, a young black bear had lumbered out of a ravine ahead of them on the trail, and again he had spent a good hour restoring calm and going after one of the cows who, terrorized by the sight of the bear, had broken loose from her halter and run blindly back in the direction of Mobile.

When Lucien brought his ponies and cows into the village, Tunkamara eagerly received him and ordered his two wives, Mahaito, a still handsome squaw of forty, and Etronala, a comely girl only a year older than Dimarte, to prepare a fine feast for his beloved son-in-law. Examining

217

the supplies Lucien had brought from Mobile, he declared himself greatly pleased and added, "My hunters have had good sport all this moon, and there will be many more pelts to take back to Mobile after you have seen your squaw and child, Lu-shee-ahn. It is good that the new commandant at Maubila turns his head the other way when the ships that fly his flag bring the fine things from England. It was a good day for Econchate when you came into our camp, oh warrior of the Bear!"

Late though it was after the lavish feast which the *Mico*'s two wives had diligently prepared and served, Lucien wanted nothing better than to row a pirogue back to the little cabin and to be reunited with Dimarte and Edmond, but it would have been unpardonable for him to show the least annoyance at having to consume at least part of every dish which the two smiling Creek squaws served him and still more so to have shown any impatience in meeting with some of the elders whom Tunkamara summoned once the meal was over.

It was nearly midnight when their meeting at last ended and Lucien was invited to sleep in the dwelling of the *Mico* himself. By then, exhausted from the long journey and the hours of answering the questions of the elders about his experiences along the trail, the attitude of the Spanish garrison at Mobile, the Spanish government's generosity to the Creeks (Lucien was able to tell them that, according to the commandant, Spain had allocated an annual expenditure of $10,000 for presents and other subsidies) and what Lucien estimated the Spanish profit to be (it was actually twenty-five percent), he had no other choice but to accept that invitation and to sleep till nearly noon of the next day.

The heavy thunderstorm which had drenched the village of Econchate and the surrounding terrain for some twenty-five miles had left pools of stagnant water in many of the irregular formations on the ground, in the ravines and in the shallow trenches between the stumps of trees which had been felled by axes. Fifty feet from Lucien's cabin and in the direction of the river, an old pine tree, dessicated by age and riddled by termites, had swayed

218

and cracked at the first angry winds of the coming storm, then toppled from its rotted stump and lay on the ground as stronger winds attacked it. The Ashanti slave had taken his axe to it after the storm and made firewood from what was salvageable. In throwing it away, he had left a shallow, trench-like outline of its length, and this, after a brief shower during the night when Lucien sat with the elders, had filled with rainwater. By dawn, a four-foot-long cottonmouth, which had recently shed its skin near the river bank, where it had hidden behind the shell of an abandoned old pirogue, wriggled slowly toward a new habitat and found the watery trench, which pleased it. It was hungry, and it had had neither frogs nor fish for days. Perhaps beyond its new hiding place there would be food.

Ben and Ellen had gone out into the cornfield, and Dimarte, assuring herself that little Edmond was lying happy and gurgling, on his back on a piece of soft doe-skin on the puncheon floor, left the cabin to pick some of the snap beans in the little patch behind the cabin and toward the side of the towering red bluff. She thought anxiously of Lucien. It was surely time for his return from Mobile and the village, where he would have gone to bring back the goods which her people needed. She longed for his arms, for the sweet way his lips touched her flesh. It was surely time for them to share their bed again. She was well now, though little Edmond had hurt her dreadfully in his warrior-like struggle to come into the world and draw first breath. Yes, she was nearly strong and well again, though it still hurt her belly if she moved too quickly or ran as she had in the old days when she was still a maiden and had never known what joy a warrior of the white-eyes could accord her. Lu-shee-ahn would want more sons. She would tell him so if he came to her today, and this night they would lie together and he would be her mate once more and she would tremble and groan and smile to the strange overpowering needs that he so well assuaged. How shameless she had become—like many of the young girls who, it was said, would creep into the hut of a guest and pleasure with him, wanting to see if he was as manly as any of the warriors of their

219

clans. How glad she was she had waited for this kind and gentle and yet so valiant and brave warrior from across the ocean!

The cottonmouth's long forked tongue flickered out, touching particles of grass, taste-smelling for food. As yet there was none, and it contracted the complicated range of muscles down either side of its backbone to move forward in its search. It attained the rough sill of the open door of the cabin, wary of enemies, and yet vaguely the emanations of human food, such as bits of cornmeal, pudding, dried meat, which had adhered to the puncheon floor, overcame its instinctive caution and it slithered on. Before it was a strange object, making sounds which it could not distinguish: the bone conducting sound from the eardrum to the inner ear of a reptile leaves it deaf to air-borne sounds, though any vibration such as a footfall can be transmitted to the inner ear by the bones of the skull. Once again its long, repulsive tongue flickered out, catching a bit of cornmeal, rejecting it as alien.

Dimarte had picked a basketful of snap beans and was hurrying back to the cabin. As she reached the door, she uttered a cry of horror and flung the basket at the yellowish reptile whose ugly head was only inches away from Edmond's waving right hand. In surprise and anger, the cottonmouth sank its fangs into the baby's thumb, as Dimarte, rushing forward, kicked with her moccasined foot at the writhing reptile. Recoiling, as she frenziedly sought some weapon, it darted its ugly head forward and sank its fangs into her slim ankle. If she had worn the ornamented boots with which she came to the council of the elders, the venom might not have reached her.

Lucien having dragged his pirogue over the river bank, stopped a moment as he saw the molted skin of the old cottonmouth. Then, not knowing exactly why but with a terrible sense of foreboding, he ran toward the cabin, his musket gripped in his right hand, his left hand at the handle of the knife which Jabez Corrigan had given him.

He came into the cabin just as Dimarte, with a scream of agony, stumbled back against the wall, glancing down at her ankle, on whose smooth tanned flesh could be seen the fatal punctures of the cottonmouth's fangs and the brackish blood drawn by them. Wielding the musket like a club, Lucien smashed the wooden stock down on the head of the squirming cottonmouth, again and again until it lay lifeless. Then swiftly kneeling down, he grasped Dimarte's ankle in his left hand, tugged out the knife with his right and slashed above and below the marks of the fangs. He put his mouth to the punctures on that soft fragrant skin and sucked and spat and sucked and spat again.

"The child—the child—" she gasped, her voice faint and husky, her head tilted back against the wall, jaws shuddering, nostrils dilating.

He turned distractedly to look at the baby and uttered an agonized cry. It lay still, its head turned to one side, its hand already black from the swiftly working venom. Sobbing, he unfastened the scabbard-belt and bound it tightly round Dimarte's ankle, tugging it as a constricting tourniquet with all his strength.

"Lu-shee-ahn—I feel the poison—the child took so much strength—I cannot fight it—oh, my husband—my beloved man—forgive me—it was my fault—I should be punished, not the—not the—ch—"

Her body sagged, and before Lucien's incredulous, agonized gaze, he saw Dimarte sway and then sink down from the wall against which she leaned. He caught her round the waist, easing her gently to the floor. Her eyes were glassy and staring, her lips moved falteringly and then no more.

His hoarse, racking sobs had brought Ben and Ellen from the cornfields. They stood in the doorway in horror, each holding the other, distraught at the tragedy which had befallen their young master, his wife and the child. Lucien did not see them. Blinded with tears, he held the inert body of his young Creek bride against his chest, kissing her throat, her face, her silent lips. And when at last he reverently eased her down onto the floor, his eyes were still unseeing, his face a tortured mask of irreparable loss.

He knelt there, an arm under Dimarte's shoulders, the tears streaming down his cheeks, for so long a time that Ellen stirred in Ben's arms and took a step toward the bereaved young Frenchman. But Ben shook his head and pulled Ellen back, holding her close, his own eyes wet with tears.

At last Lucien rose and took up the dead baby, lifting it gently as if afraid to hurt it. Then, tucking it protectively with his left arm against his chest, he moved outside the cabin and picked up a spade, and then strode slowly, head bowed, toward the high bluff.

"Can't we help him some, Ben? I feel so useless," Ellen chokingly murmured to her tall husband. But Ben shook his head: "He don't even know we're here, honey-gal. Best we stay out of his way and let him do what he means to do. 'Pears like to me, he's going to bury them both up there on the bluff. That way, the birds and the animals won't bother them, and they can sleep restful-like till Gawd calls us all to the Judgment."

Ascending the high bluff laboriously, still weeping, Lucien found a little clearing before two massive hickory trees, and there, setting the dead baby down on a bed of plantain grass, he dug a deep grave. Gently placing the infant into it, he looked up at the bright, full-mooned sky and said a wordless prayer before he filled the grave with earth, patting it solidly, smoothing the earth evenly and digging away all the grass near it so that the clearing would remain for remembrance.

Then, leaving the spade on the ground beside the grave, he went back to the cabin, without a word or nod to the grieving slaves, lifted Dimarte's body in his arms and carried her back up the bluff. This time, he dug a deeper and much wider grave, remembering the custom of the Creeks to bury their dead in a sitting position. Thus, when the Great Spirit summoned all the dead in conclave, they would be seated in council and ready to explain and defend their actions in their past lives upon this earth.

He could hardly bear to relinquish her slim body, the face so drawn and pale, the eyes closed, the sweet mouth twisted in a final grimace of agony and sorrow . . . sorrow for him, he knew, and for their little child. But at last he finished his grim task and slipped the ring off her finger and pocketed it, putting his lips to that finger as a last tribute to their love. How short it had been, the time

222

granted them, and yet how eternally long it seemed to him he had been at one with this gentle, wise girl who would have been a princess in any court if destiny had so willed. He had brought with him the little Spanish comb, and after he had climbed out of the grave and finally filled it with earth—steeling himself against another fit of desolate weeping—he pressed the teeth of the comb into the smooth earth. Later, he would use his hunting knife to carve upon a headboard the names of those two he had lost.

He moved to the edge of the bluff and, with an agonized cry, flung the spade far out into the river. From afar, there was the hooting of an owl, and it was almost as if some sympathetic spirit in the air acknowledged his anguish and sought to console him for it.

He stood for a long time looking down at those two graves, communing with his dead wife, letting his thoughts roam freely, somehow sensing that she would hear and understand them. They had been man and wife for less than a year; yet in that all too brief time, he had come to understand at last what the Greek philosopher Plato had meant when he had said that man and woman were not at all two separate entities but rather two parts of the same polarity whose fusion alone made the very oneness of life.

Dimarte had spoken of punishment—she, so guilele and so innocent of all wrongdoing, would surely be "beloved woman" in the council of her Great Spirit she had been in the village of Econchate. No, this wa punishment, this loss of all that had marked a wond new life in a new land, his punishment, perhaps, fo ing defied fate by denying his own birthright.

Had he not abandoned his family to find this freedom, that fine-sounding word which had stir as a youth, when he had first studied the histor tions ruled by despots, kingdoms sickened by bi implacable tradition? Then perhaps it was o that this agonizing loss be inflicted on him to scales. Now he had only the land and the wor his kinship with a people whose own freedom be threatened by the machinations of those

power over the land without any of his idealistic purpose, but rather out of greed and selfishness and hatred.

He retraced his steps to the cabin. Ben and Ellen had left bowls of food and water, but he did not heed these. He flung himself down on the bed that he had shared with Dimarte and surrendered himself to the aching torment in his heart.

CHAPTER EIGHTEEN

As he paddled the pirogue toward Econchate, Lucien asked himself how he could best direct his life after this cruel double tragedy. The news that he would bring to Tunkamara now would perhaps be even more crushing to the aging *Mico*: what thoughts would enter Tunkamara's mind when he learned that his only daughter, she who had been loved by all the village for her kindness and wisdom, had died before this first year of marriage to a white-eyes had passed. And, knowing the superstitions of the Creeks, Lucien thought also of the grim irony that Dimarte had died from the bite of a snake, while Shehanoy, wed to the son of the war chief of the Snake clan—the son he himself had slain—and sentenced to die by the snake, had by his own hand been given life. How would the *Windigo* interpret such an omen? Would he, Lucien, be adjudged one who came from a foreign land under an evil star to bring this sorrow to the village of Econchate? For of a certainty he had brought death with him. Death to Ecanataba, a condemnation to death for Ecanataba's beautiful young wife and finally, even though through no fault of his, this snuffing out of Dimarte's vivid young life at the very beginning of her turning from honored maiden to faithful, inspiring wife and mother. And as if that were not enough, the child of love which Dimarte had given him had followed his mother to so early a grave.

To come again to the village of Econchate, to see the red bluffs and the hill beyond and the far stretches of land, was to see the likeness of the terrain he had just left behind him, to remember how he had first seen Dimarte here and how, last night, he had laid her to her eternal rest. The Creeks believed that the spirits of the dead hovered about those places where they loved and were loved. And if that were true, then Dimarte would be with him again in Econchate just as she would remain forever near the cabin where the two of them had planned to share their enduring life as man and wife, lover and sweetheart, and, for so tragically short a time, father and mother.

After he had banked the pirogue, he circled far to the left so that he might enter the village at its other end, for he felt himself one of the lowliest ones, beneath even the *atac emittla* and the oldest squaws and the youngest, unfledged children. At the last wigwam, he came upon the blackened ashes of a little cooking fire and stooped to cup them in his hands and to smear them on his cheeks and forehead, since he was to be the harbinger of such dreadful tidings not only to the *Mico* but to all the inhabitants of this village where Dimarte had been loved and cherished. Then, sorrowfully, he walked down the open center between the opposing rows of dwellings, ignoring the few dogs which, thinking him a stranger, barked at his heels and then, seeing how little he took note of them, went back whence they had come. He came at last to the imposing house of Tunkamara and stood before the door, for one did not enter unbidden into the house of the chief of the village.

It was the *Mico*'s older wife who first saw him. Observing his blackened face, she uttered a low cry, "Aii—yeeaaa!" and turned back into the house to summon her lord. The *Mico* came toward Lucien and, understanding his wife's lamentation, uttered a low groan as he looked questioningly into the grief-swollen eyes of his son-in-law.

In the language of the Creeks, Lucien bowed his head and said, "I have lost a wife and child, oh father, but you have lost a daughter and a grandson."

"May Ibofanaga watch over their spirits! Oh my son, how did it happen?"

"A snake had come into the cabin. Dimarte tried to

226

protect the child, but both were bitten. I have buried them on the high bluff. I come to ask your forgiveness. I, a stranger, a white-eyes, to whom you gave shelter and hospitality, have robbed you of your joy." He sank down on his knees and added in a toneless voice, "It is within your right, *Mico* of Econchate, to send me to join her."

He heard Tunkamara's hoarse groan, and then he felt the *Mico*'s hands touch his head in a gesture of utmost compassion. "It was not your doing, it was so ordained. Tonight Tsipoulata will cast the signs to see what is foretold for you, my son. The village will mourn the beloved woman, I most of all, and so you and I are bound in sorrow as so little time ago we were bound in love and kinship. Rise, my son, my wives will bring you food and drink, you must nourish yourself, she would have wished it."

He did not think that he had any tears left after last night. But now, stricken by the deep compassion which the grave old *Mico* had displayed, a compassion that was so much like Dimarte's own, he felt them fall again to streak the blackening ashes of his self-imposed ritual of mourning, and he wept as a man weeps, bitterly and with tormented soul-searching.

Once again he felt Tunkamara's hands touch his head and heard the *Mico* say gently, "Go now, my son, to the house where you lived for the first time among us, where my daughter tended your hurts and learned the goodness of your heart. My wives will bring the food there to you, you will think upon the happiness you had and it will be comfort to you, and tonight we shall pray that her spirit ever remains with us here in Econchate to guide us all in the ways of friendship and of brotherhood."

That night, throughout the village, there resounded the chants of mourning for the beloved departed, and there was a ceremonial dance which besought Hisagita-imisi to guide the spirit of Dimarte into a peaceful land where she would mingle with all those before her who had been held in great esteem and love by their people. And at midnight, the old *Windigo*, Tunkamara and Lucien seated themselves before a small fire in the clearing in front of the dwelling of the *Mico* to foretell the signs. From a doe-skin pouch, Tsipoulata shook out the bones of an owl, a squirrel, a dog and a deer upon the ground, mixed them this way and that with his gnarled, stiff fingers and then, cupping them in his palms, thrice lifted them high and let them fall as they would upon the earth.

"These are bones of the friendly beasts and the birds of watch which have dwelt about us and given us food and the omens of what is to come," the *Windigo* explained to Lucien. "I cast them now in your name, and they say that the last shall be the first, and of him the first shall be the last upon the land."

"I cannot tell your meaning, Tsipoulata."

"It matters not. You will know it when the time is ful-filled, blood brother of the Bear. There is love and death, hate and vengeance, and there is also long life and a dream fulfilled at its ending. This I see now as clearly as you do the bones which lie upon our soil of Econchate."

Lucien did not speak. The old man's rheumy eyes stared beyond the fire far into the darkness and his lips moved as if in some kind of mystic incantation. Then once again he cupped up all the bones in his trembling old hands, lifted them thrice and once again let them fall as they would.

"There will be war not far distant from this soil, and it will be soaked with the blood of many warriors of the Creek Nation: And when the earth has absorbed it and forgotten, the white-eyes will build a town upon Econ-chate after the Creeks have left it to find where they must hunt and grow the crops. They will not again find such a rich land, and long after I am gone, the land they find will be found for them by the white-eyes and it will not be pleasing or fruitful to them. This, too, I see clearly, oh *Mico* and blood brother of the Bear."

Lucien at last broke the long silence which had fol-lowed the medicine man's solemn words. "Am I to dwell with all my brothers, is it so written?"

"Yes, till it is so written that you shall hunt and plant your own crops for your own bounty and for those who will be dependent upon you for it. But I see that always there will be peace between you and the warriors of the Creeks."

Lucien turned to Tunkamara. "I am ready to serve my *Mico* as I have done before, and now, even more with all my strength and purpose, if in that way I am to fulfill these signs and to show that I shall not forget her whom you gave to me as wife, oh my father."

The English settlers of Georgia, still steadfastly loyal to their British sovereign against whom the thirteen colonies had rebelled, were restless under the domination of the Spanish government and its Indian allies. A number of their more enterprising colonists petitioned Governor Edward Telfair to approve an act of the General Assembly at Savannah which authorized the conditional sale of the larger part of the territory from the Savannah to the Mississippi rivers lying between thirty-one and thirty-five degrees, declaring to him that such a disposition had been made by the charter of King Charles II. The enactment of such legislation, they urged, would people the territory and enrich the Georgia treasury immeasurably. Almost immediately, three companies were formed, and one of these, the "South Carolina Yazoo Company," purchased five million acres of the territory of the middle counties of what was to become the state of Mississippi for a paltry $60,000, while the northern counties were sold to the "Virginia Yazoo Company" for $93,000. Finally, the newly formed "Tennessee Yazoo Company" agreed to pay $46,000 for three and a half million acres of the northern counties of Alabama.

President George Washington, greatly alarmed at this undiplomatic and possibly illegal transaction, which he foresaw would involve the United States, Georgia, Spain and the Indians, issued a proclamation against the entire enterprise. The Tennessee and South Carolina companies raised troops and attempted to colonize, but were driven out by the Indians and soldiers sent by President Washington himself. The Virginia Company made no attempt to settle the lands it had purchased, and all three failed to meet the payments due Georgia for those lands. So this first venture was a failure, but it cost the lives of many innocent men, women and children who, lured by the glib promises of land speculators, sought to find new sites for peaceful homes—and found instead only armed Indians who treated them as hated enemies.

Lucien learned of this dangerous land speculation from Le Clerc Milfort, a handsome, well-educated countryman who had left France in 1775 and met Alexander McGillivray at the town of Coweta on the Chattahoochie River, eventually married the latter's sister, and was presently occupied with writing a history of the Creeks.

"I believe that the Muscogees came from Mexico and were in constant warfare with the Alibamons who had occupied this land of Alabama until the French reconciled them. Now there is a good alliance among the peoples of the Creek Nation, but if these crackers and gougers from Georgia continue to press their claims for land which does not belong to them, you will see me leading the Creeks against the invaders—yes, even if they are white like myself and even if they are my own countrymen like you.

"But, *M'sieu* Milfort," Lucien countered, "the sensible actions of President Washington's government show that this new republic does not seek war against the Creeks."

"That may well be true, but, since I am a chief among the Creeks and they look to me for counsel, I say only that this President Washington has not yet been able to control the arrogant Georgians. And there are others who have rallied to the side of the Georgians, freebooters and traitors. I think now of a certain man who I may one day be forced to put to death for what he plans to do to our leader Alexander McGillivray. But come now, *mon ami,* my condolences on your terrible loss. Still, since you and I are both French, we understand that a man may try to forget by taking, shall we say, pleasure as he finds it. There are lovely Creek maidens who would gladly drive your gloomy cares away, if only for a night."

"I could not bear to entertain such a thought, *M'sieu* Milfort."

The suave, handsome Frenchman, only a few years older than Lucien, nodded sympathetically. "Fidelity is a praiseworthy trait in a man, *Ma foi,* there are nonetheless times when a man is forced into temptation. Some few years ago, when it was seen that I was desirous of becoming a brother to the Creeks, four pretty wenches cornered me in a hut and insisted that I demonstrate my manhood to all of them, to show them that a Frenchman was the equal of a Creek brave. I came out of the combat with honor, and my adventure was soon generally known." He chuckled reminiscently, and Lucien colored, but did not answer. He knew only that he would never sully Dimarte's memory in so casual a way.

During November and the early part of December, Lucien made two more trading trips to Mobile and visited de Lanzos to inquire whether there was any news from France. No letter had yet come from *Père* Morlain, and again the gracious commandant promised that he would himself dispatch a courier to Econchate upon the arrival of any such message, as he himself had friends in New Orleans and was hopeful of settling there when his tenure in Mobile came to an end. There was, however, a letter from Eulalie Villefranche awaiting him on his arrival in Mobile the first week of December, acknowledging his thoughtful gift and flirtatiously informing him that although she was now engaged to a certain Daniel Mercier, a Creole private banker and expert gambler, she hoped that when he next came to New Orleans, he would call upon her, married or not.

After Lucien's return to the village to deliver the specific goods the *Mico* had requested, he went back to the cabin, whose emptiness only served to reinforce the brooding memories of his dual loss. How often he had reflected, during those journeys to and from Mobile, what only a few minutes' difference could have made in saving both Dimarte and Edmond. Though by no means a fatalist in emotional outlook, he had indeed begun to wonder whether his resolve to leave France had not set off a series of inexplicable misfortunes whose cumulative purpose he could not yet discern. The little poacher who had paid for a rabbit with his life after having successfully evaded his father's gamekeeper for a decade; the theft of his purse aboard the *Guerrière* and young Edmond's needless death in that heroic but misguided attempt to recover it; his parting with Arabe, whom he had loved almost as he might an inseparable companion; the death of the Creek brave which had brought in its wake the near-death and then banishment of the latter's courageous, beautiful wife; and then the unforeseen intrusion of the snake into a cabin which he and Ben had constructed with special care to prevent just such a circumstance, only to have Dimarte leave the cabin door open at the wrong moment—were these predestined happenings, or would they, somehow, have been prevented if he had sought a foothold in New Orleans, where there were other country-men to make him welcome, rather than setting forth into wilderness because of his insistence on becoming a pioneer settler in the cause of peace?

But now the die was surely cast; to admit failure, turn his back on all that had taken place since his arrival in New Orleans, would be to turn his back on the deaths of Edmond Vignon and of his wife and the infant whom he had named after that brave youth. No, it was unthinkable, and moreover, he owed a debt of honor to the *Mico* of Econchate.

And yet, when he returned to his cabin just a week before Christmas, the tall Ashanti slave had news that was, for all Ben's hesitant and apologetic telling of it, cause for reflection once again upon his own misfortunes; Ellen was with child and would have her baby by the next summer. He gripped Ben's hand and said, "Your child will be born free, I myself will go to the *Mico* and ask that as a gift in the spirit of the blessed holiday we whites celebrate, he permit me to give you and Ellen your freedom. You know that I myself have told you I have never considered you and her my slaves, but it remains for the *Mico* to help me fulfill my pledge to you both. And in the depot there are trinkets for the squaws, Ben. Take your pick of them as my present to Ellen this our second *Noël* together."

Thus, with his twenty-eighth birthday, Lucien, who had lost so much in coming to his new world in search of freedom, gave that precious gift to Ben and Ellen, for Tunkamara gravely nodded once his white son-in-law had proposed the manumission, and said, "Let it be as you have said, my son. They have served, they are good, they will serve you now more faithfully once they are free."

"As I will serve you, oh my father, because of the ties which bind us as closely as the very blood in our veins," Lucien replied.

And on that same day, the warrior Nanakota, the "beloved man," who had acted as best man in that betrothal and then the marriage ceremony, came to him in that same little house which had sheltered him on his arrival at Econchate. He gave Lucien a long bow of supple hickory wood, stained with indigo, and a doeskin quiver of sharp-pointed arrows, trophies which he himself had won for his marksmanship at the hunt and in the games of skill at the last great Corn Dance, saying, "That you may remember me, your friend, I give you this, and I pray the Great Spirit that it will serve you well when you seek game or if you must draw it against an unjust enemy. I sorrow with you, Lu-shee-ahn, but know that I was proud to stand before the *Mico* for you and Dimarte." Then, with a flash of his droll humor, which Lucien gratefully understood was meant to turn his mind from such now terribly poignant memories, Nanakota added as he patted Lucien's shoulder, "Your own gift which keeps my ugly face free from beard has indeed given me such renown in this village that if the elders were to vote for a new *Mico,* I should certainly be high on the lists of worthy candidates!"

Greatly moved, Lucien again gripped the "beloved man's" hand and murmured, "May the Great Spirit give Tunkamara yet many years, but if then it is His will that there be a new *Mico* at Econchate, I could pray for no worthier brave to take his place in the council."

At the request of Tunkamara, Lucien remained as a guest in the village through the first week of the new year of 1791 and attended two of the council meetings at which the elders discussed the plans for the spring planting, the estimated articles of trade which the village would need in the months ahead and the feasibility of enlarging the common cornfield for more extensive cultivation. Each family in the village worked the large cornfield beyond the village and first deposited a part of the crop into a common crib before filling their own. They cultivated the early corn, which they called "tanchuse," a truck patch corn which ripened in six weeks; a yellow flint corn, "tan-

233

chi hlimishko," which was used for hominy; a white corn, "tanchi tohbih," used for making bread; and popcorn, "tanchi bohanli," for the entertainment of visitors to the village. Lucien, who had already contributed his share to the common crib from his own field beyond his little cabin, offered to double the quota, a gesture which was much applauded by the elders. Also, he offered to allocate part of the produce from his truck patch to feed visitors to the village or those Creeks and traders who might stop over at his own depot.

He could not but marvel at the unity and loyalty of these Indian villagers toward the government of their council and their appointed chief. It was true that they had no written language and no method of keeping accounts, and even less concept of numbers, yet their concern for the welfare of the lowliest member of their community and their communal method of distributing provisions so that no one would starve was surely more humane than the shocking extravagances of the French court, which concerned itself not at all with the suffering of the poor. They did not number their years as the white man did, but divided each year into the four seasons, subdividing these and counting the year by lunar months. They counted the day by the three measurable differences of the sun, and subdivided it by these three standards, such as halfway between the sun's coming out of the water. To them, the year began at the first appearance of the first new moon of the vernal equinox, and each time a new moon was seen in the sky, they uttered joyful sounds and raised their arms toward it.

At such meetings, they cast aside all frivolity and assumed a laconic dignity, letting each elder speak and according him respectful silence till he had finished. Each elder spoke for the problems of his own clan, and the *Mico* acted as a kind of judicial magistrate in settling disputes and inflicting punishments.

Of these last, Lucien had occasion to observe the stern justice of the Creeks and, this time, found himself unable to prevent its execution. A handsome squaw in her mid-twenties was accused of adultery with an unmarried warrior, and her husband had petitioned the elder of their

234

clan to have judgment passed upon her. She was brought before the council and shamefacedly admitted her sin, and sentence was at once carried out. The young women and old squaws and even the children gathered switches and formed two opposing lines down the central clearing between the houses and the wigwams. Her husband brought her out, naked, her wrists thonged behind her back. He took his hunting knife and slashed off her braid, then contemptuously shoved her forward to run the gauntlet. When she reached the end, stumbling, finally crawling, groaning in her pain, her coppery skin streaked from neck to heels, he awaited her and, with his hunting knife, cropped her ears and slit her nose. Finally, it was pronounced that she should henceforth be a slave, put to the most menial and demeaning tasks, and that no man might lie with her, which would be to degrade his own manhood.

Twelve days into the new year, as Lucien prepared to return to his land and depot, David Francis rode into the village of Econchate with three pack ponies loaded with kegs of *taffai,* trinkets for the wives of the elders and gifts for the *Mico* and the war chief. Espying Lucien at the entrance of Tunkamara's dwelling, he genially called to him, "*Holà, M'sieu* Lucien, I've two letters for you. And as well, the congratulations of my master for the services you have rendered to our people."

"How kind of you to bring them!" Lucien eagerly exclaimed. "And Colonel McGillivray, how does he fare with the treaty?"

The half-breed's face was impassive as, handing the letters to Lucien, he replied, "There are those who accuse him of deception. There are those who would weaken his powers with the chiefs of the Creek Nation, but he will persevere and overcome such treacherous adversaries, have no fear of that." Then, in a gentler, sympathetic tone, he added, "Tunkamara had already sent word to us of the great sorrow that came upon you, *M'sieu* Lucien. I would add my own prayers to yours in mourning the daughter of the *Mico.*"

"You are kind again, David Francis. Will you stay long at Econchate?"

"Not so, I am to see Weatherford first, then as I return to Maubila, visit with other chiefs. It may be that I will meet you there when next you come for supplies. And now I must arrange to talk with the council on grave matters."

Lucien again warmly thanked the half-breed and shook hands with him, then went back to the little house to read his letters. One, he saw, bore the seal of Jules Ronsart from New Orleans, and he opened it and read it first. It was a genial note from the Creole, expressing the latter's delight with Arabe and thanking Lucien for the good fortune which the superb palomino had brought him: Arabe had raced four times against the fastest horses of his New Orleans rivals, had won each time and earned Ronsart nearly ten thousand dollars. He hoped that Lucien would visit him soon so that he might accord hospitality that would show his gratitude for Arabe's triumphs, since they had immeasurably added to his own prowess and reputation in New Orleans.

But the other letter bore an unfamiliar seal and had been carried from the port of Marseilles. Lucien's hands trembled as he broke the seal, opened the letter and found at last the first direct news he had had from his homeland since embarking on the *Guerrière*:

Dated the 8th day of August, in the Year of Our Lord 1790—

My Son:

Your letter to me advising of your marriage to the daughter of the Indian chief reached me only last week. As you see from the seal, I am at Marseilles, where for several months I have taken refuge with an elderly cousin who was kind enough to give me shelter. Soon I will board ship for the African coast where there are French traders and some settlers and where there is need for missionary work to bring the word of *le bon Dieu* to the natives, many of whom are distressingly being taken into bondage and shipped to the very land where you determined to begin your new life.

Earlier this year, because of the terrible revolution which has broken over all France, we of the clergy were required to take oaths to the civil authority. I could not fulfill my vows to Him who died upon the cross, and so, seeing that I could not save my flock, I resolved to go where I might be of use to comfort the poor, the oppressed in that primitive land. Many of the priests, my son, were forced to flee from their provinces because they too would not take those desecrating oaths.

I married your brother Jean to *Mademoiselle* de Courent on the last day of June of last year. Some two months later, having attained a commission at Le Havre from the factor of colonization in the West Indies, he and his wife sailed for Port-au-Prince, where he was to become *attaché* for that company's trading offices there and aid the French plantation owners in the marketing of their crops.

As you may well imagine, because of the revolution, it has been very difficult to get or send messages. You spoke of a first letter announcing your arrival at New Orleans, but that never came to me. At the time when it might have come, alas, a mob of armed peasants from the nearby town of Bolbec invaded my humble parish, and in the name of this accursed revolution, plundered and sacked and committed such deeds of violence as would make our dear Lord weep at the brutality of man. Poor Madelon was seized, repeatedly abused and mercifully died some hours after the brutes had quitted the parish—I was able to give her the last rites. Before this, I am sorry to tell you, there was much anger among the peasants over what your brother had done to her, and she bore a child which was stillborn. Perhaps that is why your brother accepted this commercial venture so readily.

And now, my dear son, I have dreadful news to give you of your father and mother. When those ruffians broke into the rectory, one of their leaders shouted that the rabble should go to the chateau and teach the damned aristocrats a lesson. I myself, trying to propitiate them, to explain that the *seigneur* de Bouchard was a just and honorable lord who had always treated the villagers with great kindness and concern, was struck down for my pains and left for dead. Later, after I had recovered, and attempted to restore what I could of the rectory itself and of my faithful flock—of whom many were killed by those godless rabble—I was asked to swear allegiance to the Revolution, and of course that is why I am now here preparing to make amends for my terrible failures in Yves-sur-lac by teaching honor and kindness and the laws of *le bon Dieu* to the unChristianized blacks in Africa.

Forgive an old man's ramblings—I am sixty-five, and my health has not been of the best since the attack upon my rectory. As I said, in spite of all my prayers and my attempts to bring them to sane reasoning, after they had done their horrid work in the village itself, they stormed toward the chateau. Your father came out upon the grounds to address them, but they would not listen. Seeing that he was dressed with his sword at his side, one of them flung a stone which struck him on the forehead, and he fell before them. Your mother, crying out in horror, rushed toward him to succor him, and finding him dead, denounced his murderers. She paid with her life—at least it was merciful, for someone in that bloodthirsty crowd fired a musket and she fell at once mortally wounded and expired nearly at that same moment—so the footman who witnessed the death of his kind master and mistress later told me.

Alas, my son, your forebodings over the storm that would break upon France were all too accurate. It will not comfort you to know—as it did not the

Greek prophetess Cassandra, to whose predictions none paid heed—that what has happened thus far in France far exceeds your worst fears. Rumor has it that the King may try to join those nobles who have already fled abroad, and equal rumor says that if he so attempts, he will be judged guilty of treason to the nation. How many virtuous men and women like your beloved parents have perished in this senseless era only because they were guilty of being aristocrats, God Himself can enumerate. I do not know what poor words of mine can cheer you, except to recall to you the story of Job, whom Satan hated because of his righteousness and love of the true God. But when Job was beset by afflictions and by the death of all those dear to him, he did not curse God and die—he lived and prayed that God would be content with his penances. And you will remember that at last a just and merciful Creator restored unto Job even more than what he had lost in his trials and tribulations.

May the blessing of such a just and all-seeing God be with you and yours in the years to come. I am, yours humbly and sorrowfully, in Christ,

Auguste Morlain, *Serviteur de Dieu*

He read the letter over and over again, as if he could not believe its dreadful message, as if by staring at the priest's words again, somehow they would be altered. Now he was truly desolate, and only his older brother and he were left alive out of all the generations which had come from that first fierce Norseman who had married a young French girl from the province which the fearful French king had given up to halt the plundering blond warriors from the cold northlands who would otherwise have conquered all of France. And more than tears now, there came an agonizing guilt of soul upon Lucien Bouchard, for he had abandoned his proud father and his gentle mother to an ignominious death at the hands of his own hate-maddened countrymen.

239

CHAPTER NINETEEN

It was a dour year, 1791, a year in which the loneliness of this new country had never seemed so vast, so desolate. There were many times when Lucien longed for delightful hours of conversation with a countryman like Jules Ronsart or the frank, honest comradeship of Jabez Corrigan. From where he was placed, it seemed that only the Creeks and the Spanish garrisons and their officers peopled the land, and above even these and ruling from afar the Spanish dignitaries, such as the Captain-General at Havana, who governed West Florida and Louisiana, and the Governor of Louisiana to whom all the commandants of the fortifications in Alabama and Mississippi were subordinate. There were only a few small American trading posts on the east upon the Oconee, while those of Spain commanded the south and the west. There were no whites as far as the distant Cumberland settlements on the north, and so it was not difficult to understand why Lucien felt that he had still no roots upon the land the Creeks had given him.

In the new republic, still struggling to rise to respectable recognition by the European powers, there were signs of vitality, however far away from Econchate. On February 25th, the American Congress passed the National Bank Act, and a week later Vermont became the fourteenth state of this new, daring union of free men. And, gradually, out of the embattled and neighboring lands of Georgia, a few white settlers fled the raiding parties of some of the Creek tribes and sought refuge not far from Lucien's little cabin and his acres of corn, beans, squash and melons.

The fomentation of trouble in Georgia was partly caused by a bold, imaginative and thoroughly amoral young man, the one whom Le Clerc Milfort had told Lucien he might have to execute one day. His name was William Augustus Bowles, a native of Maryland, who had entered the British Army as a foot soldier at the tender age of fourteen. After he had spent a year fighting his own countrymen, who were then winning their freedom from King George III, Bowles sailed with a British regiment to Jamaica in the year 1777 as an ensign. From there he went to Pensacola, where he was stripped of his rank for military insubordination. Already he had shown an ungovernable temperament and a nature that did not brook authority. Flinging his uniform into the sea as a gesture of defiance, he left Pensacola with a renegade band of Creeks and lived upon the Tallapoosa for several years, learning to speak the Creek tongue to perfection. Soon he married the daughter of a tribal chief, and was, much like Lucien Bouchard, readily accepted as one of them.

But there the similarity ended. Bowles, elegant and erect of stature, gifted with eloquent diction, with a handsome face whose expressions could change as readily as those of a great dramatic actor, together with a bold sense of military tactics—though again without discipline—was an ideal prototype of devil's advocate and treacherous Judas to the whites. Indeed, because of his theatrical presence, he actually went to New York in 1782, joined a troupe of comedians and sailed to New Providence in the Bahamas, where he alternately acted upon the stage before audiences of wealthy plantation owners and their ladies and painted portraits with astonishing skill.

He began to enter the orbit of Alexander McGillivray while he was in the Bahamas. The trading firm of Panton and Leslie of Pensacola sent to one of their associates in New Providence a schooner with a chest containing 6,000 piastres. Lord Dunmore, the arrogant British governor there, seized this chest as contraband property. Panton promptly instituted a complaint to the British Maritime Court, and the money was ordered to be returned. Vindictively, Lord Dunmore selected Bowles as an agent to establish a commercial trading house upon the Chattahoochie to check the prosperous commerce of that firm. Bowles sailed to the Florida territory, visited the Lower Creek tribes and began to preach a doctrine of hatred against Panton and particularly against Alexander McGillivray and the Georgians.

The French historian-war chief traveled to the Chattahoochee with McGillivray's order for Bowles to leave the Creek Nation within twenty-four hours on penalty of having his ears cropped. Bowles fled to the Bahamas and thence was sent on to England by Lord Dunmore together with a delegation of Creeks, Seminoles and Cherokees to enlist the aid of the English government in the cause of these Indian nations by repelling American aggression.

Bowles's persuasive eloquence and good looks won him favor before the British royal court, and he was given valuable presents and the promise of helpful alliance. Returning to New Providence, he began a piratical war upon the ships sent out by Panton, for he had taught his contingent of Creek warriors to navigate the Gulf. Capturing several of Panton's ships, which were laden with arms and ammunition, he had them sailed to desolate bayous. There, with his band of Creeks who followed him with the hope of battle and looting and massacres, as well as a crew of men who had been freed from the prisons of London to follow his unsavory enterprise, Bowles distributed the weapons to the Indians, who carried them to all parts of the Creek Nation.

This audacity, treacherous though it was, brought him much popularity among the Creeks, who admired bravery above all else. Pressing his advantage of popularity, the now twenty-nine-year-old American turncoat moved through Georgia, denouncing Alexander McGillivray as a traitor to the Creeks. It was his desire to overthrow the great spokesman and replace him. He sent his emissaries throughout the villages, contending that neither the Americans nor the Spaniards had any right to control the Creeks, that England had not yielded any part of Creek territory to either power, and that McGillivray had tried to sell out his people, first to Spain and then to the new United States.

As Lucien doggedly and sorrowfully pursued the arduous work of planting crops and tending to them, making frequent trips to Mobile to bring back trade goods for the people of the *Mico,* there thus began a Machiavellian duel between the pretender and the ruler, one which threatened to set the Creeks at war within their own nation.

Ellen had her baby, a fine sturdy boy, the second week of July. Before the baby was born, Lucien himself built an addition to her little cabin, and then invited Ben and Ellen to attend the five-day-long green corn dance, which was held in the village of Econchate the last week of that warm month. Among the Creeks, this festivity was the occasion for cleaning out the private houses and wigwams and the council house, for lighting a new fire before the entrance to the village itself and for sacrificing several kernels in gratitude for the Great Spirit's gift of corn. It was the ceremony of religious purification and Lucien, seeing Ellen's blissfully happy face as, crooning to the baby, she held it up to watch the impressive ritual of the blessing of those kernels, was glad that he had urged the *Mico* to free his two slaves. For perhaps now, just as this corn dance symbolized the beginning of a new cycle of life and fertility upon the good earth of the Creeks, so might Ellen's child break the depressing cycle of death which had pursued him ever since his departure from Yves-sur-lac.

The intense heat of this summer and the frequent heavy thunderstorms had made working with the crops a seemingly never-ending hardship, yet Lucien thrived on it. One of his first acts, after the birth of Ellen's baby, whom she had named Thomas after Ben's own father, had been to make a rude wooden cradle with large, wide rockers so that no crawling snake could reach the helpless child. Ellen's grateful thanks for the gift embarrassed him and once again sent a spasm of contrition through his mind: if only little Edmond had rested in such a cradle, might not Dimarte and his child be still alive today? And yet, though he was not a superstitious man, the words of the

Windigo and of old *Père* Morlain sometimes made him wonder if, for all the precautions a wiser man than he might take against unforeseen catastrophes, the inexplicable caprices of fate would not ultimately have the last grim joke on all such human vigilance.

One cooler, clear morning in mid-September, as he was finishing his simple breakfast of hominy, Ben entered the cabin with a worried frown. "*M'su* Lucien, (Ben's slurring *patois* combined the French he had learned in Santo Domingo and his own native African tongue) someone's been at the corn and the snap beans. Come see for yourself."

Lucien followed the tall Ashanti and saw that an entire row of ripened corn had been pulled up by the roots and nearly half the snap beans in the little truck patch behind the cabin which Ben and Ellen occupied. There was a larger field toward the bluff, those beans being reserved for the inhabitants of Econchate, but those had not been touched.

"That's human work, to be sure," Lucien agreed. "But whose? Certainly not the Creeks, and I'm sure there aren't any raiding or war parties in the vicinity. Did you hear any noise last night, Ben? As for myself, I was exhausted and I fell asleep the moment my head touched the blankets."

"No, *M'su*," "nothing last night. Whoever come, he come very late to make sure all of us are asleep."

"What we can do, Ben, is to take turns sitting up late at night and watching for prowlers. Whoever the thief is, he took enough corn and beans to feed a family."

"Maybe some new settlers find a place near here, *M'su* Lucien, start just now without enough food, come looking for it."

"That's quite possible, Ben. Just the same, we'll keep our eyes open late at night, you and I, for the next week and see if we can catch our thief."

That next Saturday evening, though it was Ben's turn to remain on guard, Lucien found that he could not sleep. He slept naked to the waist, wearing only his doeskin breeches; the comfort of the softened, well-worked animal skins had pleased him from the very first, and besides such a costume made him feel more at one with the

Creeks. He had replaced the old, worn-out boots he had brought from France with a fine new pair made in Spain and acquired in Mobile last year. They were sturdier, particularly around the calves, and they were excellent protection against the fangs of the lurking snake in the bushes or the fields or near the river bank when he worked on the depot. That orginally small and crude though sturdy storage place had been rebuilt this last spring by both himself and Ben, and it was now as solidly timbered as his own cabin and three times its size. He had whittled pinewood counters, remembering the format of the trading post in Mobile, and he kept accurate records of all transactions, using a quill pen and various vegetable dyes as ink. He foresaw that it would soon be necessary to rebuild this depot again as more ships with cargo came into Mobile; if it were one day as large as the trading post in Mobile, it would save many days of travel in bringing back supplies for Econchate.

It was well past midnight, and as he moved toward Ben's cabin, he saw the Ashanti leaning against the wall, still clutching his musket, his eyes closed, and he heard the snoring sounds of sleep. Gently touching Ben's shoulder, he wakened the Ashanti and said, "Go back to Ellen, man, I feel wide awake and I'll take your watch."

"Forgive me, massa—"

"Didn't I tell you never to use that word? And you're free now, the *Mico* made that clear."

Awkwardly the Ashanti got to his feet, sheepishly looking down at his musket and shifting it in his strong, wiry hands. "I know, I know, *M'su* Lucien. But you've been so good to Ellen and me and little Thomas, we look to you as our massa. I don't say it as a slave would, you know what I'm trying to say to you, *M'su* Lucien?"

Lucien nodded, gripped Ben's shoulder hard. "That's a compliment I'll have to live up to more than ever now. Go get your sleep."

Over his shoulder Lucien had slung the bow Nanakota had given him, the quiver of arrows fixed to the right side of his scabbard-belt with Jabez Corrigan's knife at his left. The night was still, and the faint sound of the river came clearly. On such a night as this, only a quarter moon silhouetted in a thickly clouded sky, the senses were sharpened; the cooler air from the river brushed his tanned, weather-beaten cheeks; his nostrils flared to the scent of the ripe corn and melons and all the verdant growth in every direction as far as one could see.

He heard an owl hoot from a tree high on the red bluff to his right, and he turned to stare at the top of the bluff where Dimarte and Edmond were at rest. The *Windigo* had foretold his destiny with the bones of beasts and birds who provided food and gave warning. Was that owl the harbinger of Dimarte's sweet spirit, calling to him that she would never forget, as he would never forget? Or was it a warning, indeed?

His skin twitched along the side where the bear had clawed him. His muscles tightened with an instinctive readiness, and, just as the quarter moon emerged from behind a cloud to lighten the river bank and the dark outline of the warehouse at the levee, he backed up against the wall of his cabin to hide himself in its obscurity, as an Indian might do in ambush.

There was a sound from the direction of the river, a scraping sound, and as he squinted to make out whatever movement might have caused it, he saw a shadowy, crouching figure draw a pirogue onto the bank. Then, the soft, muffled thud of an oar being carefully laid down into it.

He drew his bow, fitted an arrow from the quiver and slowly readied it, as he saw the shadowy figure more slowly. It seemed to circle away from the cabins toward the very edge of the cornfields. Then, sprinting toward the fields, he shouted, "Stand where you are, or I'll put an arrow through you!"

"No—please—" the thief's voice came back, shrill with fear.

"Walk toward me, hold your arms at your sides. I've killed many a deer with the bow and arrow, so be very careful!" Lucien called back.

Slowly the shadowy figure advanced, arms out in cross. Lucien uttered an incredulous gasp; the thief wore a man's shirt and breeches and shoes, but the face was that of a woman, even though the auburn hair was cropped.

And the high-perched, thrusting, narrowly spaced full breasts which rose and fell convulsively against the grimy shirt were final proof of the sex of Lucien's corn thief.

"A woman—are you the same one who took my corn and beans a week ago?" he demanded, lowering the bow so that the arrow pointed to the ground.

"Why—yes—I—I didn't want to or mean to, I'm sorry —I had to—please—I—I'm afraid of weapons—"

"What you need," Lucien said in a sudden flare of irritation, "is a sound thrashing with a weapon I could peel from one of those hickory or pine trees over at the bluff."

The red-haired young woman bowed her head, then uttered a bitter little laugh. "Go ahead. You might as well. I'll get whipped anyway for not bringing back what I was sent for."

"Whipped anyway?—by whom?"

She lifted her head, shrugging rounded, soft shoulders. Her face was winsome, with large, widely spaced green eyes, an impertinent snub nose, a full, generous mouth, slantingly set cheekbones. Her skin was tanned by the sun and liberally freckled. And as she shrugged, lowering her arms, he saw that she was perhaps an inch or two taller than Dimarte. "Why, by the folks who own me, that's by whom. I'm indentured."

"You, a white girl, how is that possible?"

"I—I'm English, and two years ago in London, when the press gang tried to take my brother to be a sailor in the fleet, he was sick with a bad leg. I tried to explain, but they wouldn't listen. I guess—well, I pushed one of the men down the stairs and he fell and broke his neck. They said I was to hang, but then they changed it to indenture for life in the colonies."

"Merciful God! And you mean you're bound to these people from Georgia?"

"Yes, sir. They put me on a ship and took me to Savannah, and that's where Mr. and Mrs. Wealtham bought my papers. So I have to do what they want, or they whip me. But at that, I guess it's better than hanging. I—I didn't want to take those beans and that corn, Mister, but they said I had to or they'd lace me raw. They've done that too, times enough so I know they'll do what they say."

"It's incredible! A white girl being a slave to other whites. In the Orient, I might have expected a white girl to be captured for a sultan's harem, but not in this new country, this country of freedom," Lucien incredulously declared.

"Leastways, Mister, I guess I'd rather be whipped than dangled from a rope at Tyburn. When I was waiting in Bridewell, the women there told me it was terrible slow unless you could bribe Jack Katch to have one of his boys jump on your shoulders and tighten the rope fast."

"And a British court found you guilty of murder, because you loved your brother and because he was ill and you tried to stop their taking him?"

"That's what the judge said at the Assizes, Mister. That was just before he put on the black cap. And he said it was lucky for me the Crown didn't charge me with treason too, else maybe I'd have been burned or drawn and quartered before the rope."

Lucien shook his head, appalled at what the redhaired young woman had so matter-of-factly told him. "You say you're bound to the Wealthams. What kind of family are they and exactly where have they settled?"

"Downstream, I'd say about three miles, though I don't know distance in this awful country. At least it was more civilized in Savannah—that was, till those horrible Indians started going on the warpath. Mr. Wealtham—Tobias Wealtham, he used to be an important man with some big trading company in London, and, though they don't talk about it much when I'm around, I sort of figured he'd got into trouble and had to come over here to get away from it."

"I see. What else can you tell me—and what's your name, by the way? I'm Lucien Bouchard."

The red-haired young woman gave him a wan smile. "You'd think this was London society, wouldn't you now, us introducing ourselves to each other, when here I'm like as not to get either an arrow through me or a switch to my backside after stealing what's yours. It's Amelia.

248

Amelia Duggins. My brother and I lived in Cheapside—do you know it?"

"No, I've never been to London, *Mademoiselle* Duggins."

"Là, that's real fancy—that's French, isn't it? I taught myself how to read and write mostly good enough to get by after Pa died of the gout and Ma ran off with an actor in one of those traveling companies that put on plays and such for the fancy gentry. But about the Wealthams, there's the missus, and she's a holy terror—she's the one who whips me when I have it coming. He'd like nothing better than to get at me at night, but so far, she's kept him off me. And with his two boys, I don't mind saying I wouldn't have picked being a bound servant to that special family if I'd had my druthers."

Lucien found his captured "thief" disarmingly engaging and candid, and tried to keep a smile from his lips, seeing the stolid indifference and the lackluster look in her green eyes. "Have they built a cabin at all, a place for you to stay at least?"

"Oh, they've done that well enough. Leastways, there's a big cabin for the four of them, and the mister put up a little shed and he said it was good enough for me to sleep in. It's bare ground, and I'm mortal scared of snakes and such, but I'm more scared of those boys Nat and Arnie, I can tell you straight out, Mister Lucien. They've been staying there for well nigh onto two months now, ever since some white man—real handsome and a fine talker he was, too—came into the territory and started turning the Indians against the Georgia folks. Mr. Wealtham says he's afraid that fellow'll stir up some real massacres before he's finished. But you see, Mr. Wealtham took down with river fever for a spell, and he didn't have any more flints for his musket and not much powder left either, so he told me to go scouting around and find what I could find or he'd have the missus lay it into me good."

"Does he have any money, do you know, *Mademoiselle* Duggins?"

"Some," she said doubtfully, scratching at her hip and squirming nervously. "There's bugs or skeeters or something out here. Snakes too, I bet."

249

"Yes," he said curtly, not wanting to be reminded of the dreadful image which was still engraved so vividly on his mind at the mere mention of that word. "I'll tell you what, *Mademoiselle* Duggins. You're tired, and I imagine you haven't had too much to eat yourself lately."

"That's true enough. The boys, they're the biggest eaters, which is to be expected, and the missus doesn't do so bad for herself either. I get what's left, and like as not there hasn't been much, not till I made off with that lot of corn and beans as you found out."

"Well then, I'll get you some blankets and you can sleep on the floor of my cabin—don't worry, you're perfectly safe, I'm not the kind of man to take a woman against her will."

She flushed, then looked down at her worn shoes and dirt-caked bare legs, which showed through the tatters in the legs of the breeches. "I wasn't thinking about that, Mister Bouchard. When you live in the poor side of London and you make out by yourself with just a brother to look after and no family and not many shillings to tide you both over, you know when a man's got harmful notions soon enough. No, what I was thinking was, if I don't show up until morning, she'll have me peel a couple of extra switches before she gives it to me. That's one of her cute little tricks. And the worst of it is, those awful boys stand around grinning like it's a treat and a peepshow, 'cause most times she has me drop my breeches or, when I'm staying around the cabin, pull my skirt up and let my petticoat down so she can lay it into me for fair."

"That's inhuman, monstrous! In that case, *Mademoiselle* Duggins, I myself will take you back to the Wealthams in the morning, and I'll bring along some food and try to talk them into treating you decently."

"That's might good of you, Mr. Bouchard. I don't mind admitting I could stand some real sleep and maybe, if you could just spare it, something more than green corn without the cooking. Not that corn's not tasty, you understand, but that's about all I've had the past week or so."

"I'll have Ellen get you something much more nourishing than that in the morning. Now come along. I've some extra blankets, and I'll sleep next to the door on them, and you take the thicker pile for your bed."

When Ellen brought a bowl of warmed-over rabbit stew he watched the red-haired young woman bolt it down as if she had been starved for weeks. When at last she finished and leaned back on her stool, she shook her head and with a blissful expression murmured, "Lord, but that was good! I think I can stand a lacing now. I was sort of weak these past few days. I'm mighty obliged to you, Mr. Bouchard."

"There's plenty left. I'll have Ellen fill the bowl. And I promise you that I'll have a serious talk with this Mr. Tobias Wealtham and his good wife and let them know that I don't take kindly to having anyone whipped, and especially not one of their own kind."

Amelia Duggins uttered a humorless little laugh and shook her head. "You can talk till Doomsday if you've a mind to, Mr. Bouchard, I don't think it'll do much good where that one's concerned. She's a holy terror. Preaching Scripture at me night and day when she isn't having me do all the work she can think up—not that there's much in that bare shanty they've put up for a cabin. Says I'm a murderess, that I'm not grateful for the good home they're giving me and for all the food and such and the clothes, and that if it wasn't for them I'd be dangling for the crows to peck at."

"They may not be aware, *Mademoiselle* Duggins, that they have settled in territory which is ruled by the *Mico*—that means the chief—of Econchate, which is the Creek village about twenty miles from here. Those who settle on Creek land must have permission, as I did, or they really will be in danger. And once I tell the Wealthams that the *Mico* is my good friend, I feel reasonably sure they'll be more careful in their dealings with you."

"You're good and you're kind, Mr. Bouchard. I wish I'd met someone like you back in London. Maybe I wouldn't be here now, and I surely wouldn't be stealing what you grow for yourself."

"Not altogether for myself. I share it with the Creeks. That's part of our agreement, and I do trading for them to earn the privilege of living here unmolested and on the friendliest of terms."

"You're a strange fellow. You're French, aren't you?"

As he nodded, she went on, "But you talk elegant English, though of course you've got a different way of saying those fancy words. You mean, you live here and you get along fine with those Indians?"

"I learned their language, *Mademoiselle* Duggins." He hesitated a moment, then, deciding that her candor had earned his own, added, "I was married to a Creek girl. She died last year. That's another reason I am close friends with them, because I felt that her coming to live with me in a way brought about her death."

Amelia Duggins looked at him intently, then flushed and lowered her eyes. "I know what the mister and the missus would say to that, I reckon. They'd say you were a squaw man. But I don't hold that against anyone, not in this lonely country I don't. And anyhow, if a girl was nice and loved you, what would it matter if she was an Indian? They were the first people here, weren't they?"

"From what most of the historians tell us, yes, that's true, *Mademoiselle* Duggins. Now let me bring you another bowl of stew and some of Ellen's cornbread, and when you're rested enough, we'll go back and visit with this enterprising family that appears to be my first neighbors."

CHAPTER TWENTY

Lucien loaded the pirogue with hide sacks of cornmeal, some jerky, beans, squash and a few melons and, following Amelia Duggins' directions, rowed downstream past two bends in the river until he came to a small clearing framed by towering hickory and pine trees and saw the hastily constructed, lopsided cabin of the Wealthams and, just behind and almost up against it, the shed-like hovel for the bondservant. A docile mule tethered to one of the hickory trees hardly bothered to look up at the two as they grounded the pirogue and Lucien began to lift the sacks of provisions. It went back to grazing on a scattered pile of dried corn kernels. A stout, gray-haired woman emerged from the cabin, holding an old Spanish musket, primed and ready. "So it's you, Meelie!" she snapped. "Paw said you'd likely run away, but I told him you knew what you'd git if you tried that trick. Now who's this with you, dressed like an Injun?"

"You're Mrs. Wealtham, I believe. My name is Lucien Bouchard. I brought your family some provisions, and I'd like to talk to you and your husband if you'll let me."

The woman had beady little eyes, a wen on her bulbous nose with a large, coarse gray hair sticking out of it. She shot the red-haired young woman a furious look, then grudgingly lowered the musket and stepped aside. "Come in slow and easy, Mister. My man's feeling peaked, but my boys are still spry enough to give you a tussle if you've any Injun tricks on your mind."

"As you can see, Mrs. Wealtham, all I have is my hunting knife and you've a musket. No, *Mademoiselle* Duggins didn't run away. I met her trying to bring you back some corn and beans, and I thought I'd help her," Lucien said pleasantly as he stepped into the cabin. The fat woman turned to Amelia Duggins and snarled, "You git back into your shanty, you dirty little slut, I'll tend to you later, you can depend on it."

Amelia Duggins bit her lips, cast Lucien a hopeless glance and then hurried off to the little hovel and disappeared.

The cabin had only one room, and there was a crude log and slat bed raised high above the floor, covered with old blankets, and under it a rough trundle bed. A bearded, nearly bald, potbellied man lay on the bed, his hands methodically rubbing his belly, groaning from time to time. In the corner opposite, two boys of about fourteen and sixteen, in dirty shirts and breeches and moccasins, stared sullenly at Lucien.

"Who's this stranger, Maw? He's white, but he's dressed like a redskin. Keep that musket right handy. I got the misery, stranger, but my boys and Maw killed us a couple of them damn Creeks when we had to get away from Georgia, and we'll kill some more if we have to."

"Mr. Wealtham, as I told your wife, I brought your family some food. My name's Lucien Bouchard. I'm a trader with the Creeks at Econchate and they are my friends. You have nothing to fear from them if you act decently toward them."

"Humph! I see you've kept your scalp, Mister, and I'm aiming to keep mine. But not by being friends with those murdering devils. There was a white man just like you, only better-looking, making fine speeches to all those damn redskins around where we wuz getting along just fine. Next thing you know, they come a-whooping around the cabins with their tomahawks and their muskets and they killed a lot of decent white folks. We had a little farm near the Oconee, but we had to give it up and just about everything else we owned."

"I sympathize with you, Mr. Wealtham. It looks to me as if this land beyond the river would be very good for

254

corn and other crops like potatoes and squash and beans. I'll be glad to help you get seed and the other things you'll need for the planting next spring. If you have any money, I can get supplies from Mobile where I go from time to time, and I'll charge you the very lowest prices without trying to make any profit, just to help you get started."

"Why now, that's friendly of you, Mister—you said your name was Bouchard? Who're your kinfolks?" The bearded man on the bed propped himself up on an elbow and squinted quizzically at Lucien.

"I came from France, but I've lived with the Creeks for two years now, and the chief of the village is my friend. I'll tell him that you've come here in peace and wish to farm and perhaps do some trading, once you've established yourselves here and get through the winter. But I'd advise you not to try to steal from any of the fields in this territory. Their Indian owners might not be so friendly as I was last night when your bound girl came calling on me."

"Drat the stupid bitch! I told her to make sure everybody was asleep before she skittered into the fields. Never mind, Maw'll give her a switchin' she won't soon forget."

"And that, Mr. Wealtham, I must ask you not to do to her. She doesn't deserve it, and only a week ago she did catch us all asleep at my fields and took quite a good deal."

"Say, who the devil are you to come tell me how to treat a dirty little murderess who's lucky she didn't kick her pretty legs at the end of a rope back in London?" Tobias Wealtham grumbled.

"I don't propose to argue what she did or didn't do, Mr. Wealtham. As I said, I came here to help your family, and I mean to do so. But you'd best take heed of my warning that the chief at Econchate and I are strong allies, and his warriors could very easily drive you away from here—especially since you haven't bothered to get permission to settle on this land, which is within the boundaries of Econchate."

"Well now, maybe I spoke a mite too hasty, Mr. Bouchard." The fat, flushed face attempted a wheedling smile. "Like I said, it was neighborly of you to bring us food. That's something we've been short on, since we're just about out of powder and balls for that there musket and I haven't got back my strength yet to go trapping a deer or a raccoon. And then, the boys have had to work hard finishing the cabin—it's still not strong enough against a good rain, but then we've only had a few weeks here."

"Well then, there is food enough in these sacks if you use it wisely for about a week. When you're feeling better, Mr. Wealtham, we'll talk again and you'll tell me exactly what you plan to do here, whether it's farming or trading or whatever else you've in mind."

Again the fat man on the bed scowled suspiciously at the young Frenchman. "Say now, while you kept our little gal Meelie with you all night, Mr. Bouchard, did she blab any about our business? If she did, so help me, whether your chief or you like it or not, she's for a real whipping."

"Whip her anyway, Paw," the older boy, lanky, towheaded, with lean jaws and thin sadistic mouth, sniggered.

"You shut your trap, Arnie." His father sent him a furious glare. "You see, Mr. Bouchard—" he turned to Lucien with a crafty smile on his face again—"Maw and me, we believe in the Good Book and what it says about redeemin' a sinner. Well now, Meelie having killed a British recrootin' sergeant, she was bound to swing till our good King George, bless him, had her transported. When I first saw her come up by the bailiff at Savannah, I said to Maw, if we can jist learn this bitch her place and some manners and being proper grateful for a new chance in life, why mebbe when Arnie there grows up in another six months or so, the boy can marry her."

Lucien glanced over at the two boys at the wall, and Arnie leered and winked at him. Disgustedly, he turned back to the bearded man on the bed and brusquely answered, "I'll come again next week, Mr. Wealtham, and I hope you'll be feeling better by then. You'll find some medicinal bark which the Creeks use for what you call river fever. Have your wife heat some water and crush the

256

which you, my father, have given to me. They say that they were driven from Georgia by Creek warriors who were led against the settlers by a white man, young and eloquent, and one who spoke fluently in the tongue of our people."

"Ho! That I recognize as the man who is called Bowles and who preaches rebellion against our great leader in Maubila," the *Mico* gravely responded. He had summoned a council of four elders, his war chief, and Nanakota, the "beloved man," whose knowledge of the terrain, hunting and fishing skills and great popularity with the villagers gave him high place at the council.

"If that is true, Tunkamara," Tantumito spoke up, "then it would be wise to make friends with these white-eyes, that they might tell all other settlers who try to come upon our lands by fleeing in refuge from the traitor and his murderous bands that McGillivray seeks peace ... the that back tea you .... our And I thank you. You come back like you said, when Paw's better. We'll have another palaver."

He nodded silently, took a last look around the cabin noticed Arnie's sullen insolence and went back to the pirogue. The other boy, Nat, at fourteen short and stocky like his father, followed him outside, whining, "Say, Mister, that was our canoe, now you're going back in it."

"Yes. That way, I'll make sure you don't get into my fields without permission."

"But, hey now——"

"If you need it before I come back, you can always walk to my place. It's not a long hike for a strapping lad like you, Nat." Lucien shoved the pirogue into the river, nimbly seated himself and began to paddle back upstream.

The younger boy glared after him. "Dirty Injun lover!" he hawked and spat.

"There are the man and the woman, two sons, and the white girl who is their slave under the British law," Lucien explained to Tunkamara the day after he had brought provisions to the Wealthams. "They wish permission to settle on the bend of the Alabama beyond the land bark into it, then drink down as much as you can—it's bitter, but it'll help the fever."

"I'm much obliged."

"If you want to thank me for what I've brought you, Mr. Wealtham, you can give me your promise you won't have the girl whipped. After all, you sent her out to bring back food, and as you see, she's done exactly that. Do we understand each other?"

"Why, I guess mebbe this time we can let Meelie off." Slowly, Tobias Wealtham ran his tongue over his cracked lips, a speculative glint coming into his eyes.

"I'm wise to you, Paw," his wife suddenly spoke up. "Jist don't you go forgetting what you just told Mr. Bouchard here, about mebbe Arnie's marrying up with Meelie once she's worthy. I jist don't want to catch you going out to that shed when you think I'm asleep. And that goes for both you boys too." Then, to Lucien, "I'll make that not take ... you was telling Paw about just now. friends and are honest with us."

The *Mico* grunted, then turned to Nanakota. "Speak what is in your heart, oh beloved man," he urged.

The tall, genial Creek, only two years older than Lucien, deferentially bowed his head before the council before he replied: "My chief, it was not long after the great corn dance in our village that a warrior from the Oconee came to this village on his journey through many Creek villages to bring a warning. You, Tunkamara, and all you elders heard it. Do you remember it? It was that more than ever now we must stand as one with the leader in Maubila and drive out those who would make us believe that the power of McGillivray as the spokesman for our people grows less with each new rising of the sun. He said also that the man Bowles has with him many renegades who should be banished from all Creek tribes because they do not act in honor and think only of bloodshed and plunder. And that there are also those who are agents of this white-eyes who hates McGillivray because he himself wishes to replace him and have much honor and gold. I do not trust these new white-eyes and I will not believe their story which Lu-shee-ahn has now told us till we

258

have seen them and spoken with them to learn whether they talk with a forked tongue."

"Ho, that is so. But we will not bring them here, we will go to them to see what they do on the land," Tunkamara declared, as he looked at each of the elders on the council and watched each nod approval in his turn. "So it shall be. Tomorrow when the sun has reached the middle of the heavens, we shall go to their dwelling and see for ourselves what it is they wish. You, Lu-shee-ahn, and you, Nanakota, will go with me. There will be the two braves who guard my dwelling in the other canoe. We will show them that we come in peace and we will listen to their words."

Then Tunkamara turned to Lucien. "You have told us that these white-eyes have a white slave and that it is by the law of the British. Was she a slave from birth?"

"No, my *Mico*. She had been accused of killing a British soldier who wished to take her brother to work on the tall-masted ships on the great ocean. He was ill and she tried to stop the soldiers, and one died when he fell. For this the British council said that she must hang from the tree till she was dead, but the great king of the British in mercy let her live and decreed that she should be taken on a ship to the colonies and there sold upon the auction block. And it was these people who bought her at Savannah, and she is bound to them for life by the word of the British council."

"It is very strange. I have never before known of a white-eyes who was a slave in that way. So then, it is said, tomorrow we shall see that one and those who own her. And now, my son, the elders have asked me to bid you bring back from Maubila when next you go more of the salt which is used to hold the meat of the deer and the bear and the raccoon before it can turn to carrion."

"I had thought to go to Maubila after the sun has risen and set seven times, my father," Lucien replied.

At noon of the next day, two pirogues turned down the bend of the Alabama toward the tree-framed cabin of the Wealthams. In the first, the two sturdy bodyguards of the *Mico* rode, armed with hunting knives and bows and arrows; in the one which followed, Tunkamara sat with his arms folded across his chest, while behind him, Lucien and Nanakota rode. Greatly to Nanakota's pleasure, Lucien had armed himself with the indigo-dyed bow which he had given to his blood brother after the death of Dimarte, and Nanakota's musket lay beside him, primed and ready.

As they drew near the river bank and prepared to land the pirogues, Lucien saw Amelia Duggins, barefoot and clad in a tattered calico dress, emptying a clay bowl of corn kernels for the tethered mule to eat. As she saw the two canoes, she uttered a cry of fright, dropped the bowl and hurried to the cabin, calling out, "They're coming, the Indians!"

"Out of the way, you stupid bitch!" the stout, gray-haired woman called as she appeared in the doorway of the cabin, knelt down and took careful aim with a musket.

"Look out, treachery!" Lucien cried, leaping onto the bank and notching an arrow. But before he could loose it, there was a sharp crack and the *Mico* of Econchate, who had just set foot upon the bank and begun to walk slowly toward the cabin, stopped in his tracks, lifted a hand to his mouth as blood gushed from a wound in his lungs and then toppled to the ground.

His two bodyguards, with infuriated cries, notched their bows and sent arrows whizzing toward their chief's murderess. One of them took her in the shoulder, and the other sped over her head into the cabin, and a cry of pain was heard as Arnie, raising another musket, came stumbling out of the cabin with the arrow in his right thigh. "Goddamn redskins, you killed my Maw!" he screamed at them as he leveled the musket and fired. One of the bodyguards fell back over the landed pirogue, arched convulsively, then sprawled with his head dipping below the surface of the gently lapping water. The other brave set a knee to the ground, took careful aim and sped his arrow into the older boy's chest. Arnie dropped the musket and fell over onto one side, his look of rage and his gaping mouth frozen by death.

Mrs. Wealtham frantically tried to reload her musket despite the ugly wound in her shoulder, and now her bearded husband appeared in the doorway, a hunting knife poised in his right hand. Before he could throw it at Nanakota, who stood beside Lucien, the latter sped his arrow, and the bearded man clutched his belly, uttered a gurgling cry and toppled over his kneeling wife, knocking the musket out of her trembling hands.

"Run, Nat, run for your life," she screamed, and Lucien, numb with horror at the swift, bloody tragedy which had so unexpectedly erupted, saw the younger boy emerge from Amelia's little hovel, hesitate a moment and then run into the forest.

"After him!" Nanakota angrily ordered the *Mico*'s other bodyguard.

"No, he's only a boy and he didn't have a weapon that I could see, my brother." Lucien put a restraining hand on Nanakota's shoulder.

"I heed your words, Lu-shee-ahn. But the she-wolf still lives. We shall learn from her lips why she has killed our beloved *Mico*." Then, to the surviving bodyguard of the Creek chief, Nanakota commanded, "The young white-eyes squaw—take her and bind her hands behind her, we take her to the village and she too will tell us the truth of this evil treachery!"

Amelia Duggins, pale, paralyzed with terror, had pressed herself against the side of the cabin, her eyes huge and glazed with shock. She whimpered as the stocky Creek brave approached her, but did not resist him as he seized her wrists and bound them with a rawhide thong, then angrily jerked her toward one of the pirogues.

Tobias Wealtham's wife had crawled to the side of the door of the cabin, one hand stanching the blood that flowed from the arrow buried deeply in her shoulder. With her free hand, she scrabbled in the pocket of her homespun dress, drew out a hunting knife and, even as Nanakota hurried toward her with a cry of alarm, drove it into her own heart. Her eyes fixed on the "beloved man" and her lips curled in a triumphant sneer as she gasped, "No—t—torture st—stake for me, you murdering redskin," and then slumped forward in death.

It was nightfall in the village of Econchate. There was

mourning for the kind, grave and just Tunkamara, the *Mico* who had been slain by evil white-eyes who had come upon the land of the Creeks. And old Tsipoulata had led the solemn processional to the hill at one side of the village, where the funeral mound of Tunkamara would place him beside his predecessor Iconata, the Swift Arrow and great Creek chieftain of whose exploits warriors still chanted over the fires. Now they would sing songs of the valor of Tunkamara. He had been buried in a seated position, with tobacco in his pipe that he might make council with the other dead chiefs of the Creeks when the Great Spirit should summon them all to final meeting.

And now, in that same clearing where Shehanoy had been staked out to be put to death for having violated the law of hospitality to a guest, Amelia Duggins was led out, her wrists still thonged behind her back, her elbows gripped by two tall warriors of the same clan as the war chief of Econchate. Instead of the stakes, a heavy stone slab had been placed, and in front of it stood Tantumito himself, holding a stone tomahawk, the heavy head painted in red, the wooden handle in black. It had been the sentence of the elders that the bondservant of these murderous white-eyes have her brains dashed out by the ceremonial tomahawk.

As the braves led her toward the slab, the red-haired young woman stared agonizedly at Lucien. "I swear I didn't know they were going to kill him, I swear it to you, Mr. Bouchard! Mrs. Wealtham said she'd turn me over to the boys after she'd skinned me raw if I let out a peep about what they were planning—but all he said was that he knew your chief would come calling and then they'd all be ready for him—that's all I know—I swear it is!"

Nanakota, wearing the ceremonial mantle which once Tunkamara had worn, now stepped from the dwelling of the dead chief; at twilight, the elders had appointed him to take Tunkamara's place. Lucien strode toward him and exclaimed, "I am sure she had no part in this dreadful deed, my brother. Do not let the valiant Creeks have the blood of an innocent woman upon their hands—as a slave, in fear of them, she had no choice and she did not

262

know they planned murder! She could not warn us, for she feared for her own life!"

"My brother, once before you saved the life of a woman who was condemned to death by our village. That time, it was your own life she sought. But this woman is a part of the attack upon our warriors and the death of our noble *Mico*. I know you have great compassion in your heart, my brother; you are gentle and you respect the weakness of the squaw. But you saw with your own eyes as I did how another squaw aimed the musket at great Tunkamara and gloried in her foul deed of murder when we came in peace. No, she must die."

"But she was a slave, I tell you. I myself heard those two boys ask their father and mother to let them watch her being whipped. If you see the marks upon her flesh, will you then believe that neither she nor I speak lying words, Nanakota?"

The two braves had forced Amelia Duggins to lay her head down on the stone slab, crouching and gripping her by neck and shoulders as she began to sob. Tantumito slowly lifted the heavy tomahawk and awaited the signal of the new *Mico*.

Nanakota's strong, hard-jawed face was impassive as he approached the place of execution. Dispassionately, he looked down at the kneeling bondservant, and then his dark eyes fixed Lucien's for a long moment before he spoke: "I would see the signs though they prove only that she was punished, as the white-eyes are given to punish disobedient slaves. It will not prove that she is innocent of this plot to kill our *Mico*."

Lucien turned from the new *Mico* to the war chief: "Hold your hand until the *Mico* has spoken," he pleaded. Then, moving around the slab and kneeling down behind the trembling red-haired bondservant, he murmured, "I must do this, forgive me. It is all I can think of to save your life."

Setting his hands to the neck of her crude calico dress, he ripped it down to her hips. There was a gasp from the watching villagers who had crowded to see the execution. On the pale white skin of Amelia Duggins' back and shoulders, the ugly crisscrossing welts of the switch were

263

emblazoned in reddish-purple discolorations, some of the welts disappearing under a sleazy petticoat which alone, besides the tattered dress, covered her.

"See for yourself, Nanakota. At the council, I explained how she came to be a slave, how when I visited her white-eyes owners, they talked of such punishment and delighted in it. Is it not then possible that out of her pain and her fear, and knowing that the law gave her no right to appeal it or to run away without even more terrible punishment, she was forced to silence? She has said that all she knew was that they had hoped Tunkamara would visit their cabin, nothing more. They did not speak of murder—at least not in her presence. Does this not suffice you, oh my brother?"

Nanakota scowled, as a silence fell over the thronging spectators. Compassion and justice wrestled with his fierce tribal honor: as successor to the *Mico,* his first grievous decision was to avenge Tunkamara's death. Finally, he answered, "The ways of the white-eyes are guileful. If it were you and I, my brother, who weighed the right or the wrong of what comes before us to decide, we should more quickly find the truth. How do we know that this young squaw was not in the pay of the traitor Bowles, and that indeed, she did not willingly submit herself to this punishment in order to dupe us, that we might believe her innocent of all wrongdoing?"

They had spoken in Creek, and Amelia Duggins could not understand a word. Still forced down on her knees and with her cheek pressed hard against the cold stone slab by the two braves, shaken by an uncontrollable fit of agonized trembling, she groaned, "For God's sake, I'm telling the truth, I didn't know they were going to do anything like this—all I ever heard the mister say was that he wanted to have a palaver with the chief and work things out. And he was always telling the missus about there being more gold from their friend if they got him to palaver with them."

"Don't you see, Nanakota?" Lucien anxiously exclaimed, "From what she's just said, it's evident to me that the Wealthams were in the pay of Bowles. They were talking of the money they had already got and how much more they would get if they were able to get Tunkamara to hold parley with them. Naturally, they wouldn't tell the girl, for fear she'd try to get away and warn us. I believe her, on my honor, as strongly as I believe in the blood that is between us, my brother!"

"There is by our village law only one way that you may save her, Lu-shee-ahn. You have no squaw in your lodge, nor child. If you will take her as your squaw, and make her with child, while she remains in our village guarded by our braves and our old women, she will be hostage for your bond. If she is found to be one of those murderers, she dies and you are banished forever from our land."

"I will agree to it, Nanakota. I will wed the squaw."

"So be it." The tall "beloved man" made a gesture, and Tantumito lowered the huge stone tomahawk and moved away. The two braves gripping Amelia Duggins released her and rose. Slowly, she raised her contorted, drawn face, her green eyes exorbitantly dilated. "Are they—are they going to kill me, Mr. Bouchard?" Her voice broke with her near hysteria. Her dress was ripped down to her hips in front as well as back, and he could not help seeing the full, closely set milky-sheened globes of her breasts, shudderingly swelling as she fought for breath.

"No. But I had to promise something for them to spare you, *Mademoiselle* Duggins. And I must carry out my promise if you are to keep your life. I told you that night in my cabin that I was not the kind to force a woman. But the chief has demanded, as the only way that I may save your life, that you become my wife and give me a child. You will be kept here in this village, though of course I should be free to come and look after you. It is like being a hostage, to guarantee that you are not part of that plot and that I am responsible for your actions."

The braves had lifted her to her feet now, but left the thongs still binding her slim wirsts. She glanced down at herself, suddenly conscious of her half-nakedness, and a slow, furious blush suffused her pale, tearstained cheeks. "I don't want to die. I did, for a while when I was with the Wealthams, but I don't want to now. I don't know how you can want a dirty murderess, like they called me, or a bound girl, but you can have me, wife or slave or whatever else it is you'd want, Mr. Bouchard. I owed you that much anyway when you didn't shoot me that night and when you told the Wealthams not to whip me."

"You're a brave young woman, *Mam'selle*. But I'm afraid you must call on your endurance one more time tonight. The chief wishes the ceremony to begin now."

Her blush deepened, she looked down at the ground. Biting her lips, hunching her shoulders as if to hide her naked breasts from his male eyes, she huskily murmured, "I'd sooner have you be my first than those cruel boys and that's no lie, Mr. Bouchard. And you won't be getting damaged goods. Maybe you won't believe somebody like me, who's been sentenced to hang and then indentured and being around the people who bought me as I was, but no man's lain with me yet, and that's the truth again."

Lucien Bouchard turned to Nanakota. "The squaw accepts. As I do, my brother. Prepare the marriage ceremony, and will you again stand for me as you did before our deeply mourned Tunkamara?"

On the tall Creek's face, there was a look of undisguised admiration and, more, relief that so weighty a burden had been lifted; in all previous councils where he had been heard, the "beloved man" had never raised his voice in favor of war or death to others. "It will begin. And this time, I pray to the Great Spirit that your squaw and your child will live."

"Amen to that," Lucien Bouchard murmured to himself.

They had cut away the thongs that bound Amelia Duggins' wrists, and the young women and the old squaws had scrubbed her with water from the river and their strong, biting soap and then rubbed her from head to toe with a grease of bear fat. Finally, they had garbed her in doeskin petticoat and jacket; but because she was not accepted by the village and thus aligned with no recognized and honored tribe, her feet were left bare, to symbolize her servitude to him who had saved her life and was of the Bear Clan.

As they seated themselves on the marriage ground, Lucien swiftly explained to Amelia Duggins what she must do. She forced a wry smile to her haggard though still lovely face: "I'll be honest with you, Mr. Bouchard, I haven't the strength to run, not now. I hadn't finished saying my prayers yet when I thought I was for it. All I could hope was that it wouldn't hurt as much as the rope. Besides, I'm thinking that if I try to run from you, I'll go back to that stone and that club they were going to smash my head in with. No, if it's all the same to you, I'll just wait here till it's over and then I'll go with you wherever you say."

It was done at last and with merciful swiftness, thanks to the innate compassion of the new *Mico* of Econchate. As they rose, wed by Creek law, the red-haired bondservant stared into her new husband's eyes, then lowered hers as she murmured, "At least I'm clean for you. They'd never let me so much as wash myself in the river after they bought me. And after the horrid way those boys watched me have to peel raw for a switching and the way the mister watched with his wet mouth and shifting little eyes as if he couldn't wait to get me out in the shed, I'll not mind your seeing me as God made me." Then, rallying a quick flash of humor, she added, "Besides, you just about saw all there was to me when you pulled my dress off to show my marks to the chief, didn't you?"

Trustingly, she slipped her hand into his as they walked toward the little house where first he had been lodged when he had come to the village of Econchate. Inside, the women had piled blankets and a doeskin quilt atop them for their bridal bed. No candle burned, and there was darkness and silence surrounding them as they faced each other in this strange, primitive union as strangers whose lives had become inextricably bound together.

He tried not to think of that wedding night with Dimarte. Indeed, he had almost asked Nanakota to quarter Amelia and himself in some other dwelling, so that the memory of the gentle "beloved woman" would linger and bless this little house, unsullied by a new ghost which only pity for the bound girl had evoked. For it was in pity and not love that he took her, comforting her with reassuring words as he guided her toward their rude bed. But it was she, just as Dimarte had done in what now seemed an eternity ago, who voluntarily stripped herself of her bridal garments and lay down upon the bed to await her consummation.

Amelia Duggins had not lied. No man until this moment had profaned her virginity. She shivered as he came upon her, but her arms closed over his shoulders and she held him tightly as if seeking his comfort and his strength in her maiden martyrdom. She ground her teeth to suppress the cry which the pangs of defloration drew from her, but she did not flinch from them. And when she had at last fallen into her deep, exhausted sleep, he held her tenderly in his arms and whispered into the darkness, to that gentle ghost who might even now be attending, "She does not replace you, my beloved, but she is deserving of life. Have pity on us both, and be comforted to know that you will be in my heart till my time has come."

CHAPTER TWENTY-ONE

That next morning, Lucien and two braves went back to what had been the Wealtham cabin to bury the dead and to raze the cabin. Lucien pulled the blankets off the higher bed, searching for some proof of the suspected conspiracy. There was nothing hidden in those blankets, but when he tugged the low trundle bed, in which the two boys had doubtless slept, out into the middle of the cabin, he saw a small rawhide pouch thrust up against the wall.

Opening it, he shook its contents onto the blankets of the trundle bed. A dozen gold coins clinked out, and a folded piece of paper. Opening it, he read aloud its English words to the braves in the Creek tongue:

This and twice as much more if you are successful in killing the chief at Econchate. He is one of the damned McGillivray's most loyal subjects, his death will hasten the downfall of the despot.

A sprawling, large B was the only signature—there could be no doubt that it had been penned by William Augustus Bowles. True, it did not yet clear Amelia Duggins of complicity in the assassination of Tunkamara, but it assuredly showed that the four Georgians had been hired as murderous agents by McGillivray's bitter enemy.

Perhaps it would never be known how Tobias Wealtham, his wife and two teenaged sons had come from England to Georgia, how the bearded rogue had fallen from grace with his employers and become a willing assassin for hire whose pathway had crossed that of the bold young adventurer, the white man who had turned against his own country, as he had against the flag under which he had fought his own countrymen, so that he might advance his own self-glorification as leader of the powerful Creeks. Doubtless, by sending letters back to the authorities in London and in Georgia, it would be possible after many tedious months to verify Amelia Duggins' story about her conviction and sentence and her sale at indenture as well as the warped background of the Wealthams. But Lucien, who could now read the Creek mind as he could speak the words to reach that mind, knew that Nanakota would judge by deeds. Far more convincing to the new *Mico* of Econchate than all the legal documents from London and Georgia had been Lucien's willingness to abide by the Creek law and to stake his own future with the Creeks by wedding the bondservant and leaving her as hostage.

That evening, when he showed Nanakota the contents of the pouch against the Wealtham's cabin wall, the new *Mico* spoke exactly as Lucien had foreseen he would: "What the couriers from the Oconee warned us of has come to pass, my brother. We must be more vigilant than ever before to preserve this village and to continue our loyalty to our leader in Maubila. When you journey there, take him the pledge of Nanakota, appointed by the council in Tunkamara's stead, that we do not listen to the lies of Bowles and those others who would slander his great deeds for our nation." Then, regarding Lucien with the look of a close friend and not the solemn countenance of a chief, he said gently, "Your squaw will not be harmed so long as she dwells with us. We shall teach her the skills that a woman in the lodge of a warrior must know. And if there is a child and she has not shown us treachery before its bearing, then she is free to join you in your lodge by the red bluff which marks your land as our good friend and blood brother."

It was at the end of the first week of October that Lucien and Ben steered their flatboat into the widening bay and moored it at the dock beyond which stood the trading post of Swanson and McGillivray. Ellen and little Thomas had gone to live in the village of Econchate, and Ben's young wife would act as Amelia's companion till Lucien and her husband returned from the trading trip.

But when Lucien and Ben entered the imposing plank-structured headquarters of the leader of the Creeks, they found only the black, Paro, there, for McGillivray's partner Swanson had accompanied the former to New Orleans. "David Francis has gone with his master," Paro told them. "And the traitor Bowles has learned that Colonel McGillivray has left Maubila, and he and his renegades boast that our leader will never again dare to show his face upon the Coosa and that his power is ended for all time."

"You do not believe that, Paro," Lucien smilingly declared.

The handsome, powerfully muscled black shook his head and returned Lucien's smile. "I do not. The war chief Milfort is already on the trail of the traitor, and it will not be long before he is captured and brought in chains to face the leader he has so vilely slandered. And now, what news from Econchate?"

"Sad news indeed, Paro. Tunkamara was killed by an agent in the pay of Bowles, and Nanakota is the new *Mico*. If you will dispatch word to New Orleans, let Colonel McGillivray know that Nanakota pledges unfailing loyalty."

"Truly it is sad news, for Tunkamara was a great chief. I know of Nanakota; he will keep Econchate loyal. And now, you and your man are welcome at the house of David Francis, and Kitanda will see that you are well fed. I will at once send a letter to our leader and have one of the boatmen take it at dawn tomorrow."

"Thank you, Paro. Convey also my respects to Colonel McGillivray. Thanks to his trust in me, I have prospered, but my greatest prosperity is the many friendships I have made in Econchate," Lucien replied as he shook hands with the Creek leader's trusted servant and emissary.

"Is there further news from France, Paro?" the young Frenchman inquired.

271

"Many whites come to New Orleans from your country, *M'sieu* Bouchard, because of the terror that spreads throughout France. Some come here to Maubila also, and some too from Santo Domingo. There is revolution there as in France."

"Revolution?" Lucien wonderingly echoed.

Paro nodded. "A black man likes me, *M'sieu* Bouchard, who taught himself how to read and write, and who desired freedom above all else, has united his people against the cruel plantation owners in Santo Domingo and in Haiti. Almost each week, there are ships from Port-au-Prince bringing the frightened whites to refuge here and in New Orleans."

"A black man led this revolution, Paro?"

"Yes. His name is François Dominique Toussaint, and they call him L'Ouverture because he has taught the slaves who unite with him to move swiftly against their brutal masters. They strike, they hide in the hills, and the French and the Spanish are in terror, not knowing from where the next attack will come."

"It may last a long while, that revolution," Lucien mused. "Now that France is in the throes of its own disaster, there will be few soldiers sent to Santo Domingo to help the plantation owners."

Paro's eyes narrowed and glowed with an angry fervor. "The war of L'Ouverture and his followers, *M'sieu* Bouchard, is not against soldiers who are under orders to do their duty, but rather against rich, insolent plantation owners who take joy in putting them to the whip, branding their flesh with hot irons, burying them in the sand up to their necks and using their exposed heads as pins when they bowl. Oh yes, I have heard of that last sport, and how the man who owns a sugarcane plantation will invite his friends to see how skillfully he can roll a cannonball to strike with deadly force some poor wretch who spilled his drink or fainted under the broiling sun as he worked in the fields and, wakened by the overseer's whip, had the misfortune to make a gesture of anger or revolt. Forgive me for my angry speech, *M'sieu*—I have the same skin as those poor devils, I came from the African coast long ago and I knew the whip of the slave trader and the master till the leader of the Creeks set me free. But I tell you that if I were not his loyal servant to the death, I would today be with a brave man like Toussaint."

Ben had stood silently beside Lucien all this while, and now the young Frenchman turned to him. "That was the man you met in Haiti, Ben, the man who said that no one should be called master unless he could lead his people to freedom. I do not know him as you did, but I respect him. Alas, who knows if there are leaders left in France who can bring my own countrymen to freedom out of the tyranny that has lasted for centuries, yet without shedding innocent blood? I have lost my father and mother in that struggle for freedom. Though my father was one of the aristocrats they now denounce as tyrants, I never knew him to be cruel to those who toiled on his land, and never did my mother speak a harsh word even to a clumsy footman." He sighed and shook his head. "Freedom. Over two years ago I stood before Colonel McGillivray and spoke of freedom as my dream. I have learned much since then. And mainly, something which is not inscribed in the history books at the University of Paris—that so long as men live together, no man may call himself free if he is not involved with his fellows and they are not free in a brotherhood that respects one another's right to strive and hope and dream."

Then, as if he were displeased with himself at so personal an avowal, he turned back to Paro and declared, "The new *Mico* hopes that you will have good supplies of salt when the hunters return to our village. And I need other things which I will ask of you tomorrow. It is good to see you again, Paro, and when you send your letter to New Orleans, add to it my warmest greetings to David Francis."

Since he had given his razor as a gift to Nanakota, Lucien had used his sharpened hunting knife to trim his beard and, at times, to teach himself the same Spartan discipline which the Creeks practiced. He often resorted to plucking out the hairs on his cheeks and jaws with shells that served as tweezers. At present, he wore a short, rather wide goatee, and this, together with the sun-bronzed coloration of his face, as of his arms and legs and shoulders, gave him the look of a hardy frontiersman. Leaner and more wiry than when he had left France, his reflexes had been sharpened by having lived side by side with all the elemental and primitive dangers of this new world he had chosen to make his own. Wearing as he did the doeskin jacket and breeches-leggings of a brave, he could never have been recognized as an aristocrat by the throngs of vengeful underprivileged who were even now roaming the streets of Paris and the provinces of all France to wreak a terrible and bloody reprisal for the age-old wrongs they had suffered at the hands of the arrogant nobility. In this relatively short span of two and a half years, which to him sometimes seemed a very lifetime of struggle for survival, he had taken and given life. And those acts had come not out of any scholarly convictions acquired from poring over the texts of history and philosophy, but out of impulsive reaction to the dangers which had confronted him. As he and Ben enjoyed the tasty breakfast which gracious, smiling Kitanda set before them, he reflected on the terrible scene downriver. "Ben," he asked, "have you ever killed a man?"

"No, *M'su* Lucien, but that's not because I didn't want to. Back in Santo Domingo, on *M'su* Leguin's plantation, I wanted to kill him and the overseer with my bare hands. Ellen was working in the kitchen and the cook said she'd stolen a piece of cake, and Ellen called her a liar—which was true enough—and she reported on her to *M'su* Leguin. I was in there getting orders from him on how he wanted the sugarcane thinned out, and I had to stand there and watch while they made poor Ellen lie down on a bench with her dress up and her drawers down and the overseer put a paddle to her twenty times. They called it insolence. But I knew if I tried to stop it, she'd only get worse and they'd kill me and then we could never be together. But, just like it says in the Good Book, if a man thinks of killing or hankering after a girl that isn't his in his mind, he's just about done it, *M'su* Lucien."

"God grant you may never have to do more than think about it, Ben. When I was younger and a student, I thought there was no more horrible crime than to take someone else's life, no matter what the provocation. I hated my brother because he'd taken my sweetheart away from me, and then I hated her more for having let him do it. But I tried to drive those thoughts out of my mind and to reason why all that had happened. And I found that I'd expected them to live by the same code I lived by, and of course they were different people entirely. Was I myself to blame? Were their failures really my failures? I had to come all the way across the ocean to find a girl who was good and loyal and loving and wise, only to have her die so needlessly. I'll always miss her, Ben, and now I'm afraid I'll always judge all other women by her."

He reached out to grip the Ashanti's hand, then rose from the table. "Forgive me for making you hear myself think out loud, Ben. Let's go to the trading post and see if Paro has got all our supplies ready for the journey back."

As they walked down the street of the little town, Lucien affably nodding to the Spanish soldiers who patrolled it, he suddenly stopped short and gripped Ben's wrist. "Look there—way beyond at the mouth of the bay, there's a three-master, Ben!"

"Yes, *M'su* Lucien. She's flying the *drapeau tricolore*."

"Yes, yes, Ben! But look, her prow, the shape of her masts and the way her sails are set—*mon Dieu,* it's the *Guerrière!*"

"You know that ship, *M'su* Lucien?"

"It brought me here, Ben. Yes, I know it, and I hope I'll meet once again the best friend I ever had. And there'll be news from France, maybe even—" he stopped, his face tautening as he remembered. There could be no news from France now which would have any meaning to him, not after *Père* Morlain's letter. The only news would be of the gathering momentum of that insanity which had begun out of a fine concept to level classes and restore equality among men, the kind of idea those thirteen American colonies had followed. But now ferocity and violence and hatred were unleashed, forces that could destroy the nation forever unless strong, dedicated men could force sanity to prevail.

Ben looked at his master and, understanding, simply nodded.

"They're putting out a longboat from the *Guerrière,* Ben. Let's go down to the wharf and meet them. Paro's supplies can wait. I wonder if I can still speak my own tongue as I did back in Normandy, and I'm impatient to talk to my own countrymen again!"

As he stood on the edge of the wharf, Lucien could see two wiry young seamen wearing the blue berets of the French maritime; that sign alone told him that the *Guerrière* was no longer a ship of the king and under the protection of the crown of France. They pulled vigorously at their oars and behind them sat two men, one the Spanish quarantine officer of Mobile and the other—

The other, in captain's uniform and cap, but unmistakably red-haired and stocky, the one man who had befriended and helped him to his stake in the new world, was Jabez Corrigan.

He could hardly control his impatience as the longboat neared its mooring place, one of the *matelots* nimbly leaping ashore to secure it. The Spanish officer, with a polite bow, gestured to Jabez Corrigan to precede him. With sure step and quick glance around the delta, the red-haired Irishman stood just below Lucien, then turned and peered up, his eyes widening, then slapped his thigh with a bellow of delight: "By all the saints, if it's not my old passenger with the palomino!"

"Jabez, what joy to see you again, *mon ami!* I'd never expected to see the *Guerrière* dock here in Mobile. As I came down the street and saw those great three masts of yours and made out the prow and the flag, I was hoping I'd meet you again. And you've risen in the ranks—you command this vessel now!"

"Yes, by good fortune in one sense, and bad for the man I replaced. A moment till I've finished with my declaration to the good *Capitano* Hernandez, and then we'll have much to say to each other. The fact is, it's a stroke of luck to find you here the very day I come into harbor—it saves me the trouble of trying to find you. It won't take long, Lucien, wait here and I'll be back directly. And now, *Señor Capitano,* I'm at your service."

A quarter of an hour later, Jabez Corrigan emerged from the quarters of the commandant and hurried back to the wharf, where Lucien and Ben stood waiting. He took off his cap and Lucien laughed aloud to see the same unruly shock of hair. Here and there, a becoming streak of gray marked the passing of these two and a half years. He was a few pounds stouter, too, than when Lucien had last seen him, but there was the same roguish twinkle in his blue eyes and the inimitable grin on his firm mouth. "Now, by all that's holy, you'll tell me what's happened to you." His glance swept Lucien from head to foot, and he chuckled. "You've grown a beard that would make you a devil with the ladies, and from the looks of your clothes, I'd say the Creeks had taken more than a passing fancy to you. Am I right?"

"You are indeed, my dear good friend. Yes, I met Alexander McGillivray, thanks to your suggestion, and he sent me to the Creek village of Red Ground. I learned to speak their language, and I've become a farmer and a trader for them."

"Good, good! There's more of a future for you here than back where you came from, Lucien. I've no doubt you know that the king is practically a prisoner in his own palace, the aristocrats are fleeing for their lives—I've brought a few on this vessel who wish to join friends and relatives here in Mobile, and then we'll proceed to New Orleans where I'll disembark many more. But that's not all. We stopped at Port-au-Prince over a month ago before laying over in Havana for fresh water and supplies. There's a revolution going on there too."

"So I've heard, Jabez. But it appears to be quite different from what's happening in France."

"So it is. It's the blacks against their masters, whether they be French or Spanish or English, whatever. It's an uprising against sheer inhuman cruelty, and after I'd seen a few of the ingenious punishments they thought up for the rebels they captured, I think I'm in sympathy with the blacks."

"I know. My friend Ben here—this is Jabez Corrigan of whom I've told you so much, Ben—was a slave himself on a plantation out there as was his wife. They work for me now on land just above the Creek village."

"If you're a friend of Lucien's, I'm proud to shake your

277

hand, Ben." Jabez Corrigan grinned as he clasped the tall Ashanti's hand and shook it vigorously. "Well now, the problem with my former captain was that he was a monarchist, and that's a very dangerous thing to be in the France I just left over three months ago. The port of Le Havre was taken over by the civil authorities, and all of us aboard were called in and our histories dug into until I swear I felt as if I were making my confession before a priest. But you see, since I'm common stock myself, they felt I'm on the side of the revolution of the people, and so they gave me my commission. I'm picking up cargo both in New Orleans and Mobile, but of course when some of those frightened aristocrats begged me on their knees to take them out of France and handsomely paid for their passage, I looked the other way when it came to learning their politics."

"A man has a right to life no matter what his politics are, Jabez. You did as I would have done if I had been in your place. Alas, I've already made my sacrifices to the revolution. My father and mother are dead, killed by a raging mob that invaded the province, damaged the rectory of the village, and shot my mother after she'd denounced their cowardice for flinging a stone that had killed my poor father."

"My God, I'm glad it wasn't my vessel brought you news like that, Lucien." Jabez Corrigan slowly shook his head and made the sign of the cross. "Peace to their good souls, my dear friend."

"Amen with all my heart. Have you any other news from France?"

The red-haired Irishman looked long at Lucien, then took him by the elbow. "Yes, but it's something I want to tell you in private, lad. Can you have your friend Ben occupy himself for a bit while you come back with me to the *Guerrière*?"

"Of course. Besides, Ben has to make sure that Paro's provided the exact supplies we came for. If you don't mind, Ben?"

"Of course, *M'su* Lucien. My great pleasure in meeting you, *M'su Capitaine*." The Ashanti respectfully inclined his head and then set off toward the trading post.

"There now—" Jabez Corrigan exhaled a long sigh as Lucien seated himself in the longboat. "Now, you haven't told me all your story. Don't tell me a handsome devil like you hasn't found himself a pretty squaw? Or are there any white female settlers near this Red Ground of yours whose hearts you've set afluttering?"

Lucien's smile faded. Somberly, he said, "I married the daughter of a chief of the village, Jabez. I loved her more than I thought I could love any woman. She and her child were bitten by a poisonous snake."

"You poor devil!" Jabez Corrigan hesitated, respecting his friend's sudden silence, seeing how the young Frenchman turned back to see the mouth of the bay narrow up-river along that trail which he had taken to Econchate. He waited a moment, then coughed apologetically. "Never mind, man, you're young yet, you'll have a son you can be proud of, a son you can work your land for and tell tales to, aye, and make him believe them too!" Then, keenly searching Lucien's still sober features to learn his friend's mood, he jocularly went on, "And besides, you're not going to let a fat old Irishman like me get ahead of a young dandy like yourself, not a bit of it. I've married again, you know. When we went back after leaving you here in Mobile, I had shore leave for two months, and I met a baker's daughter, right in Le Havre. Her name's Jeanne Marie, and my little son's just a year old this week, and his name's Jean."

"That's wonderful, Jabez! I wish all of you long life. Maybe you'll bring your family to America and stay for good some day."

"It's too early to tell that yet. I've taken on the job of captain and I'm honor-bound to keep my post so long as the civil authorities decide I'm fit for the job. And maybe I'd just like to lay some roots down for a change, if that damned revolution ever gets over." His face was suddenly grave. "I told you I was glad I found you, didn't I? That's the truth, Lucien. That's why I'm taking you back to the ship without Ben. You see, Lucien, when I was in Port-au-Prince, I bought the papers of an indentured bondservant. And I wanted to ask your advice about her."

Lucien, with a surprised gasp, turned to stare incredu-

279

lously at his friend. "A female bondservant? But would she not be British? I ask—well, because recently there were some Georgia settlers in our midst, English by birth, who brought with them a female bondservant from London. They bought her in Savannah, and she remains as hostage in our village because they killed the chief in a plot to undermine the strength of Colonel McGillivray."

"Some news reached me in Havana that the British, the Spanish and the Americans are vying for McGillivray's favor, each country wishing his exclusive friendship. So the idea of a plot against him doesn't surprise me, Lucien. However, to answer your question, this woman is not from England. To be frank with you, I myself bought her—that is to say, she offered herself under indenture, and, taking pity on her because of her deplorable situation, I exchanged the rights of ownership over her in return for the passage fee to a port of safety and refuge." He smiled broadly now and winked at Lucien: "I tell you, if I didn't have Jeanne Marie waiting for me back at Le Havre and with a little one that's got my own red hair and his mother's big, soft brown eyes, I'd have relished the idea of keeping this attractive creature."

"You always had an eye for a pretty girl, *mon ami*," Lucien laughed.

"I still do, I'll have you know, even though I'm wed and to a fine lass. But the thought just occurs to me, especially after the sad news you've given me about your Creek wife and child, that seeing that you're the master of land and a good friend of the Creeks, there's no reason in the world why you shouldn't own a bondservant. Out there in the wilderness, wherever you are, I imagine it grows lonely."

Lucien frowned, choosing his words with care so as not to offend his friend. "Jabez, I must be honest with you. After my wife's death, I was too stunned to think of marrying again. Indeed, if it were not that her child died with her, I should be quite content to bring up a son to continue my name and to accomplish those things upon the land which I myself may not be able to do. But, as I told you, this bondservant remains as hostage at Red Ground. Actually, she had been condemned to death because they believed she knew of the plot to kill the chief. I saved her by Creek law—and that was marrying her at once and bedding her that same night so as to get her with child. They believe that if, by the blood ties which bind me to their village, she conceives and has shown no treachery, it will be proof of her innocence. So you see, Jabez, I have a wife—though she cannot, nor will ever be what my Dimarte was to me."

Jabez Corrigan bent his head, soberly nodding, then patted Lucien's shoulder. "You'd be a man like that to a woman you loved, I could tell that from the first day I met you, Lucien. Damn it all, you're making it difficult for me. Just as you did back in New Orleans when I tried my best to ease your sorrows over that poor boy's death by sharing with me the temptations which Madame Rambouillet had to offer a man of vigor and spirit."

"What are you getting at in your whimsical Irish way?" Lucien gave him a wan smile.

"Just this. The day before we were to pull anchor from Port-au-Prince, a young woman came to me, her clothes torn and stained with the blood of her husband. She was hysterical and exhausted. She'd hidden away from the blacks who'd killed her husband and then made her way around the edge of the town to the port, without food or sleep all that night. She hadn't so much as a *sou* and no jewels—they'd been left back in the fine house she and her husband had been living in. She went down on her knees to beg me to take her away from that hell, because she'd seen what the blacks had done to some of the wives of the plantation owners who'd tortured and whipped and executed them so brutally. And so, Lucien, when she told me her name, I knew I had to save her. So I offered her that bargain and she accepted. And now, my good friend, I'm going to give you the indenture papers after I've transferred her ownership to you. I don't much care whether you reimburse me or not, to be honest with you."

He reached into the pocket of his captain's coat and drew out a neatly folded document. Opening it, he handed it to Lucien, who glanced at it, first cursorily and then with a cry of utter stupefaction.

"*Dieu du ciel!* Madame Edmée de Bouchard—she is—she was—"

"Your brother's wife," Jabez Corrigan softly finished. "And now you see why I was so anxious to trace you once I arrived in Mobile, not knowing to what part of the territory you might have gone or, for that matter, whether you were still alive."

"What fee would you have charged her as a passenger from Port-au-Prince to Mobile, Jabez?" Lucien's voice was dry and impersonal.

"In view of the circumstances and because I'm not the sort of man to profit from another's misfortunes, about fifty *piastres*."

"Then, to make such a transfer perfectly proper and legal, Jabez, I insist that you allow me to give you fifty *piastres*. I will write you a draft on my account at Swanson and McGillivray, and they will honor it at once. I have done rather well in this time, and I think I can permit myself the extravagance of fifty *piastres* for the sake of what should be a rather interesting diversion."

"Well, I'll agree that's one way to look at it. I'm not one to meddle in a family affair, not I, Lucien. But you're right about repaying me if you legally wish to own this bondservant. So when we get aboard ship, you can sign that draft for me. I'll spend it on some good rum or wine for my men on the voyage back."

"She's in that cabin near the hold, Lucien. You've only to send away the *matelot* who's guarding her and you won't be disturbed. Now that I have the permission of the quarantine officer, we'll detour paying passengers off in the longboat and then see to our supplies. Perhaps you'll have dinner with me aboard ship tonight?"

"Perhaps. I'm in your debt once again, *mon ami*. I seem eternally to be in your debt. Perhaps one day I can settle our accounts." Lucien smiled at his friend, then turned down the narrow passageway leading toward the hold. At the door of a small cabin, a squat, bearded middle-aged seaman stood stiffly at attention, shouldering a musket. Lucien spoke to him in French, jabbing his thumb in the direction of Jabez Corrigan, and the sailor nodded and left his post.

In his right hand he held the indenture papers which Jabez Corrigan a few moments before had signed over to him, acknowledging the receipt of a draft for fifty *piastres*. Now Edmée de Courent, who had become Edmée de Bouchard, belonged to him as surely as Ellen and Ben had when Tunkamara had bestowed them as slaves. By the terms of that indenture, the girl he had once loved was his to sell again if he so wished, to bed or to whip or to brand or even to put to death—for the indenture was for life. By its terms, Edmée had agreed to the unflinching and despotic bondage of servile indenture, to accept submissively and to follow obediently the orders of any man who held these papers.

He took a deep breath, put his hand to the door and opened it.

It was a small, narrow, cheerless cabin, with only the rudest, narrowest of bunks for its occupant. There was no mirror for its occupant to see herself as she was, clad in a torn white linsey-woolsey dress to her slim ankles, without shoes and the feet of both once elegant hose worn through from walking, stumbling, running. The dress was torn at one shoulder, as was the strap of the once exquisitely embroidered chemise. At her waist, the dress was stained with dried blood. The dark-brown hair, which had once been so carefully coiffured with a fringe of curls high on her forehead and a thick chignon to her shoulders, was dirty, rumpled down one tearstained, pale cheek. Her small, ripe mouth was bruised, and there was an ugly blotch on her left cheekbone, darkening and purplish. At the sight of this man in doeskin, his angular face now as dark as an Indian's from the summers in the fields and on the river, his lips thinly compressed, and the short beard and the long, sun-baked black curls to his neck, she put the back of her hand to her mouth and, whimpering, pressed herself back against the wall of the cabin beside her bunk.

"Oh *non, pas ça! Pas un sauvage rouge!*" she tearfully gasped, her eyes enormous.

"I have the honor to bid you a good morning, *Madame*

283

la Comtesse de Bouchard," Lucien said drily, with a courtly bow.

"You—you speak French——" dazed, uncomprehendingly, she stared at him, not yet recognizing him in this lean man of the wilderness who had addressed her like a gallant of the court.

"That is hardly surprising, seeing that it was my native tongue, *Madame la Comtesse.*"

"That voice—your eyes—oh no—it's not possible— you—"

"I myself, *Madame la Comtesse.* The only difference now since our last meeting is that I have dropped the 'de' of my name, while you, on the contrary, have embellished it."

"Oh, *mon Dieu,* Lucien, Lucien—you don't know—you can't—oh it's frightful—those horrible *nègres,* they came to the plantation where Jean had been meeting with the owner. He'd come back to our house, not knowing that he was in danger—oh God, how could any of us have known or dreamed that those black brutes would rise up and destroy us all like animals? And then—oh Lucien, and then after they had killed the man and his wife and the overseer, one of them told the others where they could find Jean."

She had come to him suddenly, clutching him with her arms, sobbing hoarsely, staring up into his impassive face.

"And then?"

"Lucien, Lucien, don't you understand, haven't you heard a word I've been saying to you? It's Jean—your own brother—my husband—oh, God, as long as I live, I'll never forget the horror, the nightmare of it—"

"Calm yourself, *Madame la Comtesse.* I am aware that Jean was my brother. I wish to hear of him as explicitly as you can bring yourself to tell me."

"Oh, Lucien, what has changed you, what has happened to you? Yes—Jean—oh, God, I see it now as if it were just happening all over again! We were in the garden, and suddenly three of those horrible *nègres* came over the wall and they had the machetes they use in the canefields. Jean told me to run, but I was so frightened I couldn't move. Two of them grabbed him then, but he broke away from them, tried to go for his sword, which he'd unbuckled and laid on a little table. He—they cut him down before my eyes. I ran to him, as he fell against me, bleeding, horribly hurt—dying—" She burst into uncontrollable sobs.

He stood calmly, letting her cling to him, listening, without a word.

"Then—" at last she raised her tear-stained face to him —"there was the sound of a whistle, the patrol of the plantation soldiers was coming—one of those brutes had already begun to tear off my dress and to show me the horrid machete. He—he said what he was going to do— and then the whistles grew louder and nearer, and so the three of them ran away. But the man who'd torn my dress called to me that he'd come back for me at night. And so—and so I waited and the soldiers took poor Jean's body away, and then I hid in the house of a friend until it was nearly dark, and then I made my way to the wharf— oh, Lucien—hold me—comfort me—"

"I mourn for my brother, *Madame la Comtesse*. The irony of it all is now that I am the last of the Bouchards."

"But—but how can that be?" Again she stared at him uncomprehendingly, the tears running down her cheeks.

"*Père* Morlain didn't write your husband at Port-au-Prince?"

"No. We've had no news from the *seigneur* and his dear wife—"

"But I have. They died when the peasants invaded the province. And there was hatred in the village for what my brother had done to poor little Madelon. Yes, Edmée, on the very afternoon I rode to your father's house to ask for your hand in marriage, my more worldly brother was amusing himself with an innocent peasant girl. Doubtless, not content with his own great charm with the ladies, he might have intimated that as the future Count of Normandy, she would have to submit to him because of the ancient law. But at any rate, that unworthy act inflamed the village not only against my brother but against my certainly innocent parents."

"Oh, Lucien, poor dear Lucien, if only—I was a fool— but it was you I truly loved—yes, all the time when you rode over the hill and you brought me those beautiful po-ems, and even when I was a little girl I can remember how attentive and kind you were to me—it was you al-ways, Lucien. Didn't I tell you that because of the way things were, I had to marry Jean, and that after that you and I would be lovers?"

"Yes, I remember all of it, Edmée. But it seems that you have forgotten the answer I gave you when you made just that suggestion on that very eventful afternoon. I told you that I respected your honor as much as I did mine and that I would not be party to such an arrangement."

"Yes, yes, but we were talking like two people out of one of Molière's plays, my darling Lucien!" she tearfully protested.

"But now, *Madame la Comtesse,* we meet in real life, and the realities are such as must be faced by both par-ties. Do you recall a certain indenture to which you agreed of your own free will with the captain of this vessel?"

"Yes—yes—I had no money, no jewels—but I thought —he was a kind, understanding man, this *M'sieu Capitaine* Corrigan—that when we reached Mobile or New Orleans, I could find some important official who would see to my affairs. They would send back a letter to my father, who would arrange for money to be sent to me or for my re-turn to Yves-sur-lac."

"I am sorry that I can give you no news of your parents, *Madame la Comtesse*. But the captain to whom you sold yourself has sold you in turn to me."

Her eyes widened, and then she laughed softly, hugging him, putting her bruised mouth against his, her eyes sud-denly enticing and cajoling. "Why then, my dearest dar-ling Lucien, I'm safe at last. You'll look after me, won't you? And now, now that I'm a widow, there's nothing to stop our marriage, is there? Oh, Lucien, don't you see?"

"All I see is an indentured bondservant who has the ar-rogant presumption to think that her new master would demean himself so far as to marry her," was Lucien Bouchard's glacial reply. "Shall I read you the terms of this indenture, paragraph by paragraph? I assure you its stipulations will be upheld in any British, French or Spanish court of law. And since Captain Corrigan himself speaks with the authority of the new French government, he will certainly confirm all this to you if you wish to ask."

"What—what are you trying to say to me? Lucien, Lucien, I'm your Edmée, I'm yours now, and I'm older and I've learned so much—and I can make you happy—oh, darling, let me try—we've all lost so much, you, your parents and your brother, I my husband—oh, Lucien, let's begin life again here where there's no war, no horror!"

"I am already married, Edmée. And now, my indentured bondservant, here is your first order. I wish you to strip naked before me."

She recoiled with a cry of mingled shame and consternation, a hand at her mouth: "Lucien—by the love I bore for you—"

"A love that constrained you to prefer being a countess even though it must have been evident to you from the very outset how gallantly faithful to you my brother would be. A love so chameleon-like that, after having shed tears enough for one of Corneille's heroines in relating your husband's death, you are able to look at me with soft sweet eyes and to intimate that I will find you more interesting as a widow than ever I did as a gentle virgin whom I idolized to my folly!" Now his voice again became cold and incisive: "Doubtless your husband must have told you—or perhaps you even were privileged to witness such things yourself—how a mutinous and disobedient slave is punished. It is customary to apply the lash to a recalcitrant slave. Incidentally, my wife was herself an English bondservant. When I first looked upon her body, I saw the marks of a hickory switch from neck to heels. And then, if that method is not sufficient to bring reason and submissiveness to the slave, there are other—"

"Oh, stop, stop, in the name of God in heaven—how can you talk to me this way? Doesn't my suffering, doesn't all my love for you mean anything now, now that we could be together again and be our true selves, dear Lucien?"

"But I see you now as your true self, in a way I never saw you before, Edmée. Now, I shall repeat my order a last time. If you don't obey it, I shall call the *matelot* from the passageway to bring me a stout switch or perhaps a thick leather strap or a rope's end."

"Oh, God—is this your love? I—I swear—"

"I paid fifty *piastres* to Captain Corrigan for your indenture, Edmée. With some shrewd trading, I can buy three pack ponies for that amount, and they are far more useful to me than a pampered girl who was moonstruck by a title and now blithely wishes to go back to the happy times when I was infatuated by her. *Ma foi*, I think I should have more respect for an honest *putaine*." Once again his voice hardened: "Do you intend to obey or must I call the *matelot*?"

Weeping bitterly, Edmée de Bouchard bowed her head and then slowly, with trembling hands, tugged off the tattered, bloodstained dress and let it fall to the floor of the cabin, standing in her torn chemise with its fine Alençon lace at the hems and bodice.

"The chemise, and quickly!" he curtly urged, his eyes brooding and narrowed.

Slowly she raised her head and looked at him. Her lips trembled and moved, but she could not speak. Then, with a sudden furious, hateful rage, she put both hands to the bodice of the chemise and ripped it, tearing and rending until the fragile sheath fluttered to the floor and left her naked in her bedraggled, torn hose.

Lucien caught his breath and clenched the papers in his hand at the sudden fiery lust that pervaded him. He had conjured her always as a creature of ethereal, unprofaned loveliness, and like a bedazzled schoolboy he had watched that expressive cameo which was her lovely face grow piquant and playful, gay and wonderingly feminine by turns. He had envisioned her as a kind of untouchable goddess, to be worshiped as the prototype of all that was cherishable in womanhood. But now that he saw her slim body, creamy-skinned and naked before him, the papers he clutched in his right hand flung her down from that pedestal and made her only slave-flesh in which to slake all his agonized memories. She was slim, with dainty feet and hands, her head reaching his shoulder. But there was a sensual impudence to the thrusting, high-perched rounds of her breasts tipped with carmine buds set in wide pale aureole; her slim waist set off the smooth goblet of her belly, with its wide, shallow birth-dimple, from which the eyes descended to that alluring, thick-fleeced triangle of femininity, framed by the long, gracefully rounded thighs and the sleek, sinuously high-set calves. He contemplated her, till with a groan of deepest shame Edmée pressed both palms over her sex as a sheltered virgin might.

He uttered a hoarse, nearly crazed laugh. "My bond-servant forgets that she is a widow, which is to give the lie to this touching gesture of maiden innocence. And even if you were still a virgin, Edmée, by the rights of this indenture your flesh is forfeit to mine when and as I choose. And I choose now to exercise my rights. Well, there's a certain irony in it, isn't there? Now that I'm the last of my line, the title of Count of Normandy is truly mine. Well then, why should I not imitate my older, more worldly brother, who always accused me of being a milksop? Get to that bunk and ready yourself to service your master, Edmée!"

Panting now, her face scarlet, she backed to the bunk and, without taking her eyes from him, eased herself onto it, her hands still protectively pressed against her most intimate flesh. As she saw him begin to remove his jacket, she attempted a last entreaty: "Oh, Lucien, my darling, not like this—please, Lucien—"

But her voice trailed into silence as she saw him methodically strip himself and come toward her. She twisted her face away and uttered a choking sob as she felt his hands upon her body, felt him knee apart her thighs.

The act of flesh to flesh which he wrought upon her purged him of his demons as it did of the misguided dreams by which he had idolized this inconstant, weak-willed woman.

And in his mad possessing of Edmée de Bouchard like the bond slave she had herself agreed to become, Lucien pledged himself all the more devotedly to the evergreen spirit of his late beautiful young Creek bride, Dimarte. For now at last he had been able to weigh both women he had loved, though each in a different way, and had found his first love wanting in the balance scale of trust and constancy. Nor, in another sense, was he unfaithful to the marital vows contracted with that other bondservant who remained as hostage in the village of Econchate: she had long since paid her penance and more than atoned for sins she had never really committed.

As they concluded dinner that evening in the officers' mess of the *Guerrière,* Lucien asked Jabez Corrigan for quill and ink and paper. After they had been brought to him, he quickly wrote out an instruction to the trading firm of Swanson and McGillivray, whose costs were to be debited against his by now sizeable account. Then, passing the sheet across the table to his red-haired friend, he said, "When you go ashore tomorrow, Jabez, go to the trading post with this. Paro will give you a hundred *piastres,* which I wish you to give to the woman in the cabin by the hold. I have learned that she has some small talent as a seamstress. Paro will know of some Spanish or French family in Mobile who can put that talent to use and give her the chance to earn her own livelihood. Finally, I should be grateful if you would give her these."

He took out the indenture papers, tore them neatly into several pieces and tossed the scraps before his amazed friend.

"With this, Jabez," he said softly, "all of us have settled our accounts with the former bondservant you were good enough to take on at Port-au-Prince."

CHAPTER TWENTY-TWO

Lucien and Ben returned some ten days later to Econchate, leading six pack ponies laden with bundles of salt and other supplies needed for the village. Lucien had promised his good friend Jabez Corrigan to keep in constant communication over the months ahead by leaving letters at the trading post in Mobile which would be held for the red-headed Irishman till he again dropped anchor in the great Bay. And the newly promoted captain of the *Guerrière* promised Lucien that as soon as he had returned to Le Havre, he would send back a letter by the next vessel bound for either Mobile or New Orleans to acquaint the young Frenchman with the latest developments in that ominously spreading revolution that now seemed to threaten not only the monarchical regime, but also the entire nation, and to leave France at the far from tender mercies of all her vigilant and ancient enemies.

Each time he took this winding trail which followed the Alabama River, Lucien saw in retrospect that first unforgettable journey, landmark by landmark, from the place where the water moccasin had dropped from a tree branch to frighten his pony, the ravine with the bear cub, the grassy knoll and the tree where he had rested from his wounds and where Ecanataba had found him. And this time, more than ever before, he hungrily looked his fill of these places because now all of them were fraught with the vivid memory of the gentle black-haired daughter of the dead *Mico*. Each one of them was a guidepost back into that short but gloriously blissful span fate had allowed him and Dimarte to change from strangers, each alien to the other, into trusting lovers for whom nothing mattered but their own content in each other. It was like reading a book that he loved, a book forever new and yet tragically directed to the inescapable conclusion. The bear that had clawed him and left scars he would carry for life had forced him to heroic survival; its claws had identified him to the hostile Creeks as a man of valor whose deeds they could respect even if they feared and hated the race he represented. The warrior he had had to kill or become a despised slave to squaws and an object of derision in the Indian village. And all of these had led to the little house of the honored guest of Econchate, and it was there that dark-eyed, supple young Dimarte had nursed him back to health, there he had mated with her in wordless joy and wonder and conceived their child.

And once again, as each time before, when he had made this return journey from the trading post to the village which had become a second haven to him, he asked himself again and again if somewhere along this route, somehow through the course of his words or deeds, he could not have altered that shattering conclusion to the story of the first perfect love he had ever experienced. A love still so agonizingly poignant in his mind that somehow he knew there would never be any other woman in all this world, even with the years still accorded him, who could take Dimarte's place in the deepest sanctuaries of his mind and heart.

Now he rode back to his second wife, to whom he had pledged nothing except a protection that had saved her life. She had been the innocent victim of evil forces beyond her own reckoning, and so innocent of Tunkamara's death—even though as yet the Creeks would not quickly forgive her part in it. He knew he would never force himself upon her, because, though she would surely submit, it could only be out of gratitude for his having saved her from the stone tomahawk of Tantumito.

And when he came again to the entrance of the village, he and Ben dismounting and leading the pack ponies toward the large storehouse where the supplies would be kept, he felt tears sting his eyes as he looked round at all those dwellings of the chief and the elders and, most of all, at that little house where Dimarte had stood waiting, her face demure and her eyes inscrutable, while Nanakota had spoken in his stead to ask the blessing of the *Mico* upon their marriage. Yet by the trick of fantasy and the yearning that he had for her, for just an instant it seemed to him that her sweet face was there, appearing behind the warriors and their wives, who emerged now to bid him welcome. Then again it disappeared and the past with it, and now Nanakota had emerged, a broad smile on his pleasant, homely face, to extend his hands in greeting and to welcome his blood brother back to Econchate.

"Ho, this is good, there is much salt now for the game our warriors will bring back from the great hunt. Thirty of them have left already, and this winter and this next spring will not find our bellies empty. It is good, the Great Spirit smiles upon us. And you are his chosen helper and friend to us, Lu-shee-ahn. This I thought when first you and I hunted the deer together. Come in, come in, and your companion with you. We shall eat, we shall talk, we shall smoke the pipe."

After the lavish feast prepared by the dead *Mico*'s two wives, Lucien related what he had learned from Paro of Alexander McGillivray's return to New Orleans and the expected counteraction which the Creek leader would surely take against the traitorous Bowles. Also, he told Nanakota about the *émigrés*, who were not only leaving France but also Santo Domingo. "These white settlers, my brother, are no threat to Red Ground. They will assuredly remain among their own people in either Maubila or New Orleans."

"If they are like you, Lu-shee-ahn, there will always be peace. I fear only the greedy white-eyes from the Oconee. But we shall be ready for them. Now, let us talk of more pleasant things. The squaw is well and is cared for by your companion's wife. She has shown herself grateful and useful as well, and helps many of the old women with the tasks. She has asked the squaw of your friend to teach her our language, and that is very good. If this continues,

293

when her time has come, she will be given her freedom to join you in your lodge, my brother."

"I am gateful for your kindness. But tell me, Nanakota, why have you never taken one of these lovely maidens to your own lodge? Now that you are *Mico,* there is not a girl in this village who would not willingly build your fire and bring you food."

Nanakota looked embarrassed, then scowled. Quickly Lucien added, "Will my brother forgive my meddling words? It is only that I feel such friendship for you, Nanakota, that I ask as I did."

"You have not offended me, Lu-shee-ahn. But you have made me remember why it is that no squaw shares my blanket. Do you remember, Lu-shee-ahn, many moons ago when you watched the punishment of the squaw who had been unfaithful?"

"I do."

"I have not spoken of this to any other warrior or elder, but to you, my brother, I make it known that you may understand me the better. That squaw was Emarta, and before you came to Econchate I had cast the pebbles toward her and she had not tossed them back. I had thought she would accept me, and so I made gifts to her father and mother and praised them before the council. And then, even after the maiden and I had spoken together and I had told her what was in my heart, she chose the warrior whom you saw chastise her for her sinfulness. Aiyee, you see her now despised and looked upon as lowlier than any slave; she toils in the village only that she may be fed and not die, and no man may call her to his blanket. Each time my eyes fall upon her at the end of the village where the dogs and the children and the old women gather, I see what might have been mine to do to her before all to witness. It would have given me great sorrow had I been husband to Emarta. So for me there is the ghost of happiness that never was and might never have been. My heart is sad because of it."

Lucien nodded slowly. "I too am faithful to a ghost, my brother," he murmured. "And she is dearer to me now because I have banished still another ghost about whom once I dreamed as you with your Emarta."

By the end of this eventful year, the power of Alexander McGillivray indeed seemed restored, for the young freebooter William Augustus Bowles was captured, brought to New Orleans in chains and thence sent to Madrid to be incarcerated in a Spanish prison. Le Clerc Milfort, denouncing Bowles as a scoundrel, vehemently urged the Creek leader to hang his enemy out of hand. "To let such a viper continue to draw breath even in a dungeon is to risk the chance that one day again he may be free to strike at you," he had argued. Bowles had swaggeringly boasted of his piratical escapades; to avoid pursuit by Milfort's soldiers, he had hidden in a hogshead on Pensacola Bay and lived there for several days and nights until the pursuing band had left the area. But his life was spared despite Milfort's demands for his execution, and once more the Scotch-Creek leader of this vast territory coveted by three ambitious nations was restored to power.

Amelia was with child, as she blushingly admitted to Lucien when he visited her after another trip to Mobile, which brought him back to Econchate by the end of November. And, though he could feel no abiding love for her, only an innate sense of responsibility for her well-being since he himself had pledged his entire future upon her innocence, he took her hand and brought it to his lips. "I respect and honor you, Amelia," he told her. "When the child is born, if you wish it, you may return with me to the house where first I found you. By that time, Ben and I will build another room to it so that you and the baby may have more comfort."

"I should like that very much, Mr. Bouchard," she had almost timidly replied, averting her eyes from his. "They've been very kind to me here, and Ellen's helping me learn to speak their language, you know. Just the same, it's not like living with people of your own kind. And you've been so good to me, Mr. Bouchard, I want to keep my part of the bargain and be a wife to you."

"We shall talk of that another time, Amelia. I told you that I should never force myself upon you, and I meant exactly that. I knew then as I know now that you had nothing to do with the plot to kill Tunkamara. But now that you are bearing my child, it is my duty to care for you and to make you as happy as I can, so that the child will have every chance for a good, useful life."

Then she looked up at him, studying his strong, resolute features as if she were seeing them for the first time. "You want the child very much, don't you, Mr. Bouchard? I know why, and even though I shouldn't say such a thing, I'm glad I'm carrying it for you. Maybe it'll take the place of that other one, and I'll pray that if it's a son, he'll grow up to give his father pleasure in him."

He had been so deeply moved by her unexpectedly sensitive words that he could not speak; he had permitted himself only a nod of acknowledgment, but then he had again taken her hand and brought it to his lips and kissed it as he might have kissed the hand of the queen of France herself.

As the new year of 1792 began, Lucien and Ben cheerfully busied themselves cutting down trees, splitting logs in half with the flat side upward, laying them side by side to make a puncheon floor and filling the chinks between with clay. A passageway was made between the end of Lucien's cabin and the additional little room, with a window shuttered with crude boards, and hand-split shingles for the roof. And Lucien added another room to Ben's smaller cabin so that Ellen might have more comfort in looking after her own child.

In the spring, after Lucien had worked in the fields of Econchate helping the villagers plant the new corn crop which would feed them through the fall and winter, he made another journey to Mobile and there met Francisco Luis Hector Baron de Carondelet, whom the Spanish government had appointed as governor of Louisiana and West Florida, a suave and well educated man of forty-three who had been born in Flanders. It was the genial Captain Manuel de Lanzos who introduced him to the new governor-general and who smilingly added, "Though I am desolate to leave Mobile where I have made friends like you, *Señor* Bouchard, I shall settle down to the life of a gentleman in New Orleans where I urge you to visit me." And then he added, having taken Lucien aside, "You have done well to make yourself a blood brother to the Creeks. Governor Carondelet intends to expel the

American inhabitants from the Creek Nation. This he will do by forcing them to take the oath of allegiance to Spain and to fight for the King from the headwaters of the Alabama to the sea."

"I myself have no objections to taking such an oath, *Capitaño* de Lanzos, since I am an established trader for the Creeks and know them to be under the Spanish protectorate. But those Americans who are now trading, and especially those along the Oconee, will find it a great hardship. They may even be prepared to resist by force."

"Let us hope not, for their own sakes. The Creeks are formidable foes to their enemies, and if Baron Carondelet declares these settlers as such because of their refusal to take the oath, they will be driven out of all Creek lands. But do not disturb yourself, *Señor* Bouchard. Even though there may be new trade regulations set by my replacement, the main object of the Spanish government is to maintain the best of relationships with our Indian allies."

Although they had thus parted on a cordial note, Lucien could not take comfort from de Lanzos' words. The Georgians were sure to refuse such an oath; it was as much as admitting that the Creeks were their superiors. There had already been far too many bloody forays between whites and Indians in this disputed territory, and although none of the hostilities had reached the village of Econchate, there was always that danger. It was not impossible for white settlers, driven out of Georgia, to seek refuge on the lands along the Alabama River—just as the Wealthams had falsely claimed they had been forced to. And if they were aggressive and greedy and used their weapons to repel any braves who came to learn who these new white neighbors were, then there indeed would be a far more terrible reason to call this village Red Ground than for the red clay from which it took its name.

By the last week of June, Amelia had delivered her child: a healthy boy, with wisps of hair the color of her own, and in a relatively easy labor that, with Ellen's help, had lasted only a few hours out beside the cornfields. Lucien gave Ellen the baby to wash in the river, just as Dimarte had done with little Edmond, and then he knelt down beside the bondservant who had become his wife and the mother of his child, and said tenderly, "It's a son, Amelia, and with your permission I'd like to name him Étienne after my own dead father."

Her face was still wan and wet from the agony-sweat of labor, but she forced a wry smile to her lips and huskily murmured, "But you don't need my permission, Mr. Bouchard. It's a lovely name, and I'm proud and honored that you'd name it after your own father. It makes me feel good, that maybe I'm not the low murderess the Wealthams used to call me."

"You never were. You defended your brother because it was unjust of them to take him, sick as he was. The laws of a land are not always just, especially to the unrespected poor, Amelia. That may be one of the many reasons I came to this new country, in the hope that when it is finally settled and the laws are made, those who make them will realize the need for equality and decency and integrity among all men. That's the only way to make sure that peace will bless the lands we walk upon."

He bent to kiss her forehead, a kiss of thanks and of admiration for her valor in leading this lonely yet constantly supervised life among the first people who had come upon this rich land and now held it against the growing hordes of whites who would come in the name of Christianity or commerce to take it from them. "You haven't quite learned all the Creek customs, my dear wife," he told her. "The mother is the one who decides the future of a child, who is responsible for him, not the father. This is why the father must always consult with the mother and grant her wishes."

"That's a mighty nice custom, Mr. Bouchard. Makes a girl feel right important. Do you think they'll let me go back with you now?"

"I'm sure of it, Amelia. I'll talk to Nanakota at once. In a few days, after you've rested, we'll go back together."

She groped for his hand with hers and squeezed it, giving him a grateful look from her wide green eyes. "That will be nice. A home of my own. Lord, I wanted one so bad back in London. Thank you, Mr. Bouchard."

"I'll try my best to make you happy, Amelia, that's a promise."

"You don't have to promise anything, Mr. Bouchard. I'm happy enough the way it is right now. I just didn't want you to think badly of me. And—and you know something else? I'm glad it was you who gave me my baby. Mighty glad."

"Well now, I want you to rest, and Ellen will see to all your needs, Amelia." Once again she had moved him deeply with a kind of sweet humility he had found only in Dimarte. Kissing her forehead again, he took his leave of her and went to the dwelling of the *Mico*. Nanakota at once agreed that there was no further reason to consider Amelia a hostage; whenever Lucien liked, he might return to his own little house and continue as before in the service of Econchate.

On his last journey to Mobile, just before the birth of his son Étienne, Lucien learned that King Louis XVI had tried to join the noblemen who had fled France, but had been arrested at Varennes and brought back to Paris. There he had been forced to accept the new constitution. And in the Legislative Assembly of this new government, the fiercely republican Girondists and the extreme Jacobins and Cordeliers gained the upper hand. And finally, there were new watchwords for the revolution: "liberty, equality, fraternity." And were these not the very three words, Lucien reflected to himself, which had been part of his own credo ever since his adolescence? Now he saw them bandied about in a terrible travesty, with death for the aristocrats as the penalty for all who would not subscribe to the new order.

During all this summer and early fall, Alexander McGillivray secretly caused war councils to be held throughout the Creek and Cherokee nations, but at which he appeared only in the role of interested visitor. Meanwhile William Panton, his partner and benefactor, as well as a certain Captain Don Pedro Oliver (a Frenchman who wore the Spanish military uniform and who was now stationed at the Hickory Ground upon the Coosa with a salary of $100 a month), made speeches at these council meetings and forbade the crossing of the line between them and the Georgians in the name of the king of Spain. No American trader should enter the nation, was the decision of the chiefs. To abet this decision by force, Baron Carondelet sent to the Creek Nation a large number of war-eager Shawnees, fully armed and equipped, who took up headquarters at Souvanoga on the Tallapoosa River.

McGillivray, who owned some sixty blacks by this time, moved these to Little River, gave up his house to Captain Oliver, whom he had introduced throughout the Creek Nation, and spent a good deal of time in New Orleans and Pensacola.

American agents on the Oconee were greatly alarmed by these actions, for it appeared that the Creek leader, despite being named a brigadier general of the American Army, was secretly acting against those whose honors and wages he had so eagerly accepted. Because by now it was known that through the petition of Baron Carondelet to the Spanish king (which argued against respecting the treaty of New York and which was further supplemented by Panton's protest against such granted rights), Alexander McGillivray had been named Superintendent-General of the Creek Nation at a salary of $3500 a year. Yet at the same time ostensibly he was the agent of the United States, while remaining the co-partner of William Panton as well as being virtual emperor of the Creek and Seminole nations.

News came to Econchate of Indian raids upon the settlers in the Cumberland and Georgia frontier territories. And, even more lawless than the most bloodthirsty savage who preyed upon the settlers, was an outlaw known as "Savaner Jack" who lived at Souvanoga and whose boast was that he had killed so many women and children on the Cumberland and Georgia frontiers that he could swim in their blood if it was collected in one pool!

Nanakota and the elders held councils, and they asked Lucien to attend them so that he might share his knowledge with them. "It would be well," he urged, "to send only a small number of warriors out upon the hunt this fall and winter, keeping the rest here to guard our village. As yet we have no reason to quarrel with any white settlers, since none has invaded Econchate. I cannot speak for what is in Colonel McGillivray's mind and I would not dare to do so, but I do not think that a man who loves the people of the Creek Nation as he has shown he does for so long would lead them blindly into full-scale war against all the white-eyes. It would be a war that would destroy, not strengthen, your valiant people in every territory from here through Florida."

On both sides of the Atlantic Ocean, momentous events were shaping the destinies of men, those not yet born as well as those who, far from those events, were doomed to be involved by them. On the first day of June of this year, the new United States added its fifteenth member, Kentucky, which entered as a slave state. And from a courier in Mobile, Lucien received the news that a statement issued at the castle of Pillnitz in Saxony the year before by Emperor Leopold II and Fredrick William of Prussia, which had demanded that all European powers restore Louis XVI to his full authority as king of France, had been used by the French revolutionists as a pretext for declaring war on Austria this past April. At last the hopes of the Girondists had been realized: through their machinations, they expected that a foreign war would rally all France to the republican cause and thus end the monarchy for all time.

As he worked his cornfields during this last week of September, side by side with Ben and Ellen, Lucien was often beset by gloomy thoughts. When a cooler evening breeze stirred over the fields, he shivered as if someone were walking over his grave, and he would turn to look up at the towering red bluff, where Dimarte and little Edmond were buried. He thought of that strange cold wind from the channel that May afternoon over three years ago, the wind which the old herdsmen had thought so strange for that time of year. Had that been a kind of harbinger which predicted all these quirks of fate, these unpredictable violences and now, finally, what seemed to be the imminent destruction of the land which had given him birth? Had it really been some unknown force beyond his own clear-headed reasoning which had spurred his sudden leavetaking of Yves-sur-lac, a force that went

301

beyond the inconstancy of Edmée and his shock at the poacher's useless death? What was there in his spirit so intangible that he could not name it but only vaguely sense it, which had led him along this tortuous path from peaceful Normandy to this bend in the Alabama River and already to two marriages, when the very first of those appeared to have granted him an undying love? Once again he thought of Hamlet, who had been the kind of *deus ex machina* through whose participation everything had fallen into chaotic order—and yet not at all the order that Hamlet himself would have wished. Had he then himself, he who had felt that freedom must be his at any cost, been marked by unknown and inexplicable powers to be uprooted and set down here and from that demarcation point denied the right to his own fruitful life?

They were questions which baffled him, yet at the same time stiffened his resolve to find the answers. Against those unknown, perhaps even malignant powers, he could set only his vigor and the newly acquired skill of living with an alien people, and finally his self-made promise that one day on this new land the chateau of Yves-sur-lac would rise again and that continued, purposeful life would flourish within it.

Amelia had seemed to blossom with the birth of the baby, easily and joyously nursing it. She kept it in the little cradle, rocking it and cooing to it and playing with its fingers, rapt in her pleasure in seeing it attentive to and needful of her. Lucien's respect for her grew daily, for the eagerness with which she cared for little Étienne revealed the generous warmth of her nature. He could realize that it was not only out of gratitude at being freed from her bondage as the slavey and intended bed-wench of the Wealtham sons which made her so diligently devoted to the child: it was the yearning of a decent girl who had been born to the London slums and who had been a waif given little affection through her formative years.

Yet, out of a strict sense of probity, Lucien had not again claimed his marital rights since that dramatic day in the village of Econchate. Before flinging himself down on his blankets, he would apologetically enter the additional room of the little cabin to say goodnight to Étienne and then to wish Amelia goodnight.

The second week of October was crisp and clear and augured good hunting for the warriors who had set out from the village. On this Wednesday afternoon, Ellen had looked after both little Thomas and Étienne while Amelia joined Lucien and Ben in the fields. He had brought back from Mobile on one of his last trips there a white muslin dress, simply made and fabricated in England, and given it to her as a present. Amelia's excitement over the gift and her insistence on wearing it in the fields had made him smile, so charmingly childlike had it been. And that again was another proof of her uncomplicated, genuine nature, as well as saddening evidence of how little affection she had known throughout her life.

The dress itself had been a matter of great interest to Lucien, remembering what Abram Mordecai had told him about the great potential of cotton as a profitable crop for this rich land. Elsewhere, in the Carolinas or perhaps even Georgia or again the West Indies, someone had grown cotton and processed it for shipment back to England, where a man by the name of Edmund Cartwright had invented a power loom which would fabricate material from the thread obtained from cotton so that garments might be made. Indeed, this was well worth thinking about for the future. Just as the corn plant produced food, so might the cotton plant produce the source of clothing, be exported to the European countries after these revolutionary wars had finally ended and bring great wealth and power to the settlers on this land who would raise the plant. Yes, Mordecai's words would not be forgotten, though now was certainly not the time to act upon them.

At supper, with Amelia at the little table opposite him, bending to the cradle every now and then to see to Étienne, he found himself singularly disarmed by his young wife's alacrity in serving him and even more, in the exchange of conversation between them. Tonight, she seemed to have lost the shy humility with which she had treated him all this time, relating stories of her experiences in London, the sights she had seen, her efforts to find paying work in little shops and the frugality which she had learned to live by in caring for her brother till that dreadful day when the soldiers of the press gang had come for him. He found himself telling her about Paris as he remembered it from the days at the University, the fine shops and the carriages of the nobility and the little wineshops where the students gathered at the end of the day to recite poetry and discuss politics and make eyes at the pretty girls passing by.

And at last, after he had excused himself to take a stroll outside and to sniff the night air and watch the full moon rise and look longingly over at that red bluff where his heart would always draw him, he went back to his bed of blankets and lay, arms pillowing his head, thinking of the strange destiny that had brought Amelia Duggins and himself to this cabin on the Alabama River far from all the bustling life of the great cities of London and Paris.

He had almost fallen asleep when he heard soft footsteps, and propped himself up, blinking his eyes against the cobwebs of drowsiness, he asked anxiously, "Is Étienne well?"

"Oh yes," her soft husky whisper floated to him as she moved beside him. "He's just fine, Mr. Bouchard. I—I didn't mean to waken you—truly I didn't—"

"It's quite all right, Amelia, I hadn't fallen asleep yet. I was thinking about all we talked about."

"So—so was I, Mr. Bouchard. I—I felt so good there at the table when you acted like I really was your wife and one of your own kind."

"You mustn't say a thing like that, Amelia. You're a brave girl and a kind one, and you've given me a son. A man couldn't ask for more than that."

"I—I was kind of hoping you'd say that, but you're so good and kind you'd do it anyway even if it wasn't true, Mr. Bouchard."

"Now you're making me out to sound like some sort of saint, and I assure you I'm not," he chuckled.

"Well then—" he heard her draw an uneven breath— "you're going to think me awfully shameless and maybe even a slut—and for all I know, I am—"

"No, Amelia, I've never thought that of you, never."

"Well then, please—I mean—I'm well now, and I'm your wife, and it's not right for a strong healthy man like you not to have his woman nights."

"Amelia—" he was glad there was darkness so that she could not see the sudden crimson which flooded his cheeks and the almost boyish embarrassment which took hold of him.

"That time in the village," she went on, faltering for her words, which grew huskier and softer still, "it wasn't as if it was done proper. Oh, I mean, we were married by the way they did it, I've no doubt, but it was just that once and you had to do it to stop their killing me, you said. But—well—Mr. Bouchard, I—I'm awfully fond of you and it's not just because I'm beholden—I mean—I want you to be my husband the way married folks truly are —there, I've gone and said it, though I didn't mean to make you angry, Mr. Bouchard!"

"Amelia, my dear, kind girl, of course you didn't make me angry. But you mustn't feel something that doesn't exist—you surely can't love me." He forced himself to adopt a self-mocking tone: "I've not been much of a husband to you, what with all my going off to Mobile time and again and working at the village. You haven't had time to see my bad side, and I really think you're overestimating my good."

He heard the rustle of her dress and then he suddenly felt her kneel down beside him and turn to him, and as he put his hand out, he touched her naked breast. "Amelia—" he began.

"If I was a six-penny whore, Mr. Bouchard, I'd still be in love with you. And I don't care whether you'll ever love me or not, but at least you can use me for your needs. I wouldn't feel right if you didn't, being your wife and all, having you work so hard all the time and bringing me that lovely dress and having Ben and Ellen treat me like quality. Please—just don't talk or even think who or what I am, Mr. Bouchard, I want you—you've made me say it and it's true!"

And then, frankly, sweetly, fiercely, she put her hands to his lean, sun-darkened cheeks and kissed him fervently on the mouth.

305

"Amelia, sweet, very dear Amelia!" he groaned as he strained her close to him.

How strange, how sweet it was, this gift of love and how on another night like this another girl had come unbidden to his bed to make just such a generous gift. It was not lust of the flesh alone, not this urgent communion between one who so yearningly strove for love and the other who believed he had been granted but the smallest share of a true love that transcended time itself as it had the barriers of race and creed and country. And to Amelia's soft, muted sobs of joy, in the exquisite pride of her supple, warm, ripely curved young body, in the silken caress of her long auburn hair which tumbled over her face and heaving bosom, Lucien could not but respond. So completely and deliciously did she lead him to slake all his pentup longings upon her warm eager flesh that, long moments later, drawn from appeasement into dreamless sleep, he did not hear her rise, retrieve her dress, bend to him and whisper, "Oh, I love you so, Mr. Bouchard!" and then go swiftly back to bend over the cradle and make sure that Étienne was fast asleep.

As she served him breakfast the next morning, Amelia was demurely silent, but from time to time as their eyes met, her blushes spoke more eloquently than words the joyous contentment she knew in having been accepted as a consort rather than a devoted and attentive servant. She lowered her eyes and stammered a word of thanks when he smilingly complimented her on how well the dress suited her, and as she removed the bowls which had contained the food, she hesitated a moment to touch his shoulder with a mute, shy but expressive caress before she left the cabin.

A moment later, he heard her cooing to the baby and then laughing happily as little Étienne gurgled in her arms. Lucien rose and walked outside to the patch of garden behind the cabin, wanting a moment by himself to ponder this unexpected change in what had been, when all was said and done, a marriage of convenience entered into because he could not have let her die at the hands of the Creeks, even if she had been actually involved in the murder of Tunkamara. To find himself so loved imposed a responsibility upon him which deepened the ties of this hastily arranged marriage. Beyond all else was the consideration of the child she had given him, the child who bore his own dead father's name. For that alone, he owed her a debt of fidelity and trust and kindness. Although he mourned Dimarte deeply and always would, he knew, he now found himself greatly concerned over his altered feelings for Amelia. To rebuff her would be cruel, especially after the humble, trusting devotion she had shown him. She was comely, witty and amusing, yet she had shown unsuspected depths of feeling and strong-willed character in accepting the rigorous, vigorously supervised life she had been forced to live in Econchate. No one could bring him again that first exquisite rapture which the gentle Creek girl had awakened in his heart, so tormented by the fickleness of Edmée de Courent. A stray dog that might come to him seeking a caress out of its loneliness and fear could become a devoted companion if welcomed; Amelia was that and much, much more. And perhaps, if it was meant for him to achieve the fulfillment of his quest in this New World, Amelia might well be the instrument heaven-sent in exchange for Dimarte. He must look forward to the future and work toward it, or there could be none—and then all the sacrifices would have been for nothing.

Even as Lucien began to adjust himself to this settling down anew with a girl who, in her way, proffered a loyalty and devotion not unlike Dimarte's, the news which came from Mobile grew more and more ominous. Alexander McGillivray had made several visits to Baron Carondelet and had been stricken, on his return from New Orleans late this summer, by a violent fever which kept him for some weeks inactive in Mobile. After his recovery, he went to his home at the Little Tallase, where he wrote a strangely retrospective letter to Major James Seagrove, who had been appointed agent for the Creeks by the American government. In it he deplored the unhappy disturbances which had arisen, ascribing them to the interference of the Spanish. He avowed that he had often explained the New York treaty to the chiefs of the Creek

Nation and urged them to comply with it, but that Spanish influence had defeated his recommendations.

President George Washington had already sent two agents to Madrid to renegotiate with the Spanish Secretary of Foreign Affairs. But they returned to New York without any satisfactory agreement. The Spanish government might agree, they had been told, to allow the settling of a northern boundary of the West Florida territory. Also, permission was given to establish a warehouse at the mouth of the Yazoo River in which American citizens could deposit their goods from their own boats brought down the Mississippi. But these goods were then to be taken to New Orleans in Spanish ships, sold or exported but in all instances subject to high Spanish tariffs.

And throughout all these frustrating negotiations, the Georgia settlers condemned the American authorities for the weakness and irresolution and delay shown in conducting the negotiations. They vowed that if the United States much longer neglected to drive the Spaniards from their territory, they would do it by themselves. Border warfare between Indians and the frontier settlers increased from week to week. And with the serious illness of Alexander McGillivray, there appeared to be no one who could intervene to prevent a decimating struggle between red man and white.

It was a sunny morning in early November when Amelia, rising from the table to remove the bowls of their simple breakfast, unexpectedly murmured, "I—I think I'm going to be having another baby, Mr. Bouchard."

Lucien started and looked up, seeing his young wife's cheeks turn crimson as she moved to the door of the cabin.

"Why, that's wonderful, Amelia! And this time, I hope it's a girl just like you," he cheerfully responded. Rising, he went to her, took her by the shoulders and kissed her on the forehead. "But I didn't mean for you to have to go through that ordeal again, dear. I'm very happy with our little Étienne."

She turned to look at him, then, the color still high in her pale, creamy cheeks. "You're very good to me, Mr. Bouchard. But I want this baby almost a lot more than

308

Étienne. I guess maybe it's because you let me feel like your wife last month, your real wife. I know I can't ever take *her* place, and I hope I'm not making you angry by saying what I just did."

"Of course you're not, my dear one." He kissed her this time on the mouth, gently as in a benediction. "I'm learning to give thanks for you every day of my life now, Amelia. It's not lonely any more with just the memories I had left. And I'm very much honored that you care for me as you do. I want you to know that."

She blinked away the tears which had suddenly risen to her eyes, awkwardly nodded and made her way out of the cabin. Lucien stood looking after her, watching her go down to the river to dip the bowls into the gently flowing water and then, straightening, her long, thick, glossy auburn hair flowing like a banner in the cool November breeze, come back toward him. He remembered how Edmée de Courent had looked that May afternoon in her elegant frock and furred pelisse. If they were back in France now and Amelia were as decoratively adorned, he was sure that her beauty would far outshine that of the girl he had once thought he loved above all others, a veritable lifetime ago.

But that afternoon, to help him work at the vegetable patch, Amelia changed to the doeskin petticoat and jacket which Ellen had procured for her during her stay in the village. Wearing these and beaded moccasins, she disconcerted Lucien, who, from time to time, glanced quickly over at her, and once again felt his emotions well up in him as he thought of another girl, that one black-haired, who had worn the attire of the Creeks.

He had hurried down to the river bank to draw a bucket of water, telling himself that one day very soon he must sink a well near the cabin; when Amelia's child grew burdensome within her, it would save her many steps. He walked round the cabin and toward her, then began to water the hardy snap beans.

"Mr. Bouchard, someone's got a musket—oh, my God—no—it's the Wealtham boy, the one who was left—no, no, Nat—"

She had flung herself against him, her back against his,

309

her arms outstretched, facing the cornfields. Just as Lucien twisted, trying desperately to see the assailant, there was the report of a musket. He heard Amelia utter a strangled cry of pain, and then she slumped down along his body and lay on one side, stertorously breathing.

About forty yards away, he saw a stocky, brown-haired boy of about fifteen, in the act of reloading an old musket. With a hoarse shout of blind rage, Lucien ran like one possessed, and the boy, seeing himself cornered and unable to prime the musket in time, picked it up by the barrel and swung it like a club, shouting, "You goddamn Injun-lover you, killed Arnie 'n Paw 'n Maw!" Lucien lunged to one side, evading the savage swing of the musket at him, then caught the boy round the middle and wrestled him to the ground. Ben and Ellen had run out of their cabin and were bending over the sprawled body of the red-haired bondservant.

"Oh, Gawd have mercy, she's daid!" he heard Ellen cry.

It was Nat Wealtham, the younger of the two boys who had so tormented Amelia during her bondage. A sick, agonizing hatred burst within Lucien's brain. His thumbs dug into the stocky boy's throat as Nat threshed and, clawing with dirty, jagged fingernails, tried to ease the terrible strangling pressure.

The spasm of blind fury ebbed, but it was too late; the boy was dead. Lucien found himself looking down at the hideously contorted young face, the goggling eyes, the gaping, twisted mouth and decaying, snaggled teeth. He rose, sick and weak, shaken by a violent trembling. Then slowly, stumbling, his head bowed, drawing deep sobbing breaths, he made his way back to his dead wife.

That new tragedy was not the last for either Lucien Bouchard or the Creek Nation. On February 17, 1793, Alexander McGillivray died at the home of William Panton in Pensacola of inflamed lungs and advanced gout. Panton's letter to Lachlan McGillivray, who still lived in Dunmaglass, Scotland, paid final tribute to the great leader of the Creeks:

Your son, sir, was a man that I esteemed greatly. I found him deserted by the British without pay, without money, without friends and without property, saving a few Negroes, and he and his nation threatened with destruction by the Georgians, unless they agreed to cede them the better part of their country. I had the good fortune to point out a mode by which he could save them all, and it succeeded beyond expectation. . . . No pains, no attention, no cost was spared to save the life of my friend. But fate would have it otherwise, and he breathed his last in my arms. He died possessed of sixty Negroes, three hundred head of cattle, and a large stock of horses.

I advised, I supported, I pushed him on, to be the great man. Spaniards and Americans felt his weight, and this enabled him to haul me after him, so as to establish this house with more solid privileges, than, without him I should have attained. What I intended to do for the father I shall do for his children. My heart bleeds for them, and what I can I will do. The boy, Alec, is old enough to be sent to Scotland to school, which I intend to do next year, and then you will see him.

And thus Alexander McGillivray, who had been a colonel in the British Army, a brigadier general in the American, and the superintendent-general of the Creeks for the Spanish, was buried with Masonic honors in the splendid garden of William Panton in Pensacola. There, in that land where the Seminoles had attained greatness, he would remain forever.

And in that same week of February in the year 1793, little Thomas and Étienne were stricken with river fever. Thomas recovered, but within a week, Lucien Bouchard buried his second son as he had just buried his second wife, both on the little hill beside Pintilalla Creek.

CHAPTER TWENTY-THREE

In this month of March after the death of the great Creek leader, the elements themselves seemed to presage the gathering storm that was to rage over the lands occupied by the Creeks and so avidly coveted by rival nations. There had been heavy rain all the past week over the village of Econchate, and the Alabama River had flooded near that village and just beyond the bend where Lucien had his cabin and the storage depot on the levee. Terrible wind had felled trees and cabins, even plucked up cattle from the ground and dashed them to earth far distances away, and men had died on the river and as they hunted in the forest. These winds were seen by the superstitious Creeks as a manifestation of anger and sorrow by the Great Spirit who ruled their destinies.

But now the winds of violence and age-old hatred had been unleashed in France. The news had come from Mobile that last August a mob had stormed the palaces of the Tuilleries and massacred the Swiss guards; that all power had been seized by the Paris Commune dominated by firebrands like Danton and Marat; that the Assembly had suspended the king and ordered elections for a new body to be known as the National Convention; that hundreds of royalist prisoners had been killed by reckless mobs in the September massacres. The monarchy had been abolished and a First Republic of France proclaimed. Louis XVI was on trial for his very life on the charge of treason.

Across the ocean, the nation which Lucien Bouchard had left had gone mad, and reason no longer prevailed in any province. Yet here in this terrain which was his new world between Econchate and Mobile, Lucien felt himself as powerless as if he had remained in France to face the inflamed mobs who would instantly tear to pieces any man who dared denounce their actions or proclaim himself opposed to their new government of ruthless anarchy.

At least against an enraged mob, he would have a weapon in his hand to defend himself; here he had been powerless to avert the deaths of two young women who had loved him and borne him sons who now shared their mothers' eternal sleep, the one upon a hill, the other upon a bluff. The hill and the bluff which rose to frame the valley-like land the Creeks had given him and the first sight of which had appeared to be so happy an omen in that it was almost an exact counterpart of the haven against the wind of Yves-sur-lac.

He was now thirty, at an age when most men had their families and were bringing up their sons in those precepts of decency and honor and purposeful work which to him comprised the very purpose of life itself. The Bible might well speak of a man's expectancy of three-score years and ten of life: before this revolution in France, one would be lucky to achieve half so many as his span what with plagues and diseases for which physicians had not yet found cures and the wars that inevitably threatened every powerful European land. Here in this still uncharted country, he had already seen that one could expect little better; for if there was no famine, there were serpents and animals which could destroy human life without warning. All he could learn from this most recent tragedy was that he apparently was not fated to die, or else the musket ball which Nat Wealtham had fired would have hit its intended mark. Instead Amelia had heroically shielded him with her own body, and the knowledge of her sacrifice added to his troubled thoughts and heartsick anguish. Should he not have been more vigilantly on his guard after the boy's escape and urged Nanakota to have his warriors track down the vengeful young fugitive? What bitter irony it was to have saved Amelia's life against the judgment of the council and to have held back the ceremonial tomahawk of Tantumito only to bring her out of safety in the village to become the martyred buffer against his young would-be assassin!

He was haggard, once again he had smeared his face and beard with ashes, and he sat in the dwelling of Nanakota beside old Tsipoulata. The new *Mico* reached out his hands to touch the doeskin pouch in which the *Windigo* kept the prophetic bones, and murmured, "May Ibofanaga, he who sits above, look down through the winds he has sent upon us and the drenching rain and give us a sign to ease the heart of our beloved blood brother. Show him that he is not cursed, but rather that his grief, which has come so soon upon the heels of one still greater, is meant as a trial of his great courage. Let the bones be cast, o Tsipoulata!"

"Let it be so," the white-haired little man mumbled as he shook the pouch, raising his eyes to the ceiling of the house of the chief and cast the bones forth, as one might cast dice upon a gamester's table.

"What do you see, Tsipoulata?" Nanakota asked, his voice hushed with awe.

"That which I have already seen, and part of which has already come to pass," the white-haired *Windigo* replied as he looked up at Lucien.

"Yes, I remember," Lucien slowly said as if summoning back a nearly forgotten memory. "You said that the last should be the first, and of him the first should be the last upon the land, and that I would know it when the time was fulfilled."

"It is still true, oh blood brother of the Bear."

A shiver ran through Lucien's body as he stared at the wizened medicine man of the Creeks. "You spoke, too, Tsipoulata, of love and death, of hate and vengeance. Well, you spoke truly. My beloved Dimarte was taken from me by the Great Spirit, and that was love and death. And I have had my vengeance upon the one because of whom I left my home across the great waters to come here to seek my new life."

"It is all there, all of it, and that which is to come as

314

well, oh blood brother of the Bear," the old *Windigo* nodded.

"But we who are white-eyes and who worship the Great Spirit in our own way and by our own name for Him much as you do, Tsipoulata—" Lucien's voice trembled with urgency—"believe that a man may shape his own life and that these bones of fate can be altered."

The old man smiled sadly, turning to study Lucien's face, his gaze intent and compassionate. "To every man upon this earth, Hisagita-imisi has promised a love and a death, as a birth. How these first two come to pass, that perhaps each of us may decide and it will be so—yet within our striving to change things as we would have them, we do not escape the will of the Great Spirit. It is still love and death." He turned to look at Nanakota, whose friendly face was troubled as he watched Lucien stare fixedly at the bones upon the floor of the house. "For you, my *Mico,* I see death as a welcome gift, of a gift that was welcome."

"Then it will be a good death and I will find joy in it, Tsipoulata." Nanakota bowed his head in acquiescence.

"All men are fearful of what they do not know or understand, Tsipoulata," Lucien mused aloud, half to himself. "You and I differ not perhaps in the color of our skins, but in that I cannot yet accept that all my life is written for me and that I am powerless to change it."

"But the bones do not say that, oh blood brother of the Bear," the white-haired man gently corrected. "They tell only that which happens, not how it comes about or by what means you bring the will of Hisagita-imisi to pass. You have much before you and long years to know before your time is come. Have I not already said that what was said before has come to pass?"

"Yes," Lucien wonderingly murmured, "that of vengeance. And more—the last shall be the first—for now I am indeed the only one left of our clan, now that my parents and my brother are dead. And I was the younger son, the last my mother bore."

"As I have said, you will know the meaning of the bones when the time is fulfilled, and you yourself have just now seen what has already come to pass."

"But I have had two squaws and two children, and all these too have gone to the land of the Great Spirit. If I am to have long life and a meaning to my old age, am I then to have a son who will live to carry out my work, my hopes, my dreams?"

Tsipoulata pointed a bony finger at the bones which lay strewn in a curious pattern upon the floor. "How it all shall come to pass only the Great Spirit knows. But it is there, all clearly and without shadow, that of him who is now the first shall come the first who will be the last upon these lands."

"There is comfort in your words, Tsipoulata. They lighten the burden of sorrow which is heavy upon me. I hearken to the words of your Great Spirit, because I am His servant as I am the servant of you who gave me shelter and new life," Lucien Bouchard reverently declared.

Now again the planting season had come to the village of Econchate and to the fertile fields which Lucien and Ben tilled and readied for the new crops. But along the remote frontiers of the Georgia territory, roving bands of Creeks plundered the trading posts of Robert Seagrove, who had been appointed American superintendent to the Creek Nation by President Washington himself. They killed his clerk and two settlers stopping there for supplies, captured a young woman and beat and ravished her. A few miles away from the trading post, they killed several families trying desperately to escape in their wagons to a place of refuge, and took a woman and a young girl to be prisoners reserved for greater suffering.

Incensed by these attacks, Governor Edward Telfair, determining to raise an avenging army to invade Creek country, urged President Washington to send a large supply of arms and ammunition to Augusta. After much troubled deliberation, Washington authorized the fiery Georgia leader to enlist a local militia to protect his people, but protested the contemplated invasion. It was unauthorized by law, it would embarrass the negotiations still pending between the United States and the Creeks as well as those with Spain, and it could not be justified by the deaths of a comparative handful of settlers on the remote frontiers, particularly as the Creeks who had killed them had not acted with the approval of the Creek Nation itself.

But Governor Telfair ignored Washington's plea for moderation and, refusing to accept any troops which the President had authorized him to raise, enlisted 700 mounted men under General Twiggs, who had won an accolade for his bravery in the Revolutionary War.

This improvised army marched to the Ockmulgee River, and then, because of its lack of supplies and the spreading mutiny of those who had enlisted only for a month or two, gave up the pursuit of the enemy. In return, the Indians of that area struck back at isolated settler outposts. Reassembling a new army of newly enlisted militia, Governor Telfair ordered it to scour the country between the Oconee and Ockmulgee, and for a time the Indian attacks were halted.

Hearing of the Georgia leader's audacious flouting of his warning, President Washington sent couriers to demand that Governor Telfair cease these dangerous invasions. As a consequence, many of the Georgia landholders damned the first President of the new United States for his cowardice, pinned his effigy, drawn on shingles or oiled paper, to pine trees and used them for target practice as a mark of their contempt and hatred.

Once again, as he had had to do after Dimarte's death, Lucien absorbed himself entirely in his work as trader to the village of Econchate and, since he felt closest to the soil just as in the days of his youth in Normandy, worked on his own fields as well as those of Econchate. Once again he attended the ritual corn dance in July, the consecration of the seven kernels of corn which asked the Great Spirit to bless the harvest and all those who were fed by it. As a boy, he had been brought up in the Catholic faith, and yet during these formative years of his new life with the Creeks, he found nothing blasphemous in their straightforward devotions to their deity, who was akin to his own God, and to their veneration of the elements which were surely of His creation.

There would always be those like the Georgia settlers

317

who would hate the Creeks and brand them as wanton murderers, but that was not what he had found at Econchate. Perhaps mystically the understanding that a man instinctively is really to give his life for the land on which he is born imbued him with an understanding of what impelled his blood brothers to their ways. And the oath he had taken to protect this land of Econchate to which he had been admitted had a stronger hold upon him when he reflected on how he had abandoned the land of his own birth. His thoughts were desolate through these months, and the agonizing contrition of self-blame returned again and again to torture him. Now that he was truly the last of the Bouchard line, no one except himself would say that because he had left Yves-sur-lac, his father and mother had perished in defending their estate. Only he was left to brood óver that bitter knowledge. What the *Windigo* had told him of the future, it was true, pronounced no condemnation and no guilt upon his resolve to leave France; yet with pitiless self-flagellation he excoriated his very soul as these summer months wore on.

Now, each time Lucien visited Mobile on his trading errand for the villagers, the news from France became even more terrifying. Tried for treason by the Convention, Louis XVI had been sentenced to death and courageously met his fate by the guillotine on January 21st of this momentous year of 1793. There had been royalist uprisings in the Vendee and a lawyer from Arras, Maximilien Robespierre, had become head of the Jacobins and named into the Committee of Public Safety. He had already sententiously pronounced that his religion was based upon the theories of Jean-Jacques Rousseau. And he had already been given the sobriquet of "The Incorruptible" because of his fanatical devotion to virtue.

France was at war now with the world, it seemed, but if it had a fanatical zealot as its governmental leader, it had also a hitherto unknown military genius, a little Corsican named Napoleon Bonaparte, who had just recaptured the naval city of Toulon after the loyalists had surrendered it to the English. For this heroism, this short-statured man with the brooding eyes of an Alexander the Great had been named a brigadier general.

But what was happening in France was to have a direct effect upon this southeastern part of the new American republic. George Washington had, on March 4th of this year, begun his second term as President, with Thomas Jefferson as his Secretary of State, Alexander Hamilton as the Secretary of the Treasury and Henry Knox as Secretary of War. A month after that inauguration, news of the French declaration of war on Great Britain reached New York by British packet and, only a few days later, Edmond Charles Édouard Genet, the new French minister to the United States, arrived in Charleston and had his first audience with President Washington at Philadelphia on May 18th.

This ambitious minister, known as "Citizen Genet," was welcomed by the pro-French Jeffersonians. He began at once to try to raise troops against Spanish Florida and to commission privateers against British commerce, planning an overland expedition against the Spanish at New Orleans. President Washington at once demanded his recall.

The Spanish agent, Captain Don Pedro Oliver, who appeared to have replaced the late Alexander McGillivray, rallied the tribes of the Creek Nation. The new French minister, knowing that the Creeks had lost a leader to whom they had given complete allegiance, knew also of the anger of the Georgians, who claimed all the territory between the thirty-first and thirty-fifth degrees from the Savannah to the Mississippi and viewed the exclusive occupation of the Mississippi River by the Spaniards as a great outrage. It was his belief that it would be an easy matter to make the disaffected citizens of the United States, cut off from the rest of the new republic and forced to let their corn, flour and tobacco rot at their very doors because of the arbitrary Spanish trade laws, become eager allies of France and overthrow all Spanish rule to establish a government dependent upon the new French republic.

But there was a new governor in Georgia now, Edward Matthews, far more level-headed than his predecessor. After hearing from the Governor of East Florida that Genet had been able to enlist a considerable army of

Creeks and Cherokees in the cause of the French republic, Governor Matthews issued a proclamation forbidding the people of Georgia to engage in any such treasonable act. President Washington at once issued a proclamation by which he authorized Governor Matthews to employ all United States troops then in Georgia to put down the contemplated invasion.

It was now the spring of 1794, and Baron Carondelet had strengthened New Orleans, added troops to the fort at Mobile, and erected new ones at several points below the mouth of the Ohio River, completely organizing the militia throughout Louisiana and the Floridas. Ironically, he resorted to the same scheme which had been contemplated by his French enemy and sent an English emissary among the American citizens of the territories under his jurisdiction to offer them arms, ammunition, money and free navigation if they would rally to his banner and separate themselves from the United States. This plan was aborted by the firmness of President Washington and the loyalty of the states of Georgia and South Carolina, who approved measures for the arrest of Genet and Genet's agents. The Creek superintendent, Seagrove, visited Governor Matthews in April with a contingent of Creek chiefs, who expressed a desire for peace. Thus the plan of the French—of Lucien's own countrymen—to disrupt young America was vigorously quashed.

And again Lucien Bouchard found himself part of the ironic paradox by which, having begun a new life in a thriving new republic, his own material advantages had come as a result of trading between the Creeks and the Spanish, while unscrupulous agents from his own country that had been a monarchy and was now a republic sought to destroy the very republic to which he had come in his search for freedom. At the trading post of what had now become Swanson and Strothers, to which another famous Scotch trader, the twenty-five-year-old John Forbes had come to ally that firm with Florida's Panton and Leslie, Lucien Bouchard had now amassed an account which showed $45,000 to his credit. And that stake, which many times made up for the purse of *louis d'or* his mother had given him, was all in Spanish coin.

Overshadowed by these inexorably momentous events in France and on the boundaries of the Creek Nation were two inventions which would help bring about such a tremendous colonization of and prosperity to the territory and then the state which would be named after the Alabama River, as to change the simple, almost primitive life of Lucien Bouchard. Eli Whitney, a young lawyer then living in Savannah, had fabricated a cotton engine which at last solved the problem of eliminating the seeds and preparing the cotton for processing and fabrication. At Pawtucket, Rhode Island, the wife of Samuel Slater (who had just established a Sunday school to teach writing and arithmetic to the poor children who worked in his factory), had invented cotton sewing thread.

In September of this turbulent year of 1794, Indian marauding parties along the northern frontiers of Tennessee were routed by a Major James Ore, who advanced from Nashville with 550 mountain infantry, bringing back many prisoners and a large quantity of goods and supplies which the Indians had taken from their white settler victims. In that victorious expedition, one of Major Ore's privates was a lanky, tobacco-chewing private by the name of Andrew Jackson.

Lucien Bouchard was entering upon his fifth year as a trader and farmer for the Creeks of Econchate. He had imposed the strictest discipline upon himself, utilizing all his energies to working with the villagers in the cultivation of their crops, meeting with the council of elders to determine what supplies should be brought into his depot upriver and acting, each time he journeyed to Mobile, as a courier of all news that concerned the thriving village. By now he had learned of the Reign of Terror which the despotic Robespierre had brought about in making himself a virtual dictator over all France.

He had seen Jabez Corrigan once more, this last August, when the *Guerrière* had dropped anchor in Mobile a day after he had reached the trading post. The red-haired Irishman was grayer and stouter than ever, and he had a little daughter named after her mother, Jeanne Marie, to be a playmate with his little son. He had prospered as captain of the vessel, but there was a sadness in his eyes as he related to Lucien some of the harrowing scenes he had witnessed in the relentless persecution of all aristocrats, even to the turning of friend upon friend in this insensate struggle for power. In many little towns throughout France, the grim apparatus invented by Dr. J. J. Guillotin, after whom it had been named, could be seen erected in the public square, and almost daily in every region of France the public executioners were busy at their grisly trade.

"I can only pray that one day soon reason will come to your native country, Lucien," he told his friend, "and by the time that day comes, I may take your advice and go back to the good land with my little family. Who knows?" There had been a genuine Irish twinkle in his blue eyes. "I may end my days building one of those fancy chateaux such as you yourself had back in that province you came from, Lucien."

"May God grant you that wish, as I pray He will grant mine to see one day upon my own land an exact counterpart of my once peaceful home," Lucien Bouchard solemnly replied.

There was one other piece of news Lucien learned in Mobile on the occasion of this last visit, the knowledge of which led him to believe that at last an old score had truly been settled for all time. Edmée de Bouchard, after working for the French family in Mobile as a seamstress for a little over a year, had left for New Orleans and had, two months ago, married a Creole banker named Philippe Entrevois.

CHAPTER TWENTY-FOUR

Three weeks after Lucien Bouchard's thirty-second birthday, the defiant Georgia legislature authorized the sale of thirty million acres of land, which comprised most of Alabama and Mississippi, at a cost of one and a half cents per acre under the auspices of the revived and nefarious Yazoo Land Companies. The preamble to the Yazoo bill disputed President Washington's authority to guarantee all the territory west of the Oconee to the Creeks and declared that the State of Georgia had the clear right to convey fee simple titles to all its territories, whether it be to individuals or companies. This act further stipulated that a fifth of the purchase money should be paid into the Georgia treasury prior to the passage of the bill, the remainder to be paid to Governor Matthews by the following November and to be secured by a mortgage. Payments were to be made in specie, United States bank bills, or military warrants drawn by the Governor from 1791 through 1795. If the bill was enacted and put into military effect, Lucien knew, there would be outright war between the Creek Nation and the inhabitants of that foolhardy state which would not yet adhere to the will of the new republic.

But almost immediately after the passage of this daringly ambitious act, proofs of bribery and corruption among the legislators were produced, showing that many of those who had voted for the passage of the act had received in advance from the Yazoo companies certificates of large shares of the land which they were about to vote to sell. Public acrimony rose at once, even among the very settlers who were the most anxious to obtain these lands from the Creeks.

As spring began, Lucien busied himself once more with the endless but rewarding cycle of helping prepare both his land and that of the communal fields at Econchate for the crops of corn, beans and other produce which grew in such abundance on this fertile soil. At Nanakota's invitation, the two of them, accompanied by three of the younger braves who were not yet fledged as warriors and for whom this brief hunting expedition would be invaluable, hunted deer in the forests to the northeast. Using the indigo-dyed bow the *Mico* had given him, Lucien bagged two fine bucks, but adroitly saw to it that his Creek friend felled twice as many with his own arrows. And, to make certain that he would make ever new friends among the younger men of the village—for one day they might be accepted among the "beloved men" of the council—he saw to it that each of the three young braves was able to claim a kill and thus go back to Econchate proud of his newly demonstrated skill.

On the last day of the hunt, the final week of a pleasant April, as they prepared to return to the village, Nanakota shrewdly eyed the vigorous, sun-bronzed Frenchman and remarked, "Each time you come to our village, Lu-shee-ahn, the old squaws have to cut switches for the silly young maidens who would otherwise creep into your lodge. Now you well know, my brother, that while I do not condone a squaw's forbidden mating with a brave who is not her man, there is nothing in our law which says that a squaw who has been widowed or is a maiden, if she is wise and has so been instructed by her mother, may not share your blanket and give you pleasure."

"I did not know I was so favored by the many pretty maidens in your village, my *Mico,*" Lucien smilingly responded. "If my presence here at Econchate gives you and the elders weighty problems, then I shall not come here again, but shall remain at my own lodge upriver."

"No, no, I spoke in jest," Nanakota hastily amended, a sly grin creasing his coppery cheeks. "If my brother does not come to Red Ground, it will not be the maidens alone who are sad. I am at peace and my heart is not heavy within me when my brother visits me. All of us look upon you as a man who might have become a *Mico* like myself had you but been born of a Creek mother. The great McGillivray, whom we still mourn as a faithful and devoted leader, was just such."

"But by the accident of birth, Nanakota, I am still a white-eyes, though my heart and my mind and my tongue will always be in the service of the Creeks."

"Have you not mourned her long enough now, Lu-shee-ahn? Why could you not take another maiden and get her with a fine son who would live after you? I can read what is in your heart, my brother. Yes, I too mourn Dimarte for her gentle wisdom and the more because her passing has left you sad and silent so many times when we have seen you here. You have the land, you need a son. Nor would Dimarte, looking down from the land of the Great Spirit, be saddened if she saw you with another maiden and knew that it is because we must live on so long as there is breath in our bodies."

"I have thought upon it, Nanakota. Nor is it because I should prefer to mate with one of my own race that I do not seek to toss a pebble at the feet of one like Tishenay or Kimenata."

"Aiyee, they are the two who find most favor in the eyes of the other warriors of Econchate," Nanakota chuckled. "And the parents of each girl would be honored to have you bring them gifts. I speak true, Lu-shee-ahn."

"I will think upon it again, Nanakota. But these are troubled times and I fear that many scheming men far beyond our boundaries are even now seeking to take all these lands from the people of your nation. It should best be done by treaty, if only now there were a man of the stature of Colonel McGillivray to treat with the Americans and come to a peaceful understanding so that red man and white could live side by side in friendship and in fruitful toil."

"If all white-eyes were like you, that could be done this very day, my brother. Alas, it will not be so. I still remember the words of Tsipoulata, that the land would be soaked with blood and that one day the white-eyes would build their own town upon our beloved Red Ground. For more summers than are arrows in the quivers of our three young braves, he has cast the sacred bones and spoken of their meaning to us and he has not failed us. But for that one time, Lu-shee-ahn, I pray the Great Spirit that the words are wrong, that we shall never leave our beloved Econchate."

With a long sigh, his face lifted to the sky, Nanakota rose and bade the young braves prepare for the journey back to the village.

Lucien had not been unmindful of Nanakota's frequent hints that he should seriously consider taking another wife. Both last year and this, on several occasions during his stay in the village, he had seen some of the bolder, comelier Creek girls stare smilingly at him and make signs by which he understood that they would not find his amorous advances displeasing. Once, indeed, last winter, almost as Shehanoy had done, a slim girl not more than sixteen had crept into the little house and lain down beside him, unfastening her petticoat and turning toward him to waken him. When he had discovered her, he had chided her gently but kindly, told her that his heart had turned to another who was not of this village, and then, when she was still reluctant to go, had drawn her to her feet, forced her to put back on her petticoat and then hurried her out of his house with a stinging slap on the buttocks and a playful quip to praise her charms, that she might not lose face.

This outdoor life, hardy and demanding, dedicated though it was to the trading and the farming and occasionally the hunting, had physically inured him to the same hardships which the Creek warriors endured as a natural part of their existence. He had learned to hunt or to go on horseback for a full day with only a handful of corn and a few bits of jerky and a draught of water from the river to sustain him. Taut and wiry and muscular, in the full prime of his manhood, he knew the urges of the flesh, but his rigid discipline over himself in order to abide by Creek customs and laws had taught him how to resist temptations. At Mobile, several of the Spanish soldiers had Indian mistresses, though there, either through the auspices of a priest or their commandant, they could have arranged for legitimate marriage. And that too, though it was only a subconscious thought, impelled him toward serious reflection on the theme of a third marriage.

If the *Windigo*'s prophecy that this land would one day be held by the white-eyes came true, and if he could manage to hold his land beyond the inevitable warfare waged for its control, then it was important to legitimize his heirs if he should at last seek a new wife. No priest or minister had as yet come into all of this wild territory, except in Mobile and New Orleans. He had been so spellbound by the goodness and the sweetness of Dimarte, so respectful of the religion of the Creeks, that he had willingly accepted union with her as binding. If she had lived, he would assuredly have at some later time taken her to Mobile and there had a formal marriage performed so that their children might truly be legitimate. With Amelia, on the other hand, he had had no choice; if he had suggested a marriage as the whites would have had one, she would surely have been put to death. But now, with the concern for the fraudulent claims which greedy and ruthless men were about to make upon the lands of the Creeks, it would be well for him to consider remarriage, but this time with a white girl. And there was none in this territory of Econchate, nor likely to be for some little while.

Each time Lucien visited Mobile, he could not but feel a twinge of patriotic sorrow to see the Spanish flag flying over the fort which guarded the entrance to the great bay and to be reminded that the flag of his own devastated land of birth was no longer in view, except on the mast of the *Guerrière*. And over the land where he was now settled, there was no rallying flag, no symbol by which a man might point with pride and say, "This is my country, which I will defend with my honor, my courage and my life." For the flag of the new United States had not yet been seen in this vast wilderness, though by the 1st of May Congress authorized a new flag with fifteen stars and fifteen stripes, to include the just-recognized states of Vermont and Kentucky.

In mid-June, at the request of Nanakota, Lucien again

set out for Mobile on a flatboat, this time accompanied by the devoted Ashanti. Ellen and little Thomas remained in the village for safety's sake. Little Thomas, now four years old, light-colored and with alert, intelligent features, had already found many playmates among the Creek children and had learned a few words of their language. It tore at Lucien's heart to see this thriving child enter so readily into a strange new life, while he himself had twice been cruelly deprived of the joys of fatherhood.

Nanakota saw to it that Lucien's crops would be well tended during his absence by arranging to send a dozen squaws, with four young braves to guard them. These latter would guard also the trading depot near the river bank. And, since the order for supplies this time was considerably larger than it had been over the past two years, the *Mico* sent along with Lucien and Ben four warriors armed with muskets, bows and arrows, and tomahawks to guard the returning train of pack ponies against attack by any roving parties of renegade Creeks or Choctaws.

Lucien found a warm welcome at the Mobile trading post. After the death of Alexander McGillivray, the Spanish government had promised the partners of the firm headed by William Panton full indemnification so that they would continue the profitable exchange of goods with the Creek Nation. The new factor of Indian trading, John Forbes, had become a land owner, with some small cabins on the corner of a street named St. Francis, and was present at the trading post when Lucien and Ben entered to pay their respects and to pledge the continued loyalty of the Creek tribe at Econchate.

"You come at a most welcome time, Mr. Bouchard," the twenty-six-year-old brown-haired Scot greeted him, a worried frown on his pleasant, deeply tanned face. "Two days ago, a young woman from New Orleans came here and asked directions for the trail to Fort St. Stephens. I did not return to Mobile till late last night, and, I fear, much too late to aid her. You see, sir, she was in search of her brother, an English surveyor who had gone on ahead of her to make a map of the terrain on the commission of an aide to Baron Carondelet. I do not understand

328

what the purpose of such a map would be, but it is not for me to question the governor."

"I see, Mr. Forbes. And you think that there may be some danger for the young lady?" Lucien solicitously asked.

"Damme, now that I've had a report from one of our Choctaw scouts, I do indeed! They are good people, but at times some of the traders pass out too much *taffai,* and there are always those who, when inebriated by such strong spirits, look upon any white man or woman or even child—God help us all—as legitimate prey."

"Is there a war party of Choctaws in that vicinity, then, sir?"

"No, I do not believe it is a war party, but there may be as many as a dozen braves who wandered from their village to the west of the fort in search of mischief. It may well be that the young woman's brother has already fallen prisoner or worse to them, and she would be in grave danger."

"I have with me four warriors from Econchate, and Ben and I are able warriors if it comes to that," Lucien promptly replied.

"Good! I had been told that you received from our lamented friend and partner, Colonel McGillivray, a pass into the Creek Nation. If you have it about you, that might serve. The Choctaws and the Creeks, though they have been enemies, are at the moment at peace. However, I warn you that no matter what race or creed a man may be, once he has imbibed too well, his sanity and judgment often depart."

"I do not wish to kill, but I promise you I shall do everything in my power to save the young woman and her brother."

"I could ask for no more. God go with you. Your supplies will be ready when you return. I do not think it is more than a journey of forty miles to the area where, according to Miss Wellman, her brother would be at work."

"If you have some horses you can spare us, swifter than these pack ponies, we could be there by noon of tomorrow, Mr. Forbes," Lucien volunteered.

"I shall see to it myself. I have a friend here in Mobile

who fancies swift horses and will surely be glad to lend them in so humanitarian a cause."

Lucien, Ben and his four warriors set out before twilight, and by dawn, sparing their mounts as much as was practicable, they had reached the bend of the Tombigbee River. Dismounting, one of the warriors moved along the trail, intently peering at the thick grass and shrubs which lay beyond. He turned to beckon, pointing to a tree branch hanging over a narrow dirt trail on which there were still prints of horses' hooves. From a twig, there fluttered a strip of cloth, that of a woman's dress.

"They go by not long ago," the warrior grunted to Lucien as he handed the latter the strip of torn cloth.

Here, to his left and about a hundred yards from the river, was a narrow lagoon whose surface was decorated with a wavy green plain of water-lilies larger than the palm of a man's hand and of a lemon-yellow in hue. There was a clump of magnolia trees, crested with its silver plume and fragrant blossom, and bushes of odorless wax myrtle, as well as others of evening primrose seven feet high. All around was sylvan beauty, wild and free, yet it was in just such treacherous country that an unwary man might lose his life. Timenkota, the tall, lean young warrior who had found the sign of the Choctaw raiders, primed his musket and then gobbled down a handful of maize as breakfast while Lucien, Ben and the other three Creeks watered and rested their horses as they consumed their own frugal meal. Then Timenkota, brandishing his musket, pointed toward the northwest, diagonally away from the bank of the river which found its way into the great bay of Mobile, and the six riders continued in pursuit.

"I hope we can persuade the Choctaw braves to give up the man and the woman if they've taken them prisoners," Lucien said to Ben.

The tall Ashanti dubiously shook his head. "If they drink too much *taffai,* they would rather kill than parley. A white squaw is a prize for them. They may take her back to their village as a slave or as a mate to the one who seized her, or they may put her to the torture. I do

330

not know the Choctaws, but they are fierce warriors and they are bound only to the Spanish. Now that McGillivray is no more, I do not even know if they are still loyal to his words of unity among the tribes."

After another two hours of pursuit, again Timenkota held up his musket and the others reined in their horses. They had come to a sparsely forested area, with mounds and little hills, and beyond that, vaguely seen in the distance, a sort of clearing cut through by a meandering little creek which ultimately joined the river far to the right of the pursuing riders.

"Choctaws there," Timenkota muttered. "We tie horses, we go on foot now, all be quiet."

Lucien quickly dismounted and tied the reins of his horse to a cypress tree, Ben imitating him. The four Creeks circled toward the right, taking up places of ambush behind the thickly foliaged cypress trees, with garlands of Spanish moss trailing to the ground.

Lucien and Ben had moved in the opposite direction to their four Creek companions, crouching behind the twisted, lightning-blackened husk of an old cypress tree. As Lucien knelt down, leveling his musket, he uttered a stifled gasp of horror. Across from the little creek there was a wide clearing, framed by tall trees and thick, wild bushes. Beside the bank of the creek lay a young man in buckskin jacket and breeches, face down and his arms flung out in cross on either side of him, while a Choctaw brave, hideously bedaubed in green, red and ochre paints and wearing only a breechclout and moccasins, squatted at the dead man's side, methodically removing the bloody scalp.

Beyond him, two Choctaw braves passed a leather jug of *taffai* between them, staggering and uttering shrill warwhoops as they drunkenly toasted the coup of their companion, who now rose, flourishing the bloody trophy for all to see.

An agonizing scream, a woman's, greeted this savage gesture, and Lucien ground his teeth and slowly aimed and then lowered his musket, glancing quickly at the Ashanti beside him. "I'll try to parley with them to release the girl, Ben. Cover me with your musket and kill

331

them if you have to if they seem unwilling to let the girl go," he hoarsely whispered.

Bound to a cypress tree with her arms drawn back around the gnarled trunk, her cotton dress torn from her body and ripped into haphazard shreds which lay strewn around her, her chemise tied like a sash around the waist of another Choctaw brave who crouched before her hideously grinning and brandishing his iron tomahawk, naked except for her muslin drawers, stockings and buckled shoes, was a honey-haired young woman who could not have been more than twenty. To the brave's right, three other Choctaws were kindling a fire of grass and dried twigs, one of them blowing on it with cupped hands, while two other braves stood watching the progress of the fire. They held their iron tomahawks down toward the first flickering tongues of flame.

"Oh God, kill me quickly, in the name of mercy!" the almost naked captive shrieked, beside herself. "Oh Jeremy, my poor brother, and those two blacks, you've murdered them, you dreadful savages!"

Two Negroes, undoubtedly either freemen whom the girl's dead surveyor brother had paid to aid him in his map-making, or else family slaves who had been ordered to accompany him, lay farther down the bank of the creek in the direction of the Tombigbee, dead from tomahawk wounds, already scalped.

Laying down his musket but notching an arrow to his bow, Lucien cautiously stepped out of the protective thicket behind which he and Ben had concealed themselves and called in the Creek tongue, "I come as friend, with the word of the great leader McGillivray whom we all mourn."

"Ho!" The warrior threatening the half-naked blonde captive with his tomahawk whirled and shouted across the clearing: "We too mourn him, and we take vengeance on the hated white-eyes. Leave us, the young squaw is ours to die at the torture stake. She has come without permission into our land."

"My Choctaw brother respects his land, and that is good," Lucien diplomatically called back, "but the squaw has done you no harm nor wronged your land. Her brother, whose scalp your companion has just taken, came here to draw a map at the order of the great Carondelet who rules all of this territory for the Spaniards."

"He does not rule us. Enough of parley! You, you white-eyes, you speak the Creek tongue well and I see that you are their brother, and so we have no quarrel with you. Get you gone to your own hunting grounds, the squaw is ours."

"Does the courageous Choctaw show his valor by torturing a weak white-eyes squaw? That is the work of old women, and so I have mistaken you for a warrior," Lucien taunted.

The high-cheekboned, angular face of the Choctaw twisted in a snarl of fury at this insult. Turning back to the whimpering, tethered young woman, he laid the iron blade of the tomahawk against her naked breast and snarled, "You shall watch her die, and then we shall find another tree for you. You will beg for mercy like the squaw!" Then, gesturing with his other hand to the three braves crouching around the hastily improvised fire, he called, "Take him, kill him if he does not surrender!"

In almost the same moment, he turned back to the terrified young woman, plunged his left hand into her disheveled honey-gold tresses, twisting them and pulling her head back against the trunk of the tree as he slowly lifted the tomahawk, his eyes ferociously glittering, his thin lips curved in a savage rictus of blood-lust.

As the three braves straightened and ran toward Lucien, two of them brandishing tomahawks and the third a hunting knife, the black-haired Frenchman took swift aim with the bow and released the arrow, speeding it into the Choctaw leader's back. The brave stiffened, his tomahawk dropped from his nerveless hand and he fell forward, his other hand still clutching the captive's hair. She cried out shrilly in the agony of it.

Ben's musket resounded sharply and the brave nearest Lucien, tomahawk already upraised for the throw, staggered, looked down at his bleeding belly, coughed and fell. An arrow whistled through the air from Lucien's right to sink itself deeply into the other tomahawk-wielding brave's shoulder, momentarily halting him as he cried

333

out and plucked at the shaft. But the Choctaw with the knife was already upon Lucien, and he had time only to slash at the brave's upraised arm with the wooden arc of his bow, then he drew Jabez Corrigan's knife from the scabbard-belt.

The two Choctaws who had been heating their tomahawks in the fire for the torture of their white captive came at Lucien's left, but the Creeks supporting Lucien loosed their arrows and they fell, mortally wounded. The two drunken Choctaws, sobered by the carnage about them, drew their knives and staggered forward, one of them immediately felled by Ben's second musket shot, the other by a new flight of arrows from the Creek braves.

Circling warily, one infuriated Choctaw lunged at Lucien with his knife, and the black-haired Frenchman leaped back, crouching on the balls of his feet and swinging the knife upward in a belly-aiming lunge intended as a feint.

As his enraged adversary in turn recoiled, Lucien saw two of his Creeks notching new arrows to their bows, and he cried out, "Hold your arrows! This is a fair fight between us, to decide the right!"

At once they obeyed, their eyes shining with admiration, for they admired valor, and to face a gleaming hunting knife in the hands of a Choctaw warrior was as much a test of courage as had been Lucien's encounter with the she-bear.

Now the Choctaw leaped to one side, scooped up some loose earth in his left hand and flung it into Lucien's face. A cry of warning burst from Ben, but Lucien had already anticipated that deadly ruse, and in his turn circled to the opposite side, stabbing directly out at the Choctaw's chest. Their blades clashed as the brave parried, and for a moment they stood facing each other, the brave's eyes blazing with death-lust, Lucien having caught his enemy's left wrist with his own left hand to ward off any counter blow that might decide the fight to the death—for such he now knew it would be.

To his ears there came the faint, hysterical sobbing of the half-naked blonde captive, her head bowed down by the traction impelled by the dead hand still gripping her disheveled honey-gold tresses.

Summoning all his strength, Lucien drove his right knee upward into the groin of his adversary, who let out an agonized yelp and stumbled away, but then with ferocious reflex again leaped to the charge. Once again Lucien parried a sideways stroke and again the knives clashed in the forest clearing.

He felt himself weakening, till the wiry Choctaw was easily his match; the long journey to Mobile and the night-long ride after these renegades had exhausted him. Swiftly his left hand unfastened the scabbard-belt and he swung it out like a whip just as the Choctaw lunged. It struck the warrior across the eyes, and with a cry he struck at it with his free hand, only to have Lucien crouch, lunge forward and upward with the knife, which ripped into his enemy's belly in a fatal slash.

Panting hoarsely, staggering away, Lucien watched the brave fall, roll over and over, having dropped his knife, both hands scrabbling at the bloody wound, and then stiffen in death.

He forced himself to stumble toward the tree, and with his knife slashed the rawhide thongs which bound the captive's wrists. Then, as she sank down, nearly fainting, he took her hair in both hands and with his left tugged the ends with all his strength out of the dead man's grip.

Slowly he raised his pain-racked, sweating face to stare at Ben through the blur of the nausea and fatigue which made his eyes swirl with dizziness. "Get a blanket, cover her, give her some water, Ben," he gasped.

Beyond him, the four Creek warriors were gleefully scalping the fallen Choctaws. It would be a great coup to be told over the fires of Econchate.

CHAPTER TWENTY-FIVE

It was not possible to return to Mobile by nightfall; the horses lent to Lucien and his companions had been ridden much too hard to be able to survive so swift a return journey. Moreover, Priscilla Wellman's nervous shock and exhaustion from watching the murder of her brother, and then believing herself to be marked for the same though cruelly prolonged fate, would have made such a plan manifestly impossible. Huddled beside the tree which was to have been her torture stake, shivering as with fever under the blanket with which she had wrapped herself, her face buried in her hands, the young blonde woman wept disconsolately as Lucien and Ben buried her brother as decently as they could in this verdant forest. With his hunting knife, Lucien carved the name of Jeremy Wellman on a piece of driftwood and made it serve as an upright marker. At his orders, the dead Choctaws and the blacks were buried also.

The Choctaws had come on foot from the village, some twenty miles to the northwest of this uninhabited place, and so there was no horse for Priscilla Wellman to ride back when she was able to make the journey. Taking the leather jug of *taffai*, Lucien seated himself beside her and, gently persuasive, urged her to swallow some of the potent brew as a necessary restorative. The matter of clothes, however, posed an embarrassing problem, particularly as Priscilla Wellman would have to ride side-saddle in front of Lucien, and would need to cling to him with her arm from time to time.

The black-haired Frenchman solved this by stripping one of the dead Choctaw braves of breechclout and buckskin leggings to cover himself from knee to ankle as protection against snakebite. Then, going behind a clump of bushes, he divested himself of his jacket and breeches, replacing them with the dead warrior's breechclout and leggings, and returned to the still faintly sobbing Priscilla Wellman. "It will take us a day and a half to reach Mobile, Miss Wellman," he explained as kindly as he could. "If there were another horse, you could ride it and we could make better time. But since you'll have to ride with me, it'll be easier for you if you put on my garments. I apologize for the embarrassment this and my own necessarily briefly clad person will cause you."

"You—you're very kind, sir," the honey-haired young woman stammered, looking up at him, her hazel eyes wide and clouded with tears. Her face was almost heart-shaped, with daintily upturned nose, a soft, provocatively dimpled chin, and her skin, though reddened by the hot sun and the bites of insects, was of pale carnation tint. She was of medium height, gracefully slender, with almost boyish hips but surprisingly ample, firm, tightly spaced breasts. Now, recollecting what he must have seen of her when he and his companions had come upon the clearing, she turned scarlet and lowered her eyes.

"Don't fret yourself, Miss Wellman. There's plenty of time, rest until you feel better, and we'll get you some food."

"Oh, I couldn't eat anything—when I think of poor Jeremy and David and Reuben, it's just too dreadful! Oh, whatever will I do now?"

"It might relieve your sorrow a little if you could tell me something about yourself, Miss Wellman," he gently suggested.

"It—it's all so strange and so frightening—I—I haven't even begun to thank you for what you did—I thought I was going to die—they made me watch while they killed my brother—oh my God!" She burst into a fit of sobbing, and Lucien compassionately put his arm around her shoulders. Finally she forced herself to continue, "Our parents came to Savannah when we were children. They owned a fine house and land, and then a man induced my father to begin a little plantation away from the city. For the first year, everything went well, but then the Indians came and they burned the plantation and killed my parents."

Once again, she burst into tears, and Lucien, who could sympathize with her all the more because of his own loss back in the pleasant village of Yves-sur-lac, held her close and waited until she could again regain her control.

"Then this man promised to find Jeremy a position with the authorities. Jeremy is—he—he was awfully good at maps and charts, and so we came to New Orleans. We brought very little with us, and there was almost no money. And then about a week ago Jeremy told me that this man had come to see him again and given him a commission to draw a map of the land near Fort St. Stephens. Three of our slaves followed us, because father had set them free just before he was killed. One of them went with Jeremy—he—he must have run away or been killed or captured—I don't know—oh, God, whatever shall I do?"

Again Priscilla Wellman burst into hysterical sobs, and Lucien waited, for there were no words which could assuage the young woman's bitter grief. Finally, when he saw that she was again able to speak, he asked, "But why did you try to join him? Didn't you think there might be danger, a young woman like you going alone into this wilderness?"

"No, the other two blacks came with me to protect me—and now they're dead too."

"Can you remember the name of the man who saw your father in Georgia and then came to your brother in New Orleans, Miss Wellman?" he pursued.

"He—he was Spanish, I think. I'm trying to remember —I think his name was Oliver."

"Now I begin to understand a little, Miss Wellman. From conversations I've had with John Forbes, I learned that Captain Don Pedro Oliver, who is in reality a countryman of mine, yes, a Frenchman, but wears the Spanish

338

military uniform, was an aide a few years ago to the late Colonel McGillivray, the leader of the Creek Nation. You see, the Spaniards are fighting for control of this territory and as far east as Florida. And the Georgia settlers have for the past several years been attempting to encroach upon Indian lands, not only through warfare but by the means of illegal seizure and purchase of those lands. Somehow, your unfortunate father became innocently involved with this widespread conspiracy."

Priscilla Wellman stared uncomprehendingly at him, her hazel eyes misted with glistening tears. "I—I don't understand—but why should the Indians kill my parents and my brother and try to kill me?"

"I must tell you the truth, harsh though it may seem to you and even inexplicable. Between the new United States and the Spaniards, there is a bitter duel for possession of this rich but still uncharted wilderness. And because the Creek Nation with all its tribes, which include the Choctaws in an alliance, originally occupied the land, the settlers who have come here look to their governments to protect them and to enable them to plant and grow crops and live where no white men ever lived before. Brutal though it may seem to you, I interpret what has happened as another of the schemes of the ambitious Georgia authorities to show the new Federal Government in New York that their innocent and well-meaning settlers are being attacked and murdered by the savages and that they expect the Federal Government to drive out all Indians and open the lands to colonization. The deaths of those members of your family have indirectly come about as a result of that contriving."

"Oh God, how horrible, when my father and mother and my brother never hurt a soul or wished ill to anyone!" she sobbingly burst out, then again buried her face in her hands and wept bitterly as Lucien rose and went over to bid Ben prepare some food for the distraught young woman so that she might be strengthened for the long trek back to Mobile.

It was almost twilight when they headed southward, and two hours later Lucien called a halt so that they might make camp for the night. Priscilla Wellman had ridden in front of him, turned toward him and with her arms trustingly circling his waist to support herself, her head resting against his chest, as weariness now overcame her—the natural aftermath of the emotional stress to which she had been so cruelly subjected. He gazed protectively down at her, and the feeling of her slim body against his, the sight of her in his own jacket and breeches which had been his customary attire for so many years now at Econchate, served to waken in him very recognizable instincts. There was desire, born out of the savage duel to the death he had fought with the Choctaw who had put her to the torture stake. It had been atavistic combat reduced to its most primal elements of two men battling for the life of a helpless female. It might well have taken place in the prehistoric dawn of time itself, for there had been the same obliviousness to scruples and moral conscience. He had had to kill the Choctaw or be killed; there could have been no other decision, unless he had let his companions kill the brave without danger to himself. And now that he was one of the Creeks as a blood brother of the Bear, to have let them kill the Choctaw for him would have been a great loss of esteem, powerful enough to affect even his relationship with Nanakota, whom he knew as friend as well as *Mico*. For the fourth time in his life, he had had to take a human life. And as he pondered on these violent acts, each spaced in years between with their own strange alteration of his life, he thought again of the *Windigo*'s enigmatic and paradoxical prophecy.

The old Mosaic law of which the Old Testament spoke ordained that he who took up the sword should perish by it also. Because he had killed Shehanoy's mate, he had been given Dimarte, only to have her and her child die— had that been divine retribution imposed upon him? Because he had avenged the death of Tunkamara, the fleeing teenaged boy, the only survivor of the Wealthams, had come back after a year to exact dreadful vengeance by killing Amelia, and in turn had died at his own hands. What price, then, would he be ordained to pay for having killed the Choctaw warrior?

Yet if one speculated on the master plan which guided

each taking of one of the paths at the crossroads which one encountered along the road of life, there would be indecision and doubt, which would bring about disaster too. Shaken as she was by her bereavement, Priscilla Wellman would probably never understand the devious plot which had propelled her parents, her brother and herself to this bizarre and bloody meeting in the forest clearing of the wilderness. Lucien could see it, standing aside as an impassive and disinterested spectator: there were hotheaded, war-eager factions in the Creek Nation, just as assuredly there were among the high-ranking Spanish authorities and the Tory-loving Georgians. The Wellmans had thus become unsuspecting, helpless pawns on this geographic chessboard, to be sacrificed in gambit style. They represented the faction of the Georgians, and if they were massacred by members of the Creek Nation, the already angered Georgians would ignore the warnings of President Washington's still embryonic government and plunge headlong into warfare with the Creeks. Then the Spanish, already in powerful alliance with their Indian protectorate, would have justifiable cause for reprisal and would regain the geographic frontiers to which they believed historical treaties entitled them. And the tragedy was that there was nothing in this to console the unfortunate young woman for the violent deaths of her parents, her brother and the freed slaves of her family.

In the morning, Lucien saw that the young woman was much stronger, thanks to a good night's sleep and an ample morning meal which the Ashanti had prepared. They had still some thirty-five miles before them to reach Mobile, and although he wished to bring the young woman back by the next nightfall, he did not think it practicable because of the condition of the horses. Tactfully he explained this to Priscilla Wellman, who nodded, her hazel eyes trustingly fixed on him, as she wanly replied, "I confess, Mr. Bouchard, I've nothing really to hurry back to now. Yes, I'd like to leave this wilderness because it reminds me of poor Jeremy and the others, but I've no one else left in the world now."

"Is there no one back in New Orleans to look after you, Miss Wellman?"

341

She shook her head, uttering a long sigh. "There were only the blacks, who stayed on as servants to us after they'd been freed because they loved us all. And now they're dead. Most of my father's estate was destroyed, and there's only a little money, left with a private banker in New Orleans, which Jeremy and I brought with us. He was looking forward to this work because he believed it would mean useful and profitable employment with the authorities in New Orleans. Now there's nothing. I suppose I'll have to think of finding some way to earn my livelihood. I've had some schooling, perhaps someone might be in need of a private tutoress. I play the spinet, I sew and I can prepare food acceptably enough, I think." She gave a bitter little laugh and shrugged. "I'm afraid that's all I have to offer when I take stock of myself, Mr. Bouchard."

"You couldn't return to England?"

"Oh, no! You see, father, though he was a Royalist, wasn't at all fond of the government's policies. First and foremost, he was the squire of a very fine farm in Warwickshire. He and mother believed that now that this new country had become a republic, he could prosper more as a farmer in a colony where he would find his own countrymen, and that is why we came to Savannah as we did. And then all the rest of it, so swiftly, such a nightmare of horror—no, Mr. Bouchard, there's no reason why I should go back to England either. Father intended that one day I marry a landholder like himself, and I suppose I'd have been happy enough in that kind of life. But there was no one in Savannah I cared for, and we were there so short a time before father went into the wilder country to begin a plantation. Everything he seems to have done was doomed from the start, I fear."

They sat beside the campfire, and Priscilla Wellman glanced quickly at him, then looked away, her pale cheeks reddening. Now that the hysterical shock of her experience had somewhat receded, she was suddenly conscious of the strange contrast in this man who wore only a breechclout and leggings and moccasins, his body bronzed like an Indian's, his left side marked by faint bluish scars, bearded and with hair along the edges of his cheeks down

342

nearly to his jaws, black matted hair on his sinewy chest, almost the picture of one of those red savages who had wanted to take her life. And yet his gentleness and solicitude in conversing with her, in holding her snugly with his arm as he reined his horse along the trail, violently conflicted with this almost frightening image.

And for Lucien, the contrast he saw in her between the deerskin breeches and jacket which imperfectly fitted her (for the jacket strained against the surprising amplitude of her lush round breasts) and the long, tumbled cascade of honey-gold hair which was so exquisitely feminine in its allure blended a piquant maleness of attire with the helpless and bewildered femininity which her words and features evinced. Her voice was clear and sweet, trembling with understandable enervation, and by her choice of words she was obviously gently bred.

Thus it was that a sudden, almost irrational impulse sprang into his mind, yet it was one which had been nurtured by Nanakota's words to him during their last hunt together. Priscilla Wellman was of good stock, of his own race and now, bereft and orphaned, faced the none too sanguine prospect of supporting herself. Even in New Orleans, her chances of legitimate employment would be few indeed: it had been only a fortunate coincidence that Edmée had been able to find a post as seamstress in Mobile. The chances were even more against Priscilla Wellman's luck in New Orleans, since she did not speak French or Spanish. Inevitably, she could drift into an elegant bordello, such as Madame Rambouillet had maintained. No, it would not be improper of him to propose marriage to her—not too swiftly, to be sure, lest she believe he sought to take advantage of her luckless lot. And for him, the advantages would be manifest: a mother for the heir he must have to carry out his dreams for the fruitful land and the chateau that would grace it.

He moved away as he saw that her eyelids slowly closed in sleep and stood for a moment regarding her stretched upon blankets to make a more comfortable bed than the bare ground. The campfire flickered, dwindling. Lucien walked slowly toward the river bank, listening to the sounds of the night. And then, with startling clarity, there

343

sounded the hoot of an owl, two quick calls and a third prolonged.

He started, staring toward the direction of that sound, but there were clouds and only a dim quarter moon and trees and verdant moss and foliage to obscure his vision. And then again it came, in the same cadence, as if to reassert itself and what it foretold.

There was a stillness even beyond the quiet of this night. Lucien moved toward the unseen owl and held out his arms. "Dimarte, beloved one, guide me," he whispered. "I took another to wife to save her. But now, forgive me for my selfish thoughts, for I am the last of all my line and if I do not have a son, there will be nothing left of the memory of my father and his before him. It was a noble name, in honor and goodness. This is all I ask, and I ask it in your sweet name. If what I do now is calculating, know that it is done to keep my love for you stronger than ever it was before. I shall love none other till the day I die, Dimarte. To this one, I would bring peace and kindness, safety in a land that has brought her sorrow, and if she were to give me a son, I should cherish and honor her. Tell me, my beloved, for if it offends you, I will do nothing that will destroy my love for you."

He waited, trembling, for the uncanny sharpening of all his senses in this darkness of the night recalled to him the old *Windigo*'s saying that the spirits of the blessed and the beloved and the good remain where they have been loved and seek to guide the living.

And in that stillness, came for the third time the hooting of the owl, not as alarm or the foreboding omen of peril or disaster, but gentle and faint, like a distantly murmured benediction.

After her return to Mobile by the middle of the next morning, Priscilla Wellman was at once taken to John Forbes's house to enjoy the luxury of a bath to which two Choctaw squaws brought buckets of water into which heated stones had been dropped, and then, having been provided with a nightshift, chemise and dress from the trader's English-exported stores, slept nearly till nightfall. Forbes himself had quieted the young woman's fears at

344

encountering the squaws, assuring her that they had been widowed and were employed at the trading post and were friendly to whites.

That evening, after she had wakened and dressed, Forbes invited her to dine with him, Lucien and Ben. The four braves from Econchate shared the meal, but amusingly made wry faces when they found themselves served Spanish wine in goblets instead of the customary *taffai*.

At the conclusion of the meal, Forbes turned to the young woman and solicitously declared, "Miss Wellman, if there is any further way in which I may be of service to you, you have only to ask it."

"You've been most kind, Mr. Forbes, but I suppose I shall have to go back to New Orleans and try to pick up my life. There's no one left of my family now besides myself, so I must find employment of some sort to earn my daily bread."

"I can of course find a reliable boatman to take you back to New Orleans if that is your wish, Miss Wellman. I have some friends in that city, and I shall be glad to give you letters to them which may be of aid."

"You're most kind, Mr. Forbes. I owe my life to this gentleman—" she turned toward Lucien and gave him a warm smile—"and I fear I have been a great burden to him and his party. I know so little of this part of the country, and it was very rash of me to try to find my brother as I did." Her smile vanished and she blinked her eyes to clear them of the sudden tears. "I would to God I had never gone. I shall always remember what I saw—"

"Now, now then, miss, don't fret so. Nor must you think that all Indians are bloodthirsty savages. I know it's of small consolation to know that those renegades were punished as they deserved for the awful deeds they did, but you must look on the brighter side. You're young and strong and you'll survive, and you'll meet a fine man and have babies, and it will give you back what was taken from you."

"I thank you for your kindness, Mr. Forbes. But I can't forget that my parents were killed by Indians too. Yet I have nowhere else to go but New Orleans, I fear, and so I will willingly accept whatever letters you can send in my behalf."

"I shall see to it in the morning before your departure, Miss Wellman, and my house is yours till you are ready to leave. Now, with your permission, I must go back to the trading post and see if Mr. Bouchard's supplies are ready for his journey back in the morning." He courteously took his leave of her, beckoning to the four Creeks to follow, and then Ben, seeing Lucien's scarcely perceptible nod, followed them out of the house.

At the trading post, after having brought Priscilla Wellman to John Forbes's house, Lucien had donned a waistcoat and breeches and boots, such as he had worn in France. He had also obtained a razor and shaved off his beard and the thick black sideburns down his cheeks. Throughout the meal, Priscilla Wellman had glanced at him, finding it difficult to reconcile this elegantly groomed, handsome and still youthful man with the breechclout-clad, bearded near-Indian whom she had met in the forest clearing. Remembering, too, the duel to the death which he had fought with the Choctaw leader, she had found his polished, Old World manners all the more startling. He had told her very little about himself during their two-day journey back to Mobile; despite her grief, her natural feminine curiosity had been strongly aroused. Now, finding herself alone with him at the table, she colored hotly as she observed that he was looking directly at her.

"I—I really haven't thanked you properly for what you did, Mr. Bouchard."

"You owe me no thanks, Miss Wellman. My only regret is that we did not come in time to save your brother."

She sighed, put her hands to her face and bowed her head for a moment. "Must there always be such hatred between the Indians and the white settlers, Mr. Bouchard?" she asked after a moment.

"No, not if there is truthfulness and honesty and honor between them, Miss Wellman. I have lived with the Creeks for five years, ever since I left France, and I respect and admire them. The village of Econchate is so much like the commune I once believed should be adopted in France to replace the antiquated and unjust feudal estates, and it has proved to be a sensible way of life for the Creeks. When they fight, it is for their land, and after all, history tells us that most wars are fought for just such a cause. The pity of it is that so many innocent must suffer when such wars occur."

"You—you mean you live with them of your own choice, Mr. Bouchard?"

"Yes. You see, Miss Wellman, I was the son of a nobleman of a French province just before the fall of the Bastille. For various reasons, I determined to come to this New World and find land on which I could settle and build a new life, land that would be free of politics and wars." He smiled humorlessly. "I anticipated what would happen in my country, and the reality is far worse than even my gloomiest fears. I believed that in a flourishing young republic, a man would have an opportunity to prove himself on his merits by dint of purposeful work and, above all else, decency toward his neighbors. Mind you, I have found all that at the village of Econchate. I came to New Orleans and thence to Mobile, where I met the Creek leader the late Alexander McGillivray. He sent me to Econchate and told me that if I proved myself worthy, the Creeks might employ me as a trader. So indeed they did, and they have given me some land to settle on and to farm. Thus far, the village has not been threatened by the inroads of settlers who wish to take away Indian land. Sensible treaties are in the process of being made, which, I sincerely hope, will enable the white man and the red to live side by side in amity, since each has much to learn from the other."

"You truly believe that, then?" she wonderingly asked.

"With all my heart. Weakened as she is, France can no longer hope to hold any part of her colonies in this territory, and the Spanish rule here cannot long endure. Again, I hope this can be settled through peaceful negotiation."

"You are French, yet you speak English so well, you are kind and thoughtful, yet I have seen how you can cope with danger, Mr. Bouchard. Are you truly content to live as you do? If France were at peace again, would you go back?"

He waited a moment before answering, his face grave. "It would avail me little now, Miss Wellman. My parents were killed in an uprising in the province, my brother by a rebellion in Haiti led by Toussaint L'Ouverture."

"Oh!" Her hazel eyes widened and the delicate curve of her mouth trembled in startled concern. "Then you—"

"Thus you and I, Miss Wellman," he gently interrupted, "have much in common between us. You told me that your father was a squire of a farm in Warwickshire. In a sense, I too am a squire near Econchate, and I have a house there and land on which I raise corn and other produce. By material standards, I suppose I am reasonably affluent, since my trading brings me a fair commission. So I ask you—and I apologize if I am brash or offensive at such a time—if you might not consider a less hazardous life than that of returning to New Orleans where you have no one and trying to support yourself?"

"What—what are you trying to say to me, Mr. Bouchard?" Again her lips trembled and her eyes were very wide as she waited for his answer.

"That if you would do me the honor of becoming my wife, Miss Wellman, I should do my best to protect you and give you what happiness you could find now that there is no one here to care for you. You said that you could not go back to England, just as I thought I could not go back to my country. Why could we not try to begin a new life and bring each other comfort?"

She lowered her eyes and there was new color in her cheeks as she clasped her hands, twisting her fingers, her forehead furrowing as she considered his proposal.

"I never—I could not believe that you would be in love with me, Mr. Bouchard, having known me so short a time. Are you sure it isn't pity that you feel instead?"

"Some of that, of course, because you are a good, gentle young woman who has suffered through no fault of her own."

"You are honest, and I admire that in anyone."

"Then that is a fair beginning," he smiled. "But to answer your question as honestly, it is too early to speak of love, just as I could not even begin to imagine that you would care for me. And yet, I am sure that many a man and many a woman have begun life together with less to unite them than you and I already have, Miss Wellman."

"That is certainly true. And it's true also that I owe my life to you. You risked yours to save mine, you know."

"Yes, but that was instinctive and it had no concern for your particular sensitivities, Miss Wellman. I did not do it as a romantic gesture to win you, but to save you from frightful suffering."

"You are mercilessly honest, Mr. Bouchard." Now it was her turn to utter a humorless little laugh. "This is becoming a strange sort of proposal, I think. And suppose you and your men had come upon me when they were actually—doing what they meant to do with the fire and the tomahawk—"

"If there had been no time to stop them, I should myself, out of sheer humanity, have put a merciful bullet into your heart, Miss Wellman."

"I see. I see that there are new rules and codes in this strange new country. Well then, I'll be honest with you too, Mr. Bouchard. The truth is, I should be terrified trying to make my way alone in New Orleans, and there are obvious dangers for an unmarried woman. I am disheartened because those I love are dead, and since it was you who saved my life, it seems to me that my life belongs to you in some part. If you still wish to marry me, I will say yes."

CHAPTER TWENTY-SIX

Priscilla Wellman's religion was that of her parents, who had adhered to the Church of England. Lucien had been reared in the Catholic faith. Yet, tactfully, he had proposed that they be married by the military commander of the Spanish garrison in Mobile rather than by a priest, much as a captain of a ship might marry them on the high seas, so that it would not seem that he was attempting to convert her. What was important for both of them, he delicately pointed out, was that their union be officially registered at Mobile so that if there were heirs, there would be no future legal question as to any inheritance of land, house and monies. As to their honeymoon, John Forbes had graciously offered to put his house at their disposal, since he himself would be staying in New Orleans for a week or more and would then visit the firm of Panton and Leslie in Pensacola. Ben and the four Creek braves camped for the two days of this brief "honeymoon" with a group of friendly Choctaws and their squaws employed at the trading post.

And so the records of the garrison commander for the date of June 29, 1795, bore an entry registering the marriage of Priscilla Wellman to Lucien Bouchard at an early hour of that afternoon. After the ceremony, witnessed by Ben, the four Creek braves and a platoon of Spanish soldiers and two clerks from the trading post, Lucien turned to Priscilla, a little hesitantly, to bestow the traditional kiss. Her cheeks crimsoned, and then to his pleased surprise, she trustingly put her arms around him and kissed him sweetly on the lips, whispering, "I'll try my best to be a good wife to you, Lucien. Are we going to go back at once to Econchate?"

"I thought we might leave the day after tomorrow, Priscilla dear," he whispered back as he took her hand and turned to accept the well wishes of the enthusiastic witnesses. Ben was first to shake his hand and to say, "I'm saying prayers for you, *M'su* Lucien, you and your sweet lady. And Ellen and I are going to look after her just like as if she was our own flesh and blood, I promise."

John Forbes's Choctaw squaws had prepared as festive an evening meal as provisions on hand could provide, and left the house soon after to stay with the camping group of their own tribe and Ben and the Creeks, not without casting speculative glances at the bride and bridegroom and exchanging suggestive comments with each other—which Lucien was relieved to know that Priscilla could not possibly understand—as to the groom's virility and the bride's likelihood of fertility.

When he found himself alone with her, there was a long, almost painful silence, for the squaws' words had embarrassingly turned his mind to the momentous and imminent act of union which would consummate this marriage. It was not only a sobering responsibility, this taking charge of this tragically abandoned young woman's life and bringing her to the unexciting and arduous work on a farm and trading post with no neighbors of her own kind to be her companions against the tedium. With his own merciless and introspective self-searching, he found himself uncertain how to begin to court her. A wedding night should be one of felicity and exquisite anticipation, of miraculous discoveries which each would make of the other, finding new, unsuspected communication of both mind and flesh as each shared and fulfilled the other's needs. Yet because he had married her out of what could only be regarded as cold-blooded calculation because of his burning desire for a son, and because she had accepted him out of her own desperate loneliness, he felt himself constrained not to impose upon her by any act or word. And yet, he could not forget that with Amelia, pity had been unexpectedly turned into a stronger, richer sentiment akin to love.

So it was he who forced himself to break the silence first, as with a candid smile, he began, "I've told you something about myself, my dear Priscilla. I want to be utterly honest with you. But first know that I shall demand nothing of you except the right to protect you and cherish you for as long as we both shall live."

"In the broader sense of both our original religions, Lucien, that is equally true for me, I think." Her sensitive face colored again, but she met his gaze levelly.

"From my life with the Creeks, Priscilla, I've learned that no matter what different names are given to the faith by which one lives, there's something basic about all of them. The Creeks have their own name for our God, but they are as devout in their way as you and I are in our own. And in marriage, they cling to the same principles of abiding trust, loyalty and decency which our own religions recommend. You see, Priscilla, I have been married twice before by Creek ceremony. Both my wives and the sons they gave me are dead."

"My God—you've had much more share of sorrow than I, Lucien. How—how did it happen?"

"My first wife was the daughter of the old chief of the village, Priscilla. She and the baby were bitten by a snake some few months after she had given birth. The second wife was English, like you, but a bondservant who had been brought by a family from Georgia to a place not far from my own house and land, their purpose being to kill the chief and stir up dissension and warfare. It was part of that same broad plot of which I spoke to you earlier in this greedy and unjust struggle for power over the land."

She shook her head wonderingly, and once again tears glistened in her hazel eyes. "Then once again, Lucien, you and I have much in common. But this bondservant, if she was one of those who tried to kill the chief, how did it happen that you married her?"

"No, my dear, she was innocent of all wrongdoing. But the Indians believed that she was involved, and they were about to put her to death. The only way to save her was

352

by marrying her and leaving her in the village as hostage. After the child was born, she came back with me to my house. And the boy who had survived when the Indians retaliated against his family for the murder of their chief ambushed me from the cornfield. She saw him when I did not and she gave her life to save me. And then the baby died some months later from river fever."

The tears in Priscilla's eyes now riveleted down her cheeks as she reached out a hand to take his and to squeeze it. "What unbearable sorrow you've known; more than mine, Lucien! You have had the tribulations of Job himself."

He started, for her words had brought back the final words of *Père* Morlain's letter. How strange indeed were the ways of fate, the labyrinthine convolutions of words and deeds which came out of the past into the present and even the future to alter a man's purposefully channeled life. Collecting himself, he saw how earnestly her sensitive face expressed a sincere concern for him, how she had forgotten her own misfortunes. And once again, because he had become a blood brother to the Creeks and part of his mind had been conditioned to their own inherent mysticism, Lucien thought of the gently vigilant spirit of Dimarte, his first, his undying love. Could she not have been the one who had sent him that acknowledging signal of the owl's call when he had pleaded with her to understand his yearning for an heir?

"It seems to me, Priscilla, that each of us approaches the other in a mood of sorrow. Well, it may be that pity or hate or sorrow, each in its own way, may be the beginning of deep and lasting trust between two strangers such as we are. I will not use the word 'love' lightly, and I know that you cannot. But by the vows I took before the officer of the garrison who made us man and wife, I pledge to you a husband's devotion and fidelity."

"And I myself to you, Lucien. You have been so frank with me, I—I must tell you that I have never known a man in the biblical sense. I was so reared to keep myself for the man who would be my husband. But now you are that, Lucien, and I am your wife. And it is for you to teach me how a wife can please her husband." She looked away quickly, her cheeks flaming, and rose from the table.

Profoundly moved, he walked out of the house and stood looking at the sky over the great bay of Mobile. Down the street of this still small but vital village—for it had not enough inhabitants as yet to be called a town, for all its hugely profitable commerce—a few tiny lights twinkled behind the windows of the little houses and cabins covered with oiled paper, or through the narrow, open chinks left between the battens which shielded these windows. The soft, magical sound of the gently lapping water down at the end of the wharf came faintly to him, and the sounds of the nightbirds twittering and chirping but with a hushed gentleness as if readying themselves for sleep. Across the delta, where the Spanish fort stood, there were lights also, those of the pinewood torches thrust on either side of the entry to the fort to make it loom like a squat bastion commandeering the watery channelway which led from the mighty gulf.

Could it have been only six years ago that he stood almost where he did now—the house of David Francis was only a little further up the street—wondering what adventures awaited him along the trail to Econchate? And after this night, what awaited him in the years to come? The old *Windigo* had given him the answer, though all the parts of it were not yet fulfilled and not now decipherable in his questioning mind. And yet, if thus far a part of that answer had already come to pass, was that not a kind of promise that his dream would one day be fulfilled?

Its fulfillment must depend not only upon himself, but upon the son Priscilla might give him. Yes, calculated though this union might be, he would approach it with gentleness and reverence, for she, like Dimarte and like Amelia also, was still virgin.

Beyond the act of union itself, however, Lucien compelled himself to think of their daily lives together. The absence of the cultural joys of books, music and art had not mattered with either Dimarte or Amelia, the former because she had never known of such things, the latter because her life in a squalid London slum had been entirely deprived of them. But Priscilla had been educated

354

to appreciate such rewarding and enrichening bounties, and now she would be as isolated as a prisoner from them in the house near the bend of the Alabama River. Yet to compensate, there would be the pleasure of conversation, the drawing upon reserves of enjoyable memories, the exchange of ideas to leaven the bland monotony of what was, when all was said and done, the life of a farmer and trader's wife. One day civilization as both she and Lucien had known it was certain to come to Econchate, but it might well be many years before that happened. Each, then, needs must be staunch to the other as companion and friend to stand against the chafing loneliness that could easily embitter and age a spirited young woman.

He drew a long breath and turned in the direction of northeast. There was the trail he had first taken six years ago. Now he would ride it with Ben and the four braves as escort for his new wife. There, the trail at whose end was the cabin and the depot and the thriving fields of corn and the little garden behind the cabin which would furnish food for the two of them.

Her father had been a squire back in England, she had said. Then surely he must have had a fine house, with windows from which he could command the view of the land whose master he was. One day, Lucien said to himself again, there will be a French chateau set down in the heart of this Alabama territory.

And when the chateau was built, and now his dream of building it was stronger than it had ever been before, if only because of the adversities and sorrows which had marked these six arduous years, how would he name it? Perhaps he had always known the name at the back of his mind. He had looked out from the tower toward the house of the Provost-Marshal so many times and seen the gentle little valley between the two hills and known that it was a haven against the wind. But the wind of that fateful May afternoon had not been halted by that haven in France. It had driven him across the ocean to the destiny he could only hope for and yet not be sure of ever realizing as he had dreamed it. But if those two towers of red brick would one day rise above the two stories of the house, from each of which he could see what had once

355

been rolling prairie and was now verdant cornfields, then he would name it Windhaven. For then it would mean that the May wind of such ill omen had brought him at last to a true haven of peace and fulfillment, of security in the knowledge that he had toiled well and that he would have a son to continue his plans for a kind of prosperous commune in which all the workers would be free men and work to his direction but also for their own reward.

Windhaven. He said the name aloud into the stillness and the darkness of this his wedding night. And he spoke it as one might speak a prayer, firmed by an inner strength which had known what it was to agonize and to sorrow and still to believe in the indomitable spirit which is the very essence of man's purpose upon this earth.

He turned back to the house now, like a man dedicated and strengthened by communion. So indeed it was, for he had never been so conscious before of the kind of mystical awareness of the elements of this spot on the earth where he stood so far from his native soil, of the sky and the moon and the stars and the humid smell of the air from the bay and the strength of his own body. Against his will, he had been forced to take life; now he was granted this new chance to give it and, in the giving, to give a meaningful purpose to the life of a young woman for whom death appeared to have vitiated her energy for life itself.

He went back into the house and to the darkened bedroom. Now he must think of the future, or there could be none, and that would be to deny all the reason for his dream, to deny any justice for what had happened along that trail to the northeast and what had happened at the end of it these last six years. To both his God and to the Great Spirit of the Creeks, he spoke a silent prayer that he and Priscilla might merge their disrupted lives into a strong and steady and joyous channeling.

The bed, by contrast to the pile of blankets and even the doeskin coverlet of his cabin, was a luxury, though not so fine as he had had in his own bedchamber at the chateau at Yves-sur-lac. But at least it had the semblance of a kindlier time and place, and that was a welcome thought on this so significant night.

She wore only her chemise, as he could detect when his hand groped for hers to bring it to his lips as he clambered beside her. She turned to him at once, responsive, not submissive, wonderingly innocent and yet aware. In that supple movement, there was the memory of Amelia's curious willingness, and, thankfully, not the slightest hint of wifely resignation and submission. By such means, she merited even more tenderness than he had to give any woman after Dimarte. She had asked him if there was not pity in his gesture of offering her marriage to escape the dreariness of what might have been her life alone in New Orleans. To be sure, there was a measure of pity, as there was on his part a measure of design; but her very sensitivity and intellect argued against his harsh usage of her, even granting his long-suppressed carnal needs. That was why he was content to lie beside her, holding her hand in both of his, kissing her gently, letting her understand that she was to dictate each moment of their union and quiet what timorous virginal dread she must assuredly have of even a beloved male who, for the first time, shared her chaste bed.

At last she gave a little sigh. "I can't believe, Lucien, you're the same man I saw in the clearing," she whispered, and her voice had a nuance of playful jesting.

"How so, dear Priscilla?"

"Why because, sir—" she uttered a soft little laugh— "you terrified me then when you fought that Indian. I was so afraid of you then, I even shrank from you when you came to take me down from that horrid tree. And now, sir, it seems that you're the one who's afraid of me. I'm not made of Dresden china, that you must hold back from touching me lest I break."

Taken aback by her winsome wit, he burst into laughter, and then, in the midst of it, sealed his lips on hers and drew her to him. No, it was not yet, it could not yet be love; but it was the happiest of all beginnings for two such divergent people who had come so strangely together to find a common bond.

"You're sure you're willing to go back on horseback to Econchate, Priscilla," Lucien asked his blonde wife on the second morning after their marriage as they were eating breakfast in John Forbes's house.

"Of course I can, Lucien dear. You're forgetting that I grew up on a farm in Warwickshire, and I rode horses when I was ten."

"That may be true, my dear, but it's at least a week's journey, perhaps more, because I don't propose to tax your endurance. Nearly two hundred miles, Priscilla, and with a pack train of supplies for the village, so that it might possibly take as long as ten days. That would be a rigorous experience for you."

Priscilla shot him a saucy smile which showed the delightful dimples in her cheeks and chin. "Didn't I tell you the other night that I'm not made of Dresden china, dear? Besides, it will be a new and exciting experience, I'm sure." She reached out her hand to touch his across the table. "We might call it part of our honeymoon, you know. We'll be camping at night, I imagine."

"Yes, of course." Seeing her smile deepen, he felt color rising to his sun-bronzed cheeks. Their two days in this little house had been a revelation to them both. Very much like Amelia, Priscilla was warm-hearted and generous, adapting herself with exquisite and interested curiosity to her new role as wife to a virile yet attentively considerate male. So much so, that his own self-recriminations over the calculated entry into marriage to provide an heir had been forgotten in the hours of their affectionate intimacy.

And she now delighted him with a merry little laugh and the reply, "I declare, Lucien, for a man who's fought Indians and bears singlehanded, you're blushing like a girl out of a convent!"

"What does a Church of England girl possibly know about convents?" Lucien chuckled.

"Enough to know I'm rather glad I'm here with you, Lucien, instead of in one right now," was the engaging answer in a soft, tremulous voice as Lucien once more gratefully raised Priscilla's hand to his lips.

They left that noon of the same day on the return journey to Econchate, Lucien having purchased a gentle but

358

sturdy mare for Priscilla to ride. Much to his carefully concealed amusement—and the not at all concealed surprise of the Creek braves—she insisted on riding on a saddle as a man would, and had made him procure a suitable pair of breeches and a doeskin jacket for her riding costume. Each of the braves led a pack pony behind him, as did Ben, laden with bundles containing pipes, kettles, needles, scissors, blankets, trade shirts, salt and other provisions which Nanakota had requested.

"We shall have to rebuild our storage depot before much longer, Ben," Lucien said to the Ashanti after the entourage had been ferried across on flatboats to the other side of the delta.

"That is a good idea, *M'su* Lucien. And perhaps your sweet wife will help teach the Creek squaws how to use many things which have been brought across the ocean to the trading post but are not yet known to them."

"That's also very true, Ben. I know that the Cherokees are already spinning and weaving and have a cotton engine, the new one which this man Eli Whitney invented a few years ago. I am sure that Abram Mordecai will obtain one when he thinks the time is right."

"Some of the planters tried cotton in Santo Domingo, *M'su* Lucien," Ben replied as he jogged his pony along the start of the trail which Lucien remembered so well. "There they had what they called jennies operated by horses, and there was also a hand press to take out the seed. It is said that cotton loses three-fourths of its weight with the seed, and it takes much labor to make it ready for making thread and garments."

"I have thought of that, ever since Mordecai visited Econchate, Ben," Lucien pensively replied. "I'm eager to see Mr. Whitney's device, but the problem of labor is a very difficult one. I do not think we could teach the braves in Econchate to come to work in a cotton-producing house. It is alien to their nature. They hunt and fish and till land, true enough, but that is manly and part of their most ancient heritage. But to work as laborers—no, I do not think they would take to it by nature."

Ben shrugged philosophically. "Then, *M'su* Lucien, you will have to have black slaves to do the work, just as in

359

Santo Domingo and in many of the Indian villages here and through the territory as far as Florida."

"If I have them, Ben, they may be black but they will not be slaves, any more than you are a slave now. I give you my word on that," Lucien firmly declared.

CHAPTER TWENTY-SEVEN

The journey back to Econchate actually took eleven days, a leisurely and meandering journey with long pauses over the noontime meals and watering of the horses, camping at night and, for Lucien and Priscilla, an idyllic time to become acquainted with each other. Just as he had suspected, his young blonde wife had a keen mind and vivid impressions of life on the farm back in England and sojourns with her parents in the great city of London, as well as in the thriving American city of Savannah. Her descriptions of the houses there kindled in Lucien a new eagerness to see his primitive cabin transformed into that red-brick chateau with its two imposing towers. And as she talked, with a gay animation and an ease which showed how her trust and confidence in him had dispersed the terrible shadows of her family's violent deaths, he began to believe that this time fate had smiled upon him and his hopes and dreams.

She proved to be an excellent rider and complained several times of the slowness of their pace. Twenty miles a day on a trail which Lucien knew so well was nothing, she incisively declared, and frequently smilingly twitted him on the way he was treating her like a fragile goblet of hand-blown glass, something that would break at the least touch. At night, too, when they lay together wrapped in a blanket at a distance from Ben and the four braves, who had made their own sleeping quarters at a tactful distance from the newlyweds, she showed an ever-increasing piquancy for teasing him and goading him into accepting her as an equal partner in the life they would build together. It was a blessed boon for Lucien Bouchard; his morbidly introspective concern over his selfishness in marrying her to further his ambitious plans for the future were banished by Priscilla's playful, loving and joyful acquiescence to his lovemaking. He was thus less demon-driven and more expansive than he had believed possible with this young woman whom he had rescued from a Choctaw torture stake.

Most of all, he found that she had acquired a surprising amount of knowledge of the skills of animal husbandry, improved methods of farming and irrigation, which she had carefully observed back in Warwickshire, and by pooling their knowledge thus, he foresaw that his relationship with the villagers of Econchate would be most advantageously increased. The Creeks would assuredly accord her a gracious welcome, and with this in mind, he used many of these breaks in their journey to teach her the rudiments of the Creek language. And again, the enthusiasm she showed in mastering a few simple sentences and her intelligent questions on the phrasing of some of her suggestions on agriculture and the raising of cattle—which the villagers were beginning to develop more and more—convinced him that his choice of wife had been exceedingly fortunate.

When they at last reached Econchate shortly before noon of the eleventh day, Nanakota and old Tsipoulata came out to greet them. The friendly *Mico* stared at Priscilla as she blithely dismounted from her horse and came to stand beside Lucien, in her breeches and jacket and men's sturdy boots, her honey-gold hair neatly coiled in a thick knot at the back of her head, her soft pink skin already attractively tanned from the hot summer sun. (Lucien had insisted, much to her distaste, that she anoint her forehead, cheeks and throat with the odorous bear grease to prevent intense sunburn.)

"It is good to see you again, my brother!" Nanakota exclaimed as he came forward to grasp Lucien's hand. Then, looking intently at the charming, svelte blonde, he murmured in Creek, "But who is this squaw, Lu-shee-ahn?"

"My wife, Nanakota. She came from Savannah to New Orleans with her brother, after her parents had been killed in Georgia on the lands of the Creeks. A party of renegade Choctaws killed her brother, captured her and were about to put her to death when our men came upon them and rescued her. She is alone, and we found each other agreeable, and she wishes to know our ways. But I will let her speak for herself on that, my *Mico*."

Turning to Priscilla, he smilingly said, "Introduce yourself to Nanakota as I have taught you, my dear."

With an engaging smile, the attractive young woman moved beside her husband, clasped both her hands together against her bosom, inclined her head and said in Creek, "I ask the hospitality of the mighty *Mico* for myself, who am still a stranger to him, but who wish to be as welcome as the blood brother of the Bear."

"Ho, ho, that is good, that is very good!" Nanakota slapped his thigh, his homely face wrinkled in a broad grin. "I can even understand her, though she has still much to learn of our tongue. And I know who taught her that, and who does us much honor by his presence with us again. Tell her for me that she has already won my heart with her words, and that the village of Econchate will give her shelter whenever she wishes to ask it."

Lucien chuckled and nodded, turned to his wife and, squeezing her hand, remarked, "You have made a great success, my dear. Nanakota says that the village of Red Ground is yours, and you are welcome whenever you wish to come here. And now, you must rest a little and then this evening we shall have a great feast and I must be at the council to talk over the plans for this summer and the goods my friends will need. You shall also see the green-corn dance, though that will be later this month. The tradition is to hold it for five days in the latter part of July."

"I like your friend Nanakota, Lucien dear. I begin to understand how you could find your happiness here."

"As I've told you during the evenings when we made camp, Priscilla, these people have an admirable and simple honesty in their ways. I am only sorry that you

363

had to know only the worst side of the Indians and at such a terrible cost. But it is also true that the white man has brought upon himself their fierce quickness to retaliate by his unscrupulous attempts to seize their lands."

"I can see how neat their houses are, Lucien, and how attractive this village is, as if it were actually a little city out in an English countryside. It is primitive, but clean and orderly."

"Exactly, my dear. Remember, when you show kindness to the Creeks, they reciprocate. Once you make a friend, he remains a friend for life and he does not turn upon you. So do not be afraid to say what is in your heart, because they admire truthfulness and they detest hypocrisy and lies. Well, in that respect, they are really no different from myself when all is said and done. But now, I'll take you to a little house that has been made ready for your comfort," he concluded as Nanakota made a sign to him.

A week later, Lucien took Priscilla to what was to be her new home, downriver some twenty miles from the village. Ben had gone back with Ellen and little Thomas a day after the arrival at Econchate, promising Lucien that the cabin would be in good order to receive its new mistress by the time he and Priscilla arrived. During her stay in Econchate, Priscilla had already shown sincere interest in the customs and the way of life of these people who were the blood brothers of her husband. Lucien had particularly noted how fond she seemed to be of the children, who, in their turn, thronged about her, smiling and chattering and showing her the toys they had fashioned out of bits of bark or twigs smeared with clay from the river bank. At such moments, when he saw the happy glow in her eyes, he reflected that it had been no error of judgment to save her from the morbid loneliness that would have been her lot if she had gone back to New Orleans. And more than that, her pleasure in the children augured an instinct for motherhood which, as he greatly hoped, would bring them even more closely together.

As Lucien landed the pirogue and helped his young wife onto the river bank, she excitedly exclaimed, "What a lovely place you've chosen to live in, dear Lucien! That broad stretch of green cornfields framed by the hill and the bluff, like a little valley—and with its view of this beautiful river—it's surely like a kind of Eden!"

"It will be our Eden, dear Priscilla. Do you know, the Creeks gave me this land to settle on, and although I did not know where they would send me, when I first saw it, I was struck by its similarity to my home in the province of Normandy. There, too, just beyond my father's chateau, was a little hill and then a gentle valley with a tiny lake, and then a larger hill over which—" he stopped, remembering what had drawn him to ride over that hill that never-to-be-forgotten May afternoon, and then quickly finished—"and because in those days it was a haven against the wind, *un asile du vent,* I have thought of calling it Windhaven. One day, if God so wills, you and I will live in a fine house like the one in Normandy and look out upon the land and the river from the towers on each side of it. And there will be comforts such as have not yet come to us here, to make our life more gracious and to free us from so many of the arduous tasks we now face in this still new and almost uninhabited country."

"Yes," she whispered, her hand clasping his as she looked out over the cornfields and the two cabins and saw Ellen and Ben emerge from theirs and come to greet them. "I think I know now why I wanted to marry you, Lucien. I saw in it a beginning over again for me, and I remembered how happy I was as a little girl on my father's great farm in Warwickshire. And what satisfaction it was to see the cattle and the horses and to watch the crops grow and be harvested and to know that people would be fed because of all that. I will try my best to help you to your Windhaven, my dear husband."

He drew her to him and kissed her warmly, holding her tightly and looking at her sensitive, sweetly smiling face as if he were seeing it for the first time. Then, his voice vibrant with a rich and joyous emotion, he murmured, "Come now, my dear one, let us go see my dear friends Ben and Ellen, for friends they are and more than servants and never slaves."

When he led her into the larger cabin, he uttered a cry

of surprise, for in his absence Ben had made him a draw-bed, a wooden bedstead held together with rawhide thongs, with a layer of blankets below and a doeskin cover stuffed with scalded moss which had been buried after the scalding for a time to make it softer and more pliable.

"Ben, what a marvelous coming-home present, thank you, thank you, my good friend." He turned to the tall Ashanti and shook his hand.

"I've been working on it from time to time, *M'su* Lucien." Ben looked uncomfortable at the praise.

"How very thoughtful of you, Ben. I see now why Lucien calls you his good friend." Priscilla smilingly extended her hand. "May I be yours also, Ben?"

And when she entered the other room, she colored furiously, for there was the cradle which Ben had made also for little Étienne. Glancing back at Ben, who had discreetly moved back to the door of the cabin, she whispered, "I hope I can give you a son, dear Lucien. A son to help you build your Windhaven."

A week later, Lucien and Priscilla went back to Econchate to witness the green-corn dance and enjoy the festivities which followed the mystic and symbolical ceremony which asked Hisagita-imisi to bless the crops and bring good hunting in the months ahead. And on the day that they went back to the cabin at the bend of the river, Priscilla took Lucien by the hand and led him into the room where the cradle stood and, blushing demurely, whispered, "I have missed my time, my dear husband, and I have said my own prayers that it will be our son."

And during all this time, the struggle for possession of all Indian lands went on. The second Yazoo sale had so concerned President Washington that he laid copies of the bill before the Congress, urging its members to debate the issues fully, since the consequences might deeply affect the peace and welfare of the United States. Both the Senate and the House of Representatives adopted a resolution which instructed the Attorney-General to investigate the title of Georgia to the lands sold. The four companies involved had by now paid up the entirety of the purchase money and believed themselves on the threshold of a vast fortune, since the Georgia bill had stipulated that the act of no subsequent legislature should affect their title.

But, over the past winter, the Georgia Legislature again convened with a new governor and a new body of members, which included those who had voted against the original sale. General James Jackson, who had distinguished himself in the American Revolution, introduced a bill to repeal the Yazoo sale and declare it null and void. It was so adopted and signed by the new governor of Georgia, Jared Irwin. The records of the Yazoo act were expunged and the bill itself was taken to the streets of Louisville, where a sun glass was held over the paper until it was consumed by fire as a symbolic act to proclaim that heaven itself was against such fraudulence.

Meanwhile, believing the bill to be legitimate, hundreds of settlers had emigrated to the Tombigbee and the Mississippi River territory, intending to occupy the lands which these four companies had proposed to grant them. Thus, into the wild region came a predominant population of Georgians who were destined to bring out of the wilderness towns, schools, churches and courts . . . but not without the gathering clouds of war.

Yet those clouds seemed to have been dispersed forever when, on October 27th of this momentous year of 1795, John Jay's superbly far-seeing diplomatic efforts brought about the Treaty of San Lorenzo, with Thomas Pinckney as negotiating agent. In this agreement, Spain agreed that the southern boundary of the United States should be established at the thirty-first parallel, agreed to cede the right to navigate the Mississippi to its mouth, as well as the right of deposit or warehousing of merchandise at New Orleans for three years. By this time, the Spanish had appointed Peter Olivier as commandant at Mobile. And one of Olivier's first acts was to grant a vacant lot on Royal Street running back to the river to the firm of Panton, Leslie & Company. Thus the firm which had backed the late Alexander McGillivray from its Pensacola base now formally established a vital commercial post in this Spanish-dominated town into whose great bay the Alabama and its tributaries flowed ... a water route along which, less than a generation hence, cotton would become king.

And in Lucien's homeland, turmoil, bloodshed, war and virtual anarchy had taken hold. Marie Antoinette had followed her husband to the guillotine on October 16, 1793, condemned for treason for having secretly betrayed the French campaign plans to her native Austrians. She met her death with noble and heroic courage, unlike the initiator of the reign of terror, Maximilien Robespierre, who followed her on July 28, 1794. Under the new constitution passed this very year, the Directory came into existence, a new regime marked by corruption, intrigues, disastrous inflation and bankruptcy. Meanwhile, the Committee of Public Safety had raised new armies to drive France's enemies of the First Coalition out of the provinces. French armies took the offensive in the Low Countries and forced Holland to make peace this year, and Prussia and Spain capitulated in the Treaties of Basel. And the little Corporal, Napoleon Bonaparte, was striking at Piedmont and Lombardy, crossing the Alps to join the generals from the Low Countries and South Germany.

By the end of August, when it was evident that Priscilla would surely bear Lucien a child, the black-haired Frenchman visited Ben, Ellen and their sturdy little son Thomas in their cabin to tell them the joyous news. "You have worked as a kind of overseer for me, Ben," he told the loyal Ashanti. "It is five years now, and if I had paid you wages, you would have earned some fifteen hundred *piastres*. I authorize you, whenever we go to Mobile, to draw against that amount for anything you, your wife and your son may need."

"You know that a black may not own property, *M'su* Lucien."

"Yes, because of the existing laws. Perhaps one day they will be changed. Nonetheless, Ben, you are known at the post as my assistant, and therefore, what you require will be charged against my account. In that way you will own it. It is little enough to thank you, not only for the help you have given me, but also your priceless companionship."

By fall, when her pregnancy was quite obvious, Priscilla insisted on going to Econchate with Lucien to take part in the festival harvest and the storing of supplies for the oncoming winter. She had urged Nanakota, in reasonably passable Creek (which Ellen had continued to teach her all this time), to add more cattle to the holdings of the village and to let her show the squaws how to make cheese and butter, even though in a limited way. The friendly *Mico* expressed great interest in Priscilla's suggestions and himself came to watch as the young blonde woman seated herself beside a cow and proceeded to milk it. The milk from each cow was put into clay gourds, which were then stored in a dry well. Priscilla then showed the *Mico* how she skimmed off the cream and put it into a wooden bucket to which Lucien had attached an improvised lid with plunger. She began to work this energetically until Lucien interposed, at which she teased him, "Please, dear, by now you ought to know I'm not all that delicate!" All the same, Lucien insisted on finishing the work, for it seemed to him that her belly was swollen much more than it should be in this fourth month of pregnancy.

When at last the first batch was ready for sampling, Priscilla spread a little on cornmeal cakes. Nanakota comically rolled his eyes and patted his belly to indicate his full approval of this new delicacy, and gave instructions to Tunkamara's younger wife to imitate Priscilla's chore and to see whether she could equal her white-eyes teacher.

Throughout the fall, Priscilla remained in the village practicing her growing fluency with the Creek language and helping the women practice making butter and cheese and suggesting different ways of preparing their customary dishes for the meals of their warrior consorts. Lucien and Nanakota and a dozen braves went off to hunt for ten days and returned with twenty bucks, a dozen raccoons and two bears, these last having been killed with musket fire. The deerskins would bring prime prices in Mobile, and Nanakota again expressed his gratitude for the ways in which Lucien had made himself useful to everyone at Econchate.

Then Priscilla and Lucien took their leave of Nanakota

and went back to the cabin near the bend of the river, and learned that Ellen was expecting her second child. This time, the pretty young Kru shyly expressed the hope that the child would be a girl, to be named after her own mother, Disjamilla. Her own name, she explained, had been Subarte, back in Africa; her planter master had renamed her Ellen in Santo Domingo.

The deerskins which Lucien and the *Mico* and the braves had garnered during their hunt were augmented by some fifty more by mid-November, all properly cured and treated to remain in prime condition and thus bring the highest possible values at the Mobile trading post. Lucien made the trip on the flatboat to Mobile by himself this time, for he wanted Ben to remain back at the depot to look after both his own wife and Priscilla. Despite Priscilla's enthusiasm and pleasure in the work she had done at Econchate, Lucien was more than a little concerned about her. The boyish compactness of her lithe hips was not entirely propitious for childbearing, and the advancing size of her pregnancy caused him no small anxiety. He had had a private word with Ellen before his departure, and the gentle Kru had assured him that she would look after Priscilla. "But for her to move about and do things, *M'su* Lucien, can only be good for her," she argued to reassure him. "And besides, back in Santo Domingo, I learned some of the voodoo ways. I will make a sacrifice to *Mam'zelle* Erculie, the goddess of love, so that your wife will bring forth this child without pain, you will see."

In no way would Lucien hurt Ellen's feelings by vouchsafing his personal belief that voodoo and conjuring were built on the superstitions of the fearful and easily swayed; instead, he graciously thanked her, but as he set forth on the flatboat, he addressed a prayer to the God he had worshiped ever since his boyhood.

He returned a week before Christmas, leading three pack ponies laden with trinkets and gifts for the villagers as well as for Priscilla and Ellen. At the trading post, he had found a Spanish mirror with a silver handle and had marked it at once as a *cadeau de Noël* for his courageous young wife.

This, and an exquisite Spanish fan and a box of rice

powder, together with a bolt of blue cloth from which Priscilla might make a dress or cape as she chose, made it a joyous first Christmas for Lucien and his young blonde wife. He had brought presents back for Ben and Ellen and Thomas too, and several bottles of wine so that all might toast the coming year. The year in which his child would be born, in which there might well be peace because of the treaties already signed and those in prospect, a year in which his hope to see Windhaven crystallized if only because of the birth of a son—as he fervently prayed it would be—who would, hand in hand with him, build that American counterpart of what had been his French home.

But his concern for Priscilla deepened as the winter grew upon them, for by February the child was big within her and she was often seized with false labor pains. Many a night he wakened to hear her sobs and gasps. Cradling her in his arms and kissing her sweat-beaded forehead and whispering soothing encouragements, he rued his almost obsessive yearning for a son if it was to cost this brave, loyal and lovely helpmate so dearly.

And then, the last week of a chilly March, the actual labor pains began. Haggard, her face contorted, attended by Ellen, who sat with her throughout a long, agonizing day and night, Priscilla was finally brought to term. Outside the cabin, digging his nails into his palms and swearing under his breath, Lucien stalked, knowing himself to be useless, detesting his virile urge of self-perpetuation which had brought about Priscilla's intolerable suffering. Her cries resounded, from hour to hour, till it seemed her throat must be raw and choked from them.

Then suddenly there was a frantic cry from Ellen, and Lucien flung himself into the cabin, sleepless, unshaven, eyes red and swollen with tears and exhaustion.

"It is the child, *M'su* Lucien!" Ellen gasped. "It does not breathe, but Miz Priscilla is bleeding so! See if you can make it stop while I help the poor little baby!"

She had plucked up the child, which was bluish, its eyes closed, its face wrinkled. Lucien saw his wife, her face twisted to one side, her arms flung out in cross on the rumpled bed, and saw the dark, ominous blood flowing from her. Hastily he tried his best to staunch it, ripping off his doeskin jacket and pressing it against her, sobbing prayers, endearments to the still, pale, contorted face now so dear to him. In these short months, her companionship and wit and loveliness had been an anodyne for the bleak monotony of this life of constant toil.

He glanced up at Ellen, saw her put her mouth to the baby's and breathe her own life-breath into the tiny mouth. Her fingers moved against the infant's back, and then the sides and the tiny chest, and again she blew and blew again. Finally, with a sobbing cry of joy, she exclaimed, "Now, now it lives, *M'su* Lucien!"

"Praise be unto God—Priscilla, Priscilla, praise be unto God—Priscilla, Priscilla, it's our son—"

His momentary exultation trailed off as he stared at his wife's immobile body. There was no sign of life, and she was deathly pale from the loss of blood. He put his ear to her heart, and then he uttered a strangled cry of rage and helplessness and horror to learn that once again destiny had wreaked its inexplicable will upon him.

CHAPTER TWENTY-EIGHT

Was it an evil star rather than a mysterious and unseasonal wind that had directed his course across the ocean in search of freedom, only to find disaster? He who deemed constancy as the virtue to be prized above all others, now found himself a widower for the third time in six short years. Had all this been foretold when the old *Windigo* cast the bones upon the soil of Econchate? For even Job could surely not have mourned more deeply nor more painfully than he mourned now for three dear companions, each the mother of a child, and of their issue only this tiny, black-haired son. And if malevolent destiny still held back a final, annihilating blow against all his hopes and dreams, perhaps even that son was doomed and accursed.

He had buried Priscilla on the hill not far from where Amelia and little Étienne lay, and this time he had not been able to weep. Instead, his face stony, moving dully to the small, meaningless tasks required of each day, Lucien was consumed with a bitterness that railed against whatever evil star or unseen fate had thrice let him drain the cup of joy only to taste the galling dregs at the bottom.

Ben had returned to Econchate to bring back a young squaw who had just given birth to a daughter and whose husband had died two months earlier from the bite of a copperhead lurking in a rotted hollow log over which he had stumbled while on the hunt. Her name was Shomanee, and she was quite tall and shapely, with alert, expressive features and a soft gentle voice the first hearing of which agonizedly reminded Lucien of his beloved Dimarte. The young squaw explained to the bereaved Frenchman that Nanakota had ordered her to remain with his blood brother and nurse the child until she was no longer required for that task.

Remembering how Dimarte had dipped little Edmond into the river every morning, Lucien had imitated her act with his little son. The baby was healthy and resembled him more than it did his unfortunate young English wife. How should he name the boy? Not after his dissolute brother Jean, but rather after some great personage in French history who had brought glory and honor to his native land. Yes, he knew what the child's name should be—Henry, after Henri IV, who had established religious toleration through his memorable Edict of Nantes in 1598 and who, with his minister Sully, had spent the rest of his reign restoring order, industry and trade. Although a king, he had the welfare of the common people in mind. For gallantry and wit, for concern for those far less fortunate, for conduct as a jousting knight in tourneys, his name was one to reckon with indeed. Yes, this son should be Henry Bouchard. Linked with the ancient name of a great family of the Norsemen, given a baptismal name of one of the last great French kings, this boy might at last work side by side with his father toward the fulfillment so long sought.

When the boy was old enough to travel, Lucien decided, he would take him to Mobile, there to be baptized by a priest and the event duly recorded in the town's annals. Just as he had validated his marriage to Priscilla, so he would validate his little son's future claims upon whatever inheritance he himself could bestow. And having decided all that, he walked alone toward the towering red bluff at twilight, knelt down, reverently crossed himself, and prayed that this son, unlike the two before him, would grow to manhood.

"Dimarte, my beloved, look down upon me and pray to your Great Spirit with me that this son, whom I begot in all humility and gratitude and in fidelity to our love which

374

was so short-lived, may be in spirit your own sturdy boy, touched by your gentle compassion and understanding all his life." And having uttered those words aloud in the stillness and the darkness, Lucien Bouchard at last felt the tears of grief and despair come to swollen, dry eyes and pour unchecked down his bronzed, weatherbeaten cheeks.

Now, more than ever before, he was committed and dedicated; all his energy and skill and vigilance must be expended for Henry's sake. There would be lonely years ahead, years that were already foreshadowed by the gathering storm of usurpation over the Creek lands. They were certain to involve him and his son, but he must survive them for Henry's sake. He would not again think of marriage; he did not think that he could bear another crushing deprivation. Even though Priscilla had lived with him little more than three-quarters of this tragic year, he had found in her a gift for friendship and companionship which was comforting even if they were not the ecstatic bounty of first, truest love. Besides, no one would ever take Dimarte's place, nor would he try again even for outward show or the selfish comforts that would assuage his own loneliness. No, from this moment forth, what love he had left in him was pledged to his infant son.

On the twenty-ninth of June, President Washington's commissioners and the chiefs of the entire Creek Nation concluded a treaty in which the Creeks ratified the earlier New York document and pledged themselves to carry out its provisions and assist Spain and the United States to run a territorial boundary line. The Creeks agreed also to allow the United States the right to establish trading posts upon the territory between the Ockmulgee and the Oconee, allowing to each five square miles of land, but refused to yield any of this land to Georgia. In return, the commissioners agreed to allow the Creeks two blacksmiths and two strikers, with tools and iron, and to distribute at once six thousand dollars' worth of goods to all who were present at this conclave.

The very heart of the matter went back to the Treaty of New York of 1789, in which Alexander McGillivray had held out against an acknowledgment of American sovereignty except over the parts of the Creek Nation which were within the limits of the United States. Thus the effect was to make the ultimate disposition of the Creeks depend upon the settlement of the disputed boundary between the United States and Spain. If it was found that all or part of the Creek territory lay north or east of the ultimate line, then it would be under American protection; any part south or west would be under Spanish rule, as provided by the Treaty of Pensacola in 1784. And now that Alexander McGillivray was dead, the Spanish were in no hurry to settle the boundary dispute and, wherever possible, tried to delay the American commission headed by Colonel Andrew Ellicott from completing it.

News of these disputes reached Econchate steadily as the year of 1796 drew to its close. Lucien and Ben, and often several warriors accompanying them, made frequent trips to Mobile, bringing back crude plows such as were still used in the Pyrenees and drawn at times by mules or even by humans. Salt, cloth, trinkets, hatchets and woodsmen's axes were packed in the bundles which the tireless ponies carried back along the trail to Econchate. Ellen had her child and, as she had prayed, it was a girl and accordingly named after her beloved mother. Shomanee, still nursing her own child, remained in Lucien's cabin in the room with the cradle to care for little Henry. Leaner than ever now, wiry and muscular, his eyes brooding and sad, Lucien Bouchard sought to lose his bitter memories in the arduous work of making Econchate virtually self·sufficient and at the same time, when he was admitted to the council, urging that the younger warriors think of the virtues and profits of peace rather than impulsive war against the white-eyes.

Meanwhile, the Congress of the United States had, on May 18th, passed its Public Land Act, which authorized the sale in minimum lots of 640 acres at two dollars per acre and inaugurated a credit system so that settlers would be able to meet the cost while earning it upon the land itself. It was an act which was to have considerable significance for Lucien's own land, on which he had, so far as legal tenets were concerned, only squatter's rights.

On June 1st, Tennessee entered the Union as a slave state. On November 15th, the French minister Adet pomp-ously announced the suspension of diplomatic relations with the United States, and in that same month the gawky private who had enlisted to fight Indians, Andrew Jackson, was elected as the first Congressman from the new state of Tennessee. On December 7th, electors cast their vote and proclaimed John Adams, with 71 votes President to replace George Washington, while Thomas Jefferson, to whom they had given 68 votes, became Vice-President. This new republic had established a post office for the handling of letters, and in John Adams' cabinet, Joseph Habersham replaced Washington's chosen Timothy Pickering as Postmaster General.

Through these seemingly endless months for Lucien, he could not but be aware that the attractive young widowed squaw, Shomanee, had begun to look upon him as her man, given to her by the *Mico* to replace her dead husband. Bolder than ever Dimarte was, she shared his evening meal and on many an occasion sending him provocative glances from her lustrous, dark eyes, sought to take full advantage of the proximity in which they lived. Lucien had remained strictly continent, sleeping on a pile of blankets in the original room of this enlarged cabin, according the young Creek squaw the bed which Ben had so assiduously made for Priscilla. At times, Shomanee would look away as if speaking to a third person in the cabin and say aloud in Creek, "Is it that Shomanee is not well made or too old for a mate? She has lost hers, and her mourning will be over with the coming of another year, as is the law. There is a man not far from her whom she would favor once it is her time to take another mate. Does he not find her to his liking?"

At first, Lucien turned aside these all too obvious invitations with a pleasant quip, praising Shomanee's virtues and beauty, but saying that only a warrior of her own clan was worthy of her. But as December neared, her pointed remarks about her eagerness to mate with him could no longer be so easily ignored.

On Christmas Eve, Ben and Ellen and Lucien celebrated with a well-cooked haunch of venison, maize and a sweet pudding and some Spanish wine. When the two former slaves had gone back to their cabin with little

Thomas and his baby sister, Lucien strolled along the river bank toward the red bluff where Dimarte lay. Here in silence for a long hour he communed with her, asking her spirit to bless the son who had been spared him and who would serve also to remind him constantly of her great love.

"I promise you, my beloved, that I shall take no wife again to the end of my days. In that way, I will keep your memory fresh and warm within me always. Be with me in my lonely hours, gentle Dimarte. Help me strive against the baser urges of my flesh, because I know that no other woman, however desirable her body, can approach your kindness and wisdom and the harmonious understanding of aliens and strangers which you brought to the council and won you the name of beloved woman. I long for you, and I will judge all women I shall know to the end of my life by you and they will all be lacking, my Dimarte."

Returning to the cabin, he let himself in, closed the door, and stretched out on his pile of blankets with a weary sigh. Then he heard soft, quick footsteps, and a moment later Shomanee lay beside him, naked, winding her arms around him and whispering in his ear, "I burn for you, Lu-shee-ahn, I am shameless, but do not blame me. All these months in the next room, seeing you, and with my mate so long absent from my bed, I cannot help my needs. Beat me, scorn me, but use me, you are the blood brother of the Bear and you are mighty as any warrior of Econchate—use my flesh to your own needs, Lu-shee-ahn!"

He writhed under her blandishments, and as he tried to thrust her from him, his hands felt the satiny warm flesh of her ardent, naked young body. He remembered how he had yielded to blind, lustful impulse with Shehanoy, and he strove valiantly to resist the maddening temptation of the young Creek widow.

But his very continence made the lubricious friction and violent, writhing movements of her resilient naked flesh even more of an overpowering torment. Priscilla's felicitous lovemaking—which he had considerately halted as soon as her pregnancy became obvious—had whetted his strictly disciplined virility, eased him of the remorse he had felt in what he had considered infidelity to Di-marte—just as it had been with devoted and eagerly sub-missive Amelia.

And as Shomanee struggled with him, whispering hon-eyed endearments, her warm moist lips nuzzling at his neck and ears and nose and eyes, her fingers stealthily stroking his loins and belly, his continence was undone. With a groan of carnal longing, thrusting from his mind all else, he mastered her now readily yielding body and possessed her with agonized fury, draining himself of the pent-up grief within his very being.

But that next morning, wakening her, he said gently, "Shomanee, you must go back to Econchate. I shall marry no one else now, not ever again. And you are too fine and lovely a mate for a great warrior to be enslaved as my bedwench. I will speak to Nanakota, he will find you a man who will hunt and fish and be valorous at the council. We must forget what has happened between us, Shomanee. And too, my little son has no further need of you."

She wept softly, but she obeyed. And after he had given her a horse to ride back to Econchate, he turned to Ellen and said, "I would be honored if you would nurse my little son, Ellen. Just as I grew up to believe that all of us in the eyes of *le bon Dieu* are equal, so do I wish Henry in this way to be instructed. By the source of life that you, who were once a slave and are now free, will give him, he will understand as he grows to manhood that the color of one's skin is not the designation of better or worse, of superior or inferior, but of a human being with dignity and the right to live and give life itself."

Charles Weatherford, Abram Mordecai and Lucien at-tended a council meeting in the village of Econchate shortly after the beginning of the new year of 1797, and the discussion centered around the growing problems of profitable trading, now that more white settlers were be-ginning to invade the lands of the Creeks. At the same time, the Spanish government held firm to its exorbitant tariffs on commerce, which, though still profitable to the Creeks, imposed difficult restrictions. In Lucien's opinion, until the proper boundary line was set and Spain was able to resolve its difficulties with the United States, there would be continued obstacles. He argued earnestly that the villagers develop their agricultural skills and the fabrication of goods so as to attain a degree of self-sufficiency which would enable them to survive the halting of commerce. He was remembering Priscilla's suggestions for producing butter and cheese and breeding cattle, which last he himself had already proposed to the *Mico*.

Meanwhile, Colonel Andrew Ellicott, who had remained upon the Oconee River awaiting a favorable opportunity to run the boundary line according to the original New York treaty, had been transferred to Natchez as one of the commissioners to mark the boundary between Spain and the United States. He opened negotiations with Don Manuel Gayoso de Lamos, the governor of the Natchez dependencies and Spain's delegated commissioner. But Baron Carondelet had already determined not to comply with the treaty, saying that he believed the king of Spain had agreed to it only as a gesture to begin a friendlier diplomatic relationship with the new republic and that the specific terms were as yet debatable.

Knowing that the power of his country had been seriously weakened by the war with the French, Baron Carondelet began to intrigue with groups of dissatisfied American settlers for the dismemberment of the United States, again using the Englishman Powers as his emissary, just as he had done three years before to counter the similar proposals of "Citizen" Genet. Powers was sent to Brigadier General James Wilkinson, then the ranking officer of the Army of the United States and stationed in Detroit, long the intimate friend of the Baron, who had granted him exclusive trading privileges, to urge Wilkinson's aid in maintaining the Spanish possessions. Wilkinson had been stationed at many posts on the frontier, including Fort Adams, Baton Rouge and New Orleans, and after the Jay treaty with England, Baron Carondelet had offered him pensions amounting to $20,000 as well as the opportunity to "aspire to the same position in the West that Washington entertained in the East."

Meanwhile, the star of Napoleon Bonaparte rose more

and more brightly over a disunited France, for in this year Bonaparte forced the Italians to surrender by the Treaty of Campo Formio, and now only England remained in the war against the monarchy that had become a revolution-induced republic.

Lucien's little son was thriving now, and Ellen looked after him as tenderly as she did her own Thomas and her new daughter. When Lucien and Ben traveled to Mobile, bringing back news as well as supplies and continuing the profitable trade of pelts, she stayed with the three children in the village of Econchate. On his visit toward the end of June of this year, Lucien brought back fifty head of cattle and several wooden plows. His financial worth now stood at $65,000, a heartening amount and one that would surely be sufficient to purchase the land on which he had settled, once the boundary dispute had been resolved. And yet, before he could make his dream come true of owning the land and building Windhaven upon it, there was still what seemed to be an imponderable distance between a formal treaty and the total acquiescence of the Creeks to it, since they were still masters of all this mainly uncharted, rich and beautiful land.

Lucien could only continue his dedicated work with the Creeks and doggedly await the passing of time to bring about the realization of his dreams. He and Abram Mordecai often discussed the potential of growing cotton on this rich soil around the area of Econchate, but the eccentric and still amorous trader urged him to be patient. The Whitney cotton engine had not yet come to this area, though it was known that several Georgia settlers were already using it. And then there was the matter of acquiring proper seed, and after that, sufficient labor. "I intend to be the first to use the new engine, Mr. Bouchard," Mordecai assured him, "and you will be the first I show it to when it is in operation. I, like you, believe that there is a great future for cotton—but first all of us must wait until these drearily long diplomatic hagglings between nations are at an end. And I am still not yet certain that the Creeks will agree to giving up so much land as the Americans want."

For Lucien now there was only the course of dogged, persevering work, whose only relatively minor rewards were in seeing that the villagers of Econchate were prospering, learning new skills, gaining a greater degree of self-independence than before he had first come to Red Ground. Yet there was an inescapable monotony, even though it might be briefly lightened by hunting expeditions with his good friend Nanakota and several of the peace-minded "beloved men" of the Creek village. What sustained him throughout these and the grueling years ahead was the sight of his black-haired little son, growing sturdy and now able to learn a few words of Creek to go with the English which Lucien himself had begun to teach the little boy.

Thomas, now six, slim like his father and light-colored like his mother, acted like a serious older brother to the little boy, even making little toys for him out of twigs and clay or twisting loops of plantain into the figures of birds and animals. It was a comradeship which warmed Lucien's heart, and the lesson which it would teach little Henry was better than all the polemics on tolerance and universal brotherhood. Thus Lucien's life was circumscribed within a narrow, unyielding orbit, and more and more its only warming glow came from his watching how Henry was surviving the ever-dangerous ills which threatened nearly every infant on this wilderness frontier. And he thought to himself that when at last Windhaven could be built and a prosperous plantation evolve out of its conception, Henry would inherit it and would have young Thomas as a skilled and companionable overseer with a relationship that would be far stronger than that of mere employer and laborer. In that way, his own philosophy would be justified and realized after his own days had been numbered.

By the following year, the attempt of the Spaniards to delimit as long as they could the boundary of 31 degrees came to a dramatic end when Gayoso was almost besieged in his fort by indignant American settlers. With his yielding, the boundary was settled as the southern line of the Mississippi Territory. At last Spain evacuated the land extending from the Mississippi to the Chattahoochee rivers, and in 1799 the United States, with the acquiescence of Georgia, which had also laid claim to the land, formally established the original Mississippi Territory. It was the first such organized in the southwestern part of the United States, following the pattern outlined in the Northwest Ordinance of 1787, which provided that the transition from unorganized and sparsely settled land into statehood would proceed in three stages.

First, it would be governed by a governor, secretary and three judges appointed by the President until the population reached 5003 adult males. Then the freeholders would elect a house of representatives, who in turn would nominate ten men from whom the President would choose five to form a legislative council functioning as an upper chamber. The territory would then be represented at the national capital by a delegate who sat in the House of Representatives, a kind of lobbyist looking after his constituents. And finally, when the district had a total population of 60,000, the people through their legislature could petition for statehood. It was a step that greatly heartened Lucien, for he felt that this region in which he had spent nearly a decade and endured sorrows and hardships beyond even his own practicable imaginings, might well be settled peacefully in the same judicious manner.

By the beginning of this year of 1798, Lucien had had a letter from Jabez Corrigan from Le Havre. His redhaired Irish friend had transferred to Bonaparte's French fleet as an officer of the line. He wrote that he believed in the generalship of this Corsican who was attempting to unite all France into a powerful republic not unlike the United States. And he had been given command of *La Belle Joyeuse*, with twenty cannons and a crew of the finest French seamen, some of whom had been *matelots* on the old *Guerrière*.

By 1799, Colonel Andrew Ellicott had finished running the new boundary line from the Mississippi River eastward toward Mobile, and the Spanish were distressed to find that the Fort of St. Stephens lay on the American side of the boundary line of 31 degrees. American troops marched across from Natchez and compelled the Spaniards to surrender. Ellicott's Stone, an irregular piece of brown sandstone about three feet high, was fixed on a rise between Cold Creek and Chastang's Stations; on the south side of the stone the inscription marked the dominion of His Majesty Carlos IV, and on the north side it read "U.S. Lat. 31° 1799."

Lucien and little Henry attended the green-corn festival in July, as did Ben, Ellen and their two children, and Abram Mordecai, who, still convinced that the Creeks had originated from one of the ten original tribes of the Old Testament, followed their ceremonials with great interest. As the festival was ending, a courier from Mobile entered the village of Econchate, sent by John Forbes. It was news almost a year old, but it had just reached Mobile. Bonaparte's attempt to strike at England by way of Egypt and India had failed entirely and resulted in the destruction of the French fleet at Aboukir. There was a list of warships which the enemy had destroyed or captured. And among the former was the name of *La Belle Joyeuse*. Stunned by this news, Lucien asked Nanakota if he might, in memory of his dearest friend, who had guided him, however indirectly, to Econchate, plant one of the sacred kernels of corn in the name of Jabez Corrigan, and it was done.

A new century was dawning, and there were portents of prosperity as well as disaster. Colonel Andrew Ellicott had spent three years since he had landed in Natchez, and had been only able to mark the line from the Mississippi to the Chattahoochee because of the duplicity and opposition of the Spanish authorities. In September of 1799, after his schooner had been stripped and robbed by Indians incited by Governor Gayoso of Louisiana and Governor Vicente Folch of Mobile, both of whom sought to forestall the plans of the United States in the settling of territory, Ellicott fled in his ruined schooner down the Apalachicola. When he approached the sea, he found a schooner of the British navy wrecked upon Fox Point, and in the crew was none other than William Augustus Bowles. During his incarceration in the Madrid prison which began in 1792, Bowles had been visited by many courtiers sent by the king of Spain himself with offers of military titles and pay if he would abandon his allegiance to the English interest, join that of Spain, return to the Floridas and contribute to the strength of the colonies with his warrior forces. But Bowles had spurned all such offers. Then, taking him out of prison and giving him elegant quarters, surrounding him with servants, rich food and wine, the Spanish court sought to win his favor. When he still refused, he was shackled and sent to Manila in the distant Pacific and remained there until February 1797.

Once again the king of Spain, gravely concerned over Colonel Ellicott's setting of the American boundary, had Bowles brought back to Spain. But when the bold adventurer heard of the war between Spain and England, he escaped at Ascension Island and reached Sierra Leone, whose English governor provided him with passage to London. This meeting of Bowles and Ellicott had far-reaching consequences. Ellicott supplied the perishing crew of the British schooner with vital stores, while Bowles in turn furnished Ellicott with charts and valuable directions on the navigation around the Florida peninsula. In their conversation, Bowles avowed his hatred of the Americans and the Spanish, and said, "I am determined to visit my vengeance upon the Spanish by incessant attacks upon the Florida post. I am still a general at the head of the Creeks, and they are my people."

And now it was the last year of this momentous eighteenth century, the year of 1800, when "Johnny Appleseed" began to scatter his famous tracts and appleseeds among the pioneer settlements in the Ohio valley and continued for fifty years. It was the year when the Federalists nominated John Adams for President and C. C. Pinckney for Vice-President, while the Republicans chose Thomas Jefferson and Aaron Burr. It was the year of an enforced Public Land Act, sponsored by William Henry Harrison, then governor of the Indiana territory. It authorized land sales of 320 acres at $2 an acre, with installments to be paid over four years. At its end, the Republicans had come into power, but with Jefferson and Burr tied in the count of electoral votes. On February 17, 1801, the House of Representatives, after thirty-six ballots, chose Jefferson as President and Burr as Vice-

President. At his inaugural address on March 4, 1801, Jefferson declared, "We seek peace, commerce and honest friendship with all nations, entangling alliances with none." And the following year drew Lucien Bouchard closer than ever before to his dream of owning the land and building upon it.

On April 24, 1802, Georgia ceded her western lands to the United States, and these lands were added to the Mississippi Territory. Under the Land Act, an office was opened at Fort St. Stephens that same year. And Lucien Bouchard, accompanied by Ben and Thomas, and by his own six-year-old son Henry, highly alert and intelligent for his age, journeyed to the Fort. There Lucien purchased 640 acres of the land on which he would build Windhaven for $1280, using a draft from his account at the trading post in Mobile. There would be speculators and other sales to follow, but his title would be clear and respected by even the Federal courts.

After he had gone back to what he might now call his own land and his own home, he stayed a few days and then took Henry with him to Charles Weatherford's race track, on the first eastern bluff before the junction of the Coosa and Tallapoosa. For Abram Mordecai, with the consent of the Creek chiefs, and the approval of the Creek agent Colonel Benjamin Hawkins, had established a cotton gin. It had been built by Lyons and Barnett of Georgia, who had brought their tools, gin saws and other essential materials on pack horses.

As he stood watching while Mordecai explained the operation of this ingenious device to remove cotton seeds, Lucien closed his eyes. It seemed to him that he could see vast fields of cotton growing upon his own acres, cotton processed in just such a way, baled and sent down the river to Mobile. Yes, he would always help his beloved blood brothers of Econchate, but now at last the time had come to build a prosperous and lasting stake by which his son could in turn have his own sons to make Windhaven the finest plantation of its kind in this new land.

By now, he believed that he had paid his debt to the village of Econchate. And, when he had gone to Fort St. Stephens to buy his land outright as the first step in creating Windhaven, he had tried to pay another debt, though it was one that sorrowed him to pay. He had arranged with the paymaster at the Mobile trading post to send a draft for $4000 to the wife of Jabez Corrigan, with a note offering his condolences and stating that this had been the payment of a loan Jabez had once made him. It would help Jabez's children toward their destined future, just as Jabez's advice had helped him to the stake he needed and then directed him to Econchate.

CHAPTER TWENTY-NINE

It was a time for taking stock of himself, of his achievements and of his likely future in this hot summer of 1802, for he would be forty years old the next December. It was an age in life when most men by now had already achieved their fortunes—or lack of them—and knew to what major or minor extent they had made an indelible mark upon the relentless pages of time. Perhaps now his native land would once again know peace and restoration, since the Treaty of Amiens was being signed, in which France agreed to evacuate Naples and England consented to give up most of its conquests made in the wars of this bloody revolution, which had claimed, long since, the lives of his entire family and of his very best friend, Jabez Corrigan.

His visit to Abram Mordecai's cotton gin had convinced him that here would be the future of his land. It was rich soil, and it had been planted mainly with corn, which had replenished the good earth and left it fertile for new and plentiful crops. But to plant most of his acreage in cotton was foolhardy at this time. He would need much labor and considerable transportation. And finally, so long as the Spanish kept hold of Mobile and seemed to strengthen from year to year their alliance with the Creeks, there would be only one market for that cotton. To go overland and thence by water to New Orleans was unthinkable, if only because of the time and hardships involved. No, it must be Mobile. But first he would have to experiment with the yield he could expect from a given number of acres, starting slowly, shipping perhaps as little as a bale or two a year. And if Spain were forced to give up her hold of the last possessions in this New World, there would be a period of readjustment, colonization and the re-establishment of quite different tariffs which must be considered before undertaking any major enterprise.

He, like many others, did not yet know that France had already acquired Louisiana from Spain by the secret Treaty of San Ildefonso, though he had heard rumors to that effect. And he could reason why such a rumor might indeed be fact: now that France was united under Napoleon Bonaparte, who had been elected consul for life this very year, Spain would once again fear her ancient and neighboring enemy and keep more troops along the borders than across the distant ocean in this still sparsely settled territory so far from the power of Madrid.

So, in September, Lucien made a solitary visit to the bearded Jewish trader to see for himself once again the operation of Eli Whitney's invention and to ask pointed questions, the answers to which would help shape his own plans for the oncoming year of planting crops.

"I see my gin has taken your fancy, Mr. Bouchard," Abram Mordecai affably greeted him. "Alas, such is the lack of honesty in this world that poor Mr. Whitney is busy now in the courts trying to protect his invention. As you know, our President, who was Secretary of State at the time, heard Mr. Whitney's petition and endorsed it. But when they began to make these gins, Whitney and his partner Miller, there was a mysterious fire in their shop, and at the same time, others put out both a roller gin and a saw gin. The saw gin used one of Whitney's ideas, the difference being that the teeth were cut from a continuous plate of metal instead of being inserted as wires as you see here in the one set up for me. Now that machine, therefore, is really his, but he had to go to court to force the rights of his patent. Now I understand that in the Carolinas the state legislature is imposing an annual tax of two shillings and sixpence on every saw for the benefit of Mr. Whitney. And if some of these gins contain forty saws or so, that will be a handsome windfall for the imaginative man, except that the taxes are to be collected for five years and I can only wonder if he will ultimately receive all that is his due."

"He deserves to win his case, for certain," Lucien declared.

Abram Mordecai chuckled and tugged at his beard. "One does not always get what one deserves, but you'll be knowing that yourself, Mr. Bouchard. Mr. Whitney has gone back to the manufacturing of firearms and the standardizing of muskets for the government, failing thus far to have been amply rewarded for his toil on the gin. As for me, I bless his inventiveness. But come see for yourself."

Lucien followed the Jewish trader into the large, rambling shed in which the cotton engine was enclosed. Four sturdy black workers, dressed in the breechclouts and moccasins of the Creeks, were working busily.

"You see, the one thing which has kept cotton from extensive cultivation is this knotty problem of separating the fiber from the seed. Mr. Whitney's machine does it beautifully. You see this hopper, the long box with one side perpendicular and the other diagonal. Now, this diagonal side is of iron bars about an inch wide and set with interstices about an eighth of an inch apart. The angle at the bottom is enclosed, allowing a narrow admission into a box placed below. Behind the slope of this hopper, as you will note, there are two cylinders running the entire length and revolving in the framework of the machine. One cylinder is made of good sturdy wood and has about forty circular saws of sheet iron, a foot in diameter, and these are fixed so that the teeth enter a little way into the hopper between the sloping bars."

"Most ingenious!" Lucien murmured, intently watching the dexterity and industry of Abram Mordecai's workers.

"Now, you see that Joe is throwing the cotton into the hopper from above, and Dick and Jumbo are riding mules on a water-driven treadmill which set going the wheel that gives motion to the cylinders. Now the teeth of the saws catch hold of the fibers and drag them through the interstices. The seeds fall down through that hole in the bottom. And look—the teeth of the saws come forth loaded with good cotton fiber, and this is taken off by the action of the second cylinder. It's a hollow drum, covered with brushes and made to revolve more rapidly than the saws, and in the opposite direction. Now you see the cotton brushed off and falling in all its lightness and purity to the receiver below. I tell you, with a machine such as this, a man could clear three hundred pounds of cotton a day."

"And the useless seeds?" Lucien inquired.

"They can be used as feed for animals or as fertilizer to enrich the soil, Mr. Bouchard."

"Incredible! But now as to the planting and harvesting of cotton itself. Have you any notion of the yield of such land as mine if I were to put it to cotton?"

"I am sure," Mordecai replied with a shrewd smile, "you have already been asking yourself some questions and perhaps even answering them in advance, Mr. Bouchard. Mobile is our only market from here, using the Alabama River. We have flatboats, and then we must make the long journey back by pack horse. The Spaniards pay well, but when they deduct their taxes, we may have little left, and that primarily in trade goods. You and I as traders already have ample access to the supplies we need for ourselves and for the villages we serve. But, look you, from what I have heard, it would not be unusual to expect five or six hundred pounds an acre each year if you cultivate your fields. That would be about a bale for each acre. I already have had some Georgia seeds, for which I paid about a dollar a bushel, but that will fluctuate. Then, of course, you are going to need blacks like these to work your fields. How many you have will depend upon how many acres you plant, of course."

"I had thought to start next year, Mr. Mordecai."

"You should have at least six to eight more slaves, in that case. But you will need a gin of your own."

"Perhaps I can contract with the same firm that installed yours."

"I see no reason why not. I know that the Federal Government is anxious to distribute this labor-saving device throughout this territory, because it will mean more white settlers and therefore more acquisition of land to this young nation."

"I may purchase blacks in Mobile, Mr. Mordecai, but I shall set them free."

"You are a good and honest man. I do not know if you can do that in Georgia or the Carolinas. Here, with so few whites to say you nay, and as a blood brother to the *Mico* of Econchate, you can at least begin in that humane manner."

Those last words of Abram Mordecai rang in Lucien's ears as he returned to his cabin, sobered by the magnitude of the task that faced him. No, it would not be next year or perhaps not even the one after that, for he would begin slowly, experimenting with the soil and with the formations of the rows of plants, working to achieve the finest quality of which this rich clay and limestone earth was capable. Until he could determine the productivity of the soil for cotton, it would be folly to plant too much at the outset. Besides, he meant to divide his earnings with the village of Econchate; without the original permission of Tunkamara to settle where he now was, there would have been no land for the cotton he meant to grow.

If he were to buy slaves and free them, retaining them as trusted laborers to whom he intended to pay a wage, then he would need living quarters for them. The enlarged cabin was enough for himself and little Henry, to be sure, but already Ben and Ellen had outgrown their smaller shelter, for even the small room he had added was really insufficient for sturdy, eleven-year-old Thomas, who was growing like a weed, and pretty six-year-old Disjamilla. It would be as well to go to Mobile at once to buy these slaves and set them to work through the winter building larger quarters for Ben and Ellen as well as their own cabins. Then, soon after the first of the new year, he would plant his first acres of that magical growth whose downy whiteness could become the fabric for garments, the source of thread—the source of such a prosperity as even this new republic had not yet known or dreamed of.

While Ellen stayed at the village with her son and daughter and Henry, Lucien and Ben rowed the flatboat down to Mobile to purchase six black slaves, who, as Lucien explained to the loyal Ashanti, would be manumitted as soon as they showed skill and interest in the work to be assigned them. "You are a better judge than I, Ben, of the abilities and strength of those who appear on the auction block, and so I will lean to your choices," he declared.

When they reached the trading post, they found several blacks from the Bahamas and West Indies, as well as a few who had fled Haiti after General Charles Victor Emmanuel Leclerc had been sent by Napoleon to suppress the rebellion headed by Toussaint L'Ouverture. These latter had been captured by Spanish sailors en route to Cuba, and thence brought to Mobile, part of the price they would bring at sale being set aside to compensate the Spanish captain and his crew.

Turning to Ben, Lucien declared, "These men were free under Toussaint, and my own countrymen made a peace treaty with that heroic black leader. Yet they disregarded it, seized him and took him back to France, where he is in prison. Since these men have known what it is to be free after having fought for their liberty, in my opinion they will serve with even greater loyalty if they are given a chance."

"You are right, *M'su* Lucien," Ben agreed. "I will talk to them, since I remember their gumbo dialect, and I will tell them what you have said about setting them free if they do good work."

Ultimately, Lucien chose six blacks, three of them being from Haiti, two Furlanis, and a Kru, slim, soft-spoken and from Ellen's own original village. His name was Banta, and Ben smilingly explained, "He is only in his twenties, so of course he could not know my Ellen. But she will be overjoyed to speak her own tongue once again."

The Haitians, wiry and sturdy, whose proud bearing indeed showed that they had enjoyed freedom from their plantation oppressors, were Joseph, Zebulon, and Sam; all were in their late twenties, while the two Furlanis, Jack and Lubanga, were in their early twenties. The Furlanis and the Kru spoke no English, so Ben addressed them, telling them of Lucien's offer of manumission in return for faithful toil. Lucien spoke French to the Haitians, and all six blacks enthusiastically pledged themselves to their new master. For the six, Lucien paid some 2500 *piastres*, which amount was deducted from his outstanding balance at the trading post.

In addition, he purchased a pack pony for each of the six new slaves, telling them that these horses would be gifts for them to own once they were freed, and that it would not be long before he signed the articles of manumission, since he needed their help in building cabins and enlarging the house of his overseer Ben.

Thus once again Lucien rode back along that same trail which he had taken to Econchate, and this time with steadfast purpose and high hopes. He looked forward to his annual hunting expedition with Nanakota, which would take place in the latter part of October and give him sufficient time to instruct his new workers on the duties he expected of them.

Earlier this same year, Lucien and Ben had built enclosed stalls for horses adjacent to the trading storage depot, and here the six pack ponies were comfortably tethered. The blacks, with great good humor and calling encouragements to one another, at once began to fell trees with axes from the depot and to construct a crude shelter for the night. They would build three cabins, Lucien told them, in the direction of the creek, which would serve as an excellent sentry point in the event of any unexpected ambush—he would never forget how Nat had lurked in the cornfields waiting to kill him. For this first night, they piled some logs together and covered them with blankets, which made adequate beds off the ground and away from any straying snakes.

Leaving Ben in charge, Lucien then mounted his horse and rode into Econchate, to be met by Nanakota, who had grave news. It concerned Abram Mordecai, whose amorous disposition had finally cost him dearly. Tourculla, chief of the Coosawdads, angered by Mordecai's liaison with a married squaw, had come to his house with a dozen warriors, knocked him down, thrashed him with poles until he lay unconscious, cut off his ear, and left him to the care of his sobbing wife Shulamith. After breaking up his flatboat, they burned down the cotton-gin house.

"I grieve to hear that, Nanakota." Lucien disconsolately shook his head. "I had counted on his advice and on watching the operation of that cotton engine so that I might myself begin to plant cotton and process it upon the land which the great Tunkamara so graciously gave me. Now I must buy my own cotton engine, and poor Mordecai's sufferings will delay his putting me in touch with the Georgians who have these useful machines for sale. It will delay my fulfilling my pledge, to share what profits I make with the villagers of Econchate—this is what grieves me most."

"Yes, it is sad that our brother was not more discreet," Nanakota soberly nodded. "Now perhaps you see why I have gone unwed all these years, Lu-shee-ahn. I have kept out of mischief, so that I can give all of myself to the guidance of my people here at Econchate. Do not look so unhappy, my brother. We shall have our hunt, we shall tell fine tales of the great deeds we did when we were young men who feared nothing, not even a pretty squaw, ho ho!"

But the sad look that was in the *Mico*'s eyes told Lucien that Nanakota had never forgotten his first love, Emarta, who had become a pariah, like the squaw who had brought Abram Mordecai to ridicule and suffering.

During the hunt, both Nanakota and Lucien strengthened their friendship; both shared nostalgic memories of the years since their first meeting. Moreover, for the five days of the hunt, the *Mico* had brought only two warriors with him, so he could have more time alone with his blood brother. And Lucien had worn the necklace of bear claws which Dimarte herself had fashioned, and on his ring finger was the cabochon ruby which his mother had given him. As they shared the last evening meal of the hunt with their campfire crackling softly nearby, Nanakota touched the necklace and then the ring and nodded: "These are your signs, my brother, as mine are those of the sacred Turtle of whose clan I have been honored to be named *Mico*. The turtle is slow but certain in its course. You are the blood brother of the Bear, but you mated with an Eagle—the gentle daughter of Tunka-mara. And that which you wear upon your finger I recognize as the token you gave her when I spoke for you to Tunkamara."

"Yes, Nanakota. No other woman shall ever wear it—unless perhaps the wife of my son Henry. This I have vowed. When the winter is upon us, Nanakota, I shall have seen forty summers come and go."

"And I, forty-two, my brother. It is not that the blood is sluggish and cold in my veins. Eeaiyee, I still look upon the young maidens of Econchate and find them pleasing to my eyes. But I too have made my vow, as you know. We sit here now in peace and we are brothers. As you look back, Lu-shee-ahn, do you regret the path along which the Great Spirit has set your footsteps?"

"No. Except that, and this you know without my saying, I would have remained wed all my years to her who is buried high on the red bluff which marks the boundary of the gift of land from your village, Nanakota."

"But she still lives there, and with you, and will be always. This you also know without words, my brother. Old Tsipoulata grows weaker with each passing moon, and I fear he may not see another summer. But the signs remain the same as when he first read them for us." The *Mico* shook his head again and looked up into the sky. "There are villages to the southeast of us who would not take a blood brother from among the white-eyes as Tunk-amara and I have done. This I greatly fear. There are young warriors here who have not yet blooded their tomahawks or their arrows, and one day when I am older and they are impatient, they may seek the warpath against my bidding. But this is our last night together of the hunt, my brother. And you have learned to make the deer call as cleverly as I. We shall bring back ten fine bucks and there will be meat in Econchate. Ho, it is good!"

By the end of November, three sturdy cabins stood in a protective cluster at the border of the cornfields nearest the creek, and Lucien was pleased to see that his six new workers had added a small room to Ben's cabin, so that little Disjamilla could have her privacy, just as Thomas did.

By the end of the year, Lucien had paid a sympathy call on the discomfited Abram Mordecai and was able to direct one of the partners of the Mobile trading post to place an order with the Georgia machinists who had sold the Jewish trader his Whitney cotton engine. It would be delivered by the following June, and Lucien instructed Ben and his six aides—for such he considered them—to build a large, sturdy, enclosed shed similar to Mordecai's in which to house the machine. It would be set up near the creek, so that water could be drawn to run the tread-mill on which the two mules would walk, revolving the all-essential drum. During his visit with Mordecai, he listened carefully as the bearded and still badly bruised trader explained the rudiments of cotton planting and tending. "They will sell you some seed too, and it may be from three to five dollars a bushel. You see, I have bought cotton from the Indians, ginned it and then taken it to Augusta on pack horses in small bags. In my travels, I have talked with some of the planters, and I believe that you will use about a bushel of seed for every two acres you plant. It is only a pity you will not be able to produce Sea Island cotton. All the same, this land is very rich, and the Georgia seed will do well in it. You should begin your preparations of your land in February or early March. Then by autumn you will be able to pick. Remember what I've told you about working the soil regularly so as to promote the growth of this fine plant."

"I'll remember, Mr. Mordecai. And until you can get yourself a new cotton engine, you are surely welcome to use mine if you can, and it will be my gift in friendship to you because you have taught me so well."

The year which followed Lucien's fortieth birthday was fraught with good and evil signs. England had declared war on France, and once again Lucien prayed for the salvation of his native land, which had passed from monarchy into revolution and thence into war, with still no sign of lasting peace. And meanwhile, here in the Creek Nation, the wily William Augustus Bowles, who seemed to have the nine lives of a cat, had boldly advanced into the lands still

397

occupied by the tribes. Gathering a large war party, he captured Fort St. Marks and plundered the warehouse of Panton, Leslie & Company. The Indian commissioner, Benjamin Hawkins, now united with the Spanish authorities to rid the territory of a common enemy, and a large reward was offered for Bowles's capture.

A great feast was given by the Indians at the town of Tuskegee, where the old French Fort Toulouse stood, to which Bowles and his war chiefs were invited. During the feast, the freebooter was seized by loyal Indians in hiding, who pinioned him and put him in a canoe full of armed warriors. In the night, the guard fell asleep, Bowles gnawed his ropes apart with his teeth, crept down the bank, got into a canoe, paddled across the river and fled into a thick cane swamp. In his haste to escape, he left the canoe on the opposite side of the river and the trailing Indians imprisoned him a day later. This time securely chained, he was taken to Mobile and thence to Havana, where he was to die a few years later in the prison of Moro Castle. Thus the career of one of the most dangerous enemies of the southeastern territory of the new United States—and himself American-born—came to an end.

On January 11, 1803, the very day on which James Monroe was nominated minister extraordinary to France and empowered to act with Robert Livingston to buy New Orleans and the Floridas from Napoleon Bonaparte, Lucien Bouchard began the cultivation of the ten acres of his land which would be devoted to cotton. He and his six black workers—he would never think of them by the term of "slaves"—gathered up and burned all the old cornstalks, then bedded up the ground by running one furrow and then lapping several others upon it, a process which Mordecai had called "listing" and which Lucien himself remembered from his work in the orchards and the fields of Yves-sur-lac. The iron plow, though it had already been invented and its patent applied for, was not yet available for the arduous work of digging the furrows. Lucien and his men used the crude wooden plows, with two handles, which a man would steer while a horse pulled it forward.

It was vigorous labor, and it was exhilarating for him to

work as he had worked beside his father's peasants back in France. There was a sharing here, an equality, a proud joy and dignity in labor which was to a purpose. And many a time he glanced over toward the towering red bluff, feeling that the spirit of Dimarte was looking down at him and understanding the long-range purpose which motivated such back-breaking toil. For, just as he had shared his corn and the vegetables from his little truck patch with his brothers in Econchate, so he meant, as a kind of spiritual tithe, to turn some of the profits he would make through cotton to the benefit of the villagers who had accepted him as one of them and who, indeed, had so greatly contributed to his own personal prosperity.

By February, Charles Weatherford, who had made a trip to Mobile in his own flatboat to bring skins and bear oil and medicine bark in return for his needed supplies at Wetumpka, halted his return journey by pack horse to tell Lucien that the cotton engine which he had ordered through the trading post would be delivered to him by the following June. And, greatly to Lucien's joy, Weatherford had procured for him five bushels of Georgia seed, which a colonist on his way to the land office at Fort St. Stephens had agreed to sell for the sum of $25.

By the end of February, Lucien and his blacks had plowed the ten acres reserved for cotton and began to cultivate the fields of corn, snap beans, squash and, toward the section nearest the creek, some acres of rice.

It was early in March that the seed was sown, thickly down the center of the beds. Again remembering Mordecai's instructions, Lucien covered the seeds by attaching a board with a hollow, concave surface to a plow and drawing it along the crest of the bed. There would be many months of labor before these ten acres would yield their harvest, for picking went on steadily through the fall months and well into the winter, Mordecai had told him.

Once the seeds had been planted and the first cultivation made, Lucien, Ben and the six blacks completed their work on the large, shed-like building which would house the new cotton engine. Digging a diked runway from the juncture of the river and the creek toward the shed, they were able to channel water to be used in moving the treadmill on which the mules or horses would pull the drum. Young Henry, who was already developing a stocky, well-knit body at seven, accompanied his father to the fields for an hour or two each day. Lucien was delighted to hear him ask questions and to be able to explain them: since there were no schools about, he would be his own son's teacher, but he would see to it that the boy learned from the companions around him. He had already told Henry something of his background, how he had come to live with the Creeks. One May afternoon, the boy turned to his father and asked, "Are these men here Injuns too, father?" Lucien had determined to make Henry as proficient in English as he himself was by now, and then, as the boy's intelligence could assimilate it, teach him enough Creek to make himself understood in the language, as well as a fair amount of French.

"No, my son, they are black men, some from Haiti and the Bahamas, some from far-off Africa."

"Why did they come here, father?"

Lucien pondered a moment before he spoke. "You see, Henry," he patiently explained, "once their tribes, just as with Indians who go to war against one another, were beaten by other, stronger people. And they took them away from their country and brought them here as prisoners, to make them work and earn their daily bread."

The boy looked puzzled, his dark-brown eyes narrowing as he tried to grasp the meaning of what Lucien had told him. Then he asked: "Did you beat them, father, and take them prisoners here?"

"Oh, no, Henry! When I went to Mobile, others had done that already. I bought them away so that they could come here to work and I could make them free men again. Free as you and I are, my son. Now do you understand?"

"I—I think so, father. But some of them are darker than others, like that one there—" he pointed to the Kru, Banta. "But Thomas and his sister are not so dark. Why is that, father?"

"My son, it depends on their mothers and fathers, the country from which they come and the people who lived before them. You will understand that as you grow older. But, remember always that no matter what the color of their skin or how they speak, they are free men and they are working with us to make the corn grow and the cotton, too. Soon that cotton will be turned into shirts and dresses and other useful things that people will wear; you will see, Henry. Now, the sun is quite hot, go take your nap. Tonight at supper we will talk some more about the different people in this world of ours, my son."

The cotton engine arrived as promised, and Lucien, Ben and the six others worked industriously to set it up. The men who had brought it helped them and explained its running to Lucien's satisfaction. Ben, already familiar with cotton from his days in Santo Domingo, made certain that his six new companions understood the rudiments of this seemingly complicated machinery which was destined to bring unheard-of riches to the land.

In this same year, Ohio entered the Union as a free state. On May 2nd, the Louisiana Purchase Treaty was signed, whereby France sold Louisiana to the United States for eighty million francs, an act to which the Senate (located in Washington since November 17, 1800) consented on October 20th. On December 20th, two days after Lucien's forty-first birthday, the formal transfer of Louisiana to the United States by the French took place at New Orleans. And by now, the war against Tripoli, declared by the Pasha on May 14, 1800, because he had not received sufficient tribute from American ships, entered its third year with the capture of the *Philadelphia* by the enemy in Tripoli Harbor.

On his birthday, Lucien went to the cabins occupied by his six black workers, with Ellen and Ben carrying bowls of food, and Lucien declared to them, "All of you have worked hard and well, and I am grateful. I wish to celebrate my birthday by giving you the greatest gift that any man can enjoy, one which I myself sought to win by leaving France and journeying here—freedom. I shall send dispatches to Mobile with articles of manumission to be set down in the official records, so that no one shall question from this moment forth your right to be free men. I ask you to continue with me, and I promise that each six months you shall have wages, which will be in an amount of goods such as you may wish for your personal needs or, if you prefer to have money, then certain sums will be set aside for you. The law does not yet allow me to give such wages to you, but you have my word of honor that what you have earned will be recorded in my own account at Mobile. And when the day comes that you are allowed to take possession, the money will be there for all of you."

Abram Mordecai visited Lucien several times during the late summer and early fall and was there when the first cotton from Lucien's experimental acreage was taken to be ginned. Again Lucien had remembered the Jewish trader's instructions to pick the cotton carefully over by hand for the removal of trash and yellow flakes before it went to the gin. After it emerged from the machine, there were always particles of seeds and other foreign matter which had to be removed by another picking over, or moting, as it was called. Then the cotton was handpacked into large burlap bags with slat hoops. Thus it would not be crushed, as Abram Mordecai had pointed out.

His first experiment with cotton was a good omen for the future. From the ten acres planted in early March, Lucien estimated that he had obtained nearly five thousand pounds of ginned cotton. While Ellen, Thomas and her little daughter along with Henry went to Econchate, Lucien, Ben and his six free workers made a single trip down the river to Mobile in five heavily timbered flatboats, each man poling his own boat and guarding the heavy load, which had been secured by rawhide thongs and a framework of pegged logs to brace the bags and keep them in place during the long journey.

The going price for cotton in that town which the Spanish still held was nineteen cents a pound. Thus Lucien received a little more than $900, discounting the cost of seed for his very first planting. To be sure, it would take several crops to offset the cost of the cotton engine, but there could be no doubt that this first commercial crop from what he called in his mind "Windhaven" augured great things to come.

True to his word, out of the money he received for the cotton, which was credited to his account, since by now there was beginning to be felt a shortage of Spanish silver and gold, Lucien allocated in his own ledger wages of $75 for each of his six loyal black workers, who were now officially free men and could be asked rather than ordered to work upon the land of Windhaven. That was what he had believed in back in Yves-sur-lac and, so long as this new country's laws allowed, what he would steadfastly hold to on this land which one day would be a rich plantation.

CHAPTER THIRTY

Now that the Louisiana Purchase had taken effect, the Spaniards remained in control only of what was known as Spanish West Florida, which extended from that Ellicott Line of 31 degrees to Bayou Manchac, the lakes and the Gulf of Mexico, and from the Mississippi to the Chattahoochee. The Mobile district extended as far west as Pearl River, but it was only sparsely populated and separated from the other parts of Spanish West Florida by a pine barren wilderness. Yet Spanish rule still prevailed in Mobile, although it was now greatly relaxed. Nonetheless, those who brought cotton to be sold—with the exception of commissioned traders like Lucien Bouchard himself—found that their product had lost three-fourths of its weight with the seed, and had to pay an additional twelve and one half percent in toll for the privilege of selling at Mobile. Coins became scarcer and scarcer, so that the Spanish dollars, escalins or bits, and picayunes were the principal money on both sides of the boundary line. Lucien foresaw that there would soon be territorial legislation on the subject of gins and cotton receipts, whereby the latter would furnish part of the Mississippi currency. Meanwhile, in the area of West Florida, the Spaniards used only Mexican silver.

In mid-February of the new year of 1804, New Jersey passed an act for the gradual emancipation of slaves, the news of which delighted Lucien: he believed that it was the official justification of his own personal act toward his

404

loyal workers. And he fervently hoped that when the land on which he was now settled finally was declared United States territory and then a valid state, there would be a similar law so that no man who should ever work for him or his son and his son's sons after him should know the degrading shackles of bitter bondage.

In this same month, the Republican Congressional caucus unanimously nominated Thomas Jefferson for a second term as President, with George Clinton of New York to be his Vice-President. And then came shocking news just ten days before the green-corn festival at Econchate. On July 11th, the beloved Alexander Hamilton was shot and killed by Vice-President Aaron Burr in a duel at Weehawken, New Jersey, the tragic outcome of Hamilton's exposure of Burr's complicity in the Federalist secession plot. Undoubtedly the people's anger over Hamilton's death—which many considered little short of assassination—influenced the resounding victory of Jefferson by an electoral vote of 162 to 14 for the Federalist candidate, Charles C. Pinckney, with the same overwhelming majority for his running mate over Rufus King. This marked the first election with separate ballots for President and Vice-President in the new nation's history.

It was soon after that election that Lucien, Ben and his six free men again made the flatboat journey to Mobile, this time with seven thousand pounds of ginned cotton neatly bagged. This time, the price paid was twenty cents a pound, or $1400, less the cost of some $20 for seed and $550 as the wages earmarked in Lucien's account, Ben receiving $100 as foreman, with $75 to each of the other six workers. While in Mobile, Lucien bought twenty bushels of seed for $50 and determined to devote forty acres to cotton in the year ahead. True to his promise, he generously divided his net profit of over $800 with the villagers of Econchate and used that half of the profit which he regarded as his tithe to bring back hoes, an iron plow for the village as well as one for his own fields, trinkets and ornaments and rolls of fabric for the women.

There was momentous news from France as well: Napoleon Bonaparte had proclaimed himself Emperor of the French. A surly, deaf composer named Ludwig von

Beethoven had written a symphony, which he had entitled the "Eroica," and dedicated it to Napoleon; on learning that his idol had assumed so lordly a title, he angrily tore up the dedication and growled, "He is like all other men. I shall dedicate it, therefore, to the memory of a great man."

Shortly after the Spanish had surrendered Fort St. Stephens, United States troops under Lieutenant John McClary built Fort Stoddert at Ward's Bluff in a setting of magnificent oak trees named after the then acting Secretary of War. Now it had become a revenue stop for settlers who wished to export their goods. Besides the arbitrary taxes imposed at Mobile upon American merchandise imported for American settlements, the Federal Government exacted similar duties at Fort Stoddert. And both Spanish and American taxes were heavily levied on all exported goods. A planter on the Tombigbee River, for example, who sent his produce to New Orleans by way of Mobile and exchanged it there for goods and supplies, paid by the time he reached home an *ad valorem* duty of twenty-five percent. All vessels were required to pass under the guns of Fort Charlotte and to submit to ignominious search, the Spaniards themselves appraising the cargo and imposing the onerous levy of twelve and a half percent. Already there was dissension among the American settlers over the timidity of the American government in its dealings with the Spaniards and in its own apparently greedy demands upon its own people in the name of commerce.

By the end of the year of 1805, the war with Tripoli had ended, and Lucien Bouchard had shipped twenty-four thousand pounds of ginned cotton to Mobile. This time, the price was twenty-three cents a pound, and $5520 was recorded to his increasingly prosperous account. Shortly before the green corn festival, he had gone to Mobile for goods for Econchate and had purchased two more slaves, Matiro and Simon, the former an Ashanti like Ben but in his twenties and able to speak a little English, the other a native of Haiti. These two he freed, as he had freed the others. This time, two journeys were made on ten large flatboats, each man being responsible for his own. This

406

time also, out of $4500 in profits on his cotton crop, Lucien Bouchard kept half for himself and expended the rest in necessary supplies for the Creeks who had befriended him and set him upon the land which was already promising such boundless riches for the future.

And, this same year, the day before Lucien's forty-third birthday, old Tsipoulata died peacefully in his sleep, and Nanakota and Lucien sat together, silent in their mourning for the wise old man who had seen into the future and marked them both for their intended destinies.

And these two blood brothers thought somberly upon the old *Windigo*'s prophecy that one day Econchate would be no more. For this year, the Cherokees had granted Americans the right for a mail route from Knoxville to New Orleans by way of the Tombigbee River, and the Chickasaws had ceded some 350,000 acres in the bend of the Tennessee River. At Mount Dexter, the Choctaws yielded up to the United States five million acres at a point halfway between the Alabama and the Tombigbee, running north to the Choctaw corner, thence across the Tombigbee to the Mississippi settlements, thence south to Ellicott's Line. Thus the entire southern portion of what was to be the future state of Mississippi was thrown open to American settlers, and a population of Georgians and Tennesseeans poured into the superb forests north of the Tennessee River. Natchez had already become a large town where boats going up and down the great river landed and traded, where gambling, drunkenness and debauchery had become the watchword. And all of this overshadowed the growth and prosperity of the peaceful village of Red Ground.

What gratified Lucien most of all, however, was the companionship that had grown up between his nine-year-old son Henry and Ben's son, Thomas, who acted as a kind of guiding older brother to the sturdy black-haired boy. Also, Henry appeared to be fond of Ellen's daughter, Disjamilla, who was already a charmingly pretty little girl, no darker in skin color than a mulatto and who combined a charming blend of mischievousness and helpless femininity, which called on Henry to act as a kind of dutiful

407

protector, though he might at times be irked by her pretty pranks.

It would be well, Lucien determined, to build more flatboats early in the next year for the winter transportation of his ginned cotton down to Mobile. Each flatboat, ten feet wide and twenty feet long, was capable of carrying from two thousand to 2500 pounds and had to be abandoned at the trading post once the journey downriver had been made. This next year, he would plant eighty acres, double this year's crop. At that, it had taken a full month to make the two flatboat trips down the river and return by pack horse. Until better transportation could be found, there was hardly any point in considering planting his entire acreage in cotton. Moreover, with his trading profits steadily increasing so that by now he had well over $100,000 at his disposal in supplies or cash as required, the dream of the red-brick chateau with its twin towers, the true Windhaven, was nearer realization than ever.

Yet there were so many impracticabilities against it. The tremendous difficulties of transporting building materials and furnishings upriver; the extremely large labor force such a project would require; most of all, the unavailability of any competent architect who could compose drawings from Lucien's description of a chateau and then transmit orders to what at most would be a relatively unskilled crew of workers—no, it was not yet feasible to build. Inevitably, Lucien was sure, there would be a better mode of transportation on this mighty river, and once the commerce between Europe and the new United States was restored without intervening wars, piracy and the present intervention of Spanish tariffs, then he could turn his dream into reality. Yes, by God's grace, it would be Henry Bouchard in his young manhood, who should help supervise the building of the real Windhaven that was ever in Lucien's mind whenever he looked up to the towering red bluff where Dimarte and Edmond slept forever.

But the chances for a peaceful Europe were still far off: the Third Coalition of England, Austria, Russia and Sweden was about to be joined by Prussia. Napoleon Bonaparte had defeated the Austrians at Austerlitz, and he would trounce the Prussians at Jena in this next year.

408

But even if he won all his battles against the united foes, it would be years before the ocean was free to commerce between France and the United States, years before the elegant furnishings of that chateau in Yves-sur-lac could cross the ocean and be unloaded at Mobile—which was still in the hands of the Spanish.

Yes, these were dour years, but years with a dogged purpose and a perseverance behind them to fortify Lucien Bouchard as he continued his dual life as a trader and now as a planter, half of his work dedicated to the benefit of his blood brothers, half to himself and his son and the family that Henry would have one day.

But now, as the new year of 1806 began, there was consternation among the traders, for President Jefferson had ordered the United States mint to stop the coinage of silver dollars. Now it appeared that receipts and bills of lading would be exchanged as currency in lieu of reliable coins, and that was certain to affect the balance of trade. Not for himself, since he was still recognized by the authorities at Mobile as a loyal adherent to their policy with the Creeks, but for all of the American settlers who were thronging into the southeastern part of this rapidly growing new republic which remained with its paradoxical and vital coastal port in the hands of the weakened monarchical nation.

And meanwhile, there was the even more dangerous menace of internal disunity within the nation Lucien had adopted: the threat of Aaron Burr's machinations against the United States itself. After the death of Alexander Hamilton in that ill-fated duel, a warrant for murder had prevented Burr from returning to New York, as had the strong tide of public opinion. He had gone into exile on the Carolina seacoast, then returned to Washington to preside over the Senate till the expiration of his term of office as Vice-President on March 4, 1805. For the rest of that year, he had traveled through Kentucky and Tennessee and returned to Washington the following January, spending time between Washington and Philadelphia until August of this new year of 1806. And now it was believed that he had spent that time in evolving schemes to lift him out of the morass of opprobrium into which he had fallen and satisfy his own vainglorious ego as the head of an empire itself. He had purchased a portion of the lands granted by the king of Spain to Baron Bastrop, which lay between the Sabine and Natchitoches. He had planned to colonize these lands, expel the Spaniards, conquer Texas and finally Mexico. That ambitious project would necessitate the raising of a large armed force in the Southwest. It was Burr's opinion also that a war would soon take place between the United States and Spain; and in that event, he planned to cooperate with General Wilkinson, who was in charge of the Western and Southern Armies of this new republic.

By the summer of 1806, Burr again appeared in the southwestern territory, meeting with those who could further his grand design. It was known that boats were being constructed and stored with provisions and concealed weapons, and it was equally suspected that General Wilkinson had countenanced and even aided this seemingly traitorous enterprise. President Jefferson, hearing that Burr was raising troops for the purpose of dismembering the Union, had him arrested in Lexington, where Henry Clay appeared in Burr's defense.

There was not sufficient evidence to convict him, and Burr was discharged. From there, he descended the Cumberland and Mississippi rivers with thirteen boats and sixty men, being met just above Natchez by Colonel F. L. Claiborne at the head of a detachment of 275 men. Surrendering his boats and men, Burr proceeded with Claiborne to the town of Washington, Mississippi, as a prisoner. There were balls and parties given in his honor, and he put up bond in the sum of $10,000 for his appearance in court. At the hearing, he demanded a release from his bonds, since his offenses did not come within the jurisdiction of Mississippi, though the Attorney General of the United States had insisted on his being sent to a competent tribunal. When Burr's application for a discharge was overruled by the judges, Burr fled his captors.

This *cause célèbre* greatly disturbed Lucien. Was this, he wondered, a sign of these chaotic times, and could an internecine revolution destroy his hopes and dreams of this new country as just such a rebellion against established authority—though admittedly outmoded and feudal—had done in his native land? But what disturbed him even more, a week before he, Ben and his workers were preparing to take their ginned cotton down to Mobile, was the unexpected streak of cruelty he discovered in his own little son.

Lucien had taught the ten-year-old boy how to ride horseback and had chosen a gentle little mare for him. He accompanied Henry every morning, before the sun grew too hot, to ride between the hill and the bluff and back again, near the river. On this late November morning, Henry's mare suddenly reared and whinnied in fright, and Lucien, seeing a water moccasin sluggishly crawling along the edge of the river bank, leaped from his horse and first seized the reins of Henry's mare and soothingly quieted her. Then, retrieving a piece of broken log nearby, he killed the snake. Hardly had he turned back toward his son when he saw that Henry had leaped down from the mare, picked up a withe, and begun to slash the mare across her hindquarters.

"Stop it, what are you doing, my son?" he angrily cried and ran forward to wrest the withe away from the boy and fling it out into the river. "That's cruel and unjust! Marie can't be blamed for being afraid of the snake—my heart was in my mouth when I saw it, dreading that it might strike either of you. But to beat her for that—that's unmanly and unworthy, Henry!"

The sturdy boy grasped his father's wrist and forced it away from the collar of his doeskin jacket, his eyes blazing, his face red with anger. "She almost threw me, she could have hurt me, she could have gone away from the snake! I don't trust her any more, I won't ride her again, father!"

"As you wish. But you shall never beat a horse like that again, or ride one, either, till you have learned to be kind to the dumb beasts whom we put to work for ourselves and to whom at least we owe a measure of kindness and decency. Go back into the cabin, I am displeased with you!"

Lucien stood looking as his young son angrily ran back into the cabin. Then he uttered a long sigh. Where had the boy derived this streak of cruelty? Could it be that the spirit of Jean, his dissolute older brother, had somehow been reincarnated in his own son?

This time, the price for cotton in Mobile was twenty-two cents a pound, and Lucien's controlled acreage had yielded 25,000 pounds. Thanks to his foresight in building more flatboats, he, Ben and the eight black workers, each handling his own boat and cargo, were able to negotiate the journey in a single trip downriver. Lucien had raised Ben's wages to $150 as overseer, the two newest workers receiving $75 each and the other six men $100 each. Deducting the cost of seed and the wages, Lucien had netted $4500, half of which, as was his wont, he had credited to the villagers of Econchate. And this time, Lucien took Henry along so that the boy would better understand the close companionship between his father and the black men who now had a share as free and willing workers in the profits of the venture. Thomas, almost as tall as his father despite his fifteen years, accompanied them also, on his father's flatboat. Ben was now forty-six, but did not look it; his pride in being free and Lucien's overseer and his wiry physique, which seemed to thrive on hard labor, had kept him still vigorous and youthful in outlook.

"It is my hope, Thomas," he told his son as they neared Mobile, "that when I am too old to work for *M'su* Lucien, it will be you who will become overseer. But most of all, you must watch over his boy, Henry. You see, my son, he had two boys who died like their mothers, and you know that his last wife died when little Henry was born. It is all he has left now, and he will not take another wife, I know that and he has said it as well. A son is often different from his father. You, Thomas, have pleased me as I have watched you grow to young manhood. Already you are wise and good at heart, and it may be that the young master will need to rely on you when *M'su* Lucien is not here to guide him."

"I understand, father. Perhaps it is because we do not see many settlers, and have only the Creeks as our friends, that Henry is different. His father had many

412

friends in the country from which he came, and he has been to New Orleans and to Mòbile and of course he is very wise. But the boy is still very young, father. And he likes my sister, and she likes him too."

Ben nodded soberly. "It is sometimes hard for a boy to be brought up without a mother. She will give him a love and a feeling for kindness toward others which sometimes a man cannot provide. You, my son, have my beloved Ellen, and that is why there is so much kindness in you. We are very lucky to have come to Econchate where *M'su* Lucien was guided by his star."

"He is a good man, father, and if a man had to be a slave, he could hope for no better master."

"That is true, my son. That is what I told him long ago."

On the cold night of February 18, 1807, the young lawyer Nicholas Perkins and clerk of the court Thomas Malone were playing backgammon in their cabin in the village of Wakefield in Washington County in the Alabama territory. At ten o'clock that night, two travelers rode up to the door, one of whom inquired for the tavern. The light of the fireplace illumined the face of the traveler who had asked for the tavern, and Perkins noticed that he sat upon a superb horse outfitted with a fine saddle and new holsters. Although he was dressed like a plain farmer, a pair of superb boots protruded from beneath his coarse pantaloons. No sooner had the two travelers ridden away from the cabin, than Perkins said to Malone, "That is Aaron Burr, I read a description of him in the proclamation. We must follow him to the residence of Colonel Henson, for he asked the road to that house, and we shall take measures for his arrest."

Accordingly, young Perkins rode to the house of a friend, obtained a canoe and a black to aid him, paddled down the river and arrived at Fort Stoddert at dawn. He at once told the commanding officer, Captain Edward P. Gaines, of his suspicions and Gaines placed himself at the head of a file of mounted soldiers and rode off with Perkins. At nine that morning, they met the two mysterious travelers on the descent of a hill near a wolf pen about two miles from Colonel Henson's residence.

Captain Gaines accosted the man whom Perkins had pointed out to him as Aaron Burr, identified himself as an officer of the United States Army, holding in his hands the proclamation of the President for Burr's arrest. Burr accompanied him back to the fort, and a few weeks later Captain Gaines had the illustrious prisoner rowed up the Alabama River and then into Lake Tensaw, guarded by a platoon of soldiers. There, Perkins, who had the rank of colonel in the Tennessee army, Malone, five other citizens and two soldiers escorted Burr along the Indian path, taking a route about eight miles south of Econchate. By March 30th, Aaron Burr was a prisoner in Richmond, where he was tried for treason and acquitted; he was next arraigned for misdemeanor and was again acquitted. Upon his release, he sailed to England. (He was destined to die at Staten Island on September 11, 1836, at the age of eighty, and on his deathbed swore that he had never been engaged in treasonable activity against the United States of America.) And on the evening that he passed just beyond Econchate, Lucien Bouchard and his young son Henry watched the single-file processional along the narrow Indian trail, and Lucien turned to his son and said, "That was Aaron Burr, my son. He was a great man who wished to be still greater, and that is what destroyed him. When you are older, Henry, ask yourself always if what you do is entirely to the advancement of yourself, or whether it will equally benefit those who work with you. If by advancing yourself you can help others, then you will have known ambition with honor and purpose."

Across the seas, Napoleon had defeated the Russians at Friedland, and the Peace of Tilsit left him master of the continent. Only England stood in his path, England which had defeated him on the seas at the Battle of Trafalgar in 1805. France's new emperor resolved upon economic warfare against his bitterest foe, but in this year of 1807 the United States found itself drawn close to a new conflict with that same sea power. In June, the U.S. frigate *Chesapeake* was fired upon by the British man-of-war *Leopard*, and four alleged British deserters were removed

414

from the American vessel. Two weeks later, President Jefferson closed all United States ports to British ships, and toward the end of December of this year, Jefferson signed the Embargo Act, which prohibited all ships from leaving the United States for foreign ports, in order to force the French and British withdrawal of restrictions on American trade.

Lucien learned, at about the time of Aaron Burr's acquittal in Richmond, Virginia, that Robert Fulton's steamboat, the *Clermont*, had made its first trip up the Hudson from New York to Albany in thirty-two hours. That was a bright omen for the future: if such a vessel could be brought upon the Alabama River, carrying trade goods and bags of cotton to ports that would finally be open to American goods without exorbitant tariffs, then there would be prosperity and peace for this new land which still awaited inclusion into the striving new republic.

Once again, in December, Lucien and his workers made the journey downriver to Mobile with 27,000 pounds of cotton, and this time the price paid had dropped half a cent to twenty-one and a half cents. Nonetheless, it was another substantial gain for his prospering account, one in which his workers and the villagers would share.

It could be argued that Aaron Burr's military movements had indirectly benefited the Mississippi Territory, for hundreds of his followers became permanent citizens, thereby increasing the population and the wealth of the area. Cotton replaced indigo as a principal cultivation, and several salutary laws were enacted on the toll for ginning this demanded staple. As Lucien himself had foreseen, the cotton receipts obtained from the owner of a gin were made a legal tender and passed as domestic bills of exchange.

On the gloomier side, revenue exactions upon the settlers subjected them through the Spanish custom-house at Mobile and the American at Fort Stoddert to a duty ranging from forty-two to forty-seven percent on those goods necessary for the comfort of their families. At the same time, citizens in the area of Natchez were entirely free from such exorbitant tolls, paying only four dollars a barrel for Kentucky flour while the Tombigbee planters paid four times as much. And yet these settlers remained loyal to the United States, pledging their support to avenge the wanton attack of the British upon the American ship *Chesapeake*.

By the act of Congress on March 2, 1807, the importation of slaves was prohibited after January 1st of the following year. On April 17, 1808, the Bayonne Decree of Napoleon Bonaparte commanded the seizure of all United States ships found in French ports. On July 12, 1808, the *Missouri Gazette,* published in St. Louis, became the first newspaper west of the Mississippi. And on December 7th, James Madison was elected President of the United States by the electoral vote of 122 to 47 for the Federalist Charles C. Pinckney, with George Clinton defeating Rufus King as Vice-President.

The price of cotton had begun to decline, and it would reach a low of fifteen cents by 1814. Lucien had planted sixty acres of cotton this year, using land not previously tilled, and his ginned production reached 40,000 pounds. The cotton engine had been more than paid for, there were iron plows for the villagers of Econchate and other comforts which they had not enjoyed till now. He was forty-six years old and his son was twelve and already showing a restlessness with the cyclical way of life upon the land. That was why Lucien took Henry with him to Econchate on every occasion, as well as to Mobile on the annual cotton-selling journey. Husky for his age, his black-haired son had begun to remind him a little of his older brother Jean; somehow, the boy had the same disinterest in arduous work with a purpose, but wanted always to see new sights and to enjoy new pleasures. It was a trait which disturbed Lucien more than he would admit, a trait which had been revealed in part by the boy's cruelly thoughtless beating of the mare.

In August of this new year of 1809, just after President James Madison had broken off trade relations with England because that nation had repudiated the Erskine Agreement negotiated by its own minister, Lucien had still more reason for misgivings about his son's character.

The day had been exceptionally humid and Ellen having come down with a touch of fever, took to her bed. Lucien, Ben and Thomas were in the cottonfields cultivating the new crop, as were the eight free men, tumbling the soft earth about the roots of the new plants and covering up the small young grass which had sprung up since the first working. Henry, however, had complained to his father of a listless, fatigued feeling, and Lucien, believing that the boy might have come down with a touch of river fever like Ellen, urged him to stay in bed.

Pretty Disjamilla, graceful and buddingly feminine in her thirteen years, had brought her mother a dipperful of water from the little well Ben had dug near their cabin. Out of instinctive thoughtfulness, she returned to the well to bring her playmate Henry a cool draught of water as well, and entered Lucien's cabin. Her mother had knitted her a blue woolen jacket and a bright red petticoat as a Christmas gift the previous year, and Disjamilla, out of a natural feminine vanity, was so delighted with the bright colors that she wore these garments even in the warmest weather. The petticoat was voluminous and thick, serving as dress rather than undergarment. Her glossy black hair tumbled in a thick cascade down to her shoulderblades, drawn high away from her broad forehead, accentuating the pretty, wistful features of her sensitive face.

Henry Bouchard swung his legs down off the bed and sat on its edge as she approached, his eyes glowing as they scanned her lissome figure. "I hope you feel better, M'su Henry," she solicitously exclaimed as she brought the dipper to his lips.

"Yes, much better, Milla." It was his nickname for her. He bent his head to sip from the dipper, and then put both arms around her waist and tumbled her onto the bed beside him. "Much better when you come play with me, Milla. No, it's all right, don't be afraid." For Disjamilla, startled by his unexpected, rude maneuver, had tried to rise from the bed, her dark eyes fixed on his flushed, excited face, not quite comprehending the meaning of this game.

"You're so pretty, Milla," the boy muttered, his left hand pinning her by the hip while his right stealthily for-

417

aged against the gently swelling mounds of her nubile young bosom. "Give me a nice kiss, Milla."

"Please don't—no, you mustn't—let me up, Henry, or I won't play with you any more!"

"But this is the way I want to play with you, Milla dear. Now, I won't hurt you—see?" His voice was thick and unsteady as his right hand closed over one of her small breasts.

"Don't—you mustn't touch me there, *M'su* Henry—please let me go," the girl pleaded, suddenly stricken with a nameless fear at the sight of his narrowed, gleaming eyes and his moist, twisted mouth.

Twisting away from the embarrassing and now painful pressure of his hand against her breast, Disjamilla again tried to rise, but Henry pressed her down with his right palm against her chest, his left hand tugging at her petticoat to bare her slender thighs almost to the crotch. Beside herself with shame and terror, Disjamilla uttered a piercing cry and struck at her young tormentor.

"Keep still, don't make such a fuss, I only want to love you a little, Milla," he hoarsely panted.

As she twisted and kicked, his hand forced itself against her virgin core, and again the girl uttered a frantic cry, her face scarlet and wet with the sudden tears of deepest shame.

Lucien had left the cottonfields to go to the depot storeroom for a narrower hoe when he heard the girl's shrill cry. As the cry rang out again, he hurried to his cabin and saw his son struggling to keep Disjamilla pinned beneath his stocky young body as, having rucked up her petticoat beyond her waist and liberated his turgid penis, he was attempting to mount her in the act of copulation.

"My God—Henry—let go of her, you young devil!" Lucien cried, aghast. Disjamilla had burst into tears, turning her face to one side and covering it with her trembling hands, while Henry slowly turned his congested face over his shoulder to stare angrily at his father for having interrupted his precocious attempt at mating. With an oath, Lucien strode to the bed, seized the boy by the shoulders and dragged him to his feet, then cuffed him smartly, first on one cheek and then the other till Henry cried out with pain and thrust up an arm to fend off his father's blows.

"Whatever possessed you, you young scoundrel? How could you think of treating Disjamilla like that?" Lucien's voice shook with baffled anger.

"But she's a *nègre*, father, *une esclave, n'est-ce pas?*" Henry answered in his father's native tongue. "And I'm white and her master."

Lucien fought to control the torrential rage that surged up inside him. Still gripping the boy by the left shoulder, he backhanded him across the mouth with his right hand, drawing blood and a resentful cry of pain and anger. "Never, do you understand, never again let me hear you say a filthy thing like that, Henry Bouchard! You disgrace my name and that of all your ancestors who were just and decent toward their workers. I have no slaves here on Windhaven, do you understand me? Yes, I bought the men at Mobile because I had to, but I have already freed them. As for Ben and Ellen, they were given to me by the Creeks as slaves, and I freed them also. Thus Thomas and his sister, whom you have tried to ravish, little animal that you are, are as free as you and deserving of far better treatment."

"Let go of me, father! You had no right to hit me like that! I say, she's a slave, she's the daughter of a slave and that makes her one, doesn't it, no matter what you did," Henry defiantly retorted, striking his father's hand from his shoulder and wrenching free. The sobbing young girl had scrambled off the bed and hastily smoothed down her petticoat, turning her back to them both and weeping softly in her shame.

"Who told you such lies? Not I, certainly, Henry. You have never once heard me refer to anyone here as a slave, and you never shall. Now then, who invented that filthy lie?"

"An old squaw at the village, that's who, father."

"And when did that happen and who was the squaw?"

"I think they call her Emarta. And anyway, it was the last time we were in the village, when you were talking to the chief. And I was out there at the end of the village and there was a girl, an Indian girl, who pulled me into

419

her wigwam and began to touch me and pulled my hands against her. And she said it was time I took a woman."

"Merciful God! I did not know that Emarta was still alive and in the village." He remembered Nanakota's story of how the *Mico*, when a young man, had fallen in love with that wayward maiden only to have her wed another and be condemned to public punishment for her adultery. "Well then, you will listen to me and remember what I say. That squaw is an outcast at Econchate, Henry. That is because years ago she sinned with another man after she was married. You are to forget what she told you. As for your being old enough to take a girl as you tried to do with Disjamilla, that Creek girl was wrong, and it was Emarta who told her to do what she did with you. Do you understand me?"

His eyes lowered to the floor, Henry Bouchard sullenly nodded, then shrugged.

Lucien stared at his rebellious young son, helpless before the unexpected maturity and cynicism of the boy. Yet he could not condemn him for the primitive physical instinct which had drawn him toward the nubile, pretty daughter of Ben and Ellen. It was high time his son found better occupation; what a pity there were no schools in which he could be enrolled as there would have been in France!

"Well then," he abruptly decided, "I'm going to give you an acre of land all your own, Henry. You will work on it just like the blacks, and, because you are free as they are, you will be paid for your work. I expect you to cultivate, hoe and plow and look after the plants until it is time to harvest them. In return, all the profit that comes from that acre will be yours in a special account I shall open in Mobile. That will keep you busy and perhaps it will teach you also a certain humility. Perhaps in a year or two, if I journey to New Orleans, I shall take you with me. If you are so determined to be a young animal, there are places in that city where women practice the art of teaching a young man how to give pleasure as well as take it selfishly. They will initiate you and, I hope, curb that wildness and ruthlessness in you which I both deplore and despise."

CHAPTER THIRTY-ONE

Dark clouds were gathering in this year of 1811. Napoleon Bonaparte, who had crushed the Austrian attempt to renew warfare against him at Wagram two years earlier, was now involved in the Peninsular War in Spain and was amassing a *Grande Armée* of half a million French and auxiliary troops to attack Russia, his only remaining rival on the Continent. Relations between the United States and England had worsened, partly because of the latter nation's own internal crisis. The British debt was almost a billion pounds, its exports had declined by a third in the past several years, and finally, King George III had been declared insane and his son, George Augustus Frederick had been appointed Regent. On May 16, the U.S. frigate *President* defeated the *Little Belt,* a British sloop of war off Sandy Hook. England's Orders in Council, which authorized the taking of American ships to be pressed into service in the British fleet, had not been revoked; this action alone was causing many influential Americans to demand that President James Madison declare outright war on England.

A far more immediate consequence to Lucien Bouchard was the danger of war that would involve the Creeks against the American settlers who were beginning to crowd them on either side.

President Jefferson had enforced his Embargo Act in the belief that American trade was essential to both England and France and that by denying both of them trade, he would keep his own young country out of trouble. Instead, ships from every port of the world had begun to pour into the Florida territory, and slaves and supplies had been smuggled into Georgia in defiance of the act forbidding the importation of slaves. And Spain, weakened by its costly war against Napoleon, was unable to protect the territory and the people it still controlled.

That was why in January of this ominous New Year, President Madison gave Congress a secret message to prompt a resolution which would ease the tremendous tensions building along the southern border of the United States. In that resolution, the wording of the Congress was that "the United States cannot, without serious inquietude, see any part of the Floridas pass into the hands of any foreign power." And by that resolution, Congress authorized President Madison to take temporary possession of East Florida. In April, James Monroe was appointed Secretary of State and selected Colonel John McKee, an Indian agent, and General George Matthews, ex-governor of Georgia and a veteran of the Revolutionary War, to meet with Governor Vicente Folch of West Florida in an attempt to get that territory yielded to the United States in an amicable fashion. President Madison had already, on October 27, 1810, issued a proclamation declaring the Spanish province of West Florida annexed to the United States, after receiving a declaration of Independence by a large group of American settlers who had migrated into that territory. He had acted thus to prevent England's use of the Gulf ports as a base to which to treat with hostile Indians, as well as to eliminate Spanish influence; with French and English armies fighting over the throne of Spain, leaving this vital territory in Spanish hands would be foolhardy to the future welfare of the new republic.

After Governor William G. Claiborne of the Territory of Orleans took formal possession of the country as far east as the Pearl River, the newly acquired Spanish province was joined to the governor's territory and, on April 30, 1812, would become the state of Louisiana, a slave state.

In negotiations with the Americans, Vicente Folch, the Spanish governor of the West Florida territory, offered to surrender Mobile as well as the rest of Florida if he were not relieved by his government by the first of January of this new year. That offer, too, encouraged President Madison to take his forthright step in annexing the territory. Governor Folch offered also to abolish all duties paid on American goods passing up and down the river; because of his eagerness to compromise, American authorities put off the vital question of Mobile till a later time.

But throughout all these negotiations, British agents in Canada and the Floridas tried to bring about the cooperation of the entire southwestern Indian tribes, and devoted most of their persuasive efforts toward the Creeks; these were the most powerful in number, in arms and in military tactics, of all the Indians remaining on the lands which American settlers so eagerly sought.

At the green corn festival this summer, Lucien and Nanakota spent long hours pondering the ultimate result of the negotiations between England, Spain and the United States, but most of all the potentially explosive meetings of the secret British envoys to the tribes. "I have heard, my brother," Nanakota gravely declared, "that many of the Creek tribes are becoming dissatisfied with the good Colonel Hawkins, who has managed them with so much wisdom for so long. They are resentful that he was able to get their chiefs to grant a public road which runs from Mims' Ferry upon the Alabama River to the Chattahoochee. And now there are white-eyes coming along that Federal Road, as it is now called, to settle upon the land and to be neighbors of those Creeks who have as yet no love in their hearts for the white-eyes who hunger for the good, rich land. The Georgians will hem our people in from one side and those from the Tombigbee on the other. And the Spanish, who have been good to us all these long years, as you know yourself, my brother, hate these settlers who have driven them from their forts and seek to take over their trading posts."

"Your words are spoken straight, my *Mico*. But do you not see the advantage in having only one nation to deal with? As it stands, your people may be besieged not only by the Americans and the Spanish, but by the English as well. It would be far better to live in peace with the Americans and to make all of this southern country a single, unified nation in which the red man and the white can walk together with dignity and honor."

"Your words come from your heart, and in your heart there is peace for all men. Ho, already my youngest warriors tell me I am growing old and that I seek peace as a toothless squaw might, content to sit by my fire and smoke my pipe and dream of the days when I could draw the bow and send the arrow speeding to the heart of the strongest buck at the greatest distance. My elders at the council urge peace too, and they are of your view, Lu-shee-ahn, that we do not make war upon the white-eyes whose flag shows the stars and stripes. But word has come to me that there is a Shawnee whose father and mother were born upon the Tallapoosa and thence moved to the great forest of Ohio, where he was born. His name is Tecumseh and he has fought many times against the Americans and he hates them. The British have sought him out, and it is certain that he will use his influence with the Cherokees and the Creeks and the lesser tribes to hold the land against the Americans. This is what I fear most.

"I remember what Tsipoulata said, and now as I grow older, I begin to see more clearly that the Red Ground we love and which has been our home will pass from us and we shall be forgotten like the ashes of a dead campfire that has no warmth or life."

Over these past two years, since Lucien had come upon his precocious son in the act of trying to force Disjamilla, Lucien had ridden strict herd on the sturdy youth. The experiment of putting him to work on an entire acre and holding him completely responsible for the crop had proved to be a fortunate one; young Henry Bouchard had managed to produce 750 pounds of cotton, which, discounting the cost of seed, had netted him $142 in last year's journey to Mobile. He had asked Lucien if he might have the money to take back with him, and Lucien had found it somewhat difficult to collect enough of the rapidly disappearing silver coin to total the amount owed to his son. Lucien himself had been paid either in bank notes or in bills of lading and receipts which served as legal tender at the trading post.

Out of his first earnings, the boy had purchased a scrolled walnut box, brought the box back to his room in the cabin and covered it with a blanket in the corner. At first, Lucien had ascribed this miserly gesture to his son's excitement at having earned his very first dollars by diligent labor. But this past February, after he had told Henry that he would give him two acres whose profits would be his to keep, the black-haired youth's brown eyes sparkled as he retorted, "I want the money in silver, father, to put with the rest of it in my savings box." And when Lucien had countered, "But money, my son, is simply a medium of exchange, it should be used to trade for the things you want," Henry had swiftly rejoined, "The more silver there is in the box, father, the more I shall know I'm becoming a man and making my own way. That's what you want from me, isn't it?" And Lucien, nonplused, could only shake his head and sigh, wondering if this avariciousness was still another disturbing sign in the character of the heir to his ultimate Windhaven.

He had tactfully broached the subject of Henry's erotic initiation to Nanakota just before setting down the river for Mobile with this most abundant of all his crops— eighty acres under careful cultivation and favored by excellent weather throughout most of the year had brought 60,000 pounds of cotton from the gin. Even at the expected lowering price of seventeen cents per pound that represented over $10,000 in receipts at Mobile. And after he had told the *Mico* how much this harvest would mean to the villagers of Econchate, he looked at his old friend and added, "My son has worked hard the last two years, and he thinks now of the dollars that he can earn from the land. He is still too young to wish to share them with others, as I learned long ago to do. This is the best kind of wealth, in which one man may help his neighbors to build a prosperous community in which there will be no poverty, for that creates unrest and envy, which lead to bloodshed. Still, though he has shown the strength of a young man in his work at the fields, I think that it will not be long before he must take a wife. On this new frontier, to marry young is desirable, so that a father may grow up with his children and be a companion to them and work in harmony. I did not have such a chance, and Henry has had no mother. But I see already that he covets the pleasures of the flesh and that if he were not carefully watched, he might indulge lustful ways among the maidens of your village."

"The blood of the young grows hot by turns, and cools and grows hot again, Lu-shee-ahn," Nanakota smilingly replied. "I know there are young squaws here who would willingly share the fever which comes upon a sturdy fledgling, the more so because his countenance and his body are pleasing to gaze upon in their eyes."

"Two years ago, Nanakota, one such young squaw did approach him, and it was at the bidding of her before whom you once tossed your pebble."

"Emarta—aiyeee, I might have guessed as much. She has never forgiven me for not having begged mercy for her before our beloved Tunkamara. And now that she is gray and old, I have not the heart to banish her from this village. But your son has now seen fifteen summers come and go, and at that age one wishes quickly to become a man, is it not so, my brother?"

"Yes. That is why I plan to take him to New Orleans after we have brought the cotton to Mobile, Nanakota. I have had a letter from my old friend Jules Ronsart, the Creole who bought my beautiful horse when I came to this country so long ago. And the horse, Arabe, still lives and has bred many times with the finest mares, and now enjoys peaceful grazing after his long useful life. Yes, I shall take Henry with me, and I will let him look upon white-eyes of his own kind for the first time. For when he marries, it would be best that way. Perhaps some day he will find a French girl to marry, a girl from my own native land, and in that way the cycle of life which began with me across the ocean will continue on this other side. Perhaps that was what old Tsipoulata meant."

"Perhaps, my brother. But because you did not buy slaves last year, I will lend you some of my own, and they will build the boats to take all this cotton down to Mobile so that you need not make more than one long journey. I will give orders at once to have them built, and I will send ten of our strongest and youngest slaves on them to pole them down the river and to watch after the cargo which, thanks to you, has made Econchate one of the fairest and happiest of all Creek villages."

In the twenty-two years since Lucien had first seen New Orleans, it did not seem to have changed as the boatman poling him and his son from Mobile on the barge-like raft entered the river and moved toward the willow-crowned levee. The river was filled with as many different vessels as it had been when the *Guerrière* had first dropped anchor, except that there were more now. He could make out Kentucky broadhorns all the way down to the lower fort, and saw whiskey bottles raised on some of their poles, a sign that the skippers were ready to sell their often contraband cargo. And there were the non-descript schooners which flew no flag and which might well be smugglers from the Baratarian stronghold in the Gulf. He could see the wild rivermen's section of the city, and the floating brothels along the Tchoupitoulas levee, which fronted the American quarter. But beyond all that, there were newer buildings, stately and more durable than those he had viewed when the gig had brought him and Jabez Corrigan to the wharf.

"We'll stop at a tailor's stall, Henry," he told his excitedly gawking son. "For an evening or two, at any rate, we'll try to look like French gentlemen taking our ease. Ah, here's something they didn't have when I first came to New Orleans, a hackney carriage with a driver to take us where we wish to go. That way, you'll keep your boots from being muddied, my son." He called out to the wiry little hunchback with a silken hat and a long stock whip with knotted string end driving a starved-looking mare, *"Ici! Arrêtez, m'sieu!"*

"You're French then, are you?" The hunchbacked driver squinted warily at the tall, bronzed man whose black hair was streaked with gray at the temple and sides, and at the stockier, wide-eyed black-haired boy beside him. For both wore buckskin jackets and the trouser-leggings of the Creeks, as well as dirty knee-length boots.

"*N'ayez pas peur, mon ami,*" Lucien chuckled. "*Je ne suis pas un sauvage rouge, parce que je suis Normand.*"

The hunchback almost dropped his whip, shook his head and spat to show his surprise. "*Quelle blague!* I, Jean-Pierre Moursonnet, I came from Brittany, before the Revolution."

"And now there is an emperor where there was a king," Lucien replied in French.

"So what would you? With my hump and my ugly face, they'd have hanged me as well under King Louis as under the Little Corporal. Now then, how may I serve you fine gentlemen?"

"First, if there is a stall along the way where we can get some hand-me-downs to fit us and to convince you that we're your countrymen, I'd be obliged to you, *mon ami,*" Lucien chuckled. "After that, you may take us to the counting house of *M'sieu* Jules Ronsart on the *Rue de Toulouse, ça va?*"

"*Ça va bien, mais oui!*" the little driver cackled as he flicked the long but harmless whip, useful only for flicking off flies, and the mare started down the now partly cobbled street. Yes, this too was new after twenty-two years. And so were the fashions, for Lucien saw that tight breeches had given way to colorful pantaloons of gaudy purples and greens in broadcloth weave, with fine white shirts adorned with ruffles down the fronts and at the collars and cuffs; cockaded hats, multi-colored beavers, and stovepipe hats as well. And as the little carriage clattered on, he caught sight of several handsome young women, not at all aristocrats and more than likely *filles de joie*, whose flouncy dresses were slimmed at the waist by whalebone, and whose half-bared bosoms seemed to spill out into low bodices above the stays. Coquettishly they waved and winked at this striking pair of newcomers to New Orleans, and Henry turned to look back at them, his eyes now sparkling with a sudden new desire. A desire which Lucien recognized, but tempered with calculation this time, where it had not been with pretty little Disjamilla.

"They're doxies, my son," he reprovingly murmured.

"With that kind, to use a French proverb, *une heure de Venus, ça compte sept ans de maladie* (one hour of Venus can often lead to seven years of illness). No, for your first experience, it will be with a *demi mondaine*, still young enough to take your fancy, yet wise enough to let you leave her bed in the best of health."

The hackney driver, glancing back from his open seat, had eavesdropped on this parental-filial conversation, and now slyly interposed, "If it's companionship you two fine gentlemen are seeking, there's rare sport to be had at Madame Ducroit's establishment. If you like, I can come calling for you wherever you're staying, and once she sees it's Jean-Pierre who brings you, you'll have your pick of the house. They've some new beauties there this week, take my word for it. Now here's the stall you might be looking for, they've some elegant waistcoats and pantaloons, yes, and silver-buckled shoes for both you fine gentlemen. It's not crowded at this hour, so I'll wait for you till you make your choice, *n'est-ce pas?*"

A quarter of an hour later, Lucien emerged in waistcoat and pantaloons of green broadcloth, a fine silk shirt and triple cravats flowing down his ruffles, and with a broad-brimmed brown hat. His son seemed older indeed by virtue of lavender broadcloth waistcoat and pantaloons and as equally fancy a shirt with its fashionable triple cravats. And both wore silver-buckled shoes, the boy wiggling his feet tentatively to test the feel of them in place of customary boots or moccasins. Then, looking up at his father, he managed a broad, smug grin and nodded.

"Pleased with yourself, are you, *mon gars?*" Lucien smiled back. "Now we'll pay a visit on an old friend and perhaps see that palomino of mine. What memories Arabe brings back—I must tell you about them tonight when we dine. And I'll admit that the prospect of a real feast tonight after our usual rations back at the village makes my mouth water. Come along now, my son!"

On the way to the counting house, Lucien leaned forward and inquired of the hunchbacked driver, "Do you know, perhaps, the house of a Madame Rambouillet on Isola Street?"

The driver cackled and winked as he looked back at

Lucien. "Now I believe you are truly a countryman, *m'sieu*. And that you've been to New Orleans before. Everyone knows her house, but now it's on Rampart Street. And she has a dozen girls, of the finest quality, and one pays dearly to spend an evening there. Do you wish me to take you there tonight? Of course, I shall lose the commission from Madame Ducroit, but I'm sure that a discriminating gentleman like yourself will reward me."

"First we must finish our business with *M'sieu* Ronsart. And I have other matters to attend to, Jean-Pierre. We'll see about tonight."

The little driver tugged at the reins to halt the mare before the counting house, and Lucien and Henry dismounted. Lucien paid the driver with a silver dollar, which drew garrulous and flowery thanks and promises that guaranteed so generous a patron devoted service to his every need. Then the hack clattered down the cobbled street, and Lucien and his son entered the counting house. There were clerks seated at desks scribbling busily with quills, others behind a counter to one side stacking bank notes into one pile and bills of lading and cargo and gin receipts into another. At the rear of the counting house, a tall, wiry man stood genially chatting with a fat, mustachioed, ornately dressed Creole, and despite all these years, Lucien at once recognized the man who had bought Arabe. The latter turned and, catching sight of Lucien, whispered something to his fat companion and then strode forward, his alert, intelligent face animatedly glowing. "Do my eyes deceive me? Is this the same man who sold me a palomino?"

"The same, a little the worse for wear. And you, Jules, *mon Dieu*, except for your white hair, you've not changed at all. Still as tall and straight and full of life as ever!"

"By all the saints, it's good to see you, *mon vieux!*" Jules Ronsart turned, to smile at stocky black-haired Henry. "And this is your son, I'd guess, from the hair and the eyes, though he's likely to be a bit stouter than his father."

"Yes, my son Henry Bouchard. Henry, this is *M'sieu* Jules Ronsart. If it hadn't been for his aid twenty-two years ago, the chances are that you might never have been born," Lucien affably explained as he put his arm around the boy's shoulders.

"A privilege to meet you, *M'sieu* Ronsart," Henry dutifully murmured as he accepted the Creole banker's enthusiastically extended hand.

"Well now, if you'll spare me just a moment or two with *M'sieu* Duclos, who's claiming a mortgage due on a ship that was beset by those damned pirates out of the gulf and all its cargo taken and the vessel so badly damaged it had to limp into port, I'll be at your service. And of course you'll dine with me tonight, I shan't take no for an answer."

"I was hoping you'd invite us, Jules, we've much to say to each other."

A few moments later, after the frock-coated and bewigged client had left the counting house, Jules Ronsart led Lucien and Henry into a little cubicle which was his private office and had one of his clerks bring in an extra chair for Lucien's son. "Now then, you'll want to see Arabe, of course. I tell you, that horse of yours helped make me a rich man. I raced him thirty times and lost only a single race, and that because of a foul against him which the stupid judges didn't notice. Then I studded him with some of the finest mares that could be found, and I kept two of the finest foals and sold the others at a tidy profit. Now Arabe takes life easy in a stable beside my country house—a few miles on the outside of this monstrously growing city. Yes, I still see that he gets a reward of a carrot as frequently as I can take time off from my affairs to visit him."

"I'll take him a carrot too, if I may."

"I shouldn't be surprised if he recognizes his old master just as quickly as I recognized you now, Lucien. You've had my letters from time to time, and I've had several from you over all these years. But now tell me all that's happened to you, things you didn't put in those letters."

Lucien glanced at his son, rather hesitant to plunge into the nostalgic recollections of the past before this old friend who was, after all, only a stranger to his son. But Henry had turned to stare at the clerks behind the counter, raptly observing their swift separations of bank notes, their alignment of the stacks of receipts, bills of lading and the rest of the commercial papers which Jules Ronsart's prosperous house handled. He suavely interposed, "Jules, my boy is fascinated by the way your clerks are handling these transactions. Perhaps, if it's not too much to ask, you could let him take a closer view, and maybe one of them would be good enough to explain to him the operation of a counting house."

"Of course, of course, it would be my pleasure, Antoine, *viens ici, je t'en prie,*" Jules Ronsart called to a pleasant-featured, light-brownhaired clerk in his late twenties, who promptly rose from his desk and hurried to the Creole. "This is Henry Bouchard, the son of a dear old friend of mine, *M'sieu* Lucien Bouchard. The young man admires the skill of your fingers. I myself have often said, have I not, that if you weren't so indispensable to me, Antoine, you could make your fortune at one of the gaming houses on Rampart Street." Then, turning to Lucien with a wink, he added, "The fact is, Antoine does so well here that he's able to afford a *petite maîtresse* from Rampart Street itself, and the two of them, while they are not whiling away the time making *l'amour,* play baccarat."

The young clerk's cheeks flushed and he looked sheepish, then joined his master in a hearty laugh.

Lucien watched his son go back with Antoine to the latter's desk, the boy standing there watching intently as Antoine began to talk to him. Then he turned back to Jules Ronsart. "He's all I've left now, Jules. I'd written you, you remember, about Dimarte and Amelia, and how those two other sons died also. He's of good stock, his mother was a gently bred young English girl who'd come to Savannah with her parents and brother, only to become unsuspecting pawns in the Georgians' plot to take the land away from the Creeks. She was the only survivor, and she died giving me my son."

"He's a sturdy fellow, and he looks like a hard worker. You'll have reason to be proud of him, I'm sure."

"It's my fondest dream, Jules. He's going to help me build the old chateau I had back in Normandy, when the time's right."

"It's certainly not right now, Lucien. Here in New Orleans, there are fifty-to-one odds that we'll be at war with England before next summer. And from what I've heard of the stirring-up of the Indians by English agents, I shouldn't at all be surprised if there'll be a bloody war, either along with the one with the English or right after. I hope I'm wrong, for the sake of you and your son at least."

"I, too, Jules. And also, because the people of Econchate, particularly the young warriors who look upon doing battle as a way to glory, would be called on to join their blood brothers against the whites. But now, tell me about yourself," Lucien earnestly asked.

"I've made a great deal of money, I've built this fine mansion which I'll expect you to visit this evening, but I lost both my plantation and my pretty sweetheart back in Haiti when that magnificent rebel Toussaint drove out his white oppressors. I can't help feeling a great admiration for him, even if he cost me dearly. It was then I decided to devote full time to my counting house, though I still spend a few hours racing some of Arabe's descendants for an occasional stake when one of my friends grows too boastful."

"And you've never married?"

"No, *mon ami*, because I'm too set in my ways and too selfish for my creature comforts. Not that I don't still keep a *maîtresse*, and in this case, it's a stunning octoroon in a little house of her own not far from Isola Street—and I've a buxom Juno as a housekeeper, an indentured English wench who clawed her master when he tried to abuse her and whom I saved from a sound flogging at the Cabildo. That was fifteen years ago, and she's past forty now, but still devoted to me." He winked knowingly. "Now then, it's nearly four o'clock and I've done with business for the day. Let me see to my clerks for a moment, and then I'll have my coachman bring you both to my new house. You'll want a bath again, just as you did that first time you came from Mobile, I'll be bound."

"It would be a luxury I'd enjoy, Jules. One question, if I may?"

"Of course."

"Are you acquainted with two Creole bankers, named Daniel Mercier and Philippe Entrevois, by any chance?"

The tall, wiry, white-haired Creole frowned, pursing his lips as he strove for recollection. "Mercier—ah yes, he married the charming Eulalie Villefranche. They had a daughter who, I'm told, is even lovelier than her mother. I've done business with Mercier, he's a good, reliable man, a bit stodgy and not at all of the Gallic temperament we Creoles most usually possess. But the other one, this Entrevois, his mother was a *griffe*. He has a touch of black blood in him, though it's hardly noticeable at all. He occasionally dines with me when we stay in the city, since we do a great deal of business together. He has a much larger house than Mercier and an attractive wife too, a French girl, Edmée."

"I see." Lucien found himself agreeing without the slightest feeling of emotion.

"Yes," Jules Ronsart went on with a reminiscent smile, "they've just the one little girl, though not so little, since she's just about fifteen. But such an enchanting face, such soulful brown eyes to go with her warm brown hair and her white skin, and the soft sweet voice of an angel—it won't be long before our young gallants will be fighting duels for her favor."

"You say that this Entrevois has a touch of black blood to him. But he's not a slave?"

"Here in New Orleans, we are perhaps more tolerant than in other parts of this still uncivilized country. First of all, as I recall the story, his grandmother was a beautiful West Indian black who was freed by his grandfather, a nobleman and the owner of a large plantation. Whatever conjure spells she set upon him, I don't know, but he married her. Naturally, having manumitted her first, there could be no question of the succession of the line. But the fact remains that if *M'sieu* Entrevois should ever have the misfortune to go bankrupt and his wife and daughter be held liable for his debts, they would be accused of that taint and they could be sold as slaves. Mind you, I say it is only a remote possibility, for he's far too wealthy and too sensible in his business judgment to let such a catastrophe occur. Now then, I see my coachman Duval awaits us, and if you can pry your absorbed young son away from Antoine's desk, we'll enjoy what poor comforts this pesthole of a city can provide."

Several miles outside the city and well back of the bend of the river stood Jules Ronsart's manor house, made of red bricks, with three majestic wide white Doric columns fronting the entrance and a veranda to one side. There had been little rain in the past ten days, which, as the Creole banker indicated, made the road from the city accessible by carriage. When there was heavy rain, unless one did not worry about having one's breeches spattered with mud to the waist, one might ride horseback or else come slowly on foot along narrow planks set down to make a kind of pathway.

But for Lucien, humble though this manor house looked beside his own chateau at Yves-sur-lac, it was already a good omen. To be sure, New Orleans was a port to which ships came readily from across the ocean, bearing glass from Venice, fine woods from Spain and England, four-postered canopied beds and the most elegant fabrics from Flanders and France. Slaves had built this house three years ago, Jules Ronsart informed him. Well, free men could build Windhaven in the years ahead.

Inside, the furnishings bespoke the Creole banker's wealth and good taste. Tapestries hung on the plaster walls from wooden frames, French tapestries with scenes of bucolic landscapes and nymphs and satyrs which caused a sudden surge of homesickness in Lucien's heart as he recognized the creative source. An overstuffed sofa, and a costly Sèvres vase on a marble stand beside the entrance to the salon. Candles in glass chimneys cast an intimate yet adequate light throughout the rooms, and in the Creole's study, Lucien recognized the magnificent rosewood writing desk with its scrolled legs and the still serviceable divan with its damask covering. He paused to look into the bedroom, momentarily envious of the massive, four-postered, muslin-canopied bed which dominated the room, and Jules Ronsart, an arm about his shoulders, chuckled softly, "Though I approach the biblical threescore and ten, *mon ami,* I thank *le bon Dieu* that I am still able to expend some little homage to the pagan goddess of love. Ah, Juno has come to tell us that we are ready to dine, *n'est-ce pas, ma belle déesse?*"

Lucien turned to see the buxom housekeeper, her pale blonde hair coquettishly set in spitcurls along her ' road forehead and falling in a luxuriant sweep of upturned curls at her sturdy round shoulders. It was hard to believe that she was well past forty, and the red crinoline dress with its widely flaring skirt accentuated her ripely bovine charms. The bodice was cut low, though not quite so low as he had seen those flirtatious women of the street wear on his way to the Creole's counting house.

Juno herself served her master and his two guests, and Lucien covertly observed that young Henry could not take his eyes from her, especially when she bent toward the table to replenish the wine in Jules Ronsart's cut-glass goblet or his own. But most of all, the boy's eyes laved her with a sensual appraisement as she moved to fill his own glass, for Lucien on this gala occasion saw no reason why Henry should not have his first real taste of vintage wine.

"You'll spend the night with me, of course, *mon vieux*," the Creole urged as they sipped their brandy, the sturdy black-haired boy making a wry face at his first encounter with this potent finale to the sumptuous repast, which had included turtle soup, baked red snapper with Juno's own marvelously spicy sauce, fruits and little cakes she herself had baked.

"It's kind of you, Jules, but I promised Henry a night on the town. And I'm anxious to visit the house of Madame Rambouillet."

"*Tiens, je comprends!*" the elderly Creole chuckled. "That was where our lamented and mutual friend Jabez Corrigan took you after your first night in my little place in town, wasn't it? Oh yes, how well I remember! He'd taken me back to Haiti, you see, and he told me how you'd saved that lovely niece—now I begin to catch your drift, and why you asked me about the banker Daniel Mercier. Why of course, the very same!"

As in his salad days, Lucien felt his cheeks reddening as he met Jules Ronsart's slyly mocking gaze. "Come now, you know me better than that!" he bantered, trying to hide his embarrassment and at the same time not edify his now curiously attentive son. "In the Creek village which I serve, the woman is severely punished for adultery—though I personally regard it as unjust not to mete out equal chastisement to the guilty male. I assure you, however, Jules, I had no thought of disrupting the Mercier household."

"I was only jesting, *bien sur*," Jules Ronsart mischievously grinned. "But you see, the widow Rambouillet has really prospered. She has what is without exception the finest *maison de plaisir* on all Rampart Street. And it's there you wish to initiate this fine strapping heir of yours. Of course I understand. I'll have Duval take you both into town. And you, you'll stay at the house as well?"

"To safeguard my son only." Lucien inwardly cursed himself for feeling the hot flush spread even more deeply on his sun-bronzed cheeks.

CHAPTER THIRTY-TWO

He had gone out to the huge stable behind the manor house while Duval was hitching up two spirited stallions to the carriage to take him and his son out to the house on Rampart Street, and Jules Ronsart had handed him a lantern and opened the stable door, saying, "Of course he'll recognize me, *mon vieux*, so that won't be a test. I'll just stay out here till you've had your reunion with Arabe. Juno gave you the carrots, I presume?"

Lucien had smilingly nodded and then entered. Holding the lantern high, he moved into the tidy, spacious stable, seeing the young fillies and stallions prick up their ears at his coming, knowing that Arabe was back at the very last stall, the largest of all, with plenty of oats and water as befitted the illustrious palomino who had sired such fine stock and earned his reward many times over.

Henry, moving slowly behind his father, eyeing the horses in the first stalls with that same covetous glint which he had shown over the handling of bank bills this afternoon, stumbled over a riding crop half-hidden in the straw under his feet. He bent, retrieved it, flexed it between his strong young hands, and smiled to himself, then deftly thrust it under his waistcoat and moved on behind his father.

The great palomino stood in the darkness, and as the lantern light suddenly plucked him out of the shadows, he whinnied nervously. He was heavier, but his head was high, his nostrils flaring as when Lucien had ridden him

438

over the fields of Yves-sur-lac. He waited now, his eyes fixed on the gray-haired man who moved toward him, holding out a carrot.

"Arabe, *mon ami*," Lucien said in the huskily vibrant tone he had always used when mounted on the Palomino, "do you remember? *C'est moi*, Lucien. Do you remember how we rode over the hill and down into the little valley with the lake on our way to see a beautiful young lady? And how I said to you, *'Va vite, mon ami*, stretch out those long legs of yours and bring me to her quickly!'— now do you remember?" He took out one of the carrots Juno had given him and held it out to the palomino.

The old horse whinnied again, tossed his head, whisked his tail, pawed the straw with his front hooves, reaching his muzzle over the gate of the stall toward Lucien. He took the carrot, chewed it, tossed his head again and stomped one front hoof, and Lucien patted the beautiful head, stroking Arabe's nose, then rubbing his knuckles between the palomino's eyes, a secret caress between them which he had applied after a long course run swiftly and well. "My old friend, we meet again!" Lucien's voice was choked. "Yes, you've had a happier life than I could have given you. You've had a good master, a kind one, and he's grateful to you for all the triumphs you've brought him. And you've left heirs to remember you by, Arabe. And that's the greatest reward of all. God give you yet many happy years, and may you think of Lucien and his carrots always."

"I'd love to have a horse like that, father," Henry said as he clambered into the carriage beside his father.

"My father gave him to me on my twenty-sixth birthday, Henry. Perhaps on yours, if you've given me a grandson by then, I'll try to make you a similar gift. But you can't use a whip on a spirited animal like that, my son. And I haven't forgotten how you treated poor little Marie. It's true, you've been gentler since then with the pack pony I showed you how to load and ride, but I hope you've remembered just one thing from my seeing Arabe again—he remembers me with love after all these years just because I treated him as I would anyone who was loyal to me. You don't buy loyalty with your hoarded sil-

439

ver, Henry, nor with the kind of cruel mastery that only breeds fear and hatred and rebellion. And that's why I don't own slaves."

"You've told me, father, but things are changing so. In New Orleans, such a huge city, they can't be the way they are in our fields and our cabin."

"They could be if all men would treat one another like brothers. I'll admit that's a kind of utopia that won't be realized in our lifetimes. But I only wish the warmongers and the malcontents could spend some time at Econchate and see how decently the Creeks live together in a commune that I'm sure even Rousseau or Voltaire would have approved of."

"Yes, yes, father." Henry made no attempt to conceal his impatience at this sermonizing. "Are you actually taking me to one of those places you spoke about? And I'll have my own girl and can do what I like with her?"

Lucien stared sharply at his stocky, eager-eyed son. "You don't take a woman the way you went rutting after poor little Disjamilla. I've told you that love is the greatest gift a man can receive from a woman. Yes, even on such an occasion as this, when one might speak of love for hire. A *maison de luxe* is nothing like the cheap coupling you'd find on one of those riverboats down on the American sector. Besides, you'd likely get the pox. Look upon this as a kind of initiation, an education and a lesson, as I hope you really will, Henry. Pretend that you and the young woman who will escort you to her bedchamber tonight are two strangers meeting for the first time, perhaps never to meet again. Within the little hour of your making love, if you're patient and tolerant and let yourself be guided by her, the experience can become a kind of romantic revelation, a dream of love which is neither grotesque nor animal. Don't look at me so scornfully, my son. Ah, yes, my brother Jean, if he were here beside me now, would laugh at me and call me a poetic idiot. But I tell you, Henry, loving is sharing, and even in the act of union, for all its animalism, there can be poetry and beauty and gratitude. I've learned that, and I've cherished my memories of my learning. I only hope tonight your first experience equals mine."

The Haitian coachman turned back to Lucien as he drew the two stallions to a halt in front of the iron railing which enclosed the house and, at the back, the flowery courtyard. "Do you wish me to call for you later tonight, *M'sieu*?" he deferentially asked.

"No, my friend, would you tell your master for me that I'll see him tomorrow at the counting house. I may stay another day or so in New Orleans, but I've no wish to be a burden to him. And this is for your pains, Duval." He handed the coachman a silver coin.

"But you needn't have, *M'sieu*, it was my duty to my master."

"But I'm not your master, Duval, and you've done me a real service and driven us both most expertly. My compliments. Perhaps I'll see you again before I leave for Mobile, and a pleasant good night to you."

Lucien unlatched the gate and Henry eagerly followed, glancing down the sidewalk. Farther down the street, there were frontiersmen in buckskin talking loudly and profanely, some intent on conversations with a perfumed, daringly dressed woman of the evening, and just then two carriages went by, driven by silk-hatted coachmen, with a well-groomed elderly man inside each—no doubt en route to his own mistress in a little house beyond Rampart Street. There was an iron railing, curved out as a kind of balcony, on the second floor, and from behind the drawn shutters could be seen the occasional glimmering of light. Lucien lifted the heavy brass knocker and smiled, for, appropriately enough, it had been wrought in the figure of a naked nymph, and struck three times.

The door was opened almost at once by a smiling light-colored negress, dressed in a pretty blue muslin frock which left her shoulders bare, and she curtsied low, an act which showed off the impudently thrusting pear-shaped globes of her half-revealed bosom in the low-cut bodice. "Welcome to *Plaisir,* good masters. Does you come in and seat yourselves, Madame be with you presently."

She escorted Lucien and his son into an ornately furnished salon and gestured to them to make themselves comfortable on a thickly upholstered, spidery-legged couch. From a sideboard, she deftly opened a decanter of Canary wine, filled two silver goblets as elegant as any Lucien had seen back in France, and, with a low curtsy to each of them, offered them the brimming goblets.

The floors were covered with fur pelts which had been nailed onto the boards. Henry shoved his silver-buckled shoe back and forth, testing the thickness and softness, then glanced quizzically at his father.

"Can I have a girl like that, father?" he hoarsely whispered.

"She's a maid, my son, and I doubt that she's in service. Never fear, we'll choose a pleasing companion for you tonight. And try to remember what I told you. You're sitting so stiffly, as if you were going to your own execution. Sit back, be at your ease, like a gentleman."

A moment later, the negress reappeared behind the proprietress of *Plaisir*. The years had dealt kindly with Marthe Rambouillet, Lucien observed as he gallantly rose to his feet and proffered her a courtly bow. Henry rose, his face sullen, his left hand pressed over his waistcoat as he imitated his father with a quick, short inclination of his head and shoulders.

Though she must be surely fifty-five by now, Lucien estimated, the chestnut wig she wore and the same round, sweet face with artful rice powder and just the proper touch of rouge banished the thought of age. So did the flouncy emerald-green silk gown and the pretty white satin slippers. She was wise enough, however, to wear full sleeves and a high neckline, but if he had not met her twenty-two years ago and known her age then, Lucien would have sworn that she had not aged a day since their first meeting.

"May I welcome you to New Orleans and to *Plaisir*, messieurs?" Her voice was soft and gracious. "You are newcomers to my house, I believe—or are you?" Her voice trailed off as she stared intently at Lucien. He was clean-shaven as he had been his first night in New Orleans as the guest of Jules Ronsart. And, though he had not yet had time for the bath to which he had looked forward, he had managed to borrow the Creole's razor and shave before dinner so as to appear presentable at his host's table.

"Oh, no—it's not possible—" she began, a hand to her cheek and her eyes very wide.

"It's possible, Madame Rambouillet. Yes, I'm Lucien Bouchard, and this is my son, Henry."

"Mais c'est incroyable!" she burst out, coming forward to clasp his outstretched hand in both of hers and then to kiss him warmly on the cheek. "Who would have thought it after so long? And how fit, how strong and young you look, *M'sieu* Lucien." Then, turning, with a radiant smile to the scowling black-haired youth, she went on, "And this is your son, yes, except that he's a bit sturdier I would have guessed it at once, the eyes, the hair, and so self-contained!"

Then, turning back to Lucien, she exclaimed, "My niece has never forgotten you, and your gift was in exquisite taste, *M'sieu* Lucien."

"She's well, I trust, and living in New Orleans?"

"Oh, yes, very well. Except that she and Daniel are visiting Daniel's cousin in Pensacola. What a pity she couldn't be here to see you again and to thank you for what you did, as I thank you again. My sweet Eulalie might never have lived to know the happiness she now has if it hadn't been for you that night."

"It was nothing, madame, you make too much of it. Anyone would have done as much—"

"But only you did, and so bravely, without a weapon to defend yourself!" Impulsively, she turned to Henry. "Your father, *M'sieu* Henry, is a kind, brave man, who thinks of others constantly. If you follow in his footsteps, you couldn't have a better model and you will be very dearly loved, I promise you that." Then, as if ashamed of herself over such a display of emotion, she drew back and, with a faint smile, asked, "But now, my house is at your disposal. If there is any way in which I may serve you—"

"I—well, madame, it's my son. He's fifteen, but as you see, quite mature. And the fact is—" Lucien found himself suddenly at a loss for words.

"Je comprends tout," Marthe Rambouillet softly mur-

mured, appraisingly glancing at the glowering boy, who still sat stiffly, one hand pressed against his waistcoat. "The first time must be *tout à fait exquis, naturellement.* And I think that he will like Honorine. May I first serve you a small collation—Daphne, my lovely mustee maid, will bring it in and more wine, of course—and then, when you are both at your ease, I shall have Daphne escort the young gentleman to Honorine's chamber."

"I'm grateful for your understanding, madame."

She lingered a moment. "And yourself—"

"Frankly, if I might put you to the trouble, I'm in dire need of a bath. I was able to shave but not to bathe, and a flatboat journey from Mobile to New Orleans is hardly conducive to cleanliness," Lucien explained with a self-deprecating smile.

"But of course! I'll have the collation brought in for the young gentleman at once, you shall have your bath and then something to eat and drink, and perhaps we shall chat about old times, if that pleases you?"

"It would, very much, Madame Rambouillet."

"If you'll come this way then, I've a marble tub, a rarity in this city, and obtained for me by the good graces of a very grateful patron who, like you, brought his two young sons here for their first education in *l'amour.* The fact is, it was a part of his plantation in Haiti, which he no longer owns, a misfortune he shared with many other plantation owners."

"That too I understand. And again I'm in your debt."

"No, no, *M'sieu* Lucien, it's the other way around. Now, here we are, the bath chamber all to yourself. And I'll have one of my girls bring in the water. It will be as hot as we can heat the stones."

The pink marble bathtub would have tempted a sybarite, much less a man who had ridden ten days on horseback with perhaps a dip in the river as his only ablutions Lucien sighed nostalgically, remembering the chateau of Yves-sur-lac. Decidedly, when Windhaven was built to his specifications, there would be just such a tub as this!

On the brightly painted plaster walls, which were red and green and blue in a riotous melange to suggest the entire erotic tone of this establishment of carnal gratification, some Creole artist had daubed three water colors on heavy linen paper and attached them with resin gum to the walls. One of them was a reproduction of Watteau's *Embarkation for Cythera,* the original of which hung in the Louvre. The other two were highly scabrous yet witty, showing nymphs and satyrs making love in a little lagoon where leering Pan played his pipes and watched the lubricious scene with sparkling gaze. And in the opposite corner from the tub was a low, wide, thickly upholstered couch covered in red velvet. To the other side of the tub there was a tall stool on which, Lucien supposed, he might drape his clothes as he undressed, which he now began to do.

At the tailor stall, he had purchased a pair of cotton *caleçon de bain,* and he now removed waistcoat and pantaloons and ruffled shirt cravats, gaitered hose and the silver-buckled shoes, and stood in these alone. He glanced down at his body, grateful for its wiry strength. Along his side, the faint discolorations of the bear's claws still remained, ineffaceable, but not disfiguring. His legs were long and lean and vigorously muscled, his chest expansive. The black hair which matted it was thicker than it had ever been in France. Now the door opened, and his eyes widened to see a slim young woman, surely no more than twenty, clad in a green crepe de chine dress with neckline slashed to the waist and the edges held together with little silver clasps that permitted tantalizing glimpses of milky flesh. It swathed and outlined her voluptuous body at the flaring hips and lithe sleek thighs, and he could see just the glimpses of the inner round curves of surprisingly sumptuous firm breasts. Her hair was russet, drawn to the back and formed into a thick knot to leave her nape bare. Her face was broadly oval, exquisite and provocative, with large narrowly spaced hazel eyes, diminutive upturned nose, soft ripe mouth and delicately rounded chin. "*Bon soir, M'sieu,*" she softly murmured, then moved outside to bring in a large wooden bucket of water and set it beside the tub and then another.

"Let me do that, *m'amselle,*" he stammered, flushing

hotly as he saw her eyes quickly study his almost nakedness.

"But it is for me to do, *m'sieu*. I am Virginie, at your service. I shall bring you a glass of wine directly, the stones are heating and Sally, who is our cook, will bring them as they are ready."

"Well then, I'll drink a toast to your health, *m'amselle*." He gave her a half-bow, hugely embarrassed. Their eyes met and her moist red lips curved in a charming little smile as she left the room, returning a moment later with a glass of excellent Madeira, which he sipped, lifting the glass to toast her, and then watched as the plump, beaming black cook in a gay red calico dress and white apron round the front, waddled in with a leather sling of rocks and dumped them with a sizzling hiss into the first bucket. "Nothah batch heatin', massa suh, ready in a jiffy," she announced, and disappeared.

"If you'll get into the tub, I'll pour the water, *M'sieu* Lucien," the russet-haired girl proffered.

"Why, the buckets are much too heavy for you to lift," he protested.

"But I'm in service, and Madame would be vexed if I didn't do my duty. Please make yourself comfortable in the tub, *M'sieu* Lucien."

Self-consciously, Lucien clambered into the tub and watched as the young woman lifted the heavy bucket and carefully moved to the edge of the tub to empty it. It was pleasantly warm, and the sensation was good against his naked flesh. With it, came the inevitable twinge of physical desire, which he sought to quell, tightening his knees together and sitting as stiffly as if he were back at the council of Econchate. Virginie lifted the other bucket and poured it into the tub, then took both with her to fill them with water for the next sling of oven-heated rocks.

After six buckets, Lucien had ample water for his bath and scoured himself vigorously. Virginie had left him to his ablutions, for which he was indeed grateful. But as he clambered out of the tub, drying himself with a piece of soft, doubly thick toweling, the door opened again and then closed as she stood watching. "Would you like the

446

collation now, or would you prefer to have it in the little salon, *M'sieu* Lucien?"

"Why, I dined very well tonight, and there's really no need," he apologetically replied.

The light in the room came from a candle in an ornate glass chimney placed on a tabouret beside the couch. Its flickering glow intensified the warmth of her fresh milky skin, of the moist curves of her enticing mouth, of the intriguing glow in her hazel eyes. "In that case, let me massage you a little. You've had a long journey, Madame tells me, and it will help you sleep. Please, I wish to do it."

He could hardly refuse so gracious an offer, and, moreover, the thought of being ministered to by an attractive female was not at all unpleasant after the strict continence he had observed since Priscilla's death. Obligingly, he stretched himself out on his belly on the couch, closed his eyes and surrendered himself to the gentle, caressing touch of her soft, slim fingers. A drowsy languor took possession of him, plunged him into a kind of reverie in which dream and the reality of past events inseparably merged. Then, half-drowsy, he felt her hands draw away and he waited. There was a soft rustling sound, so faint and imperceptible that he did not distinguish it from the luxurious relaxation of his entire body and his senses.

"Do turn over now, dear *M'sieu* Lucien," he heard her voice entreat him, and unthinkingly obeyed. Then he lifted his head, startled, incredulous. The daring dress, its silver clasps unfastened, had dropped to her feet and she was naked, the smooth, deep-dimpled belly evasively curving down to the crisp dark *mons* framed by the warm milky-sheened thighs. Her beautiful round full breasts, spacious and yet flawlessly proportioned, rose and fell with her quickened breathing as she dropped down to her knees beside him on the couch.

"No—I didn't wish madame—" he began, his voice hoarse and faltering.

She put a finger to his lips, shook her head, with a sweet, beguiling smile. "Shhh, dear *M'sieu* Lucien. This is not a service of the house, but my own. I'm Eulalie's daughter, and I've been staying with my great-aunt while

447

my parents are in Pensacola, you see. You don't know how often my mother has told me of what you did that night so long ago. Why——" and now, most uncharacteristically, she giggled like a very young girl finding amusement in the discomfiture of her elders——"if it hadn't been for you, I might not ever have been born. Don't you see, dear *M'sieu* Lucien? And besides, both *maman* and my *grande-tante* Marthe have instructed me in such things. I'm to be wed to a very nice boy next month, and we've already been lovers, so you're not to think you're spoiling me for him——now won't you please make me stop talking so much and let me love you, *M'sieu* Lucien?"

"Little Virginie, so lovely, as sweet and gracious as her mother——yes, my dear one, oh yes!" Lucien murmured as he drew the smiling naked girl down to him. And it was as if all the yesterdays had been rolled back to that night in the little house on Isola Street, and it was once again for Lucien Bouchard the priceless gift of unexpected love.

She had stolen away, leaving him bemused and dreaming, when he was suddenly torn out of his euphoric haze by a shrill scream, which reverberated down the hallway. Then another, and then excited voices. Struggling to his feet, he hastily donned waistcoat and pantaloons and hastened out into the hallway. Marthe Rambouillet was there already, her face tear-stained, reaching for his hand: "Oh, please, *M'sieu* Lucien, come with me——it's Honorine! Your son——he's hurt her——oh, I didn't believe it——not your son, you, so gentle——hurry!"

He took the stairs in a bound and stood on the threshold of the room whose door was partly open. The pretty girl who had admitted him and his son was crouching against the wall just inside, a hand to her mouth. And on the canopied bed, a stately, buxom light-brownhaired young woman in her mid-twenties, naked save for clockwork stockings, sprawled on her belly, her face buried in her hands, her shoulders heaving with hysterical sobs, her pale carnation-tinted skin viciously striped with the angry, darkening weals from the riding crop which young Henry Bouchard clutched in his right hand, as he stood naked in

448

his silver-buckled shoes and gaitered hose, his face twisted, his eyes glittering with sadistic concupiscence.

"What the devil—you depraved beast—is this your notion of love?" Lucien angrily shouted as he strode to the boy, tore the crop away and slashed him across the cheek with it. "I should leave your skin in tatters for what you've done to this poor girl!"

"She wouldn't do as I asked her, father—I paid for her, not you—I took some of my silver from the box so that I could—when a man pays in a house like this, he has a right to be treated as he wants, doesn't he?" Henry growled, rubbing the burning welt which ran from jaw nearly to temple. "I wanted her to play at being my slave, and at first she did, and then she started to insult me—"

"Close your mouth, before I forget myself and thrash you as you've thrashed her," Lucien panted. "Get your clothes on, you disgusting little animal! In God's name, why does this obsession with slavery twist your young brain? You surely didn't inherit it from me!"

"But in France, where you came from, father, the peasants were slaves, weren't they?"

"Yes, damn you, and they overthrew their king because of it. And they killed innocent people like your grandfather and grandmother because they'd been brutalized by those whose cruelty is akin to yours! Enough, I say, get yourself out of my sight. We'll go back to *M'sieu* Ronsart's house and then back to Mobile as fast as possible. Take your clothes, I say, and get yourself into some empty room and make yourself decent, if you can. Leave me with this poor girl."

When Henry hesitated, Lucien lifted the riding crop, his eyes narrowed and cold. With a shrug, the sturdy, naked black-haired youth gathered up his clothes and strode defiantly out of the room. On the bed, Honorine was still sobbing.

"My deepest apologies, *M'amselle*. I didn't dream my son could treat any woman this way. I'll have Madame tend to your hurts and I'll leave something to console you as my gift—it's little enough, and I can only hope you'll forgive me," he murmured.

Marthe Rambouillet and two of her girls had already

come into the room, and with ointments and soaked cloths and soothing words they did their best to comfort the anguished Honorine.

Lucien stood alone in the hallway, staring down at the riding crop which he still brandished in his hand. Then, with an imprecation, he flung it to the floor and said softly, for only himself and her to whom he addressed those words to hear, "Dimarte, out of all my sorrows, is this boy to be the heir who builds my Windhaven as a memorial to you who were the soul of gentleness and kindness? Oh, God, I have waited so long, do not destroy my dreams, but cleanse the strange evil in my only son's young heart!"

CHAPTER THIRTY-THREE

There was a restlessnesss in this southeastern part of the new country, not only because of the imminent threat of war with England and the fear of simultaneous attacks upon the white settlers by the aroused Creeks and other tribes, but also because the right to settle upon the land itself was now in suspended question. In the year of 1809 the Supreme Court of the United States, in the case of *Fletcher* vs. *Peck*, declared that the repeal of the Yazoo grants was a breach of contract and therefore forbidden by the Constitution. Claimants under the separate Yazoo companies at once appealed to Congress for relief, but John Randolph of Roanoke had made the case his personal concern and was to block all action until 1814.

In the very year in which Lucien had visited New Orleans for the second time, many titles to the land in the Mississippi Territory were threatened by the Yazoo claimants, while others were endangered by a conflict between British and Spanish grants. Many settlers held tracts under Spanish grants which had been superseded by grants under the British rule. While these British claims had never been established, the entire matter was subject to judicial determination, and so those who lived upon the land began to wonder if all their toil was to be in vain once the courts heard the claims. Indeed, it was the dread of federal courts as well as of British and Yazoo claimants which caused many of the settlers to oppose Mississippi's admission to statehood.

Lucien and his son had gone back to Econchate, there to render an accounting to Nanakota and the elders of the profits made from this last year's bounteous crop and to bring back the goods which the villagers had ordered. Between Lucien and his son, too, there was an uneasy truce after the boy's inexplicably sadistic behavior at the house of Marthe Rambouillet. What most concerned Lucien was the proximity of Disjamilla, who would be his son's own age of sixteen this summer. She was even more attractive now than her mother, who was entering her forty-third year of life and still as hardworking and vigorous as when she and Ben had been given to Lucien as slaves. He had already spoken to Ellen about the potential danger, and the gentle Kru woman had understandingly nodded and said, "My hope is that soon my girl will be spoken for by a warrior of Econchate. You know very well, *M'su* Lucien, that she spends much time at the village and speaks Creek as well as the villagers, and they are all drawn to her because of her goodness. I myself would favor such a marriage, and it would not be like leaving us forever, since she would be only a few miles from us."

This news greatly relieved Lucien's concern, for he had felt himself impelled to tell both Ben and Ellen of Henry's attempt to force their daughter three years ago. They had been most sympathetic with him in his anguish that his own son had caused such a breach between them all, but he had felt as guilty as if he himself had lusted after the young girl. If Disjamilla were married, that would be a happy solution to this pressing problem, and the second would be Henry's own marriage as soon as that was feasible.

But now there was work to be done with the new cotton crop, for on his previous trip to Mobile and New Orleans, he had purchased four new slaves, strong, capable field workers in their mid-twenties, men from Dahomey who had been smuggled in on a Portuguese slaver harboring off the Florida coast and thence through Georgia and on to Mobile. He had paid $2000 for them, and had Ben tell them as he had told all the others that freedom awaited them and the chance to earn their own wages, which would be held in trust for them. And when these four, Djarta, Kimbayo, Jaspar and Moses, had talked to the others who had once been slaves as they were now, they showed an eagerness to learn the cultivation of this rich crop in which they would have a recognized part under so benevolent a master, who, as Ben solemnly assured them, had never used a whip and never would.

There was one more piece of unfinished business which Lucien Bouchard had transacted in Mobile before returning with his son to Econchate. Jules Ronsart's prediction of a war with the British could mean embargo and blockade, and it could also mean financial disaster. Many planters along the Tombigbee bought seed on credit, relying on their crop at the end of the year to pay for it and to repeat the process the following year. Receipts and scrip were being used as legal tender, but their value could be obliterated overnight in the event of a serious war between two great powers. And so, after he had taken Henry back to Mobile and before setting forth on the return journey to Econchate, Lucien Bouchard had paid a call on the principal factors of the Mobile trading post to review his account and to see what part of it could be transferred in bank notes and specie to Jules Ronsart's New Orleans counting house. The Creole operated a private bank which, Lucien had quickly learned from reliable sources, was in an enviably solvent position. And the Creole had told him that it would be an honor to handle his business and that he would take it on the basis of an especially low discount because they were such good friends.

Lucien's account at Mobile showed a credit of $148,000 less the $2000 he had just spent for the four new slaves from Dahomey. He was able to arrange for the transfer of $94,000 to Jules Ronsart's private bank, the balance to be carried on the ledgers in Mobile for the acquisition of goods for Econchate. This time, sensing his father's subdued anger with him, Henry did not ask for his profits to be given him in silver coin—and besides, silver had virtually disappeared.

As summer approached, Jules Ronsart's prediction appeared certain of fulfillment: the "Young Warhawks" headed by John C. Calhoun of South Carolina and

Speaker of the House of Representatives Henry Clay of Kentucky were foremost in urging President Madison to declare war on England. Madison was nominated by the Congressional Caucus of Republicans on May 18th for a second term, with John Langdon refusing the nomination of Vice-President and Elbridge Gerry replacing him. Eleven days later, a caucus of the Republican members of the New York legislature met in Albany to nominate DeWitt Clinton to run against Madison for the illustrious office of President of the United States.

It was on June 1st that President Madison sent his war message to Congress, and three days later the Territory of Missouri was established. On that same day, the House voted 79 to 49 for war with England, and two weeks later the Senate concurred by a vote of 19 to 13. The next day, President Madison approved the declaration of war and proclaimed it on June 19, 1812.

The irony was that England revoked its notorious Orders in Council on June 23rd, unaware that the United States had already issued its declaration of war. President Madison accordingly authorized Jonathan Russell, the American *chargé d'affaires* in London, to negotiate an armistice on conditions stipulating the revocation of those Orders in Council and the abandonment of all impressment of American sailors as well.

But the war was not unanimously popular. Twice a mob attacked the offices of the *Federal Republican* in Baltimore for that newspaper's denunciation of the declaration of war, and in August the Friends of Liberty, Peace and Commerce held a mass meeting in New York City to oppose the war. In this same month, Fort Dearborn, on the site of what was to become the great city of Chicago, surrendered to the British, and Indians massacred American settlers. A day later, General William Hull surrendered Detroit to the British.

These American defeats, coupled with the July 17th surrender of Michilimackinac, the American outpost on upper Lake Huron, acted as a goad to the increasing belligerence of the Indian tribes. They reasoned that if the military power of these hostile white-eyes could be thus weakened by defeat against the British, whom Tecumseh

454

was continuing to laud as their natural allies, the time might be ripe for a confederation of strength throughout the southeast which would once and for all drive out the aggressive Georgians as well as the settlers along the Tombigbee. And in October, when American troops were severely defeated in an attack upon Canada at Queenstown and lost a thousand men, their hopes were further aggrandized. In November, General Henry Dearborn's campaign against Montreal ended and at the Canadian boundary militia refused to leave the United States. True, there were naval victories like that of Stephen Decatur's capture in his frigate *United States* over the British frigate *Macedonian* off the Madeira Islands and the victory of the *Constitution* over the British frigate *Java* off the coast of Brazil, but the British fleet was blockading the Delaware and Chesapeake bays.

On December 2nd, President Madison was re-elected by the electoral vote of 128 to 89 against DeWitt Clinton, who ran as the Federalist candidate, and Elbridge Gerry defeated Jared Ingersoll for the office of Vice-President by a vote of 131 to 86. The program of the "Young Warhawks" was now in full swing.

But this war was a personal disaster for Lucien Bouchard and the villagers of Econchate: his cotton crop, out of 150 acres planted, had brought him 112,500 pounds of prime ginned cotton, which should have netted, at the prevailing price of 15 cents a pound, $16,875. But because the ports were blockaded, including Mobile, the burlap bags lay on the wharf until they rotted, and other planters at Natchez and other points along the newly opened and settled territory of the southeast suffered as well.

On December 18th, Lucien's fiftieth birthday, Disjamilla was married in the village of Econchate by Creek ritual to a twenty-year-old unfledged brave, Eisquayaw, a youth who had shown no interest in warfare or hunting, but who preferred to work in the fields and whose gentle nature had attracted the pretty Kru girl. Lucien enacted the role of relative at the wedding ceremony and brought Henry to observe it. "Remember that although these unions are made without priest or Holy Book, my son," he told the sturdy black-haired youth, "they endure and there is harmony and discipline and understanding. There is much you can learn from these people, and you can see for yourself what loyal friends they have proved to be since I first came here as a stranger and intruder on their land."

"But, father, you've told me about the history of this new country, this America. And I'm an American now, born here and not in France, isn't that so?"

"Yes. I don't want you to forget the tradition of your name, Henry, for it is one of the oldest in France. But you are quite right, we are both of us now Americans."

"Then," the boy scornfully declared, "I want to think about the future, because one day soon there will be white men here and they will drive these Indians away. I've learned all I care to from them, father."

Lucien gave his son a long, hard look. "You're wrong," he said softly, as he watched Disjamilla hold hands with her young husband and saw the happy smile on her lips. "You want to domineer people, to prove yourself superior to them. And you won't be able to do that with white settlers when they do come to this country. What you still have to learn from the Creeks is how to give and not to take, and that's a lesson that will prevail with anyone you meet in the future." And he uttered a faint sigh of disapproval as he saw his son shrug with indifference.

Now that Disjamilla had gone to live in Econchate with her young husband, Lucien could devote himself to teaching his son more and more of the work of running the cotton engine, cultivating the fields and helping build the flatboats that would take the cotton crops downriver to Mobile once the port would be open again to commerce. He had given Henry fifteen acres to cultivate in this new year of 1813, and although last year's crop had been lost because of the war, he had told Henry that he would make good out of his own pocket the boy's loss. There could be no question about young Henry's stamina and intensity in his toil, but Lucien was quick to observe that the black free men were rarely as communicative with Henry as they were with him when he took his own place in the fields at their side.

Instinctively, there was a resentment in this glowering, strong adolescent, now nearing his sixteenth birthday, a resentment which proclaimed itself as selfish ego. To Lucien it was one of the seven deadly sins, but he did not know how it could be eradicated. Perhaps only time would do it and perhaps, too, the sobering responsibilities of marriage. Yes, marriage might be the answer; Henry would then feel that he had achieved his manhood and was independent of his father and could thus begin to shape his own life. And yet Lucien could not forget the scene at the house of Marthe Rambouillet, nor the boy's treatment of the mare and of Disjamilla before that.

Spanish rule in Mobile was mild, and even the British had come there to live. By now, there were some twenty-five white families, of French, Spanish, American and English nationality, building the town more permanently and raising cattle and hogs, as well as rice and vegetables. They had oysters and fish to eat, and in winter there were wild geese and ducks, with venison in abundance throughout the year. So plentiful, indeed, that a quarter of a deer was sold for twenty-five cents to the town's inhabitants. Some cotton had been planted at Mobile, too, but there was little labor to cultivate it, though the land was wonderfully rich because of its constant moisture from the gulf.

There was more access about the area of Mobile, too, for American soldiers had built a road and bridges from Baton Rouge on the Mississippi to Fort Stoddert, and from Fort Stoddert on to Georgia, so that many carriages bringing settlers from Savannah to Fort Stoddert could find a swifter, unbroken journey, which hitherto had been impossible.

There was news from France which made Lucien again wonder over the fate of his native land. Napoleon Bonaparte had had to retreat from Moscow because of lack of supplies, and the Russians had practiced a scorched-earth policy and an harassment of his army throughout the long retreat. The *Grande Armée* was annihilated and Napoleon had hastened to Paris to raise a new army. And now a new coalition, which comprised

Russia, Prussia, England, Sweden and Austria, had come into existence and defeated the Corsican usurper at Leipzig and pursued him into the very heart of France itself.

President James Madison saw that the British were using only such armies as they could spare from the bitter contest with Napoleon, and decided to take possession of Mobile. Under an act of Congress in this spring of 1813, he directed General James Wilkinson, then commanding at New Orleans, to occupy that vital port.

With six hundred men and five cannon against only sixty men in Fort Charlotte and no provisions for the Spaniards, Captain Cayetano Perez surrendered without hostility on April 13, 1813. Without the shedding of a single drop of blood, as General Wilkinson himself expressed it, the occupation of the United States was now extended to the Perdido River, the boundary which the Americans had always claimed under the terms of the Louisiana Purchase. The Stars and Stripes now waved from Fort Stoddert to Mobile, from Fort Charlotte to Fort Bowyer: Mississippi Territory had at last reached the mighty gulf.

But the couriers of Tecumseh had done their work and given the British renewed hope of winning the war against the United States.

Throughout the Creek Confederacy, belligerence toward the white-eyes grew. Peter McQueen, a half-breed of Tallase, led a war party of 350 Creeks toward Pensacola with many pack horses to collect arms and ammunition for a savage attack upon the white settlers. General Wilkinson had been transferred to Canada and replaced in New Orleans and Mobile by General Flournoy, who refused to send any regular or volunteer troops to protect the inhabitants of the Tombigbee and the Tensaw. The British fleet had been seen off the coast, and from its ships supplies, arms, ammunition and Indian emissaries were being sent to Pensacola and the other remaining Spanish ports in Florida.

Now the American settlers in the Alabama territory were completely isolated and defenseless. Colonel James Caller ordered out the militia to intercept McQueen's war party, raising 180 mounted men. He overtook them on a peninsula of low pine barren, formed by the windings of Burnt Corn Creek. The Creeks had camped and were preparing their noontime meal when the militia attacked. Unhappily, after forcing the Creeks to retreat, many of the militia remained behind and sought to capture the Indian packhorses and the booty which they carried. Colonel Caller was forced to order a retreat to the rising heights overlooking the peninsula, but a hundred of his men fled in confusion, still driving the captured pack horses before them. McQueen's warriors surged out of the swamp and routed the Americans. And when news of this defeat, which had become a victory for the Creeks, reached the tribal villages, the American capture of Mobile was forgotten: in its place, the Indians believed that the greedy settlers could at last be driven forever from their lands.

A courier from Tecumseh came to Econchate in the first week of August. He demanded to be heard by the council and by the *Mico*, Nanakota; and Lucien was present also.

Lucien heard with growing horror the bold plans which Tecumseh's courier swaggeringly revealed. There were traitors in the tribes, who believed in peace; they would be put to death, and then all the Creeks would unite in a common cause against the hated Americans. Those tribes upon the Coosa, Tallapoosa and the Black Warrior would attack the settlements upon the Tensaw and the Tombigbee; those near the Cherokees, with the assistance of the latter, were to attack the Tennesseeans; the Georgians would be exterminated by the fierce depredations of the Lower Creeks and the Seminoles; and the Choctaws would exterminate the white settlers of Mississippi.

"In every Creek village," the emissary boasted, "the people have gone into the woods, dancing and preparing for war. Our *Windigos*, all, without exception, proclaim that the white-eyes' blood will stain the land and that scalps will hang from the tentpoles of all the lodges. Once again the mighty Creeks will rule, with no intruders to halt their power. Unite with us, you braves of Econchate!

459

Come with your muskets and your bows and arrows and your tomahawks, you will count many coups!"

Nanakota turned to Lucien, who wore about his neck the bear-claw necklace which Dimarte had fashioned for him, buckskin jacket and breeches and moccasins. "What say you, oh blood brother of the Bear?" he gravely asked.

"To the courier of the valiant Tecumseh—" Lucien turned to speak at the scowling, paint-bedaubed warrior who faced the council—"I say the ways of peace are the ways of life, and if the Creeks go upon the warpath now against the Americans, they will most surely be defeated. There will be weeping in all the lodges, and the children and the widows will starve and they will be driven like wild dogs from the villages. It is wiser to make peace with the stronger force, and to live in peace, for the land will provide rich harvests for red man as well as white."

"Who dares speak so to mighty Tecumseh?" the half-naked warrior arrogantly sneered, brandishing his tomahawk. "You are a white-eyes. How come you by this council?"

"Because he is my friend, because he is of the clan of the Bear, and he has proved his valor over many more summers than you have scalps at your tentpole," Nanakota at once angrily replied. "The great Tunkamara thought so well of this blood brother that he gave him his daughter to wed."

"I did not wish to offend the mighty *Mico* of Econchate." The emissary inclined his head with a fawning smile toward Nanakota and a sudden look of hatred toward Lucien. "But the words of your blood brother are those of an old fearful squaw who does not know what it is to take an enemy's scalp."

"Again you speak with a forked tongue," Nanakota scowlingly interrupted, pointing toward Lucien's throat. Do you not see this necklace? With a knife, he slew the she-bear and in single-handed combat took the life of the son of the war chief who was sent to bring him here in bondage as a slave. More than that, when Tunkamara was foully slain by white-eyes in the pay of the traitor Bowles, this blood brother of mine slew with his own hands their leader. And armed with a knife alone, he fought a renegade Choctaw who had taken an innocent white-eyes squaw to the torture stake and slew him in fair fight. Do not speak of cowardice, oh emissary of Tecumseh, not in my presence or before our elders, who know well what Lu-shee-ahn has done to make Econchate prosper in the eyes of the Great Spirit!"

"I go, then, mighty *Mico*." Again the emissary made a gesture of homage to the stern-faced Nanakota. "But I call upon those warriors whose courage and whose loyalty to the great Creek Nation forces them to take up arms with us against the white-eyes who would rob all of you of your land. There can be no peace with them, they make treaties and they lie, they promise but they do not keep their promises. Once they are driven out, then we shall be the masters. Tecumseh has said it. Let those who believe in him and his destiny follow, for I will lead them to great victories!"

Again he bowed low to the council, then strode defiantly out of the meeting house. But by the end of the next day, a hundred warriors from Econchate had followed him, spurning Nanakota's entreaties to keep the peace that Econchate might continue its prosperity upon the good land.

And when the *Mico* saw the youngest and fiercest of his warriors mount their horses and ride out of the village without a backward look, he turned to Lucien and said sadly, "Did not old Tsipoulata say that there would be war not far distant from this soil, soaked with the blood of many warriors of our great Creek Nation? And did he not say also that when the earth has absorbed and forgotten it, the white-eyes will build a town upon Econchate after we have left it to find where we must hunt and grow the crops? Aiyee, now I believe that his words begin to come true, Lu-shee-ahn. And when you spoke to the courier of the powerful sachem Tecumseh, you remembered those words too, but he would not listen. I pray that the Great Spirit has not turned His face from us here at Econchate. Let us go now and each in our own way beg Him to look with mercy upon our weakened village."

461

General Ferdinand Leigh Claiborne, brother of the ex-governor of the Mississippi Territory and a veteran of Wayne's army on the northwestern frontier which had won resounding victory over a far larger force of Indians, had been appointed by General Wilkinson to be in charge of volunteers and to take command of the post of Baton Rouge. By the end of this July, he had been ordered by General Flournoy to march with his entire command to Fort Stoddert and defend Mobile. His troops numbered seven hundred men, whom he had chiefly sustained by supplies raised by mortgages upon his own estate, for the quartermaster at Baton Rouge had provided him with a small sum of $200 for his provisions. Learning of the disastrous Burnt Corn expedition, he set to work to distribute his troops for the greatest protection of the settlers. Two hundred of his men under Colonel Carson were sent to Fort Glass, where they began the construction of Fort Madison. Another company was sent to Fort St. Stephens to occupy the old Spanish blockhouse, while another contingent of mounted dragoons scoured the countryside in reconnaissance missions to determine whether hostile Indians were in the vicinity.

Meanwhile the settlers had begun the construction of a fort around the residence of Samuel Mims, who lived on Lake Tensaw, a mile east of the Alabama River. His house was a large, one-story frame building with spacious shed-rooms, and pickets were driven around it with fence rails placed between. Five hundred portholes were made, three and a half feet from the ground. The stockade enclosed an acre of ground in a square form and was entered by two heavy gates. They began to build a blockhouse at the southwest corner, but it was never finished. Woods intervened between the picketing and the lake, while from the north one saw dense cane swamps. On the east, the flatlands continued for several miles, interspersed with cane marshes and ravines, an ill-chosen place for a fort.

Before the defenses could be completed, settlers poured in with their provisions and effects. On August 7th, General Claiborne himself arrived at Fort Mims and ordered Major Daniel Beasley to strengthen the picketing, build two more blockhouses, send out frequent scouts and give all who needed them provisions, whether they were whites or friendly Indians.

There were now 553 whites, Indians, soldiers and blacks congregated in this inadequate fort, in hot August, and sickness broke out. Meanwhile, the Creeks warriors were on their way back from Pensacola with heavy supplies of weapons and ammunition. And warriors from sixteen Creek villages joined them in a planned attack.

Besides Peter McQueen and the prophet Josiah Francis, William Weatherford, the son of the trader Charles Weatherford, was in command. And it was he who led the Creeks against the Tensaw settlers, among whom were his own brother, his half-brother David Tait and several sisters.

By noon of August 30th, a thousand Creek warriors lying on the ground in a thick ravine 400 yards from the eastern gate of Fort Mims waited for the sound of the drum which summoned the soldiers of the garrison to their noonday meal. The prophets of these Indian villages, dancing and calling out incantations, led the attack, having assured the braves that American bullets would split upon their sacred persons without harm, but five of them were immediately shot down. This only momentarily halted the charge of the Creeks, while the settlers, many of whom had never done battle before, were disorganized and stricken with terror at the sight of the circling Indians who attacked from all sides. By five that evening, all of the occupants of Fort Mims were dead except a few halfbreeds who had been made prisoners, some blacks taken to serve as slaves, and about fifteen soldiers and settlers who escaped.

The British agents at Pensacola had offered a reward of five dollars for every American scalp, and the Creeks jerked the skin from the entire head, collected all the possessions which the fire had not consumed, and returned to the east a mile from the ruins to spend the night, to smoke their pipes, to trim and dry their bloody trophies. William Weatherford had implored the warriors to spare the women and children and reproached them for their barbarism, but his own life was threatened for interposing. Tomahawks were raised over his head and he had to yield to their bloodthirsty desire for total vengeance against the white-eyes.

Fate had enjoyed its moment of grim irony over the tragic destiny of Fort Mims. Major Beasley had sent dispatches to General Claiborne almost daily, and just two hours before the Creeks entered the gate of the doomed fort, had sent a letter to General Claiborne declaring his ability to maintain the post against any number of the enemy. Indeed, a black slave who had gone out to scout and reported that there were Indians had been sentenced to a whipping because the soldiers could not see them and was undergoing his punishment at the very moment the Creeks charged out of the ravine.

Meanwhile, Josiah Francis, the prophet, heading a hundred warriors, was ravaging settlers along the fork of the Alabama and Tombigbee, and the settlers were in terror. A British war schooner had anchored at Pensacola with a large supply of ammunition and arms, and Gonzales Minique, the governor of Pensacola, addressed a letter to William Weatherford and his chiefs to congratulate them on their victory at Fort Mims. He assured them of his unflagging aid, but urged them not to set fire to Mobile, since that town properly belonged to the king of Spain and would soon be reoccupied.

But not all Indians hated the American settlers, and at this critical time, Pushmatahaw, the enlightened chief of the Choctaws, rode to Fort St. Stephens and offered to enlist several companies of his warriors in the American cause. This was declined by General Flournoy, who then changed his mind after the aroused citizens harangued him and cursed him for his folly. Colonel John McKee, agent of the Chickasaws, raised a large force of their warriors to march to Tuscaloosa Falls to attack the Creek town at that place, but found it reduced to ashes, for the Indians had fled. George S. Gaines met with Pushmatahaw at the council ground where over 5000 Choctaws were encamped, and their chief urged them to defeat the bloodthirsty plan of Tecumseh. But Tecumseh's own days were numbered; he was killed on October 5, 1813, near Chatham on the Thames River in southern Ontario,

Canada, leading forces against General William Henry Harrison, an American victory which restored control of the vital Northwest.

Gaines sent letters to General Andrew Jackson detailing the massacre at Fort Mims, and Jackson, at the head of a large volunteer force of Tennesseeans, inflicted an overwhelming defeat on the Creeks at Talladega on November 10th, a battle in which over 300 Indians were killed as against only fifteen Americans. Colonel John Coffee, with 600 horsemen, destroyed the town of Black Warrior and, promoted to the rank of brigadier general by Jackson, advanced with a thousand men to inflict another overwhelming defeat on the Creeks at Tallushatchee. On November 29th, Brigadier General John Floyd of Georgia, with an army of 950 militia soldiers and 400 friendly Creeks guided by none other than Abram Mordecai, fought a savage and victorious battle at the Creek town of Auttose on the east bank of the Tallapoosa.

At last, General Flournoy gave the order which permitted General Claiborne to advance with his southern army to the Alabama River and by the end of this bloody month of November, he built a strong stockade defended by three blockhouses and a half-moon battery commanding the Little River, which was named in his honor.

There was no chance for Lucien Bouchard, with warfare raging on all sides, to send his cotton down the river to Mobile. Instead, he gave orders to Thomas and Ben to plow it under and let the land lie fallow till next year, turning all his attention to corn for the needy villagers. For of those hundred warriors who had left Econchate, only ten had returned, all wounded and unfit for further battle.

General Andrew Jackson had thus won international renown for his campaigns against the Red Sticks, the war party headed by William Weatherford. He had risen from his bed at the news of Fort Mims, his left shoulder shattered by a slug with a bullet imbedded in the upper arm, both the result of a duel with the younger brother of Thomas Hart Benton with whom he had had a long-standing feud. In his company were other Indian fighters destined to become immortals: Davy Crockett, and Sam Houston.

The Alabama winter had begun, and Jackson had to cope with wholesale desertions among his troops, inadequate and even at times nonexisting supplies, insufficient forces to guard what supplies he had as well as to care for the wounded, and throughout all this to keep Tennessee's Governor Willie Blount, under whose command he was, convinced that the campaign against the Red Sticks should not be abandoned. "I will perish before I will retrograde," he wrote the wavering Blount.

In December, General Claiborne moved in a northeastern direction until he reached the high land south of Double Swamp, where he built a depot. Thirty miles further brought him into the area of the Holy Ground, Econachaca, a fort strongly fortified in Creek manner, and erected by Weatherford after the prophets had assured him that here no white man could approach without instant destruction by the gods of war. It was situated on a bluff on the eastern side of the Alabama River, just below Powell's Ferry ... and not many miles from the land on which Lucien Bouchard toiled.

Nanakota, who, like his white blood-brother, was determined to fight only for the cause of peace, sent his younger braves with supplies of corn to the warring Creeks as an act of loyalty. But he would send no warriors to take part in the slaying of white settlers, he told Weatherford's courier.

As Claiborne's troops advanced within sight of the sacred Creek town, Weatherford's prophets ordered the executions by fire of their white prisoners and the half-breeds and Creeks whom they considered traitors. Others awaited execution as Claiborne's troops attacked. Before the battle began, Indian women and children had been conveyed across the river and hidden in the thick forest. As the Creeks began to retreat, Weatherford mounted a gray stallion and raced along the banks of the Alabama below the town till he reached a perpendicular bluff fifteen feet over the surface of the river. As Claiborne's soldiers knelt to fire their rifles at him (for by now breech-loading carbines had been invented to replace the antiquated muskets), Weatherford mockingly lifted his own rifle in his right hand and shook it, then with a tug at the reins, made his horse leap into the river. When they rose, Weatherford still gripped his rifle with one hand and his horse's mane with the other, and both swam to the Autauga side.

In January of 1814, Jackson again met the Creeks at Emuckfaw and Enolochopco and defeated them each time, pressing onward toward Horseshoe Bend on the Tallapoosa River, where he knew the Creeks were concentrating their forces. The Red Sticks had assembled here to make a desperate defense, where nature had provided an excellent and seemingly unassailable fortress. A hundred acres of land was bordered by the Tallapoosa River, forming a small peninsula. Across the neck of the bend, the Creeks set up a breastwork of logs, so arranged as to expose any advancing enemy troops to a murderous crossfire. The houses of the village stood on low ground at the bottom of the bend, where hundreds of canoes were tied to the banks of the river. The friendly Cherokees under General Coffee, swimming the river, seized the canoes and returned with them to the opposite bank, where they loaded them with friendly Indians and American militia. General Jackson ordered his troops to storm the breastwork behind which all the warriors had posted themselves. After a desperate battle, the Tennesseeans mounted the breastwork, while Coffee's troops attacked the Red Sticks from behind.

This battle had begun at dawn on the morning of March 27, 1814, and ended late at night. The Red Sticks left 557 warriors of their contingent of a thousand dead upon the field of battle, while the Americans lost thirty-two men with ninety-nine wounded. Among the heroic dead were Major Lemuel Purnell Montgomery, born in Virginia in 1786 and blood kin of General Richard Montgomery, who had died December 3, 1775, in the battle of Quebec. Major Montgomery had been the first man to mount the breastworks and, as he waved his sword to urge his men forward, a rifle ball killed him at once. When the battle was at an end, General Jackson stood over his body and, tears running down his cheeks, exclaimed, "I have lost the flower of my army, a brave man whose twenty-eight short years were scarcely half enough for the valorous deeds he did!"

Deputations of Creek chiefs came now to Horseshoe Bend to surrender, and William Weatherford, on the same superb gray stallion which had carried him over the bluff at the Holy Ground, rode to the new Fort Jackson, where the victorious Tennesseean had planted his colors on the very spot where the Sieur de Bienville, a century before, had erected Fort Toulouse, at that head of the peninsula formed by the confluence of the Coosa and Tallapoosa rivers, within 600 yards of each other, then diverging to unite four miles below.

As Weatherford neared the fort, a deer crossed his path and he killed it with his rifle. Reloading it with two balls and with the avowed intention of killing General Jackson if any hostility be shown him, he tied the deer behind his saddle and rode up to the tent of his victorious rival.

"I fear no man, for I am a Creek warrior. You can kill me if you desire, but I come to beg you to send for the women and the children of the war party who are now starving in the woods. I am now done fighting. The Red Sticks are nearly all killed. Kill me, if the white people want it done."

His brave words were angrily echoed by soldiers and settlers who shouted, "Yes, kill him, kill him!"

But General Jackson sternly raised his hand and declared, "Any man who would kill as brave a man as this would rob the dead." They drank a glass of brandy together; Weatherford gave him the deer as a present, and then rode off to Fort Claiborne. There, afraid that angry settlers might kill the leader of the Red Sticks, the commanding officer gave Weatherford a horse and bade him escape.

And thus the power of the Creeks was broken, and now the Americans could concentrate on the war against the English. For on August 9, 1814, the Creeks signed a treaty at Fort Jackson, turning over to the United States most of their vast lands. The day before, American peace commissioners, among whose number was John Quincy Adams, met the British commissioners at Ghent to talk of peace. In the next month, Commodore Thomas Macdonough resoundingly defeated the British fleet at the battle of Plattsburg on Lake Champlain. On September 14th, Francis Scott Key wrote the words of the *Star Spangled Banner* during the bombardment of Fort McHenry, and saw the British land and naval attack upon Baltimore turned back by his courageous countrymen.

On November 7th, Andrew Jackson took Pensacola and thus cleared East Florida of the British, after which he turned toward New Orleans to take command there on the first of December. Two days before Christmas, he halted a British attack about seven miles below that city to which Lucien Bouchard had first come in his quest for freedom on the land.

On December 24th, the Treaty of Ghent was signed with Great Britain to end the War of 1812, a treaty which was no more than an end to hostilities on the basis of the *status quo* before the outbreak of that conflict. But because the news from Ghent could not possibly reach General Jackson in time, there was a final and conclusive triumph for the Stars and Stripes. On January 8, 1815, General Jackson, with his troops, pirates under Jean LaFitte, blacks and free citizens of the city, defeated the British under General Edward Pakenham, inflicting losses of 700 dead and 1400 wounded.

And now the wars were over, and peace would begin, and there would be settlers on the Creek lands at last, and the prophecy of old Tsipoulata would come to pass.

CHAPTER THIRTY-FOUR

There was at last peace in Europe, too. Napoleon Bonaparte, who had abdicated on April 12, 1814, and had been exiled to Elba, which the allies gave him as sovereign principality, escaped and landed with a handful of followers in France on March 1, 1815. His conquerors were still deliberating over the division of the spoils at the memorable Congress of Vienna, and the news of his return to seize power consternated them all. Once again France rallied to him and Louis XVIII, the brother of the martyred Louis XVI and hitherto Count of Provence until the *émigrés* had proclaimed him king in 1795, fled the throne on which the allies, with the help of Talleyrand, had placed him. But Napoleon enjoyed his rule only a legendary Hundred Days, as he was irrevocably defeated at Waterloo. Once again he had to abdicate, surrendering to a British warship in his hope to find asylum in England, but instead he was taken to Saint Helena to spend the rest of his dreary exile dictating memoirs.

But if at last there was peace on both sides of the ocean, there began a dangerous bickering over the lands which the Creeks had yielded by the treaty of Fort Jackson, since now hundreds of settlers poured into these ceded lands and squatted upon them despite the law and the government. The Congress had established a policy to prevent intrusion until proper surveys could be made and the lands offered for sale at auction. Attempts were made to remove these squatters; troops were called in and ordered to burn the cabins of those who refused to leave, but it was all to no avail. For most of these settlers did not come to seek wealth, but only to gain a subsistence or enjoy the freedom of the forest. They built simple cabins, they planted their crops of corn between trees which they killed by girdling, and their greatest immediate problem was to survive until the first crop was made.

Lucien and his free workers had at once set to work planting cotton along with their corn in this early spring of the year of 1815. The English mills would buy heavily to make up for these lost years, and the price of cotton was certain to rise. But the village of Econchate was in dire straits; not only had the wars against the Creeks and the British prevented free trading, but many of the hunters and the warriors of the village were gone forever, and there were widowed squaws and children who needed food, blankets, simple utensils, salt and other primal needs. Nanakota had visibly aged, and his hair had turned white in the last year alone. As he told Lucien when the latter visited him during the middle of February to give accounting of the planning of crops and the restoration of trade at Mobile, "There are still many braves at Econchate who look upon their *Mico* as a traitor, as a coward. You and I know that the war was ruinous, that we could not win against the white-eyes, and that we are no longer a nation. Soon we shall be forced to leave even this village and find unwelcome home near the settlers who rush to the lands our nation has had taken from it by greater force of arms. Then will the prophecy of Tsipoulata be truly fulfilled, my brother."

"Have courage, Nanakota. I am still loyal to you, and my workers and my son pledge themselves to you also. I must work harder this year than ever before, for the account at Mobile has been wiped out. I had counted on it to pay for all the clothing and the food and the salt and the other things your people need for this year and other years to come, but those profits were not in coin and therefore the war has erased them as the wind erases a footprint in the sand. But you have my pledge, my brother, that by the end of this year there will be much food and much clothing in every lodge."

"Your pledge is truth itself, my brother Lu-shee-ahn. It lightens the burden of sorrow in my heart. And may this year bring you, too, and your son the happiness and the peace you have so long sought."

It was a warm July, and the cotton was thriving on 200 acres of newly planted land. Nanakota had ordered the widowed squaws of Econchate to help his blood brother in the cottonfields. They would thus repay the white-eyes trader-farmer who had brought such prosperity to the village and who now had promised to keep it from starvation. Moreover, by such work, they would do homage to the spirits of their warrior husbands, who would thus look down and see them prepare for a harvest of peace to compensate for the supreme sacrifices which had been made to save Red Ground.

Lucien was not entirely happy with this offer of supplemental labor, because several of the squaws were still young and attractive and he knew only too well his son's inflammatory nature. Now that Henry was nineteen, and he himself fifty-three, he was more aware than ever of the disparity between them quite apart from their ages; at Henry's age, he had been an absorbed romantic and idealist, but his own son was the direct opposite. Yes, he too had had the agonizingly blinding passions of the flesh during his young manhood, but he had known how to quell them and to divert them through study and through arduous work side by side with his father's peasants. Henry, too, was able to work as assiduously as the strongest black, but Lucien sensed that this almost defiantly dogged labor was aimed at sheer material gain. The gulf between them was widening, and somehow it must be bridged before much longer if Windhaven was ever to be built.

He watched Thomas with pleasure, seeing how ably and effortlessly the light-colored twenty-four-year-old son of Ben mingled with the workers, encouraged them, corrected their faults with such encouraging words that they were not demeaned before their companions. Yes, Thomas must be the overseer of this great plantation. He must stand beside Henry and, with his gifts for diplomacy and graciousness, know how to give the soft answers that would turn away this strange, implacable wrath which appeared to consume the soul of his only son and heir.

During the last week of July, Lucien rode to Econchate to confer with Nanakota on the necessity of an immediate trip to Mobile. A new merchant, Lewis Judson, originally from Connecticut, had come to Mobile and was establishing himself with his own trading house, which would one day surpass that of John Forbes. It would be good to establish amicable relations with Judson, to acquaint him with the long and highly satisfactory relationship which the Creeks and Econchate had always enjoyed at the trading post. Also, Lucien intended to offer his cotton and to determine what price he might expect at the year's end.

This time he went alone on a small flatboat, laden with a few pelts and deerskins, after first having instructed Ben and Thomas to supervise Henry with extreme vigilance and to make certain that the youth did not approach any of the squaws. For these, Ben and Lucien and the other blacks had built small cabins, locating them at a distance from Lucien's and near the lodgings of the other workers, with the same protective idea in mind.

As he set out down the river, Lucien started with surprise to see a small cabin and a clearing of land on which corn had already been planted located about ten miles away from his own holdings. This was strange indeed. It could only be a family of settlers who had moved in to obtain squatter's rights on the ceded Creek land before the Federal land office could openly offer it for sale. He poled his flatboat over to the bank and grounded it, then walked slowly toward the cabin, his rifle lowered to the ground in sign of peace.

A heavily set, nearly bald man in his mid-forties came slowly out of the cabin, holding his own rifle at the ready, squinting suspiciously at Lucien. "Who might you be, neighbor? Ain't looking for no trouble, but I'm primed for it if you've a mind."

"No trouble at all, just introducing myself to a new neighbor. I'm Lucien Bouchard, upriver aways from you."

"Oh, sure now!" The man wore a buckskin jacket and old, muddied breeches and heavy, knee-length black boots. "You'd be that fellow with all the cotton land. Say now, mebbe your dropping in here unexpected like 'll save me a trip. Care to sell your land, Mr. Bouchard? My name's Carl Trask. Me and my daughter Dora and our nigger slaves came from Georgia soon as we heard the Injuns got wiped out round these parts. You see, Mr. Bouchard, I bought me into the Yazoo Land deal some years back, and I've got my certificate. 'Pears like now the highest court of the land says it's good, so I aim to squat here first and worry later."

"I understand your point of view, Mr. Trask. But the land hasn't been opened for survey yet, so you really don't hold title. As for my own, I went to Fort St. Stephens right after the Land Act and paid down hard cash, and I've got my title."

"Smart feller, I can see that just by talking with you, Mr. Bouchard." Trask grinned crookedly, showing decaying teeth, and tugging at his straggly graying beard as he lowered the rifle muzzle to the ground. "Now y'see, Mr. Bouchard, my old daddy back in Savannah left me a nice windfall of cash, and I'm prepared to make you a mighty handsome offer. What you got there, round 500 acres?"

"Six-hundred and forty, to be exact. But it's not for sale at any price."

"Look, if you paid just $2 an acre, I'll give you $25, and there's a nice tidy profit just for a morning's conversation, I'd say right off."

"It would be if I were inclined to sell. But I've been on that land a good many years, Mr. Trask, and I've been a trader with the Creeks and done farming with them, and after the war, they need my help more than ever."

"I see. One of them damned Injun-lovers, eh?" Trask hawked and spat close to Lucien's boots. "No offense meant, y'unnerstan'. Well now, you on your way to Mobile?"

"Yes, I've some supplies to bring back to the village."

"You got any kin back up at your place? My little gal Dora's plumb pinin' to meet some nice strapping feller and hitch up with him. Takes after her maw, she does. Hey now, Dora, quit hidin' in there, git yourself out here and let Mr. Bouchard look you over good."

"I'm not a prospect for your daughter, I'm sorry to say, and with all due respect to her, Mr. Trask."

An attractive girl, her long hair the color of moist sand, dressed in a linsey-woolsey dress, her feet thrust into moccasins and her legs bare to the lower thigh, sidled out of the door of the cabin, casting Lucien a simpering look, then giggled and hid her face in both hands.

"Dora, straighten up and quit actin' like a baby," her father sharply reprimanded her. "She's just turned seventeen, and she was sparkin' with a fine upstanding young feller back in Savannah when I took the notion to use my certificate real fast before any other settlers picked this spot. Right on the river, and that means a good market at Mobile now, doesn't it?"

"Yes, now that we're at peace with the English and the Creeks, it'll be a very good market, especially for cotton."

"I plan to raise a little myself, once I get settled down here good. Corn's enough for a starter, though. You see, maw—that's my wife—took sick of lung fever and passed just before Dora and I and the niggers made our plans to move out here. That's another reason I aim to git Dora off my hands soon as I can. Well now, if you're not in the market for a wife, know any likely prospects?" At this, the girl giggled again, but was silenced by a snarling oath from her father, who then turned back to regard Lucien with an ingratiating smile.

"I have a son, but I'm not sure that she'd take a fancy to him," Lucien frowningly replied. Quickly he had appraised the teen-aged girl and instantly dismissed her as a potential wife for Henry: what the boy needed was certainly not a passive, pallid girl without a mind of her own.

"Oh, if he's a husky feller like you, Mr. Bouchard, don't you worry none about Dora's not fancying him," Trask sniggered. Then, delving into the frayed pocket of his muddied breeches, he brought out a wallet thick with banknotes. "Now, seeing as how we're good neighbors and such, why not think it over about my little offer? Tell you what, $30 an acre. Now that's as high as I'll go. Might have something left to buy some of your niggers, if you've a mind to sell."

"I have no slaves, they're all free workers, Mr. Trask.

And as I told you before, my land is not for sale. On my way back from Mobile, I'll stop by and pay my respects to you and your daughter. By the way, if there are any supplies you'd like me to get there for you, it will be my pleasure to bring them on pack horse."

"Why now, that's real friendly! Isn't it now, Dora? Told you we wuz gonna make out in this nice rich land, once they kicked the Injuns out of where us whites belong." Dora only nodded and giggled softly again. Trask continued, "Now that you mention it, we could use a little salt. Maybe some flour, if you got any. I'm sorta sick of cornmeal cakes. Mighty tasty venison and raccoon in these parts, though."

"I'll bring back some salt and flour for you at a fair price, Mr. Trask. Well, I'd best be getting downriver. Good to have met you."

He shook hands courteously with the Georgian, inclined his head respectfully toward Dora, who tittered and then clapped both hands over her mouth after another of her father's withering looks. Then he pushed the flatboat out into the river and poled it down the rapidly flowing current and was soon out of sight around the next bend.

Carl Trask squinted after him till he was out of sight, then muttered, "Goddamn Injun-lover, think I'll take me a little ride over and see if I can't talk to that boy of his. Mebbe he'll listen to banknotes talkin'. You, Dora, tidy yourself up a mite and put on that blue dress your maw laid out for you in Savannah 'fore she took to her bed sick to die. Mebbe we'll go sparkin' too. Might as well kill two birds with one stone, I allus say."

"Daddy, there's a fellow on horseback coming along that trail at the end of the cornfields." Thomas stopped hoeing his row of stalks and called to his gray-haired father, who was examining a furrow in the next row. The tall Ashanti straightened, put his hand to his eyes to shield them from the blazing sun, then nodded. "You're right, Thomas boy. There's a man, and a girl in a blue dress and two blacks. Never saw them before. Wonder where they came from?"

"We better tell Mr. Henry right off, Pa. He's over at the gin. I'll go fetch him."

"You do that, Thomas. I'll just mosey down to the end of the fields and see what these strangers have in mind," Ben agreed.

The other blacks working the cottonfields looked up, glad for a break in their sweating labors, as they saw the four riders pull up and Ben approach the heavily set, almost bald lead rider.

"Afternoon, sir," Ben said graciously. "Can I help you folks?"

"This is Mr. Bouchard's land, is it?" the Georgian demanded.

"That's right, sir. But he's gone down to Mobile."

"I know. Met him on his way the other day. You the foreman, the overseer, nigger?"

The tall Ashanti's pleasant smile wavered an instant, but returned. "Yes, I guess you might say I'm that, sir."

"Uppity nigger, ain't you, boy?" Carl Trask sneered. "Bet you ain't had a taste of the whup in a coon's age. If you wuz my nigger, you'd sure as hell catch it, snotty-like talking to a white man. Well, can't you see I'm thirsty? And my daughter there, she's plumb parched. Go get some water in a dipper and make it damned fast, nigger!"

"Yes, sir. I'll bring you water right away."

Henry Trask turned back to leer triumphantly at the pallid, giggling teenager behind him, then squinted at the two black slaves, both in their early thirties, who wore only ragged cotton breeches. "Rastus, Abe, you niggers look right sharp now. Got your knives handy, just in case there's trouble?"

"Yassuh, mastuh, sho' nuff has," they chorused.

Henry Bouchard came out of the shed which housed the cotton engine, holding a rifle in his right hand, Thomas hurrying along beside him. Ben's tall, light-colored son had picked up a heavy cudgel in the shed, for the presence of strangers in this still uncharted land always carried with it the foreboding of possible danger.

Ben had gone to the creek and filled two clay dippers, returning to the four riders. He handed one up to Carl Trask, only to have the Georgian snarl, "You stupid nigger, ain't you never been taught how to act round white folks? Take care of my daughter Dora first, then me! Wuz you my nigger, I'd lace you raw first day I owned you!"

"Then, sir, I've reason to be grateful," Ben gently replied as he lifted one of the dippers up to the young girl.

With an oath, Carl Trask lifted his rifle, pulled the trigger and Ben stumbled back, his eyes wide in shock, dropped the other dipper and then sank to his knees, blood staining his breeches from an ugly wound just under the heart.

"Paw, Paw, why'd you go and shoot the nigger, why, Paw?" Dora Trask wailed, suddenly shaken out of her apathy by her father's callous brutality.

"Rastus, Abe, git those knives ready, we're gonna have some trouble—" he quickly called to his two slaves; then, as Henry Bouchard and Thomas came hurrying up, he lifted his left hand and ingratiatingly called, "Now, don't get hasty about this, you men! This here nigger sassed me real mean, he did, then started to lift his hoe to clobber me one—couldn't very well sit here on my horse and take nuttin' like that—"

"He—he lies—Thomas—I never lifted my hoe," Ben gasped, his face twisted in mortal agony.

With a sobbing cry, the young Ashanti leaped at Carl Trask, dragging him down off his horse, wresting away the rifle and flinging it into the rows of cottonstalks. Then, sobbing hoarsely, he lifted his cudgel and struck, and struck and struck again.

"Don't you niggers budge off those horses, put those knives away, or I'll shoot you down," Henry Bouchard cried as he leveled his rifle.

"We ain't gwine to, we won't do nuttin', don't shoot, mastuh!" the stockier, older black wailed as he dropped his clasp knife to the ground and lifted both hands, his face congealed in terror.

"You killed my paw! His head, it's all bloody, the nigger killed him!" Dora screamed, as she pulled at the reins of her horse and tried to turn out of the fields and back onto the trail.

But Henry Bouchard leaped forward and seized the reins, brought the horse to a halt, and then roughly with

478

his other hand dragged her down onto the ground. "You just stay where you are, missy," he said roughly. "We'll see what this is all about and who you are. Thomas, is your father bad?"

Thomas was kneeling down now trying to staunch his father's bleeding wound with his bare hands, tears running down his cheeks.

"You take—you take good care of your mother and *M'su* Lucien, you hear me, boy?" Ben panted, grimacing as a wave of pain wrenched his wiry body. "And *M'su* Henry, too—"

"I promise, I promise, father!" Thomas groaned, cradling his father's head against his chest.

"You help—" the Ashanti's words came now with an effort, were fainter, almost incomprehensible as the young man leaned down to hear them, "you build—you help *M'su* Henry build that Windhaven for his daddy, promise me, boy—"

"I promise, father, oh God, I promise—"

Ben shuddered, his eyes closed, and Thomas slowly let him lie back upon the earth which was red with his blood.

"Get some of our blacks to take those slaves into the cabin where we can talk to them, Thomas," Henry directed. Then, his eyes sweeping the cowering girl, he said softly, "And you and I are going to have a talk, little missy, and you better be ready to tell the truth, or you'll wish to God you had!"

CHAPTER THIRTY-FIVE

"In you go, missy." Henry Bouchard pushed the sobbing teen-aged girl into the cabin, then swung the door shut behind him. He put a hand into the pocket of his breeches and pulled out the bulging wallet which he had retrieved from the sprawled body of Carl Trask. In the man's death struggles, it had fallen out of his waistcoat pocket and gone unnoticed.

"What—what're you gonna do with me, M-mister?" Dora tearfully quavered.

"Shut up and let me see what your father's got in here." The surly, glowering black-haired young man made her shiver and she thrust herself against the wall as, still dazed from the violent scene, she watched him open the wallet and take out a sheaf of dirty banknotes and a folded bit of paper. "Now then, you better start telling me what this is all about, missy, or you'll be in real trouble. What's your pa doing with all this money and this certificate for land, eh?" Henry stared balefully at the frightened teenager.

"I—I don't know—"

"You're a lying little bitch, missy! But I'll get the truth out of you. Where did you and that murdering pa of yours come from, anyhow?"

"S-Savannah—please—I didn't do nuttin'—"

"Maybe not, but you were in it, and here's where you are and here's where you're going to stay till I find out a lot more," he grimly declared. "Where'd your pa get all this money? Stop looking around like that, nobody's going to help you. I'm the master here, now that my father's gone to Mobile."

"I—I know—we—we saw him at the river yesterday—"

"Oh ho, you did, did you?" He grinned savagely. "Did that father of yours talk to him any?"

"Yes—but I don't know—"

"You're lying—want me to beat it out of you, you tricksy little bitch, you?" He took a step toward the frightened girl, his eyes narrowing and gleaming. The blue dress clung to her graceful, ripening young body by the sweat of the ride from the Trask cabin downriver, and it emphasized the tempting, high-perched rounds of her bosom, the sensual flare of her ripening hips and the long but delightfully sculptured columns of her thighs.

"Please—you got to let me go—I didn't do nuttin'," she tearfully repeated, putting out a grimy hand toward him in a pathetically appealing gesture.

"There's close to $4000 in your pa's wallet, missy. And this certificate says he works for the Georgia Yazoo Company—but you know that, don't you?"

"No, honest, I don't know nuttin' 'bout what paw did, you gotta believe me, mister!" she helplessly sobbed.

"But I don't have to believe anything if I don't want to. Not till you make me believe it, missy. When did you and your pa come to these parts?"

"About—about a month ago. Honest, I don't—"

"My father told me about the Yazoo Companies," Henry Bouchard said slowly, his eyes never leaving the trembling, terrified young girl. "He was a speculator, wasn't he? Working for the land company and coming here and trying to make the settlers give up prime land for a price. And I'll bet he'd just show them a little cash and give them sweet talk about how they'd get the rest once they moved off—wasn't that it, missy?"

"No—please—" her eyes, like a frightened animal's, turned this way and that, as if seeking salvation from the stocky, menacing black-haired youth who confronted her, his booted feet planted firmly apart in the attitude of a victorious conqueror.

481

"I've had enough of your whining—what's your name, anyhow?"

"D-Dora—please, please lemme go—I didn't know he was gonna k-kill your n-nigger—"

"But he did, and you were there to see it, so you're as much guilty as he is. Why—" Henry Bouchard cruelly grinned—"if I was to take you down to Mobile now and turn you in to the soldiers, they'd stretch your pretty neck and watch you kicking in the air, that's for certain, Dora girl!"

"Oh my G-Gawd!" Dora hysterically ejaculated, her eyes huge and glazed with tears.

"But if you tell the truth, maybe I won't turn you in, understand? And I mean the truth, Dora. Now let's have it!" he snapped.

The sandy-haired teen-aged girl gnawed her lower lip, furtively glancing around again, but when he took a menacing step toward her, she uttered a frantic cry and held out her hand again: "No, don't, I'll tell, I'll tell! He—yes, he was a spec'lator, just like you said—and he—he's my uncle, not my paw!"

"That's better," Henry Bouchard triumphantly chuckled. "Now let's have the rest of it."

Pocketing the wallet, he loosened the heavy rawhide thong which served as belt for his breeches and swept it meaningfully through the air like a whip. Dora Trask's eyes goggled at the sight, and she tried to press herself back into the wall of the cabin as she began to whimper: "N-no—please don't—don't l-lick me—I said I'd tell—"

"Be quick about it, then. Well?"

"He—he's my uncle, see? My paw died 'bout ten years ago, and Uncle C-Carl brung me up in Savannah. He—he ran a store there, and the men who ran that land company, they—they gave him a job and said he could make lots of money—just like you said, waiting till the Injuns got cleared out and then talkin' to the folks who squatted on the best land—he—he'd pay them some money and write a paper out. But he didn't put his right name on it, see, and then he'd get the land for the company and he could sell it over again and get a good price—that's the truth—"

"I think you're telling it for once, Dora girl. Now, you got any kinfolks left back in Savannah?"

Terrified, the girl could only shake her head and continue to stare at him with fearful, unwavering gaze.

"Did your uncle have any papers back at his cabin, any more stuff that proves what you've been telling me?" he pursued, and this time Dora Trask numbly nodded.

"That's fine. I'll go there with you and we'll find it. And those two slaves who rode along with him—does he own them for sure?" Once again came the frightened nod. Dora Trask had pressed the back of her hand against her mouth, and was trembling as with ague.

Henry Bouchard lowered the rawhide thong to the floor of the cabin, his eyes lustfully appraising the shrinking teen-aged prisoner. "You ever get poked by a man, Dora girl?" His voice was husky and unsteady now.

"Oh no—not ever, I'm a good girl—I know—Uncle—Uncle Carl wanted to do it to me, but I wouldn't ever let him, no, please, can I go now?"

"Go where, Dora? Down to Mobile and let the soldiers string you up by that pretty neck? You wouldn't want that, now, would you?"

"Please—don't—don't talk that way—it plumb scares me awful," she moaned.

"All right then—" now his voice was breathless with excitement, his eyes glittering with the sudden, audacious plan of it as he moved toward her. "Here's what you're going to do if you don't want to get hanged, you sniveling little bitch. I need me a wife, and I want my own land too. You're going to marry me, Dora Trask, and we'll get it done at Econchate, Creek style. It'll be binding, don't you worry any, and the next time we go to Mobile, we'll have it written down there in the records for everybody to know about. And I'll just keep hold of this money and those two slaves and the land your thieving uncle settled down on, because it doesn't belong to him yet till there's a proper survey and title sale, understand?"

"I—I don't know what you mean—m-marry you—"

"Don't you now? Well, then, guess I'll just have to show you what I mean, Dora. Take off that dress and be quick about it!" He raised the thong, his face red and congested with passion.

"Oh Gawd—no—I'm decent—I ain't never done that—I won't—"

"Didn't I say I was going to marry you and make it nice and legal and proper, you ornery bitch? Would you rather go down to Mobile for a hanging, then? I didn't think so." He saw her face contort with terror at the threat, and a low, hoarse chuckle of triumph escaped him as he moved inexorably toward her.

"Oh don't—oh no—I—I don't want to—ahrrr! Please, don't lick me—oh Gawd, it hurts—stop—oh it hurts!" she screamed as he slashed the rawhide thong over her ripening young breasts. She flung herself down on her knees, huddling against him, her arms clutching round his thighs. His face insensate with rutting fury, Henry Bouchard slashed the thong down over her back again, again and pitilessly again as she squirmed and twisted, crying out in torment under the rain of blows.

"Had enough, or want me to strip you bare and tan your ornery hide raw, Dora?" he panted, lifting the thong again.

"Please—oh no more—I can't—I just can't stand it— I'll do what you want—don't hit me any more—oh please—m-mister, please don't!" she blubbered.

"Then take that damned dress off before I rip it off you, bitch!"

Stumbling to her feet, her body shaking with choking sobs, Dora Trask despondently tugged off the blue dress and let it drop from trembling fingers, huddling before him in only a sleazy, ripped petticoat. He sucked in his breath at the sight of her glossy-smooth, pale-pink skin, the shudderingly uplifting rounds of her naked breasts. "That too," he grated, lifting the thong slowly above her.

With a sobbing cry, Dora Trask fairly ripped the petticoat from her and then, bowing her head, covering her tear-stained face with her hands, wept in her wretched shame and helplessness.

"Now," he gloatingly muttered, "I'll show you what being married is like, Dora honey!" Dropping the rawhide thong, he seized her by the elbows and forced her down on the blankets of Lucien's bed, then yanked down his breeches and drawers and flung himself on her. Dora Trask, her eyes rolling, her mouth gaping in a shrill scream of agony, arched and struggled under his brutal penetration. His hands clutched her heaving breasts, his moist sensual mouth silencing her sobbing cries of shame, terror and suffering as he thrust and mercilessly thrust till he had spent his blazing lust and left her sprawled, half-fainting, on his father's bed.

The next evening, Lucien's rebellious son sat opposite the cowed young girl whose eyes were still swollen from weeping, with Thomas taking the role of relative for Henry and the gray-haired squaw Tumishma, who had been Tunkamara's younger wife, the same proxy for Dora. Ellen did not attend the ceremony; prostrated with grief at Ben's violent death, she mourned in the house of a squaw who had lost her man at Horseshoe Bend, and like the squaw, had shorn off her hair and blackened her face with ashes. Thomas himself, silent and impassive, did his best to hide his own sorrow; he had buried his murdered father on the hill, beyond where Amelia and Priscilla Bouchard rested in their eternal sleep and, with them, little Étienne.

This morning before the wedding, Henry had rowed Dora in a pirogue to the Trask cabin and ransacked it, finding the purchase deeds by which Dora's conniving uncle had acquired Abe and Rastus as slaves. There was also a pouch of hoarded silver coins which he confiscated, but best of all was his discovery that Abe and Rastus each had wives who had been included with their purchase by Carl Trask: Abe's wife was a light-colored Kru girl, about sixteen, as light and almost as pretty as Disjamilla, named Mary; the wife of Rastus was twenty-two, much darker, a Furlani, named Molly. He found them cowering in a little shanty built well behind the Trask cabin and threateningly ordered them to remain there until he could come for them again.

Nor did Henry Bouchard linger over the wedding feast which Nanakota gave in honor of the union of his blood brother's only son; as soon as he had eaten his fill, he muttered some half-apologetic words to the greatly troubled *Mico,* and grasping his teen-aged, terrified young wife by the wrist, led her out of the village and down to the pirogue at the riverbank. Once back at the Trask cabin, on her uncle's rude bed, he ruthlessly possessed her, and when he had done with her, chuckled, "I hope I've got you with child, you scared little bitch! That's all I want from you, a son, because then my fine, proud father will see that I've my own life to live and am my own master. And one thing more, Dora—you'd best not fuss if I take Mary or Molly to bed instead of you, I've a notion they can give a man more pleasure than you, always crying and whining like a baby."

When Lucien returned to Econchate nearly two weeks later, bearing the good news that trading would indeed be profitable this year, he was thunderstruck to learn what his son had done. But the ruthless audacity with which it had been done, had, perhaps, a saving grace: at least his son had a wife to care for and slaves of his own, though Lucien intended to demand that Henry free them once they had proved their worth. As soon as the land on which Carl Trask had feloniously settled had been surveyed and opened to public bidding, Lucien would purchase it in his son's name. And in return for that, in forging this bond between them, it was Lucien's hope that Henry would join him in the project of building the red-brick chateau with its twin towers, the Windhaven toward which he strove now with greater zeal than ever because still another life so dear to him—that of Ben, the faithful Ashanti—had been added to the grievous cost.

CHAPTER THIRTY-SIX

On the day of his fifty-third birthday, Lucien, Thomas, his eight free workers and a number of unfledged braves whom Nanakota had ordered to help their blood brother transport the profitable cotton crop downriver arrived at Mobile. Over 80,000 pounds of ginned cotton was sold at the excellent price of twenty-one cents a pound, a profit of over $14,000 after Lucien had deducted his cost of seed and wages for his men. Thomas was now overseer at a salary of $200 a year, and Lucien introduced him to the factors of the trading post so that the young overseer might be granted the power of ordering supplies and effecting trades in his absence.

Once again, Lucien divided his profit in half, so that the villagers of Econchate would have ample tools, clothing and goods of which they were in sore need. He sent a letter of Christmas greetings to old Jules Ronsart, who had already dispatched back to him a current accounting of the money which Lucien had deposited in his private bank.

But this time, Henry Bouchard did not make the journey with his father. He had given up his acreage on Lucien's plantation and busied himself on the hundred acres which Carl Trask had usurped, for he now considered it his own. Abe and Rastus had first been put to building a larger, more comfortable cabin for Dora and himself and were given the Trask cabin as their own quarters. And he had put the banknotes from Carl Trask's wallet into the box with his hoarded silver coins, burying them at the side of the new cabin in the dead of night so that only he would know where his treasure lay hidden.

He had, however, made a token reconciliation with his father by agreeing to take Dora to Mobile after the first of the new year of 1816. She was already pregnant, listless and self-effacing, and Lucien could not but have misgivings over the dominated lot she now had to endure. Yet he pointed out to Henry that it would be wise to have a marriage performed by a priest in Mobile to legitimize their issue, so that when his own time had come, there would be no legal obstacle to Henry's inheritance of all the land and the dwellings on it. And so Henry and Dora rode a flatboat to Mobile early in January and returned on horseback, though the young girl was now in her sixth month of pregnancy and found the journey arduous and painful.

While he was in Mobile, Henry bought ten bushels of cotton seed, which he at once instructed Abe and Rastus to plant by February and to clear twenty acres in readiness for his crop. He had compelled Dora to produce the purchase papers of the two slaves at the office of the Mobile registrar and testify that as Carl Trask's only heir their ownership had passed to her. Since no female could inherit such property, her marriage to Henry Bouchard conveyed full title to Abe and Rastus over to her husband. And with this new document, Henry returned with his apathetic, completely subjugated young wife to the new cabin as not only a husband but also master of slaves . . . and their two wives as well.

A week after he had returned, he reprimanded pretty young Mary for the tasteless food she had served Dora and him and, with a thin-lipped smile, declared, "Now that I'm master here, Mary, all of you are going to know what obedience means. Go out to the shanty, I'm going to give you a whipping." And when her husband Abe, startled at the cruel order, stared uncomprehendingly at him, he growled, "She's just a slave, nigger, just like you, and don't forget it for a minute. Slaves aren't married properly, they just live with each other, so there's no cause for you to think the two of you are free and equal because you've bedded each other. I'll whip you too if you give me another surly look, you black bastard!"

The sturdy black slave lowered his eyes as Henry Bouchard grasping Mary by the elbow, pushed her out into the shanty and banged the door behind him. "Now peel down fast, you pretty black bitch, I'm going to learn you your place," he commanded as he unfastened his rawhide belt. The young girl, trembling with fright, hesitated a moment, then as he moved closer to her, uttered a whimpering cry and tugged off the shapeless cotton garment, cowering naked before him. Henry Bouchard's eyes glistened as they swept her lissome body, and he saw in his mind's eye Disjamilla. "Kneel down and cover your face so's I can thrash you, bitch," he ordered.

The terrified young girl obeyed, huddling her body and tightening her muscles against the cruel anticipation of the rawhide thong. His face a mask of lust, the sturdy black-haired young man began to stripe her smooth shoulders and softly dimpled back, as she crouched forward, shielding her face with her arms and sobbing plaintively as the cadence of the whipping accelerated.

"Now, you think you can please your master better from now on, Mary?" he hoarsely demanded as he applied a final slash across the smooth satiny light-brown-sheened globes of her trembling buttocks.

"Oh, oww, yassuh, mastuh, please, don't whup me no moah, I'll be a good slave!" Mary wailed.

He flung aside the belt, bent to her, gripped her shoulders, twisted her onto her back and flung her down on the floor of the shanty. Mary uttered a poignant cry of shame and anguish, closing her eyes and twisting her head to one side to shut out the sight of his flushed, lust-contorted face. Panting with exultant pleasure, he took her brutally and quickly. After he had assuaged his needs, he got to his feet and snarled, "Now dress yourself and go fix us a proper breakfast tomorrow, or you'll get a double dose of my belt!"

A week later, with a similar pretext, Lucien's ruthless son marched Molly out to the shanty, forced her to strip naked and kneel down and beg for the whipping she deserved, and after he had inflicted it till her plump thighs

489

and buttocks were cruelly welted, he then sated his furious passion upon her shuddering body.

By the middle of April, Dora gave birth to a blond, healthy baby boy. A week after its birth, Henry mounted his horse and rode with the infant to Lucien's land, meeting his father in the cottonfields. "My first son, father," he exultantly exclaimed as he dismounted and showed Lucien the baby wrapped in a soft doeskin swaddling cloth. "I mean to name him after you, if you'll let me. I want to call him Luke."

Lucien Bouchard's eyes softened. "It's thoughtful of you, my son." He looked down at the gurgling infant; his weatherbeaten face creased in a tender smile. "Soft blue innocent eyes, Henry. Pray God they'll have only good things to look upon as he grows to manhood. And how's Dora?"

Henry Bouchard shrugged. "Well enough, I daresay. She had an easy time, Mary and Molly tending to her the way they did. Well, it's done then, I'll name him Luke and sprinkle water from the river on his head, and that'll do till he's grown enough to go to Mobile for the priest to baptize him. I'd best be getting back now, father. Some evening, why don't you come for supper? Dora's no cook at all, but Mary and Molly put up a right smart meal, now that I've taught them how."

Henry Bouchard carefully mounted his horse, took the reins in his right hand, cradling his son in his left arm, nodded to Lucien and started back toward his cabin downriver. As he neared it, he could see Mary and Molly and Abe and Rastus standing by the river bank, and he dismounted and hurried toward them.

"What's the matter here?" he angrily called. "Why aren't you out in the fields tending the cotton?"

"It's Missy Dora, Mastuh suh," Abe exclaimed. "She done throwed herself in the rivah, just now, when she woke up and found the baby gone!"

Henry Bouchard looked down at the baby in his arms, his eyes cold, his face expressionless. "We'll manage, Luke and I. We'll manage well enough. Here, Mary, take the baby. Abe and Rastus, get back to the field. I'll go back to Econchate and find a squaw that can nurse my son."

This was the year in which there was no summer in New England. On June 6, 1816, the snow was ten inches deep in the Berkshires, Vermont and New Hampshire, and in July and August ice was half an inch thick. There was little corn for the settlers along the Eastern seaboard of this new republic. But in the territory where Lucien and his son toiled, the weather was good and the corn crop plentiful, except that the influx of immigrants was so great that there was not enough corn for the would-be settlers who were swarming in from every side, eager to register their claims upon the ceded Creek lands. Corn was bringing $4 a bushel along the road from Huntsville to Tuscaloosa, and Lucien minimized his planting of cotton to favor corn so that the villagers of Econchate would have enough through the long year.

In August, Lucien received a letter, brought by a friendly Choctaw from the Mobile trading post, which bore the inscription of Jules Ronsart's counting house. When he opened it, he uttered a cry of grief, for it was from Antoine Rigalle, the young clerk who had shown his son Henry how bank notes and receipts and bills of lading were handled. "I deeply regret to tell you that our beloved founder, Jules Ronsart, passed away quietly in his sleep on the last day of July. He had no living kin, but my humble services had pleased him to such an incredible extent that he bequeathed his estate to me and also the position of administrator of the counting house. He was always attached to you, *Monsieur* Bouchard, and bade me show the utmost diligence to your private account with his house. I should therefore welcome the opportunity to meet with you and render you a current accounting and to discuss at your convenience your plans for the usage of these funds."

Lucien at once called Thomas to him and explained, "I shall take Henry with me to New Orleans, Thomas. I should be greatly obliged if you would ask your mother to look after little Luke while we are gone. The young squaw from Econchate continues to nurse him, and since

491

Ellen has remained in the village to help the squaws work the corn, she will find it convenient to have the squaw there with the baby instead of at Henry's cabin."

"Of course, *M'su* Lucien. Helping to look after your first grandson may ease her grief over the loss of my father, whom I still mourn."

Lucien clasped the young Ashanti's hand. "I too mourn him as deeply as you, Thomas. And in many ways, you are like a son to me. I only wish Henry could have your kindness and tolerance toward others. He's still young, and perhaps working his own land will help mature him."

Thomas looked intently at the man whom he still respected as a true master, and slowly replied, "If I may be so bold as to speak my mind, *M'su* Lucien, I think his restlessness and his selfishness come because he is envious of you, seeing how dearly you are loved by the Creeks as by all who know you. He is proud and alone, and he wants to succeed swiftly while he is still very young."

"Perhaps you are right, Thomas," Lucien sighed. "And he must marry again, I'm convinced of it. But this time, to a woman of character and strength who can show him no sign of weakness, or he will try to make a slave of her as he did of poor Dora."

Lucien had persuaded his son to bring along his hoarded money box and open his own account at the New Orleans counting house, and Henry, much to his father's surprise, enthusiastically agreed. "Perhaps I can find a wife in New Orleans besides, father," he cheerfully declared. And then, seeing Lucien's face grow somber, he cynically added, "Please, no sermons, if you don't mind. What would have happened to that pathetic creature Dora if I hadn't taken pity on her and married her? Like as not, that damned speculator would have made a whore out of her. She fulfilled her purpose, she gave me Luke."

"I can't for the life of me understand where you got your attitude about the uselessness of human life, Henry. But, as you ask, I shan't belabor you with sermons. You have your life to live, and all I ask of you is your help in building Windhaven when the time is right for it. And when it's built, my son, I want you and little Luke and

492

your wife, too, if you've found the proper one by then, to come live with me."

"I can promise you that. I'm heartily sick unto death of living in a wretched cabin. And the land, father?"

"There's news that next year the government will open a land office in Milledgeville, Georgia, by next August, and that this office will dispose of lands along the headwaters of the Alabama River. At that time, we can both go there and acquire legal title to Trask's hundred acres, and more if you so desire. The thought occurs to me that it might not be a bad idea to build a cotton engine and shed as well as a storage warehouse and levee by the bank of the river. Some day soon, I hope, there'll be better transportation than a flatboat. The Alabama is high in the winter months, but during the summer it's torturingly low and the trip to Mobile takes two weeks then, if the flatboat is heavily loaded with trading goods."

"And that will be part of Windhaven too, father?"

"Yes, if it's agreeable to you, my son. Remember, when I'm gone, you will inherit all of it, and Luke after you. So I can understand your passion for acquisition—though I can't say I always countenance the means by which it's done."

"There you go again, father, sermonizing," his black-haired son slyly taunted.

"What a pleasure to see you again, *M'sieu* Bouchard—and your son Henry, as sturdy and strong as you, *ma fois!*" Antoine Rigalle came forward from his office, ornately groomed in elegant frockcoat with a flowery cravat and ruffles at the collar of his silk shirt. "Come in, do come in, it's good to see you both again!"

"And you too, Antoine. How I regret I couldn't attend Jules's funeral," Lucien said as he followed the suave, handsome new head of the Ronsart counting house into his office.

"At first, *M'sieu* Lucien," Antoine Rigalle began, "let me advise you that the Second Bank of the United States, with a twenty-year charter, was incorporated by an act of Congress this past April. It will go into operation early next year. The value of this is that many banknotes previously circulated have been of uncertain value, and profits have been wiped out for many investors. But there is a resolution that government will accept only specie-paying paper, so that the banks of issue will have to cut down circulation to all except solvent notes. This will strengthen your own account."

"A very sound policy. And I daresay that when more of this southeastern territory is admitted to statehood, this new bank will help solidify matters even more," Lucien smilingly conjectured.

"Precisely. Last year, we had a panic because the wars against the Creeks and the English prevented cotton and other crops from leaving ports here and in Mobile, as you know. The smaller planters were greatly harmed. Fortunately, *M'sieu* Lucien, your transfer of funds here came at a most propitious time for you as well as us."

"It's exactly because of the confidence I have in the Ronsart house, *M'sieu* Antoine—do let me call you that—that I have brought my son Henry here to open his own account with you."

"It will be my pleasure and my honor to do that for your son. You may not know that the Republicans have nominated James Monroe for President over William H. Crawford of Georgia. Crawford is a sound man on financing, and I suspect that he may be nominated to a high post. Many of us in New Orleans believe that Monroe's election will mean greater prosperity than we've known in years."

"I'm glad for that, because it means that I can share my good fortune with my Creek friends," Lucien Bouchard smilingly said.

"The new tariff, *M'sieu* Lucien, will maintain most of the duties which took place during the War of 1812, a piece of legislation which has the interest of American industries at heart. All of this, together with the rising price of cotton, which was to be expected, augurs well for the future. Ah, if you will pardon me a moment, I believe— yes, *M'sieu* Entrevois and his lovely daughter are honoring us with a visit. As you know, my late employer did a great deal of business with him, and it's naturally being continued. Do come along, both of you, I'd like you to

494

meet them!" Antoine Rigalle rose and walked swiftly toward the entrance of the counting house, beckoning Lucien and Henry to follow him.

Lucien Bouchard stiffened, then incredulously stared at the dazzlingly attractive young woman on the arm of a tall, gray-haired Creole in his early fifties, attired in elegant green waistcoat and pantaloons and with a silk hat soberly set on his leonine head. For that young woman, about twenty now, was almost the living image of Edmée de Courent, who had become Edmée de Bouchard soon after his departure from France. The same sensitive oval face, the highset cheekbones, the same dainty little Grecian nose, the small ripe mouth and creamy skin which had so bewitched him in his youth . . . those charms which he had only once and finally seen revealed in the hold of the *Guerrière* when that same fickle beauty whom he had so idolized stood before him as an indentured bondservant.

"What's the matter, father? You look as if you'd seen a ghost." He scarcely heard Henry's anxious voice and recollected himself with an effort.

"Perhaps in a way I have, my son," he said softly, almost to himself, as he went forward to be introduced to the Creole banker and his daughter.

He observed a black band on the left sleeve of Philippe Entrevois' waistcoat, and the tall Creole somberly explained, "My beloved wife Edmée died a month ago of yellow fever, *M'sieu* Bouchard. Now that another Louis is on the throne of France and the danger of that accursed Corsican is forever removed, my daughter Louisette and I are leaving soon to visit *La belle France*."

A few moments later, after Antoine Rigalle had had a private conversation with the rival banker, the latter and his daughter took their leave. And once Lucien and Henry in their turn had left the counting house, Henry turned to his father and exclaimed, "Now there's a woman I'd like to marry, father!"

Lucien stopped, grasped his sturdy son's elbow and stared fiercely into his eyes. "And that, my son," he corrected, "is a woman I shall see to it you never marry."

495

"But why? She's beautiful, and Antoine says her father's almost as rich as old Ronsart was."

"Why then," Lucien Bouchard said with a kind of sarcastic scorn, "knowing you as I do and your insistence upon the purity of your blood and your superiority to others who had not been quite so fortunate as you in being born with a white skin, I need tell you only that you would find such a marriage tainted. You see, Henry, Philippe Entrevois has black blood in him from several generations back. So obviously this beautiful daughter of his would have it too."

"Damnation! What a pity—what a woman, I'd have enjoyed wedding and bedding her all the same, father!" Henry Bouchard enviously declared.

CHAPTER THIRTY-SEVEN

As Antoine Rigalle had predicted, James Monroe was elected President of the United States by an electoral vote of 183 to 34 for Rufus King, the Federalist candidate, with Daniel T. Thompkins his Vice-President. A week later, in the last month of this year of 1816, Indiana entered the Union as a free state. And also as Ronsart's successor at the New Orleans counting house had been convinced, W. H. Crawford of Georgia was named as Secretary of the Treasury, with the redoubtable John Quincy Adams chosen as Secretary of State.

But now the momentous matter of the division of the Mississippi Territory was before the Congress in this new year of 1817; northern Congressmen were inclined to let it come in as one state; southern ones insisted on division, and even the residents themselves were in disagreement over the matter. At last on March 3, 1817, the act establishing the Alabama Territory was approved and William Wyatt Bibb of Georgia was appointed governor. Bibb had just previously resigned his seat in the United States Senate because his vote for a bill increasing the salaries of senators had aroused a storm of indignation among his constituents. The territorial line was fixed so as to run due north from the Gulf to the northwest corner of Washington County, thence directly to the point where Bear Creek flows into the Tennessee River, and along the course of that river to the Tennessee line. It would be two years later when the Alabama enabling act changed the line so as to make it run southeastward from the north-west corner of Washington County and to strike the Gulf at a point ten miles east of the mouth of the Pascagoula.

Lucien Bouchard and his son Henry greeted this territorial decision with enthusiasm. It would soon mean statehood, it would mean a development of transportation and of freer trade than had ever before been known on this rich land. He hoped that it would mean also a fair allowance of land for the villagers of Econchate. As to transportation, on the very same day that the Alabama Territory was formed, the *Washington,* a steamboat with stern paddlewheels and Henry Shreve as captain, left Louisville for New Orleans on a round trip, thus marking the first steam navigation on the mighty Mississippi. The possibilities of shipping cotton in huge quantities, safely and swiftly to retain the prime quality of the yield, kindled Lucien's always industrious imagination as to the future. Now surely Windhaven could be turned from hopeful dream to structural reality!

To prepare for this new planting season, Lucien had purchased four slaves from Nanakota, crediting the villagers with $2000 in his newly re-established account in Mobile, four blacks who were originally Gullahs, in their mid-twenties and hard workers, all speaking passable Creek. This time, he planted cotton on two hundred acres which had hitherto been used only for corn and had lain fallow the previous year to enrich the soil. The cotton engine was still bearing up well, but in Lucien's opinion would need replacement within another year or two at the most; the process of moting—that of removing the foreign particles from the lint—was not yet perfect and necessitated much manual examination of the ginned cotton before it could be packed and sent downriver. There was talk, too, of vastly improved seed being brought in by many of the Georgia settlers, who had already squatted on the land in anticipation of their opportunity to acquire it when the land office finally announced its readiness to deal in hitherto Indian-controlled territory.

As for Henry, he put fifty of his hundred acres into cotton cultivation and himself purchased two slaves in Mobile, Daniel, a Furlani of twenty-seven, good-natured and hard working, and Steven, a twenty-two-year-old Kru whose Georgia master had died of a stroke and whose property had been foreclosed by his debtors. And he continued to satisfy his carnal needs by summoning Mary and Molly to his bed whenever he desired. His idea of compensating Abe and Rastus was by buying them an occasional keg of *taffai* and increasing their allowance of meat. Yet these two blacks had their own occasional solace, for at times when they visited the village of Econchate on an errand for their self-centered young master, they enjoyed the sexual favors of the younger widowed squaws whose warrior-mates had perished in the great Creek War.

As Lucien and Henry rode their horses toward the Georgia town of Milledgeville early in August, he turned to his stocky black-haired son and asked, "Will you free your slaves, Henry, as I have done?"

He saw his son's lips tighten and his eyes grow cold, as Henry brusquely replied, "I do not propose to, and I think I have sound economic reasons. You've taught me how to make use of the land and its natural resources, and I respect you for that, father. But these are changing times. Why, the settlers from Georgia are pouring in here and they've more black slaves, more niggers, than children of their own. It won't be long before this new territory has fewer whites than blacks, and I don't propose to be inferior to them."

"But by being humane, by accepting them as equals, you're sure to get more labor from them. Don't my own accomplishments mean anything to you, Henry?" Lucien pleaded.

"You're too sentimental, father," came the cynical answer. "You had to make friends with the Indians to keep alive, and I'd have done the same thing in your place. But that was long ago, and the Indians are being driven out and it's high time."

"How can you speak so callously of the people of Econchate, my son? Without them, I couldn't have prospered, I'd never have had the land which has made me wealthy. Understand, I don't judge my life by the wealth I've accumulated, only so much as it can bring the things I've dreamed of to pass. One of them is Windhaven, so

499

that one day you and I will see a red-brick chateau as it was back in Yves-sur-lac, with two great towers from which we can see the river and the bluff where Dimarte sleeps. But I see more than that, I see a family, a brotherhood of men, black as well as white, working together in harmony and peace and understanding."

"Then you're still looking back into the past, father," Henry Bouchard impatiently retorted. "You'll see, there'll be laws passed to regulate these niggers, and you can be sure they won't be given freedom by the legislature. Why, you've got slaveholders on it already, and the territorial governor himself knows what it is to run a plantation with niggers on it. You have my word that I'll build your Windhaven for you, father. But let me live my own life."

"I always have, my son, and I've raised my voice and my hand to you only when I was appalled at your cruelty. It's a cruelty I saw only in my older brother Jean, and seeing it and its counterpart among so many of the thoughtless aristocrats of France was one of the reasons that I came to this good land."

"Look, father, Abe and Rastus aren't appalled, to use your word, when I want Mary or Molly for the night. Why should they be? Their marriages don't hold with the church, there was just an understanding, or maybe a Creek ceremony. Besides, they have their sport with some of those pretty squaws, and I don't give a damn if they do that so long as they don't stir up trouble with your Indian friends. For that matter, why don't you take yourself one of those good-looking squaws, father, or go to New Orleans and get yourself an octoroon? Maybe someone like that Louisette Entrevois I told you I wouldn't mind marrying."

"We'll not discuss that further, Henry." Lucien was pale with anger. "I'm no saint, God knows, but I've more respect for myself than to rut like a boar with any sow that passes by."

"Thank you for your flattery, father," Henry Bouchard scowlingly countered.

The land was paid for, and Henry Bouchard had clear title to his hundred acres. But Lucien's despondency over his son's arrogant philosophy was deepened when he overheard two well-dressed Georgians talking in the land office about an Easterner's purchase of land perilously near the village of Econchate.

One of the men, a bluff, red-faced planter, declared, "I wanted that land myself, damn the luck. It seems Andrew Dexter, nephew of that Massachusetts senator who lost his shirt on a building venture which he called a sky-scraper—what a zany idea, to build a house more than two stories!—beat me to it. He and John Falconer from South Carolina went into partnership on this deal, but that's not the worst."

"What can it be, then, Lawrence?" His companion, a lanky long-bearded planter in a black frockcoat and new boots, questioned him.

"This Dexter fellow must have picked up some ideas from his uncle. Do you know what he's doing? Offering free lots to get some traders in to join the venture, and he's talking of laying out a town on the crest of the tallest hill. He's going to build a two-room house, with glass windows, no less! Doesn't that beat all?"

Lucien felt a sudden chill of presentiment. There was already another white man near Econchate, an Arthur Moore, who had built a cabin on the bluff which over-looked the Indian village. He was a gentle man who hunted and fished, and Nanakota had visited him and brought him a side of venison as a gift of welcome. But if there would be a town, what would happen to Econchate?

The answer to that question came even earlier than Lucien Bouchard feared. For as he and Henry rode toward the village after they had finished their business at the land office, they saw the booted surveyors and a few uni-formed soldiers chatting with them near the entrance to Econchate. Nanakota and two of his elders were there also, talking to one of the soldiers.

"Ho, it is good that my blood brother returns to help us," the *Mico* anxiously exclaimed. "These white-eyes tell me that our land is to be marked off and that it is even now being sold to settlers."

"That's right, mister," a young, black-bearded surveyor spoke up to Lucien. "This chief speaks English, and he

501

seems to be friendly, but maybe you can help tell him that we don't want any trouble and that it's all legal."

"Nanakota understands what you are doing, my friend," Lucien sadly replied as he dismounted. But Henry sat astride his horse, glowering at the *Mico* and the two white-haired elders, and as Lucien glanced back at his son, he was disconsolate to see so hostile and triumphant a look on that handsome, impassive young face. It was as if Henry Bouchard had awaited just such a *dénouement* as this to declare his open hatred for those who were not white like himself, just as he had already shown his adversion to the blacks.

"It is so, my *Mico*," Lucien spoke in Creek to the aging Creek leader. "My son and I have just come from the Georgia land office, where all of this land is being offered to the bidders. It is being marked off by these men, whom we call surveyors, so that no one can take more than his rightful share, for which he must pay. But you and your people may still remain upon land which will not be sold. These settlers will of course want the lands bordering the great Alabama River, and they are already planning to build a town here."

"Aiyeee, it is as Tsipoulata foretold," Nanakota wearily sighed. "Tell the soldiers there will be no trouble. I have never wished for bloodshed, and the lodges are still filled with squaws who lost their mates in the battle against the great Jackson. I will give orders to my people to take their belongings and to come with me to find land where we may be permitted to live and not interfere with the white-eyes."

"There's a parcel about thirty miles east, mister," the bearded young surveyor told Lucien after the latter had communicated Nanakota's pledge of peaceful submission to the federal order. "Chances are no one's likely to claim that for a spell. I've been through it myself, and there's good hunting there."

"Yes, the *Mico* and I have hunted deer there in years past," Lucien agreed. Then, turning to Nanakota, he said in Creek, "Where the soldiers suggest you take your people, my blood brother, is not far from where you and I hunted the swift deer in the days of our youth. Perhaps it is a good omen, not an ill one, and you know that no matter where you are, I will bring supplies to feed and clothe you. In Mobile now the new account is good, and your people will not starve this winter."

"If we are not separated except by land which the speedy hooves of a horse can cover between two risings of the sun, Lu-shee-ahn, then my heart will not be so heavy. It is done, then. Tell the soldiers that by the time the sun rises again, my people will have gone."

By the end of this year of 1817, Lucien and his workers and some of the younger braves who had declared their desire to help the *Mico*'s blood brother in the ways of peace and harvesting took 160,000 pounds of ginned cotton on flatboats down to Mobile, where the price had risen to 26½ cents per pound. Thus Lucien netted over $42,000, of which he estimated some $4000 for his costs of seed and labor. And, constant to his pledge, he allocated $19,000 for the village of Econchate and as much for his own personal account.

The return journey was longer this time, not only because it was bound for the new location of the Econchate villagers, but also because the pack ponies carried clothing, hunting and planting implements, much salt and some flour, as well as presents which Lucien himself had purchased out of his own account to give to Nanakota, the elders and to the squaws of the village.

As he and his riders passed by what had been Econchate, he could see the beginning of the new town, with its cabins set off in individual lots. He dismounted at one of these and introduced himself to a ruddy-faced, stockily built South Carolinan who had the first cabin in the center of this new town. "We're starting new here, Mr. Bouchard," the newcomer chuckled, gesturing to the other cabins. "We're calling this place New Philadelphia. I took my axe and cut down the very first tree. My name's John G. Klinck. And by next year, we'll have a mile or two downstream two towns, one adjoining the other. There's talk of calling the one Alabama Town and t'other East Alabama Town."

"I wish all of you the best of fortune, Mr. Klinck. And

you needn't worry about the Creeks. You may have heard that I've lived with them for a good many years, and I'm on my way to take their supplies to them eastward. Nanakota, the chief, wants peace, as do all of us."

"I'll say Amen to that, Mr. Bouchard." The enthusiastic South Carolinan vigorously shook Lucien's hand.

So perhaps, Lucien thought to himself as he rode toward the new home of the villagers of Econchate, the old *Windigo*'s prophecy had been softened by the passing of the years. Yes, there had been blood upon the ground where the Creeks had fought their last great battle, but not in Econchate. Yet in this new home, the hunting would be good, even though the *Windigo* had said the land would not be as rich as here at Red Ground. But by the strength of his vow to these people who were his blood brothers, Lucien resolved that they should want for nothing and thus the ominous words of old Tsipoulata might yet be gently turned aside.

CHAPTER THIRTY-EIGHT

On November 20, 1817, just a few weeks before Lucien Bouchard had made his highly profitable journey to Mobile with his crop of ginned cotton, the Seminole War began, initiated by an attack of white settlers upon Indians just above the Florida border. That act of aggression was immediately followed by Indian reprisal against the Georgia backwoodsmen. John C. Calhoun, whom newly inaugurated President James Monre had only just appointed as Secretary of War, authorized General Andrew Jackson, the hero of the victorious Creek War, to take strong measures to bring this new hostility with the Indians to a swift conclusion. On December 10th, Mississippi entered the Union as a slave state. Now there was little left of the original Spanish possessions on this southeastern part of the thriving young republic.

As the new year of 1818 began, the first of a series of petitions for the admission of Missouri as a state was presented in Congress. On April 4th, Congress adopted the design for the flag of the United States, with thirteen alternate red and white stripes and a white star for each state appearing in blue background. Three days after that patriotic decision, General Jackson seized the Spanish fort at St. Marks, Florida. And three weeks later, he approved the court martial verdict and execution of Alexander Arbuthnot and Robert C. Ambrister, British citizens, on the charge of having incited the Seminoles against the United States. Because of that action, there took place a long debate in Congress on the question of censuring General Jackson for such high-handed measures. Yet, in his opinion, he was doing only what Secretary of War Calhoun had told him in a directive worded: "Adopt the necessary measures to terminate this conflict."

On May 24th, Jackson seized Pensacola from the Spanish, not only ending the Seminole War, but also stripping Spain of virtually her last holding in this new nation, whose flag flew so proudly now from so many forts and bastions.

Lucien Bouchard again plunged himself into arduous work on his land, for the previous winter had been difficult indeed for his blood brothers of what had once been Econchate. His little grandson Luke had gone with Ellen, who was caring for the healthy little boy, to that new village thirty miles to the east. Strangely enough, Henry seemed delighted to leave the care of his son to Ellen, even if it meant that he would rarely see the boy. He too was busy on his hundred acres, and he had bought two more black slaves at Mobile to build a shed for the new cotton engine, which was now on order and was to be delivered by summer of this new year of 1818.

There was nostalgia in the heart of Lucien Bouchard when he heard, via a letter from Antoine Rigalle, that many of his own countrymen were coming to the Alabama Territory as Napoleonic refugees. Some of them had already settled on the banks of the Tombigbee last year, and many had read William Darby's *Emigrant's Guide,* which empirically declared that extensive vineyards could successfully be planted upon the dry slopes of the Alabama River if anywhere in the United States and that the olive would find a congenial soil upon the banks of the Alabama, Cahawba, Coosa and Tallapoosa rivers.

William Lee and Henry Clay had induced Congress to grant the French emigrants 92,160 acres of public land on the Tombigbee River, at a price of $2 per acre, and with fourteen years in which to pay off their indebtedness. They had come to Philadelphia, and thence to Mobile, and the leader of the expedition was none other than Count Charles Lefebre Desnouettes, who had been a lieutenant-general of cavalry and had accompanied Napoleon in his march to Russia and rode back with him in his carriage in that disastrous retreat. There was Colonel Nicholas Rooul, who had commanded the advance guard of two hundred grenadiers when Napoleon had left Elba and marched to Paris to regain his throne and who, like Napoleon, had confronted the King's troops under Marshall Ney and valiantly defied Ney to fire. How gallant, how romantic it had been when Ney's troops instead shouted *"Vive l'Empereur!"* and Napoleon had marched at their head through the very gates of Paris!

And finally there was Maurice Peniers, a member of the National Assembly who had voted for the death of Louis XVI, a vote which, if evidence can be believed, may have been the deciding one in ending the monarchy of France and creating the seeds of war which Napoleon was fated to harvest to the near-decimation of all Europe and assuredly of the very flower of French manhood. These illustrious refugees who, now that monarchy was restored to France, were condemned as proscribed traitors liable to execution if they again set foot upon French soil, founded the town of Demopolis, "the city of the people."

It was in October, the month in which the Chickasaws signed a treaty ceding to the United States all their remaining lands between the Mississippi River and the northern course of the Tennessee River, that Lucien and Henry Bouchard, after visiting Nanakota in the new Creek village, returned to what had once been Econchate and was now New Philadelphia. Bluff, friendly John Klinck greeted them, invited them to take refreshment with him, and then jovially declared, "Mr. Bouchard, our little town is growing by leaps and bounds, as you can see for yourself with all these cabins rising. Just a few weeks ago, we got ourselves a lawyer in our midst, with a mighty good-looking daughter. Maybe you'd like to meet them? They're in the third cabin north from mine. His name's Grover Mason, and he comes from Boston, just like Senator Samuel Dexter. That nephew of Dexter's is as smart as his uncle, judging by the way he's planning to make this town really boom, Mr. Bouchard!"

"Well," Lucien chuckled, "I have no doubt that with

all these land sales, we'll have need for a good lawyer in our midst to avoid angry disputes."

"That's the long and the short of it, Mr. Bouchard, you hit the nail right on the head!" Klinck grinned as he filled his clay mug with rum and refilled Lucien's and Henry's to brimming measure. "Now, whyn't I take you round to Lawyer Mason directly after we've drunk a toast to our new town, to cotton and prosperity!"

Klinck led them toward the lawyer's cabin and greeted his Boston neighbor, who was standing in the doorway, "We were just coming to pay you a visit, Grover! Here's Mr. Bouchard and his fine son. I've told you how he's been the one who's kept Nanakota's braves off the warpath and what he's done with cotton already."

"Indeed you have, my friend, and I'm certainly eager to meet a man of such talents." Grover Mason beamed as he stepped forward to shake hands with Lucien and then with Henry. He was a fussy little man, in brown waistcoat and pantaloons and brass-buckled shoes, in his mid-forties, with a straggly dark-brown and somewhat graying beard, shrewd little pale-blue eyes that swiftly appraised both Lucien and his son at first glance. "Come in, come in both of you. Sybella's just fixing our supper. You'll stay and have a bite with us, I do hope?"

"My thanks for your hospitality, Mr. Mason, but we're on our way back to our own cabins and want to get there before the dead of night. Perhaps you and your daughter would be good enough one day to accept my invitation," Lucien smilingly countered.

Henry Bouchard stood like one transfixed, staring at a slim, auburn-haired girl in a plain white muslin dress who was setting two pewter plates on the rough-hewn table in the center of the cabin's larger room. Behind her was a stone fireplace in which an iron kettle of stew was simmering.

"Syb, honey, come and meet Mr. Bouchard and his son Henry," her father called to her.

Sybella Mason, though she could not have been more than seventeen, had a quality of stately poise and self-assurance which was evidenced by the way she deftly

508

straightened, without the least hurry, and came forward to offer both visitors a short curtsy.

"Her mother died last year, so Syb's been cook and housekeeper for her helpless old father ever since," Grover Mason affably explained.

"Mr. Klinck tells me that you come from Boston, Mr. Mason," Lucien said.

"Quite right, sir, quite right. I had the pleasure of being associated with Senator Dexter in his lamentably unrecognized building venture. Mind you, it was a stupendous idea, but perhaps too far ahead of these benighted times. But his nephew, sir, has the same foresight and acumen, mark my words. One day this town is going to be the very capital of what will soon be the state of Alabama. And remember, sir, it was Grover Mason who first told you that," the pompous little lawyer vehemently assured them.

"And you hope to pursue your practice here, I take it?" Lucien went on.

"I do indeed, sir. I was able to put away a considerable part of my savings—which I am bound to tell you I did not entirely invest with the Senator—and so Sybella and I are comfortably off. But I foresee, sir, that for some years you're going to have a problem here with the squatters on the land, with the Indian treaties which will mean constant surveying, and of course the notorious land speculators, who descend like locusts upon any new land offered up. Oh yes, they'll be needing legal counsel, and it's to Grover Mason they'll have to turn. I should be most privileged, Mr. Bouchard, to have you avail yourself of my services whenever that comes necessary."

"I'll remember your kind offer, Mr. Mason. As it happens, both my son and I have clear title to our lands, and they're on the river and most advantageously placed."

"Then you too, sir, are a man of acumen and foresight. It won't be long before we have the steamboat down the Alabama, and then you'll see what it'll mean in the way of profits on your crop, once you can go straight to Mobile, load at the levee from your engine house and deal directly with the biggest factors there." Grover Mason rubbed his hands as if he himself were anticipating a sizable share in the coming new enterprise.

Henry Bouchard had drawn away from his father and moved closer to Sybella, seeing that the two men were absorbed in their discussion. "Miss Sybella," he murmured, "that's a most fetching dress you're wearing."

"La, sir, it's an old one, though clean. I have several much more elegant which I brought from Boston." She gave him a pert smile, cool and entirely self-possessed. What most fascinated Henry Bouchard, quite apart from her haughty dignity, which seemed so out of place in a teen-aged girl, was the calm, insolent loveliness of her face. It was oval, with high-set, spacious forehead, her cheekbones prominent, her chin firm, even aggressive, but disarmingly matched to a full, sensual mouth, delicate, aquiline nose and large, intense dark-blue eyes. Her tawny skin was freckled, and the rich luster of her auburn hair, set with two large curls on each side of her forehead and a thick bun-shaped knot at the back of her neck, evoked in him an almost hypnotic appeal. It was exactly as if Henry Bouchard, for all his feral cruelty and carnal dominance, had never before seen a female he desired—and at this exact moment, that was exactly the case.

"We'd best be going now, Henry." Lucien Bouchard had not missed the effect which Sybella Mason had made on his son. "And do remember to accept my invitation, you and Miss Mason, to visit us. You'll always be welcome."

And when they were on the trail again, Henry Bouchard, who had been silent for many miles as he rode beside his father, suddenly looked at Lucien and said, "Suppose I were to pick that one as a wife, would you have any objections this time?"

"So soon, Henry? No, though she's still quite young."

"I know that, father. But there's something about her, something that tells me she's got strength and a mind of her own. It would be fun trying to bend her to my way."

"If by that you mean treating her like Dora, then it's better you forget marriage entirely."

"But, father—" Henry Bouchard gave him a thin-lipped smile—"you're forgetting about my son Luke. He'll need a mother. Ellen's getting old, and I don't want Luke brought up in an Indian village for the rest of his

510

life, you know. I've made my mind up. I'm going to go calling on her. You'll see, father."

And in December, while his slaves carried 50,000 pounds of his newly ginned cotton down to Mobile on flatboats, cotton that brought a record high of thirty-four cents a pound, Henry Bouchard and Sybella Mason rode that same trail up which his father had come for the first time nearly thirty years ago. At Mobile, they crossed the delta on the flatboat, and on the day before Christmas, 1818, were married by the priest. Henry's attractive bride gave as the date of her birth, March 14, 1802, the knowledge of which made her domineering young husband even more surprised by the quite convincing maturity she had exhibited toward him during their courtship.

But he was to have a still greater surprise when, that night, after a festive wedding supper which Lewis Judson gave for the young couple and then announced that he would stay the night at a friend's house so he might be in New Orleans for Christmas night with a dear friend, Sybella and Henry found themselves beginning their honeymoon in the comfortable bedroom of the trader. Lucien, who had already brought his 200,000 pounds of ginned cotton to this flourishing town and was on his way back to his own cabin, could have told his son of a similar happy coincidence when he had married Priscilla Wellman; for on the very night that Henry had been conceived, his father and that gentle English girl had begun their married life in the house of John Forbes. But there the similarity entirely ended. For between Priscilla's trusting surrender and Sybella's acceptance of her role as wife, there was to be a world of emotional difference which even Henry Bouchard could not possibly have anticipated.

In his excited anticipation of their wedding night, the sturdy, black-haired young man had shown what was for him a surprising consideration for his new bride's feelings. After an excellent dinner, which had been laid out for them by Judson's manservant (who had left with his master for New Orleans), Henry had downed a glass of wine and then abruptly risen from the table. "I'll go smoke a pipe outside and look at the stars, Sybella," he had gruffly declared. "You will wish to be by yourself for a bit, I've

511

no doubt. Then blow out the candle and I'll come to you."

But to his utter stupefaction, the auburn-haired girl he had just married shrugged and replied in a tone of amused derision, "I can't for the life of me think why you should be afraid to see me with the candle burning, my dear husband. I'm really not so ill-made as all that, you know."

Henry Bouchard gulped, momentarily at a loss for words. Then an ugly suspicion manifested itself by a scowl on his sun-tanned face. "By the eternal, that's brazen, Sybella! If I find you've been——"

She blithely interrupted: "Bedded with another man? Alas, I fear not, dear Mr. Bouchard. But that, you see, is why I'm all the more eager to see and learn all that is expected of me. I do confess, sir, to a most unmaidenly interest in the matter. Please do not think it unhealthy of me. After all, we are now man and wife, and papa once said to me that it was a female's duty to cleave unto her husband."

He scratched his head, nonplussed, for Sybella's proclamation of her virginal state in the same breath as her bold offer to watch him strip down and he in turn watch her do the same simply did not jibe with his notions of respectable womanhood. She was not like that Honorine, that was for certain; all the same, that bitch had most unashamedly peeled herself down raw and begun to cozen him, until she had enraged him by refusing to kneel and grovel like a slave when he had bade her do so.

"Well, if you're shy, Mr. Bouchard, I'll help you, then," Sybella then declared in her cool sweet voice. Half-turning away from him and standing beside the bed, she proceeded to pull off her pretty blue dress and fold it neatly over the back of a nearby chair, standing in chemise and batiste drawers, elegant silk stockings which had ladders in them from the journey on horseback, and sturdy, brass-buckled shoes. His face reddened as he watched her lift her hands toward the lace-trimmed straps of the chemise, a movement which wantonly thrust out the startlingly full round globes of her closely spaced breasts. But instead, she reached back further still to un-

512

knot the bun of auburn hair and let it fall just past her shoulderblades, then tossed her head and let the curls dance as they would as she regarded him with an impish, challenging smile: "La, Mr. Bouchard, I would think you are even more virginal than I, sir, seeing how you blush. If you were gallant, you would assist me."

His face was violently flushed, and his fingers trembled as he approached her, inflamed as much by her beauty in déshabillé as by the mocking challenge of her dark-blue eyes. He took the chemise at the neck and tore it with his strong hands, flinging it to the floor, and let her stand there in her drawers, hose and, to his further amazement, a pair of flouncy, ruffled garters high on her ripplingly muscled thighs.

"Where the devil did you get anything like that, Sybella?" he pointed, almost outraged, at the offending garters: they would not have been out of place in Marthe Rambouillet's bordello, but now they affronted his virtue as a husband.

"Silly, papa took me to New York last year, and when he wasn't looking I bought them in a fancy goods shop. Don't you like them, Mr. Bouchard?" she archly inquired, stooping a little and brushing her thighs with the palms of her hands.

"Damn it, Sybella, if I find you've had other men—" he began in a choked voice.

"Well, Mr. Bouchard, you'll find out if you'll just get undressed and get me into bed as respectable married folks ought to be by now, don't you think?" was her confounding answer.

He had not believed that any female could stand up to him and defy him so wantonly. With a lecherous grin, he stepped back and began to undress. *If she wanted to be shocked, the pretty little bitch, he'd oblige her!* But she continued to stand looking at him with those contemplative, coolly mocking eyes as he divested himself of everything save hose and gaiters, and then her eyes calmly appraised him, as if he were a male slave on the auction block at Mobile. Deliberately, she looked at his vigorous chest, already matted with a heavy growth of black hair, at the strong hips and sinewy thighs, and then, almost embarrassing him who had never believed any woman could manage that, regarded his almost fully erect generative organ.

"Well, I'm glad to see you really are a man after all, Mr. Bouchard," was her calm remark as, while he stood there with mouth agape, she very deliberately took hold of her batiste drawers, unfastened them, tugged them down and let them slither about her ankles, scuffed off her shoes and kicked away her final garment and moved like a tawny-sheened young nymph to their bridal bed.

With a hoarse cry, he flung himself down beside her, seizing her ruthlessly, and heard her softly little satisfied laugh which he silenced with a savage, crushing kiss. But even this did not disconcert the precocious auburn-haired girl: with a feline, intuitive movement of her supple naked body, she arched to him, her fingernails digging into his sturdy shoulders, and offered herself with a fierce eagerness that met his own.

Though she winced and gasped at the moment of defloration, she did not shrink in the least from his violent ardor. Her legs enlaced him, her nails raked his neck and back and shoulders as she strove with him. And when it was done, Henry Bouchard stared down in a kind of awestricken delight at his new wife and muttered, "I can't believe you really were a virgin, after all!"

Flushed and quivering, Sybella pertly whispered back, "Well, Mr. Bouchard, I should think by now you've found out that you were the first ever with me. Such conceit, to think that it's only a man who's interested in making love. Now, please tidy us up, and then come back and love me nicely."

CHAPTER THIRTY-NINE

On September 28, 1819, Sybella Bouchard was easily delivered of a seven-pound black-haired boy which her infatuated young husband promptly named Mark. Henry had brought along as a souvenir of his brief honeymoon in Mobile some of that city's first issue of banknotes, in denominations of fifty, twenty-five and twelve-and-a-half cents, having in the left margins an ox, horse, and eagle respectively, and redeemable in specie, Louisiana, Mississippi or United States bank notes. The day after the baby's birth, Henry fatuously held one of each of these small-change notes over the cradle, and with a cooing sound, the baby reached up for the one closest to him—the fifty-cent note. "You see, Syb," Henry exultantly crowed, "he goes for the biggest denomination. That boy's going to make his mark, see if I'm not right—and that's exactly what we are going to call him—Mark!"

This was the year of President James Monroe's visit to Huntsville in June, a visit which was part of the President's tour of territory newly acquired by the United States to examine the situation of the fortifications and to select suitable sites to be put in a state of defense against foreign aggression. He declared that he conceded the duty of the chief magistrate of the new Union to acquaint himself with knowledge of the interior country over which he presided, and as far as it was practicable to ascertain the state of society and improvement in agriculture, manufactures, as well as to inquire into the condition of the Indian tribes dispersed through the western portion of the Union. And he drank a toast to the admission of the Territory of Alabama, hoping that it would be speedily admitted as a state to augment the national strength and prosperity.

Such a wish appeared to be close to realization when, this same year, steamboats began to ply between Mobile and St. Stephens and made the first trip up to the new French town of Demopolis. There were other good signs as well. On February 22, 1819, the United States signed a treaty with Spain in which Spain gave up East and West Florida, defined the western boundary of the Louisiana Purchase to the 42nd parallel and designated that parallel as the northern limit of all Spanish territorial claims. In return, the United States renounced its claim to Texas. The following month, Arkansas was organized as a territory. But on the darker side, the Senate rejected James Talmadge's amendment to the Missouri Bill which would prohibit the further introduction of slavery and free all children after the age of twenty-five who were born after the admission of Missouri, which was now drafting its constitution and preparing for statehood. The veto of this amendment was to precipitate the great slavery struggle, and it marked the gathering of the storm that would one day descend upon the entire nation and rend it asunder in internecine warfare.

But the telltale sign that this year was not to fulfill President Monroe's expectations of great prosperity came with the descending price of cotton at the year's end. When Lucien and Henry brought their ginned cotton to Mobile, they found that they could net only twenty-four cents a pound, a drop of ten cents from the previous year. Correspondingly, the value of slaves on the open market at Mobile and New Orleans dropped as well.

On the other hand, Lucien's by now almost obsessive dream of building Windhaven seemed closer than ever; on May 26th of this year, the *Savannah* left Savannah, Georgia, for Liverpool, crossing mainly under steam, to mark the first trans-Atlantic passage of a steamship. If this venture proved successful and other ships were built to cross the stormy Atlantic, they could bring back glass, furnishings, linen and silverware such as had graced the stately

516

and durable chateau at Yves-sur-lac. Yet the costs of such importation were still outlandishly high, and even Lucien's thriving personal account in the Ronsart bank at New Orleans would not presently be enough to duplicate that edifice which represented his former life and whose counterpart would stand as his memorial to the life he had built here in Alabama, the life inspired by the gentle young girl who slept in the towering bluff nearby.

Yet to counter his impatience at the tediously slow passage of the years before he could achieve his dream, Lucien was granted a measure of happiness in observing how skillfully young Sybella adapted herself to his dominant and selfish son and, best of all, easily became as good a mother to little blond Luke as she did to Mark, whom she nursed at her breast and brought through the first critical year of infancy in the very best of health. At times, when he eagerly accepted invitations to dine with his new daughter-in-law and son—which, even had there been greater constraint between himself and Henry, he would have done if only to see his two grandsons—he never failed to marvel at Sybella's ready wit and her ability to give as well as take in the sometimes cynically unguarded domestic arguments which sprang up between her and Henry, even across the supper table. Thomas, invaluable overseer on Lucien's own flourishing acreage, had often visited Henry's cottonfields and the shed-enclosed engine, mingled with Henry's slaves and had been able to report that their young master seemed to be absorbing himself in the operation of this small adjunct to Lucien's plantation without resuming his carnal depredations upon Mary and Molly. Evidently, Lucien thought with satisfaction, the physical charms of auburn-haired young Sybella coupled with her shrewd sagacity for managing so unruly and self-willed a husband were bearing bountiful fruit.

Four days before Lucien's fifty-seventh birthday, Alabama entered the Union as a slave state. That evening, Lucien dined in his son's cabin, with Sybella herself the cook, and the gray-haired Frenchman sat at the head of the table with his grandson Luke at his right and the baby Mark in an ingeniously contrived high chair which Thomas himself had designed and hewn out of pinewood.

"I begin to believe that I have contributed something to this rich land which Tunkamara gave me so long ago," he said slowly as he lifted a glass of wine to his lips to respond to the birthday toast which Henry had proposed. "Here is my son and here are my two grandsons; my son works his land as I have worked mine, and it is clear for both of us. I do not feel my age tonight, Henry. Instead, I feel as young as when I wed my beautiful Dimarte. May God grant that very soon the chateau of Normandy will be erected on this Alabama soil, with its tower toward the bluff from which I shall talk to her as I did in those sweet golden days when this land was young and new and uncharted."

"Amen to that, father." Henry Bouchard touched his glass to his lips. And then he wryly added, "But don't forget, the legislators of Alabama, this fine new state of ours, celebrated your birthday in advance by entering this rich land as a state where freeholders own slaves and where slavery is now a recognized institution. You see, father, they were more practical than you."

Lucien Bouchard bowed his head and set down his glass. After a long pause he said, "Once I told Alexander McGillivray that I had come from France to seek a land where neither politics nor religious bias could halt a free man's ambition to build a purposeful life in which freedom would be the ultimate goal. I meant it then, I mean it still today in the face of your legislators, Henry. This desire to possess, to own, to hold in bondage is to my mind a shadow on the bright sun of our new state of Alabama. And if Tsipoulata were still alive today, he would say that one day that shadow may very well blot out the sun itself."

Econchate was no more, except as a memory in the mind of Lucien Bouchard. On December 3, 1819, New Philadelphia and East Alabama Town were united in one town called Montgomery, which was named after the general who had died in the Battle of Quebec. It was now part of the county of the same name, but that county had been named after the heroic Major Lemuel Purnell Montgomery, who had been the first man to fall on the breast-

518

works of the Battle of Horseshoe Bend. Now it was a bustling little frontier town, with a population of about six hundred, a fledgling newspaper called the *Republican,* which carried advertisements for the barter of a gun and a rifle in exchange for planks and shingles, or saddle horses for bricks and mortar. Even a school was established, and one of the first steamboats brought up the Alabama River from Mobile such educational texts as Murray's *Grammar,* Webster's *Speller,* and Watts's *Psalms and Hymns.* A town ordinance was passed to impose a tax of fifty cents for every dog a family kept, except the first one, which was free. The stores of the merchants were in a kind of valley, and the city streets were laid out like a spider web. Dexter Avenue, named after the far-sighted cofounder of this thriving little town, became the very center of Montgomery.

And to reach the red bluff on which once Tunkamara had stood, peering out over the land and finding it a good site for this village of Red Ground, one ascended a steep hill. All that was left of the Creek village were remnants of campfires, buried in the ground on which cabins now stood, and soon more sturdy houses modeled on those which many of the Eastern settlers had lived in before seeking a pioneer horizon in this southeastern part of the flourishing new republic.

And yet, in spite of this seeming prosperity in the new state of Alabama, there was financial disaster brewing. Instead of a currency of uniform value resting upon the credit of the government, there were only bank notes, whose value depended upon the credit of the issuing banks. The first Bank of the United States had done a great deal to stabilize the solvency of the currency, but it had gone out of operation in 1811. By the end of the War of 1812, the country was flooded with paper money which was no longer redeemed in specie by the banks which issued it. And it was during this time that settlers had begun to find their way into the Alabama Territory in increasing numbers, with the only money permeating this vast frontier consisting of the depreciated notes of the banks of Georgia.

The Second Bank of the United States had obliged the

state banks to resume specie payments in 1817, and immigrants to Alabama were supplied with funds by the numerous new banks which had sprung up in Tennessee and Kentucky in 1818. But this year of 1819, which marked the birth of Lucien's second grandson, was one of dire financial stress, for these new banks closed their doors and left their notes circulating at depreciated value in the western country.

This section of the country was considered the West and it was a debtor section: it owed for lands, slaves and goods. The affluent East was creditor and had to be paid. But when the banks of Tennessee suspended their specie payments, their notes were no longer available for remittance to the East. In 1816, the legislature of the Mississippi Territory had chartered the Merchant's and Planter's Bank of Huntsville, and Huntsville notes were purchased with the Tennessee notes and drew specie on the former. But this put so great a drain on the specie reserve of the Huntsville bank that it was obliged to suspend payments by the new year of 1820. Though the notes continued to be used, they fell below par and circulated at the same value as notes from Tennessee. Specie and the notes of specie-paying banks, now at an exorbitant premium, ceased to pass from hand to hand; thus North Alabama was left with depreciated currency. And there was a further problem: although both gold and silver were legal tender by law, market prices of the metals put a higher value on the gold dollar than on the silver. Thus silver passed from hand to hand, while gold began to be withdrawn from circulation and a premium had to be paid to obtain it.

President Jefferson had suspended the coinage of silver dollars in 1806 because there had been a profit made out of sending silver dollars to Latin American countries and exchanging them in equal terms for Spanish dollars, or pieces of eight *reales,* which were somewhat heavier. These foreign coins had been brought back and melted down because the silver in them was worth slightly more than a dollar by American monetary standards, so all that was left for circulation were the Spanish dollars, far too light to afford a profit on the bullion market, and a certain amount of fractional Spanish coin. The change tickets, as these bits of paper worth twenty-five, fifty or twelve and a half cents were called, were signed by the issuer and were supposed to be redeemable for specie. Forgeries were easy, and the country soon became flooded with the papers of various uncertain houses.

Those Alabama planters who had cotton to sell were affected not only by local conditions, but by national and international trade relations as well. Mobile and New Orleans merchants sold almost all of Alabama's cotton crop, disposing of the bulk of it, directly or indirectly, in the British market. The American merchant collected his account by drawing a bill of exchange on the British purchaser and then disposing of this to some other American merchant who was in need of funds to remit to England. And, just as Grover Mason had shrewdly guessed, speculation, land grabbing and graft of all kinds were the stock in trade of scores of new settlers who scrambled for a place and where the strong could use their cunning to merciless advantage against the weak.

Lucien Bouchard and his son Henry, as cotton planters, were regarded as men of prestige, since theirs was the only occupation which brought profits not extorted from their neighbors. But the merchants who used their capital to carry the small land-holding settlers, who were constantly in debt and had to depend on their crops, made their profits out of their community and often made too much. And thus it was that even part of Lucien Bouchard's newly negotiated account with the trading house of Lewis Judson in Mobile suffered depreciation from this general financial panic. Of the sum which he had privately marked to be at the disposal of the villagers of Econchate, now in this year of 1820 there was only a scant $10,000 left. Yet ironically, in the private bank of Jules Ronsart, now operated by Antoine Rigalle, all of his own personal money remained intact.

He had made a pledge to Tunkamara and renewed it with Nanakota. He would not build Windhaven until he had paid his debt to the Creeks, who had given him this chance at a new life which had brought him wealth, a son and two healthy grandsons—and to Luke and Mark would fall the real future of the Bouchard inheritance. It would be those two boys, when they were full grown to manhood, who would profit from the arduous work he and Henry had initiated, knowing by then how to profit from the errors he and his son had made and how to take inspiration from the best of their endeavors.

In this same new year of 1820, in which Lucien was entering his fifty-eighth year of life, a steamboat line was established between New York and New Orleans, a further step forward in making his Windhaven possible. Yet discovering the severe loss of paper profits from his Mobile account had made him grimly resolve to put that dream out of his mind even if it took another few years, until he could make certain that Nanakota and the villagers wanted for nothing and would be fairly dealt with when the time came—as it most assuredly would—for them to leave Alabama altogether. The year began with the famous Taylor amendment to a bill in the House of Representatives admitting Maine as a slave-free state while prohibiting slavery in Missouri as well.

In February, Senator J. B. Thomas of Illinois submitted to the Senate an amendment to the bill for Maine's admission, prohibiting slavery in territory of the Louisiana Purchase north of 36°30′, except Missouri, during the territorial period. On March 3rd, the bill for the admission of Maine to the Union was approved by President Monroe, and three days later he approved the Missouri Enabling Bill, which adopted the Thomas compromise provision. In the following month, the Public Land Act authorized the purchase of 80-acre lots at $1.25 an acre for cash and abolished the credit system. Now those settlers who had paid only a fractional part of their land costs down and had hoped to meet their payments with future crops were placed in jeopardy and many of them sold their land to greedy speculators, who reaped a windfall.

On May 15th, foreign slave trade was declared to be piracy and punishable by death by the act of Congress. And twelve days before Lucien's fifty-eighth birthday, James Monroe was re-elected President with 231 electoral votes, all but one of which was given by New Hampshire to John Quincy Adams. Daniel D. Thompkins was re-elected his Vice-President.

But the controversy over slaveholding continued to gain greater momentum. The Missouri Constitution, adopted by a convention of the legislators of that territory, and containing a clause which forbade free Negroes to enter the state, was submitted to the Senate. In this act Henry Bouchard saw his steadfast belief that slavery was a virtual necessity for those who worked the land to a profit vigorously confirmed by the legislators of the land. For Lucien, it was a dour realization that the very swiftness with which former Indian land was being settled was bringing about a materialistic and wholly utilitarian way of life that might well influence the future of his grandchildren. Perhaps, he thought sadly to himself, they would one day be embroiled in this clearly drawn issue between slavery and freedom for the black workers upon the soil which gave them sustenance and hope.

And as a further ominous indication of the business panic which had gripped not only Alabama but also the entire nation, he found that his cotton brought only seventeen cents a pound in Mobile, exactly half of what he had been paid only two years before.

A month before his birthday, he rode to the new village of the Creeks, there to spend a week hunting with Nanakota, who was now sixty, vigorous as ever, but with a sadness to his face and a whiteness to his hair which spoke more eloquently than any words of the soul-anguish which the *Mico* endured in leaving the beloved Red Ground. Each of them killed two fine bucks, and the venison was welcome for those squaws whose husbands had long since died and who had no man to bring meat to their lodges. Lucien had loaded four pack ponies with corn from his own fields to be distributed to the villagers.

As they sat before their fire on the last night of the hunt, Nanakota said slowly, "I grow old and tired, and the young men of my village are restless. They do not know how long we shall be permitted to stay here where the soldiers told us to go. Yes, the hunting has been good, and we can fish and you bring us corn and the goods from Maubila. But what, Lu-shee-ahn, will become of us if the

Great Spirit summons you to join the beloved woman whom you still mourn? Who will then be friend and blood brother to us? The young men will leave, they may take up the tomahawk and the rifle in their despairing hatred of the white-eyes, who have made us leave our land, even though we have signed the treaty and we are at peace. I cannot control them now as I once did. My elders and I pray nightly to the Giver of Breath that he will grant our disturbed young warriors the wisdom which we have learned with the weight of our years, the wisdom you had in your heart even when you were young and came to become one of us."

"I pray that too, Nanakota. And I have told my son to see that your people do not starve. Even if Henry should be too selfish to think of his father's blood brothers, my overseer Thomas knows how I wish the crops of my good land bestowed. I pledge you this with my heart and my life and by the words I have spoken to those whom I trust and who will live after me, my *Mico*."

The old chief nodded slowly and he put one hand upon Lucien Bouchard's heart and the other upon his forehead and he said in Creek, "I will speak the truth to you, my brother. When I was the age of your son, in me was a hatred of all the white-eyes. I had seen them kill my mother and father—no, I have not told you this before. I swore an oath of vengeance, and even when you came to Econchate that first time and Tunkamara welcomed you, I found hatred for you in my heart. Then you came among us, and when I saw how just you were with Shehanoy and how you spoke of honesty and honor, my heart warmed toward you. This I say to you now, my brother: I thank the Great Spirit that He turned my heart from the thoughts of war and hatred and let me be your friend. It is because of this that I am not ashamed of what I have done as *Mico* for my people."

Lucien was too deeply moved to speak. Instead, he put his hands upon Nanakota's forehead and heart, and he was not ashamed of the tears that blinded his vision.

The price of both cotton and slaves continued to drop. Ginned cotton commanded only fourteen cents a pound in

Mobile in 1821, and two years later it reached bottom at about eleven cents a pound. On August 10, 1821, Missouri was admitted to the Union by proclamation of President Monroe, after a joint resolution of Congress had approved Missouri's admission on the condition that nothing in its constitution would ever be construed to deny to a citizen of any state—including any free Negro—the privileges he was entitled to under the Constitution. And in this year, the steamboat *Harriett* ascended the Alabama River from Mobile to Montgomery. Now, Lucien knew, the means of transportation was at hand to bring to his land the materials and the furnishings he foresaw as part of Windhaven. And yet, by fate's own irony, never was the dream less practicable than during these years of the business panic.

Yet there were improvements which could be made in the cultivation and the very processing of cotton itself, and such industry would occupy his strength and his mind until the time was right for the fulfillment of that dream. An improved cotton engine had just been introduced in Mississippi, and the claims were that the new machine did not tear the fiber when removing it from the seed, thereby improving the quality of the staple. At the same time, also in Mississippi, an apparatus was introduced to mote the cotton as it came from the gin. In Whitney's original device, fiber was removed from the seed by means of revolving saw-teeth, with revolving brushes eliminating the fiber from the saws. The innovation now supplied fans to the arms of the revolving brushes, blowing the issuing cotton through a horizontal wooden flue with a latticed bottom. As the lint passed through the flue, the particles of foreign matter dropped through the grating into a trough below, saving many hours of slave labor.

Also, the "Mexican" variety of seed had been introduced, which produced larger pods to open wider than the old variety, allowing the fiber to hang from the bolls and making picking an easier process. Lucien experimented and found that his workers were able to pick two hundred pounds a day, whereas one hundred had formerly been an excellent average.

Henry's slaves had built additional rooms to his own

cabin, so that Luke and Mark might share a room, with another reserved for Sybella's second child, which was expected in the spring of 1824. Luke, now seven, was thin and slender, like his grandfather, shy and soft-spoken, with pale-blue eyes and an inquisitive look almost always on his serious young face. Mark, cheerful and robust at four, would one day be as stocky as his father. And it was naturally Mark to whom Henry seemed to show the most affection. His occasional boisterous displays of affection toward Luke seemed to make the boy withdraw more and more. Early in March of 1824, on the very day that Andrew Jackson was nominated for President and John C. Calhoun for Vice-President at the state nominating convention in Harrisburg, Pennsylvania, while at dinner Henry said contemptuously to Lucien, "Father, I don't want to show preference, but I find I can't help myself. The boy I named after you shrinks away from me; yes, whenever I pat him or say something nice to him. He's forever at his speller and just the other day he asked me when he could go to school."

"I think that's highly commendable, my son. What's wrong with an education? We can't all be planters and farmers. Some of us, like Grover Mason, have to use our brains to settle the disputes that men of the soil are bound to engage in."

"Oh, that's all very well for you to say, father," Henry Bouchard impatiently declared. "Though I'll admit my father-in-law's been very useful to me. He's about to help me foreclose on old Granville Murton—you know, the doddering old fool who bit off more than he could chew with that fifty acres about five miles downriver. He's in debt, and Grover's got hold of his notes and I'm taking them over next week."

"Why do you want the extra land?"

"Because this low price of cotton isn't going to prevail forever. And if we get old Andy Jackson in as President, he'll chase all the rest of the Indians out and then we can really work the soil."

"I've told you repeatedly, Henry, that if you plant nothing but one crop year after year, you're going to ruin the soil. I never planted the same acreage in cotton more than two or three years in a row at the most; I used beans or I used corn, or I plowed under and let it lie fallow, so that all of my acreage is still about as rich as when I got my deed to it."

"That's all very well for you to say, father, but you're getting old, after all, and now that the steamboats are here and towns are booming, I'm going to raise more cotton than ever. That's why I want Murton's land, and, when I can afford it, even more. No, I haven't forgotten, I'm going to help build you that chateau of yours. But you can see for yourself how this money crisis is cutting down our profits—why, it even wiped out some that you so generously gave away to the Creeks."

"I gave nothing away to the Creeks," Lucien angrily corrected. "I repaid them a debt, and what I've given them is little enough for all they've done for me over these years. Besides which, my son, you apparently still haven't learned that there are things like friendship and trust which banknotes will never buy."

"Neither of us is going to change our views at this late date, father. But, to indulge you, I've no objection to Luke's studying. But you can't expect him to go to school, it's twenty-five miles from here."

"I've books myself, and I can teach him. I'll teach him to ride a horse, too."

"If you like, by all means do. As for myself, I think I can give Mark what he needs by way of education, and in a few years more, he'll be working beside me in the fields or going downriver to Mobile to make money for me."

"Very well, my son," Lucien soberly replied. "Let us see if a combination of book learning and natural curiosity about life will make my older grandson as useful a man as I hope Mark will learn to be from your own guidance."

Sybella set down a plate of hot cornmeal biscuits before them, and shrewdly eyed her stocky black-haired husband. "If Mark isn't the man you hope he'll be, Henry, it'll be your own fault and nobody else's. Grandfather's right—there's no reason to be ashamed of book learning. Look what it did for my father."

Henry Bouchard shot her a venomous look. "Please,

527

Sybella, this conversation doesn't concern you. Do you mind?"

Planting her hands on her hips, the handsome auburn-haired young woman defiantly stared at him, a mocking smile on her sensuous mouth. "I do mind, and it does concern me, since it's about Mark. My son as well as yours, if you'll remember, Henry. I say you give him his head too much, just as if he were a wild horse. And one day he'll throw you, watch and see if I'm not right. As for me, I think your father's quite right. Luke is the quiet type, but still waters run deep. They do in me too, Henry, if you'd sometimes take the trouble to notice." With this, she left the room with an emphatic flounce of her skirts that said better than words that her mind was made up on the matter.

"Women," Henry Bouchard said with a heavy sigh. "There's no doing without them, but sometimes there's no doing with them either."

Lucien permitted himself a wry smile. "That's because, my son, you fail to give them credit for as much intelligence as you."

CHAPTER FORTY

Eight arduous years had passed, and the new year of 1831 was dawning. Andrew Jackson had been elected President on December 3, 1828, by the electoral vote of 178 to 83 for John Quincy Adams. Jackson, elected as a Democrat, had failed of election in 1824, though he had received 99 electoral votes to the 84 of John Quincy Adams: with no electoral majority, the House of Representatives had on February 9, 1825, voted for John Quincy Adams to hold the highest office. On the very first ballot, thirteen of the states had voted for Adams, seven for Jackson, and four for W. H. Crawford. A few days later in that same year of 1825, there had been a treaty signed at Indian Springs in which the Creek leaders yielded up all their Georgia lands to the United States and promised to leave for the West by September 1, 1826. It was a treaty that was at once repudiated by most of the Creek tribes. And, in Alabama, the capital was moved from Cahawba to Tuscaloosa.

John C. Calhoun, who had been Vice-President under John Quincy Adams, was re-elected to hold the same office under the hero of Horseshoe Bend. On July 4, 1826, two great ex-Presidents, John Adams and Thomas Jefferson, had died on the fiftieth anniversary of the Declaration of Independence and on January 24th of that same year, the Treaty of Washington with the Creeks replaced the previous year's agreement, taking a smaller portion of land for the United States and permitting the Creeks to remain on their lands until January 1, 1827.

In 1829, Governor Stephen D. Miller, in his message to the South Carolina legislature, declared, "Slavery is not a national evil; on the contrary, it is a national benefit." The address, printed in the Montgomery *Journal,* made Henry Bouchard exultant and he made certain that his aging father read it. In that same year, President Jackson offered to buy Texas from Mexico, an offer which was refused. To counter it, Mexico's President Gauerreo declared Texas exempt from his Mexican anti-slavery decree.

A year later, the town of Chicago was laid out at Fort Dearborn, which had been a Federal post since 1803. The first covered wagons from the Missouri River to the Rockies broke new ground toward an ever-increasing American frontier. In this year, too, Louis A. Godey founded *Godey's Lady's Book* in Philadelphia, a publication which was to influence the fashions of American men and women for generations to come. But also in this same year, there came about a growing rupture between President Jackson and his Vice-President, an outgrowth of Calhoun's advocacy of the censure of Jackson's action in Florida in 1818 when Calhoun was then Secretary of War under President Monroe.

On May 28, 1830, President Jackson signed the Indian Removal Act, for the general removal of Indians to lands west of the Mississippi, and, twelve days before Lucien Bouchard's sixty-eighth birthday, delivered an annual message which attacked the Bank of the United States, confirming his support of the principal of protection and arguing for the proposed distribution of surplus revenue among the states for internal improvements.

Now Lucien Bouchard had a pretty little granddaughter, Arabella, born April 27, 1824, a black-haired, already flirtatious little girl who idolized her virile, dominant father. Henry Bouchard had been quite content with Sybella, and apart from an occasional clandestine conquest with one of the more promiscuous Creek maidens and younger squaws as well as an equally occasional easing of his vigorous lusts on the still attractive Mary and

Molly, had been faithful to his auburn-haired wife. Sybella wholesomely enjoyed their mating, and often took the initiative, particularly when she observed his ardors waning—a sure sign that he would seek diversion elsewhere.

The new cotton engines had been installed on Lucien's land as well as on Henry's and were producing a far better quality of cotton for the market than had ever been offered before. Yet the price at Mobile, though improving to fifteen cents a pound in 1824 and twenty-one cents in 1825, dropped to nine and a half cents in 1827 and averaged about ten and a quarter cents per pound thereafter.

Now, because of regular steamboat service between Montgomery and Mobile, both Henry and Lucien Bouchard could convey the ginned cotton to their levees on the river, packing them in bales averaging from 400 to 425 pounds. These bales were made as nearly square as possible, pressed until the side seams were well closed or a little lapped, and secured with six sturdy ropes, the heads neatly sewn in, so that when completed and turned out of the press, no cotton would be exposed. Yet Lucien soon discovered that baling cotton compressed it and often deteriorated its prime quality. Henry, on the other hand, was more concerned with quantity shipped, particularly because of the low price offered at the market. By now, after having added old Murton's fifty acres to his holdings, and another seventy-five further downriver which his father-in-law had ingeniously managed to foreclose upon, he had purchased eight more slaves at Mobile, three of them having wives in their late twenties. Sybella noted this last purchase, which occurred in December of 1830, and resolved to occupy her husband with another child.

Blond Luke, now fifteen, and black-haired Mark, twelve, both attended the same rural school which had been built about two miles east of their grandfather's land. Though Luke rode horseback ably, Henry Bouchard still showed obvious preference to his younger son as well as to his charming and mischievous seven-year-old daughter Arabella. In July, when the cotton season was at its height, Luke often joined his grandfather in the fields, asking questions which delighted the now white-haired Frenchman. And Luke's gentleness toward his sister and unassuming manner toward Lucien's free black workers delighted him even more.

Late one afternoon, as Lucien walked with his grandson down the tall stalks of cotton, the boy suddenly asked, *"Grandpère,* Mark says I'm wrong to talk to the Indians and the *nègres* as if they were my equals. Do you think I am?"

Lucien stopped and studied his blond grandson, observing the boy's earnest face, the intent, sincere look in his eyes. "No, Luke. You see, there are different people throughout this world of ours, descended from other races in other lands. So their skin color, their language, their ways of doing things are necessarily different. Yet if we take time to know them and talk with them, we find that all of us have the same essential beliefs and decency. We call our Creator God or *le bon Dieu.* The Creeks call him Ibofanaga or Hisagita-imisi. The Hindus pray to Buddha, the Moslems to Allah and Mohammed as His Prophet. And yet, Luke, this is the brotherhood of mankind, that each of those supreme beings is, when all is said and done, the same. So, too, are we, no matter what the color of our skin or our creed. You have already learned the greatest lesson of life, that of tolerance toward all people. Yes, there will be those who will hate you for it, but in return, there will be many more who will love you, as I do."

Luke took his grandfather's hand and squeezed it hard as he replied, "So long as you think I'm right, *Grandpère,* that's all that matters to me."

Mark, on the other hand, bullied his father's slaves, autocratically demanding that one of them stop work to bring him a dipper of water or to whittle him a new toy. Old Abe and Rastus, who foresaw that catering to the preferred son of their self-willed master might somewhat ease their lot, had vied with each other in making wooden figures of animals and soldiers. Mark accepted these as his rightful due, often upbraiding the two blacks when any of the toys broke or its form did not please him. And he often sent Arabella crying to her mother by tiptoeing up behind her and pulling her hair, jealous that his father showed her so much attention.

This year of 1831 was to be more momentous than either Lucien or Henry dreamed. On March 18th, the Supreme Court, in the case of *Cherokee Nation* vs. *Georgia*, denied the right of any Indian tribe to sue in Federal courts, since it was not a foreign nation. A few weeks later, Secretary of War John H. Eaton resigned from President Jackson's cabinet, and by summer the hero of Horseshoe Bend had chosen a complete new cabinet. His feud with John C. Calhoun led to the latter's nomination for President at a public meeting in New York on August 9th.

But twelve days after that, Nat Turner led a slave insurrection in Southhampton, Virginia, killing fifty-five whites and arousing a fomentation of public opinion on the potential danger from rebellious slaves.

"Don't you see, father, it's what I've been telling you all these years!" Henry Bouchard exploded as he flung the *Republican* to the floor. "We've got to have laws that will keep the whites in power, laws so strong that no uppity nigger will dare even dream of taking a weapon against his master. That's what your education does. Nat Turner could read and write. Why, we ought to pass a law here in Alabama forbidding any plantation owner to let his slaves learn how to read and write. A little knowledge is a dangerous thing—isn't that a quotation from one of the authors you're always throwing at me, father?"

"Perhaps," Lucien Bouchard drily retorted, "but a little prejudice is even more dangerous. Because one oppressed or unfortunately advised black rises against his master does not mean that all the whites will be massacred. That will happen still less if slavery is abolished and men are free. Have I once in all these years had the slightest argument with any of my workers?"

"You spoil them, father. Next thing, those men of yours will be wanting to take white wives—and damn it all, if that ever happens, I'll fight you in the highest court of the land to prevent such an abomination!"

"I see," his father grimly smiled. Noticing that Sybella had gone out to the shed which enclosed the stone oven to bring in a roast turkey, he added softly, so that neither Mark nor Luke nor Arabella would hear, "But you wouldn't want a law that would keep you from taking your slaves' wives to bed, now would you?"

Henry Bouchard turned livid with fury and glared at his father. Then, suddenly expansive, he leaned back and shrugged. "I'm going to New Orleans to check our accounts with Rigalle, father. I wrote him several weeks ago asking him to put me in touch with an architect."

Lucien's anger swiftly ebbed as he stared at his black-haired son. "An—an architect, Henry?"

Henry Bouchard nodded. "To build Windhaven for you. I've made some money on land speculation myself, father, and I'm going to buy about thirty more slaves when I'm in New Orleans. They can work on the construction of that famous chateau of yours. And I'll admit I haven't done too badly, even though cotton prices have been miserable of late. I'll ask the architect to give me an estimate on what he thinks it will cost to duplicate your chateau."

Lucien Bouchard drew a kerchief from his frockcoat and blew his nose. He blinked his eyes and reached for the mug of strong black tea which he had learned to enjoy these past few years after finding it in a salvaged cargo of spices which had been reclaimed in Mobile two years ago. Henry Bouchard watched his father with an amused little smile. "I didn't mean to upset your digestion, father, with my bit of news."

Now again in control of himself, the dignified white-haired Frenchman leaned back and, his eyes half-closed, with nostalgic remembrance of the past, mused aloud, "Just a few months more than forty-two years ago, my son, I sat at a supper table like this back in Yves-sur-lac. And my father spoke of my digestion, too, as you've just done. And I told him that it wasn't the pheasant which I found too rich for my plebeian tastes, but rather the price of a very small rabbit."

"A rabbit, father?" Despite his usual impatience with Lucien's anecdotes, Henry Bouchard leaned forward with interest; this was one he had not previously heard.

"Yes, a rabbit," Lucien repeated. "A rabbit in a snare

which a poor little poacher had set. He paid with his life for setting it, because my father's gamekeeper killed him. And I told my father that evening that I wanted to find a country where such intolerable laws did not exist. The next morning, I set out for Le Havre to sail to New Orleans. I looked back and I saw that red-brick sturdy chateau with its high tower rising above the roof at each side, flanking it like watchful sentinels to look out over the fields and the valley on the other side of the hill and that little lake from which our village took its name. All these years, Henry, I've seen that chateau in my mind's eye. And now at last it's going to be built—do you wonder that I've something of a lump in my throat now, my son?" He held out his hand to Henry Bouchard, and a look of profound understanding passed between them, perhaps for the first time.

CHAPTER FORTY-ONE

It was the first week of November, 1831, and Henry Bouchard marveled at the changes that had taken place in New Orleans in the twenty years since he had first seen it in the company of his father. Now it was a city of nearly fifty thousand, so Antoine Rigalle had written him. Now there were sidewalks of brick which clung close to the façades of the brick and plaster houses, often protected from rain by overhanging balconies railed with wrought iron. Between the sidewalk and the road were deep ditches lined with cypress wood, in which water stood at all times. The open gutters were cleaned every day by the prisoners from the jails, who were mostly black slaves, Ronsart's successor had chattily added in his letter. At the street corners, one could see wagons selling drinking water, brought in from the river and sold in barrels, the vendor pouring the water into large jars into which alum and charcoal had been dropped to purify it. There were imposing buildings now, constructed of brick covered with stucco, the roofs attractively shielded with slate or tile. There were no cellars in these buildings, for the dampness of the ground made them impossible.

At night, New Orleans was guarded by fifty men, who patrolled in groups of two or three, carrying lanterns. By the Ordinance of 1825, it was required that the night watchman be able to speak both French and English. On every corner, there swung a large oil lamp lighted before sunset and remaining lit through the night. From heavy iron hooks on the angles of houses directly opposite hung the chains which supported these lamps, and the cost of this innovation was maintained by a special chimney tax, for every property owner in New Orleans was taxed a dollar a year for each chimney in his house.

At eight o'clock at night, a cannon was fired to signal all sailors, soldiers or blacks to get off the streets. Those who were found on them after the cannon had been fired required a pass from their employers or masters, or they were taken to the Calaboose. By the sound of the cannon also, all groceries and taverns were bidden to close.

"I do hope, my dear Henry," Rigalle had written, "that you will have time to spend an extra evening or two in our beautiful city, particularly to visit the famous quadroon balls at the New Orleans Theater. Ever since old Governor Miro passed the law back in 1788 that any unmarried women of color living in the little houses near the ramparts would be found guilty of misconduct and could be punished if they walked abroad in silk, jewels or plumes, these dark-tinted beauties have worn the madras handkerchief, or what we call *tignon*. But when their mothers chaperone them at the balls to which only white men are admitted—so that their daughters may find suitable protectors, *ca va sans dire!*—they come forth resplendent like birds of plumage!"

Yes, it was an exciting city now, a city to which six years ago the great Marquis de Lafayette had come to renew acquaintances with those patriotic countrymen of his, who, though transplanted in this new world, would never forget *la belle France*. Henry had already seen the houses of the fencing masters along Exchange Alley which ran from Canal to Conti between Royal and Bourbon Streets. These *maîtres d'armes* had a society all their own, gave elaborate suppers for their pupils, with much roistering and swordplay.

And there were also the attractively furnished auction rooms of the slavedealers, to say nothing of the even more luxuriously furnished bordellos. Antoine Rigalle had added a postscript to his letter: "Since you have French blood in you, my dear Henry, I do not doubt that when you come alone to New Orleans you will avail yourself of

537

the opportunities afforded your sanguine temperament. You must particularly visit the establishment of a certain Armand Duvalier. Some say he was a French privateer who flew the black flag at the beginning of his career. Regardless of that, he now has one of the finest and most talked-of slave marts and *maisons de joie* which one could find anywhere in these United States. His assistant, Pierre Lourat, though younger than yourself by far—he is just twenty-one, to be exact—acts as Duvalier's aide and managerial assistant at both establishments."

Well, Henry Bouchard told himself, there was no reason why he shouldn't treat himself to a little amusement. After all, here he was seeing to it that his father got what he'd always wanted. There was money enough in both their accounts to do much more than build that chateau, quite a good deal more. A pity that his father's share put aside for those flea-bitten, dirty Indians of his living near Tuskegee had been wiped out in the panic which had followed all the land speculation. Father had been in his dotage to think of taking money out of his own personal account to replace what had been set aside for the Creeks, he thought irritably.

But as he entered the counting house and saw Antoine Rigalle come forward in the most resplendent bottle-green coat, gay flowered vest, and tan-colored pantaloons, which proclaimed him a true dandy conscious of the latest fashion mode, all his annoyance vanished and he shook hands with the one-time clerk who had shown him what banknotes and bills of lading were and was now manager of one of the wealthiest private banks in all New Orleans.

"How good it is to see you, Antoine! And you've asked this *M'sieu* Arnaut to have dinner with us this evening?"

"Yes, of course. He's been here three years, and he's already designed one of our finest restaurants and a new hotel. Your father will like him, Henry. He comes from Provence, the very heart of the French countryside. I know he'll be able to help your father actualize that dream he's had so long. And then, *mon ami*—" Antoine Rigalle amicably steered his esteemed client into his private office—"perhaps the three of us will have a night on the town. Arnaut himself has remained a widower since

538

his young wife died a decade ago, but that's not to say he doesn't fancy one of those *jolies filles* at the house of Armand Duvalier."

Maurice Arnaut proved to be a witty conversationalist, a gourmand and a thorough man of the world after Henry Bouchard's heart. Just forty-five, tall and slender, he insisted on ordering a Lucullan dinner for them at Moreau's fine restaurant near the St. Charles Hotel, where the chef was a personal friend of his and a former countryman, who provided the most delicious red snapper and turtle soup imaginable and who, in honor of his friend's guests, concocted a very special dessert of rich cake with fruits soaked in various wines and cognacs, all of these courses being accompanied with separate wines.

Thus fortified, the trio was taken by carriage to the handsomely furnished auction rooms of Armand Duvalier on Chartres Street. Henry Bouchard quivered with feverish erotic desire as, taking his place in a chair near the front of the large rectangular platform at the very forefront of the room, he watched a sleek, elegantly attired black-haired young man exhibit two extremely attractive young mulatto girls, who, although illegitimate daughters of a New Orleans merchant, were being sold to satisfy the dead merchant's creditors. They were presented covered with silken capes from head to toe, and at the young auctioneer's gesture, each was obliged to drop the cape to her feet and, putting her hands at the back of her neck, slowly turn round and round until commanded to stop, so that every prospective bidder in the room might view her naked charms sufficiently to whet his bidding.

"That's Pierre Lourat, Duvalier's celebrated aide," Antoine Rigalle whispered to Henry Bouchard. "Some say he's from Cuba, some call him a Spaniard and a fop because he dresses like an aristocrat—just look at that silk shirt with all the ruffles, would you! But he's as deadly with the rapier and the *épée* as any of those fencing masters you'll find in Exchange Alley. Rumor has it that he's already fought four duels and sent two of his opponents to the brick sepulchers where we of New Orleans bury

539

our reputable dead. And, of course, he's a devil with the ladies."

"Those girls are damnably attractive, Antoine," Henry Bouchard muttered between his teeth.

"I assure you he has even more desirable ones and of lighter color, too, in the house around the corner, Henry, *mon ami*. After the sale is over for this evening, the three of us will have a glass of wine with him and then choose our partners for the evening. His prices are dear, but then the merchandise is of prime quality."

Half an hour later, Henry Bouchard shook hands with Pierre Lourat. There was perhaps something effeminate about the dark eyes and the ripe, sensual lips and the delicately winged nostrils of this personable young man, but from the steely grip he accorded Henry at their introduction, the latter divined that appearances could well be deceiving: the firmness of that handshake suggested a dexterity with the sword which would fatally rebuke any of his detractors.

"One day I may buy a slave from you, *M'sieu* Lourat," he told the young auctioneer.

Pierre Lourat bowed. "It would be my pleasure to serve you, and I promise that you won't regret your choice. And now, since we've quite finished here, let me take you to *Les Extases*."

"Now that is a most appropriate name for the sweet delights of the flesh one encounters there," Antoine Rigalle laughed. *"Allons-y, vite!"*

"It was good of you to come all this way, *M'sieu* Arnaut." Lucien Bouchard beamed as he shook hands with the suave New Orleans architect. After three nights of exciting debauchery—good food and wine, gambling and, to top it all off, a visit to *Les Extases* each of those three nights—Henry Bouchard had paid the architect's passage on the steamboat *Mobile* and a retainer out of his own money to compensate him for the time he would spend away from his affairs in New Orleans. "My son tells me you're from that beautiful country of Provence about whom the troubadors and the minstrels sang their immortal *chansons*. Then you know the architecture of Normandy as well."

"I do, and I still cherish it. In New Orleans, as you understand, the Spanish influence was greatest after that fire before the turn of the century. Under Spanish rule, however tolerant, it was to be expected. But we are rebuilding year by year. And now, if you'll outline to me this idea of yours for the chateau which you are to call Windhaven, I will tell you how long it will take, what must be done, and what my fee will be."

"I've thought of it so long, *M'sieu* Arnaut, that I could almost recite every detail from my memory," Lucien Bouchard happily sighed. "Two stories, of red brick, almost square and durable, with the flavor of our ancient Norse vigor—for of course, as you well know, *M'sieu* Arnaut, a king of France once gave our province to these fierce fighting men of the North lest they destroy all his country. And then, at each side, flanking that building, a pointed tower rising about half a story higher than the roof, which must be as heavy as we can make it. *Hélas*, the Alabama rains are sometimes more driving and destructive than what we had in Yves-sur-lac. Glass windows in the towers, and the towers themselves to have stairways of stone—mind you, accessible only from inside at the first floor, and of course from the second as well. At the back, a great kitchen with a superb flue and chimney so that none of the smoke from the cooking will offend our guests. On the first floor, a superb salon, a drawing room, if you please, and *naturellement* a sumptuous dining room. A library as well and a study and two bedrooms. On the second floor, bedrooms and guest rooms, and a gallery along the stairway on whose walls one might hang paintings and *objets d'art* if one so fancies. Do you begin to grasp my concept, *M'sieu* Arnaut?" His eyes blazed with youthful excitement and he leaned forward to grip the architect's wrist.

"I quite comprehend, *mon cher M'sieu* Bouchard. Now, as to bricks, I have already inspected the soil, and you have some magnificent clay and enough of it so that you can have your slaves make your own kiln and the bricks you will need. First, of course, we build the

541

foundation. I shall be here to supervise. Have you an overseer you can entrust with delegating the work?"

"Yes, a man called Thomas who is as dear to me as a son."

"Excellent! I should judge—mind you, this is only a random guess until we figure all the essentials and the costs—that it would take you from eighteen months to two years to build to completion. And your son tells me you wish a building also for the cotton engine and a sturdier one for your levee from which you ship your cotton—that's a very minor problem. But as I say, first the foundation, made solid with rubblestone and bricks; then the first-floor joists, the walls, the second-floor joists, the roof and the towers. Gradually, filling solidly with brick, we complete the floors and sections so that you and your family can be comfortably ensconced well before the completion of the entire project."

"I wish only to ask that you build one of the towers first, the tower which faces that great red bluff downriver," Lucien Bouchard said in a voice that shook with emotion.

"You will doubtless order your glass from Italy or England, depending on your preference," the architect went on, Lucien Bouchard's excitement now beginning to infect his own usually bland nature from the very scope of this project. "While you can undoubtedly order beds and tables from France, I may say that there are excellent furniture fabricators in the eastern United States who can make what you desire to order. It will be of top quality, and it will also be less costly when one assumes that even by steamboat there will be high tariffs and always the danger of damage in so long a journey from across the ocean."

"Well, I'm an American now, and so long as we retain the outer counterpart of my French chateau, where I was born, I shan't be overly critical if some of the furnishings inside are American-made." Lucien Bouchard smiled gently. "How many slaves do you think it will take to build all this?"

"I should like to think of a crew of at least fifty, directed by a capable overseer, *M'sieu* Bouchard. Slaves you

542

could spare from the planting of your crops and their harvesting, of course."

"So many?" Lucien Bouchard frowned. "I have perhaps about twenty—and they are free men."

"I will lend you some of mine, father," Henry Bouchard put in. "The rest, we can buy. I can get good field hands at about $400 apiece and of course, ever since 1820, our legislators have held that slaves can be emancipated only by voted legislative acts. Grover Mason was telling me the other day that it was held in the case of *Lilinam* vs. *Johnson* that if a slave is freed in any other way, he can be seized as derelict from the old law of 1800. So, father, if you want to free the slaves you're going to have to buy to build Windhaven, you'll have to go before the Alabama legislature—there's no help for it otherwise. And since that Nat Turner uprising, all the other states have even more severe laws—we've discussed that all too often to bother *M'sieu* Arnaut with it now."

"Very well." Lucien Bouchard uttered a doleful sigh and shook his head. "I shall buy the slaves, not you. It will be I who will appear before the legislators when the time is better than now—there are still too many grievous outcries because of poor Nat Turner's ill-advised example for me to attempt to do what I always did in the days of Econchate. And the cost, *M'sieu* Arnaut?"

"Yes. Well now, I'm plain to say that this chateau of yours enchants me, *M'sieu* Bouchard. I should spend at least a month at the outset to get your men started. Then of course I'd have to make a trip at least once a month, perhaps more often as the work progresses. I'd say $25,000 for my fee, and if you can make your own bricks and quarry your own stone, then the interior furnishings will be your major cost. Totally, and this is only a very quick guess, I should say that from outside and inside you should expect to spend close to $175,000."

Henry Bouchard whistled under his breath and shook his head. But white-haired Lucien gravely smiled as he answered: "I have that and more in the bank in New Orleans. I've always said that money was a medium of exchange. One barters for what one wants. Besides, it isn't only a selfish dream, this Windhaven of mine. It's for you,

Henry, and for Luke and Mark and Arabella and the new child your sweet Sybella is bearing even now." He rose from the table, straight and erect as in the days of his youth. "Let it commence, *M'sieu* Arnaut. The sooner it does, the better chance I shall have to see it and to stand in the top of the tower to remember—to remember the most beautiful dream of all I ever had."

CHAPTER FORTY-TWO

In 1830, the Treaty of Dancing Rabbit Creek had arranged for the final removal of the Choctaws from Alabama to the west. And even as Lucien Bouchard gave the order to build Windhaven to the exact specifications which had dwelt in his mind with imperishable clarity since that last morning when he had turned to look back at the red-brick chateau on his way to bid adieu to *Père* Morlain, President Jackson was preparing to move out the rest of the Indian tribes in keeping with his national policy. This coming year of 1832 would be marked by a new Presidential election, and already, on December 12, 1831, the National Republican Party had met in convention in Baltimore to nominate Henry Clay as Jackson's successor and John Sergeant of Pennsylvania as Clay's running mate. On that same day, John Quincy Adams presented in the House of Representatives fifteen petitions from Pennsylvania demanding the abolition of slavery in the District of Columbia. And a few weeks later, the New England Anti-Slavery Society was founded.

On this January morning of the new year of 1832, Lucien Bouchard dressed himself in the buckskin jacket and breeches, the boots and the bearclaw necklace which he had worn so long in Econchate and mounted the horse which Thomas had saddled for him to ride toward the new village of the Creeks. No one looking at him as he set the stallion to galloping along the trail would have believed that he was entering his seventieth year of life.

Thomas, wiry and energetic as always, himself now turned forty, stood looking after the white-haired rider on the dappled stallion and turned back toward the fields with a smile on his lips. Here was work closest to his heart, here was his way at last to keep his final promise to his murdered father. Even *M'su* Henry had come at last to a more sympathetic understanding of his father, and that was heartening for all who toiled for Windhaven. There would be many new slaves to supervise, and *M'su* Arnaut had spent several hours with him outlining the work that would have to be done to build the chateau just as *M'su* Lucien wished it. His mind was already full of plans for the selection of the best workers who could be most swiftly trained to carry out their duties. The timber could be cut at the nearby sawmill, the floor joists keyed so that the walls would not cant. The glass would be shipped in from England, and the architect had promised to bring a diamond-cutter on his next visit so that the panels could be properly cut to size. There would be hinged casement windows in the towers and special wood dividers to hold the glass securely. And already, young *M'su* Luke had come to him, shaken him by the hand and, his serious young face bright with eagerness, had declared, "I want to work with the others, even if it's only making bricks. I want to have a part in Grandfather's Windhaven."

Yes, there was so much to do, and *M'su* Lucien, even though he rode so vigorously in his saddle, would be seventy next December. He, Thomas, would work night and day if need be to make certain that the only man whom his father had called worthy of being a master of others should know in his final years the peace and joy of living in this beautiful new dwelling which meant so much to him.

The roofs would be of glazed tile, and he, Thomas, would have to show the workers how to make a special earthen glaze. And the tower which would look toward that towering red bluff had to be finished most urgently of all—and he understood why.

The rain had begun to fall as Lucien Bouchard dismounted and entered the lodge of Nanakota. The old

Mico wore the colorful mantle of his rank, but he sat with head bowed and shoulders slumped, his wrinkled face abject and sorrowful. And the lodge did not have the warmth or the sturdiness of construction as in the days of Econchate. It was made of logs and mud and there were many chinks through which the rain entered. And there were fewer tepees and wigwams and little houses in the Creek village than there had ever been before. So many had died, many of them having joined the Seminoles to do battle against the white-eyes who wanted the land without payment.

"I greet my blood brother," Lucien Bouchard said softly as he seated himself beside his brooding friend.

"Ho, it is good to see you again, Lu-shee-ahn. This morning, an agent from the white-eyes has come to tell me that soon a treaty will be signed with the remaining chiefs of the Creeks. He spoke the words and he smiled, but I read in his eyes the meaning. Like the Choctaws, who fear water and cannot swim, we too shall be moved to the west, away from this beloved river of the Alibamon. It is said that each head of a family and each orphan child shall receive 320 acres of land. Each of the chiefs is to have 640, and then, the agent says, we shall be given 16,000 more acres which can be sold to benefit what is left of the Creek Nation."

"It sounds fair, Nanakota, and it will be done without bloodshed or hatred."

"Aiyeee, you have never lied to me, my blood brother. But you are wise with the years as I have learned to be. Can you tell me that this does not mean what I fear it does? It is at last the prophecy of Tsipoulata, that we shall go to lands which will not be good for hunting, and there the Creek Nation will at last perish from the good earth to which Ibofanaga sent us in the beginning."

Lucien bowed his head and was silent, for there were no words.

"The agent says that each of us will be given a certificate which tells of the new land we shall own, and the chiefs of the white-eyes will send another agent to us to help us find this land. In my heart I know it will not be within the borders of the Alibamon."

547

"If only I had the power to give you some of my land so that you and the villagers would have a home to the end of your days, Nanakota!"

Nanakota slowly raised his head and stared at his white-haired friend. "Then you have already said it, and the words of Tsipoulata are truly to be fulfilled before many more moons, Lu-shee-ahn. For I know that if your laws allowed, you would keep that promise as you have kept every other that you have ever made to the Creeks. But the great soldier Jackson who defeated us at Horseshoe Bend, where so many of my brave young men laid down their lives for the Nation, has no wish to see our faces mingle with those of the settlers. Well, I cannot blame him. If I were in his place, perhaps I too would banish the white-eyes. Ho, ho, if only that had been written, my blood brother!"

"But I have made sure that the goods and the money held at Mobile will be distributed to your people, Nanakota, no matter where you may go."

"Yes, and the villagers give you thanks as I do. But now this is a matter which passes beyond the two of us who sit here as blood brothers and old friends who have shared the hunt and the green corn festival and the marriage feast."

"Yes, Nanakota."

"We are proud and we were once strong and took pride in our strength. Now there are few of us left in the villages, and the white-eyes look upon us with hatred they no longer bother to conceal, and, what is far worse, Lu-shee-ahn, contempt—as they would look upon skulking dogs that crawl to the edge of their campfires to steal a bone they have thrown away. To whatever land we go, it can never be as it was. And I do not speak of warfare—this you know well."

"Yes, my brother."

"I speak of the ending of one life as of the ending of all the Nation. What will it mean when the Taker of Breath above us stills us forever? What will be left of the Creeks except the thoughts of the old like you and perhaps the tales that will be told to those who come after you? Not even the wind will remember who and what we were, and the earth will consume the bones of our dead, and there will be nothing to mark that we once lived and were proud and strong."

"I will remember, and my grandsons, who are still young enough to look upon life with curiosity and eagerness and joy and who will not be taught what hatred is among men, they will remember, Nanakota. I go now, and I will have Thomas send you more supplies from my own store room."

Nanakota slowly rose to his feet, stared long into the face of his old friend and clasped both of Lucien's hands in his and touched them to his heart. "I read in your eyes that you had other news to tell me, but you knew that I was sad and thus did not wish to intrude upon my old and sorrowful thoughts. But if there is joy in that news, and it must be, then there will be joy for me also."

"Yes, it is joyful news for me, but it is saddened by knowing that I cannot share it with you. I have begun to build the house that I had in that far country across the great ocean, Nanakota. And there will be a tower from whose top I shall look toward Dimarte and tell her that I have not forgotten and that when my time is come, I pray my God that I shall join her."

"May the Giver of Breath allow you moons without end to see where she lies in sleep as the beloved woman, my brother."

"I shall visit my brother again to make sure that he and his people are well cared for," Lucien Bouchard said gently, as he released the old chief's hands and turned to the entrance of the lodge.

The old *Mico* walked slowly outside of his lodge and, as the rain again began to fall, watched his friend mount his horse and ride away. He looked up at the dull, ominous sky, and then he went back into his lodge. From under a blanket, he drew the case in which he had kept Lucien Bouchard's French razor. Seated tailor-fashion on the bare ground, oblivious to the spatter of rain which fell upon him through the chinks in the roof, Nanakota intoned the death chant of the Creeks, the prayer of the warrior who goes into battle with the foreknowledge that his time has come. And when he had finished it, in so

549

low a voice that none even outside the lodge could have overheard him, he opened the case and took out the gleaming razor.

"Oh, Tsipoulata, do you remember the words you spoke to me after the death of Tunkamara? They were true words, oh, *Windigo*. Death as a welcome gift of a gift that was welcome—those were your words, Tsipoulata. And, wherever your spirit may be now, you remember well what I said to you—that it would be a good death and I would joy in it. And so I do. To Ibofanaga, I give back my breath and my spirit. And let the blood I shed be the last upon this land which we must leave forever. This is my prayer—and now my time is upon me. Tunkamara, Dimarte, my father and my mother, aiyeee, even you, faithless Emarta, I come to join you."

His trembling hand lifted the sharp blade to his throat.

CHAPTER FORTY-THREE

It was a starry evening in late November, 1834, and the Alabama River was high and swift. As the tall, still erect, white-haired man carefully and slowly ascended the broad stone steps of the red-brick tower, he could hear the mournful tooting of the steamboat whistle as its paddle-wheels churned the dark water on its way to Mobile. The air was cool and good and it wafted in from the open casement windows at the very top. He paused to get his breath, put his hand to the gleamingly polished wooden guardrail and ascended. He wore buckskin jacket and breeches, leggings and moccasins and a necklace of bear claws. The moon had risen, a full bright moon that made even the many stars dwindle in their luster as he faced the towering red bluff.

Two years ago, before even the Treaty of Cusseta by whose terms the remaining Creeks yielded up all their lands east of the Mississippi, he had forced himself to climb that steep bluff to its very peak. Groping at times on all fours, strengthened by the timeless love that waited for him there, he had found her grave. Only a few fragments of that Spanish comb were on the earth, but even that was not needed to tell him who slept here and whose spirit hovered amid the majestic pines and firs which rose so proudly above the winding river below. He had wept for Nanakota then, and for all those others who, in pitiful, ragged groups, beleaguered by scornful agents, tricked by greedy white and half-breed settlers, were being led

551

toward the west, even past Arkansas, carrying their pitifully few belongings with them. They had left the beloved land forever. But she still remained and would throughout the end of time itself, for even though his years were numbered, his descendants would remember. Surely of these, it would be young Luke, who already now at eighteen reminded him so poignantly of the way he had been at that same idealistic age.

It was accomplished. Only last week Maurice Arnaut had supervised the placement of the portico, that handsome triangulated roof supported by white-oak Ionic columns which rose from the top of the heavy stone steps to frame the door of the chateau. And Luke, like the lowliest of the black slaves whom Lucien's son Henry had purchased in Mobile, had helped lift one of those heavy columns into place.

Lucien had thanked God for having spared the life of Maurice Arnaut. In the fall of 1832, at the exact time the architect had been here supervising the construction of the walls and floor joists, a deadly plague of yellow fever followed by Asiatic cholera had taken the lives of six thousand of New Orleans' thirty-five thousand inhabitants. And Arnaut's own house had been located in the very area where the epidemic had wrought its most terrible decimation.

This tower at whose top he now stood staring through the open window toward the red bluff had been completed the day before his seventieth birthday, and he had indignantly refused his son's aid in accompanying him up these steps to the top. By God, he could still ride a horse even today! And he had remained there at the open window till, having lost all consciousness of time, he had been brought back from the reveries of the dear, so deeply mourned past, by the anxious voice of Luke calling, "*Grandpère,* please, I'm worried for you—please come down!"

And all through the ensuing months, like a child who wakens from deep sleep to hurry down to the fireplace to see the magical remembrances of Christmas awaiting him, he had stood at the levee to watch the steamboat unload its precious cargo: the glass from England, an exact du-

552

plicate of the goat-legged writing table with its Watteau panels and silver encrustation which had graced his own father's study, the canopied beds and the tapestries from France—all that his vividly restored memories of boyhood and young manhood had summoned back from his days at the chateau of Yves-sur-lac. And now, as he walked through every room, it seemed to him that he had never left France at all.

Yet, far beyond the acres of corn and cotton were the cabins of black slaves. Slaves whom he could not yet free because here in this new land those who had taken it from the Creeks and the other tribes feared it might be taken in turn from them once there was freedom for all men. Now, where there had been red men, there were white and black; the fifteen remaining Seminole chiefs had given up their Florida lands by treaty and moved far across the mighty Mississippi.

So much had happened during these two years of the building of Windhaven. At the end of 1832, Andrew Jackson had been reelected President by an electoral vote of 219 to 49 for Henry Clay, with solid, reliable Martin Van Buren his new Vice-President. The following year, there had been wild speculation in public lands, roads, canals, banks, buildings and cotton throughout the entire nation. Yet last year America's arch enemy, England, had abolished slavery in her colonies. What irony that slavery should now be the law of this land on which Windhaven stood with all its heritage and memories! And on this last Independence Day, a meeting of the Anti-Slavery Society in New York had been broken up by rioters because they had discovered blacks in the audience, and churches and houses had been destroyed during a week of insensate madness. Only last month, a similar riot had taken place in Philadelphia, but this time directed against the blacks, and forty of their houses had been destroyed. Would this new conflict between black and white be even more terrible than between white man and red? He turned again to look out through the open window at the bluff where she lay. She, the beloved woman, with whose spirit he communed, knew all his thoughts.

But now that Windhaven was built, what of the future?

Now he had four grandchildren, for Sybella had had another daughter, born in April of 1832, Fleurette, auburn-haired like her beautiful, now buxom and mature mother, and surely destined to be just as beautiful. Sybella had taken Fleurette to Montgomery yesterday for a visit with her father, who was leaving for Philadelphia, but she and the little girl would be back in the morning. Lucien was glad of that, for Sybella seemed to exert a strong influence on Henry. When she was home, she often let him feel the edge of her sharp tongue when his behavior did not suit her. And Henry's philandering seemed to have been checked to a great extent, too. At least, Lucien smilingly thought to himself, Henry found a woman he had vastly underestimated, one capable enough to see to all the details of running this great new plantation without giving way to the vapors, like so many young women her age. Indeed, if Sybella had been born a man, she could have matched Henry for energy and purpose; yet her very femininity, which kept him bound to her if only by the ties of the flesh, had a subtlety and cunning which counterbalanced his own deviousness.

Luke was in his first term at the new Lowndesboro Advanced Academy for Young Gentlemen, equivalent to what in France would be the first year of college after the *lycée*. Old Dr. Peter Martin, the founder of the institution, had only last week sent Lucien a letter complimenting him on his grandson's keen, inquisitive mind and modest behavior. "He is quiet and reflective, thinks out his projects carefully and logically, Mr. Bouchard," Dr. Martin had written, "and is always ready to learn more about a particular subject without thinking he has the answer once and for all. Besides all this, he has tact wedded to manly strength; he rides a horse as well as any of our rowdier pupils, and though he is not given to fisticuffs or loud argument, I am certain he could more than hold his own if any test of his physical prowess were made upon him."

Yes, here was a grandson to be proud of and to welcome on the occasion of his forthcoming seventy-second birthday. Luke had shown great respect and consideration for Sybella, treating her as if she were his own mother.

That was undoubtedly why Sybella had flared up at Henry's disparaging remarks on Luke's self-effacing nature that evening a decade ago, and why, ever since then, she had gone out of her way to praise Luke to Henry, much to the latter's irritation.

It would be a joyous reunion of them all here at Windhaven this coming December 18th. Lucien smiled happily as he thought of the prospect. They would talk of the year ahead, and then he and Henry would sensibly discuss the cultivation of the new crops. Henry would be wise to let some of his land lie fallow. Overplanting cotton would wear out even the richest land, he was certain. And then there was the problem of the Creeks, always close to his heart: without them, none of this could have come to pass.

He had had a factor from the trading house in Mobile bring supplies and money to the handful of Creeks who were left in that nearly abandoned village near Tuskegee. After Nanakota's death, many of the younger braves had deserted. He did not know where they were now, but it was certain that eventually they would be banded together in yet another wretched processional across the borders of this state which had been their home for longer than the white man knew.

He uttered a deep sigh and slowly shook his head. Tomorrow night he would climb the steps of the other tower and think of Amelia and Priscilla, yes, and of Ben and his Ellen, who had sickened and died just a year after Henry had married Sybella. Now she was united with the father of Thomas, whom he could never repay for the latter's skillful and dedicated work as overseer of Windhaven.

Thomas was forty-two now, and surely he should think of marrying and having a child of his own. What worried Lucien was Henry's insistence that, now that the plantation was built, a brick shed for the cotton engine, a superbly spacious and well-protected storage depot on the levee, it was high time they had a white overseer. They had quarreled about it only last week, before Henry had gone off to New Orleans to inspect the ledgers in Antoine Rigalle's bank. There was still so much of his dead brother Jean that he could see in Henry, and some in

Henry's son Mark as well. Just yesterday and in his very presence, that black-haired fifteen-year-old boy had slapped one of the black slaves for having inadvertently brushed some of Mark's silverware onto the floor while serving a tureen of soup to the arrogant boy. And he had not liked the way young Mark had looked at some of the more attractive black women whom Henry had trained to serve as maids and kitchen help at Windhaven. Mark had little use for books, and even in his speech had begun to imitate his father, even to the use of that hateful word "nigger."

There came to Lucien's ears the distant hooting of an owl. His wrinkled face, so brown from the sun, so weatherbeaten, that one would have thought him a true brother of the Creeks, was suddenly wet with tears as he pronounced her name: "Dimarte, beloved. I am here, I am ever faithful. Can you, like old Tsipoulata, see the future for us here at Windhaven?"

Henry Bouchard stood, twisting a black leather riding crop between his strong hands, near the platform where Pierre Lourat had just drawn off the cape from a trembling eighteen-year-old mulatto named Celia. Her head was bowed, her right knee bent, an arm crossed over her uptilting, firm round breasts, her left hand clenched in a gesture of bleak despair and shame. Around him, the other planters hoarsely exchanged their ribald and lecherous comments on her sleek brown-skinned nakedness and stared enviously at him. He had just bought her for $2500, and he shot a triumphant, mocking little smile at Peter Denson, a neighbor fifty miles downriver from him, who had finally dropped out of the bidding.

Money was tight for the smaller planters, but not for him, Henry Bouchard. Even with cotton at an all-time low, even with the depreciation of banknotes, yes, even with the fortune that had been spent for Windhaven—most all of it spent by his dreamer of a father—he was still well off and could afford to buy a bedwench. Hadn't he done enough already, hadn't he kept all his promises to the old man? Well, to be sure, how could his father begrudge him a little pleasure now? Sybella was still damnably capable in bed, but there were times when a hot-blooded man in his prime hungered for the soft untouched flesh of a dark-skinned bitch like this, especially one who'd never been bedded. When Denson and himself had been the only bidders left, that young rascal of a Lourat had invited them both to attest Celia's virginity. Well, he'd be home tomorrow night, and Celia would be sent straight to a room where he'd find her without Sybella's knowledge. They slept in separate bedrooms anyway, so he'd wait till Sybella was fast asleep. Then he'd bathe and shave, take along a bottle of Madeira, and he and Celia would make a rare night of it!

"See what a fancy house I've brought you to live in, Celia girl?" Henry Bouchard affably stroked the young girl's hair, done up just like a white woman's with a big psyche knot at the back. Why, dress the bitch up in marcellines and chine silks, or organdies stamped in the flowery designs you could find in *Godey's Lady's Book,* or one of those fancy imported French calicos, and you could almost pass her for white. And the delicious pleasure of knowing that she was just a nigger once you peeled off all those frilly clothes and underthings, a frightened little virgin bitch of a nigger, made it all the more exciting.

"Yassum, masta." The girl quavered, hanging her head and biting her lips.

"You'll be grateful, you'll see, girl. Now listen, I'm goin' to take you in to see Mammy Clorinda, the housekeeper here. She'll get you a room for the night—yes, honey, you're worth enough, by God, to be put up in the house, not like a cheap field nigger. I paid top price for you, Celia, so just remember you're special—and you're mine, understand? Now let's go find Mammy Clorinda."

Glancing down the hallway as he stood in the spacious foyer of this replica of his father's French chateau, Henry Bouchard exhaled a sigh of relief to see no one except the footman, Benjamin, a lanky Kru in red livery. "I'm back, Benjy," he said affably, pushing the frightened young girl ahead of him with a proprietary gesture. "No need to tell

557

the mistress, I'll be up directly to see her—she's in her bedchamber, I suppose?"

"Yassh, mastah, she go there right aftah supper, mastah." The footman deferentially inclined his head.

"Perfect! You can go to bed now, Benjy. No one else'll be coming this late. Come along, girl."

In the kitchen, in a calico dress which her obese bulk threatened to split at any moment, Mammy Clorinda, forty-five but still, in her own words, "spry enuff foah any black buck thinks he kin still stud a wench," was cleaning the pots and pans with the help of two teen-aged black girls whom she had herself elected as kitchen apprentices but who were relegated to the slave cabins at the far back of the fields. She turned and clapped her hands, "Sukey, Dulcy, you look sharp now, de mastah's come home! Clean dem things good now, you heah?" Then, to Henry Bouchard, a wide grin on her broad, gleaming face, "Good to have you home, suh. Disyeah a new gal from N'Awleans?"

"That's right, Mammy Clorinda. This is Celia. I had in mind an upstairs maid—light cleaning, dusting, polishing—you know." He gave the fat Negress a broad wink.

"Hee hee hee, dass right, mastah. Mighty purty gal, too."

"Her name's Celia. Now give her a bite to eat, then find a room upstairs for her. The right wing would be satisfactory." He pursed his lips, frowned a moment. Sybella and he had bedrooms on the opposite wing of the second floor, adjacent to each other and with a connecting door between. There had been times, especially after he had quarreled with Luke over the latter's continued acceptance of these niggers as equals—was ever a father so plagued by so obstinate and unworldly a son?—that his outspoken auburn-haired wife locked that door to him. Well, that was still another reason for his having Celia accessible, whenever her ladyship took it into her head to have those high and mighty airs toward him. As if he didn't know she was as hotblooded as any of the girls at Pierre Lourat's bordello when the mood came on her. "Yes, Mammy Clorinda, I'm sure you can find her a small room in that wing."

"Ah'll tend to dat right off, mastah, you kin depen' on it shonuff," the waddling housekeeper assured him. "Come 'long, chile, set yoahself down, ah'll git you some vittles, then we'll see you gits a nice soft bed to sleep in aftah dat long trip from N'Awleans."

With a motherly gesture, she put an arm around the young girl's waist, soothing her as she might a restive mare. Henry Bouchard grinned, highly pleased with his stratagem. Then he went back up the stairs and knocked at Sybella's door.

"Syb? It's Henry, just got back from New Orleans," he murmured as he entered the darkened room.

"Oh? That's fine, Henry. I had a headache all evening, so I went to bed early. Please let me sleep. I'll see you in the morning."

"Of course, my dear. I'm sorry to have disturbed you. Just wanted to let you know I was back." He went toward the canopied bed, bent and kissed her forehead. Sybella uttered a little sigh and turned onto her side. His face darkened, his lips tightened, he then turned on his heel and closed the door behind him. Then, rubbing his hands with anticipation, he hurried back down the stairs. There was sure to be some of Mammy Clorinda's famous chicken and biscuits left. . . .

Timidly, the young girl entered the room. She shuddered as she saw the canopied bed loom before her. No candle had been lit, because Henry Bouchard had not told the slaves exactly on what date he would return from New Orleans. But, docile, having already tasted the whip from the hand of Pierre Lourat, who had coached her into how to present herself before these avid white buyers, she knew better than to protest or argue. Biting her lips, she unfastened the cape Henry Bouchard had bought for her in New Orleans, then doffed the plain cotton dress and the shift beneath it, removed shoes and stockings and, shiveringly naked, crept into the huge bed and cowered there.

The door stealthily opened, and a half-naked figure moved swiftly toward the bed. "Is—is dat you, mastah?" Celia quavered at the sound of soft quick footsteps.

559

"Keep your mouth shut, you sweet little bitch. Just yell once, and I'll have you out to the whipping shed in the morning, see if I don't," the shadowy figure hissed.

Tugging the covers from her, he flung himself down, his mouth greedily crushing hers, his hands coveting the round satiny turrets of her young bosom.

Her eyes rolled, her mewling sound of anguish was muffled by her ravisher's hoarse chuckle of triumph. . . .

He had shaved and bathed, and ascended the stairway to the second floor wearing only a robe, drawers and boots. Pierre Lourat had told him that a young black wench was most impressed when her master wore only his boots to bed: it was a symbol of dominance, of power, and even the strongest female would quail before the mastery which that symbol implied over her palpitating flesh. With each step toward his bedroom, he felt his virility agonizingly swell, an exquisite torment and one he had learned from his many visits to *Les Extases*. What a remarkable young devil Pierre Lourat was, how much he knew about women; yet he was only a few years older than that milksop of a son, Luke. Lourat had been the one who'd counseled him on the joys of prolongation, of putting off, of dalliance and delaying, to tauten the nerves of the female partner until she was ready to grovel and beg for fulfillment. By God, he'd wear Celia out tonight!

As he put his hand to the knob of the door, he fancied he heard muffled weeping. Well, that was to be expected. It was also still another proof that the little bitch hadn't ever been bedded before—not that he hadn't himself verified it at Lourat's invitation. Celia had been the issue of a Creole and a handsome black girl from the West Indies. They'd been married there, somehow, and come to New Orleans. Celia's father had been wealthy enough at the time, so it hadn't mattered too much. But then he'd lost everything he had at gambling, and his debtors had foreclosed on him. So much the worse for her father, and so much the better for him right now, Henry Bouchard avariciously thought as he swung the door open and in his harsh, domineering voice exclaimed, "Here I am at last,

Celia. Are you ready for me, girl? Pull back the covers and invite me to bed, that's a good slave."

The weeping was louder now, almost hysterical. He swore under his breath; he should have remembered to fetch a candle or a lantern with him. No matter, darkness would do this first time, it would augment Celia's fears. Tomorrow night, there'd be time enough for making her parade in a pair of high-heeled slippers, taking all the poses his lubricious fancies could conjecture.

"Didn't you hear me, Celia?" he angrily repeated, taking a step toward the bed.

"She can hear you, father. You needn't shout so."

"Damnation—Mark—what in hell are you doing here?"

"Why, just what you planned on doing, I guess father." The black-haired boy eased himself out of bed and came forward, naked but for his ruffled shirt.

"You—you're telling me you bedded Celia?" Henry Bouchard could scarcely speak, his face purpling with a savage fury.

"Why not, father? She's a slave, isn't she? I didn't think you'd mind if I shared her with you."

"You filthy little bastard! You'd dare to do that to me?" Henry Bouchard clenched his fists and struck at the taunting young face before him. Then he cried out in pained consternation; Mark had returned the blow so forcefully to the pit of his stomach that he'd doubled up in agony, groaning and sobbing with rage and pain.

"Nobody hits me, father, not even you," his son coldly informed him.

"I'll kill you for this—you dirty little guttersnipe—where the devil did you learn how to go whoring at fifteen?" Henry Bouchard gasped as he slowly, wincingly straightened.

"Why, from you, father. And I'm old enough to do it too, just ask Celia. I had her twice, father. She's nice. If you wanted her all to yourself, why didn't you buy me one in New Orleans, too?"

Goaded beyond control, Henry Bouchard seized Mark by the collar of his shirt, dragging him out of the room and toward the stairway. "Bastard, filthy young scum—

561

I'll teach you a lesson you won't soon forget—in my own house, my own son—oh, you little swine—" he hoarsely panted.

Mark Bouchard struck again and again at his father's congested, twisted face, but Henry ignored the jolting pain of those blows and continued to drag his stocky young son toward the top of the landing. Then, releasing the boy, he drew back his fist to smash it into that mocking young face, preparing to deliver it with all his strength. With a taunting laugh, Mark Bouchard shoved him in a sudden bound with both hands thrust against his father's chest, and with a frantic cry, Henry Bouchard toppled and fell down the stairs.

"Oh Christ, my leg, my leg, it's broken—I'll kill you for this—oh you little bastard—my God, how my leg hurts—don't stand there, you young swine, go get help—oh Jesus, to think I've raised a son like you—"

Lucien Bouchard was slowly descending from the top of the tower. At the door which connected the second-floor landing with the enclosed tower, he heard angry voices, and as he opened it, he was just in time to see his son hurtle down the stairs and hear Henry's frenzied bellow of agony.

He saw young Mark standing gloatingly at the top of the landing, his arms folded across his chest, contemplating the injured man. And then he heard his son cry out, almost hysterically in his suffering, "Oh you just wait, Mark—damn your soul to hell, taking my bed wench, daring to raise your hand to me, breaking my leg—you wait till I'm well, you mangy pup, we'll have our accounting!"

As he watched, stupefied, horrified, he saw Sybella come down the hallway from her bedroom, a wrapper over her nightgown. The beautiful auburn-haired matron stared at both her son and her fallen husband, then looked down the hall and saw the open door from which both had come. Swiftly she hurried down the hall into the bedroom, and in the darkness heard the sound of muffled weeping. "Who's that? Who are you? Speak up!" she hissed.

"Aw, please, m'am, it warn't my fault, honest—de

mastah, Mista Henry, he brought me here from N'Awleans, 'n Mammy Clorinda, she bring me up to disyeah room'n tell me to get into bed and stay there. Den—oh Gawd—it warn't my fault!"

"I see," Sybella Bouchard said grimly. "I'm sure it wasn't your fault, girl. We'll talk about it later."

Then, swiftly, she went back to the stairway and stood looking down at Henry. Mark had retreated at the sight of his mother, hurrying back to his room.

"For God's sake, get someone to help me, I've broken my leg, Syb," Henry groaned, grimacing with pain.

"I will, Henry." Her voice was quiet and assured. "So you bought yourself a pretty little filly in New Orleans and sneaked her into the house, did you? No wonder you were in such a hurry to say goodnight to me. You might have tried to cure my headache the way you were going to cure that girl's homesickness, you know."

"Damn you, woman, have you no heart?" he raged.

"Much more than you, Henry. I'll get Benjy and Oscar to help you to your room and get Doctor Lorimer for your leg. You won't die of a broken leg. It will put you out of action for a while, though. And I'm going to look after you myself, Henry, the way a good wife should."

"All right, all right, I'll admit I—God, my leg's killing me—"

"I'll call for help in a minute, Henry. Yes, as I say, I'll look after you properly. And you're going to take my advice for a change. When Luke comes back from school for the Christmas holidays, you're going to give him a chance to show what his mind can do, a mind full of book learning as you've always so scornfully pointed out to me. Perhaps it's time his young alert mind and mine worked together to keep this plantation on an even keel, Henry. Just remember that. And now I'll get help for you."

Lucien, who had heard and seen everything, slowly closed the door and turned back to the stone steps. His breath escaping him in panting sobs, he attained the open casement window. He turned to the bluff just as the moonlight bathed it in a luminous glow that showed its steep, almost perpendicular rise.

"Oh, Dimarte, Dimarte, is this my heritage of Windhaven? Already I have lived to see my own son turn against me, and now my grandson turns against him in his turn! You, beloved woman, you the good spirit of all my waking days and dream-filled nights to the end of my life, banish the malignant spirit of Jean, which must surely, like some evil incubus, have touched the soul of my son and my younger grandson. Yes, my son's wife seems strong and enduring—but can she turn him from his course of self-destruction and folly, one which Mark already seems eager to pursue? Oh, beloved one, have I come to the fulfillment of my dream? have I built this memorial in your sweet name, only to have the lingering ghost of Jean, who destroyed whatever he touched, come back to haunt it through my own blood by the blood of my only living son and of his own favored son?"

As he watched the moonlight bathe the side of the bluff in its silver luminosity, the distant hooting of an owl was heard. And as he waited, it seemed to say, "Luke . . . Luke . . . Luke . . . take heart, it will be Luke who dreams your dream, who takes your heritage and brings it to the fulfillment you have pledged."

. . . and so ends the first book in the saga of the Bouchard family, and their magnificent home, Windhaven. The story continues in the next novel by Marie de Jourlet, Storm Over Windhaven. In the following pages we offer you a preview sampling of this sequel. It will be published in September 1977, be sure to watch for it.

—**THE EDITORS**

Preview

Storm over Windhaven

by Marie de Jourlet

"Enough of your fine-sounding talk about not freeing a slave, Henry," Sybella burst out in a tone of suppressed fury as she abruptly rose from the table, pushing aside the little sweater she had been crocheting for Fleurette. "What it really amounts to is that you mean to punish that poor girl Celia, all because your fine, young son Mark got to bed with her before you did!"

"Sybella, that's not true—" he began, his face mottled with anger.

The handsome auburn-haired matron sent him a scathing look in which contempt and secret anguish were equally mingled. "And you're punishing Mark too, though I can't blame the boy for his profligacy, not when he has his own father's illustrious examples to follow."

"Stop it, damn you!" he growled.

"Yet you could solve everything by letting Thomas marry Celia, and thus little Prissy would be legitimate. Don't you see, Henry, by refusing, you're turning an innocent little baby into a slave who, one day, God forbid, may have to submit to some white plantation owner—just as you intended Celia to submit to you?"

"I'm warning you, Sybella!" he rose, glowering with fury, fists clenched.

She shrugged. "Go ahead, beat me, Henry, why don't you? That's your customary way of wooing a woman, I suppose. Only remember, I'm not your slave and never will be. And now I'm going for a ride on Dulcy. Maybe the fresh air will clear my thoughts about you, Henry. And you'd best do some self-searching yourself while I'm gone."

She flung out of the drawing room, leaving her black-haired, florid-faced husband standing with mouth agape, stunned at her intensity. She went out through the kitchen, scarcely noticing Mammy Clorinda's obsequious curtsy and greeting, heading directly for the stable just ahead of the rows of slave cabins. The sky had turned an ominous gray and the wind was rising, tugging at her long flowing skirt, at the ruffles on her bodice, but she paid it no heed. As the skinny sixteen-year-old Kru stableboy Jimmy emerged, she snapped at him, "Saddle Dulcy, boy, and quickly!"

"Yes, Missy. Only looks mighty lak a storm comin' up, Missy—maybe it better—" he uneasily said.

"You heard what I said, boy! Do it—or would you rather have a whipping?" her lips curled with anger. *My God she told herself, Henry's cruelty's starting to affect even me. I'd never have thought of saying such a thing to anyone, not even a slave, before I married him.*

"Oh no 'm, I'll saddle her, yes'm!" the boy fearfully bobbed his head and disappeared into the stable. A few moments later, he came out leading the spirited chestnut mare, and helped his mistress mount side-saddle, tendering her the reins. At a distant rumble of thunder, Dulcy whinnied and pawed the ground.

"Easy, girl!" Sybella jerked on the reins, then patted the mare's neck to soothe her. "Better hand me my riding crop too, Jimmy."

"Yes'm. Here it be—" he hesitantly held it up to Sybella. Snatching it from him, her lips compressed, her forehead creased with exasperation, she directed the mare toward the narrow, cleared path which led through a clump of thickets, emerging beyond it into a wide stretch of grassy field as yet uncultivated. Miles beyond, it would eventually connect with the old Federal Road, one of her favorite riding jaunts. Her mind swirled with the rift that had grown between Henry and herself, with her awareness of how much young Mark was emulating his father, in a kind of fierce blood rivalry to prove himself a man despite his precocious fifteen years. Could she and Henry ever go back to those joyous days and nights of comradeship and sharing at the outset of their marriage? Yes, she was thirty-three, but still vital, still attractive, she knew. And men were not the only ones with deep, underlying needs, even if it was a man's world.

Back in the stable, the tall sturdy Mandingo Djamba scowled at the timid stableboy. "Which way she go, Timothy?" he demanded.

"That way, to the old road," the boy gestured. As he spoke, there was another rumble of thunder. With an imprecation in his own tongue, Djamba hurried to one of the stalls where a black stallion pawed its straw, swiftly applied bridle and reins and, vaulting bareback astride it, urged it in the direction Sybella had taken.

Again, thunder growled in the darkening sky and there was a sudden spattering of rain. Sybella flicked Dulcy's haunch with the crop, commanding, "Steady, girl, I said!"

But the mare had sensed her mistress' inner raging discontent, and suddenly, as a shaft of jagged lightning illumined the sullen sky, bolted. Sybella uttered a cry of fear and strove with all her strength to draw on the reins, but the mare had taken her head and would not stop.

Jostled, panting, in danger of losing her balance, Sybella called as soothingly as she could, but to no avail. As the thunder growled again, the mare gave a frightened whinny and galloped on.

"Oh my God," Sybella groaned as, in her heedless gait, the mare brushed her helpless rider against the overhanging branch of a small oak tree which tore the crop out of Sybella's nerveless hand.

Sybella's lips moved in prayer and she closed her eyes. *Please God, let it be quick.* And then suddenly there was a shout beside her, and Djamba, reaching out with both hands seized her by the waist and lifted her out of the side-saddle, setting her down in front of him as he called out a command she could not understand, and the great stallion obediently slackened its pace and came to a gradual halt.

"Oh—th—thank God—oh Djamba—you—you've saved me," she gasped, her arms clinging round his dusky, sweating waist.

"Missy safe now. Dulcy, she run herself out, she be quiet soon," he consoled her.

Now he gently disengaged her arms, slid from the stallion and helped her down. Sybella tottered, weak with reaction. A sudden flash of lightning drew a terrified little cry from her and again she clung to him.

"We hide down here from de lightnin', Missy," he urged, guiding her down into a deep wide ravine whose overhanging sides formed a kind of shelter from the storm. She could not know that, long years ago, it was in just such a ravine that Henry's father Lucien had taken shelter from a violent thunderstorm on his way to Econchate and his rendezvous with the destiny that awaited him in the Creek village.

There, huddling against the sturdy Mandingo slave, Sybella Bouchard trembled now, but not from fear of the raging storm. Rather, from the sudden inexplicable yearning that had seized her. He was a slave, yet he had once been the chief of his tribe; most of all, he was a man of indomitable courage and strength.

She stared up at him and she read in his dark eyes a devotion and steadfastness that quieted her fears. Gently he murmured, "Missy safe now. Storm soon over, then I find Dulcy and we ride back home to Massa Henry, Missy."

And Sybella knew with a flash of feminine intuition that in that instant Djamba had sensed her momentary yearning, acknowledged it with his own, and yet had resolution and wisdom enough to ignore it for them both. . . .